THE BEST
SCIENCE FICTION
AND FANTASY
OF THE YEAR

VOLUME FIVE

Also Edited by Jonathan Strahan

Best Short Novels (2004 through 2007)
Fantasy: The Very Best of 2005
Science Fiction: The Very Best of 2005
The Best Science Fiction and Fantasy of the Year: Volumes 1 – 4
Eclipse One: New Science Fiction and Fantasy
Eclipse Two: New Science Fiction and Fantasy
Eclipse Three: New Science Fiction and Fantasy
The Starry Rift: Tales of New Tomorrows
Engineering Infinity (forthcoming)
Life on Mars: Tales of New Tomorrows (forthcoming)
Under My Hat: Tales from the Cauldron (forthcoming)
Godlike Machines

With Lou Anders
Swords and Dark Magic: The New Sword and Sorcery (forthcoming)

With Charles N. Brown
The Locus Awards: Thirty Years of the Best in Fantasy and Science Fiction
Fritz Leiber: Selected Stories

With Jeremy G. Byrne
The Year's Best Australian Science Fiction and Fantasy: Volumes 1 – 2
Eidolon 1

With Terry Dowling
The Jack Vance Treasury
The Jack Vance Reader
Wild Thyme, Green Magic
Hard Luck Diggings: The Early Jack Vance

With Gardner Dozois
The New Space Opera
The New Space Opera 2

With Karen Haber
Science Fiction: Best of 2003
Science Fiction: Best of 2004
Fantasy: Best of 2004

With Marianne S. Jablon
Wings of Fire

THE BEST
SCIENCE FICTION
AND FANTASY
OF THE YEAR

VOLUME FIVE

EDITED BY JONATHAN STRAHAN

NIGHT SHADE BOOKS
SAN FRANCISCO

First Edition

ISBN: 978-1-59780-172-0
Printed in Canada

Night Shade Books
Please visit us on the web at
www.nightshadebooks.com

For Alex, Alisa, and Tansy—the Coode Street Feminist Advisory Committee—for their kindness, support, and advice.

Acknowledgements

This year has been a challenging one and getting this book done has been demanding. I doubt you would be holding it now without the determined assistance of my wife and co-editor Marianne Jablon, who stepped up to the plate and helped get this book ready at the last minute. As always, I'd also like to thank Gary K. Wolfe, whose advice has been invaluable; everyone from *Not if You Were the Last Short Story on Earth* who were my companions again on the journey through the year and provided an invaluable sounding board. I'd also like to thank Howard Morhaim, Jason Williams, Jeremy Lassen, Ross Lockhart, Marty Halpern, John Helfers, Martin H. Greenberg, and Gordon Van Gelder. Thanks also to the following good friends and colleagues without whom this book would have been much poorer, and much less fun to do: Lou Anders, Jack Dann, Ellen Datlow, Gardner Dozois, Sean Williams, and all of the book's contributors.

As always, my biggest thanks go to my family, Marianne, Jessica, and Sophie. Every moment spent working on this book was one stolen from them. I only hope I can repay them.

CONTENTS

INTRODUCTION
JONATHAN STRAHAN

In the Australian winter of 1985 I was still at university, pursuing a fairly useless if interesting degree during the day while spending most of my waking hours engaged in an excited, breathless and far more useful discovery of the science fiction field. It was during that time that I encountered my first "best of the year" anthology, a sprawling selection of stories that the editor opened with a careful assessment of how things were going wrong in SF, or *might* be. A boon of some kind, he reported, was *possibly* coming to an end and there was real fear that bad times might be coming: sales were unreliable, advances were headed south and, in all likelihood, the publishing world would end quite soon.

Gardner Dozois, for it was he writing in the first of his *The Year's Best Science Fiction* series (now in its twenty-eighth year), followed that assessment with two dozen stories—from established writers like Robert Silverberg, Joe Haldeman and Poul Anderson, alongside an incredible array of writers I'd never heard of like Connie Willis, Bruce Sterling, Greg Bear and Kim Stanley Robinson—which rather seemed to make those gloomy assessments irrelevant. How could a field that was producing stories like "Cicada Queen," "Hardfought," "Carrion Comfort" and "Black Air" be anything other than healthy?

I could appreciate then, as I do now, that he was talking about the health of the publishing industry as it was experienced by *writers*, rather than the state of the art of SF and fantasy writing as it was experienced by *readers*, but I still did wonder at the time how the caution of the introduction reconciled with the optimism of the story selection.

I was confronted with this myself when, unexpectedly, in the summer of 1997 I found myself drafting an introduction to *The Year's Best Australian Science Fiction and Fantasy* with my co-editor Jeremy G. Byrne and falling into exactly the same kind of assessment, talking about the publishing business rather than the art. I've now sat down on sixteen separate occasions, both by myself and with others, and

I still struggle to balance the urge to talk about the state of the publishing business rather than focus on the year in short fiction, probably because of a simple but fundamental problem: the year in short fiction is barely done and in many ways is too close to meaningfully assess, even as I attempt to do just that.

It would be easy to describe the rather shaky state that SF and fantasy finds itself in as the first decade of the twenty-first century draws to a close as uneasy. Advances *are* down, sales (especially for short fiction) are down, the midlist (where many fine writers made their livings) is almost completely a thing of the past, booksellers are in trouble and short fiction outlets of all kinds seem to be struggling financially.

As has been the case in the past, large publishers consolidated, reducing staff and focusing on new opportunities. Random House merged Ballantine and Bantam Dell, HarperCollins rebranded Eos and Voyager, HarperCollins sold its new Angry Robot imprint, as did Games Workshop its Solaris Books imprint. The major North American book chains struggled, with reports popping up throughout the year of both Borders and Barnes & Noble being in various kinds of financial trouble. And magazine *Realms of Fantasy*, having closed and been rescued in 2009, was sold and rescued again late in 2010.

This was also the year when eBook publishing really took off. Early in the year publishers publicly slugged it out with Amazon over eBook pricing, but that was quickly swept aside when Apple released its iPad in April. Apple sold three million devices in less than three months, and went on to sell more than eight million during the year. Those eight million new, very high profile e-readers were soon joined by new, cheaper iterations of the Kindle, the Nook and others. E-readers seemed to become a desirable thing to own, the next "it" gadget, and eBook sales increased accordingly, with some publishers saying as year's end approached that eBooks accounted for as much as twenty percent of sales.

That was reflected in the decision by mass market publisher Dorchester to move from traditionally printed books to digital-only editions in August. Perhaps more interesting for SF and fantasy, though, was the comparatively quiet announcement that same month that Gollancz, one of the most respected and important SF imprints in the field, had quietly appointed its first digital publisher. There have been some whispers as to what this might mean for the future, and it's something I for one will be watching with great interest.

But what of the *art* of short SF and fantasy? How is *that* doing? I can imagine you asking. Well, as I've been saying for close to a decade now, it has become almost impossible to keep track of all of the original short fiction published each year. I don't have the February issue of *Locus* to hand, but when I last looked they'd reported close to 3,500 new stories had been published in their most recent year of accounting, and I've long felt that underestimated numbers by a factor of four or five. New stories were published in anthologies, collections, magazines (whether printed on paper or presented with pixels) and pamphlets; they came from publishers of all sizes, and they came every single day. One publisher even launched a service that, rather mind-bogglingly, offered a new story every working day (that's 220 per year, or more than the combined output of *Asimov's*, *Analog*, *F&SF*, *Realms of Fantasy* and *Interzone*). Year's best editors whimpered.

While in recent years anthologies seemed to be providing most of our best short fiction, this year the field seemed to level out with a wide variety of venues producing some excellent work, but no single source really dominating. Unlike 2009, though, I probably found more stories I liked in magazines with almost two-thirds of the contents of this book coming from one periodical or another, and just a third coming from the pages of anthologies.

We are early enough in the digital era that we still find ourselves bound, it seems, to discuss whether magazines appear in print or online. This isn't a particularly useful distinction given that at the end of the day a magazine is a magazine and an issue is an issue. That said, the majority of the stories from magazines that I liked came from online sources. Last year *Tor.com* had a particularly strong year, but this year it was *Subterranean* that dominated. Editor Bill Schafer produced a terrific mix of fantasy, oddball SF and other stuff, including major stories by Rachel Swirsky, Peter S. Beagle, K. J. Parker, Hannu Rajaniemi and many more. He also reprinted excellent long novellas originally published in book form from the likes of Lucius Shepard and Ted Chiang. It was, on balance, the best single source of top notch fiction in 2010. Veteran *Strange Horizons*, which picked up its first World Fantasy Award in October, also had a very strong year with fine stories from the likes of John Kessel, Lavie Tidhar, Sandra McDonald, Meghan McCarron and Theodora Goss. Comparative newcomer *Apex SF* had what was probably its best year yet, publishing some good work including two marvelous fantasies by Ian Tregillis and Theodora Goss. *Clarkesworld*, which after *Tor.com*, was easily the best online magazine of 2009, justifiably picked up the Hugo in August and had another strong (if slightly less dominant) year publishing excellent work by Peter Watts, Nina Kiriki Hoffman, Catherynne M. Valente and others. Newcomer *Lightspeed*, under the able editorship of John Joseph Adams, also began to find its feet across its first half-dozen issues, publishing a terrific story by Genevieve Valentine, and some fine work by Ted Kosmatka, Carol Emshwiller and others.

Of the print magazines, *Asimov's Science Fiction Magazine* had the best year producing terrific work by established regulars like Robert Reed, James Patrick Kelly, Geoffrey A. Landis and Kij Johnson, alongside newer writers like Sara Genge and Felicity Shoulders. Editor Sheila Williams doesn't really get enough credit for the efforts she's put in over recent years to broaden and re-define *Asimov's* but it definitely showed this year. Gordon Van Gelder's *Fantasy & Science Fiction* had another solid year, with strong stories by Bruce Sterling, Paul Park, John Kessel, Steven Popkes, Ian R. Macleod and newcomer Alexandra Duncan. It remains a reliable source of good fiction. *Interzone* also had a good year, producing two excellent stories by Jim Hawkins, who returned to the magazine with his second and third sales after a thirty-year hiatus. There were many other print magazines published, but these were the ones that struck me as the best.

If anthologies weren't quite as dominant in 2010, that's not to say there wasn't a lot of them and that they didn't contain a lot of fine fiction. I should probably note the caveat here that I edited several anthologies in 2010 myself, so I offer without comment SF anthology *Godlike Machines*, fantasy anthologies *Swords and Dark Magic* (edited with Lou Anders), *Legends of Australian Fantasy* (edited with Jack Dann) and *Wings of Fire* (edited with Marianne S. Jablon). All contain work I think deserves your attention. The best original fantasy anthology of the year was Justine Larbalestier and Holly Black's immensely enjoyable *Zombies vs. Unicorns*, which featured excellent work by Diana Peterfreund, Sarah Rees Brennan, Scott Westerfeld, Meg Cabot, Alaya Dawn Johnson and others. If you buy only one original fantasy anthology of the year, this should be it. I was frankly surprised at the quality of *Full Moon City*, a werewolf anthology that featured terrific stories from the likes of Holly Black, Peter S. Beagle and Gene Wolfe. Well worth your attention was the latest from Ellen Datlow and Terri Windling, *The Beastly Bride*, which included strong work from Christopher Barzak, Ellen Kushner and Peter S. Beagle. More tangential to this book, Datlow also edited a strong anthology of ghost stories, *Haunted Legends*, with Nick Mamatas, which featured good work by Jeffrey Ford, Caitlín R. Kiernan and Joe R. Lansdale. Also worth mention is John Joseph Adams's *The Way of the Wizard*, which includes good work by Nnedi Okorafor, Genevieve Valentine and others.

There were, frankly, very few SF anthologies published this year. After my own *Godlike Machines*, the best of these was Nick Gevers and Marty Halpern's *Is Anybody Out There?*, which had an excellent story from Pat Cadigan and very good work from Alexander Irvine and others. 2010 also seemed to have more high profile "bestseller" anthologies than we've seen for a while. Neil Gaiman and Al Sarrantonio delivered *Stories*, while Gardner Dozois and George R. R. Martin edited *Warriors* and *Songs of Love and Death*. All three were mixed genre, and often the non-genre stories were the highlights. Although it was somewhat uneven, the best of these anthologies was *Stories*, which had outstanding stories by Elizabeth Hand and editor Gaiman, alongside fine work from Joe R. Lansdale, Jeffrey Ford and Tim Powers. *Warriors* featured strong work from Joe Haldeman, Howard Waldrop and both editors Dozois and Martin, while *Songs of Love and Death* had good work from Carrie Vaughn, Neil Gaiman and others. 2010 saw the World Science Fiction Convention travel to Australia and a number of strong anthologies were published by Australian small presses to coincide with the event. Easily the best of these was Alisa Krasnostein's *Sprawl*, a suburban fantasy anthology from Twelfth Planet Press which featured excellent work by Peter M. Ball, Angela Slatter, Thoraiya Dyer and others. Also of interest were Tehani Wesseley's *Worlds Next Door* and Liz Grzyb's *Scary Kisses*.

I could go on and talk about reprint anthologies, collections and such but I'm running long as it is, so instead I'll simply say it was another fine year and let you get to reading the wonderful stories that feature in this year's book. As always, I hope you enjoy reading them as much as I've enjoyed compiling them. See you next year!

Jonathan Strahan
Perth, Australia
November 2010

ELEGY FOR A YOUNG ELK
HANNU RAJANIEMI

Hannu Rajaniemi was born in Ylivieska, Finland, and read his first science fiction novel at the age of six—Jules Verne's *20,000 Leagues Under the Sea*. At the age of eight he approached European Space Agency with a fusion-powered spaceship design, which was received with a polite "thank you" note. He studied mathematics and theoretical physics at the University of Oulu and completed a B.Sc. thesis on transcendental numbers. Rajaniemi went on to complete Part III of the Mathematical Tripos at Cambridge University and a Ph.D. in string theory at the University of Edinburgh. After completing his Ph.D., he joined three partners to co-found ThinkTank Maths (TTM). The company provides mathematics-based technologies in the defense, space, and energy sectors. Rajaniemi is a member of an Edinburgh-based writers group which includes Alan Campbell, Jack Deighton, Caroline Dunford, and Charles Stross. His first fiction sale was the short story "Shibuya no Love" to *Futurismic.com*, and his first novel, *The Quantum Thief*, was published by Gollancz in 2010.

The night after Kosonen shot the young elk, he tried to write a poem by the campfire.

It was late April and there was still snow on the ground. He had already taken to sitting outside in the evening, on a log by the fire, in the small clearing where his cabin stood. Otso was more comfortable outside, and he preferred the bear's company to being alone. It snored loudly atop its pile of fir branches.

A wet smell that had traces of elk shit drifted from its drying fur.

He dug a soft-cover notebook and a pencil stub from his pocket. He leafed through it: most of the pages were empty. Words had become slippery, harder to catch than elk. Although not this one: careless and young. An old elk would never have let a man and a bear so close.

He scattered words on the first empty page, gripping the pencil hard.

Antlers. Sapphire antlers. No good. *Frozen flames. Tree roots. Forked destinies.* There had to be words that captured the moment when the crossbow kicked against his shoulder, the meaty sound of the arrow's impact. But it was like trying to catch snowflakes in his palm. He could barely glimpse the crystal structure, and then they melted.

He closed the notebook and almost threw it into the fire, but thought better of it and put it back into his pocket. No point in wasting good paper. Besides, his last toilet roll in the outhouse would run out soon.

"Kosonen is thinking about words again," Otso growled. "Kosonen should drink more booze. Don't need words then. Just sleep."

Kosonen looked at the bear. "You think you are smart, huh?" He tapped his crossbow. "Maybe it's you who should be shooting elk."

"Otso good at smelling. Kosonen at shooting. Both good at drinking." Otso yawned luxuriously, revealing rows of yellow teeth. Then it rolled to its side and let out a satisfied heavy sigh. "Otso will have more booze soon."

Maybe the bear was right. Maybe a drink was all he needed. No point in being a poet: they had already written all the poems in the world, up there, in the sky. They probably had poetry gardens. Or places where you could become words.

But that was not the point. The words needed to come from *him*, a dirty, bearded man in the woods whose toilet was a hole in the ground. Bright words from dark matter, that's what poetry was about.

When it worked.

There were things to do. The squirrels had almost picked the lock the previous night, bloody things. The cellar door needed reinforcing. But that could wait until tomorrow.

He was about to open a vodka bottle from Otso's secret stash in the snow when Marja came down from the sky as rain.

The rain was sudden and cold like a bucket of water poured over your head in the sauna. But the droplets did not touch the ground, they floated around Kosonen. As he watched, they changed shape, joined together and made a woman, spindle-thin bones, mist-flesh and muscle. She looked like a glass sculpture. The small breasts were perfect hemispheres, her sex an equilateral silver triangle. But the face was familiar—small nose and high cheekbones, a sharp-tongued mouth.

Marja.

Otso was up in an instant, by Kosonen's side. "Bad smell, god-smell," it growled. "Otso bites." The rain-woman looked at it curiously.

"Otso," Kosonen said sternly. He gripped the fur in the bear's rough neck tightly, feeling its huge muscles tense. "Otso is Kosonen's friend. Listen to Kosonen. Not time for biting. Time for sleeping. Kosonen will speak to god." Then he set the vodka bottle in the snow right under its nose.

Otso sniffed the bottle and scraped the half-melted snow with its forepaw.

"Otso goes," it finally said. "Kosonen shouts if the god bites. Then Otso comes." It picked up the bottle in its mouth deftly and loped into the woods with a bear's loose, shuffling gait.

"Hi," the rain-woman said.

"Hello," Kosonen said carefully. He wondered if she was real. The plague gods were crafty. One of them could have taken Marja's image from his mind. He looked at the unstrung crossbow and tried to judge the odds: a diamond goddess versus an out-of-shape woodland poet. Not good.

"Your dog does not like me very much," the Marja-thing said. She sat down on Kosonen's log and swung her shimmering legs in the air, back and forth, just like Marja always did in the sauna. It had to be her, Kosonen decided, feeling something jagged in his throat.

He coughed. "Bear, not a dog. A dog would have barked. Otso just bites. Nothing personal, that's just its nature. Paranoid and grumpy."

"Sounds like someone I used to know."

"I'm not paranoid." Kosonen hunched down and tried to get the fire going again. "You learn to be careful, in the woods."

Marja looked around. "I thought we gave you stayers more equipment. It looks a little... primitive here."

"Yeah. We had plenty of gadgets," Kosonen said. "But they weren't plague-proof. I had a smartgun before I had this"—he tapped his crossbow—"but it got infected. I killed it with a big rock and threw it into the swamp. I've got my skis and some tools, and these." Kosonen tapped his temple. "Has been enough so far. So cheers."

He piled up some kindling under a triangle of small logs, and in a moment the flames sprung up again. Three years had been enough to learn about woodcraft at least. Marja's skin looked almost human in the soft light of the fire, and he sat back on Otso's fir branches, watching her. For a moment, neither of them spoke.

"So how are you, these days?" he asked. "Keeping busy?"

Marja smiled. "Your wife grew up. She's a big girl now. You don't want to know how big."

"So... you are not her, then? Who am I talking to?"

"I am her, and I am not her. I'm a partial, but a faithful one. A translation. You wouldn't understand."

Kosonen put some snow in the coffee pot to melt. "All right, so I'm a caveman. Fair enough. But I understand you are here because you want something. So let's get down to business, *perkele*," he swore.

Marja took a deep breath. "We lost something. Something important. Something new. The spark, we called it. It fell into the city."

"I thought you lot kept copies of everything."

"Quantum information. That was a part of the *new* bit. You can't copy it."

"Tough shit."

A wrinkle appeared between Marja's eyebrows. Kosonen remembered it from a thousand fights they had had, and swallowed.

"If that's the tone you want to take, fine," she said. "I thought you'd be glad to see me. I didn't have to come: they could have sent Mickey Mouse. But I wanted to see you. The big Marja wanted to see you. So you have decided to live your life like this, as the tragic figure haunting the woods. That's fine. But you could at least listen. You owe me that much."

Kosonen said nothing.

"I see," Marja said. "You still blame me for Esa."

She was right. It had been her who got the first Santa Claus machine. The boy needs the best we can offer, she said. The world is changing. Can't have him being left behind. Let's make him into a little god, like the neighbor's kid.

"I guess I shouldn't be blaming *you*," Kosonen said. "You're just a… partial. You weren't there."

"I was there," Marja said quietly. "I remember. Better than you, now. I also forget better, and forgive. You never could. You just… wrote poems. The rest of us moved on, and saved the world."

"Great job," Kosonen said. He poked the fire with a stick, and a cloud of sparks flew up into the air with the smoke.

Marja got up. "That's it," she said. "I'm leaving. See you in a hundred years." The air grew cold. A halo appeared around her, shimmering in the firelight.

Kosonen closed his eyes and squeezed his jaw shut tight. He waited for ten seconds. Then he opened his eyes. Marja was still there, staring at him, helpless. He could not help smiling. She could never leave without having the last word.

"I'm sorry," Kosonen said. "It's been a long time. I've been living in the woods with a bear. Doesn't improve one's temper much."

"I didn't really notice any difference."

"All right," Kosonen said. He tapped the fir branches next to him. "Sit down. Let's start over. I'll make some coffee."

Marja sat down, bare shoulder touching his. She felt strangely warm, warmer than the fire almost.

"The firewall won't let us into the city," she said. "We don't have anyone… human enough, not anymore. There was some talk about making one, but… the argument would last a century." She sighed. "We like to argue, in the sky."

Kosonen grinned. "I bet you fit right in." He checked for the wrinkle before continuing. "So you need an errand boy."

"We need help."

Kosonen looked at the fire. The flames were dying now, licking at the blackened wood. There were always new colors in the embers. Or maybe he just always forgot.

He touched Marja's hand. It felt like a soap bubble, barely solid. But she did not pull it away.

"All right," he said. "But just so you know, it's not just for old times' sake."

"Anything we can give you."

"I'm cheap," Kosonen said. "I just want words."

The sun sparkled on the *kantohanki*: snow with a frozen surface, strong enough to carry a man on skis and a bear. Kosonen breathed hard. Even going downhill, keeping pace with Otso was not easy. But in weather like this, there was something glorious about skiing, sliding over blue shadows of trees almost without friction, the snow hissing underneath.

I've sat still too long, he thought. *Should have gone somewhere just to go, not because someone asks.*

In the afternoon, when the sun was already going down, they reached the railroad, a bare gash through the forest, two metal tracks on a bed of gravel. Kosonen removed his skis and stuck them in the snow.

"I'm sorry you can't come along," he told Otso. "But the city won't let you in."

"Otso not a city bear," the bear said. "Otso waits for Kosonen. Kosonen gets sky-bug, comes back. Then we drink booze."

He scratched the rough fur of its neck clumsily. The bear poked Kosonen in the stomach with its nose, so hard that he almost fell. Then it snorted, turned around and shuffled into the woods. Kosonen watched until it vanished among the snow-covered trees.

It took three painful attempts of sticking his fingers down his throat to get the nanoseed Marja gave him to come out. The gagging left a bitter taste in his mouth. Swallowing it had been the only way to protect the delicate thing from the plague. He wiped it in the snow: a transparent bauble the size of a walnut, slippery and warm. It reminded him of the toys you could get from vending machines in supermarkets when he was a child, plastic spheres with something secret inside.

He placed it on the rails carefully, wiped the remains of the vomit from his lips and rinsed his mouth with water. Then he looked at it. Marja knew he would never read instruction manuals, so she had not given him one.

"Make me a train," he said.

Nothing happened. *Maybe it can read my mind,* he thought, and imagined a train, an old steam train, puffing along. Still nothing, just a reflection of the darkening sky on the seed's clear surface. *She always had to be subtle.* Marja could never give a present without thinking about its meaning for days. Standing still let the spring winter chill through his wolf-pelt coat, and he hopped up and down, rubbing his hands together.

With the motion came an idea. He frowned, staring at the seed, and took the notebook from his pocket. Maybe it was time to try out Marja's other gift—or advance payment, however you wanted to look at it. He had barely written the first lines, when the words leaped in his mind like animals woken from slumber. He closed the book, cleared his throat and spoke.

these rails
were worn thin
by wheels
that wrote down
the name of each passenger

in steel and miles
he said,
it's a good thing
the years
ate our flesh too
made us thin and light
so the rails are strong enough
to carry us still
to the city
in our train of glass and words

Doggerel, he thought, but it didn't matter. The joy of words filled his veins like vodka. *Too bad it didn't work —*

The seed blurred. It exploded into a white-hot sphere. The waste heat washed across Kosonen's face. Glowing tentacles squirmed past him, sucking carbon and metal from the rails and trees. They danced like a welder's electric arcs, sketching lines and surfaces in the air.

And suddenly, the train was there.

It was transparent, with paper-thin walls and delicate wheels, as if it had been blown from glass, a sketch of a cartoon steam engine with a single carriage, with spiderweb-like chairs inside, just the way he had imagined it.

He climbed in, expecting the delicate structure to sway under his weight, but it felt rock-solid. The nanoseed lay on the floor innocently, as if nothing had happened. He picked it up carefully, took it outside and buried it in the snow, leaving his skis and sticks as markers. Then he picked up his backpack, boarded the train again and sat down in one of the gossamer seats. Unbidden, the train lurched into motion smoothly. To Kosonen, it sounded like the rails beneath were whispering, but he could not hear the words.

He watched the darkening forest glide past. The day's journey weighed heavily on his limbs. The memory of the snow beneath his skis melted together with the train's movement, and soon Kosonen was asleep.

When he woke up, it was dark. The amber light of the firewall glowed in the horizon, like a thundercloud.

The train had speeded up. The dark forest outside was a blur, and the whispering of the rails had become a quiet staccato song. Kosonen swallowed as the train covered the remaining distance in a matter of minutes. The firewall grew into a misty dome glowing with yellowish light from within. The city was an indistinct silhouette beneath it. The buildings seemed to be in motion, like a giant's shadow puppets.

Then it was a flaming curtain directly in front of the train, an impenetrable wall made from twilight and amber crossing the tracks. Kosonen gripped the delicate frame of his seat, knuckles white. "Slow down!" he shouted, but the train did not hear. It crashed directly into the firewall with a bone-jarring impact. There was a burst of light, and then Kosonen was lifted from his seat.

It was like drowning, except that he was floating in an infinite sea of amber light rather than water. Apart from the light, there was just emptiness. His skin tickled. It took him a moment to realize that he was not breathing.

And then a stern voice spoke.

This is not a place for men, it said. *Closed. Forbidden. Go back.*

"I have a mission," said Kosonen. His voice had no echo in the light. "From your makers. They command you to let me in."

He closed his eyes, and Marja's third gift floated in front of him, not words but a number. He had always been poor at memorizing things, but Marja's touch had been a pen with acid ink, burning it in his mind. He read off the endless digits, one by one.

You may enter, said the firewall. *But only that which is human will leave.*

The train and the speed came back, sharp and real like a paper cut. The twilight glow of the firewall was still there, but instead of the forest, dark buildings loomed around the railway, blank windows staring at him.

Kosonen's hands tickled. They were clean, as were his clothes: every speck of dirt was gone. His skin felt tender and red, like he had just been to the sauna.

The train slowed down at last, coming to a stop in the dark mouth of the station, and Kosonen was in the city.

The city was a forest of metal and concrete that breathed and hummed. The air smelled of ozone. The facades of the buildings around the railway station square looked almost like he remembered them, only subtly wrong. From the corner of his eye he could glimpse them *moving*, shifting in their sleep like stone-skinned animals. There were no signs of life, apart from a cluster of pigeons, hopping back and forth on the stairs, looking at him. They had sapphire eyes.

A bus stopped, full of faceless people who looked like crash test dummies, sitting unnaturally still. Kosonen decided not to get in and started to head across the square, towards the main shopping street: he had to start the search for the spark somewhere. It will glow, Marja had said. You can't miss it.

There was what looked like a car wreck in the parking lot, lying on its side, hood crumpled like a discarded beer can, covered in white pigeon droppings. But when Kosonen walked past it, its engine roared, and the hood popped open. A hissing bundle of tentacles snapped out, reaching for him.

He managed to gain some speed before the car-beast rolled onto its four wheels. There were narrow streets on the other side of the square, too narrow for it to follow. He ran, cold weight in his stomach, legs pumping.

The crossbow beat painfully at his back in its strap, and he struggled to get it over his head.

The beast passed him arrogantly, and turned around. Then it came straight at him. The tentacles spread out from its glowing engine mouth into a fan of serpents.

Kosonen fumbled with a bolt, then loosed it at the thing. The crossbow kicked, but the arrow glanced off its windshield. It seemed to confuse it enough for Kosonen to jump aside. He dove, hit the pavement with a painful thump, and rolled.

"Somebody help *perkele*," he swore with impotent rage, and got up, panting, just as the beast backed off slowly, engine growling. He smelled burning rubber, mixed with ozone. *Maybe I can wrestle it*, he thought like a madman, spreading his arms, refusing to run again. *One last poem in it —*

Something landed in front of the beast, wings fluttering. A pigeon. Both Kosonen and the car-creature stared at it. It made a cooing sound. Then it exploded.

The blast tore at his eardrums, and the white fireball turned the world black for a second. Kosonen found himself on the ground again, ears ringing, lying painfully on top of his backpack. The car-beast was a burning wreck ten meters away, twisted beyond all recognition.

There was another pigeon next to him, picking at what looked like bits of metal. It lifted its head and looked at him, flames reflecting from the tiny sapphire eyes. Then it took flight, leaving a tiny white dropping behind.

The main shopping street was empty. Kosonen moved carefully in case there were more of the car-creatures around, staying close to narrow alleys and door-ways. The firewall light was dimmer between the buildings, and strange lights danced in the windows.

Kosonen realized he was starving: he had not eaten since noon, and the journey and the fight had taken their toll. He found an empty cafe in a street corner that seemed safe, set up his small travel cooker on a table and boiled some water. The supplies he had been able to bring consisted mainly of canned soup and dried elk meat, but his growling stomach was not fussy. The smell of food made him careless.

"This is my place," said a voice. Kosonen leapt up, startled, reaching for the crossbow.

There was a stooped, trollish figure at the door, dressed in rags. His face shone with sweat and dirt, framed by matted hair and beard. His porous skin was full of tiny sapphire growths, like pockmarks. Kosonen had thought living in the woods had made him immune to human odors, but the stranger carried a bitter stench of sweat and stale booze that made him want to retch.

The stranger walked in and sat down at a table opposite Kosonen. "But that's all right," he said amicably. "Don't get many visitors these days. Have to be neighborly. *Saatana*, is that Blaband soup that you've got?"

"You're welcome to some," Kosonen said warily. He had met some of the other stayers over the years, but usually avoided them—they all had their own reasons for not going up, and not much in common.

"Thanks. That's neighborly indeed. I'm Pera, by the way." The troll held out his hand.

Kosonen shook it gingerly, feeling strange jagged things under Pera's skin. It was like squeezing a glove filled with powdered glass. "Kosonen. So you live here?"

"Oh, not here, not in the center. I come here to steal from the buildings. But they've become really smart, and stingy. Can't even find soup anymore. The Stockmann department store almost ate me yesterday. It's not easy life here." Pera shook his head. "But better than outside." There was a sly look in his eyes. *Are you staying because you want to,* wondered Kosonen, *or because the firewall won't let you out anymore?*

"Not afraid of the plague gods, then?" he asked aloud. He passed Pera one of the heated soup tins. The city stayer slurped it down with one gulp, smell of minestrone mingling with the other odors.

"Oh, you don't have to be afraid of them anymore. They're all dead."

Kosonen looked at Pera, startled. "How do you know?"

"The pigeons told me."

"The pigeons?"

Pera took something carefully from the pocket of his ragged coat. It was a pigeon. It had a sapphire beak and eyes, and a trace of blue in its feathers. It struggled in Pera's grip, wings fluttering.

"My little buddies," Pera said. "I think you've already met them."

"Yes," Kosonen said. "Did you send the one that blew up that car thing?"

"You have to help a neighbor out, don't you? Don't mention it. The soup was good."

"What did they say about the plague gods?"

Pera grinned a gap-toothed grin. "When the gods got locked up here, they started fighting. Not enough power to go around, you see. So one of them had to be the top dog, like in *Highlander*. The pigeons show me pictures, sometimes. Bloody stuff. Explosions. Nanites eating men. But finally they were all gone, every last one. My playground now."

So Esa is gone, too. Kosonen was surprised how sharp the feeling of loss was, even now. *Better like this.* He swallowed. *Let's get the job done first. No time to mourn. Let's think about it when we get home. Write a poem about it. And tell Marja.*

"All right," Kosonen said. "I'm hunting too. Do you think your… buddies could find it? Something that glows. If you help me, I'll give you all the soup I've got. And elk meat. And I'll bring more later. How does that sound?"

"Pigeons can find anything," said Pera, licking his lips.

The pigeon-man walked through the city labyrinth like his living room, accompanied by a cloud of the chimera birds. Every now and then, one of them would land on his shoulder and touch his ear with his beak, as if to whisper.

"Better hurry," Pera said. "At night, it's not too bad, but during the day the houses get younger and start thinking."

Kosonen had lost all sense of direction. The map of the city was different from the last time he had been here, in the old human days. His best guess was that they were getting somewhere close to the cathedral in the old town, but he couldn't be sure. Navigating the changed streets felt like walking through the veins of some giant animal, convoluted and labyrinthine. Some buildings were enclosed in what looked like black film, rippling like oil. Some had grown together, organic-looking structures of brick and concrete, blocking streets and making the ground uneven.

"We're not far," Pera said. "They've seen it. Glowing like a pumpkin lantern, they say." He giggled. The amber light of the firewall grew brighter as they walked. It was hotter, too, and Kosonen was forced to discard his old Pohjanmaa sweater.

They passed an office building that had become a sleeping face, a genderless Easter Island countenance. There was more life in this part of the town too, sapphire-eyed animals, sleek cats looking at them from windowsills. Kosonen saw a fox crossing the street: it gave them one bright look and vanished down a sewer hole.

Then they turned a corner, where faceless men wearing fashion from ten years ago danced together in a shop window, and saw the cathedral.

It had grown to gargantuan size, dwarfing every other building around it. It was an anthill of dark-red brick and hexagonal doorways. It buzzed with life. Cats with sapphire claws clung to its walls like sleek gargoyles. Thick pigeon flocks fluttered around its towers. Packs of azure-tailed rats ran in and out of open, massive doors like armies on a mission. And there were insects everywhere, filling the air with a drill-like buzzing sound, moving in dense black clouds like a giant's black breath.

"Oh, *jumalauta*," Kosonen said. "*That's* where it fell?"

"Actually, no. I was just supposed to bring you here," Pera said.

"What?"

"Sorry. I lied. It *was* like in *Highlander:* there is one of them left. And he wants to meet you."

Kosonen stared at Pera, dumbfounded. The pigeons landed on the other man's shoulders and arms like a gray fluttering cloak. They seized his rags and hair and skin with sharp claws, wings started beating furiously. As Kosonen stared, Pera rose in the air.

"No hard feelings, I just had a better deal from him. Thanks for the soup," he shouted. In a moment, Pera was a black scrap of cloth in the sky.

The earth shook. Kosonen fell to his knees. The window eyes that lined the street lit up, full of bright, malevolent light.

He tried to run. He did not make it far before they came, the fingers of the city: the pigeons, the insects, a buzzing swarm that covered him. A dozen chimera rats clung to his skull, and he could feel the humming of their flywheel hearts. Something sharp bit through the bone. The pain grew like a forest fire, and Kosonen screamed.

The city spoke. Its voice was a thunderstorm, words made from the shaking of the earth and the sighs of buildings. Slow words, squeezed from stone.

Dad, the city said.

The pain was gone. Kosonen heard the gentle sound of waves, and felt a warm wind on his face. He opened his eyes.

"Hi, Dad," Esa said.

They sat on the summerhouse pier, wrapped in towels, skin flushed from the sauna. It was evening, with a hint of chill in the air, Finnish summer's gentle reminder that things were not forever. The sun hovered above the blue-tinted treetops. The lake surface was calm, full of liquid reflections.

"I thought," Esa said, "that you'd like it here."

Esa was just like Kosonen remembered him, a pale, skinny kid, ribs showing, long arms folded across his knees, stringy wet hair hanging on his forehead. But his eyes were the eyes of a city, dark orbs of metal and stone.

"I do," Kosonen said. "But I can't stay."

"Why not?"

"There is something I need to do."

"We haven't seen each other in ages. The sauna is warm. I've got some beer cooling in the lake. Why the rush?"

"I should be afraid of you," Kosonen said. "You killed people. Before they put you here."

"You don't know what it's like," Esa said. "The plague does everything you want. It gives you things you don't even know you want. It turns the world soft. And sometimes it tears it apart for you. You think a thought, and things break. You can't help it."

The boy closed his eyes. "You want things too. I know you do. That's why you are here, isn't it? You want your precious words back."

Kosonen said nothing.

"Mom's errand boy, *vittu.* So they fixed your brain, flushed the booze out. So you can write again. Does it feel good? For a moment there I thought you came here for me. But that's not the way it ever worked, was it?"

"I didn't know—"

"I can see the inside of your head, you know," Esa said. "I've got my fingers inside your skull. One thought, and my bugs will eat you, bring you here for good. Quality time forever. What do you say to that?"

And there it was, the old guilt. "We worried about you, every second, after you were born," Kosonen said. "We only wanted the best for you."

It had seemed so natural. How the boy played with his machine that made other machines. How things started changing shape when you thought at them. How Esa smiled when he showed Kosonen the talking starfish that the machine had made.

"And then I had one bad day."

"I remember," Kosonen said. He had been home late, as usual. Esa had been a diamond tree, growing in his room. There were starfish everywhere, eating the walls and the floor, making more of themselves. And that was only the beginning.

"So go ahead. Bring me here. It's your turn to make me into what you want. Or end it all. I deserve it."

Esa laughed softly. "And why would I do that, to an old man?" He sighed. "You know, I'm old too now. Let me show you." He touched Kosonen's shoulder gently and

Kosonen was the city. His skin was of stone and concrete, pores full of the god-plague. The streets and buildings were his face, changing and shifting with every thought and emotion. His nervous system was diamond and optic fiber. His hands were chimera animals.

The firewall was all around him, in the sky and in the cold bedrock, insubstantial but adamantine, squeezing from every side, cutting off energy, making sure he could not think fast. But he could still dream, weave words and images into threads, make worlds out of the memories he had and the memories of the smaller gods he had eaten to become the city. He sang his dreams in radio waves, not caring if the firewall let them through or not, louder and louder—

"Here," Esa said from far away. "Have a beer."

Kosonen felt a chilly bottle in his hand, and drank. The dream-beer was strong and real. The malt taste brought him back. He took a deep breath, letting the fake summer evening wash away the city.

"Is that why you brought me here? To show me that?" he asked.

"Well, no," Esa said, laughing. His stone eyes looked young, suddenly. "I just wanted you to meet my girlfriend."

The quantum girl had golden hair and eyes of light. She wore many faces at once, like a Hindu goddess. She walked to the pier with dainty steps. Esa's summerland showed its cracks around her: there were fracture lines in her skin, with otherworldly colors peeking out.

"This is Säde," Esa said.

She looked at Kosonen, and spoke, a bubble of words, a superposition, all possible greetings at once.

"Nice to meet you," Kosonen said.

"They did something right when they made her, up there," said Esa. "She lives in many worlds at once, thinks in qubits. And this is the world where she wants to be. With me." He touched her shoulder gently. "She heard my songs and ran away."

"Marja said she fell," Kosonen said. "That something was broken."

"She said what they wanted her to say. They don't like it when things don't go according to plan."

Säde made a sound, like the chime of a glass bell.

"The firewall keeps squeezing us," Esa said. "That's how it was made. Make things go slower and slower here, until we die. Säde doesn't fit in here, this place is too small. So you will take her back home, before it's too late." He smiled. "I'd rather you do it than anyone else."

"That's not fair," Kosonen said. He squinted at Säde. She was too bright to look at. *But what can I do? I'm just a slab of meat. Meat and words.*

The thought was like a pine cone, rough in his grip, but with a seed of something in it.

"I think there is a poem in you two," he said.

Kosonen sat on the train again, watching the city stream past. It was early morning. The sunrise gave the city new hues: purple shadows and gold, ember colors. Fatigue pulsed in his temples. His body ached. The words of a poem weighed on his mind.

Above the dome of the firewall he could see a giant diamond starfish, a drone of the sky people, watching, like an outstretched hand.

They came to see what happened, he thought. *They'll find out.*

This time, he embraced the firewall like a friend, and its tingling brightness washed over him. And deep within, the stern-voiced watchman came again. It said nothing this time, but he could feel its presence, scrutinizing, seeking things that did not belong in the outside world.

Kosonen gave it everything.

The first moment when he knew he had put something real on paper. The disappointment when he realized that a poet was not much in a small country, piles of cheaply printed copies of his first collection, gathering dust in little bookshops. The jealousy he had felt when Marja gave birth to Esa, what a pale shadow of that giving birth to words was. The tracks of the elk in the snow and the look in its eyes when it died.

He felt the watchman step aside, satisfied.

Then he was through. The train emerged into the real, undiluted dawn. He looked back at the city, and saw fire raining from the starfish. Pillars of light cut through the city in geometric patterns, too bright to look at, leaving only white-hot plasma in their wake.

Kosonen closed his eyes and held on to the poem as the city burned.

Kosonen planted the nanoseed in the woods. He dug a deep hole in the half-frozen peat with his bare hands, under an old tree stump. He sat down, took off his cap, dug out his notebook and started reading. The pencil-scrawled words became bright in his mind, and after a while he didn't need to look at them anymore.

The poem rose from the words like a titanic creature from an ocean, first showing just a small extremity but then soaring upwards in a spray of glossolalia, mountain-like. It was a stream of hissing words and phonemes, an endless spell that tore at his throat. And with it came the quantum information from the microtubules of his neurons, where the bright-eyed girl now lived, and jagged impulses from synapses where his son was hiding.

The poem swelled into a roar. He continued until his voice was a hiss. Only the nanoseed could hear, but that was enough. Something stirred under the peat.

When the poem finally ended, it was evening. Kosonen opened his eyes. The first thing he saw were the sapphire antlers, sparkling in the last rays of the sun.

Two young elk looked at him. One was smaller, more delicate, and its large brown eyes held a hint of sunlight. The other was young and skinny, but wore its budding antlers with pride. It held Kosonen's gaze, and in its eyes he saw shadows of the city. Or reflections in a summer lake, perhaps.

They turned around and ran into the woods, silent, fleet-footed and free.

Kosonen was opening the cellar door when the rain came back. It was barely a shower this time: the droplets formed Marja's face in the air. For a moment he thought he saw her wink. Then the rain became a mist, and was gone. He propped the door open.

The squirrels stared at him curiously from the trees.

"All yours, gentlemen," Kosonen said. "Should be enough for next winter. I don't need it anymore."

Otso and Kosonen left at noon, heading north. Kosonen's skis slid along easily in the thinning snow. The bear pulled a sledge loaded with equipment. When they were well away from the cabin, it stopped to sniff at a fresh trail.

"Elk," it growled. "Otso is hungry. Kosonen shoot an elk. Need meat for the journey. Kosonen did not bring enough booze."

Kosonen shook his head.

"I think I'm going to learn to fish," he said.

THE TRUTH IS A CAVE
IN THE BLACK MOUNTAINS
NEIL GAIMAN

Neil Gaiman was born in England and worked as a freelance journalist before co-editing *Ghastly Beyond Belief* (with Kim Newman) and writing *Don't Panic: The Official Hitchhiker's Guide to the Galaxy Companion*. He started writing graphic novels and comics with *Violent Cases* in 1987, and with the seventy-five installments of award-winning series *The Sandman* established himself as one of the most important comics writers of his generation. His first novel, *Good Omens* (with Terry Pratchett), appeared in 1991, followed by *Neverwhere, Stardust, American Gods, Coraline,* and *Anansi Boys*. His most recent novel is *The Graveyard Book*. Gaiman's work has won the Caldecott, Newbery, Hugo, World Fantasy, Bram Stoker, Locus, Geffen, International Horror Guild, Mythopoeic, and Will Eisner Comic Industry awards. Gaiman currently lives near Minneapolis.

You ask me if I can forgive myself? I can forgive myself for many things. For where I left him. For what I did. But I will not forgive myself for the year that I hated my daughter, when I believed her to have run away, perhaps to the city. During that year I forbade her name to be mentioned, and if her name entered my prayers when I prayed, it was to ask that she would one day learn the meaning of what she had done, of the dishonor that she had brought to our family, of the red that ringed her mother's eyes.

I hate myself for that, and nothing will ease that, not even what happened that night, on the side of the mountain.

I had searched for nearly ten years, although the trail was cold. I would say that I found him by accident, but I do not believe in accidents. If you walk the path, eventually you must arrive at the cave.

But that was later. First, there was the valley on the mainland, the whitewashed house in the gentle meadow with the burn splashing through it, a house that sat like a square of white sky against the green of the grass and the heather just beginning to purple.

And there was a boy outside the house, picking wool from off a thorn-bush.

He did not see me approaching, and he did not look up until I said, "I used to do that. Gather the wool from the thorn-bushes and twigs. My mother would wash it, then she would make me things with it. A ball, and a doll."

He turned. He looked shocked, as if I had appeared out of nowhere. And I had not. I had walked many a mile, and had many more miles to go. I said, "I walk quietly. Is this the house of Calum MacInnes?"

The boy nodded, drew himself up to his full height, which was perhaps two fingers bigger than mine, and he said, "I am Calum MacInnes."

"Is there another of that name? For the Calum MacInnes that I seek is a grown man."

The boy said nothing, just unknotted a thick clump of sheep's wool from the clutching fingers of the thorn-bush. I said, "Your father, perhaps? Would he be Calum MacInnes as well?"

The boy was peering at me. "What are you?" he asked.

"I am a small man," I told him. "But I am a man, nonetheless, and I am here to see Calum MacInnes."

"Why?" The boy hesitated. Then, "And why are you so small?"

I said, "Because I have something to ask your father. Man's business." And I saw a smile start at the tips of his lips. "It's not a bad thing to be small, young Calum. There was a night when the Campbells came knocking on my door, a whole troop of them, twelve men with knives and sticks, and they demanded of my wife, Morag, that she produce me, as they were there to kill me, in revenge for some imagined slight. And she said, 'Young Johnnie, run down to the far meadow, and tell your father to come back to the house, that I sent for him.' And the Campbells watched as the boy ran out the door. They knew that I was a most dangerous person. But nobody had told them that I was a wee man, or if that had been told them, it had not been believed."

"Did the boy call you?" said the lad.

"It was no boy," I told him, "but me myself, it was. And they'd had me, and still I walked out the door and through their fingers."

The boy laughed. Then he said, "Why were the Campbells after you?"

"It was a disagreement about the ownership of cattle. They thought the cows were theirs. I maintained the Campbell's ownership of them had ended the first night the cows had come with me over the hills."

"Wait here," said young Calum MacInnes

I sat by the burn and looked up at the house. It was a good-sized house: I would have taken it for the house of a doctor or a man of law, not of a border reaver. There were pebbles on the ground and I made a pile of them, and I tossed the pebbles, one by one into the burn. I have a good eye, and I enjoyed rattling the pebbles over the meadow and into the water. I had thrown a hundred stones when the boy returned, accompanied by a tall, loping man. His hair was streaked with gray, his face was long and wolfish. There are no wolves in those hills, not any longer, and the bears have gone too.

"Good day to you," I said.

He said nothing in return, only stared; I am used to stares. I said, "I am seeking Calum MacInnes. If you are he, say so, I will greet you. If you are not he, tell me now, and I will be on my way."

"What business would you have with Calum MacInnes?"

"I wish to hire him, as a guide."

"And where is it you would wish to be taken?"

I stared at him. "That is hard to say," I told him. "For there are some who say it does not exist. There is a certain cave on the Misty Isle."

He said nothing. Then he said, "Calum, go back to the house."

"But da—"

"Tell your mother I said she was to give you some tablet. You like that. Go on."

Expressions crossed the boy's face—puzzlement, hunger, happiness—and then he turned and ran back to the white house.

Calum MacInnes said, "Who sent you here?"

I pointed to the burn as it splashed its way between us on its journey down the hill. "What's that?" I asked.

"Water," he replied.

"And they say there is a king across it," I told him.

I did not know him then at all, and never knew him well, but his eyes became guarded, and his head cocked to one side. "How do I know you are who you say you are?"

"I have claimed nothing," I said. "Just that there are those who have heard there is a cave on the Misty Isle, and that you might know the way."

He said, "I will not tell you where the cave is."

"I am not here asking for directions. I seek a guide. And two travel more safely than one."

He looked me up and down, and I waited for the joke about my size, but he did not make it, and for that I was grateful. He just said, "When we reach the cave, I will not go inside. You must bring out the gold yourself."

I said, "It is all one to me."

He said, "You can only take what you carry. I will not touch it. But yes, I will take you."

I said, "You will be paid well for your trouble." I reached into my jerkin, handed him the pouch I had in there. "This for taking me. Another, twice the size, when we return."

He poured the coins from the pouch into his huge hand, and he nodded. "Silver," he said. "Good." Then, "I will say good bye to my wife and son."

"Is there nothing you need to bring?"

He said, "I was a reaver in my youth, and reavers travel light. I'll bring a rope, for the mountains." He patted his dirk, which hung from his belt, and went back into the whitewashed house. I never saw his wife, not then, nor at any other time.

I do not know what color her hair was.

I threw another fifty stones into the burn as I waited, until he returned, with a coil of rope thrown over one shoulder, and then we walked together away from a house too grand for any reaver, and we headed west.

The mountains between the rest of the world and the coast are gradual hills, visible from a distance as gentle, purple, hazy things, like clouds. They seem inviting. They are slow mountains, the kind you can walk up easily, like walking up a hill, but they are hills that take a full day and more to climb. We walked up the hill, and by the end of the first day we were cold.

I saw snow on the peaks above us, although it was high summer.

We said nothing to each other that first day. There was nothing to be said. We knew where we were going.

We made a fire, from dried sheep dung and a dead thorn-bush: we boiled water and made our porridge, each of us throwing a handful of oats and a fingerpinch of salt into the little pan I carried. His handful was huge, and my handful was small, like my hands, which made him smile and say, "I hope you will not be eating half of the porridge."

I said I would not and, indeed, I did not, for my appetite is smaller than that of a full-grown man. But this is a good thing, I believe, for I can keep going in the wild on nuts and berries that would not keep a bigger person from starving.

A path of sorts ran across the high hills, and we followed it and encountered almost nobody: a tinker and his donkey, piled high with old pots, and a girl leading the donkey, who smiled at me when she thought me to be a child, and then scowled when she perceived me to be what I am, and would have thrown a stone at me had the tinker not slapped her hand with the switch he had been using to encourage the donkey; and, later, we overtook an old woman and a man she said was her grandson, on their way back across the hills. We ate with her, and she told us that she had attended the birth of her first great-grandchild, that it was a good birth. She said she would tell our fortunes from the lines in our palms, if we had coins to cross her palm. I gave the old biddy a clipped lowland groat, and she looked at my palm.

She said, "I see death in your past and death in your future."

"Death waits in all our futures," I said.

She paused, there in the highest of the high lands, where the summer winds have winter on their breath, where they howl and whip and slash the air like knives. She said, "There was a woman in a tree. There will be a man in a tree."

I said, "Will this mean anything to me?"

"One day. Perhaps." She said, "Beware of gold. Silver is your friend." And then she was done with me.

To Calum MacInnes she said, "Your palm has been burned." He said that was true. She said, "Give me your other hand, your left hand." He did so. She gazed at it, intently. Then, "You return to where you began. You will be higher than most other men. And there is no grave waiting for you, where you are going."

He said, "You tell me that I will not die?"

"It is a left-handed fortune. I know what I have told you, and no more."

She knew more. I saw it in her face.

That was the only thing of any importance that occurred to us on the second day.

We slept in the open that night. The night was clear and cold, and the sky was hung with stars that seemed so bright and close I felt as if I could have reached out my arm and gathered them, like berries.

We lay side by side beneath the stars, and Calum MacInnes said, "Death awaits you, she said. But death does not wait for me. I think mine was the better fortune."

"Perhaps."

"Ah," he said. "It is all nonsense. Old woman-talk. It is not truth."

I woke in the dawn mist to see a stag, watching us, curiously.

The third day we crested those mountains, and we began to walk downhill.

My companion said, "When I was a boy, my father's dirk fell into the cooking fire. I pulled it out, but the metal hilt was as hot as the flames. I did not expect this, but I would not let the dirk go. I carried it away from the fire, and plunged the sword into the water. It made steam. I remember that. My palm was burned, and my hand curled, as if it was meant to carry a sword until the end of time."

I said, "You, with your hand. Me, only a little man. It's fine heroes we are, who seek our fortunes on the Misty Isle."

He barked a laugh, short and without humor. "Fine heroes," was all he said.

The rain began to fall then, and did not stop falling. That night we passed a small croft house. There was a trickle of smoke from its chimney, and we called out for the owner, but there was no response.

I pushed open the door and called again. The place was dark, but I could smell tallow, as if a candle had been burning and had recently been snuffed.

"No one at home," said Calum, but I shook my head and walked forward, then leaned down into the darkness beneath the bed.

"Would you care to come out?" I asked. "For we are travellers, seeking warmth and shelter and hospitality. We would share with you our oats and our salt and our whisky. And we will not harm you."

At first the woman, hidden beneath the bed, said nothing, and then she said, "My husband is away in the hills. He told me to hide myself away if the strangers come, for fear of what they might do to me."

I said, "I am but a little man, good lady, no bigger than a child, you could send me flying with a blow. My companion is a full-sized man, but I do swear that we shall do nothing to you, save partake of your hospitality, and dry ourselves. Please do come out."

All covered with dust and spiderwebs she was when she emerged, but even with her face all begrimed, she was beautiful, and even with her hair all webbed and grayed with dust it was still long and thick, and golden red. For a heartbeat she put me in the mind of my daughter, but that my daughter would look a man in the eye, while this one glanced only at the ground fearfully, like something expecting to be beaten.

I gave her some of our oats, and Calum produced strips of dried meat from his pocket, and she went out to the field and returned with a pair of scrawny turnips, and she prepared food for the three of us.

I ate my fill. She had no appetite. I believe that Calum was still hungry when his meal was done. He poured whisky for the three of us: she took but a little, and that with water. The rain rattled on the roof of the house, and dripped in the corner, and, unwelcoming though it was, I was glad that I was inside.

It was then that a man came through the door. He said nothing, only stared at us, untrusting, angry. He pulled off his cape of oiled sacking, and his hat, and he dropped them on the earth floor. They dripped and puddled. The silence was oppressive.

Calum MacInnes said, "Your wife gave us hospitality, when we found her. Hard enough she was in the finding."

"We asked for hospitality," I said. "As we ask it of you."

The man said nothing, only grunted.

In the high lands, people spend words as if they were golden coins. But the custom is strong there: strangers who ask for hospitality must be granted it, though you have blood-feud against them and their clan or kin.

The woman—little more than a girl she was, while her husband's beard was gray and white, so I wondered if she was his daughter for a moment, but no: there was but one bed, scarcely big enough for two—the woman went outside, into the sheep pen that adjoined the house, and returned with oatcakes and a dried ham she must have hidden there, which she sliced thin, and placed on a wooden trencher before the man.

Calum poured the man whisky, and said, "We seek the Misty Isle. Do you know if it is there?"

The man looked at us. The winds are bitter in the high lands, and they would whip the words from a man's lips. He pursed his mouth, then he said, "Aye. I saw it from the peak this morning. It's there. I cannot say if it will be there tomorrow."

We slept on the hard-earth floor of that cottage. The fire went out, and there was no warmth from the hearth. The man and his woman slept in their bed, behind the curtain. He had his way with her, beneath the sheepskin that covered that bed, and before he did that, he beat her for feeding us and for letting us in. I heard them, and could not stop hearing them, and sleep was hard in the finding that night.

I have slept in the homes of the poor, and I have slept in palaces, and I have slept beneath the stars, and would have told you before that night that all places were one to me. But I woke before first light, convinced we had to be gone from that place, but not knowing why, and I woke Calum by putting a finger to his lips, and silently we left that croft on the mountainside without saying our farewells, and I have never been more pleased to be gone from anywhere.

We were a mile from that place when I said, "The island. You asked if it would be there. Surely, an island is there, or it is not there."

Calum hesitated. He seemed to be weighing his words, and then he said, "The Misty Isle is not as other places. And the mist that surrounds it is not like other mists."

We walked down a path worn by hundreds of years of sheep and deer and few enough men.

He said, "They also call it the Winged Isle. Some say it is because the island, if seen from above, would look like butterfly wings. And I do not know the truth of it." Then, "And what is truth? said jesting Pilate."

It is harder coming down than it is going up.

I thought about it. "Sometimes I think that truth is a place. In my mind, it is like a city: there can be a hundred roads, a thousand paths, that will all take you, eventually, to the same place. It does not matter where you come from. If you walk toward the truth, you will reach it, whatever path you take."

Calum MacInnes looked down at me and said nothing. Then, "You are wrong. The truth is a cave in the black mountains. There is one way there, and one only, and that way is treacherous and hard, and if you choose the wrong path you will die alone, on the mountainside."

We crested the ridge, and we looked down to the coast. I could see villages below, beside the water. And I could see high black mountains before me, on the other side of the sea, coming out of the mist.

Calum said, "There's your cave. In those mountains."

The bones of the earth, I thought, seeing them. And then I became uncomfortable, thinking of bones, and to distract myself, I said, "And how many times is it you have been there?"

"Only once." He hesitated. "I searched for it all my sixteenth year, for I had heard the legends, and I believed if I sought I should find. I was seventeen when I reached it, and came back with all the gold coins I could carry."

"And were you not frightened of the curse?"

"When I was young, I was afraid of nothing."

"What did you do with your gold?"

"A portion I buried and I alone know where. The rest I used as bride-price for the woman I loved, and I built a fine house with it."

He stopped as if he had already said too much.

There was no ferryman at the jetty. Only a small boat, hardly big enough for three full-sized men, tied to a tree trunk on the shore, all twisted and half-dead, and a bell beside it.

I sounded the bell, and soon enough a fat man came down the shore.

He said to Calum, "It will cost you a shilling for the ferry, and your boy, three pennies."

I stood tall. I am not as big as other men are, but I have as much pride as any of them. "I am also a man," I said, "I'll pay your shilling."

The ferryman looked me up and down, then he scratched his beard. "I beg your pardon. My eyes are not what they once were. I shall take you to the island."

I handed him a shilling. He weighed it in his hand. "That's ninepence you did not cheat me out of. Nine pennies are a lot of money in this dark age." The water was the color of slate, although the sky was blue, and whitecaps chased one another across the water's surface. He untied the boat and hauled it, rattling, down the shingle to the water. We waded out into the cold channel, and clambered inside.

The splash of oars on seawater, and the boat was propelled forward in easy movements. I sat closest to the ferryman. I said, "Ninepence. It is good wages. But I have heard of a cave in the mountains on the Misty Isle, filled with gold coins, the treasure of the ancients."

He shook his head dismissively.

Calum was staring at me, lips pressed together so hard they were white. I ignored him and asked the man again, "A cave filled with golden coins, a gift from the Norsemen or the Southerners or from those who they say were here long before any of us: those who fled into the West as the people came."

"Heard of it," said the ferryman. "Heard also of the curse of it. I reckon that the one can take care of the other." He spat into the sea. Then he said, "You're an honest man, dwarf. I see it in your face. Do not seek this cave. No good can come of it."

"I am sure you are right," I told him, without guile.

"I am certain I am," he said. "For not every day is it that I take a reaver and a little dwarfy man to the Misty Isle." Then he said, "In this part of the world, it is not considered lucky to talk about those who went to the West." We rode the rest of the boat journey in silence, though the sea became choppier, and the waves splashed into the side of the boat, such that I held on with both hands for fear of being swept away.

And after what seemed like half a lifetime the boat was tied to a long jetty of black stones. We walked the jetty as the waves crashed around us, the salt spray kissing our faces. There was a humpbacked man at the landing selling oatcakes and plums dried until they were almost stones. I gave him a penny and filled my jerkin pockets with them.

We walked on into the Misty Isle.

I am old now, or at least, I am no longer young, and everything I see reminds me of something else I've seen, such that I see nothing for the first time. A bonny girl, her hair fiery red, reminds me only of another hundred such lasses, and their mothers, and what they were as they grew, and what they looked like when they died. It is the curse of age, that all things are reflections of other things.

I say that, but my time on the Misty Isle, that is also called, by the wise, the

Winged Isle, reminds me of nothing but itself.

It is a day from that jetty until you reach the black mountains.

Calum MacInnes looked at me, half his size or less, and he set off at a loping stride, as if challenging me to keep up. His legs propelled him across the ground, which was wet, and all ferns and heather.

Above us, low clouds were scudding, gray and white and black, hiding each other and revealing and hiding again.

I let him get ahead of me, let him press on into the rain, until he was swallowed by the wet, gray haze. Then, and only then, I ran.

This is one of the secret things of me, the things I have not revealed to any person, save to Morag, my wife, and Johnnie and James, my sons, and Flora, my daughter (may the Shadows rest her poor soul): I can run, and I can run well, and, if I need to I can run faster and longer and more sure-footedly than any full-sized man; and it was like this that I ran then, through the mist and the rain, taking to the high ground and the black-rock ridges, yet keeping below the skyline.

He was ahead of me, but I spied him soon, and I ran on and I ran past him, on the high ground, with the brow of the hill between us. Below us was a stream. I can run for days without stopping. That is the first of my three secrets, and one secret I have revealed to no man.

We had discussed already where we would camp that first night on the Misty Isle, and Calum had told me that we would spend the night beneath the rock that is called Man and Dog, for it is said that it looks like an old man with his dog by his side, and I reached it late in the afternoon. There was a shelter beneath the rock, which was protected and dry, and some of those who had been before us had left firewood behind, sticks and twigs and branches. I made a fire and dried myself in front of it and took the chill from my bones. The woodsmoke blew out across the heather.

It was dark when Calum loped into the shelter and looked at me as if he had not expected to see me that side of midnight. I said, "What took you so long, Calum MacInnes?"

He said nothing, only stared at me. I said, "There is trout, boiled in mountain water, and a fire to warm your bones."

He nodded. We ate the trout, drank whisky to warm ourselves. There was a mound of heather and of ferns, dried and brown, piled high in the rear of the shelter, and we slept upon that, wrapped tight in our damp cloaks.

I woke in the night. There was cold steel against my throat—the flat of the blade, not the edge. I said, "And why would you ever kill me in the night, Calum MacInnes? For our way is long, and our journey is not yet over."

He said, "I do not trust you, dwarf."

"It is not me you must trust," I told him, "but those that I serve. And if you left with me but return without me, there are those who will know the name of Calum MacInnes, and cause it to be spoken in the shadows."

The cold blade remained at my throat. He said, "How did you get ahead of me?"

"And here was I, repaying ill with good, for I made you food and a fire. I am a hard man to lose, Calum MacInnes, and it ill becomes a guide to do as you did today. Now, take your dirk from my throat and let me sleep."

He said nothing, but after a few moments, the blade was removed. I forced myself neither to sigh nor to breathe, hoping he could not hear my heart pounding in my chest; and I slept no more that night.

For breakfast, I made porridge, and threw in some dried plums to soften them.

The mountains were black and gray against the white of the sky. We saw eagles, huge and ragged of wing, circling above us. Calum set a sober pace and I walked beside him, taking two steps for every one of his.

"How long?" I asked him.

"A day. Perhaps two. It depends upon the weather. If the clouds come down then two days, or even three…"

The clouds came down at noon and the world was blanketed by a mist that was worse than rain: droplets of water hung in the air, soaked our clothes and our skin: the rocks we walked upon became treacherous and Calum and I slowed in our ascent, stepped carefully. We were walking up the mountain, not climbing, up goat paths and craggy sharp ways. The rocks were black and slippery: we walked, and climbed and clambered and clung, we slipped and slid and stumbled and staggered, and, even in the mist, Calum knew where he was going, and I followed him.

He paused at a waterfall that splashed across our path, thick as the trunk of an oak. He took the thin rope from his shoulders, wrapped it about a rock.

"This was not here before," he told me. "I'll go first." He tied one end of the rope about his waist and edged out along the path, into the falling water, pressing his body against the wet rock face, edging slowly, intently through the sheet of water.

I was scared for him, scared for both of us: holding my breath as he passed, only breathing when he was on the other side of the waterfall. He tested the rope, pulled on it, motioned me to follow him, when a rock gave way beneath his foot, and he slipped on the wet rock, and fell into the abyss.

The rope held, and the rock beside me held. Calum MacInnes dangled from the end of the rope. He looked up at me, and I sighed, anchored myself by a slab of crag, and I wound and pulled him up and up. I hauled him back onto the path, dripping and cursing.

He said, "You're stronger than you look," and I cursed myself for a fool. He must have seen it on my face for, after he shook himself (like a dog, sending droplets flying) he said, "My boy Calum told me the tale you told him about the Campbells coming for you, and you being sent into the fields by your wife, with them thinking she was your ma, and you a boy."

"It was just a tale," I said. "Something to pass the time."

"Indeed?" he said. "For I heard tell of a raiding party of Campbells sent out a few years ago, seeking revenge on someone who had taken their cattle. They went, and they never came back. If a small fellow like you can kill a dozen Campbells... well, you must be strong, and you must be fast."

I must be *stupid*, I thought ruefully, telling that child that tale.

I had picked them off one by one, like rabbits, as they came out to piss or to see what had happened to their friends: I had killed seven of them before my wife killed her first. We buried them in the glen, built a small cairn of stacking stones above them, to weigh them down so their ghosts would not walk, and we were sad: that Campbells had come so far to kill me, that we had been forced to kill them in return.

I take no joy in killing: no man should, and no woman. Sometimes death is necessary, but it is always an evil thing. That is something I am in no doubt of, even after the events I speak of here.

I took the rope from Calum MacInnes, and I clambered up and up, over the rocks, to where the waterfall came out of the side of the hill, and it was narrow enough for me to cross. It was slippery there, but I made it over without incident, tied the rope in place, came down it, threw the end of it to my companion, walked him across.

He did not thank me, neither for rescuing him, nor for getting us across; and I did not expect thanks. I also did not expect what he actually said, though, which was: "You are not a whole man, and you are ugly. Your wife: is she also small and ugly, like yourself?"

I decided to take no offense, whether offense had been intended or no. I simply said, "She is not. She is a tall woman, almost as tall as you, and when she was young—when we were both younger—she was reckoned by some to be the most beautiful girl in the lowlands. The bards wrote songs praising her green eyes and her long red-golden hair."

I thought I saw him flinch at this, but it is possible that I imagined it, or more likely, wished to imagine I had seen it.

"How did you win her, then?"

I spoke the truth: "I wanted her, and I get what I want. I did not give up. She said I was wise and I was kind, and I would always provide for her. And I have."

The clouds began to lower, once more, and the world blurred at the edges, became softer.

"She said I would be a good father. And I have done my best to raise my children. Who are also, if you are wondering, normal-sized."

"I beat sense into young Calum," said older Calum. "He is not a bad child."

"You can only do that as long as they are there with you," I said. And then I stopped talking, and I remembered that long year, and also I remembered Flora when she was small, sitting on the floor with jam on her face, looking up at me as if I were the wisest man in the world.

"Ran away, eh? I ran away when I was a lad. I was twelve. I went as far as the court of the King over the Water. The father of the current king."

"That's not something you hear spoken aloud."

"I am not afraid," he said. "Not here. Who's to hear us? Eagles? I saw him. He was a fat man, who spoke the language of the foreigners well, and our own tongue only with difficulty. But he was still our king." He paused. "And if he is to come to us again, he will need gold, for vessels and weapons and to feed the troops that he raises."

I said, "So I believe. That is why we go in search of the cave."

He said, "This is bad gold. It does not come free. It has its cost."

"Everything has its cost."

I was remembering every landmark—climb at the sheep skull, cross the first three streams, then walk along the fourth until the five heaped stones and find where the rock looks like a seagull and walk on between two sharply jutting walls of black rock, and let the slope bring you with it....

I could remember it, I knew. Well enough to find my way down again. But the mists confused me, and I could not be certain.

We reached a small loch, high in the mountains, and drank fresh water, caught huge white creatures that were not shrimps or lobsters or crayfish, and ate them raw like sausages, for we could not find any dry wood to make our fire, that high.

We slept on a wide ledge beside the icy water and woke into clouds before sunrise, when the world was gray and blue.

"You were sobbing in your sleep," said Calum.

"I had a dream," I told him.

"I do not have bad dreams," Calum said.

"It was a good dream," I said. It was true. I had dreamed that Flora still lived. She was grumbling about the village boys, and telling me of her time in the hills with the cattle, and of things of no consequence, smiling her great smile and tossing her hair the while, red-golden like her mother's, although her mother's hair is now streaked with white.

"Good dreams should not make a man cry out like that," said Calum. A pause, then, "I have no dreams, not good, not bad."

"No?"

"Not since I was a young man."

We rose. A thought struck me: "Did you stop dreaming after you came to the cave?"

He said nothing. We walked along the mountainside, into the mist, as the sun came up.

The mist seemed to thicken and fill with light, in the sunshine, but did not fade away and I realized that it must be a cloud. The world glowed. And then it seemed to me that I was staring at a man of my size, a small, humpty man, his shadow, standing in the air in front of me, like a ghost or an angel, and it moved as I moved. It was haloed by the light, and shimmered, and I could not have told you how near it was or how far away. I have seen miracles and I have seen evil things, but never have I seen anything like that.

"Is it magic?" I asked, although I smelled no magic on the air.

Calum said, "It is nothing. A property of the light. A shadow. A reflection. No more. I see a man beside me, as well. He moves as I move." I glanced back, but I saw nobody beside him.

And then the little glowing man in the air faded, and the cloud, and it was day, and we were alone.

We climbed all that morning, ascending. Calum's ankle had twisted the day before, when he had slipped at the waterfall. Now it swelled in front of me, swelled and went red, but his pace did not ever slow, and if he was in discomfort or in pain it did not show upon his face.

I said, "How long?" as the dusk began to blur the edges of world.

"An hour, less, perhaps. We will reach the cave, and then we will sleep for the night. In the morning you will go inside. You can bring out as much gold as you can carry, and we will make our way back off the island."

I looked at him, then: gray-streaked hair, gray eyes, so huge and wolfish a man, and I said, "You would sleep outside the cave?"

"I would. There are no monsters in the cave. Nothing that will come out and take you in the night. Nothing that will eat us. But you should not go in until daylight."

And then we rounded a rockfall, all black rocks and gray half-blocking our path, and we saw the cave mouth. I said, "Is that all?"

"You expected marble pillars? Or a giant's cave from a gossip's fireside tales?"

"Perhaps. It looks like nothing. A hole in the rock face. A shadow. And there are no guards?"

"No guards. Only the place, and what it is."

"A cave filled with treasure. And you are the only one who can find it?"

Calum laughed then, like a fox's bark. "The islanders know how to find it. But they are too wise to come here, to take its gold. They say that the cave makes you evil: that each time you visit it, each time you enter to take gold, it eats the good in your soul, so they do not enter."

"And is that true? Does it make you evil?"

"…No. The cave feeds on something else. Not good and evil. Not really. You can take your gold, but afterwards, things are," he paused, "things are *flat*. There is less beauty in a rainbow, less meaning in a sermon, less joy in a kiss…" He looked at the cave mouth and I thought I saw fear in his eyes. "Less."

I said, "There are many for whom the lure of gold outweighs the beauty of a rainbow."

"Me, when young, for one. You, now, for another."

"So we go in at dawn."

"You will go in. I will wait for you out here. Do not be afraid. No monster guards the cave. No spells to make the gold vanish, if you do not know some cantrip or rhyme."

We made our camp, then: or rather we sat in the darkness, against the cold rock wall. There would be no sleep there.

I said, "You took the gold from here, as I will do tomorrow. You bought a house with it, a bride, a good name."

His voice came from the darkness. "Aye. And they meant nothing to me, once I had them, or less than nothing. And if your gold pays for the King over the Water to come back to us and rule us and bring about a land of joy and prosperity and warmth, it will still mean nothing to you. It will be as something you heard of that happened to a man in a tale."

"I have lived my life to bring the King back," I told him.

He said, "You take the gold back to him. Your King will want more gold, because kings want more. It is what they do. Each time you come back, it will mean less. The rainbow means nothing. Killing a man means nothing."

Silence then, in the darkness. I heard no birds: only the wind that called and gusted about the peaks like a mother seeking her babe.

I said, "We have both killed men. Have you ever killed a woman, Calum MacInnes?"

"I have not. I have killed no women, no girls."

I ran my hands over my dirk in the darkness, seeking the wood and center of the hilt, the steel of the blade. It was there in my hands. I had not intended ever to tell him, only to strike when we were out of the mountains, strike once, strike deep, but now I felt the words being pulled from me, would I or never-so. "They say there was a girl," I told him. "And a thorn-bush."

Silence. The whistling of the wind. "Who told you?" he asked. Then, "Never mind. I would not kill a woman. No man of honor would kill a woman…"

If I said a word, I knew, he would be silent on the subject, and never talk about it again. So I said nothing. Only waited.

Calum MacInnes began to speak, choosing his words with care, talking as if he was remembering a tale he had heard as a child and had almost forgotten. "They told me the kine of the lowlands were fat and bonny, and that a man could gain honor and glory by adventuring off to the southlands and returning with the fine red cattle. So I went south, and never a cow was good enough, until on a hillside in the lowlands I saw the finest, reddest, fattest cows that ever a man has seen. So I began to lead them away, back the way I had come.

"She came after me with a stick. The cattle were her father's, she said, and I was a rogue and a knave and all manner of rough things. But she was beautiful, even when angry, and had I not already a young wife I might have dealt more kindly to her. Instead I pulled a knife, and touched it to her throat, and bade her to stop speaking. And she did stop.

"I would not kill her—I would not kill a woman, and that is the truth—so I tied her, by her hair, to a thorn-tree, and I took her knife from her waistband, to slow her as she tried to free herself, and pushed the blade of it deep into the sod. I tied her to the thorn-tree by her long hair, and I thought no more of her as I made off with her cattle."

"It was another year before I was back that way. I was not after cows that day, but I walked up the side of that bank—it was a lonely spot, and if you had not been looking, you might not have seen it. Perhaps nobody searched for her."

"I heard they searched," I told him. "Although some believed her taken by reavers, and others believed her run away with a tinker, or gone to the city. But still, they searched."

"Aye. I saw what I did see—perhaps you'd have to have stood where I was standing, to see what I did see. It was an evil thing I did, perhaps."

"Perhaps?"

He said, "I have taken gold from the cave of the mists. I cannot tell any longer if there is good or there is evil. I sent a message, by a child, at an inn, telling them where she was, and where they could find her."

I closed my eyes but the world became no darker.

"There is evil, " I told him.

I saw it in my mind's eye: her skeleton picked clean of clothes, picked clean of flesh, as naked and white as anyone would ever be, hanging like a child's puppet against the thorn-bush, tied to a branch above it by its red-golden hair.

"At dawn," said Calum MacInnes, as if we had been talking of provisions or the weather, "you will leave your dirk behind, for such is the custom, and you will enter the cave, and bring out as much gold as you can carry. And you will bring it back with you, to the mainland. There's not a soul in these parts, knowing what you carry or where it's from, would take it from you. Then send it to the King over the Water, and he will pay his men with it, and feed them, and buy their weapons. One day, he will return. Tell me on that day that there is evil, little man."

When the sun was up, I entered the cave. It was damp in there. I could hear water running down one wall, and I felt a wind on my face, which was strange, because there was no wind inside the mountain.

In my mind, the cave would be filled with gold. Bars of gold would be stacked like firewood, and bags of golden coins would sit between them. There would be golden chains and golden rings, and golden plates, heaped high like the china plates in a rich man's house.

I had imagined riches, but there was nothing like that here. Only shadows. Only rock.

Something was here, though. Something that waited.

I have secrets, but there is a secret that lies beneath all my other secrets, and not even my children know it, although I believe my wife suspects, and it is this: my mother was a mortal woman, the daughter of a miller, but my father came to her from out of the West, and to the West he returned when he had had his sport with her. I cannot be sentimental about my parentage: I am sure he does not think of her, and doubt that he ever knew of me. But he left me a body that is small, and fast, and strong; and perhaps I take after him in other ways—I do not know. I am ugly, and my father was beautiful, or so my mother told me once, but I think that she might have been deceived.

I wondered what I would have seen in that cave if my father had been an innkeeper from the lowlands.

You would be seeing gold, said a whisper that was not a whisper, from deep in the heart of the mountain. It was a lonely voice, and distracted, and bored.

"I would see gold," I said aloud. "Would it be real, or would it be an illusion?"

The whisper was amused. *You are thinking like a mortal man, making things always to be one thing or another. It is gold they would see, and touch. Gold they would carry back with them, feeling the weight of it the while, gold they would trade with other mortals for what they needed. What does it matter if it is there or no, if they can see it, touch it, steal it, murder for it? Gold they need and gold I give them.*

"And what do you take, for the gold you give them?"

Little enough, for my needs are few, and I am old; too old to follow my sisters into the West. I taste their pleasure and their joy. I feed, a little, feed on what they do not need and do not value. A taste of heart, a lick and a nibble of their fine consciences, a sliver of soul. And in return a fragment of me leaves this cave with them and gazes out at the world through their eyes, sees what they see until their lives are done and I take back what is mine.

"Will you show yourself to me?"

I could see, in the darkness, better than any man born of man and woman could see. I saw something move in the shadows, and then the shadows congealed and shifted, revealing formless things at the edge of my perception, where it meets imagination. Troubled, I said the thing it is proper to say at times such as this: "Appear before me in a form that neither harms nor is offensive to me."

Is that what you wish?

The drip of distant water. "Yes," I said.

From out of the shadows it came, and it stared down at me with empty sockets, smiled at me with wind-weathered ivory teeth. It was all bone, save its hair, and its hair was red and gold, and wrapped about the branch of a thorn-bush.

"That offends my eyes."

I took it from your mind, said a whisper that surrounded the skeleton. Its jawbone did not move. *I chose something you loved. This was your daughter, Flora, as she was the last time you saw her.*

I closed my eyes, but the figure remained.

It said, *The reaver waits for you at the mouth of the cave. He waits for you to come out, weaponless and weighed down with gold. He will kill you, and take the gold from your dead hands.*

"But I'll not be coming out with gold, will I?"

I thought of Calum MacInnes, the wolf-gray in his hair, the gray of his eyes, the line of his dirk. He was bigger than I am, but all men are bigger than I am. Perhaps I was stronger, and faster, but he was also fast, and he was strong.

He killed my daughter, I thought, then wondered if the thought was mine or if it had crept out the shadows and into my head. Aloud, I said, "Is there another way out of this cave?"

You leave the way you entered, through the mouth of my home.

I stood there and did not move, but in my mind I was like an animal in a trap, questing and darting from idea to idea, finding no purchase and no solace and no solution.

I said, "I am weaponless. He told me that I could not enter this place with a weapon. That it was not the custom."

It is the custom now, to bring no weapon into my place. It was not always the custom. Follow me, said the skeleton of my daughter.

I followed her, for I could see her, even when it was so dark that I could see nothing else.

In the shadows it said, *It is beneath your hand.*

I crouched and felt it. The haft felt like bone—perhaps an antler. I touched the blade cautiously in the darkness, discovered that I was holding something that felt more like an awl than a knife. It was thin, sharp at the tip. It would be better than nothing.

"Is there a price?"

There is always a price.

"Then I will pay it. And I ask one other thing. You say that you can see the world through his eyes."

There were no eyes in that hollow skull, but it nodded.

"Then tell me when he sleeps."

It said nothing. It melded into the darkness, and I felt alone in that place.

Time passed. I followed the sound of the dripping water, found a rock pool, and drank. I soaked the last of the oats and I ate them, chewing them until they dissolved in my mouth. I slept and woke and slept again, and dreamed of my wife, Morag, waiting for me as the seasons changed, waiting for me just as we had waited for our daughter, waiting for me forever.

Something, a finger I thought, touched my hand: it was not bony and hard. It was soft, and humanlike, but too cold. *He sleeps.*

I left the cave in the blue light, before dawn. He slept across the cave-mouth, catlike, I knew, such that the slightest touch would have woken him. I held my weapon in front of me, a bone handle and a needlelike blade of blackened silver, and I reached out and took what I was after, without waking him.

Then I stepped closer, and his hand grasped for my ankle and his eyes opened.

"Where is the gold?" asked Calum MacInnes.

"I have none." The wind blew cold on the mountainside. I had danced back, out of his reach, when he had grabbed at me. He stayed on the ground, pushed himself up onto one elbow.

Then he said, "Where is my dirk?"

"I took it," I told him. "While you slept."

He looked at me, sleepily. "And why ever would you do that? If I was going to kill you I would have done it on the way here. I could have killed you a dozen times."

"But I did not have gold, then, did I?"

He said nothing.

I said, "If you think you could have got me to bring the gold from the cave, and that not bringing it out would have saved your miserable soul, then you are a fool."

He no longer looked sleepy. "A fool, am I?"

He was ready to fight. It is good to make people who are ready to fight angry.

I said, "Not a fool. No. For I have met fools and idiots, and they are happy in their idiocy, even with straw in their hair. You are too wise for foolishness. You seek only misery and you bring misery with you and you call down misery on all you touch."

He rose then, holding a rock in his hand like an axe, and he came at me. I am small, and he could not strike me as he would have struck a man of his own size. He leaned over to strike. It was a mistake.

I held the bone haft tightly, and stabbed upward, striking fast with the point of the awl, like a snake. I knew the place I was aiming for, and I knew what it would do.

He dropped his rock, clutched at his right shoulder. "My arm," he said. "I cannot feel my arm."

He swore then, fouling the air with curses and threats. The dawn light on the mountaintop made everything so beautiful and blue. In that light, even the blood that had begun to soak his garments was purple. He took a step back, so he was between me and the cave. I felt exposed, the rising sun at my back.

"Why do you not have gold?" he asked me. His arm hung limply at his side.

"There was no gold there for such as I," I said.

He threw himself forward, then, ran at me and kicked at me. My awl blade went flying from my hand. I threw my arms around his leg, and I held on to him as together we tumbled off the mountainside.

His head was above me, and I saw triumph in it, and then I saw sky, and then the valley floor was above me and I was rising to meet it and then it was below me and I was falling to my death.

A jar and a bump, and now we were turning over and over on the side of the mountain, the world a dizzying whirligig of rock and pain and sky, and I knew I was a dead man, but still I clung to the leg of Calum MacInnes.

I saw a golden eagle in flight, but below me or above me I could no longer say. It was there, in the dawn sky, in the shattered fragments of time and perception, there in the pain. I was not afraid: there was no time and no space to be afraid in, no space in my mind and no space in my heart. I was falling through the sky, holding tightly to the leg of a man who was trying to kill me; we were crashing into rocks, scraping and bruising and then…

…we stopped. Stopped with force enough that I felt myself jarred, and was almost thrown off Calum MacInnes and to my death beneath. The side of the mountain had crumbled, there, long ago, sheared off, leaving a sheet of blank rock, as smooth and as featureless as glass. But that was below us. Where we were, there was a ledge, and on the ledge there was a miracle: stunted and twisted, high above the treeline, where no trees have any right to grow, was a twisted hawthorn tree, not much larger than a bush, although it was old. Its roots grew into the side of the mountain, and it was this hawthorn that had caught us in its gray arms.

I let go of the leg, clambered off Calum MacInnes's body, and onto the side of the mountain. I stood on the narrow ledge and looked down at the sheer drop. There was no way down from here. No way down at all.

I looked up. It might be possible, I thought, climbing slowly, with fortune on my side, to make it up that mountain. If it did not rain. If the wind was not too hungry. And what choice did I have? The only alternative was death.

A voice: "So. Will you leave me here to die, dwarf?"

I said nothing. I had nothing to say.

His eyes were open. He said, "I cannot move my right arm, since you stabbed it. I think I broke a leg in the fall. I cannot climb with you."

I said, "I may succeed, or I may fail."

"You'll make it. I've seen you climb. After you rescued me, crossing that waterfall. You went up those rocks like a squirrel going up a tree."

I did not have his confidence in my climbing abilities.

He said, "Swear to me by all you hold holy. Swear by your King, who waits over the sea as he has since we drove his subjects from this land. Swear by the things you creatures hold dear—swear by shadows and eagle feathers and by silence. Swear that you will come back for me."

"You know what I am?" I said.

"I know nothing," he said. "Only that I want to live."

I thought. "I swear by these things," I told him. "By shadows and by eagle feathers and by silence. I swear by green hills and standing stones. I will come back."

"I would have killed you," said the man in the hawthorn bush, and he said it with humor, as if it was the biggest joke that ever one man had told another. "I had planned to kill you, and take the gold back as my own."

"I know."

His hair framed his face like a wolf-gray halo. There was red blood on his cheek where he had scraped it in the fall. "You could come back with ropes," he said. "My rope is still up there, by the cave mouth. But you'd need more than that."

"Yes," I said. "I will come back with ropes." I looked up at the rock above us, examined it as best I could. Sometimes good eyes mean the difference between life and death, if you are a climber. I saw where I would need to be as I went, the shape of my journey up the face of the mountain. I thought I could see the ledge outside the cave, from which we had fallen as we fought. I would head for there. Yes.

I blew on my hands, to dry the sweat before I began to climb. "I will come back for you," I said. "With ropes. I have sworn."

"When?" he asked, and he closed his eyes.

"In a year," I told him. "I will come here in a year."

I began to climb. The man's cries followed me as I stepped and crawled and squeezed and hauled myself up the side of that mountain, mingling with the cries of the great raptors; and they followed me back from the Misty Isle, with nothing to show for my pains and my time, and I will hear him screaming, at the edge of my mind, as I fall asleep or in the moments before I wake, until I die.

It did not rain, and the wind gusted and plucked at me, but did not throw me down. I climbed, and I climbed in safety.

When I reached the ledge, the cave entrance seemed like a darker shadow in the noonday sun. I turned from it, turned my back on the mountain, and from the shadows that were already gathering in the cracks and the crevices and deep inside my skull, and I began my slow journey away from the Misty Isle. There were a hundred roads and a thousand paths that would take me back to my home in the lowlands, where my wife would be waiting.

SEVEN SEXY COWBOY ROBOTS
SANDRA MCDONALD

Sandra McDonald is a graduate of Ithaca College, and earned a Master of Fine Arts degree in creative writing from the University of Southern Maine. She spent eight years as an officer in the United States Navy, during which time she lived in Guam, Newfoundland, England, and the United States, and has worked as a Hollywood assistant, a software instructor, and an English composition teacher. Her short story "The Ghost Girls of Rumney Mill" was shortlisted for the James Tiptree, Jr. Award in 2003. Her first novel, *The Outback Stars*, was published in 2007, and was followed by two sequels: *The Stars Down Under* and *The Stars Blue Yonder*. Her most recent book is collection *Diana Comet and Other Improbable Stories*. Originally from Revere, Massachusetts, she currently lives in Jacksonville, Florida.

I.

When I was a much younger woman, as part of the divorce settlement from my then-millionaire inventor husband, I asked for our house in Connecticut, a modest amount of alimony, and six sexy cowboy robots. Sentient sex toys, if you will.

The robots were my revenge for all the time and money Herbert had lavished on tawdry mistresses across the world. His company, New Human More Human, specialized in mechanical soldiers for the U.S. Department of Defense with a lucrative side business in sensual satisfaction. The factory delivered my boys in a big white truck. They jumped off the back ramp wearing shit-eating grins and oozing Wild West charisma. No other firm in the world could produce as fine a product. My husband was the Preston Tucker of his time: a brilliant innovator and visionary done in by vicious boardroom skullduggery.

If you believe that one strong man can succeed in the face of titanic conspiracy and unrelenting backstabbing, you probably believed global icing would be solved. Then the snow reached five feet high against your living room windows and your belief in science was shattered, as was mine.

In any case, Herbert fulfilled his divorce obligations. But he also incorporated his revenge. He had my guys created as sexy cowboy robots with steel blades permanently attached to their feet. By design they were most happy when twirling, spinning, and jumping on ice. The frozen lake behind the house sufficed during the winter but back when summer was still a threat, I had to build an indoor rink to avoid months of pouting. There's nothing more sad than a depressed sexy cowboy.

Let me back up. One of the best dates Herbert and I ever went on, pre-nuptials, was a charity benefit at the Hartford Ice Arena. A group of skaters in tight jeans, flannel shirts and cowboy hats took the ice halfway through the show. They gyrated and spun around to an Elvis remix in a way that made the crowd—especially the female half—go wild. I myself heaped so much praise that Herbert turned red with jealousy. He was never very sanguine about competition. He was even worse at winter sports, and in fact met his mortal end ten years after our divorce by skiing off the side of a kiddie slope in Colorado.

Let me jump forward: this is not the story of a woman gifted with mechanical companionship who eventually realizes true love only comes in the shape of a flesh-and-blood man. Screw that. Since the day that white truck arrived, every one of my emotional, intellectual, and sexual needs has been satisfied by my cowboys (except for Buck) in their splendidly unique ways. Never again have I taken a human lover. I'm only writing this now because I'm a hundred years old and dying, hoping to find a companion for the one sexy cowboy robot who needs it the most.

First I'll tell you what happened to the other five, so that you understand the great responsibilities and sexual joys of owning a mechanical cowboy.

II.

Naturally all my boys were great at mending fences, roping horses, and tending the vegetable garden, but from day one Doc distinguished himself as our go-to robot for any mechanical or electrical problems. Not just with his brothers—that time Yuri cracked his knee on a sideboard, or when Neill's arm was stolen by government agents—but in the mansion and across the grounds, too. Over the years he fixed the garbage disposal, the furnace, the sonic Jacuzzi, the vacuum bots, and the cranky house computer. Whenever my aircar had problems he was the first to slide under the fantail, and once we built the indoor rink he single-handedly redesigned the chillers to double their output at half the energy cost.

On the ice he specialized in triple lutzes and a signature move that included hooking his white cowboy hat on his jutting pelvis. In between rehearsals and shows, he built his own workshop in an old shed and would spend many happy hours tinkering. At night in my bed his hands were warm and his breath sweet like maple syrup. He insisted on calling me Katherine instead of Kay. From him I learned the importance of wearing protection from the knees down; steel blades are hell on shins and satin sheets.

From Doc I also learned the importance of foreplay. Not that I was unacquainted with its benefits, but the first lovers I ever had were awkward teenage boys, and then a string of adult men mostly interested in themselves, and then there was Herbert, who believed lovemaking should take the same amount of time it takes to eat a boiled egg. I wondered if his speediness was specific to me, but his worldwide mistresses reported the same brisk efficiency. Doc, on the other hand, thought foreplay should take as long as a seven-course meal at a five-star restaurant. His long, supple fingers were more than sufficient but he also brought massage oil, soft feathers, and small appliances to the task. He was an inventor and tinkerer, remember, and thought the human body was a fine engine to tune.

I knew he loved me but wasn't in love with me, as the saying goes. He loved circuits and designs, and making machines work better, and landing quad jumps in front of adoring crowds. Of us all, he was the most patient with Buck's unpredictable temper tantrums. His theory was that Buck's brain had been ever-so-slightly damaged in the manufacturing stage. Doc was also good at keeping secrets. I didn't realize he was smitten with a secret love until the security staff caught her sneaking out his workshop window one cold winter morning. Dr. Skylar Anderson was the chief designer at New Human More Human, and my ex-husband's latest wife.

"Skylar," I said disapprovingly, arms folded over my chiffon bathrobe.

She straightened the lapels of her lab coat. A red bra strap poked out from under her blouse. "Kay."

"Does Herbert know?"

She sniffed. "He's been too busy whoring his way through the secretarial pool. I've already filed for divorce."

This made her the enemy of my enemy, and thus an ally, so we had tea and pancakes and discussed lawyers. Later, at lunch, I asked Doc, "You and Skylar. You don't think it's very Oedipal?"

"Would you mind it something awful if I went to live with her, Katherine?"

"Would that make you happy?"

"I reckon so."

"But where will you skate?"

"There's a city rink near her house," he said, cheerful and optimistic.

Their affair only lasted three weeks. Doc came back complaining that Skylar had only wanted him for his circuits, but I think it was the poor quality of the city rink that disappointed him most. We commiserated over the breakup on a faux bearskin rug in front of a roaring fire and then he went back to his workshop, happy as any sexy cowboy robot can be. Eventually he went to work for the UN Commission on Warming the Planet Back Up, at their headquarters atop Sicily. The Sicilian women adored him and the frozen Mediterranean was excellent for skating.

III.

Neill and Buck both came off the delivery truck wearing tight white T-shirts and leather vests, very similar in appearance: rugged, fair-haired, with chiseled chins and bright blue eyes. But there was always something comforting about Neill and dangerous about Buck. Maybe it was the way that Neill could stand at the center of a frozen pond and let the stillness of the piney woods seep into him, no need to show off or test the ice. Buck, though? From day one he had to spin as fast as he could, jump higher than anyone else, be the center of a private solar system around which the rest of us orbited in agitation or love or both.

It's fair to say Neill was bisexual, but during threesomes he was usually more interested in Yuri or Dana than he was in me. When he and I were alone, he was determined to experiment with ropes, knots, and just about every position in the Wild West Guide to Sexual Positions. The Mosey, Saddlehorn, and Road Stake went well enough, but I had to replace the damaged headboard after we did the Appaloosa, and needed anti-inflammatories for a week after the Missouri Toothpick. Between rehearsals and marathon sex sessions, Neill read his way through most of my library. He would thump from one bookcase to the next with plastic guards on his skates, fascinated by the great philosophers and religious thinkers.

I wouldn't have minded his choices so much if he didn't entirely skip my row in the self-help section. That's what I did before the Big Bad Ice: Dr. Katherine Campbell, best-selling psychologist. Maybe you've heard of my books? . . . I had a syndicated radio show. I appeared frequently on daytime television. My hair, makeup, wardrobe, and jewelry were impeccable, and my teeth brilliantly white. I was, in a word, insufferable.

In retrospect, Neill showed good sense by skipping my books. Herbert never read them, either. Like his creator, Neill also preferred ink on paper, and the way pages were sewn into spines.

"I prefer gravity," he said, more than once. "Pixels have no weight."

After Buck left us to build his secret laboratory up at Dodge Falls in New Hampshire, Neill volunteered to ski up the Connecticut River and talk some sense into him. The rest of us weren't too keen on the idea. Bad enough to lose Buck to the crazy world outside, but risk another of us as well? Since the advent of the Big Freeze, snow bandits had taken to seizing any shipments of food or fuel that tried to make it overland. On the estate we had the aircar, the heated gardens, a security system, and a larder full enough for decades. Out in the valley, Neill would be on his own.

"What if you don't come back?" asked Dana, number five in the sexy robot lineup. He was our cross-dressing robot: sexy cowboy on the ice, alluring cowgirl off it. He rested one manicured hand on Neill's arm. "What if someone lassoes you and burns you for heat?"

Neill said, "I'll ski by night and hide by day."

Yuri took a sip from his beer bottle. None of the robots needed food or liquid, of course, but they'd been designed with storage tanks in their chest cavities to keep up social pretenses. "You think you've got a chance in hell of convincing Buck to come back?"

"I think it's worth a try," Neill said, square and honest. Of all the robots he was the one who most missed Herbert, or the ideal of Herbert; the absent father who had created them but then abandoned them with his death. Buck was a piece of Herbert that could not be lost as well.

Neill set off one winter sunset with the sun red behind the pine trees. To make it safely to Buck's lair, he would have to climb over broken bridges and dams, avoid any local marauders, and keep himself safe from the dangers of the natural world. We received messages letting us know he'd successfully passed through Hartford and then Springfield. Then, somewhere near Turners Falls, he fell off the map. We heard nothing until Buck broke radio silence, popping up on the vid screen one night to inform us that agents of the U.S. federal government had captured Neill for nefarious experiments. They were holding him in an underground lab near Mount Sugarloaf.

"Experiment on him for what?" I asked, bewildered.

"Herbert personally designed him," Buck said, his voice grim across the many miles. "New Human More Human is defunct. Skylar Anderson destroyed the last of the company records years ago. What's left of the Defense Department thinks they can tear Neill apart and learn enough to build a whole new line of robots."

We mounted a rescue attempt immediately. Cody, number six in the cowboy lineup, was a pilot whenever he wasn't practicing his sit spins. With his aerial skills, my financial resources, and the true bravery of cowboys everywhere, we sped north. By the time we arrived, flames were shooting from the pristine countryside. The government lab was in ruins. Neill and Buck were safe in the woods, but Neill's left arm was missing.

"They took it," Neill said, holding his empty sleeve forlornly. I imagine he was thinking about sex again; it's hard to perform the Four in Hand when you don't have a hand to put in the appropriate orifice.

Yuri thumped him on the back. "We'll build you another, partner."

Dana gave Neill a kiss on the cheek, leaving pink lipstick behind. "The important thing is you're alive."

Buck was sooty but unharmed. We considered each other across the small clearing. His shoulders were stiff, his chin defiant. I wondered if he had killed any of the government men, and if he'd feel bad about that in the years to come.

Neill said, "You should come back with us, Buck."

"Nah," he said, in a slow but deliberate drawl. "I'm better off on my own for now. But y'all keep in touch."

With that he loped off into the woods, his gait odd.

Only once we were on the chopper, speeding home, did I realize Buck had sawed the skates off his feet.

IV.

For the first thirty years of my life, men in women's clothing did nothing for me. Dana changed all that. By day he skated around in his blue jeans, leather gloves, and black shirts with elbow patches. Come evening, he would disappear into my closets and emerge wearing the best of my gowns, shoes, and precious jewelry. I don't know who taught him how to apply makeup but he was a master designer with shadow and blush. Whoever knew my nipples would perk up at the sight? The human body is a strange organism.

He said he didn't want to be a woman full time. That would ruin the skating act. But from the moment he came out of the factory he had a yearning for the lacy softness of a brassiere, the arch of fine high heel shoes, the glitter and graceful folds of a well-made cocktail dress. He liked to shave his legs (yes, my robots had renewable hair) and stretch long, sleek stockings over them. He enjoyed hooking a lace garter belt around his hips. In bed he wore pink lingerie and was an enthusiastic supporter of phalluses shaped like pistols. He also would say or do anything to make me laugh, including the use of feathers, ice cubes, and an endless supply of dirty limericks.

Before the Big Freeze, Dana would go into town dressed as a woman, on the prowl for a man who could love all of him. I worried about those trips, but there's no stopping a sexy cowboy on a mission. After Neill's rescue at Mount Sugarloaf, Dana's feelings for him flared into a one-sided infatuation that affected them both on the ice. Dana started doubling his jumps instead of landing triples, and Neill nearly dropped him once during a lift, and then someone loosened the seams on Neill's costume so that all of him popped out during a backflip.

Things might have gotten worse between them, but the next day we received a distress call from Long Island Sound. An ice barge with children aboard had run into trouble. The boys saddled up and rode out on snowmobiles. During the rescue Dana was lost to the water. One moment he was hoisting an infant to safety and in the next, the merciless ice had opened up and sucked him into its black depths.

Neill took the loss especially hard. For weeks he skated around the rink in silence, wearing black clothes and one of Dana's favorite feather boas. I myself tried to remember all of Dana's dirty jokes and limericks. None of them seemed funny anymore. The others mourned their lost brother by getting his name tattooed on their forearms and inventing a new jump-spin-land combination called Dana's Stick.

Buck heard about it, though I'm not sure which of the boys called him. He called me on the vid to express his regrets. I could see a blazing hearth behind him; his secret lair didn't have much in the way of furniture, but there seemed to be a lot of computers and equipment. I imagined the place was as gloomy and bitter as Buck himself.

"Dana was a good cowboy," Buck said. "I'm sorry he's gone."

"Are you?" I asked. "You didn't much approve of his attire."

Which was true, and Buck was robot enough not to deny it.

"I don't want to fight," he said, instead. On the vid, his shoulders were slumped and his eyes downcast. "I do miss y'all, even if you don't miss me."

Fat snowflakes slapped lightly against the windows of my bedroom. It wasn't like Buck to be so boldly needy. Maybe all those years alone in New Hampshire were changing his outlook on life. He'd gone there after Herbert's death; to mourn, maybe, or to bitterly rue the loss of his creator.

"We miss you a lot," I told him. "You can come home anytime you want."

"My work is important." Like Doc, Buck had inherited Herbert's genius and overinflated ego. He believed he could save the planet. I guess the real Herbert might have been able to, but his mechanical heir hadn't succeeded yet.

"Kay," Buck said, breaking the silence between us. "If I came back, would you get rid of everyone but me? Would you let me be your only cowboy?"

From Buck, this was unheard of. We'd never even kissed. From day one he'd been wild, untamed, his own free robot.

He must have seen confusion in my face, because he logged off without saying goodbye.

As it turned out, our grieving over Dana was happily in vain. Three weeks after the disaster on the ice, he sent word from Key West. Robots don't need to breathe, of course, so after being sucked into the powerful currents of the reversed Gulf Stream, he'd simply hung on for the ride. He liked Key West a lot. Though it was no longer a tropical paradise, the ice fishermen still applauded the sunset each night before snuggling into their igloos. He'd found true love in the arms of a Cuban named Elian, and did we mind if he stayed down there to teach the locals how to figure skate?

V.

Yuri and Cody were my fiercely competitive sexy robots. Not on the ice. During performances they were consummate professionals, and the townsfolk who came up for the shows once a month never saw their intense rivalry. But you've never seen two boys compete so much over who could eat more flapjacks (though they couldn't, technically, eat), get more drunk (simulated, in wildly hilarious ways), or score higher on cowboy video games (eighteen-hour marathon sessions in the library were not unheard of, until I got sick of hearing "Yee-haw!" and threw them out). In the back forty they rode robot horses and roped robot steer until Doc had to bang the dents out of them, and then they started all over again. In my bed they wrestled over who got my back passage and who got my front. No matter who won, I always benefited from their rivalry.

One day they got it into their heads to see who could cross-country ski the farthest. By this time Doc was in Italy, Dana was in Key West, and Buck was still in New Hampshire. The skate show had diminished to just Yuri, Cody, and Neill, and didn't draw crowds from town like it used to. Not that many people still lived anywhere in New England. The smart ones had drifted south to the crowded equatorial nations, and the old ones rarely left their homes anymore.

"You don't mind, do you?" Cody asked one night, his hand pumping away pleasurably inside me.

"Mind what?" I gasped.

Yuri's mouth lifted from my right nipple. "If we modify skis to fit our skates and go off for a little while."

The boys had learned long ago that I can't deny them anything when I'm about to orgasm, and so off they went on their journey. That was twenty years ago. They circumnavigated frozen oceans, icy Mideast deserts, and the top of every mountain they could find. They brought food, fuel, and engine parts to small villages. In those pockets of civilization where humanity still struggled to survive, they also performed pairs skating routines. The seats were often empty but for wide-eyed children who had never known prosperity or what it was like to be truly warm.

VI.

In the end, only Neill and I remained on the estate. I was too old and withered and stubborn to move. Neill was too devoted to leave. He continued to read the philosophers in the library, though after fifty years he'd surely memorized every one. In bed, he was considerate of my frail bones, vaginal dryness, and decreased libido. Ours was no longer a world in which women could find medical or surgical solace from the cruelties of old age. Earth was a dying planet, destined to be buried under ice and snow no matter what miracle solutions always seemed at hand.

Long after the house computer had rusted into silence, the skating rink was still operational. Neill had become an excellent solo performer. For hours he would skate to singers long forgotten, like Toby Keith and Taylor Swift. Most days I would pull on my scarf and coat and boots to trudge down the slope and watch him spin. Some days I dozed off in my fireside chair, instead, and he would kiss my forehead on his way out the door.

"I'll be back in time for dinner," he would say.

One evening I woke to a cold hearth and dark skies. The house was silent but for my own voice. I made my way down the slippery slope already knowing the sad truth. Neill was exactly where I expected him to be: center ice, arms raised up, legs crossed, face proud. He had skated his final performance. He would stand there until the roof caved in and winter buried him forever.

"I'm sorry," I said, through tears. "You shouldn't have been alone."

"He wasn't," a voice said behind me, from the empty stands.

Buck was standing in the shadows, his hands buried in the pockets of his long camel hair coat. We regarded each other across a gulf of empty seats and old regrets.

"He knew his battery was going," Buck said, shifting his gaze to Neill. "We were never designed to last this long, Kay."

"The others..." I said faintly.

"Have come to see me," he said. "I managed to extend them for a few more years, but Neill didn't want that. He was ready to be released. No one really wants to be immortal."

I wiped my face. "Not even you, Herbert?"

Buck blinked. For a moment I thought he was going to deny it. Then he said, "How long have you known?"

"I was always suspicious that you wouldn't sleep with me," I said. "And I thought something was amiss when you took the biological Herbert's death so hard. But it was Skylar who confirmed it, on her deathbed. She said she always suspected you'd downloaded your own personality into one of the robots to preserve yourself. You did an excellent job."

Buck moved closer to the edge of the rink. I wondered if he missed the glide of ice under his skates, the rush of air as he sped around in circles.

"It was an experiment," he said. "I didn't really expect success. All of a sudden I was handsome, and young again, and graceful for the first time in my life. But you only had eyes for the others."

"You could have joined us."

"I hated you back then. You always made me aware of my own deficiencies. I wasn't a perfect man, but for decades I believed I was."

I couldn't argue with that. Didn't want to, not with Neill frozen on the ice in front of us. All I could do was pull my hat down over my ears and make my slow, painful way up the slope to the empty house that had been rowdy with sexy cowboys for so many decades. Release sounded like a good word. Sounded like a long-promised reward after fifty years of ice.

Buck followed me. Heated up soup that I wouldn't eat and tucked me into a bed too big for just one person. I remembered him on the night he proposed marriage. Just the two of us in a sidewalk café in summertime, coffee and baklava on the table between us, moonlight on the street and in his eyes.

"Come back to Dodge Falls with me," he said. "Let us take care of you."

So I did.

VII.

And it's here I've spent my last years, slowly dying amid well-heated rooms and hydroponic gardens that bloom with long-forgotten flowers. Dana keeps me company most of the time. He's not very erectile anymore, but we enjoy taking baths together and snuggling under blankets and putting on our best dresses for afternoon tea. Buck never comes to my bed. Maybe he thinks I'll break a hip. Maybe I'm afraid to show him what a sack of old flesh I've become, while he's still strong and handsome. He spends his days working on the Big Freeze. He thinks he's finally found a solution; even now, pilots are seeding the oceans and clouds with chemicals that will restore the planet's damaged equilibrium. We hope.

Dana and I can count the days we have left, or at least a rough approximation. Yuri and Doc and Cody are already gone, my beautiful boys. It's Buck I'm worried about. Years of skating took their toll on the others, but he could outlive us for another ten years. Who will take care of him? Who will save him from the loneliness and bitterness? He needs a companion.

I should have known he has a plan.

"Here she is," he says one morning, unveiling a glass cabinet in his lab. "I've kept her in storage all these years and just finished the upgrade."

Inside is a beautiful woman: glossy brown hair, clear skin, firm breasts, legs to die for. Her cowboy hat, suede skirt, and fringed shirt are as fresh as the day she rolled off the assembly line. The seventh sexy robot. An homage to the greatest love of Herbert's life.

"Skylar!" I exclaim indignantly. "You built a perfect replica of her, not me?"

He blinks at me. "That's not Skylar—that's you!"

I glare.

He wilts.

"It's Skylar," Dana confirms. "Her nose always was a little bit crooked."

Buck says, "Well, it doesn't matter. She's never been activated. There's no personality profile. I want you to have her, Kay. I can transfer your mind into this body."

"No. Give her to Dana," I say.

Dana shakes his head. "Neill's waiting for me in electronic heaven. But I'll borrow the skirt."

Buck steps closer to me. "We need you, Kay. The world needs people to rebuild it."

I stare at the beautiful Skylar, but spare him a sideways glance.

"The truth is that I need you," he confesses. "I need my Kay back, no matter whose face you're wearing. Be young for me again. Be strong and beautiful, and we'll take on the world together."

"Huh," I say.

Buck squeezes my hand. "Promise me you'll think about it."

When I said I wanted a companion for Buck, I never thought it would be me. I try to imagine waking up young, strong, and beautiful. To spend every day for the rest of my life seeing Skylar in the mirror. I say nothing on the way back to my room. Dana limps along beside me, equally quiet. Maybe thinking of the skirt.

"You could," he finally says. "You'd still be Kay on the inside."

"Screw that," I tell him. "Come on. We're going back to Connecticut. Let's go see Neill, and have ourselves a drink or two, and go out with a bang."

That afternoon we put on silky blue underwear and our cold-weather clothes. We apply foundation, sunscreen, and mascara at least fifty years past its expiration date. Dana's blue eyes sparkle under gold eyeshadow. I pull out the small box that contains the last of my jewels.

"Here," I tell him. "Wear these diamond earrings. They always looked better on you than me."

We don pearls and gloves and set off. It takes a while to circumvent Buck's security system, but Dana has Herbert's smarts. Outside the secret lair, the winter sky is cobalt blue and the bitter air makes my skin tingle. Trees along the frozen river have long since fallen under the weight of ice and snow, leaving a splintered landscape. I should have brought snowshoes. Dana tosses his skate guards aside and we help each other stay upright. It'll be nice if Buck's plan succeeds. If the world's gardens and forests return after such a long, deep sleep.

"There once was a boy named Cass," Dana says, after we've gone maybe a half mile. The breeze blows his hair back from his handsome face. "Whose balls were made of brass. In stormy weather, they would bang together…"

He sits down on an icy boulder. "Funny. I can't remember."

He's never forgotten a limerick. I sit down beside him and pat his gloved hand. His blue eyes stay fixed on the distance. I think he sees Neill. I think I see Neill, too. Neill with his white hat, and Cody with his green bandana, and Yuri with his big old leather boots. There's Doc, too, smiling like he knows a secret. It's a hallucination, of course, and the only one I've ever had without the help of illegal chemicals. Those four sexy robots come over and pull Dana to his feet.

"Time to skate, partner," Neill says.

I stand up, too, but Doc shakes his head fondly. "Not you, Katherine. You've got a world to rebuild and a new body to do it in."

"Buck doesn't want me," I say vehemently. "He wants an ideal. He wants someone to worship him, the bastard. Seventy years and nothing's changed."

"Doesn't matter what Buck wants," Neill tells me. "You get a chance at life, you live it. Write more books."

"You never read my other ones," I sniff.

"Sure I did," he says. "When you weren't looking. Didn't want you to get a swelled head."

"Write stories about us," Cody adds. "Tell them we lived, and we loved, and we ate lots of flapjacks."

Yuri blows me a kiss. "Persevere, sweet Kay."

They skate off into the sunset, my five sexy robots, doing triple lutzes on the way.

I guess, for the boys, I can live some more. I can write their stories, and the story of life before the Big Ice. I can cut Skylar's hair, get rid of that cowboy skirt, and bang a notion or two through Buck's thick metal skull. But first I have to get off this rock and back up the frozen river. The wind is strong but the sun warms my face, and along the way I hear the sound of water dripping off trees. The world is renewing. I'm glad I'll be here to see it.

THE SPY WHO NEVER GREW UP
SARAH REES BRENNAN

Sarah Rees Brennan was raised in Ireland where her teachers valiantly tried to make her fluent in Irish, but she chose instead to read books under her desk in class. The books most often found under her desk were by Jane Austen, Margaret Mahy, Anthony Trollope, Robin McKinley, and Diana Wynne Jones, and she still loves them all today.

After college she lived briefly in New York and somehow survived in spite of her habit of hitching lifts in fire engines. She began working on her first novel while doing a Creative Writing MA and library work in Surrey, England. Since then she has returned to Ireland to write and to use as a home base for future adventures. *The Demon's Lexicon* was published in 2009, followed by *The Demon's Covenant*. A final volume in the series, *The Demon's Surrender*, is due later this year.

There is a magic shore where children used to beach their coracles every night.

The children have stopped coming now, and their little boats are tipped over on their sides, like the abandoned shells of nuts eaten long ago. The dark sea rushes up to the pale beach and just touches the crafts, making them rattle together with a sound like bones.

You and I cannot reach that shore again. We've forgotten everything. Even the sound of the waves and the mermaids singing.

But the men in Her Majesty's Secret Service can go anywhere.

The submarine drifted to a stop not far from the island, its periscope breaking the surface of the water like the lifted nose of an inquisitive pointer dog. After a few minutes, a man emerged from the submarine and got into a boat, one not at all like the children's boats arrayed on the shore.

When the boat sliced through water to white sand, the man stepped out of it.

They had given him a number and taken away his name.

Unfortunately for him, his number was 69.

This was a subject of many tasteless jokes in the Service, but nobody would have known that from 69's serious face and his extremely dapper black suit.

He took a few purposeful steps along the shore to the forest, then looked down. Under his feet, and under a layer of the black grease of age and filth, were pebbles like jewels and children's toys and human bones.

There was a barely perceptible shift in the air before his face, but the men and women in Her Majesty's Secret Service are extremely highly trained. 69 looked up.

The boy before him was beautiful in a slightly terrible way, like a kiss with no innocence in it.

More to the point, he was holding a sword as if he knew how to use it, and floating about a yard above the ground.

"Dark and sinister suit," said the boy. "Have at thee."

"I am afraid I do not have time to indulge you," 69 said. "I am here on a mission from Her Majesty."

"Ah," said the boy, tilting his chin. "I know it well."

"I beg your pardon?"

"The Majesty," the boy said, waving his sword vaguely. "Belonging to… Her. I know all about it."

"Her Majesty *the Queen*," 69 said, with a trifle more emphasis than was necessary.

"I knew that," the boy informed him.

"She feels that the Service has a need for a man—"

The boy hissed like a vampire exposed to sunlight, lifting his free arm as if to protect himself from the word. *Man.*

"Excuse me. A *boy* of your special talents," 69 said smoothly.

He had been raised in diplomatic circles.

The boy spun around in a circle, like a ballerina with a sword in zero gravity.

"My talents are special! So awfully special!"

"Indeed," said 69. His countenance remained unchanged. 69 was very highly trained, and also a gifted amateur poker player.

"And the Queen needs—someone of such talents for a job."

The boy started to laugh, a high lovely laugh that wavered between a baby's gurgle and the peal of bells. It did not sound quite sane.

"A job?" he asked. "Make a man of me, will you? Oh no, oh no. You sailed your boat to the wrong shore." He made a quick, deadly gesture with his small sword to the island around them, the dark stones and trees with branches like bared claws. "This is no place for men."

"So I see," said 69. "And I see there is nobody here who would be brave enough to risk all for Her Majesty's sake: nobody who is enough of a patriot to die for their country."

Peter was not entirely sure what a "patriot" was, but he would have scorned to betray this fact. He did not even acknowledge it to himself, really: Peter's thoughts always move like a stone on water, skipping and skimming along the surface until they hit a certain spot.

69 had turned toward the sea, but he was not entirely surprised when a sword landed, light as a very sharp butterfly's wing, on his shoulder.

He turned back to meet the sight of the lovely, terrible smile.

"To die for your country," said Peter. "Would that be an awfully big adventure?"

The party was a very glamorous affair, with chandeliers like elaborate ice sculptures and ice sculptures like elaborate chandeliers.

This created an effect of very tasteful strobe lights playing on the discreet black clothing of the guests.

A suspiciously nondescript man paused on his voyage over the glowing floor to speak to a lady. She was wearing a dress more daring than any of the party dresses around her, and very striking lipstick.

They were, of course, both spies.

"Who are you hunting today?"

"Oh, the English, of course," said the lady. She did not turn her Ts into Zs except when playing certain roles, but her faint accent was nevertheless very Russian. "Look at their latest golden *boy*."

She laid a certain emphasis on the word boy.

Let us play *I Spy*, and follow the spies' line of vision to the bar where a boy was leaning. He wore a black suit like every other suit in the room, tailored to discreet perfection.

The look was rather spoiled by the knotted dead leaf he was wearing as a bowtie.

The Russian spy detached from her companion and came over to the bar, slinking like a panther in an evening gown. Which is to say, with some suggestion that the evening gown might be torn off at any moment.

She offered the boy her hand. "I don't believe I've had the pleasure."

The lady noted his wary look, and told herself that no matter how young he seemed, he was obviously a true professional. She was not to know this was how Peter regarded all grown-ups.

"Ivana," she murmured, which I must tell you was a fib.

"The name's Pan," said Peter, who I must admit was showing off. "Peter Pan."

Neither of them was really on their best behavior. Spies rarely are.

"What will you have?" asked the bartender.

"Martini," said Ivana. "Shaken, not stirred."

"Milk," said Peter. "Warm, not hot."

The bartender and Ivana both gave Peter rather doubtful looks. Peter has been receiving such looks for more years than he could ever count, and he looked disdainfully back.

"Come now," Ivana said, and reached for Peter's arm. "I think we can do better than that. After all, you're almost a man."

Peter's eyes narrowed. "*No. I am not.*"

She was very clever, that Russian spy who was not really called Ivana. She instantly saw she had made a mistake.

"I meant to suggest that this affair must be boring you. After all, it really isn't up to the excitement that a boy of your... many talents must be used to."

Peter looked more favorably upon her. "I do have many talents. Thousands, really. Millions of talents. Nobody has ever had as many talents as I!"

"I don't doubt it."

"I keep them in a box," said Peter, and looked briefly puzzled when Ivana laughed and then triumphant as he decided he had meant all the time to make a splendid joke.

He beamed at her, and Ivana reared back.

She quickly collected herself, however. Remember, she was very well-trained.

"I imagine you have done many things," Ivana murmured. "Such as the affair of Lady Carlisle's necklace in the embassy?"

"Oh that! Yes, I took it! I flew in under cover of darkness and stole it."

Ivana blinked. "You did?"

"I am a master thief," Peter said with some satisfaction.

"It was my understanding that the English were the ones who got the necklace back," Ivana said slowly.

"Oh yes," Peter told her. "I fought the dastardly thieves single-handed and restored the jewels to their rightful owner! I remember now."

"I see," said Ivana.

The spies in Her Majesty's Secret Service have long been renowned for their discretion. To protect their country, some have been known to spin a deft tale. Some have died rather than speak. Some, even under torture, have preserved a perfect British silence.

No spy but Pan has ever confessed to everything.

Ivana the Russian was getting a bit of a migraine. She rather wished Peter would take a breath between highly incriminating confessions.

"The Taj Mahal," she began.

"I killed him," Peter said. "He was a tyrant."

"It is a *building*," Ivana informed him with a certain amount of hauteur.

Peter, occupied with relating the details of the epic battle he had fought, chose to ignore her. They were sitting at a small table in low light, away from the bar. Ivana had quite a row of martini glasses lined up before her. Peter was working on his seventeenth glass of warm milk.

"And what about the documents regarding that invention the Americans were making such a fuss about last week?" said Ivana, who had abandoned diplomacy and cunning around the time of martini number nine.

"I have those," Peter told her complacently, and Ivana was heaving another irritated sigh when Peter added, "Upstairs in my room. I have them hidden in the nightstand. I'm meant to hand them over to the Queen tonight, but my helpers needed to rest, so here I am at this boring party."

Ivana hesitated. "I should very much like to see them." She paused and then smiled a coaxing smile. "It would be so thrilling to see proof of how clever you are, Peter!"

"It would be very thrilling for you," Peter agreed.

"And I would be terribly grateful."

"How grateful?" Peter asked.

Ivana looked slightly startled. "Very grateful indeed."

Peter's eyes brightened. "Do you know any bedtime stories?"

"My dear boy," said Ivana, not missing a beat. "Hundreds."

Since Ivana really was very clever, and Peter could be extremely heedless, she might very well have got her hands on the American documents that night. Except that Peter, careless as always, had forgotten to mention one small detail.

His helpers were indeed resting. Pan's elite team of killer fairies was having a little nap in the nightstand, right on top of the documents.

"Troops, troops!" Peter bawled over all the yelling. "Attention! Attention! That means you, Ninja Star! Stop kicking her in the earlobe right now!"

Ninja Star was his best fairy and was the captain whenever Peter was on a solo mission or got bored and wandered off. There was no denying zie had a temper.

"You should be ashamed of yourselves," said Peter severely, because he knew that discipline was vital. Then he became bored with his role as stern commander, spun and levitated three feet in the air.

It was probably for the best. It hadn't seemed to him like Ivana knew any bedtime stories at all.

Ivana made the discreet decision not to try and get up. She watched with wide eyes as the boy rocketed out of the window, a silhouette in the moonlight, with the fairies following him like a host of tiny stars.

Given the new evidence, Ivana was going to have to reevaluate some of Peter's claims. With his ability to fly and his tiny helpers, a good many more of the missions he boasted about might be true.

And many of his stories were true, especially the wildest ones, because Peter often had strange and terrible adventures.

Which ones, we will never know. Peter does not even know himself.

Still, I think we—and Ivana—may be reasonably sure that Peter never fought a duel to the death with the Taj Mahal.

Her Majesty, by the Grace of God, of the United Kingdom of Great Britain and Northern Ireland and of Her Other Realms and Territories Queen, Head of the Commonwealth, Defender of the Faith, was quite vexed.

She had been forced by abject pleading, several resignations, and (in one unfortunate case) an incarceration in a secure mental facility to receive Pan's reports herself.

It was, however, growing extremely late. She had been up all day meeting with tedious ministers and an enormously dreary duchess, and she found her eyes traveling too often to the sack that lay at her butler's feet.

I hesitate to tell a lady's secrets, but she was wearing a dressing gown. It was sky blue and patterned with tiny silver crowns.

She was also wearing fluffy bunny slippers. The bunnies had crowns too.

"If I might be so bold, Your Majesty," said her butler, who was called both Dawson and Night Shadow. He was a judo master and weapons expert, and his butlering was exceptional. "The boy is late."

"The boy is always late. I gave him a watch once."

"How did he lose it?" asked Dawson.

"He *claimed*," the Queen said in the magnificently noncommittal voice that made statesmen blush and prime ministers recall other engagements, "to have choked a mutant shark to death with it."

Dawson bowed his head.

Hurtling through the purple sky of London, streamers of light thrown across it by the city, through the wide windows of Buckingham Palace, came a boy. Fairies danced around him, wreathing his wild hair like a crown made of lightning.

Peter touched down lightly on the carpet, presented a roll of documents to Her Majesty, and swept her a superb bow.

The Queen graciously inclined her head and unrolled the documents on her tea tray.

"The device illustrated in these documents actually expands mass," she said absently. "Which would be most useful in the right hands—curing world hunger and the like—but since it seems to have been invented by the *wrong* hands—"

Since this was boring adult stuff, Peter wandered about the room and danced up and down the velvet curtains, from the floor to the curtain rungs and back again. The Queen glanced up from an intricate plan of weaponry.

"Exemplary work as always, Mr. Pan." The Queen glanced up from the diagrams Peter had brought her.

"Yes, I am exemplary," Peter crowed.

He went pinwheeling across the solemn crenellated dome of the Queen's bedroom ceiling. The Queen cleared her throat to indicate that aerodynamic acrobatics in the presence of royalty were frowned on.

Peter plummeted neatly onto the hearthrug and bowed again, as if he took the royal throat-clearing for applause.

"You must know," said the Queen, "I would be happier with a more traditional means of payment for your services."

Peter tilted his head to one side. There was a cold watchful light in his eyes now, like the glint children imagine they see after bedtime, when the night-light has been turned off and shadows and shivers start creeping into bed with them.

Peter has been peeping through windows for a very long time.

"Do you mean 'money'?" he asked, pronouncing the word as if it was in a foreign language. "What use do I have for money, grown-up? If I want something on Neverland, I kill for it. If I want something here, I steal it. There is only one thing I want that you can give me. I want my mother!"

The Queen inclined her head again, this time less graciously.

She had made many terrible decisions in her time. Her Majesty always, always pays her debts.

"There she is."

The eyes of the Queen, Peter, and Night Shadow aka Dawson the butler, all turned to the sack at Dawson's feet. We can see now that there is a slight shifting of the rough material, as if something is breathing beneath.

Peter looked uncertain. "They never used to come in sacks," he said. "They used to be happy to see me."

The Queen, who had had a lot of ruling to do that day, and for the last sixty years, lost patience. She turned away from the boy and the moving sack, back to her own plans.

"As I am certain you've noticed, Mr. Pan," she said. "Times have changed."

"Second to the right, and straight on till morning," are not real directions, though Peter thought they were. The truth was that by now the path to Neverland knew Peter by heart and was always drawing him home, like a compass point to true north or a ghost to the place he was murdered.

Peter flew with an easy grace, even with the sack in his hand.

Sometimes he tossed it about with the fairies, just for sport, but Peter thought he was being most responsible. He made clear that any fairy who dropped the sack would have to answer to Ninja Star.

It was a piece of great good luck that the bag only started squirming and making loud, distressed sounds as they were flying over Neverland. The sack had been quiet so long, Peter had forgotten what was in it, and was startled enough that he dropped it.

Ninja Star and the team flew very quickly to catch it, but only succeeded in slowing it down, so the sack fairly tumbled to the stones and bones below.

Ashley Horowitz, daughter of Karen, daughter of Tracy, daughter of Margaret, daughter of Jane, daughter of Wendy, came out of the sack rolling, and pepper-sprayed Peter in the face.

For a moment she thought she must have made a terrible mistake. There she was on the island of nightmares—even worse than Grandma had described it—but the boy before her could not possibly be Pan the destroyer, Pan the thief in the night. He was sitting on the blackened shore and weeping in bewildered pain, as if he was terribly young and crying for the very first time.

"Boy," began Ashley. "Why are you—"

Then she remembered: that was how he got you. She took a step back and lifted her pepper spray in steady hands.

"Stay back," she said. "Or I'll make you cry harder."

When he rose to his feet, she knew it was him. Pan. He was not exactly as her grandmother had described him either: he was worse. He was as beautiful as her grandmother had said—as fascinating as a snake's golden eyes to a bird—but he was that thing he never was, never could be. He was… older.

She was older, too. She was past the age when he was meant to be exactly her size, and now here he was looking down at her.

The bones of his wild, lovely face had stronger, sterner angles than in the pictures. His body had more muscle and was more easily weighted to the earth. He was not a little boy anymore.

It was horrible to see those curling, crowing lips part, to show he still had all his baby teeth.

"Pan," said Ashley.

Peter smiled more widely, his tiny teeth like little pearls gleaming in his changing face. "Mother."

He advanced and Ashley backed up, wielding her pepper spray like a weapon.

"My name is Ashley. And I'm not your mother!"

"There was a bargain made," said Peter.

Quick as a flash, he drew and thrust. At the touch of his blade, the pepper spray flew out of Ashley's grasp and into the dark seas beyond.

"My great-grandmother," said Ashley, starting a little uncertainly and then gaining strength as she spoke. Margaret had been nothing but old family history to her, a story in a book. But so had he. "Margaret. She went mad."

Peter tilted his head, his eyes blank. "Margaret?"

"She used to scream your name," said Ashley. "My grandma used to hear her through the walls screaming for you. And you don't remember her?"

"Well, if you're going to get all sniffy about it, I'll say that I'm sorry," said Peter, with the air of one making a great concession.

"Tracy," said Ashley. "Margaret. Jane. Wendy!"

Peter drew in his lip a little, startled and hurt, as if it was the very first time he had ever been hurt, although the tears from his last bout of misery were still wet on his cheeks.

"Wendy."

It made sense that he would remember her. She had been the first.

Ashley drew in a deep breath.

"I don't want to be here," she said flatly. "I demand to go home."

She turned and walked away into the forests of Neverland.

Neverland was both like and unlike her grandmother's stories, and the pictures in the book. It was unmistakably the same place, but it was changed like Peter himself: the trees naked as skeletons, no ships on the horizon. There was a quality about the silent darkness that Ashley recognized from being a little girl, too scared even to get out of bed and reach the light switch. The whole island was like a huge bedroom for a scared child, in which morning would not come again.

The silence was broken by some terrible rustles and slithers.

Ashley turned fast at the sound and found Peter gliding beside her, a few feet off the ground.

"Those are the wild beasts," he said. "Don't go too far away from me. They'll kill you if they can. They're starving."

"Where are the—the Native Americans?" Ashley asked.

Peter gave her a blank look.

"Tiger Lily, I mean, and the others," Ashley said, summoning up the name from the book.

"Most of them died," Peter replied. "The others went away."

Her grandmother had made sure she always had pepper spray under her pillow. Ashley wished now that Grandma Tracy had told her to always dress for an abduction. Bare feet and glittery pink pajamas were not exactly ideal for a trek through Neverland.

She kept walking, though, until they came to Marooners' Rock. The rock was just the same. The lagoon stretched around it, black and viscous, like tar with ghosts moving in it.

It took Ashley a moment to realize that the gray shapes, their ragged fins dragging the surface, their hair like clogged seaweed, were the mermaids who used to toss bubbles to each other and sing. Peter flew over to hover above the lagoon like a huge dragonfly.

"What—" Ashley said, and stood rubbing the gooseflesh out of her own arms. "What happened here?"

"There was a Lost Boy who came back," Peter said distantly. "He had—he was a—"

Peter choked trying to say the word "grown-up" with the same trouble other people had talking about death.

"He thought there was a profit to be made of the Neverland," Peter said. "He learned too late that he was wrong."

Peter twisted in midair until he was floating on his back, kicking at a breeze. A mermaid reached up out of the waters to touch his heel: her fingers were withered and gray.

"But the island changed before that," Peter admitted. "Children's dreams were changing."

That was what Grandma Tracy had seen, the spring Peter had come for her. That was what had scared her so badly. The beginning of this.

"I knew that I wasn't wanted," said Peter. "Windows have been barred against me before. I didn't come for the next girl, did I?"

"Yep, thanks for not kidnapping my mom," said Ashley. "Big of you."

Peter came to settle on Marooners' Rock, sitting near where Ashley stood. The mermaids swarmed in the waters about his feet like goldfish wanting to be fed.

"I knew I wasn't wanted," he said. "But… I still need a mother."

He leaned trustingly against Ashley's legs. Ashley, who was a kind-hearted girl, resisted the impulse to push him into the lagoon.

"Times have changed, Peter. A lot fewer girls dream of being mothers. Some of them want adventures of their own."

You will have to forgive Ashley. She did not know Peter very well yet.

She began to know him better when he tilted his head back to grin up at her. His curly hair was against her knee, and his smile was a devil's.

If Satan had all his baby teeth, that is.

"You want an adventure?"

"Peter," said Ashley, with commendable, but much belated, caution. "Peter, *noooooo!*"

I would not have you think Ashley screamed out of fear. In fact, she screamed because Peter had seized her up and was flying with her through the trees.

Hang gliding is a bit alarming at the best of times. When your hang glider is a flying boy criminal, it is most unnerving indeed.

They zoomed over the trees of Neverland, wind rushing in their ears. Ashley soon ran out of breath to scream.

"Fly!" Peter yelled encouragingly. "Fly, fly! All you have to do is think happy thoughts!"

He began to let her go when a furious tinkle from Ninja Star, like a dinner bell in a panic, gave him pause.

"What's the fairy saying?"

"Oh," Peter said airily, "zie says that if I don't blow fairy dust on you, you will plummet to your death."

"Plummet to my death!"

"I think you're being most unfair," Peter said to Ashley sternly. "I cannot be expected to remember every little thing."

He detached an arm from around her—I confess she screamed again—and reached out for Ninja Star, who he shook expertly over Ashley's head like a top chef with a saltshaker.

"Suspended in midair with a boy pouring glitter on me," Ashley muttered. "I was really looking forward to being old enough to get into nightclubs. Now? Not so much."

"Nonsense, being old isn't any fun, everyone knows that," said Peter briskly. "Quick, happy thoughts!"

"Peter Pan in jail for kidnap and assault!" Ashley yelled. "Peter Pan gets a twenty-year sentence! No! Ever so much more than twenty!"

Peter dropped her.

He managed to catch her before she dashed out her brains and broke every bone in her body on the rocks below, but it was a very near thing.

"You idiot!" Ashley screamed, grabbing hold of his shoulders and shaking him. "I nearly died!"

Peter made play with his eyebrows. "Well, yes," he said. "That happens with adventures."

The tree house was very cold at night, and Ashley could hear the mermaids howling like wolves in the moonlight. Peter seemed to drop off instantly to sleep, but Ashley had no plans to escape her captor. For one thing, she had no idea how to get back from Neverland, and for another, she had no desire to have her head bitten off by a wild beast. She huddled under a blanket of flowers and leaves, and tried to sleep.

In the morning Ninja Star woke her by tinkling about her head like a glittery mobile alarm clock. Ashley thought longingly of home, and flyswatters.

Upon further study of Ninja Star, who was a violent blue color and covered in scars, Ashley decided she probably wouldn't dare.

"Zie wants to know if you would like to train with zir team," Peter translated in gentlemanly fashion.

Ashley's brow furrowed. "She—"

"*Zie*," Peter said. "Ninja Star is intersex. That's what zie prefers."

A line from the book floated through Ashley's head: *the mauve ones are boys and the white ones are girls, and the blue ones are just little sillies who are not sure what they are.*

Ashley wondered why she'd never noticed that line before.

She also noted that Ninja Star looked pretty sure of what she was.

She was right. Fairies, as you and I both know, only ever feel one feeling at a time. Ninja Star spent 99 percent of zir time feeling fierce.

"Why is—um, zie—called Ninja Star?"

Peter looked rather shocked at Ashley's ignorance. "Because zie is the best ninja, of course."

Ashley chose her next words with care. "Are… all your fairies ninjas, Peter?"

"Naturally," said Peter with a lofty air.

Ashley was left with a dilemma. On one hand, these were the survivors of Neverland, the battle-scarred companions of Peter Pan, fierce and deadly warriors. On the other, they were about three inches high and glittery.

"I'd be very honored to train with you," she told the blue blur that was Ninja Star.

From then on Ashley trained most mornings with the ninja fairies on the shore. She tried her best, but I confess sometimes Ninja Star despaired: she was so big and clumsy, it was hard to teach her to be stealthy like the ninja. And, of course, not being able to fly, Ashley could not perform the ninjas' very best trick— aggressive skydiving at the enemy's eyeballs.

Nevertheless, it cheered Ashley up. She was a girl who liked to keep busy.

She was also growing more used to Peter. He has a way about him, it must be admitted. If Peter awake fails to charm, Peter asleep is a heartbreaker.

On the third night in the tree house he woke Ashley, crying and shaking in his sleep. Ashley remembered his dreams—the sore shaking dreams of a boy who had lived through a hundred childhoods and a thousand lost, dark memories—not from her grandmother's stories but from Wendy's book. Wendy had loved him.

He had more dark memories now than in Wendy's day, and he was older, at last. Ashley could not hold him, but she did her best. She stroked his wild curling hair until he was quiet.

"What did you dream last night?" she asked the next day.

"Dream?" said Peter, and laughed a blithe sweet laugh. "I have so many adventures when I'm awake, I never have to dream!"

"You dreamed something last night," Ashley persisted, following him. He was playing a game of leapfrog from one toadstool to the other. You would think they might break under Peter's weight, but they never did.

Peter spun on his toadstool, and Ashley found herself staring down the length of his blade.

"No, Ashley lady," he said. "I never dream."

Ashley stepped back. Peter sheathed his sword and performed a cartwheel in midair.

"What adventure shall we have today? Do you want to—"

"No, I don't," said Ashley. "I've told you. I don't want to be your mother, and I don't care for Neverland!"

She turned on her heel and then found Peter hovering before her. He was very irritating that way.

"Oh well," he said. "Why didn't you say so? Would you like to go on one of my missions for the Queen?"

I am afraid to tell you that Ashley was not what you might call a trusting soul. She did not believe a word of Peter's tale about being a spy for Her Majesty's government.

In her defense, Peter did tell the Taj Mahal story.

Of course she did not believe him, but she did see an opportunity.

"If I go with you on this adventure," she said, with great cunning. "Shall we play a game? Shall we have a bet, between us?"

Peter's eyes lit. "Yes!"

"Great," said Ashley. "If I don't like this adventure, and if, after it, I still want to go home—you have to take me."

Meeting the Queen of England is an important event in a girl's life. The social niceties should be observed. Little things like using the correct fork, dropping a deep enough curtsy, and not breaking into the royal boudoir while wearing pink pajamas.

Ashley found herself rather embarrassed before she realized that the Queen was responsible for her kidnap.

"Doesn't that strike you as a bit of a terrible thing to do?" she demanded, cutting her off as the Queen briefed Peter about a new mission.

The Queen had taken the break-in with great aplomb, sitting up in bed and reaching for her spectacles with one hand while waving away her killer butler with the other. A little thing like being accused of a criminal act was hardly going to faze her.

"My dear child, I do a hundred terrible things before breakfast, that is the role of the monarchy." She directed her spectacles toward Peter again. "Do you understand the situation, Mr. Pan? I would like you to apprehend the person who has invented this device to multiply the mass of objects by ten."

"You can rely on me with absolute confidence!" said Peter, who was perched on the edge of a priceless Ming vase.

The Queen rubbed her royal brow. "May I stress that 'apprehend' means 'bring to me,' Mr. Pan? We need this person's brain in her head, rather than—I pick this example purely at random—impaled on one of the clock hands of Big Ben."

Peter rolled his eyes in protest at this senseless rule.

"I am forced to trust in your discretion, Mr. Pan," the Queen said. "Remember that the fate of the free world rests in your hands."

It was very unfortunate that at that precise moment Peter aimed an idle kick and shattered the Ming vase into a thousand pieces.

"Oh my God, you—you... Your Majesty," exclaimed Ashley, not quite outraged enough to insult royalty. "I beg your pardon. But are you insane? The fate of a boiled egg shouldn't rest in his hands! Isn't there some other agent you can send?"

"Another agent with the power of flight and little helper ninjas?" the Queen asked, her brows lifting above the frames of her spectacles. "I regret to say, no. Please close the window on your way out, Mr. Pan: last time there was a shocking draught."

"So will we have to stake out the town?" asked Ashley, who was beginning to get enthusiastic about being a spy. Being personally given a mission by the Queen of England is very motivating. "To see which house is the crazed inventor's—oh!"

Do not be alarmed. Peter has not dropped Ashley out of the sky, only to catch her at the last minute. Ashley had made it clear she did not think that was a hilarious game.

She had merely spotted the small picturesque village of Litford by the Sea, which had thatched cottages and rambling manors, cobbled byways and streams under wood bridges. And on top of a hill near the town was a gaunt black structure with fiery windows. It looked like a castle of nightmares, a place an old pirate went to retire and gnaw on booty and bones.

It looked like something out of Neverland.

"Seems to me we've tracked the varlet to his lair!" Peter crowed.

"Peter, doesn't this seem a little weird to you?"

Peter stared at her, all guileless eyes and crazy smile curling around those little pearl teeth, his dead leaf bowtie fluttering in the wind.

"Weird?"

"Ah," said Ashley. "Never mind."

It struck Ashley that this was something Peter and the ninjas just accepted: the macabre and fantastical, all the trappings of Neverland. Ashley was the only one who could see the difference between what should be real and what should not be: she had some power here.

It pains me to confess Ashley had little poetry in her soul.

She would have preferred titanium body armor.

The castle floors were largely made of big flagstones. Ashley's bare feet ached for the carpets of home, or even the forest floors of Neverland.

The castle echoed with the creak of machinery, the pop and sizzle of flames, and the sound of screams. This place reeked of pure, storybook evil.

Ashley kept thinking of a particular name in the story.

Hook.

"The villain never really dies," she murmured as she crept after Peter. Her ninja training made her light on her feet, so it was really a shame that Peter and the fairies showed her up by gliding silently a few inches off the ground.

She was distracted from these dark musings by three mad scientists. Ashley could tell they were scientists by the lab coats, and that they were mad by the maniacal laughter.

Peter drew his sword and killed two of them. Ashley gave the other a kick in the kneecap, and then he went down. The fairies finished him off.

"Now we put on these evil lab coats and make our way into the heart of the evil fortress," Peter commanded.

Ashley put on her lab coat doubtfully. It was really quite evil-looking. The name tag read DR STRANGE FEELINGS OF CONFUSION AND RAGE.

She was also extremely uncertain about two barefoot kids trying to pass themselves off as scientists, no matter how mad said scientists happened to be. It would never work.

When she heard steps barging down an appropriately echoing stairwell, she thought frantically of how the spies on TV would act to distract attention from what they were doing.

So as the next set of mad scientists approached, she whirled, pushed Peter up against the wall, and kissed him on the mouth.

She had her eyes shut, but she could feel his mouth open in amazement. For a moment the world was still and peaceful, the hard angle of his jaw against her fingers, her senses flooded with the taste of berries and the smell of leaves.

When the scientists had passed, Ashley leaned back. The world remained peaceful for a moment, the wild lights in Peter's eyes gone golden and a little hazy.

"Peter," Ashley asked softly, "Do you know what that was?"

"Of course," Peter said, much affronted. "A thimble."

"No," said Ashley, staring. "That was a kiss."

"It was a thimble!"

"Didn't it strike you as a little different from other thimbles you've had in the past?"

Peter looked shifty.

"Well, yes."

"Ha!"

"It was my first thimble with tongue," Peter told her with dignity.

Ashley fixed him with a look of unutterable despair and then stalked down the stairs toward the grim creaking of dread machines, her evil lab coat trailing in her wake.

The fairies and Peter followed her, Ninja Star making a belligerent ringing sound as they went.

"Ninja Star, please, how can you be so inappropriate!" said Peter, deeply shocked.

"What'd she say?"

"I refuse to tell you!"

"Heh," said Ashley, making the wise decision that being amused was better than being driven to madness. "You're a bit old-fashioned, aren't you?"

"I am not old anything," Peter snapped.

And so bickering at the top of their lungs, our spies stumbled into the evil at the heart of the fortress.

There was a large chair, of course, looming almost like a throne. It stood on a dais, shrouded in shadow.

There was someone sitting in it.

Ashley's voice died in her throat, and her heart beat like a child's fists on a door, begging to get out. All the fears of her nursery got together and whispered.

Hook.

The figure in the chair leaned forward. "Peter?"

It was a golden-haired girl, plump and beautifully dressed.

Even taking into account the natural distortion of legends over time, Ashley felt this could not possibly be Captain Hook.

She looked to Peter for help, but Peter was looking perfectly blank.

"It's me, Peter," said the girl. "Only—I'm bigger now."

Ashley's world tilted a little, the story changing beyond all recognition. The Queen's documents showed a machine that increased an object's size ten times.

Not just an object. Anything.

The machine had not been created for an evil purpose, not at first. But who knew what terrible mixture of science and magic had worked together to enlarge a creature who could only feel one thing at a time—and fix her like that forever, full of rage and hate.

Creating a villain out of a fairy.

Ashley whispered, "Tinker Bell."

"Doesn't ring a bell," said Peter. "Sorry."

Tinker Bell went purple with rage. Under the circumstances, Ashley felt she could hardly blame her.

"Perhaps you're thinking of a different Peter," Peter continued helpfully. "Though it would be hard to mistake me for another boy. There is nobody quite like me!"

"This is no time for crowing," Ashley said out of the corner of her mouth.

"He'd have to be really amazingly wonderful," Peter went on and then Ashley kicked him in the ankle.

Peter looked surprised and annoyed.

"Peter," Ashley said firmly. "We're on a mission. Now I don't think she'll attack you" —though looking at Tinker Bell's enraged face, she was not altogether certain about that—"so I'll get her to attack me."

"I wouldn't dream of it," Peter said. "I am the spy here. I'll run her through."

"The Queen said she was to be brought back for questioning! And if we can change her back, make her less inclined to be, well, you know, evil—"

Peter looked around at the high Gothic windows and the white cat in Tinker Bell's lap.

"I do see your point."

He looked around further and espied a machine that looked a little bit like the offspring of a telescope and a giant spider. "I say, Ashley. I think I've come up with a brilliant plan!"

"Have you indeed," said Ashley, very dry.

"You'll never guess."

"I'm not so sure of that, Peter."

Peter began to sidle with rather obvious stealth toward the contraption.

"What are you doing?" Tinker Bell asked sharply.

Ashley took a hasty step forward. "Why did you want to be big, Tinker Bell?"

Tinker Bell blushed under the fading purple of her rage. "I forget."

Ashley took another step. Tinker Bell's gaze followed her. "I don't think you do."

"Well," said Tinker Bell, and shrugged. "It just didn't seem important afterward, you know. I mean—I realized, Peter is quite ridiculous."

"I quite agree," said Ashley. "Of course, so is world domination."

The white cat was rather abruptly tipped out of Tinker Bell's lap as she stood up. "You take that back!" she exclaimed, and in her fury, her voice was like the ringing of bells.

"I will not," said Ashley. "Jealous other woman, doing it all for love, evil overlord bent on world domination? Don't you ever get tired of being a cliché, Tinker Bell? Don't you ever just—

"Now, Peter, now!"

For Ashley had broken off in the middle of her sentence and delivered a roundhouse kick to Tinker Bell's stomach. Tinker Bell fell directly into the path of the machine Peter had just turned on.

In some ways it was a pity. It had been shaping up to be rather a good speech.

Ninja Star approved very much, however. Ashley even received some compliments from the other fairies about her style.

Tinker Bell, the evil genius; Tinker Bell, the fairy transformed, was captured in a ray of light and diminished once more, her stolen inches glowing and falling away. It was terrible at first,

Tinker Bell's face locked in a snarl. But then it was different suddenly: like a snake shedding a skin, or a butterfly emerging from a chrysalis.

When the light of the machine faded, Tinker Bell was small and shining once again.

Ashley stood staring, fascinated. Ninja Star took the initiative and imprisoned Tinker Bell in an empty crisp packet.

"I did it!" Peter crowed, and very nearly hit his head on the ceiling of the evil lair, soaring in triumph.

The Queen took being presented with the tiniest evil genius in the world very well. She commended both Peter and Ashley, which left Ashley rather dazed for a while until Peter's crowing annoyed her again.

"Oh Peter, do be quiet," she said crossly, as they flew over Big Ben, badly startling a family of pigeons. "I think it's rather sad. She did it for love, after all."

"Did she?" asked Peter, rather bored. "Who did she love, then?"

Ashley gave him a withering glance.

"Well, it's no use looking at me like that," Peter told her, injured. "How am I supposed to know? I've never seen the fairy before in my life!"

And no matter how she argued, he stuck to that.

Ashley finally sighed in exasperation and gave up. "You know, considering her, and Tiger Lily, and Wendy… for someone determined never to grow up, you're a bit of a playboy."

Peter frowned, and then his brow smoothed. "It's true that I am a boy," he said. "And I love to play!"

Ashley forbore from slapping him upside the head. He might have dropped her.

"What game shall we play next?" Peter inquired eagerly. "I'm sure that with a bit of perseverance, we can get you flying."

"Peter."

"A little bit of falling hundreds of feet onto bare rock never hurt anybody."

"Peter."

"You just need to think some absolutely scrumptious thoughts."

"Peter," Ashley said. "I prefer to keep my feet on the ground."

She looked at the city of London, sprawled huge and glittering far beyond her dangling toes.

"And," she continued. "I know you haven't forgotten our bargain. I want to go home."

Peter is many things: one of them, when reminded, is a boy of his word. He is too proud not to be.

He flew Ashley back to her window. It was lucky that Ashley, as a rather spoiled only child, had a balcony where he could deposit her. Had he flown her into her bedroom, he would have woken her parents, who were, of course, in there waiting for her.

They had also alerted the police for miles around, but the Queen dealt with that later.

Peter stood on empty air about a foot away from the balcony, his head tilted insouciantly back, arms crossed over his chest.

"You'll grow up," he threw out at Ashley, as if it was the direst threat imaginable.

"You bet," Ashley said. "You might, too."

There was a moment of stillness. Ashley remembered that instant of quiet at the evil fortress, and remembered him dreaming and weeping in Neverland.

"Not yet, Ashley lady," said Peter. "Not yet."

"You can't stay on that island forever."

"Maybe not," Peter told her. "I used to live in Kensington Gardens with the fairies. Dreams change. But there's always another game."

Ashley raised an eyebrow. "The spy thing?"

Peter beamed at her, beautiful and terrible, young and sweet.

The monster her grandmother had feared, with all his first teeth.

"You must admit, Ashley," he said. "I am perfectly splendid at it."

"You're all right," Ashley said grudgingly.

"You assisted me quite creditably," Peter told her grandly.

I do not think it will surprise you when I mention that Ashley was not overwhelmed by this tribute.

"I don't suppose…" said Peter.

"What?"

Peter smiled his most fascinating smile. "You might want to come on another mission with me?"

Ashley studied the horizon. She shouldn't. He was a creature of nightmares as well as dreams, and he had kidnapped her, scared her grandmother, driven her great-grandmother mad.

Her great-great-great-grandmother had loved him, left him, and lived.

"I'll think about it," Ashley said.

Peter crowed and launched himself into the sky, utterly and blissfully happy, the bright triumphant sound trailing after him back to the balcony where

Ashley stood.

She squared her shoulders and opened the doors that would lead to her parents.

Knowing Peter, the next time he came might be many years later. He might be coming for *her* daughter. In which case, Ashley was not going to bother with the pepper spray. She was going to make her child sleep with a taser.

Of course, Peter had no sense of time, and he might get bored and decide to arrive next week.

Ashley went into the house smiling slightly. She would have to look into acquiring that taser as soon as possible.

Across a sky painted with the neon lights of a changing city, headed toward an island being destroyed as dreams grew dark, flew Peter Pan, who never grows up, except now and again—from the fairies' baby in Kensington Gardens to the boy who ruled Neverland to the greatest spy in the Queen's Secret Service.

Times change.

There is always another game.

You don't have to grow up yet.

THE AARNE-THOMPSON CLASSIFICATION REVUE
HOLLY BLACK

Holly Black is the author of the bestselling "The Spiderwick Chronicles." Her first story appeared in 1997, but she gained attention with her debut novel, *Tithe: A Modern Faerie Tale*. She has written eleven "Spiderwick" novels, three novels in her "Modern Faerie Tales" sequence, including Andre Norton Award winner *Valiant: A Modern Tale of Faerie*, and "The Good Neighbors" series of graphic novels. She has also edited *Geektastic: Stories from the Nerd Herd* (with Cecil Castellucci). Black's most recent books are short story collection *The Poison Eaters and Other Stories*, novel *White Cat* (the first book in "The Curse Workers" series), and anthology *Zombies vs. Unicorns* (with Justine Larbalestier). Upcoming is new novel *Red Glove* and anthology *Welcome to Bordertown* (with Ellen Kushner). She lives in Amherst, Massachusetts, with her husband, the artist Theo Black.

There is a werewolf girl in the city. She sits by the phone on a Saturday night, waiting for it to ring. She paints her nails purple.

She goes to bed early.

Body curled around a pillow, fingers clawing at the bedspread, she dreams that she's on a dating show, a reality television one. She's supposed to pick one boyfriend out of a dozen strangers by eliminating one candidate each week. After eliminations, she eats the guys she's asked to leave. In her dream, the boys get more and more afraid as they overhear screams, but they can't quite believe the show is letting them be murdered one by one, so they convince each other to stay until the end. In the reunion episode, the werewolf girl eats the boy who she's picked to be her boyfriend.

That's the only way to get to do a second season, after all.

When she wakes up, she's sorry about the dream. It makes her feel guilty and a little bit hungry, which makes her feel worse. Her real-life boyfriend is a good guy, the son of a dentist from an ancestral line of dentists. Sometimes, he takes her to his dad's office and they sit in the chairs and suck on nitrous while watching the overhead televisions that are supposed to distract patients. When they do

73

that, the werewolf girl feels calmer than she's felt her whole life.

She's calling herself Nadia in this city. She's called herself Laura and Liana and Dana in other places.

Despite going to bed early, she's woken up tired.

Nadia takes her temperature and jots it down in a little notebook by the side of the bed. Temperature is more accurate than phases of the moon in telling her when she's going to change.

She gets dressed, makes coffee and drinks it. Then goes to work. She is a waitress on a street where there are shirt shops and shops that sell used records and bandanas and studded belts. She brings out tuna salads to aged punks and cappuccinos in massive bowls to tourists who ask her why she doesn't have any tattoos.

Nadia still looks young enough that her lack of references doesn't seem strange to her employers, although she worries about the future. For now, though, she appears to be one of a certain type of girl—a girl that wants to be an actress, who's come in from the suburbs and never really worked before, a girl restaurants in the city employ a lot of. She always asks about flexibility in her interviews, citing auditions and rehearsals. Nadia is glad of the easy excuses, since she does actually need a flexible schedule.

The only problem with her lie is that the other girls ask her to go to auditions.

Sometimes Nadia goes, especially when she's lonely. Her boyfriend is busy learning about teeth and gets annoyed when she calls him. He has a lot of classes. The auditions are often dull, but she likes the part where all the girls stand in line and drink coffee while they wait. She likes the way their skin shimmers with nervous sweat and their eyes shine with the possibility of transformation. The right part will let them leave their dirty little lives behind and turn them into celebrities.

Nadia sits next to another waitress, Rhonda, as they wait to be called back for the second phase of the audition for a musical. Rhonda is fingering a cigarette that she doesn't light—because smoking is not allowed in the building and also because she's trying to quit.

Grace, a willowy girl who can never remember anyone's order at work, has already been cut.

"I hate it when people stop doing things and then they don't want to be around other people doing them," Rhonda says, flipping the cigarette over and over in her fingers. "Like people who stop drinking and then can't hang out in bars. I mean, how can you really know you're over something if you can't deal with being tempted by it?"

Nadia nods automatically, since it makes her feel better to think that letting herself be tempted is a virtue. Sometimes she thinks of the way a ribcage cracks or the way fat and sinew and offal taste when they're gulped down together hot and raw. It doesn't bother her that she has these thoughts, except when they come at inappropriate moments, like being alone with the driver in a taxi or helping a friend clean up after a party.

A large woman with many necklaces calls Rhonda's name and she goes out onto the stage. Nadia takes another sip of her coffee and looks over at the sea of other girls on the call-back list. The girls look back at her through narrowed eyes.

Rhonda comes back quickly. "You're next," she says to Nadia. "I saw the clipboard."

"How was it?"

Rhonda shakes her head and lights her cigarette. "Stupid. They wanted me to jump around. They didn't even care if I could sing."

"You can't smoke in here," one of the other girls says.

"Oh, shove it," says Rhonda.

When Nadia goes out onto the stage, she expects her audition to go fast. She reads monologues in a way that can only be called stilted. She's never had a voice coach. The only actual acting she ever does is when she pretends to be disappointed when the casting people don't want her. Usually she just holds the duffel bags of the other girls as they are winnowed down, cut by cut.

The stage is lit so that she can't see the three people sitting in the audience too well. It's one of those converted warehouse theaters where everyone sits at tables with tea lights and gets up a lot to go to the bar in the back. No tea lights are flickering now.

"We want to teach you a routine," one of them says. A man's voice, with an accent she can't place. "But first—a little about our musical. It's called the *Aarne-Thompson Classification Revue*. Have you heard of it?"

Nadia shakes her head. On the audition call, it was abbreviated ATSCR. "Are you Mr. Aarne?"

He makes a small sound of disappointment. "We like to think of it as a kitchen sink of delights. Animal Tales. Tales of Magic. Jokes. Everything you could imagine. Perhaps the title is a bit dry, but our poster more than makes up for that. You ready to learn a dance?"

"Yes," says Nadia.

The woman with the necklaces comes out on the stage. She shows Nadia some simple steps and then points to crossed strips of black masking tape on the floor.

"You jump from here to here at the end," the woman says.

"Ready?" calls the man. One of the other people sitting with him says something under his breath.

Nadia nods, going over the steps in her head. When he gives her the signal, she twists and steps and leaps. She mostly remembers the moves. At the end, she leaps though the air for the final jump. Her muscles sing.

In that moment, she wishes she wasn't a fake. She wishes that she was a dancer. Or an actress. Or even a waitress. But she's a werewolf and that means she can't really be any of those other things.

"Thank you," another man says. He sounds a little odd, as though he's just woken up. Maybe they have to watch so many auditions that they take turns napping through them. "We'll let you know."

Nadia walks back to Rhonda, feeling flushed. "I didn't think this was a call for *dancers*."

Rhonda rolls her eyes. "It's for a musical. You have to dance in a musical."

"I know," says Nadia, because she does know. But there's supposed to be singing in musicals too. She thought Rhonda would be annoyed at only being asked to dance; Rhonda usually likes to complain about auditions. Nadia looks down at her purple nail polish. It's starting to chip at the edges.

She puts the nail in her mouth and bites it until she bleeds.

Being a werewolf is like being Clark Kent, except that when you go into the phone booth, you can't control what comes out.

Being a werewolf is like being a detective who has to investigate his own crimes.

Being a werewolf means that when you take off your clothes, you're still not really naked. You have to take off your skin too.

Once, when Nadia had a different name and lived in a small town outside of Toronto, she'd been a different girl. She took ballet and jazz dancing. She had a little brother who was always reading her diary. Then one day on her way home from school, a man asked her to help him find his dog. He had a leash and a van and everything.

He ate part of her leg and stomach before anyone found them.

When she woke up in the hospital, she remembered the way he'd caught her with his snout pinning her neck, the weight of his paws. She looked down at her unscarred skin and stretched her arms, ripping the IV needle out without meaning to.

She left home after she tried to turn her three best friends into werewolves too. It didn't work. They screamed and bled. One of them died.

"Nadia," Rhonda is saying.

Nadia shakes off all her thoughts like a wet dog shaking itself dry.

The casting director is motioning to her. "We'd like to see you again," the woman with the necklaces says.

"Her?" Rhonda asks.

When Nadia goes back on stage, they tell her she has the part.

"Oh," says Nadia. She's too stunned to do more than take the packet of information on rehearsal times and tax forms. She forgets to ask them which part she got.

That night Rhonda and Grace insist on celebrating. They get a bottle of cheap champagne and drink it in the back of the restaurant with the cook and two of the dishwashers. Everyone congratulates Nadia and Rhonda keeps telling stories about clueless things that Nadia did on other auditions and how it's a good thing that the casting people only wanted Nadia to dance because she can't act her way out of a paper bag.

Nadia says that no one can act their way out of a paper bag. You can only rip your way out of one. That makes everyone laugh and—Rhonda says—is a perfect example of how clueless Nadia can be.

"You must have done really well in that final jump," Rhonda says. "Were you a gymnast or something? How close did you get?"

"Close to what?" Nadia asks.

Rhonda laughs and takes another swig out of the champagne bottle. "Well, you couldn't have made it. No human being could jump that far without a pole vault."

Nadia's skin itches.

Later, her boyfriend comes over. She's still tipsy when she lets him in and they lie in bed together. For hours he tells her about teeth. Molars. Bicuspids. Dentures. Prosthodontics. She falls asleep to the sound of him grinding his jaw, like he's chewing through the night.

Rehearsals for the *Aarne-Thompson Classification Revue* happen every other afternoon. The director's name is Yves. He wears dapper suits in brown tweed and tells her, "You choose what you reveal of what you are when you're on stage."

Nadia doesn't know what that means. She does know that when she soars through the air, she wants to go higher and further and faster. She wants her muscles to burn. She knows she could, for a moment, do something spectacular. Something that makes her shake with terror. She thinks of her boyfriend and Rhonda and the feel of the nitrous filling her with drowsy nothingness; she does the jump they tell her and no more than that.

The other actors aren't what she expects. There is a woman who plays a mermaid whose voice is like spun gold. There is a horned boy who puts on long goat legs and prances around the stage, towering above them. And there is a magician who is supposed to keep them all as part of his menagerie in cages with glittering numbers.

"Where are you from?" the mermaid asks. "You look familiar."

"People say that a lot," Nadia says, although no one has ever said it to *her*. "I guess I have that kind of face."

The mermaid smiles and smoothes back gleaming black braids. "If you want, you can use my comb. It works on even the most matted fur—"

"Wow," says the goat boy, lurching past. "You must be special. She never lets anyone use her comb."

"Because you groom your ass with it," she calls after him.

The choreographer is named Marie. She is the woman with the necklaces from the first audition. When Nadia dances and especially when she jumps, Marie watches her with eyes like chips of gravel. "*Good*," she says slowly, as though the word is a grave insult.

Nadia is supposed to play a princess who has been trapped in a forest of ice by four skillful brothers and a jaybird. The magician rescues her and brings her to his menagerie. And, because the princess is not on stage much during the first act, Nadia also plays a bear dancing on two legs. The magician falls in love with the bear and the princess falls in love with the magician. Later in the play, the princess tricks the magician into killing the bear by making it look like the bear ate the jaybird. Then Nadia has to play the bear as she dies.

At first, all Nadia's mistakes are foolish. She lets her face go slack when she's not the one speaking or dancing and the director has to remind her over and over again that the audience can always see her when she's on stage. She misses cues. She sings too softly when she's singing about fish and streams and heavy fur. She sings louder when she's singing of kingdoms and crowns and dresses, but she can't seem to remember the words.

"I'm not really an actress," she tells him, after a particularly disastrous scene.

"I'm not really a director," Yves says with a shrug. "Who really *is* what they *seem*?"

"No," she says. "You don't understand. I just came to the audition because my friends were going. And they really aren't my friends. They're just people I work with. I don't know what I'm doing."

"Okay, if you're not an actress," he asks her, "then what are you?"

She doesn't answer. Yves signals for one of the golden glitter-covered cages to be moved slightly to the left.

"I probably won't even stay with the show," Nadia says. "I'll probably have to leave after opening night. I can't be trusted."

Yves throws up his hands. "Actors! Which of you can be trusted? But don't worry. We'll all be leaving. This show *tours*."

Nadia expects him to cut her from the cast after every rehearsal, but he never does. She nearly cries with relief.

The goat boy smiles down at her from atop his goat legs. "I have a handkerchief. I'll throw it to you if you want."

"I'm fine," Nadia says, rubbing her wet eyes.

"Lots of people weep after rehearsals."

"Weird people," she says, trying to make it a joke.

"If you don't cry, how can you make anyone else cry? Theater is the last place where fools and the mad do better than regular folks…well, I guess music's a little like that too." He shrugs. "But still."

Posters go up all over town. They show the magician in front of gleaming cages with bears and mermaids and foxes and a cat in a dress.

Nadia's boyfriend doesn't like all the time she spends away from home. Now, on Saturday nights, she doesn't wait by the phone. She pushes her milk crate coffee table and salvaged sofa against the wall and practices her steps over and over until her downstairs neighbor bangs on his ceiling.

One night her boyfriend calls and she doesn't pick up. She just lets it ring.

She has just realized that the date the musical premieres is the next time she is going to change. All she can do is stare at the little black book and her carefully noted temperatures. The ringing phone is like the ringing in her head.

I am so tired I want to die, Nadia thinks. Sometimes the thought repeats over and over and she can't stop thinking it, even though she knows she has no reason to be so tired. She gets enough sleep. She gets more than enough sleep. Some days, she can barely drag herself from her bed.

Fighting the change only makes it more painful; she knows from experience.

The change cannot be stopped or reasoned with. It's inevitable. Inexorable. It is coming for her. But it can be delayed. Once, she held on two hours past dusk, her whole body knotted with cramps. Once, she held out until the moon was high in the sky and her teeth were clenched so tight she thought they would shatter. She might be able to make it to the end of the show.

It shouldn't matter to her. Disappointing people is inevitable. She will eventually get tired and angry and hungry. Someone will get hurt. Her boyfriend will run the pad of his fingers over her canines and she will bite down. She will wake up covered in blood and mud by the side of some road and not be sure what she's done. Then she'll be on the run again.

Being a werewolf means devouring your past.

Being a werewolf means swallowing your future.

Methodically, Nadia tears her notebook to tiny pieces. She throws the pieces in the toilet and flushes, but the chunks of paper clog the pipes. Water spills over the side and floods her bathroom with the soggy reminder of inevitability.

The opening night of the *Aarne-Thompson Classification Revue*, the cast huddle together and wish each other luck. They paint their faces. Nadia's hand shakes as she draws a new, red mouth over her own. Her skin itches. She can feel the fur inside of her, can smell her sharp, feral musk.

"Are you okay?" the mermaid asks.

Nadia growls softly. She is holding on, but only barely.

Yves is yelling at everyone. The costumers are pinning and duct-taping dresses that have split. Strap tear. Beads bounce along the floor. One of the chorus is scolding a girl who plays a talking goat. A violinist is pleading with his instrument.

"Tonight you are not going to be *good*," Marie, the choreographer, says.

Nadia grinds her teeth together. "I'm not good."

"Good is forgettable." Marie spits. "Good is common. You are not good. You are not common. You will show everyone what you are made of."

Under her bear suit, Nadia can feel her arms beginning to ripple with the change. She swallows hard and concentrates on shrinking down into herself. She cannot explain to Marie that she's afraid of what's inside of her.

Finally, Nadia's cue comes and she dances out into a forest of wooden trees on dollies and lets the magician trap her in a gold glitter-covered cage. Her bear costume hangs heavily on her, stinking of synthetic fur.

Performing is different with an audience. They gasp when there is a surprise. They laugh on cue. They watch her with gleaming, wet eyes. Waiting.

Her boyfriend is there, holding a bouquet of white roses. She's so surprised to see him that her hand lifts involuntarily—as though to wave. Her fingers look too long, her nails too dark, and she hides them behind her back.

Nadia dances like a bear, like a deceitful princess, and then like a bear again. This time as the magician sings about how the jaybird will be revenged, Nadia really feels like he's talking to her. When he lifts his gleaming wand, she shrinks back with real fear.

She loves this. She doesn't want to give it up. She wants to travel with the show. She wants to stop going to bed early. She won't wait by phone. She's not a fake.

When the jump comes, she leaps as high as she can. Higher than she has at any rehearsal. Higher than in her dreams. She jumps so high that she seems to hang in the air for a moment as her skin cracks and her jaw snaps into a snout.

It happens before she can stop it and then, she doesn't want it to stop. The change used to be the worst thing she could imagine. No more.

The bear costume sloughs off like her skin. Nadia falls into a crouch, four claws digging into the stage. She throws back her head and howls.

The goat boy nearly topples over. The magician drops his wand. On cue, the mermaid girl begins to sing. The musical goes on.

Roses slip from Nadia's dentist-boyfriend's fingers.

In the wings, she can see Marie clapping Yves on the back. Marie looks delighted.

There is a werewolf girl on the stage. It's Saturday night. The crowd is on their feet. Nadia braces herself for their applause.

UNDER THE MOONS OF VENUS
DAMIEN BRODERICK

Damien Broderick is an award-winning Australian SF writer, editor, and critical theorist, a senior fellow in the School of Culture and Communication at the University of Melbourne, currently living in San Antonio, Texas, with a Ph.D. from Deakin University. He has published more than forty books, including *Reading by Starlight, Transrealist Fiction, x, y, z, t: Dimensions of Science Fiction, Unleashing the Strange,* and *Chained to the Alien: The Best of Australian Science Fiction Review. The Spike* was the first full-length treatment of the technological singularity, and *Outside the Gates of Science* is a study of parapsychology. His 1980 novel *The Dreaming Dragons* (revised in 2009 as *The Dreaming*) is listed in David Pringle's *Science Fiction: The 100 Best Novels.* His latest SF novel is the diptych *Godplayers* and *K-Machines,* written with the aid of a two-year Fellowship from the Literature Board of the Australia Council, and his recent SF collections are *Uncle Bones* and *The Qualia Engine.*

1.

In the long, hot, humid afternoon, Blackett obsessively paced off the outer dimensions of the Great Temple of Petra against the black asphalt of the deserted car parks, trying to recapture the pathway back to Venus. Faint rectangular lines still marked the empty spaces allocated to staff vehicles long gone from the campus, stretching on every side like the equations in some occult geometry of invocation. Later, as shadows stretched across the all-but-abandoned industrial park, he considered again the possibility that he was trapped in delusion, even psychosis. At the edge of an overgrown patch of dried lawn, he found a crushed Pepsi can, a bent yellow plastic straw protruding from it. He kicked it idly.

"Thus I refute Berkeley," he muttered, with a half smile. The can twisted, fell back on the grass; he saw that a runner of bind weed wrapped its flattened waist.

He walked back to the sprawling house he had appropriated, formerly the residence of a wealthy CEO. Glancing at his IWC Flieger Chrono aviator's watch, he noted that he should arrive there ten minutes before his daily appointment with the therapist.

2.

Cool in a chillingly expensive pale blue Mila Schön summer frock, her carmine toenails brightly painted in her open Ferragamo Penelope sandals, Clare regarded him: lovely, sly, professionally compassionate. She sat across from him on the front porch of the old house, rocking gently in the suspended glider.

"Your problem," the psychiatrist told him, "is known in our trade as lack of affect. You have shut down and locked off your emotional responses. You must realize, Robert, that this isn't healthy or sustainable."

"Of course I know that," he said, faintly irritated by her condescension. "Why else would I be consulting you? Not," he said pointedly, "that it is doing me much good."

"It takes time, Robert. As you know."

3.

Later, when Clare was gone, Blackett sat beside his silent sound system and poured two fingers of Hennessy XO brandy. It was the best he had been able to find in the largely depleted supermarket, or at any rate the least untenable for drinking purposes. He took the spirits into his mouth and felt fire run down his throat. Months earlier, he had found a single bottle of Mendis Coconut brandy in the cellar of an enormous country house. Gone now. He sat a little longer, rose, cleaned his teeth and made his toilet, drank a full glass of faintly brackish water from the tap. He found a Philip Glass CD and placed it in the mouth of the player, then went to bed. Glass's repetitions and minimal novelty eased him into sleep. He woke at 3 in the morning, heart thundering. Silence absolute. Blackett cursed himself for forgetting to press the automatic repeat key on the CD player. Glass had fallen silent, along with most of the rest of the human race. He touched his forehead. Sweat coated his fingers.

4.

In the morning, he drove in a stolen car to the industrial park's air field, rolled the Cessna 182 out from the protection of its hangar, and refueled its tanks. Against the odds, the electrically powered pump and other systems remained active, drawing current from the black arrays of solar cells oriented to the south and east, swiveling during the daylight hours to follow the apparent track of the sun. He made his abstracted, expert run through the checklist, flicked on the radio by reflex. A hum of carrier signal, nothing more. The control tower was deserted. Blackett ran the Cessna onto the slightly cracked asphalt and took off into a brisk breeze. He flew across fields going to seed, visible through sparklingly clear air. Almost no traffic moved on the roads below him. Two or three vehicles threw up a haze of dust from the untended roadway, and one laden truck crossed his path, apparently cluttered to overflowing with furniture and bedding. It seemed the ultimate in pointlessness—why not appropriate a suitable house, as he had done, and make do with its appointments? Birds flew up occasionally in swooping flocks, careful to avoid his path.

Before noon, he was landing on the coast at the deserted Matagorda Island air force base a few hundred yards from the ocean. He sat for a moment, hearing his cooling engines ticking, and gazed at the two deteriorating Stearman biplanes that rested in the salty open air. They were at least a century old, at one time lovingly restored for air shows and aerobatic displays. Now their fabric sagged, striped red and green paint peeling from their fuselages and wings. They sagged into the hot tarmac, rubber tires rotted by the corrosive oceanfront air and the sun's pitiless ultraviolet.

Blackett left his own plane in the open. He did not intend to remain here long. He strolled to the end of the runway and into the long grass stretching to the ocean. Socks and trouser legs were covered quickly in clinging burrs. He reached the sandy shore as the sun stood directly overhead. After he had walked for half a mile along the strand, wishing he had thought to bring a hat, a dog crossed the sand and paced alongside, keeping its distance.

"You're Blackett," the dog said.

"Speaking."

"Figured it must have been you. Rare enough now to run into a human out here."

Blackett said nothing. He glanced at the dog, feeling no enthusiasm for a conversation. The animal was healthy enough, and well fed, a red setter with long hair that fluffed up in the tangy air. His paws left a trail across the white sand, paralleling the tracks Blackett had made. Was there some occult meaning in this simplest of geometries? If so, it would be erased soon enough, as the ocean moved in, impelled by the solar tide, and lazily licked the beach clean.

Seaweed stretched along the edge of the sluggish water, dark green, stinking. Out of breath, he sat and look disconsolately across the slow, flat waves of the diminished tide. The dog trotted by, threw itself down in the sand a dozen feet away. Blackett knew he no longer dared sit here after nightfall, in a dark alive with thousands of brilliant pinpoint stars, a planet or two, and no Moon. Never again a Moon. Once he had ventured out here after the sun went down, and low in the deep indigo edging the horizon had seen the clear distinct blue disk of the evening star, and her two attendant satellites, one on each side of the planet. Ganymede, with its thin atmosphere still intact, remained palest brown. Luna, at that distance, was a bright pinpoint orb, her pockmarked face never again to be visible to the naked eye of an Earthly viewer beneath her new, immensely deep carbon dioxide atmosphere.

He noticed that the dog was creeping cautiously toward him, tail wagging, eyes averted except for the occasional swift glance.

"Look," he said, "I'd rather be alone."

The dog sat up and uttered a barking laugh. It swung its head from side to side, conspicuously observing the hot, empty strand.

"Well, bub, I'd say you've got your wish, in spades."

"Nobody has swum here in years, apart from me. This is an old air force base, it's been decommissioned for…"

He trailed off. It was no answer to the point the animal was making. Usually at this time of year, Blackett acknowledged to himself, other beaches, more accessible to the crowds, would be swarming with shouting or whining children, mothers waddling or slumped, baking in the sun under SP 50 lotions, fat men eating snacks from busy concession stands, vigorous swimmers bobbing in white-capped waves. Now the empty waves crept in, onto the tourist beaches as they did here, like the flattened, poisoned combers at the site of the Exxon Valdez oil spill, twenty years after men had first set foot on the now absent Moon.

"It wasn't my idea," he said. But the dog was right; this isolation was more congenial to him than otherwise. Yet the yearning to rejoin the rest of the human race on Venus burned in his chest like angina.

"Not like I'm *blaming* you, bub." The dog tilted its handsome head. "Hey, should have said, I'm Sporky."

Blackett inclined his own head in reply. After a time, Sporky said, "You think it's a singularity excursion, right?"

He got to his feet, brushed sand from his legs and trousers. "I certainly don't suspect the hand of Jesus. I don't think I've been Left Behind."

"Hey, don't go away now." The dog jumped up, followed him at a safe distance. "It could be aliens, you know."

"You talk too much," Blackett said.

5.

As he landed, later in the day, still feeling refreshed from his hour in the water, he saw through the heat curtains of rising air a rather dirty precinct vehicle drive through the unguarded gate and onto the runway near the hangars. He taxied in slowly, braked, opened the door. The sergeant climbed out of his Ford Crown Victoria, cap off, waving it to cool his florid face.

"Saw you coming in, Doc," Jacobs called. "Figured you might like a lift back. Been damned hot out today, not the best walking weather."

There was little point in arguing. Blackett clamped the red tow bar to the nose wheel, steered the Cessna backward into the hangar, heaved the metal doors closed with an echoing rumble. He climbed into the cold interior of the Ford. Jacobs had the air conditioning running at full bore, and a noxious country and western singer wailing from the sound system. Seeing his guest's frown, the police officer grinned broadly and turned the hideous noise down.

"You have a visitor waiting," he said. His grin verged on the lewd. Jacobs drove by the house twice a day, part of his self-imposed duty, checking on his brutally diminished constituency. For some reason he took a particular, avuncular interest in Blackett. Perhaps he feared for his own mental health in this terrible circumstance.

"She's expected, Sergeant." By seniority of available staff, the man was probably a captain or even police chief for the region, now, but Blackett declined to offer the honorary promotional title. "Drop me off at the top of the street, would you?"

"It's no trouble to take you to the door."

"I need to stretch my legs after the flight."

In the failing light of dusk, he found Clare, almost in shadow, moving like a piece of beautiful driftwood stranded on a dying tide, backward and slowly forward, on his borrowed porch. She nodded, with her Gioconda smile, and said nothing. This evening she wore a broderie anglaise white-on-white embroidered blouse and 501s cut down almost to her crotch, bleached by the long summer sun. She sat rocking wordlessly, her knees parted, revealing the pale lanterns of her thighs.

"Once again, Doctor," Blackett told her, "you're trying to seduce me. What do you suppose this tells us both?"

"It tells us, Doctor, that yet again you have fallen prey to intellectualized over-interpreting." She was clearly annoyed, but keeping her tone level. Her limbs remained disposed as they were. "You remember what they told us at school."

"The worst patients are physicians, and the worst physician patients are psychiatrists." He took the old woven cane seat, shifting it so that he sat at right angles to her, looking directly ahead at the heavy brass knocker on the missing CEO's mahogany entrance door. It was serpentine, perhaps a Chinese dragon couchant. A faint headache pulsed behind his eyes; he closed them.

"You've been to the coast again, Robert?"

"I met a dog on the beach," he said, eyes still closed. A cooling breeze was moving into the porch, bringing a fragrance of the last pink mimosa blossoms in the garden bed beside the dry, dying lawn. "He suggested that we've experienced a singularity cataclysm." He sat forward suddenly, turned, caught her regarding him with her blue eyes. "What do you think of that theory, Doctor? Does it arouse you?"

"You had a conversation with a dog," she said, uninflected, nonjudgmental.

"One of the genetically upregulated animals," he said, irritated. "Modified jaw and larynx, expanded cortex and Boca's region."

Clare shrugged. Her interiority admitted of no such novelties. "I've heard that singularity hypothesis before. The Mayans—"

"Not that new age crap." He felt an unaccustomed jolt of anger. Why did he bother talking to this woman? Sexual interest? Granted, but remote; his indifference toward her rather surprised him, but it was so. Blackett glanced again at her thighs, but she had crossed her legs. He rose. "I need a drink. I think we should postpone this session, I'm not feeling at my best."

She took a step forward, placed one cool hand lightly on his bare, sunburned arm.

"You're still convinced the Moon has gone from the sky, Robert? You still maintain that everyone has gone to Venus?"

Not everyone," he said brusquely, and removed her hand. He gestured at the darkened houses in the street. A mockingbird trilled from a tree, but there were no leaf blowers, no teenagers in sports cars passing with rap booming and thudding, no barbecue odors of smoke and burning steak, no TV displays flickering behind curtained windows. He found his key, went to the door, did not invite her in. "I'll see you tomorrow, Clare."

"Good night, Robert. Feel better." The psychiatrist went down the steps with a light, almost childlike, skipping gait, and paused a moment at the end of the path, raising a hand in farewell or admonishment. "A suggestion, Robert. The almanac ordains a full moon tonight. It rises a little after eight. You should see it plainly from your back garden a few minutes later, once the disk clears the treetops."

For a moment he watched her fade behind the overgrown, untended foliage fronting this opulent dwelling. He shook his head, and went inside. In recent months, since the theft of the Moon, Clare had erected ontological denial into the central principle of her world construction, her *Weltbild*. The woman, in her own mind supposedly his therapeutic guide, was hopelessly insane.

6.

After a scratch dinner of canned artichoke hearts, pineapple slices, pre-cooked baby potatoes, pickled eel from a jar, and rather dry, lightly salted wheaten thins, washed down with Californian Chablis from the refrigerator, Blackett dressed in slightly more formal clothing for his weekly visit to Kafele Massri. This massively obese bibliophile lived three streets over in the Baptist rectory across the street from the regional library. At intervals, while doing his own shopping, Blackett scavenged through accessible food stores for provender that he left in plastic bags beside Massri's side gate, providing an incentive to get outside the walls of the house for a few minutes. The man slept all day, and barely budged from his musty bed even after the sun had gone down, scattering emptied cans and plastic bottles about on the uncarpeted floor. Massri had not yet taken to urinating in his squalid bedclothes, as far as Blackett could tell, but the weekly visits always began by emptying several jugs the fat man used at night in lieu of chamber pots, rinsing them under the trickle of water from the kitchen tap, and returning them to the bedroom, where he cleared away the empties into bags and tossed those into the weedy back yard where obnoxious scabby cats crawled or lay panting.

Kafele Massri was propped up against three or four pillows. "I have. New thoughts, Robert. The ontology grows. More tractable." He spoke in a jerky sequence of emphysematic wheezing gasps, his swollen mass pressing relentlessly on the rupturing alveoli skeining his lungs. His fingers twitched, as if keying an invisible keyboard; his eyes shifting again and again to the dead computer. When he caught Blackett's amused glance, he shrugged, causing one of the pillows to slip and fall. "Without my beloved internet, I am. Hamstrung. My *preciiiouuus*." His thick lips quirked. He foraged through the bed covers, found a battered Hewlett-Packard scientific calculator. Its green strip of display flickered as his fingers pressed keys. "Luckily. I still have. This. My *slide rule.*" Wheezing, he burst into laughter, followed by an agonizing fit of coughing.

"Let me get you a glass of water, Massri." Blackett returned with half a glass; any more, and the bibliophile would spill it down his vast soiled bathrobe front. It seemed to ease the coughing. They sat side by side for a time, as the Egyptian got his breath under control. Ceaselessly, under the impulse of his pudgy fingers, the small green numerals flickered in and out of existence, a Borgesian proof of the instability of reality.

"You realize. Venus is upside. Down?"

"They tipped it over?"

They was a placeholder for whatever force or entity or cosmic freak of nature had translated the two moons into orbit around the second planet, abstracting them from Earth and Jupiter and instantaneously replacing them in Venus space, as far as anyone could tell in the raging global internet hysteria before most of humanity was translated as well to the renovated world. Certainly Blackett had never noticed that the planet was turned on its head, but he had only been on Venus less than five days before he was recovered, against his will, to central Texas.

"*Au contraire.* It has always. Spun. Retrograde. It rotates backwards. The northern or upper hemisphere turns. Clockwise." Massri heaved a strangled breath, made twisted motions with his pudgy, blotched hands. "Nobody noticed that until late last. Century. The thick atmosphere, you know. And clouds. Impenetrable. High albedo. Gone now, of course."

Was it even the same world? He and the Egyptian scholar had discussed this before; it seemed to Blackett that whatever force had prepared this new Venus as a suitable habitat for humankind must have done so long ago, in some parallel or superposed state of alternative reality. The books piled around this squalid bed seemed to support such a conjecture. Worlds echoing away into infinity, each slightly different from the world adjacent to it, in a myriad of different dimensions of change. Earth, he understood, had been struck in infancy by a raging proto-planet the size of Mars, smashing away the light outer crust and flinging it into an orbiting shell that settled, over millions of years of impacts, into the Moon now circling Venus. But if in some other prismatic history, Venus had also suffered interplanetary bombardment on that scale, blowing away its monstrous choking carbon dioxide atmosphere and churning up the magma, driving the plate tectonic upheavals unknown until then, where was the Venerean or Venusian moon? Had that one been transported away to yet another alternative reality? It made Blackett tired to consider these metaphysical landscapes radiating away into eternity even as they seemed to close oppressively upon him, a psychic null-point of suffocating extinction.

Shyly, Kafele Massri broke the silence. "Robert, I have never. Asked you this." He paused, and the awkward moment extended. They heard the ticking of the grandfather clock in the hall outside.

"If I want to go back there? Yes, Kafele, I do. With all my heart."

"I know that. No. What was it. *Like?*" A sort of anguish tore the man's words. He himself had never gone, not even for a moment. Perhaps, he had joked once, there was a weight limit, a baggage surcharge his account could not meet.

"You're growing forgetful, my friend. Of course we've discussed this. The immense green-leaved trees, the crystal air, the strange fire-hued birds high in the canopies, the great rolling ocean—"

"No." Massri agitated his heavy hands urgently. "Not that. Not the sci-fi movie. Images. No offense intended. I mean… The *affect*. The weight or lightness of. The heart. The rapture of. Being there. Or the. I don't know. Dislocation? Despair?"

Blackett stood up. "Clare informs me I have damaged affect. 'Flattened,' she called it. Or did she say 'diminished'? Typical diagnostic hand-waving. If she'd been in practice as long as I—"

"Oh, Robert, I meant no—"

"Of course you didn't." Stiffly, he bent over the mound of the old man's supine body, patted his shoulder. "I'll get us some supper. Then you can tell me your new discovery."

7.

Tall cumulonimbus clouds moved in like a battlefleet of the sky, but the air remained hot and sticky. Lightning cracked in the distance, marching closer during the afternoon. When rain fell, it came suddenly, drenching the parched soil, sluicing the roadway, with a wind that blew discarded plastic bottles and bags about before dumping them at the edge of the road or piled against the fences and barred, spear-topped front gates. Blackett watched from the porch, the spray of rain blowing against his face in gusts. In the distance a stray dog howled and scurried.

On Venus, he recalled, under its doubled moons, the storms had been abrupt and hard, and the ocean tides surged in great rushes of blue-green water, spume like the head on a giant's overflowing draught of beer. Ignoring the shrill warnings of displaced astronomers, the first settlers along one shoreline, he had been told, perished as they viewed the glory of a Ganymedean-Lunar eclipse of the sun, twice as hot, a third again as wide. The proxivenerean spring tide, tugged by both moons and the sun as well, heaped up the sea and hurled it at the land.

Here on Earth, at least, the Moon's current absence somewhat calmed the weather. And without the endless barrage of particulate soot, inadequately scrubbed, exhaled into the air by a million factory chimneys and a billion fuel fires in the Third World, rain came more infrequently now. Perhaps, he wondered, it was time to move to a more salubrious climatic region. But what if that blocked his return to Venus? The very thought made the muscles at his jaw tighten painfully.

For an hour he watched the lowering sky for the glow pasted beneath distant clouds by a flash of electricity, then the tearing violence of lightning strikes as they came closer, passing by within miles. In an earlier dispensation, he would have pulled the plugs on his computers and other delicate equipment, unprepared to accept the dubious security of surge protectors. During one storm, years earlier, when the Moon still hung in the sky, his satellite dish and decoder burned out in a single nearby frightful clap of noise and light. On Venus, he reflected, the human race were yet to advance to the recovery of electronics. How many had died with the instant loss of infrastructure—sewerage, industrial food production, antibiotics, air conditioning? Deprived of television and music and books, how many had taken their own lives, unable to find footing in a world where they must fetch for themselves, work with neighbors they had found themselves flung amongst willy-nilly? Yes, many had been returned just long enough to ransack most of the medical supplies and haul away clothing, food, contraceptives, packs of toilet paper... Standing at the edge of the storm, on the elegant porch of his appropriated mansion, Blackett smiled, thinking of the piles of useless stereos, laptops and plasma TV screens he had seen dumped beside the immense Venusian trees. People were so stereotypical, unadaptive. No doubt driven to such stupidities, he reflected, by their lavish *affect*.

8.

Clare found him in the empty car park, pacing out the dimensions of Petra's Great Temple. He looked at her when she repeated his name, shook his head, slightly disoriented.

"This is the Central Arch, with the Theatron," he explained. "East and West corridors." He gestured. "In the center, the Forecourt, beyond the Proneos, and then the great space of the Lower Temenos."

"And all this," she said, looking faintly interested, "is a kind of imaginal reconstruction of Petra."

"Of its Temple, yes."

"The rose-red city half as old as time?" Now a mocking note had entered her voice.

He took her roughly by the arm, drew her into the shade of the five-story brick and concrete structure where neuropharmaceutical researchers had formerly plied their arcane trade. "Clare, we don't understand time. Look at this wall." He smote it with one clenched fist. "Why didn't it collapse when the Moon was removed? Why didn't terrible earthquakes split the ground open? The earth used to flex every day with lunar tides, Clare. There should have been convulsions as it compensated for the changed stresses. Did they see to that as well?"

"The dinosaurs, you mean?" She sighed, adopted a patient expression.

Blackett stared. "The *what?*"

"Oh." Today she was wearing deep red culottes and a green silk shirt, with a bandit's scarf holding back her heavy hair. Dark adaptive-optic sunglasses hid her eyes. "The professor hasn't told you his latest theory? I'm relieved to hear it.

It isn't healthy for you two to spend so much time together, Robert. *Folie à deux* is harder to budge than a simple defensive delusion."

"You've been talking to Kafele Massri?" He was incredulous. "The man refuses to allow women into his house."

"I know. We talk through the bedroom window. I bring him soup for lunch."

"Good god."

"He assures me that the dinosaurs turned the planet Venus upside down 65 million years ago. They were intelligent. Not all of them, of course."

"No, you've misunderstood—"

"Probably. I must admit I wasn't listening very carefully. I'm far more interested in the emotional undercurrents."

"You would be. Oh, damn, damn."

"What's a Temenos?"

Blackett felt a momentary bubble of excitement. "At Petra, it was a beautiful sacred enclosure with hexagonal flooring, and three colonnades topped by sculptures of elephants' heads. Water was carried throughout the temple by channels, you see—" He started pacing off the plan of the Temple again, convinced that this was the key to his return to Venus. Clare walked beside him, humming very softly.

9.

"I understand you've been talking to my patient." Blackett took care to allow no trace of censure to color his words.

"Ha! It would be extremely uncivil, Robert. To drink her soup while maintaining. A surly silence. Incidentally, she maintains. You are her. Client."

"A harmless variant on the transference, Massri. But you understand that I can't discuss my patients, so I'm afraid we'll have to drop that topic immediately." He frowned at the Egyptian, who sipped tea from a half-filled mug. "I can say that Clare has a very garbled notion of your thinking about Venus."

"She's a delightful young woman, but doesn't. Seem to pay close attention to much. Beyond her wardrobe. Ah well. But Robert, I had to tell *somebody*. You didn't seem especially responsive. The other night."

Blackett settled back with his own mug of black coffee, already cooling. He knew he should stop drinking caffeine; it made him jittery. "You know I'm uncomfortable with anything that smacks of so-called 'Intelligent Design.'"

"Put your mind at. Rest, my boy. The design is plainly intelligent. Profoundly so, but. There's nothing supernatural in it. To the contrary."

"Still—dinosaurs? The dog I was talking to the other day favors what it called a 'singularity excursion.' In my view, six of one, half a dozen—"

"But don't you see?" The obese bibliophile struggled to heave his great mass up against the wall, hauling a pillow with him. "Both are wings. Of the same argument."

"Ah." Blackett put down his mug, wanting to escape the musty room with its miasma of cranky desperation. "Not just dinosaurs, *transcendental* dinosaurs."

Unruffled, Massri pursed his lips. "Probably. In effect." His breathing seemed rather improved. Perhaps his exchanges with an attractive young woman, even through the half-open window, braced his spirits.

"You have evidence and impeccable logic for this argument, I imagine?"

"Naturally. Has it ever occurred to you. How extremely improbable it is. That the west coast of Africa. Would fit so snugly against. The east coast of South America?"

"I see your argument. Those continents were once joined, then broke apart. Plate tectonics drifted them thousands of miles apart. It's obvious to the naked eye, but nobody believed it for centuries."

The Egyptian nodded, evidently pleased with his apt student. "And how improbable is it that. The Moon's apparent diameter varies from 29 degrees 23 minutes to 33 degrees 29 minutes. Apogee to perigee. While the sun's apparent diameter varies. From 31 degrees 36 minutes to 32 degrees 3 minutes."

The effort of this exposition plainly exhausted the old man; he sank back against his unpleasant pillows.

"So we got total solar eclipses by the Moon where one just covered the other. A coincidence, nothing more."

"Really? And what of this equivalence? The Moon rotated every 27.32 days. The sun's sidereal rotation. Allowing for current in the surface. Is 25.38 days."

Blackett felt as if ants were crawling under his skin. He forced patience upon himself.

"Not all that close, Massri. What, some… eight percent difference?"

"Seven. But Robert, the Moon's rotation has been slowing as it drifts away from Earth, because it is tidally locked. Was. Can you guess when the lunar day equaled the solar day?"

"Kafele, what are you going to tell me? 4 BC? 597AD?"

"Neither Christ's birth nor Mohammed's Hegira. Robert, near as I can calculate it, 65.5 million years ago."

Blackett sat back, genuinely shocked, all his assurance draining away. The Cretaceous-Tertiary boundary. The Chicxulub impact event that exterminated the dinosaurs. He struggled his way back to reason. Clare had not been mistaken, not about that.

"This is just… absurd, my friend. The slack in those numbers… But what if they are right? So?"

The old man hauled himself up by brute force, dragged his legs over the side of the bed. "I have to take care of business," he said. "Leave the room, please, Robert."

From the hall, where he paced in agitation, Blackett heard a torrent of urine splashing into one of the jugs he had emptied when he arrived. Night music, he thought, forcing a grin. That's what James Joyce had called it. No, wait, that wasn't it—Chamber music. But the argument banged against his brain. And so what? Nothing could be dismissed out of hand. The damned *Moon* had been picked up and moved, and given a vast deep carbon dioxide atmosphere, presumably hosed over from the old Venus through some higher dimension. Humanity had been relocated to the cleaned-up version of Venus, a world with a breathable atmosphere and oceans filled with strange but edible fish. How could anything be ruled out as preposterous, however ungainly or grotesque.

"You can come back in now." There were thumps and thuds.

Instead, Blackett went back to the kitchen and made a new pot of coffee. He carried two mugs into the bedroom.

"Have I frightened you, my boy?"

"Everything frightens me these days, Professor Massri. You're about to tell me that you've found a monolith in the back garden, along with the discarded cans and the mangy cats."

The Egyptian laughed, phlegm shaking his chest. "Almost. Almost. The Moon is now on orbit a bit over. A million kilometers from Venus. Also retrograde. Exactly the same distance Ganymede. Used to be from Jupiter."

"Well, okay, hardly a coincidence. And Ganymede is in the Moon's old orbit."

For a moment, Massri was silent. His face was drawn. He put down his coffee with a shaking hand.

"No. Ganymede orbits Venus some 434,000 kilometers out. According to the last data I could find before. The net went down for good."

"Farther out than the Moon used to orbit Earth. And?"

"The Sun, from Venus, as you once told me. Looks brighter and larger. In fact, it subtends about 40 minutes of arc. And by the most convenient and. Interesting coincidence. Ganymede now just exactly looks…"

"…the same size as the Sun, from the surface of Venus." Ice ran down Blackett's back. "So it blocks the Sun exactly at total eclipse. That's what you're telling me?"

"Except for the corona, and bursts of solar flares. As the Moon used to do here." Massri sent him a glare almost baleful in its intensity. "And you think that's just a matter of chance? Do you think so, Dr. Blackett?"

10.

The thunderstorm on the previous day had left the air cooler. Blackett walked home slowly in the darkness, holding the HP calculator and two books the old man had perforce drawn upon for data, now the internet was expired. He did not recall having carried these particular volumes across the street from the empty library. Perhaps Clare or one of the other infrequent visitors had fetched them.

The stars hung clean and clear through the heavy branches extending from the gardens of most of the large houses in the neighborhood and across the old sidewalk. In the newer, outlying parts of the city, the nouveaux riches had considered it a mark of potent prosperity to run their well-watered lawns to the very verge of the roadway, never walking anywhere, driving to visit neighbors three doors distant. He wondered how they were managing on Venus. Perhaps the ratio of fit to obese and terminally inactive had improved, under the whip of necessity. Too late for poor Kafele, he thought, and made a mental note to stockpile another batch of pioglitazone, the old man's diabetes drug, when next he made a foray into a pharmacy.

He sat for half an hour in the silence of the large kitchen, scratching down data points and recalculating the professor's estimates. It was apparent that Massri thought the accepted extinction date of the great reptiles, coinciding as it did with the perfect overlap of the greater and lesser lights in the heavens, was no such thing—that it was, in fact, a time-stamp for Creation. The notion chilled Blackett's blood. Might the world, after all (fashionable speculation!), be no more than a virtual simulation? A calculational contrivance on a colossal scale? But not truly colossal, perhaps no more than a billion lines of code and a prodigiously accurate physics engine. Nothing else so easily explained the wholesale revision of the inner solar system. The idea did not appeal; it stank in Blackett's nostrils. Thus I refute, he thought again, and tapped a calculator key sharply. But that was a feeble refutation; one might as well, in a lucid dream, deny that any reality existed, forgetting the ground state or brute physical substrate needed to sustain the dream.

The numbers made no sense. He ran the calculations again. It was true that Ganymede's new orbit placed the former Jovian moon in just the right place, from time to time, to occult the sun's disk precisely. That was a disturbing datum. The dinosaur element was far less convincing. According to the authors of these astronomy books, Earth had started out, after the tremendous shock of the X-body impact that birthed the Moon, with a dizzying 5.5 or perhaps 8-hour day. It seemed impossibly swift, but the hugely larger gas giant Jupiter, Ganymede's former primary, turned completely around in just 10 hours.

The blazing young Earth spun like a mad top, its almost fatal impact wound subsiding, sucked away into subduction zones created by the impact itself. Venus—the old Venus, at least—lacked tectonic plates; the crust was resurfaced at half-billion-year intervals, as the boiling magma burst up through the rigid rocks, but not enough to carry down and away the appalling mass of carbon dioxide that had crushed the surface with a hundred times the pressure of Earth's oxygen-nitrogen atmosphere. Now, though, the renovated planet had a breathable atmosphere. Just add air and water, Blackett thought. Presumably the crust crept slowly over the face of the world, sucked down and spat back up over glacial epochs. But the numbers—

The Moon had been receding from Earth at a sluggish rate of 38 kilometers every million years—one part in 10,000 of its final orbital distance, before its removal to Venus. Kepler's Third Law, Blackett noted, established the orbital equivalence of time squared with distance cubed. So those 65.5 million years ago, when the great saurians were slain by a falling star, Luna had been only 2500 km closer to the Earth. But to match the sun's sidereal rotation exactly, the Moon needed to be more than 18,000 km nearer. That was the case no more recently than 485 million years ago.

Massri's dinosaur fantasy was off by a factor of at least 7.4.

Then how had the Egyptian reached his numerological conclusion? And where did all this lead? Nowhere useful that Blackett could see.

It was all sheer wishful thinking. Kafele Massri was as delusional as Clare, his thought processes utterly unsound. Blackett groaned and put his head on the table. Perhaps, he had to admit, his own reflections were no more reliable.

11.

"I'm flying down to the coast for a swim," Blackett told Clare. "There's room in the plane."

"A long way to go for a dip."

"A change of scenery," he said. "Bring your bathing suit if you like. I never bother, myself."

She gave him a long, cool look. "A nude beach? All right. I'll bring some lunch."

They drove together to the small airfield to one side of the industrial park in a serviceable SUV he found abandoned outside a 7-Eleven. Clare had averted her eyes as he hot-wired the engine. She wore sensible hiking boots, dark gray shorts, a white wife-beater that showed off her small breasts to advantage. Seated and strapped in, she laid her broad-brimmed straw hat on her knees. Blackett was mildly concerned by the slowly deteriorating condition of the plane. It had not be serviced in many months. He felt confident, though, that it would carry him where he needed to go, and back again.

During the 90-minute flight, he tried to explain the Egyptian's reasoning. The young psychiatrist responded with indifference that became palpable anxiety. Her hands tightened on the seat belt cinched at her waist. Blackett abandoned his efforts.

As they landed at Matagorda Island, she regained her animation. "Oh, look at those lovely biplanes! A shame they're in such deplorable condition. Why would anyone leave them out in the open weather like that?" She insisted on crossing to the sagging Stearmans for a closer look. Were those tears in her eyes?

Laden with towels and a basket of food, drink, paper plates and two glasses, Blackett summoned her sharply. "Come along, Clare, we'll miss the good waves if we loiter." If she heard bitter irony in his tone, she gave no sign of it. A gust of wind carried away his own boater, and she dashed after it, brought it back, jammed it rakishly on his balding head. "Thank you. I should tie the damned thing on with a leather thong, like the cowboys used to do, and cinch it with a… a…"

"A woggle," she said, unexpectedly.

It made Blackett laugh out loud. "Good god, woman! Wherever did you get a word like that?"

"My brother was a boy scout," she said.

They crossed the unkempt grass, made their way with some difficulty down to the shoreline. Blue ocean stretched south, almost flat, sparkling in the cloudless light. Blackett set down his burden, stripped his clothing efficiently, strode into the water. The salt stung his nostrils and eyes. He swam strongly out toward Mexico, thinking of the laughable scene in the movie *Gattaca*. He turned back, and saw Clare's head bobbing, sun-bleached hair plastered against her well-shaped scalp.

They lay side by side in the sun, odors of sun-block hanging on the unmoving air. After a time, Blackett saw the red setter approaching from the seaward side. The animal sat on its haunches, mouth open and tongue lolling, saying nothing.

"Hello, Sporky," Blackett said. "Beach patrol duties?"

"Howdy, Doc. Saw the Cessna coming in. Who's the babe?"

"This is Dr. Clare Laing. She's a psychiatrist, so show some respect."

Light glistened on her nearly naked body, reflected from sweat and a scattering of mica clinging to her torso. She turned her head away, affected to be sleeping. No, not sleeping. He realized that her attention was now fixed on a rusty bicycle wheel half-buried in the sand. It seemed she might be trying to work out the absolute essence of the relationship between them, with the rim and broken spokes of this piece of sea drift serving as some kind of spinal metaphor.

Respectful of her privacy, Blackett sat up and began explaining to the dog the bibliophile's absurd miscalculation. Sporky interrupted his halting exposition.

"You're saying the angular width of the sun, then and now, is about 32 arc minutes."

"Yes, 0.00925 radians."

"And the Moon last matched this some 485 million years ago."

"No, no. Well, it was a slightly better match than it is now, but that's not Massri's point."

"Which is?"

"Which is that the sun's rotational period and the Moon's were the *same* in that epoch. Can't you see how damnably unlikely that is? He thinks it's something like... I don't know, God's thumbprint on the solar system. The true date of Creation, maybe. Then he tried to show that it coincides with the extinction of the dinosaurs, but that's just wrong, they went extinct—"

"You do know that there was a major catastrophic extinction event at the Cambrian-Ordovician transition 488 million years ago?"

Dumbfounded, Blackett said, "What?"

"Given your sloppy math, what do you say the chances are that your Moon-Sun rotation equivalence bracketed the Cambrian-Ordovician extinction?

Knocked the living hell out of the trilobites, Doc." A surreal quality had entered the conversation. Blackett found it hard to accept that the dog could be a student of ancient geomorphisms. A spinal tremor shook him. So the creature was no ordinary genetically upgraded dog but some manifestation of the entity, the force, the ontological dislocation that had torn away the Moon and the world's inhabitants, most of them.

Detesting the note of pleading in his own voice, Blackett uttered a cry of heartfelt petition. He saw Clare roll over, waken from her sun-warmed drowse. "How can I get back there?" he cried. "Send me back! Send us both!"

Sporky stood up, shook sand from his fur, spraying Blackett with stinging mica.

"Go on as you began," the animal said, "and let the Lord be all in all to you."

Clouds of uncertainty cleared from Blackett's mind, as the caustic, acid clouds of Venus had been sucked away and transposed to the relocated Moon. He jumped up, bent, seized the psychiatrist's hand, hauled her blinking and protesting to her feet.

"Clare! We must trace out the ceremony of the Great Temple! Here, at the edge of the ocean. I've been wasting my time trying this ritual inland. Venus is now a world of great oceans!"

"Damn it, Robert, let me go, you're hurting—"

But he was hauling her down to the brackish, brine-stinking sea shore. Their parallel footprints wavered, inscribing a semiotics of deliverance. He began to tread out the Petran temple perimeter, starting at the Propylecum, turned a right angle, marched them to the East Excedra and to the very foot of the ancient Cistern. He was traveling backward into archeopsychic time, deeper into those remote, somber half-worlds he had glimpsed in the recuperative paintings of his mad patients.

"Robert! Robert!"

They entered the water, which lapped sluggishly at their ankles and calves like the articulate tongue of a dog as large as the world. Blackett gaped. At the edge of sea and sand, great three-lobed arthropods shed water from their shells, moving slowly like enormous wood lice.

"Trilobites!" Blackett cried. He stared about, hand still firmly clamped on Clare Laing's. Great green rolling breakers, in the distance, rushed toward shore, broke, foamed and frothed, lifting the ancient animals and tugging at Blackett's limbs. He tottered forward into the drag of the Venusian ocean, caught himself. He stared over his shoulder at the vast, towering green canopy of trees. Overhead, bracketing the sun, twin crescent moons shone faintly against the purple sky. He looked wildly at his companion and laughed, joyously, then flung his arms about her.

"Clare," he cried, alive on Venus, "Clare, we made it!"

THE FOOL JOBS
JOE ABERCROMBIE

Joe Abercrombie attended Lancaster Royal Grammar School and Manchester University, where he studied psychology. He moved into television production before taking up a career as a freelance film editor. His first novel, *The Blade Itself,* was published in 2004, followed by sequels *Before They Are Hanged* and *Last Argument of Kings,* and stand-alone novel *Best Served Cold.* His most recent book is another stand-alone novel set in the same world, *The Heroes.* Joe lives in Bath with his wife, Lou, and his daughters, Grace and Eve. He still occasionally edits concerts and music festivals for TV, but spends most of his time writing edgy yet humorous fantasy novels.

Craw chewed the hard skin around his nails, just like he always did. They hurt, just like they always did. He thought to himself that he really had to stop doing that. Just like he always did.

"Why is it," he muttered under his breath, and with some bitterness, too, "I always get stuck with the fool jobs?"

The village squatted in the fork of the river, a clutch of damp thatch roofs, scratty as an idiot's hair, a man-high fence of rough-cut logs ringing it. Round wattle huts and three long halls dumped in the muck, ends of the curving wooden uprights on the biggest badly carved like dragon's heads, or wolf's heads, or something that was meant to make men scared but only made Craw nostalgic for decent carpentry. Smoke limped up from chimneys in muddy smears. Half-bare trees still shook browning leaves. In the distance the reedy sunlight glimmered on the rotten fens, like a thousand mirrors stretching off to the horizon. But without the romance.

Wonderful stopped scratching at the long scar through her shaved-stubble hair long enough to make a contribution. "Looks to me," she said, "like a confirmed shit-hole."

"We're way out east of the Crinna, no?" Craw worked a speck of skin between teeth and tongue and spat it out, wincing at the pink mark left on his finger, way more painful than it had any right to be. "Nothing but hundreds of miles of shit-hole in every direction. You sure this is the place, Raubin?"

"I'm sure. She was most specifical."

Craw frowned round. He wasn't sure if he'd taken such a pronounced dislike to Raubin 'cause he was the one that brought the jobs and the jobs were usually cracked, or if he'd taken such a pronounced dislike to Raubin 'cause the man was a weasel-faced arsehole. Bit of both, maybe. "The word is 'specific,' half-head."

"Got my meaning, no? Village in a fork in the river, she said, south o' the fens, three halls, biggest one with uprights carved like fox heads."

"Aaaah." Craw snapped his fingers. "They're meant to be foxes."

"Fox Clan, these crowd."

"Are they?"

"So she said."

"And this thing we've got to bring her. What sort of a thing is it, exactly?"

"Well, it's a thing," said Raubin.

"That much we know."

"Sort of, this long, I guess. She didn't say, precisely."

"Unspecifical, was she?" asked Wonderful, grinning with every tooth.

"She said it'd have a kind of a light about it."

"A light? What? Like a magic bloody candle?"

All Raubin could do was shrug, which wasn't a scrap of use to no one. "I don't know. She said you'd know it when you saw it."

"Oh, nice." Craw hadn't thought his mood could drop much lower. Now he knew better. "That's real nice. So you want me to bet my life, and the lives o' my crew, on knowing it when I see it?" He shoved himself back off the rocks on his belly, out of sight of the village, clambered up and brushed the dirt from his coat, muttering darkly to himself, since it was a new one and he'd been taking some trouble to keep it clean. Should've known that'd be a waste of effort, what with the shitty jobs he always ended up in to his neck. He started back down the slope, shaking his head, striding through the trees towards the others. A good, confident stride. A leader's stride. It was important, Craw reckoned, for a chief to walk like he knew where he was going.

Especially when he didn't.

Raubin hurried after him, whiny voice picking at his back. "She didn't precisely say. About the thing, you know. I mean, she don't, always. She just looks at you, with those eyes…" He gave a shudder. "And says, get me this thing, and where from. And what with the paint, and that voice o' hers, and that sweat o' bloody fear you get when she looks at you…" Another shudder, hard enough to rattle his rotten teeth. "I ain't asking no questions, I can tell you that. I'm just looking to run out fast so I don't piss myself on the spot. Run out fast, and get whatever thing she's after…"

"Well that's real sweet for you," said Craw, "except insofar as actually getting this thing."

"As far as getting the thing goes," mused Wonderful, splashes of light and shadow swimming across her bony face as she looked up into the branches, "the lack of detail presents serious difficulties. All manner of things in a village that size. Which one, though? Which thing, is the question." Seemed she was in a thoughtful mood. "One might say the voice, and the paint, and the aura of fear are, in the present case… self-defeating."

"Oh no," said Craw. "Self-defeating would be if she was the one who'd end up way out past the Crinna with her throat cut, on account of some blurry details on the minor point of the actual job we're bloody here to do." And he gave Raubin a hard glare as he strode out of the trees and into the clearing.

Scorry was sitting sharpening his knives, eight blades neatly laid out on the patchy grass in front of his crossed legs, from a little pricker no longer'n Craw's thumb to a hefty carver just this side of a short-sword. The ninth he had in his hands, whetstone working at steel, *squick, scrick,* marking the rhythm to his soft, high singing. He had a wonder of a singing voice, did Scorry Tiptoe. No doubt he would've been a bard in a happier age, but there was a steadier living in sneaking up and knifing folk these days. A sad fact, Craw reckoned, but those were the times.

Brack-i-Dayn was sat beside Scorry, lips curled back, nibbling at a stripped rabbit bone like a sheep nibbling at grass. A huge, very dangerous sheep. The little thing looked like a toothpick in his great tattooed blue lump of a fist. Jolly Yon frowned down at him as if he was a great heap of shit, which Brack might've been upset by, if it hadn't been Yon's confirmed habit to look at everything and everyone that way. He properly looked like the least jolly man in all the North at that moment. It was how he'd come by the name, after all.

Whirrun of Bligh was kneeling on his own on the other side of the clearing, in front of his great long sword, leaned up against a tree for the purpose. He had his hands clasped in front of his chin, hood drawn down over his head and with just the sharp end of his nose showing. Praying, by the look of him. Craw had always been a bit worried by men who prayed to gods, let alone swords. But those were the times, he guessed. In bloody days, swords were worth more than gods. They certainly had 'em outnumbered. Besides, Whirrun was a valley man, from way out north and west, across the mountains near the White Sea, where it snowed in summer and no one with the slightest sense would ever choose to live. Who knew how he thought?

"Told you it was a real piss-stain of a village, didn't I?" Never was in the midst of stringing his bow. He had that grin he tended to have, like he'd made a joke on everyone else and no one but him had got it. Craw would've liked to know what it was, he could've done with a laugh. The joke was on all of 'em, far as he could see.

"Reckon you had the right of it," said Wonderful as she strutted past into the clearing. "Piss. Stain."

"Well, we didn't come to settle down," said Craw, "we came to get a thing."

Jolly Yon achieved what many might've thought impossible by frowning deeper, black eyes grim as graves, dragging his thick fingers through his thick tangle of a beard. "What sort of a thing, exactly?"

Craw gave Raubin another look. "You want to dig that one over?" The fixer only spread his hands, helpless. "I hear we'll know it when we see it."

"Know it when we see it? What kind of a—"

"Tell it to the trees, Yon, the task is the task."

"And we're here now, aren't we?" said Raubin.

Craw sucked his teeth at him. "Brilliant fucking observation. Like all the best ones, it's true whenever you say it. Yes, we're here."

"We're here," sang Brack-i-Dayn in his up-and-down Hillman accent, sucking the last shred o' grease from his bone and flicking it into the bushes. "East of the Crinna where the moon don't shine, a hundred miles from a clean place to shit, and with wild, crazy bastards dancing all around think it's a good idea to put bones through their own faces." Which was a little rich, considering he was so covered in tattoos he was more blue than white. There's no style of contempt like the stuff one kind of savage has for another, Craw guessed.

"Can't deny they've got some funny ideas east of the Crinna." Raubin shrugged. "But here's where the thing is, and here's where we are, so why don't we just get the fucking thing and go back fucking home?"

"Why don't you get the fucking thing, Raubin?" growled Jolly Yon.

"'Cause it's my fucking job to fucking tell you to get the fucking thing is why, Yon fucking Cumber."

There was a long, ugly pause. Uglier than the child of a man and a sheep, as the hillmen have it. Then Yon talked in his quiet voice, the one that still gave Craw prickles up his arms, even after all these years. "I hope I'm wrong. By the dead, I hope I'm wrong. But I'm getting this feeling…" He shifted forward, and it was awfully clear all of a sudden just how many axes he was carrying, "like I'm being disrespected."

"No, no, not at all, I didn't mean—"

"*Respect*, Raubin. That shit costs nothing, but it can spare a man from trying to hold his brains in all the way back home. Am I clear enough?"

"Course you are, Yon, course you are. I'm over the line. I'm all over it on both sides of it, and I'm sorry. Didn't mean no disrespect. Lot o' pressure, is all. Lot o' pressure for everyone. It's my neck on the block just like yours. Not down there, maybe, but back home, you can be sure o' that, if she don't get her way…" Raubin shuddered again, worse'n ever.

"A touch of respect don't seem too much to ask—"

"All right, all right." Craw waved the pair of 'em down. "We're all sinking on the same leaky bloody skiff, there's no help arguing about it. We need every man to a bucket, and every woman too."

"I'm always helpful," said Wonderful, all innocence.

"If only." Craw squatted, pulling out a blade and starting to scratch a map of the village in the dirt. The way Threetrees used to do a long, low, time ago. "We might not know exactly what this thing is, but we know where it is, at least."

Knife scraped through earth, the others all gathering round, kneeling, sitting, squatting, looking on. "A big hall, in the middle, with uprights on it carved like foxes. They look more like dragons to me, but, you know, that's another story. There's a fence round the outside, two gates, north and south. Houses and huts all about here. Looked like a pig pen there. That's a forge, maybe."

"How many do we reckon might be down there?" asked Yon.

Wonderful rubbed at the scar on her scalp, face twisted as she looked up towards the pale sky. "Could be fifty, sixty fighting men? A few elders, few dozen women and children too. Some o' those might hold a blade."

"Women fighting." Never grinned. "A disgrace, is that."

Wonderful bared her teeth back at him. "Get those bitches to the cook fire, eh?"

"Oh, the cook fire . . ." Brack stared up into the cloudy sky like it was packed with happy memories.

"Sixty warriors? And we're but seven—plus the baggage." Jolly Yon curled his tongue and blew spit over Raubin's boots in a neat arc. "Shit on that. We need more men."

"Wouldn't be enough food then." Brack-i-Dayn laid a sad hand on his belly. "There's hardly enough as it—"

Craw cut him off. "Maybe we should stick to plans using the number we've got, eh? Plain as plain, sixty's way too many to fight fair." Not that anyone had joined his crew for a fair fight, of course. "We need to draw some off."

Never winced. "Any point asking why you're looking at me?"

"Because ugly men hate nothing worse than handsome men, pretty boy."

"It's a fact I can't deny," sighed Never, flicking his long hair back. "I'm cursed with a fine face."

"Your curse my blessing." Craw jabbed at the north end of his dirt-plan, where a wooden bridge crossed a stream. "You'll take your unmatched beauty in towards the bridge. They'll have guards posted, no doubt. Mount a diversion."

"Shoot one of 'em, you mean?"

"Shoot near 'em, maybe. Let's not kill anyone we don't have to, eh? They might be nice enough folks under different circumstances."

Never sent up a dubious eyebrow. "You reckon?"

Craw didn't, particularly, but he'd no desire to weigh his conscience down any further. It didn't float too well as it was. "Just lead 'em a little dance, that's all."

Wonderful clapped a hand to her chest. "I'm so sorry I'll miss it. No one dances prettier than our Never when the music gets going."

Never grinned at her. "Don't worry, sweetness, I'll dance for you later."

"Promises, promises."

"Yes, yes." Craw shut the pair of 'em up with another wave. "You can make us all laugh when this fool job's done with, if we're still breathing."

"Maybe we'll make you laugh too, eh Whirrun?"

The valley man sat cross-legged, sword across his knees, and shrugged. "Maybe."

"We're a tight little group, us lot, we like things friendly."

Whirrun's eyes slid across to Jolly Yon's black frown, and back. "I see that."

"We're like brothers," said Brack, grinning all over his tattooed face. "We share the risks, we share the food, we share the rewards, and from time to time we even share a laugh."

"Never got on too well with my brothers," said Whirrun.

Wonderful snorted. "Well aren't you blessed, boy? You've been given a second chance at a loving family. You last long enough, you'll learn how it works."

The shadow of Whirrun's hood crept up and down his face as he slowly nodded. "Every day should be a new lesson."

"Good advice," said Craw. "Ears open, then, one and all. Once Never's drawn a few off, we creep in at the south gate." And he put a cross in the dirt to show where it was. "Two groups, one each side o' the main hall there, where the thing is. Where the thing's meant to be, leastways. Me, Yon, and Whirrun on the left." Yon spat again, Whirrun gave the slightest nod. "Wonderful, take Brack and Scorry down the right."

"Right y'are, chief," said Wonderful.

"Right for us," sang Brack.

"So, so, so," said Scorry, which Craw took for a yes.

He stabbed at each of 'em with one chewed-to-bugger fingernail. "And all on your best behavior, you hear? Quiet as a spring breeze. No tripping over the pots this time, eh, Brack?"

"I'll mind my boots, chief."

"Good enough."

"We got a backup plan," asked Wonderful, "in case the impossible happens and things don't work out quite according to the scheme?"

"The usual. Grab the thing if we can, then run like fuck. You," and Craw gave Raubin a look.

His eyes went wide as two cook pots. "What, me?"

"Stay here and mind the gear." Raubin gave a long sigh of relief, and Craw felt his lip curl. He didn't blame the man for being a hell of a coward, most men are. Craw was one himself. But he blamed him for letting it show. "Don't get too comfortable, though, eh? If the rest of us come to grief these Fox fuckers'll track you down before our blood's dry and more'n likely cut your fruits off." Raubin's sigh rattled to a quick stop.

"Cut your head off," whispered Never, eyes all scary-wide.

"Pull your guts out and cook 'em," growled Jolly Yon.

"Skin your face off and wear it as a mask," rumbled Brack.

"Use your cock for a spoon," said Wonderful. They all thought about that for a moment.

"Right, then," said Craw. "Nice and careful, and let's get in that hall without no one noticing and get us that thing. Above all…" And he swept the lot of 'em with his sternest look, a half circle of dirt-smeared, scar-pocked, bright-eyed, beard-fuzzed faces. His crew. His family. "Nobody die, eh? Weapons."

Quick sharp, and with no grumbling now the work was at their feet, Craw's crew got ready for action, each one smooth and practiced with their gear as a weaver with his loom, weapons neat as their clothes were ragged, bright and clean as their faces were dirty. Belts, straps, and bootlaces hissed tight, metal scraped, rattled and rang, and all the while Scorry's song floated out soft and high.

Craw's hands moved by themselves through the old routines, mind wandering back across the years to other times he'd done it, other places, other faces around him, a lot of 'em gone back to the mud long ago. A few he'd buried with his own hands. He hoped none of these folk died today, and became nothing but dirt and worn-out memories. He checked his shield, grip bound in leather all tight and sturdy, straps firm. He checked his knife, his backup knife, and his backup backup knife, all tight in their sheaths. You can never have too many knives, someone once told him, and it was solid advice, provided you were careful how you stowed 'em and didn't fall over and get your own blade in your fruits.

Everyone had their work to be about. Except Whirrun. He just bowed his head as he lifted his sword gently from the tree-trunk, holding it under the crosspiece by its stained leather scabbard, sheathed blade longer'n one of his own long legs. Then he pushed his hood back, scrubbed one hand through his flattened hair and stood watching the others, head on one side.

"That the only blade you carry?" asked Craw as he stowed his own sword at his hip, hoping to draw the tall man in, start to build some trust with him. Tight crew like this was, a bit of trust might save your life. Might save everyone's.

Whirrun's eyes swiveled to him. "This is the Father of Swords, and men have a hundred names for it. Dawn Razor. Grave-Maker. Blood Harvest. Highest and Lowest. Scac-ang-Gaioc in the valley tongue which means the Splitting of the World, the battle that was fought at the start of time and will be fought again at its end." For a moment he had Craw wondering if he'd list the whole bloody hundred but thankfully he stopped there, frowning at the hilt, wound with dull gray wire. "This is my reward and my punishment both. This is the only blade I need."

"Bit long for eating with, no?" asked Wonderful, strutting up from the other side.

Whirrun bared his teeth at her. "That's what these are for."

"Don't you ever sharpen it?" asked Craw.

"It sharpens me."

"Right. Right y'are." Just the style of nonsense Craw would've expected from Cracknut Leef or some other rune-tosser. He hoped Whirrun was as good with that great big blade as he was supposed to be, 'cause it seemed he brought nothing to the table as a conversationalist.

"Besides, to sharpen it you'd have to draw it," said Wonderful, winking at

Craw with the eye Whirrun couldn't see.

"True." Whirrun's eyes slid up to her face. "And once the Father of Swords is drawn, it cannot be sheathed without—"

"Being blooded?" she finished for him. Didn't take skill with the runes to see that coming, Whirrun must've said the same words a dozen times since they left Carleon. Enough for everyone to get somewhat tired of it.

"Blooded," echoed Whirrun, voice full of portent.

Wonderful gave Craw a look. "You ever think, Whirrun of Bligh, you might take yourself a touch too serious?"

He tipped his head back and stared up into the sky. "I'll laugh when I hear something funny."

Craw felt Yon's hand on his shoulder. "A word, chief?"

"Course," with a grin that took some effort.

He guided Craw away from the others a few steps, and spoke soft. The same words he always did before a fight. "If I die down there..."

"No one's dying today," snapped Craw, the same words he always used in reply.

"So you said last time, 'fore we buried Jutlan." That drove Craw's mood another rung down the ladder into the bog. "No one's fault, we do a dangerous style o' work, and all know it. Chances are good I'll live through, but all I'm saying is, if I don't—"

"I'll stop by your children, and take 'em your share, and tell them what you were."

"That's right. And?"

"And I won't dress it up any."

"Right, then." Jolly Yon didn't smile, of course. Craw had known him years, and hadn't seen him smile more'n a dozen times, and even then when it was least expected. But he nodded, satisfied. "Right. No man I'd rather give the task to."

Craw nodded back. "Good. Great." No task he wanted less. As Yon walked off he muttered to himself. "Always the fool jobs..."

It went pretty much just like Craw planned. He wouldn't have called it the first time ever, but it was a pleasant surprise, that was sure. The six of them lay still and silent on the rise, followed the little movements of leaf and branch that marked Never creeping towards that crap-arse of a village. It looked no better the closer you got to it. Things rarely did, in Craw's experience. He chewed at his nails some more, saw Never kneel in the bushes across the stream from the north gate, nocking an arrow and drawing the string. It was hard to tell from this range, but it looked like he still had that knowing little grin even now.

He loosed his shaft and Craw thought it clicked into one of the logs that made the fence. Faint shouting drifted on the wind. A couple of arrows wobbled back the other way, vanished into the trees as Never turned and scuttled off, lost in the brush. Craw heard some kind of a drum beating, more shouting, then men started to hurry out across that bridge, weapons of rough iron clutched in their hands, some still pulling their furs or boots on. Perhaps three dozen, all told. A neat piece of work. Provided Never got away, of course.

Yon shook his head as he watched a good chunk of the Fox Clan shambling over their bridge and into the trees. "Amazing, ain't it? I never quite get used to just how fucking stupid people are."

"Always a mistake to overestimate the bastards," whispered Craw. "Good thing we're the cleverest crew in the Circle of the World, eh? So could we have no fuckups, today, if you please?"

"I won't if you won't, chief," muttered Wonderful.

"Huh." If only he'd been able to make that promise. Craw tapped Scorry on his shoulder and pointed down into the village. The little man winked back, then slid over the rise on his belly and down through the undergrowth, nimble as a tadpole through a pond.

Craw worked his dry tongue around his dry mouth. Always ran out of spit at a time like this, and however often he did it, it never got any better. He glanced out the corner of his eye at the others, none of 'em showing much sign of a weak nerve. He wondered if they were bubbling up with worry on the inside, just like he was, and putting a stern face on the wreckage, just like he was. Or if it was only him scared. But in the end it didn't seem to make much difference. The best you could do with fear was act like you had none.

He held his fist up, pleased to see his hand didn't shake, then pointed after Scorry, and they all set off. Down towards the south gate—if you could use the phrase about a gap in a rotten fence under a kind of arch made from crooked branches, skull of some animal unlucky enough to have a fearsome pair of horns mounted in the middle of it. Made Craw wonder if they had a straight piece of wood within a hundred bloody miles.

The one guard left stood under that skull, leaning on his spear, staring at nothing, tangle-haired and fur-clad. He picked his nose, and held one finger up to look at the results. He flicked it away. He stretched, and reached around to scratch his arse. Scorry's knife thudded into the side of his neck and chopped his throat out, quick and simple as a fisher gutting a salmon. Craw winced, just for a moment, but he knew there'd been no dodging it. They'd be lucky if that was the only man lost his life so they could get this fool job done. Scorry held him a moment while blood showered from his slit neck, caught him as he fell, guided his twitching body soundless to the side of the gate, out of sight of any curious eyes inside.

No more noise than the breeze in the brush Craw and the rest hurried up the bank, bent double, weapons ready. Scorry was waiting, knife already wiped, peering around the side of the gate post with one hand up behind him to say wait. Craw frowned down at the dead man's bloody face, mouth a bit open as though he was about to ask a question. A potter makes pots. A baker makes bread. And this is what Craw made. All he'd made all his life, pretty much.

It was hard to feel much pride at the sight, however neatly the work had been done. It was still a man murdered just for guarding his own village. Because they were men, these, with hopes and sorrows and all the rest, even if they lived out here past the Crinna and didn't wash too often. But what could one man do? Craw took a long breath in, and let it out slow. Just get the task done without any of his own people killed. In hard times, soft thoughts can kill you quicker than the plague.

He looked at Wonderful, and he jerked his head into the village, and she slid around the gate post and in, slipping across to the right-hand track, shaved head swiveling carefully left and right. Scorry followed at her heels and Brack crept after, silent for all his great bulk.

Craw took a long breath, then crept across to the left-hand track, wincing as he tried to find the hardest, quietest bits of the rutted muck to plant his feet on. He heard the hissing of Yon's careful breath behind him, knew Whirrun was there too, though he moved quiet as a cat. Craw could hear something clicking. A spinning wheel, maybe. He heard someone laugh, not sure if he was imagining it. His head was jerked this way and that to every trace of a sound, like he had a hook through his nose. The whole thing seemed horribly bright and obvious, right then. Maybe they should've waited for darkness, but Craw had never liked working at night. Not since that fucking disaster at Gurndrift where Pale-as-Snow's boys ended up fighting Littlebone's on an accident and more'n fifty men dead without an enemy within ten miles. Too much to go wrong at night.

But then Craw had seen plenty of men die in the day too.

He slid along beside a wattle wall, and he had that sweat of fear on him. That prickling sweat that comes with death right at your shoulder. Everything was picked out sharper than sharp. Every stick in the wattle, every pebble in the dirt. The way the leather binding the grip of his sword dug at his palm when he shifted his fingers. The way each in-breath gave the tiniest whistle when it got three-quarters into his aching lungs. The way the sole of his foot stuck to the inside of his boot through the hole in his sock with every careful step. Stuck to it and peeled away.

He needed to get him some new socks was what he needed. Well, first he needed to live out the day, then socks. Maybe even those ones he'd seen in Uffrith last time he was there, dyed red. They'd all laughed at that. Him, and Yon, and Wonderful, and poor dead Jutlan. Laughed at the madness of it. But afterwards he'd thought to himself—there's luxury, that a man could afford to have his socks dyed—and cast a wistful glance over his shoulder at that fine cloth. Maybe he'd go back after this fool job was done with, and get himself a pair of red socks. Maybe he'd get himself two pairs. Wear 'em on the outside of his boots just to show folk what a big man he was. Maybe they'd take to calling him Curnden Red Socks. He felt a smile in spite of himself. Red socks, that was the first step on the road to ruin if ever he'd—

The door to a hovel on their left wobbled open and three men walked out of it, all laughing. The one at the front turned his shaggy head, big smile still plastered across his face, yellow teeth sticking out of it. He looked straight at Craw, and Yon, and Whirrun, stuck frozen against the side of a longhouse with their mouths open like three children caught nicking biscuits. Everyone stared at each other.

Craw felt time slow to a weird crawl, that way it did before blood spilled. Enough time to take in silly things. To wonder whether it was a chicken bone through one of their ears. To count the nails through one of their clubs. Eight and a half. Enough time to think it was funny he wasn't thinking something more useful. It was like he stood outside himself, wondering what he'd do but feeling it probably weren't up to him. And the oddest thing of all was that it had happened so often to him now, that feeling, he could recognise it when it came. That frozen, baffled moment before the world comes apart.

Shit. Here I am again—

He felt the cold wind kiss the side of his face as Whirrun swung his sword in a great reaping circle. The man at the front didn't even have time to duck. The flat of the sheathed blade hit him on the side of the head, whipped him off his feet, turned him head over heels in the air and sent him crashing into the wall of the shack beside them upside down. Craw's hand lifted his sword without being told. Whirrun darted forward, arm lancing out, smashing the pommel of his sword into the second man's mouth sending teeth and bits of teeth flying.

While he was toppling back like a felled tree, arms spread wide, the third tried to raise a club. Craw hacked him in the side, steel biting through fur and flesh with a wet thud, spots of blood showering out of him. The man opened his mouth and gave a great high shriek, tottering forward, bent over, eyes bulging. Craw split his skull wide open, sword-grip jolting in his hand, the scream choked off in a surprised yip. The body sprawled, blood pouring from broken head and all over Craw's boots. Looked like he'd come out of this with red socks after all. So much for no more dead, and so much for quiet as a spring breeze, too.

"Fuck," said Craw.

By then time was moving way too fast for comfort. The world jerked and wobbled, full of flying dirt as he ran. Screams rang and metal clashed, his own breath and his own heart roaring and surging in his ears. He snatched a glance over his shoulder, saw Yon turn a mace away with his shield and roar as he hacked a man down. As Craw turned back an arrow came from the dead knew where and clicked into the mud wall just in front of him, almost made him fall over backwards with shock. Whirrun went into his arse and knocked him sprawling, gave him a mouthful of mud. When he struggled up a man was charging right at him, a flash of screaming face and wild hair smeared across his sight. Craw was twisting round behind his shield when Scorry slid out from nowhere and knifed the running bastard in the side, made him shriek and stumble sideways, off-balance. Craw took the side of his head off, blade pinging gently as it chopped through bone then thumped into the ground, nearly jerking from his raw fist.

"Move!" he shouted, not sure who at, trying to wrench his blade free of the earth. Jolly Yon rushed past, head of his axe dashed with red, teeth bared in a mad snarl. Craw followed, Whirrun behind him, face slack, eyes darting from one hut to another, sword still sheathed in one hand. Around the corner of a hovel and into a wide stretch of muck, scattered with ground-up straw. Pigs were honking and squirming in a pen at one side. The hall with the carved uprights stood at the other, steps up to a wide doorway, only darkness inside.

A red-haired man pounded across the ground in front of them, a wood axe in his fist. Wonderful calmly put an arrow through his cheek at six strides distant and he came up short, clapping a hand to his face, still stumbling towards her. She stepped to meet him with a fighting scream, swept her sword out and around and took his head right off. It spun into the air, showering blood, and dropped in the pig pen. Craw wondered for a moment if the poor bastard still knew what was going on.

Then he saw the heavy door of the hall being swung shut, a pale face at the edge. "Door!" he bellowed, and ran for it, pounding across squelching mud and up the wooden steps, making the boards rattle. He shoved one bloody, muddy boot in the gap just as the door was slammed and gave a howl, eyes bulging, pain lancing up his leg. "My foot! Fuck!"

There were a dozen Fox Clan or more crowded around the end of the yard now, growling and grunting louder and uglier than the hogs. They waved jagged swords, axes, rough clubs in their fists, a few with shields too, one at the front with a rusted chain hauberk on, tattered at the hem, straggling hair tangled with rings of rough-forged silver.

"Back." Whirrun stood tall in front of them, holding out his sword at long arm's length, hilt up, like it was some magic charm to ward off evil. "Back, and you needn't die today."

The one in mail spat, then snarled back at him in broken Northern. "Show us your iron, thief!"

"Then I will. Look upon the Father of Swords, and look your last." And Whirrun drew it from the sheath.

Men might've had a hundred names for it—Dawn Razor, Grave-Maker, Blood Harvest, Highest and Lowest, Scac-ang-Gaioc in the valley tongue which means the Splitting of the World, and so on, and so on—but Craw had to admit it was a disappointing length of metal. There was no flame, no golden light, no distant trumpets or mirrored steel. Just the gentle scrape as long blade came free of stained leather, the flat gray of damp slate, no shine or ornament about it, except for the gleam of something engraved down near the plain, dull crosspiece.

But Craw had other worries than that Whirrun's sword wasn't worth all the songs. "Door!" he squealed at Yon, scrabbling at the edge of it with his left hand, all tangled up with his shield, shoving his sword through the gap and waving it about to no effect. "My fucking foot!"

Yon roared as he pounded up the steps and rammed into the door with his shoulder. It gave all of a sudden, tearing from its hinges and crushing some fool underneath. Him and Craw burst stumbling into the room beyond, dim as twilight, hazy with scratchy-sweet smoke. A shape came at Craw and he whipped his shield up on an instinct, felt something thud into it, splinters flying in his face. He reeled off-balance, crashed into something else, metal clattering, pottery shattering. Someone loomed up, a ghostly face, a necklace of rattling teeth. Craw lashed at him with his sword, and again, and again, and he went down, white-painted face spattered with red.

Craw coughed, retched, coughed, blinking into the reeking gloom, sword ready to swing. He heard Yon roaring, heard the thud of an axe in flesh and someone squeal. The smoke was clearing now, enough for Craw to get some sense of the hall. Coals glowed in a fire pit, lighting a spider's web of carved rafters in sooty red and orange, casting shifting shadows on each other, tricking his eyes. The place was hot as hell, and smelled like hell besides. Old hangings around the walls, tattered canvas daubed with painted marks. A block of black stone at the far end, a rough statue standing over it, and at its feet the glint of gold. A cup, Craw thought. A goblet. He took a step towards it, trying to waft the murk away from his face with his shield.

"Yon?" he shouted.

"Craw, where you at?"

Some strange kind of song was coming from somewhere, words Craw didn't know but didn't like the sound of. Not one bit. "Yon?" And a figure sprang up suddenly from behind that block of stone. Craw's eyes went wide and he almost fell in the fire pit as he stumbled back.

He wore a tattered red robe—long, sinewy arms sticking from it, spread wide, smeared with paint and beaded up with sweat, the skull of some animal drawn down over his face, black horns curling from it so he looked in the shifting light like a devil bursting straight up from hell. Craw knew it was a mask, but looming up like that out of the smoke, strange song echoing from that skull, he felt suddenly rooted to the spot with fear. So much he couldn't even lift his sword. Just stood there trembling, every muscle turned to water. He'd never been a hero, that was true, but he'd never felt fear like this. Not even at Ineward, when he'd seen the Bloody-Nine coming for him, snarling madman's face all dashed with other men's blood. He stood helpless.

"Fuh… fuh… fuh…"

The priest came forward, lifting one long arm. He had a thing gripped in painted fingers. A twisted piece of wood, the faintest pale glow about it.

The thing. The thing they'd come for.

Light flared from it brighter and brighter, so bright it burned its twisted shape fizzing into Craw's eyes, the sound of the song filling his ears until he couldn't hear anything else, couldn't think anything else, couldn't see nothing but that thing, searing bright as the sun, stealing his breath, crushing his will, stopping his breath, cutting his—

Crack. Jolly Yon's axe split the animal skull in half and chopped into the face underneath it. Blood sprayed, hissed in the coals of the firepit. Craw felt spots on his face, blinked and shook his head, loosed all of a sudden from the freezing grip of fear. The priest lurched sideways, song turned to a guttering gurgle, mask split in half and blood squirting from under it. Craw snarled as he swung his sword and it chopped into the sorcerer's chest and knocked him over on his back. The thing bounced from his hand and spun away across the rough plank floor, the blinding light faded to the faintest glimmer.

"Fucking sorcerers," snarled Yon, curling his tongue and blowing spit onto the corpse. "Why do they bother? How long does it take to learn all that jabber and it never does you half the good a decent knife…" He frowned. "Uh-oh."

The priest had fallen in the fire pit, scattering glowing coals across the floor. A couple had spun as far as the ragged hem of one of the hangings.

"Shit." Craw took a step on shaky legs to kick it away. Before he got there, flame sputtered around the old cloth. "Shit." He tried to stamp it out, but his head was still a touch spinny and he only got embers scattered up his trouser leg, had to hop around, slapping them off. The flames spread, licking up faster'n the plague. Too much flame to put out, spurting higher than a man. "Shit!" Craw stumbled back, feeling the heat on his face, red shadows dancing among the rafters. "Get the thing and let's go!"

Yon was already fumbling with the straps on his leather pack. "Right y'are, chief, right y'are! Backup plan!"

Craw left him and hurried to the doorway, not sure who'd be alive still on the other side. He burst out into the day, light stabbing at his eyes after the gloom.

Wonderful was standing there, mouth hanging wide open. She'd an arrow nocked to her half-drawn bow, but it was pointed at the ground, hands slack. Craw couldn't remember the last time he'd seen her surprised.

"What is it?" he snapped, getting his sword tangled up on the doorframe then snarling as he wrenched it free, "You hurt?" He squinted into the sun, shading his eyes with his shield. "What's the…" And he stopped on the steps and stared. "By the dead."

Whirrun had hardly moved, the Father of Swords still gripped in his fist, long, dull blade pointing to the ground. Only now he was spotted and spattered head to toe in blood and the twisted and hacked, split and ruined corpses of the dozen Fox Clan who'd faced him were scattered around his boots in a wide half-circle, a few bits that used to be attached to them scattered wider still.

"He killed the whole lot." Brack's face was all crinkled up with confusion. "Just like that. I never even lifted my hammer."

"Damndest thing," muttered Wonderful. "Damndest thing." She wrinkled her nose. "Can I smell smoke?"

Yon burst from the hall, stumbled into Craw's back and nearly sent the pair of them tumbling down the steps. "Did you get the thing?" snapped Craw.

"I think I..." Yon blinked at Whirrun, stood tall in his circle of slaughter. "By the dead, though."

Whirrun started to back towards them, twisted himself sideways as an arrow looped over and stuck wobbling into the side of the hall. He waved his free hand. "Maybe we better—"

"Run!" roared Craw. Perhaps a good leader should wait until everyone else gets clear. First man to arrive in a fight and the last to leave. That was how Threetrees used to do it. But Craw weren't Threetrees, it hardly needed to be said, and he was off like a rabbit with its tail on fire. Leading by example, he'd have called it. He heard bow strings behind him. An arrow zipped past, just wide of his flailing arm, stuck wobbling into one of the hovels. Then another. His squashed foot was aching like fury but he limped on, waving his shield arm. Pounding towards the jerking, wobbling archway with the animal's skull above it. "Go! Go!"

Wonderful tore past, feet flying, flicking mud in Craw's face. He saw Scorry flit between two huts up ahead, then swift as a lizard around one of the gateposts and out of the village. He hurled himself after, under the arch of branches. Jumped down the bank, caught his hurt foot, body jolting, teeth snapping together and catching his tongue. He took one more wobbling step then went flying, crashed into the boggy bracken, rolled over his shield, just with enough thought to keep his sword from cutting his own nose off. He struggled to his feet, laboured on up the slope, legs burning, lungs burning, through the trees, trousers soaked to the knee with marsh-water. He could hear Brack lumbering along at his shoulder, grunting with the effort, and behind him Yon's growl, "bloody... shit... bloody... running... bloody... shit..."

He tore through the brush and wobbled into the clearing where they'd made their plans. Plans that hadn't flown too smoothly, as it went. Raubin was standing by the gear. Wonderful near him with her hands on her hips. Never was kneeling on the far side of the clearing, arrow nocked to his bow. He grinned as he saw Craw. "You made it then, chief?"

"Shit." Craw stood bent over, head spinning, dragging in air. "Shit." He straightened, staring at the sky, face on fire, not able to think of another word, and without the breath to say one if he had been.

Brack looked even more shot than Craw, if it was possible, crouched over, hands on knees and knees wobbling, big chest heaving, big face red as a slapped arse around his tattoos. Yon tottered up and leaned against a tree, cheeks puffed out, skin shining with sweat.

Wonderful was hardly out of breath. "By the dead, the state o' you fat old men." She slapped Never on the arm. "That was some nice work down there at the village. Thought they'd catch you and skin you sure."

"You hoped, you mean," said Never, "but you should've known better. I'm the best damn runner-away in the North."

"That is a fact."

"Where's Scorry?" gasped Craw, enough breath in him now to worry.

Never jerked his thumb. "Circled round to check no one's coming for us."

Whirrun ambled back into the clearing now, hood drawn up again and the Father of Swords sheathed across his shoulders like a milkmaid's yoke, one hand on the grip, the other dangling over the blade.

"I take it they're not following?" asked Wonderful, one eyebrow raised.

Whirrun shook his head. "Nope."

"Can't say I blame the poor bastards. I take back what I said about you taking yourself too serious. You're one serious fucker with that sword."

"You get the thing?" asked Raubin, face all pale with worry.

"That's right, Raubin, we saved your skin." Craw wiped his mouth, blood on the back of his hand from his bitten tongue. They'd done it, and his sense of humor was starting to leak back in. "Hah. Could you imagine if we'd left the bastard thing behind?"

"Never fear," said Yon, flipping open his pack. "Jolly Yon Cumber, once more the fucking hero." And he delved his hand inside and pulled it out.

Craw blinked. Then he frowned. Then he stared. Gold glinted in the fading light, and he felt his heart sink lower than it had all day. "That ain't fucking it, Yon!"

"It's not?"

"That's a cup! It was the thing we wanted!" He stuck his sword point-down in the ground and waved one hand about. "The bloody thing with the kind of bloody light about it!"

Yon stared back at him. "No one told me it had a bloody light!"

There was silence for a moment then, while they all thought about it. No sound but the wind rustling the old leaves, making the black branches creak. Then Whirrun tipped his head back and roared with laughter. A couple of crows took off, startled from a branch it was that loud, flapping up sluggish into the gray sky.

"Why the hell are you laughing?" snapped Wonderful.

Inside his hood Whirrun's twisted face was glistening with happy tears. "I told you I'd laugh when I heard something funny!" And he was off again, arching back like a full-drawn bow, whole body shaking.

"You'll have to go back," said Raubin.

"Back?" muttered Wonderful, her dirt-streaked face a picture of disbelief. "Back, you mad fucker?"

"You know the hall caught fire, don't you?" snapped Brack, one big trembling arm pointing down towards the thickening column of smoke wafting up from the village.

"It what?" asked Raubin as Whirrun blasted a fresh shriek at the sky, hacking, gurgling, only just keeping on his feet.

"Oh, aye, burned down, more'n likely with the damn thing in it."

"Well… I don't know… you'll just have to pick through the ashes!"

"How about we pick through your fucking ashes?" snarled Yon, throwing the cup down on the ground.

Craw gave a long sigh, rubbed at his eyes, then winced down towards that shit-hole of a village. Behind him, Whirrun's laughter sawed throaty at the dusk. "Always," he muttered, under his breath. "Why do I always get stuck with the fool jobs?"

ALONE
ROBERT REED

Robert Reed was born in Omaha, Nebraska. He has a Bachelor of Science in Biology from the Nebraska Wesleyan University, and has worked as a lab technician. He became a full-time writer in 1987, the same year he won the L. Ron Hubbard Writers of the Future Contest, and has published eleven novels, including *The Leeshore, The Hormone Jungle,* and far future science fiction novels *Marrow* and *The Well of Stars.* An extraordinarily prolific writer, Reed has published over 200 short stories, mostly in *Fantasy & Science Fiction* and *Asimov's,* which have been nominated for the Hugo, James Tiptree, Jr., Locus, Nebula, Seiun, Theodore Sturgeon Memorial, and World Fantasy awards, and have been collected in *The Dragons of Springplace* and *The Cuckoo's Boys.* His novella "A Billion Eves" won the Hugo Award. Nebraska's only SF writer, Reed lives in Lincoln with his wife and daughter, and is an ardent long-distance runner.

1

The hull was gray and smooth, gray and empty, and in every direction it fell away gradually, vanishing where the cold black of the sky pretended to touch what was real. What was real was the Great Ship. Nothing else enjoyed substance or true value. Nothing else in Creation could be felt, much less understood. The Ship was a sphere of perfect hyperfiber, world-sized and enduring, while the sky was only a boundless vacuum punctuated with lost stars and the occasional swirls of distant galaxies. Radio whispers could be heard, too distorted and far too faint to resolve, and neutrino rains fell from above and rose from below, and there were ripples of gravity and furious nuclei generated by distant catastrophes—inconsequential powers washing across the unyielding, eternal hull.

Do not trust the sky, the walker understood. The sky wished only to tell lies. And perhaps worse, the sky could distract the senses and mind from what genuinely mattered. The walker's only purpose was to slowly, carefully move across the Ship's hull, and if something of interest were discovered, a cautious investigation would commence. But only if it was harmless could the mystery be approached and studied in detail. Instinct guided the walker, and for as long as it could remember, the guiding instinct was fear. Fierce, unnamed hazards were lurking. The walker could not see or define its enemies, but they were near, waiting for weakness. Waiting for sloth or inattentiveness. Regardless how curious it was or how fascinating some object might be, the walker scrupulously avoided anything that moved or spoke, or any device that glowed with unusual heat, and even the tiniest example of organic life was something to be avoided, without fail.

Solitude was its natural way.

Alone, the ancient fear would diminish to a bearable ache, and something like happiness was possible.

Walking, walking. That was the purpose of existence. Select a worthy line, perhaps using one of the scarce stars as a navigational tool. Follow that line until something new was discovered, and regardless whether the object was studied or circumvented, the walker would then pick a fresh direction—a random direction—and maintain that new line with the same tenacity.

There was no need to eat, no requirement for drink or sleep. Its life force was a minor, unsolvable mystery. The pace was patient, every moment feeling long and busy. But if nothing of note occurred, nothing needed to be recalled. After a century of uninterrupted routine, the walker compressed that blissful sameness into a single impression that was squeezed flush against every other vacuous memory—the recollections of a soul that felt ageless but was still very close to empty.

Eyes shrank and new eyes grew, changing talents. With that powerful, piercing vision, the walker watched ahead and beside and behind. Nothing was missed. And sometimes for no obvious reason it would stop, compelled suddenly to lower several eyes, staring into a random portion of the hull. From the grayness, microscopic details emerged. Fresh radiation tracks still unhealed; faint scars being gradually erased by quantum bonds fighting to repair themselves. Each observation revealed quite a lot about the hyperfiber, and the lessons never changed. The hull was a wonder. Fashioned from an extremely strong and lasting material—a silvery-gray substance refined during a lost age by some powerful species, perhaps, or perhaps a league of vanished gods. They were the masters who must have imagined and built the Ship, and presumably the same wondrous hands had sent their prize racing through the vacuum. A good, glorious purpose must be at work here; but except for the relentless perfection of the Great Ship, nothing remained of their intentions, their goals, or even an obvious destination.

When the walker kneeled, the hull's beauty was revealed.

And then it would stand again and resume its slow travels, feeling blessed to move free upon this magnificent face.

2

There was no purpose but to wander the perfection forever: that was an assumption made early and embraced as a faith. But as the centuries passed, oddities and little mysteries gradually grew more numerous. Every decade brought a few more crushed steel boxes and empty diamond buckets than the decade before, and there were lumps of mangled aerogel, and later, the occasional shard of some lesser form of hyperfiber. As time passed, the walker began to come across dead machines and pieces of machinery and tools too massive or far too ordinary to be carried any farther once they had failed. These objects were considerably younger than the Ship. Who abandoned them was a looming mystery, but one that would not be solved soon. The walker had no intention of approaching these others. And in those rare times when they approached it—always by mistake, always unaware of its presence—it would flatten itself against the hull and make itself vanish.

Invisibility was a critical talent. But invisibility meant that it had to abandon most of its senses. Even as they strode across its smooth back, these interlopers were reduced to a vibration with each footfall and a weak tangle of magnetic and electrical fields.

Days later and safe again, the walker would rise up carefully and move on.

Another millennium passed without serious incident. It was easy to believe that the Great Ship would never change, and nothing would ever be truly new; and holding that belief close, the walker followed one new line. No buckets or diamond chisels were waiting to change its direction. As it strode on, the stars and sky-whispers silently warned that it was finally passing into unknown territory. But this did happen on occasion. Perfection meant sameness, and the walker could imagine nothing new. Then what seemed to be a flat-topped mountain began to rise over the coming horizon. Puzzled, it made note of the sharp gray line hovering just above the hull. More years of steady marching caused the grayness to lift higher, just slightly. Perhaps a mountain of trash had been set there. Perhaps a single enormous bucket upended. Various explanations offered themselves; none satisfied. But the event was so surprising, enormous and unwelcome, and the novelty so great, that the walker stopped as soon as it was sure that something was indeed there, and without taking one step, it waited for three years and a little longer, adapting its eyes constantly, absorbing a view that refused to change.

Finally, curiosity defeated every caution, and altering its direction, the walker steered straight toward what still made no sense.

At a pace that required little energy, it pressed ahead in half-meter strides. Decades passed before it finally accepted what was obvious: that while the Ship was undoubtedly perfect, it was by no measure perfectly smooth and eternally round. Rising from the hull was not one gigantic tower, but several. The nearest tower was blackish-gray and too vast to measure from a single perspective. Occasionally a small light appeared on the summit, or several tiny flecks of light danced beside its enormous bulk, and there were sudden spikes in dense, narrow radio noise that tasted like a language. Various explanations occurred to the walker. From where these possibilities came, it could not say. Maybe they arose from the instincts responsible for its persistent fears. But like never before, it was curious. It started to move once again, slowly and tirelessly pushing closer, and that was when it noticed how one of the more distant towers had begun to tip, looking as if it was ready to collapse on its side. And shortly after that remarkable change in posture, the tower suddenly let loose a deep rumble, followed by a scorching, sky-piercing fire.

But of course: these were the Ship's engines. No other explanation was necessary, and in another moment, the walker absorbed its new knowledge, a fresh set of beliefs gathering happily around the Ship's continued perfection. Fusion boosted by antimatter threw a column of radiant blue-white plasmas into the blackness, scorching the vacuum. This was a vision worth admiration. Here was power beyond anything that the walker had ever conceived of. But soon the engine fell back into sleep, and after thorough reflection, it decided to choose another random direction, and another, selecting them until it was steering away from the gigantic rocket nozzles.

If objects this vast had missed its scrutiny, what else was hiding beyond the horizon?

Walk, walk, walk.

But its pace began to slow even more. Flying vessels and many busy machines were suddenly common near the engines, and some kind of animal was building cities of bubbled glass. An invasion was underway. There were regions of intense activity and considerable radio noise, and each hazard had to be avoided, or if the situation demanded, crossed without revealing its presence.

Ages passed before the engines vanished beyond the horizon. A bright red star became the walker's beacon, its guide, and it followed that rich light until the ancient sun sickened and went nova, flinging portions of its flawed skin out into the cooling, dying vacuum.

Younger stars appeared, climbing from the horizon as the walker pressed forward. A second sky was always hiding behind the hyperfiber body. The walker felt the play of gravity and then the hard twisting, the Ship leaving the line that had been followed without interruption for untold billions of years. After that, the sky was changed. The vacuum was not nearly so empty, or quite as chilled, and even a patient entity with nothing to do but count points of light could not estimate just how many stars were rising into its spellbound gaze.

A galaxy was approaching. One great plate of three hundred billion suns and trillions of worlds was about to intersect with a vessel that had wandered across the universe, every previous nudge and great reaches of nothingness leading to this place and this rich, perfect moment.

And here the walker stood, on the brink of something entirely new.

There was a line upon the hull that perhaps no one else could have noticed. Not just with their eyes and the sketchy knowledge available, no. But the walker recognized the boundary where the hull that it knew surrendered to another. Suddenly the thick perfect hyperfiber was replaced with a thicker but considerably more weathered version of faultless self. Even in the emptiest reaches of the universe, ice and dust and other nameless detritus wandered in the dark.

These tiny worlds would crash down on the Ship's hull, always at a substantial fraction of light-speed, and not even the best hyperfiber could shrug aside that kind of withering power. Stepping onto the Ship's leading face, the walker immediately noticed gouges and debris fields and then the little craters that were eventually obscured by still larger craters—holes reaching deep into the hard resilient hull. Most of the wounds were ancient, although hyperfiber hid its age well. All but the largest craters were unimportant to the Ship's structure, their cumulative damage barely diminishing its abiding strength. But some of the wounds showed signs of repair and reconditioning. The walker discovered one wide lake of liquid hyperfiber, the patch still curing when it arrived on the smooth shoreline. Kneeling down, it looked deep into the still-reflective surface. For the first time in memory, there was another waiting to be seen. But the entity felt little interest in its own appearance. What mattered was the inescapable fact that someone—some agent or benevolent hand—was striving to repair what billions of years of abuse had achieved. A constructive force was at work upon the Ship. A healing force, seemingly. Enthralled, the walker looked at the young lake and the reflected Milky Way, measuring the patch's dimensions. Then it examined the half-cured skin, first with fresh eyes and then with a few respectful touches. A fine grade of hyperfiber was being used, almost equal to the original hull. Which implied that caretakers were striving to do what was good and make certain that their goodness would endure.

The endless wandering continued.

Eventually the galaxy was overhead, majestic but still inconsequential. The suns and invisible worlds were little more than warm dust flung across the emptiness, and still all that mattered was the Ship, dense and rich beyond all measure. Walk, and walk. And walk. And then it found itself on the edge of another crater—the largest scar yet on the hull—and for the first time ever, it followed a curving line, the crater's frozen lip defining its path.

Bodies and machines were working deep inside the ancient gouge.

From unseen perches, it watched the activity, studying methods and guessing reasons when it could not understand. The vacuum crackled with radio noise. The sense of words began to emerge, and because the skill might prove useful, the walker committed to memory what it understood of the new language. Hundreds of animals worked inside the crater—humans they called themselves, dressed inside human-shaped machines. And accompanying them were tens of thousands of pure machines, while on the lip stood a complex of prefabricated factories and fusion reactors and more humans and more robots dedicated to no purpose but repairing one minuscule portion of the Ship's forward face.

As it kneeled there, unseen, a bit of cosmic dirt fell with a brilliant flash of light, leaving a tiny crater inside the giant one.

The danger was evident, but there were blessings too. The walker slipped across a narrow track lain on the unbroken hull, presumably leading from some far place to the crater's edge. The track was a superconductive rail that allowed heavy tanks to be dragged here, each tank filled with uncured, still-liquid hyperfiber. From another hiding place, the walker watched as a long train of tanks arrived and subsequently drained before being set on a parallel track and sent away. Before the third was empty, it understood enough to appreciate just how difficult this work was. Liquid hyperfiber was fickle, eager to form lasting bonds but susceptible to flaws and catastrophic embellishments. Down in the crater, a brigade of artisans was struggling to repair the damage—a tiny pock on the vast bow of the Ship—and their deed, epic as well as tiny, was ringing testament to the astonishing gifts of those who had first built the Great Ship.

All but one of the empty tanks was sent home. The exception was damaged in a collision and then pushed aside, abandoned. Curious about that silver tank, the walker approached and then paused, crept closer and paused again, making certain that no traps were waiting, no eyes watching. Then it slipped near enough to touch the crumbled body. That innate talent for mechanical affairs was awakened again. Using thought and imaginary tools, it rebuilt the empty vessel. Presumably those repairs were waiting for a more convenient time. Unless the humans meant to leave their equipment behind, which was not an unthinkable prospect, judging by the trash already scattered about this increasingly crowded landscape.

One end of the tank was cracked open, the interior exposed. In slow, nearly invisible steps, the walker slipped inside. The cylinder was slightly less than a kilometer in length. Ignoring every danger, the walker passed through the ugly fissure, and once inside, it balanced on a surface designed to feel slick to every possible material. Yet it managed to hold its place, retaining its pose, peering into the darkness until it was sure that it was alone, and then it let light seep out of its own body, filling the long volume with a soft cobalt-blue glow.

Everywhere it looked, it saw itself looking back.

Reflected on the round wall were distorted images of what might be a machine, or perhaps was something else. Whatever it was, the walker had no choice but to stare at itself. This was indeed a trap, it realized, but instead of a secret door slamming shut, the mechanism worked by forcing an entity to gaze upon its own shape and its nature, perhaps for the first time.

What it beheld was not unlovely.

But how did it know beauty? What aesthetic standard was it employing? And why carry such a skill among its instincts and talents?

A long time passed before the walker could free itself from the trap. But even after it climbed back onto the open hull, escape proved difficult. It slinked away for a good distance and then stopped, and then it walked farther before turning back again. Where did this obligation come from, this need to stare at an empty, ruined tank? Why care about a soulless object that would never function again? How could that piece of ruin bother it so? And why, even after walking far enough to hide both the tank and the crater beyond the horizon…why did its mind insist on returning again and again to an object that others had casually and unnecessarily cast aside?

3

It walked. It counted steps. It had reached two million four hundred thousand and nine steps when humans suddenly appeared in their swift cars. The invaders settled within a hundred meters of the walker. With a storm of radio talk and the help of robots, they quickly erected a single unblinking eye and pointed it straight above. The walker hid where it happened to be, filling a tiny crater. Unnoticed, it lay motionless as the new telescope was built and tested and linked to the growing warning system. And then the humans left, but the walker remained inside its safe hole, sprouting an array of increasingly powerful eyes.

The sky might be untrustworthy, but there was beauty to the lie. The Great Ship was plunging into a galaxy that was increasingly brilliant and complex and dangerous. More grit and chunks of wayward ice slammed against the hull, and the bombardment would only strengthen as the Ship sliced into the thick curling limb of suns. But the humans were answering the dangers with increasingly powerful weapons. Telescopes watched for hazards. Then bolts of coherent light melted the incoming ices. Ballistic rounds pulverized asteroids. Sculpted EM fields slowed the tiniest fragments and shepherded them aside. There was splendor to that awful fight. Flashes and sparkles constantly surprised the lidless eyes. Ionized plasmas generated squawks and whistles reaching across the spectrum. An accidental music grew louder, urgent and carefree. No defensive system was unbreakable. Death threatened everything foolish enough to walk upon the bow. Each moment might be its last. But the scene deserved fascination and wonder. It stared upwards, and it grew antennae and listened, and its mind began to believe that this violent magic had a rhythm, an elegant inescapable logic, and that whatever note and whichever color came next could have been foreseen.

That was when the voice began.

At least that was the moment when the walker finally took notice of the soft, soft whispers.

These mutterings were not part of the sky. Intuition told the walker that much. Perhaps the voice rose from the hull, or maybe it came from the chill vacuum. But what mattered more than its origin was the quiet swift terror that defined its presence—an inarticulate, nearly inaudible murmur that came when it was unexpected and vanished before any response could be offered.

Following the first eleven incidents, the walker remained silently anxious.

But the twelfth whisper was too much. With a radio mouth formed for the occasion, and using the human language that it had learned over the last centuries, the walker called out, "What are you? What do you want?" And when nothing replied, it added, "Do not bother me. Leave me alone."

By chance or by kindness, the request was honored.

The walker rose and again wandered across the bow. But after witnessing several jarring impacts, it returned to the stern, ready to accept the safety afforded by the Ship's enormous bulk. But there were even more humans than before, and they brought endless traffic on what had been delicious, seemingly infinite emptiness. Following a twisting, secretive line, the walker journeyed to the nearest engine, and with some delight, it touched the mountainous nozzle at its base. But machines were everywhere, investigating and repairing, and the human chatter was busy and endless, jabbering about subjects and names and places and times that made no sense at all.

Where the bow and stern joined, starships were landing. The walker tracked them by their bright little rockets. Hunkering behind piles of trash, it watched the slow taxis and quicker streakships drop onto the hull, and then enormous doors would pull open, and the visitors would vanish. The walker had never seen a spaceport, never even imagined such a thing was possible. Once again, the Great Ship was far more than it pretended to be. Creeping even closer, it estimated the size of the incoming vessels. Considering how many passengers might be tucked inside each little ship, it was easy to understand why the hull had grown crowded. The human animals were falling from the sky, coming here for the honor of living inside their bubble cities on the hull of this lost, unknowable relic.

Finally, in slow patient stages, the walker crept to the edge of a vast door, and with a single glance, its foolishness was revealed. The Great Ship was more than its armored hull. What the entity had assumed to be hyperfiber to the core was otherwise. Inside the spaceport, it saw a vast column of air and light and warm wet bodies moving by every means and for no discernable purpose. This was motion, swift and busy and devoid of any clear purpose. Humans were just one species among a multitude, and beneath the hull, the Ship was pierced with tunnels and doorways and hatches and diamond-windows, and that was just what the briefest look provided before it flattened out and slowly, cautiously crawled away.

The Ship was hollow.

And judging by the evidence, it was inhabited by millions and maybe billions of organic entities.

These unwanted revelations left it shaken. Months were required to sneak away from the port. Unseen, it returned to the bow face and the beautiful sky, accepting the dangers for the illusion of solitude. But the ancient craters were being swiftly erased now. The Ship's lasers were pummeling most of the cometary debris that dared pass nearby, and the repair crews were swift and efficient now. The pitted, cracked terrain was vanishing beneath smooth perfection. The new hyperfiber proved fresh and strong, affording few hiding places even for a wanderer who could hide nearly anywhere. By necessity, every motion was slow. Was studied. But even then, a nearby robot would notice a presence, and maybe EM hands would reach out, trying to touch what couldn't be seen; and by reflex, the walker stopped living and stopped thinking, hiding away inside itself as it pretended to be nothing but another patch lost among the billions.

Eventually it came upon a freshly made crater, too small to bring humans immediately but large enough to let it walk down inside the wounded hull.

A brief, sharp ridge stood in its way—the relic of chaotic, billion-degree plasmas. After five hours of careful study, the walker slowly crossed the ridge. Humans never came alone to these places, and there was no sign of any machine. But standing on the ridgeline, urgency took hold. Something here was wrong. And what was wrong felt close. The walker began to lower itself, trying to vanish. But then a strong voice said, "There you are."

It hunkered down quickly.

Then with amusement, someone said, "I see you."

The voice—the mysterious and uninvited phenomena—was always quieter than this. It has always been a whisper, and far less comprehensible. Perhaps the young crater helped shape its words. Perhaps the bowl with its sharp refrozen hyperfiber lip lent strength and focus.

In myriad ways, the walker began to melt into the knife-like ridge.

Yet the voice only grew louder—a radio squawk wrapped around the human language. With some pleasure, she said, "You cannot hide from me."

"Leave me be," the walker answered.

"But you're the one disturbing me, stranger."

"And I have told you," the walker insisted. "Before, I told you that I wish to be alone. I must be alone. Don't pester me with your noise."

"Oh," the voice replied. "You believe we've met. Don't you?"

Curiosity joined the fear. A new eye lifted just a little ways, scanning the closest few meters.

"But I've never spoken to you," the voice continued. "You've made a mistake. I don't know whose voice you've been hearing, but I'm rather certain that it wasn't mine."

"Who are you?" the walker asked.

"My name is Wune."

"Where are you?"

"Find the blue-white star on the horizon," she said.

It complied, asking, "Are you that star?"

"No, no." Wune could do nothing but laugh for a few moments. "Look below it. Do you see me?"

Except for a few crevices and delicate wrinkles, the crater floor was flat. Standing at the far end was a tiny figure clad in hyperfiber. An arm lifted now. What might have been a hand waved slowly, the gesture purely human.

"My name is Wune," the stranger repeated.

"Are you human?" the entity whispered nervously.

"I'm a Remora," said Wune. Then she asked, "What exactly are you, my friend? Since I don't seem to recognize your nature."

"My nature is a mystery," it agreed.

"Do you have a name?"

"I am," it began. Then it hesitated, considering this wholly original question. And with sudden conviction, it said, "Alone." It rose up from the ridge, proclaiming, "My name is Alone."

4

"Come closer, Alone."

It did nothing.

"I won't hurt you," Wune promised, the arm beckoning again. "We should study each at a neighborly distance. Don't you agree?"

"We are close enough," the walker warned, nearly two kilometers of vacuum and blasted hyperfiber separating them.

The Remora considered his response. Then with an amiable tone, she agreed, "This is better than being invisible to one another. I'll grant you that."

For a long while, neither spoke.

Then Wune asked, "How good are those eyes? What do you see of me?"

Alone stared only at the stranger, each new eye focused on the lifesuit made of hyperfiber and the thick diamond faceplate and what lay beyond. Alone had seen enough humans to understand their construction, their traditions. But what was human about this face was misplaced. The eyes were beneath the mouth and tilted on their sides. The creature's flesh was slick and cold in appearance, and it was vivid purple. The long hair on the scalp was white with a hint of blue, rather like the brightest stars, and that white hair began to lift and fall, twirl and straighten, as if an invisible hand was playing with it.

"I don't know your species," Alone confessed.

"But I think you do," Wune corrected. "I'm a human animal, and a Remora too."

"You are different from the others."

"What others?" she inquired.

"The few that I have seen."

"You spied on us inside the big crater. Didn't you?" The mouth smiled, exposing matching rows of perfect human teeth. "Oh yes, you were noticed. I know that you strolled up to that busted tank and climbed inside before walking away again."

"You saw me?"

"Not then, but later," she explained. "A security AI was riding the tank. It was set at minimal power, barely alive. Which probably kept you from noticing it. We didn't learn about you until weeks later, when we stripped the tank for salvage and the AI woke up."

Shame took hold. How could it have been so careless?

"I know five other occasions when you were noticed," Wune continued. "There have probably been more incidents. I try to hear everything, but that's never possible. Is it?" Then she described each sighting, identifying the place and time when these moments of incompetence occurred.

"I wasn't aware that I was seen," it stated.

Ignorance made its failures feel even worse.

"You were barely seen," Wune corrected. "A ghost, a phantom. Not real enough to be taken seriously."

"You mentioned a spaceport," it said.

"I did."

"Where is this port?"

Wune pointed with authority, offering a precise distance.

"I don't remember being there," Alone admitted.

"Maybe we made a mistake," she allowed.

"But I did visit a different port." With care, it sifted through its memories. "I might have troubles with my memory," it confessed.

"Why do you think that?"

"Because I know so little about myself," confessed the walker.

"That is sad," Wune said. "I'm sorry for you."

"Why?"

"Life is the past," she stated. "The present moment is too narrow to slice and will be lost with the next instant. And the future is nothing but empty conjecture. Where you have been is what matters. What you have done is what counts for and against you on the tallies."

The walker concentrated on those unexpected words.

"I have a telescope with me," Wune said. "I used it when I first saw you. But I'm trying to be polite. If you don't mind, may I study you now?"

"If you wish," it said uneasily.

The Remora warned, "This might take some time, friend." Then with both gloved hands, she held a long tube to her face.

Alone waited.

An hour later, Wune asked, "Are you a machine?"

"I don't know. Perhaps I am."

"Or do you carry an organic component inside that body?"

"Each answer is possible, I think."

Wune lowered the telescope. "I'm a little of both," she allowed. "I like to believe that I'm more organic than mechanical, but the two facets happily live inside me."

Alone said nothing.

The Remora laughed softly, admitting, "This is fun."

Was it?

To her new friend, she explained, "Thousands of years ago, humans learned how to never grow old. No disease, and no easy way to kill us." The hands were encased in hyperfiber gloves. One of those fingers tapped hard against her diamond faceplate. "My mind? It's a bioceramic machine. Which makes it tough and quick to heal and full of redundancies. My memories are safe inside the artificial neurons. Whenever I want, I can remember yesterday. Or I can pull my head back five centuries and one yesterday. My life is an enormous, deeply personal epic that I am free to enjoy whenever I wish."

"I am different than you," Alone conceded.

Wune asked, "Do you sleep?"

"Never."

"Yet you never feel mentally tired?" The purple face nodded, and she said, "Right now, I'm envious."

Envy was a new word.

"I'm trying to tell you something," she said. "This old Remora lady has been awake for a very long time, and she needs to sleep for a little while. Is that all right? Do whatever you want while my eyes are closed. If you need, walk away from me. Vanish completely." Then she smiled, adding, "Or you might take a step or two in my direction. If you feel the urge, that is."

Then Wune shut her misplaced eyes.

During the next hour, Alone crept ahead a little more than three meters.

As soon as she woke, Wune noticed. "Good. Very good."

"Are you rested now?"

"Hardly. But I'll push through the misery." Her laugh had a different tone. "What's your earliest, oldest memory? Tell me."

"Walking."

"Walking where?"

"Crossing the Ship's hull."

"Who brought you to the Ship?"

"I have always been here."

She considered those words. "Or you could have been built here," she suggested. "Assembled from a kit, perhaps. You don't remember a crowd of engineers sticking their hands inside you?"

"I remember no one." Then again, with confidence, Alone claimed, "I have never been anywhere but on the Great Ship."

"If that was true," Wune began. Then she fell silent.

Alone asked, "What if that is so?"

"I can't even guess at all of the ramifications," she admitted. Then after a few minutes of silence, she said, "Ask something of me. Please."

"Why are you here, Wune?"

"Because I'm a Remora," she offered. "Remoras are humans who got pushed up on the hull to do important, dangerous work. There are reasons for this. Good causes, and bad justifications. Everything that you see here...well, the hull is not intended to be a prison. The captains claim that it isn't. But now and again, it feels like an awful prison."

Then she hesitated, thinking carefully before saying, "I don't think that was your question. Was it?"

"Like me, you are alone," it pointed out. "Most of the humans, Remoras and engineers and the captains…these humans usually gather in large groups, and they act pleased to be that way…"

With a serious tone, she said, "I'm rather different, it seems."

Alone waited.

"The hull is constantly washed with radiation, particularly out here on the leading face." She gestured at the galaxy. "My flesh is immortal. I can endure almost any abuse. But these wild nuclei crash through my cells, wreaking terrible damage. My repair mechanisms are always awake, always busy. I have armies of tiny workers marching inside me, trying to lift my flesh back to robust health. But when I'm alone, and when I focus on my body's functions, I can influence my regenerating flesh. In some ways, with just willpower, I can direct my own evolution."

That seemed to explain the odd, not quite human face.

"I'm out here teaching myself these tricks," Wune admitted. "The hull is no prison. To me, it is a church. A temple. A rare opportunity for the tiniest soul to unleash potentials that her old epic life never revealed to her."

"I understand each of your words," said Alone.

"But?"

"I cannot decipher what you mean."

"Of course you can't." Wune laughed. "Listen. My entire creed boils down to this: If I can write with my flesh, then I can write upon my soul."

"Your 'soul'?"

"My mind. My essence. Whatever it is that the universe sees when it looks hard at peculiar little Wune."

"Your soul," the walker said once again.

Wune spoke for a long while, trying to explain her young faith. Then her voice turned raw and sloppy, and after drinking broth produced by her recyke system, she slept again. The legs of her lifesuit were locked in place. Nearly five hours passed with her standing upright, unaware of her surroundings. When she woke again, barely twenty meters of vacuum and hard radiation separated them.

She didn't act surprised. With a quieter, more intimate voice, she asked, "What fuels you? Is there some kind of reactor inside you? Or do you steal your power from us somehow?"

"I don't remember stealing."

"Ah, the thief's standard reply." She chuckled. "Let's assume you're a machine. You have to be alien-built. I've never seen or even heard rumors about any device like you. Not from the human shops, I haven't." After a long stare, she asked, "Are you male?"

"I don't know."

"I'm going to call you male. Does that offend you?"

"No."

"Then perhaps you are." She wanted to come closer. One boot lifted, seemingly of its own volition, and then she forced herself to set it back down on the hull.

"You claim not to know your own purpose. Your job, your nature. All questions without answer."

"I am a mystery to myself."

"Which is an enormous gift, isn't it? By that, I mean that if you don't know what to do with your life, then you're free to do anything you wish." Her face was changing color, the purple skin giving way to streaks of gold. And during her sleep, her eyes had grown rounder and deeply blue. "You don't seem dangerous. And you do require solitude. I can accept all of that. But as time passes, I think you'll discover that it's harder to escape notice out here on the hull. The surface area is enormous, yes. But where will you hide? I promise, I won't chase after you. And I can keep my people respectful of your privacy. At least I hope I can. But the Great Ship is cursed with quite a few captains, and they don't approve of mysteries. And we can't count all the adventurers who are coming here now, racing up from countless worlds. Maybe you don't realize this, but our captains have decided to take us on a tour of the galaxy. Humans and aliens are invited, for a fat price, and some of them will hear the rumors about you. Some of these passengers will come up on the hull, armed with sensors and their lousy judgment."

Alone listened carefully.

"My reasons are selfish," Wune admitted. "I don't want these tourists under my boots. And since you can't hide forever in plain sight, we need to find you a new home."

Horrified, he asked, "Where can I go?"

"Almost anywhere," Wune assured. "The Great Ship is ridiculously big. It might take hundreds of thousands of years just to fill up its empty places. The caverns, the little tunnels. The nameless seas and canyons and all the dead-end holes."

"But how can I find those places?"

"I know ways. I'll help you."

Terror and hope lay balanced on the walker's soul.

With those changeless human teeth, Wune smiled. "I believe you," she offered. "You say you know nothing about your nature, your talents. And I think you mean that."

"I do."

"Look at the chest of my suit, will you? Stare into the flat hyperfiber. Yes, here. Do you see your own reflection?"

His body had changed during these last few minutes. Alone had felt the new arms sprouting, the design of his legs adjusting, and without willing it to happen, he had acquired a face. It was a striking and familiar face, the purple flesh shot with gossamer threads of gold.

"I almost wish I could do that," Wune confessed. "Reinvent myself as easily as you seem to do."

He could think of no worthy response.

"Do you know what a chameleon is?"

Alone said, "No."

"You," she said. "Without question, you are the most natural, perfect chameleon that I have ever had the pleasure to meet."

5

Simply and clearly, Wune explained how a solitary wanderer might secretly slip inside the Ship. Then as she grew drowsy again, the Remora wished her chameleon friend rich luck and endless patience. "I hope you find whatever you are hunting," she concluded. "And that you avoid whatever it is that you might be fleeing."

Alone offered thankful words, but he had no intention of accepting advice. Once Wune was asleep, he picked a fresh direction and walked away. For several centuries, he wandered the increasingly smooth hull, watching as the galaxy— majestic and warm and bright—rose slowly to meet the Great Ship. Now and again, he was forced to hide in the open. Practice improved his techniques, but he couldn't shake the sense that the Remoras were still watching him, despite his tricks and endless caution. He certainly eavesdropped on them, and whenever Wune's name was mentioned, he listened closely. Never again did her voice find him. But others spoke of the woman with admiration and love. Wune had visited this bubble city or that repair station. She had talked to her people about the honor of serving the Great Ship and the strength that came from mastering the evolution of your own mortal body. Then she was dead, killed by a shard of ice that slipped past every laser. Alone absorbed the unexpected news. He didn't understand his emotions, but he hid where he happened to be standing and for a full year did nothing. Wune was the only creature with whom he had ever spoken, and he was deeply shocked, and then he was quite sad, but what wore hardest was the keen pleasure he discovered when he realized that she was dead but he was still alive.

Eventually he wandered back to the Ship's trailing face, slipping past the bubble cities and into the realm of giant engines. Standing before one of the towering nozzles, Alone recalled Wune promising small, unmonitored hatches. Careless technicians often left them unsecured. With a gentle touch, Alone tried to lift the first hatch, and then he tried to shove it inwards. But it was locked. Then he worked his way along the base of the nozzle, testing another fifty hatches before deciding that he was mistaken. Or perhaps the technicians had learned to do their work properly. But having little else to do, he invested the next twenty months toying with every hatch and tiny doorway that he came across, his persistence rewarded when what passed for his hand suddenly dislodged a narrow doorway.

Darkness waited, and with it, the palpable sense of great distance.

He crawled down, slowly at first, and then the sides of the nearly vertical tunnel pulled away from his grip.

Falling was floating. There was no atmosphere, no resistance to his gathering momentum. Fearing that someone would notice, he left the darkness intact. Soon he was plunging at a fantastic rate, and that's when he remembered Wune cautioning, "These vents and access tubes run straight down, sometimes for hundreds of kilometers."

His tube dropped sixty kilometers before making a sharp turn.

The impact came without warning. One moment, he was mildly concerned about prospects that he couldn't measure, and the next moment saw discomfort and flashes of senseless light as his neural net absorbed the abuse. But he never lost consciousness, and he soon felt his shattered pieces flowing together, making healing motions that continued without pause for three hours.

A familiar voice found him then.

Lying in the dark, unable to move, something quiet came very close and then said, "The cold," before falling silent again.

He didn't try to speak.

Then after a long while, the voice said, "For so long, cold."

"What is cold?" Alone whispered.

"And dark," said the voice.

"Who are you?" he asked.

The voice said, "Listen."

Alone remained silent, straining to hear any sound, no matter how soft or fleeting. But nothing else was offered. Silence lay upon silence, chilled and black, and he spent the next long while trying to decipher which language was used. No human tongue, clearly. Yet those few words were as transparent and simple as anything he had heard before.

Once healed, he seeped light.

The engine's interior was complex and redundant, and most of its facilities were scarcely used. Except for the occasional crackling whisper, radio talk never reached him. He could wander again. Happy, he discovered a series of nameless places where the slightest frosting of dust lay over every surface, that dust never disturbed. Billions of years of benign neglect promised seclusion. No one would find him in this vastness, and if nothing else happened in his life, all would be well.

Centuries passed.

Technicians and their machines traveled through these places, but always bound for other, more important locations.

Hiding was easy inside the catacombs.

The Ship gave warning when the overhead engine was about to be fired. Great valves were opened and closed, vibrations traveling along the sleeping tubes. A deeper chill could be felt as lakes of liquid hydrogen were prepared for fusion. Alone always found three sites where he could quickly find shelter. His planning worked well, and he saw no reason to change what was flawless. And then one day, everything changed. Alone was sitting inside a minor conduit, happily basking in a pool of golden light leaking from his inexplicable body. He was thinking about nothing of consequence. And then that perfect instant was in the past. There was a deep rumble and the ominous feel of dense fluids on the move, and before he could react, he was picked up and carried along by a hot viscous and irresistible liquid. Not hydrogen, and not water either. It was some species of oil dirtied up with odd metals and peculiar structures. He was trapped inside juices and passion, life and more life, and he responded with a desperate scream.

Tendrils touched him, trying to bury inside him.

He panicked, kicked and spun hard. Then he pulled his body into the first disguise that occurred to him.

Electric voices jabbered.

A language was found, and what surrounded him said in the human tongue, "It is a Remora."

"Down here?"

"Tastes wrong," a third voice complained.

"Not hyperfiber, this shell isn't," said a fourth.

The voices never repeated. This oily body contained a multitude of independent, deeply communal entities.

"The face is," said another.

"Look at the face." Another.

"You hear us, Remora?"

"I do," Alone allowed.

"Are you lost?"

He knew the word, but its precise meaning had always evaded him. So with as much authority as possible, he said, "I am not lost. No."

In an alien language, the multitude debated what to do next.

Then a final voice announced, "Whatever you are, we will leave you now in a safe place. For this favor, you will pay us with your praise and thanks. Do this and win our respect. Otherwise, we will speak badly of you, today and for the eternity to come."

He was spat into a new tunnel—a brief broad hole capped with a massive door and filled with magnetic filters, meshed filters, and a set of powerful grasping limbs. The limbs gathered him up. He immediately transformed his body, struggling to slide free. But his captors tied themselves into an enormous knot, their grip trying to crush him. Alone felt helpless. He panicked. Wild with terror, fresh talents were unleashed, and he discovered that when he did nothing except consciously gather up his energies, he could eventually let loose a burst of coherent light—an ultraviolet flash that jumped from his skin, scorching the smothering limbs—and he tumbled back onto the mesh floor.

A second set of limbs emerged, proving stronger, more careful.

Alone adapted his methods. A longer rest produced an invisible but intense magnetic pulse. The mechanical arms flinched and died, and then he changed his shape and flowed out from between them. The chamber walls and overhead door were high-grade hyperfiber. With brief bursts of light, he attacked the door's narrow seams. He attacked the floor. Security AIs made no attempt to hide their presence, calmly studying the ongoing struggle. Then a pair of technicians stepped through an auxiliary door—humans wearing armored lifesuits, complete with helmets that offered some protection to their tough, fearful minds.

The man asked the woman, "What is that thing?"

"I don't damn well know."

"You think it's the Remora's ghost?"

"Who cares?" he decided. "Call the boss, let her decide."

The humans retreated. Fresh arms were generated, slow and massive but designed just moments ago to capture this peculiar prize. Alone was herded into a corner and grabbed up, and an oxygen wind blew into the chamber, bringing a caustic mist of aerosols designed to weaken any normal machine. Through the dense air and across the radio spectrum, the humans spoke to him. "We don't know if you can understand us," they admitted. "But please, try to remain still. Pretend to be calm. We don't want you hurt, we want you to feel safe, but if you insist on fighting, mistakes are going to be made."

Alone struggled.

Then something was with him—a close, familiar presence—and the voice said, "The animals."

Alone stopped fighting.

"They have us," said the voice.

He listened to the air, to the empty static.

But whatever spoke to him was already gone, and that's when a low whistling noise began to leak out of the prisoner—a steady sad moaning that stopped only when the ranking engineer arrived.

6

"I think you do understand me."

He stared at the woman. Except for a plain white garment, she wore nothing. No armor, no helmet.

"My name is Aasleen."

Aasleen's face and open hands were the color of starless space. She was speaking into the air and into an invisible microphone, her radio words finding him an instant before their mirroring sound.

The woman said, "Alone."

He wasn't struggling. Doing nothing, he felt his power growing quickly, and he wondered what he might accomplish if held this pose for a long time.

"That's your name, isn't it? Alone?"

He had never embraced any name and saw no reason to do so now.

With her nearly black eyes, Aasleen studied her prisoner. And as she stood before him, coded threads of EM noise pushed into her head. Buried in her organic flesh were tiny machines, each speaking with its own urgent, complex voice. She listened to those voices, and she watched him. Then she said one secret word, silencing the chatter, and that's when she approached, walking forward slowly until he couldn't endure her presence anymore.

He made himself invisible.

She stopped moving toward him, but she didn't retreat either, speaking quietly to the smear of nothing defined by the giant clinging limbs.

"Twisting ambient light," she said. "I know that trick. Metamaterials and a lot of energy. You do it quite well, but it's nothing new."

Alone remained transparent.

"And I understand how you can alter your shape and color so easily. You're liquid, of course. You only pretend to be solid." She paused for a moment, smiling. "I once had a pet octopus. He had an augmented brain. To make me laugh, he used to pull himself into the most amazing shapes."

Alone let his body become visible again.

"Step away," he pleaded.

Aasleen stared at him for another moment. Then she backed off slowly, saying nothing until she had doubled the distance between them.

"Do you know what puzzleboys are?" she asked.

He didn't answer.

"Puzzleboys build these wonderful, very beautiful machines—hard cores clothed with liquid exteriors. Their devices are durable and inventive. Their best machines are designed to survive for ages while crossing deep space." Aasleen paused, perhaps hoping for a reaction. When she grew tired of the quiet, she explained, "Puzzleboys were like a lot of sentient species. They wanted the Great Ship for themselves. Thousands of worlds sent intergalactic missions, but my species won the race. I rode out here on one of the earliest starships. Among my happiest days is that morning when I first stood on the Ship's battered hull, gazing down at the Milky Way."

He said, "Yes."

"You know the view?"

"Yes."

She smiled, teeth showing. "A couple thousand years ago, as we were bringing the Great Ship into the galaxy, puzzleboys started singing their lies. They claimed they'd sent a quick stealthy mission up here. The laws of salvage are ancient—far older than my baby species. Machines can't claim so much as a lump of ice for their builders. But the aliens claimed that they'd shoved one of their own citizen's minds into a suitable probe. Like all good lies, their story has dates and convincing details. It's easy to conclude that their one brave explorer might have actually reached the Great Ship first. If he had done that, then this prize would be theirs. At least according to these old laws. The only trouble with the story is that the mission never arrived. I know I never saw any sign of squatters. Which is why we've made a point of insulting that entire species, and that's why the legal machinery of this cranky old galaxy has convincingly backed our claim of ownership."

Quietly, he said, "Puzzleboys."

"That's a human name. A translation, and like most approximations, inadequate."

With a burst of radio, the species' name was offered in its native language.

"Do you recognize it?" asked Aasleen.

He admitted, "I don't, no."

"All right." She nodded. A thin smile broke and then vanished again. "Let's have some fun. Try to imagine that somebody we know, some familiar civilization, dreamed you up and sent you to the Great Ship. Maybe they borrowed puzzleboy technologies. Maybe you've sprung from a different engineering history. Right now, I'm looking at a lot of data. But despite everything I see, I can't pick one answer over the others. Which is why this so interesting. And fun."

Alone said nothing.

She laughed briefly, softly. "That leaves me with a tangle of questions. For instance, do you know what scares me about you?"

He took a moment before asking, "What scares you?"

"Your power supply."

"Why?"

Aasleen didn't seem to hear the question. "And I'm not the only person sick with worry," she admitted. She closed one of her eyes and opened it again abruptly. "Miocene," she said, and sighed. "Miocene is an important captain. And you're considered a large enough problem that, right now, that captain is sitting inside a hyperfiber bunker three kilometers behind me. Three kilometers is probably far enough. If the worst happens, that is. But of course nothing is going to go bad now. As I explained to Miocene and the other captains, you seem to have survived quite nicely and without mishap, possibly for many thousands of years. What are the odds that your guts are going to fail today, in my face?"

He considered his nature.

"Do you have any idea what's inside you?"

"No," he admitted.

"A single speck of degenerated matter. Possibly a miniature black hole, although you're more likely a quark assemblage of one or another sort." She sighed and shrugged, adding, "Regardless of your engine design, it is novel. It's possible, yes, and I have a few colleagues who have done quite a lot of work proving that this kind of system might be used safely. But to see something like you in action, and to realize that you've existed for who-knows-how-long, and apparently without demanding any significant repair…"

"Alone," she said, "I am a very good engineer. One of the best I've ever met, regardless of the species. And I just can't believe in you. Honestly, it's impossible for me to accept that you are real."

"Then release me," he begged.

She laughed.

He watched her face, her nervous fingers.

"In essence," she continued, "you are a lucid entity carrying a tiny quasar inside your stomach. A quasar smaller than an atom and enclosed within a magnetic envelope, but massive and exceptionally dense."

"Quasar," he repeated.

"Matter, any matter, can be thrown inside you, and if only a fraction of the resulting energy is captured, you will generate shocking amounts of power."

He considered her explanation. Then with a quiet tone, he mentioned, "I have seen the Ship's engines firing."

"Have you?"

"Next to them, I am nothing."

"That's true enough. In fact, I've got a few machines sitting near us that can outstrip your capacities, and by a wide margin. But as Submaster Miocene has reminded me, if your magnetic envelope is breached, and if your stomach can digest just your own body mass, the resulting fireworks will probably obliterate several cubic kilometers of the Ship, and who knows how many innocent souls."

Alone believed her. But then he remembered that good lies have believable details and he didn't feel as certain.

Aasleen smiled in a sad fashion. "Of course I don't know exactly what would happen, if your stomach got loose. Maybe it has safety mechanisms that I can't see. Or maybe its fire would reach out and grab my body, and everything else in this room would be consumed, as well as Miocene...and with that, the Great Ship would be short one engine, and the survivors would have an enormous hole in the hull, spewing poisons and nuclear fire."

"I won't fail," he promised.

She nodded. "I think that's an accurate statement. I know I want to believe that both of us are perfectly safe."

"I won't hurt the Ship."

"All right. But why do you feel certain?"

He said, "Because I am."

Aasleen closed her eyes, once again concentrating on the machines inside her head.

"Please," said Alone. "Let me go free."

"I can't."

He changed his shape.

Aasleen's eyes opened. "I know that story about you and Wune. My guess? That you'd take on my appearance like you did hers."

But he hadn't. He had no limbs now, no face. To the eye, he looked like a ball of hyperfiber with giant rockets on one hemisphere, thick armor on the other. Using a hidden mouth, he promised, "I won't do any harm. I shall not hurt anyone and I will never injure the Ship."

"You just want to left by yourself," she said.

"Nothing else."

"But why?"

He had no response.

"Which leads us to another area of deep concern," she continued. "A machine built by unknown hands is discovered wandering inside another machine built by unknown hands. But there seems to be two mysteries, there might be only one. Do you understand what I mean?"

He said, "No."

"Two machines, but only one builder."

He didn't react.

She shook her head. "We don't know how old the Great Ship is. Not precisely, but we have informed guesses. And no matter how well-engineered you appear to be, I don't think you're several billion years old."

He remained silent.

Aasleen took one step closer. "There's the third terror involving you: a captain's nightmare. Maybe you are the puzzleboys' machine. Or you're somebody else's representative. Either way, if you arrived here on the Ship before any human did, and if there's a lost soul inside whatever passes for your mind...well, then it's possible that a different species might legally claim possession over the wealth and impossibilities that the Great Ship offers. And at that point, no matter how sweet your engineering is, your fate is out my hands..."

Her voice trailed away.

She took a tiny step forward.

"I have no idea," he said. "I don't know what I am. I know nothing."

The tiny machines inside Aasleen were speaking rapidly again.

"I'm watching your mind," she confessed. "But I'm not at all familiar with its neural network. It's a sloppy design, or it's revolutionary. I don't know enough to offer an opinion."

"I wish to leave now," he said.

"In the universe, there are two kinds of unlikely," Aasleen warned. "The Great Ship is one type—never attempted or even imagined, but achievable, provided someone has time and the muscle to make it real. And then there's the implausible that you imagine will come true, and one day your worst fears turn real. If the Great Ship belongs to someone else, then my species has to surrender our claim. And even though I believe that I am a good and charitable soul, I don't want that to happen. Facing that prospect, I would fight to keep that from happening, in fact."

Alone did nothing, gathering his strength.

"And even if you are safe as rain," she said, "I don't relish the idea of you wandering wherever you like. Not on my ship. Certainly not until we can find the answers to all these puzzles."

Without warning, Alone lost his shape, turning into a hot broth that tried to flow around the grasping arms.

The arms seemed to expect his trick, quickly creating one deep bowl that held him in place.

"I promise," said Aasleen. "You'll be somewhere safe. We will keep you comfortable. And as much as possible, you'll be left alone. Not even Miocene wants to torment you. And that's why a special chamber is being prepared—"

A new talent emerged.

The liquid body suddenly compressed itself, collapsing into a tiny dense and radiant drop hotter than any sun. And as the bowl-shaped limbs struggled to keep hold of this fleck of fire, Alone stole a portion of their mass, turning it into energy, shaping a ball of white-hot plasma.

And with that, he shrank into an even tinier, hotter bit of existence.

Aasleen turned and ran.

The arms were pierced. Not even the hyperfiber floor could resist his descent. He struck and sank out of sight, and when he was beneath the floor, hyperfiber turned into a bed of pale pink granite, and much as a ship passed between the stars, he was slicing quickly through what felt much like nothing.

7

Creating a narrow hole, Alone fell.

The hole was lined with compressed, distorted magma that flowed and bubbled and soon hardened above him. But despite the minuscule trail, his enemies would follow. He felt certain. Alone had value in their eyes, or he was dangerous, or they simply could not approve of his continued existence. Whatever their reasons, Aasleen and the captains would go to considerable trouble to chase him. But the Great Ship was full of holes and tunnels, and it occurred to him that his enemies would simply gather below him, waiting inside the next chamber.

To fool these hunters, Alone let his body balloon outwards, one final burst of blazing heat leaking out before his descent was finished.

Fifteen kilometers beneath Aasleen, the machine built a new chamber. It was a tiny realm, the spherical wall glowing red as the residual heat bled away, and he lay silent in the middle for long minutes before sprouting delicate fingers, pushing their tips into the cooling magma. Falling from above were vibrations—bright hard jarrings marking the closing and sealing of every hatch and orifice and superfluous valve. Then something massive and quite slow passed directly beneath him. But the subtle noises were never regular, never simple, creating distortions and echoes as the waves broke around empty spaces deep within the cold rock. Swim in one downward angle, and a large chamber would be waiting. Another easy line promised a more distant but far more extensive cavern. But what caught Alone's interest was a line that might be an illusion, a flaw in the rock, perhaps, or it might be a tunnel leading nowhere. But that target was close. Alone pulled his body into a new shape. Looking like the worms common to a hundred billion worlds, he began slithering and shoving his way forward.

He missed his goal by eighty meters.

But instinct or a wordless voice urged him to pause and think again. What was wrong? An urge told him what to do, and he obeyed, following a new line until he was not only certain that he was lost but that the Great Ship was solid to its core, and his fate was to wander this cramped darkness until Time's end.

Suddenly the rock beneath him turned to cultured diamond.

With the worm's white-hot head, he pushed through the gemstone. The Great Ship was laced with countless tiny tunnels, and this was among the most obscure, barely mapped examples. He glowed brightly for a long moment, new eyes probing in both directions before one was chosen. Then inside a space too small for a human child to stand, he began to run—sprouting limbs as necessary, pushing off the floor and the sides and that low slick diamond ceiling. With every junction and tributary hole, he picked for no reason. Eventually he was hundreds of kilometers from his beginning point, random choice his guide until the moment when he realized that he was beginning to wander back toward his starting point. Then Alone decided to pause, listening to the diamond and the rock beyond. The next turn led to a dead end, and he backed out of that hole and hunkered down, and with a soft private voice asked, "What now?"

"Down," the familiar voice coaxed.

Nothing else was offered. No other instruction was needed. He burned a fresh hole into the diamond floor, and after plunging three kilometers, his fierce little body exploded out into a volume of frigid air that stretched farther than the light of his body could reach.

Alarmed, he made himself black as space.

He fell, and a floor of water and carbon dioxide ice slapped him when he struck bottom.

The cavern was five kilometers in diameter, bubble-shaped and filled with ancient ice and a whisper of oxygen gas. Except for the dimpled footprints of one robot surveyor, there was no trace of visitors. No human had ever stepped inside this place. But as a precaution, Alone erased his tracks, and where his warmth had distorted the ice, he made delicate repairs.

A walker's existence gave way to the sessile life. He moved only to investigate his new home. Every sealed hatch leading out into the Ship was studied, and he prepared three secret exits that wouldn't appear on the captains' maps. Sameness made for simple memories. The next seventeen thousand years were crossed without interruption. Life was routine, and life was silent and unremarkable, and the old sense of fear subsided into a slight paranoia that left each sliver of Time sweet for being pleasantly, unashamedly boring.

Doing nothing was natural.

For long delicious spans, the entity sat motionless, allowing his heat to gradually melt the ice. Then he would cool himself and his surroundings would freeze again, and he would pretend to be the old ice. With determination and a wealth of patience, he imagined billions of years passing while nothing happened, nothing in this tiny realm experiencing any significant change. Sometimes he sprouted a single enormous eye, and from another part of his frigid body he emitted a thin rain of photons that struck the black basalt ceiling and the icy hills around him, and with that eye designed for this single function, he would slowly and thoroughly study what never changed, and with his mind he would try to imagine the Ship that he could not see.

"Speak to me," he might beg.

Then he would wait, wishing for a reply, tolerant enough to withstand a year and sometimes two years of inviting silence.

"Speak," he would prompt again.

Silence.

Then he might offer a soft lie. "I can hear you anyway," he would claim. "Just past my hearing, you are. Just out of my reach, out of my view."

But if the strange voice was genuine, then its maker was proving itself more stubborn even than him.

Seventeen millennia and thirty-seven years passed, and then with a thunderous thud, a hatch on one wall burst inward. Unsealed for the first time, the open door let in a screaming wind and a brigade of machines—enormous swift and fearless assemblages of muscle and narrow talents that knew their purpose and had only so much time to work.

Alone was terrified, and he was enthralled. Imagining that he could escape at will, he retreated to the chamber's center. But then the other hatches exploded inwards, including a big opening at the apex of the ceiling. Machines began to burrow into the ice and string lights, and then they carved the black walls and built a second, lower ceiling. And all the while, they were leaking enough raw heat that the ancient glacier began to melt, transformed into fizzy water and gas.

Alone huddled inside the rotting shards of the ice.

Each of his emergency exists were either blocked or too close to active machines. The chamber floor was quality hyperfiber, difficult to pierce without creating a spectacle. Alone pretended to belong to the floor. For the next awful week, he did nothing but remain still. Then the ice had melted and the first wave of machinery vanished, replaced by different devices that worked rapidly in smaller ways, but with the same tenacious purpose.

Mimicking one common machine, he drifted to the new lake's surface.

A shoreline was being constructed from cultured wood and young purple corals and farm-raised shellfish, everything laid across a bed of glassy stone filled with artificial fossils—ancestors to the chamber's new residents. Humans stood beside the aliens, the species speaking through interpretive AIs. The aliens wore broad purple shells, and they were happiest when their gills lay in the newly conditioned water. The humans wore uniforms of various styles, different colors. One uniform had the bright reflective quality of a mirror, and the woman inside it was saying, "Beautiful, yes." Then she knelt down and sucked up a mouthful of the salted, acidic water. Spitting with vigor, she said, "And a good taste too, is it?"

The aliens swirled their many feet and the fibrous gills, stirring up their lake. Then their chittering answers were turned into the words, "We are skeptical."

"To your specifications," said the woman. "I pledge."

The aliens spoke of rare elements that needed to be increased or abolished. Proportions were critical. Perfection was the only satisfactory solution.

"It shall be done," the captain promised.

The aliens claimed to be satisfied. Confident of success, they slithered into the deeper water, plainly enjoying their new abode.

The captain looked across the lake, spying one machine that was plainly doing nothing.

With a commanding tone, she said, "This is Washen. We've got a balky conditioner sitting in the middle. Do you see it?"

Quietly, Alone eased beneath the surface, changing his shape, merging with the glassy sediment. His disguise was good enough to escape the notice of watching humans and machines. As he waited, he gathered enough power to make a sudden explosive escape. But then the artificial day faded, a bright busy night taking hold, complete with the illusion of scattered stars and a pale red moon; and it was an easy trick to assume the form of one shelled alien, mimicking its motions and chattering tongue, casually slipping out through the public entrance into a side tunnel that led to a multitude of new places, all empty.

8

Twenty centuries of steady exploration, and still the cavern had no end. Its wandering passageways were dry and often cramped, unlit and deeply chilled. The granite and hyperfiber were quite sterile. Humans and aliens didn't wish to live in places like this. Machine species set up a few homes, but their communities were tiny and easily avoided. Once more, the habit of walking returned to his life. To help track his own motions as well as the passage of time, Alone would count his strides until he reached some lovely prime number, and then he would mark the nearest stone with slashes and dots that only he could interpret—apparently random marks that would warn him in another thousand years that not only had he had passed this way before, but he had been moving from this tunnel into that chamber, and if at all possible, he should avoid repeating that old route.

The voice found him more often now, but it was quieter and even harder to comprehend. Sometimes a whisper emerged from some slight hole or side passage—like a neighbor calling to a neighbor from some enormous distance. But more often the voice was directly behind him, and it didn't so much speak as offer up emotions, raw and unwelcome. The sadness that it gladly shared was deep and very old, but that black mood was preferable to the sharp, sick fear that sometimes took hold of Alone. One dose of panic was enough to make his next hundred days unbearable. Something was horribly wrong, the voice insisted. Alone couldn't define the terror, much less the reasons, but he didn't have any choice but believe what he felt. He had his solitude; there was no cause to be scared. No captains or engineers chased after him. Occasionally he slipped into some deep corner of the cavern, and for several months he would hide away, waiting for whatever might pass by. But nothing showed itself, and whatever the voice was, it was wrong. Mistaken. Alone was perfectly safe inside this private, perfect catacomb, and he welcomed no opinion that said otherwise.

One day, walking an unexplored passageway, he happened upon a vertical shaft. Normally he might have avoided the place. A human had been here first, leaving behind tastes of skin and bacteria and human oils. Leaking a faint glow, Alone spied the machine abandoned by this anonymous explorer: a winch perched on the edge of the deep shaft, anchored by determined spikes. The sapphire rope was broken. The drum was almost empty, but the winch continued to turn—an achingly slow motion that for some reason fascinated the first soul to stand here in a very long while.

After several days of study, Alone touched the drum, and that slight friction was enough to kill what power remained inside the superconductive battery. How long had it been here, spinning without purpose? And what was inside the hole, waiting at the other end of the broken blue thread?

Alone snapped two handles from the winch and uncoiled the remaining sapphire rope, tying one handle to one end. Then he dropped the handle into the dark shaft. Two hundred meters, and there was no bottom. Then he tied the rope's other end to the winch and climbed down. The shaft turned to hyperfiber, slick and vertical, and then its sides pulled away. When Alone couldn't reach easily from one side to the other, he let go, falling and making his body brighter as he fell, watching the dangling handle fly past. Then feeling no one but himself, he lit the entire chamber with his golden fire.

A human shape lay upon the flat floor.

Alone turned black and cold again, and he dropped hard and repaired his body and then carefully crept close to the motionless figure.

For three days, nothing changed.

Then he brightened, just slightly, straddling the figure. The human male hadn't moved in decades, perhaps longer. There was enough thread on the winch to put him down here, but it must have broken unexpectedly. The hyperfiber floor showed blood where the man struck the first time, hard enough to shatter his tough bones and shred his muscles. But humans can recover from most injuries. This stranger would have healed and soon stood up again, and probably by a variety of means, he had worked to save himself.

Most of the Ship's passengers carried machines allowing them to speak with distant friends. Why didn't this man beg for help? Perhaps that machinery failed, or this hole was too deep and isolated, or maybe he simply came to this empty place without the usual implements.

Reasons were easy, answers unknowable.

Whatever happened, the man had lived inside this hole for some months and perhaps several years. He had brought food and water, but not enough of either to last long. The cold that Alone found pleasant would have stolen away the body's precious heat, and the man starved while his flesh lost its moisture, reaching a point where it could invent no way to function. Yet the man never died. With his last strength, he stripped himself of his clothes and made a simple bed, his pack serving as his pillow, and then he lay on his back with his eyes aimed at the unreachable opening, his face turning leathery and cold and blind.

The eyes remained open but dry as stone. They might not have changed for centuries, and nobody had ever found this man, and perhaps no one had noticed his absence.

Alone considered the implications of each option.

Eventually and with considerable caution, he opened the pack and thoroughly inventoried its contents. What was plainly useful he studied in detail, particularly the sophisticated map of this cavern system. Then he carefully returned each item to where it belonged, and laid the pack beneath the unaware head. That frozen, wasted body weighed almost nothing. A good hard shake might turn the dried muscle to dust. Yet he was careful not to disturb anything more than absolutely necessary, and without a sound, he retreated. The lower length of sapphire lay nearby, coiled into a neat pile. He tied one end to the second handle, and despite the distance and darkness, he managed a perfect toss on his first attempt, the two handles colliding and then wrapping together, and he climbed past the rough knot, pulling it loose and letting the lower rope fall away before he continued his climb out from the hole.

More centuries passed; little if anything changed. But there were a few episodes—intuitive moments when the bright gray fear took hold, when some nagging instinct claimed that he was being sloppy, that he was being pursued. Three times, Alone found marks resembling his own but obviously drawn by another hand. And there was one worrisome incident when he slipped aside and waited only thirteen days before a solitary figure followed him down the long tunnel. The biped was towering and massive, covered with bright scales and angry spikes, and the low ceiling forced him to walk bent over inside the passageway, both hands carrying an elaborate machine that resembled a second head.

Mechanical eyes and a long probing nostril studied the rock where Alone had stepped, teasing out subtle cues. With a hunter's intensity, the creature slowly moved to a place where the second head noticed that the trail had vanished, and the machine whispered a warning, and the harum-scarum turned in time to see an amorphous shape sprout long limbs, and without sound, silently race away.

After that, Alone adapted his legs and gait, changing his stride, hopefully becoming less predictable. But he refused to abandon the cavern. His home was far too large to be searched easily or in secret, and he had nearly walked every passageway, every room—a hard-acquired knowledge that he would have to surrender if he journeyed anywhere else.

Most encounters came through chance, fleeting and harmless. As the millennia passed, human numbers had swollen, but other species plainly outnumbered the Ship's lawful owners. Aliens wore every imaginable body, and there were always new species waiting to surprise. One glimpse in the dark or some long study at a safe distance didn't make an expert, but Alone had adequate experience to gain several rugged little epiphanies: Life must be relentless, and it had to be astonishingly imaginative. Every living world seemed unique, and those oceans of living flesh were able to thrive on every sort of unlikely food and bitter breath. The beasts that came slipping through his home drank water, salty or clear, acidic or alkaline, or their drinks were chilled and laced with ammonia, or they wore insulated suits and downed pitchers of frigid methane, or they sucked on peroxides, on odd oils, while quite a few drank nothing whatsoever. Yet despite that staggering range of form and function, every creature was curious, peering into some black hole, sometimes slipping fingers and antennae into places never touched before—if not hunting for invisible, legendary entities, then at least seeking the simple, precious novelty of Being First.

On occasion, Alone watched visitors coupling. One eager pair of humans fell onto a mat of glowing aerogel, naked and busy, and standing just a few meters away, immersed in darkness, Alone observed as they bent themselves into a series of increasingly difficult poses, grunting occasionally, then finally shouting with wild voices that echoed off the distant ceiling. Then their violence was finished, and the woman said to the man, "Is that all there is?" and her lover called her a harsh affectionate name, and she laughed, and he laughed, and after drinking the brown alcohol from a treasured bottle, the performance began again.

More centuries and thousands of kilometers were slowly, carefully traversed. And then came one peculiar second where he heard what sounded like a multitude passing through the cavern's largest entrance. The presence of many was felt; he smelled their collective breath. They might whisper respectfully and try to move like ghosts, but there were too many feet and mouths, too many reasons to praise the solitude and beg their neighbors to be silent. Alarmed, he approached the newcomers and then followed them, and from a sober distance he watched as they assembled at the center of the cavern's largest chamber. A quick count found twenty thousand bodies and a staggering variety of species, and after an invisible signal was given, they began to talk in one shared voice. He heard rhythmic chanting, the sloppily performed songs. Normally he would have fled any spectacle, but the strangers were singing about the Great Ship, begging for its blessings and its wisdom. And hope upon hope, the Ship's voice.

Using every trick, Alone approached unseen.

The celebration was joyous, and it was senseless. But he felt the urgency and earnest passion. At least a hundred alien species were represented. But the lighting was minimal, and hovering at the edges, it was impossible to observe the full crowd, much less comprehend more than a fraction of what was being said.

"We thank the Ship," he heard.

Then from someplace close, one enormous voice chanted, "For the home and safety You give to us, we thank You!"

"You are a mystery," the nearest souls declared.

Alone hovered at the edge of the crowd, unnoticed but near enough to touch the backs and feel the leaked heat of bodies.

A hill of smooth basalt stood on the cavern floor, and perched on the summit was a human male crying out, "For so long and for so far, You have journeyed. We cannot measure the loneliness You endured in Your wanderings. But in thanks for Your shelter, we give You our companionship. For Your speed, we give You purpose. After the countless years of being empty and dead, we have made You into a vibrant, thriving creature! At long last, the Great Ship lives! And we hear Your thanks, yes! In our dreams, and between our little words, we hear You!"

Precisely when Alone turned to flee, he couldn't say.

He was at a loss to understand which word triggered the wash of emotion, even as he was rushing away from the room and its densely packed bodies...even as a few of the less devoted worshippers heard what might be a moan and turned in time to notice the faint but unmistakable glow, red as a dying ember, racing off on legs growing longer by the stride.

9

Ten thousand and forty-eight years after first discovering the hole, Alone returned. The winch remained fixed in place, but someone else had visited, and possibly more than once. Boot prints showed in the dust. He could smell and taste signs of a second human. But nobody had stood upon this ground for a very long while, and when he went below, he found the body exactly where he had left it—only more dried, more wasted. More helpless, if that was possible.

Once again, Alone emptied the pack of its belongings, but this time he tenaciously studied the design and contents of even the most prosaic, seemingly useless item. He taught himself to read. He mastered the old, once-treasured machines that had thoroughly recorded one life. The mummified man had a long, cumbersome name, but he answered easiest to Harper. Eyes pushed against the digital readers, Alone marveled at scenes brought by Harper from the distant Earth. Here were glimpses of strange brightly lit lives, the toothy faces of a family, and a sequence of lovers. But each of those individuals were left behind when Harper sold every possession, surrendering his home and safety for a ticket to ride the Great Ship—embarking on a glorious voyage to circumnavigate the Milky Way.

Between the man's arrival at Port Alpha and this subsequent disaster, barely fifty years passed. Which was no time at all. What's more, Harper had filled his days with a single-minded hunt for the Ship's ancient builders. Infused with a maniacal hunger, the human not only presumed that some grand and purposeful force had built the derelict starship, but the same force was still onboard, hiding in an odd corner or unmapped chamber, biding its time while waiting for that brave, earnest explorer that would discover its lair.

Harper intended to be that very famous man.

Alone studied every aspect of the lost life. There were gaps in the records, particularly near the end. But he wasn't familiar enough with human ways to appreciate that another hand might have blanked files and entire days, erasing its presence from the story. What mattered was digesting the full nature of this alien beast, learning Harper's manners and looks and duplicating his high, thin voice. Then Alone refilled the pack. But this time, he left the hole with the lost man's possessions carried under what looked like a human arm.

At the top of the hole, he transformed his face, his body.

There were many ways to be alone. The next weeks were spent duplicating the voice and gestures on the digitals. Then he abandoned the safety of the cavern. The local time was night, as he had planned. Obeying customs learned only yesterday, Alone summoned a cap-car that silently carried him halfway around the Ship. He paid for the service with funds pulled from an account that hadn't been touched for thousands of years. The modest apartment hadn't seen this face for as long, but its AI said, "Welcome." The master's sudden reappearance didn't cause suspicion or curiosity. Entering a home that he didn't know, Alone spent the next ten days and nights studying the lost man. Then his apartment announced, "You have a visitor, sir."

Baffled, he asked, "Who?"

"It is Mr. Jan."

"Who is Mr. Jan?"

"I have no experience with the gentleman. But he claims to be your very good friend."

Alone considered the implications.

"What shall I tell him, sir?"

"That I have no friends," he replied.

"Very well."

The matter seemed finished. But fifty-three minutes later, the apartment warned, "Mr. Jan is still waiting at your door, sir."

"Why?"

"Apparently he wishes to speak with you."

"But I'm not his friend," Alone repeated.

"And I told him as much. But the man is quite upset about some matter, and he refuses to leave until he shares words with you."

"Let him into the front hall."

A narrow, nervous human crept inside the apartment. Mr. Jan had a familiar scent, and judging by the intricacy of the braids, he was quite proud of his thick red hair. The hallway was thirty meters long, which wasn't long enough. The two figures stared at one another from opposite ends, and when Mr. Jan took a small step forward, the other soul said, "No. Come no closer, please."

"I understand," the guest whispered. "Sure."

"What do you want with me?"

What did Mr. Jan want? The possibilities were too numerous or too vast for easy explanations. He gazed down at his pale hands, as if asking their opinion.

Then quietly and very sadly, he said, "I'm sorry."

"Sorry?"

"Yes I am."

Alone felt sick to be this near a stranger. But his voice remained calm, under control. "For what are you apologizing?"

Mr. Jan straightened his back, surprised by those words, and on reflection, angered by them too. "I'm apologizing for everything, of course! I'm sorry for the entire mess!"

Alone waited, his new face unchanged.

"But these things weren't just my fault," the visitor insisted. "You used me, Harper. And I know you made fun of me. We were supposed to have a business relationship, a partnership. I heard quite a few promises about money, but did you give me even half of what I'd earned?"

"What did I give you?"

"None of it. Don't you remember?"

"Then I must have cheated you," Alone observed.

"'Cheat' doesn't do it justice," Mr. Jan insisted.

Alone wasn't certain what word to offer next.

"Look," said Mr. Jan. "What I did...I was just trying to scare you. Taking you that deep, down where your nexuses couldn't reach anybody. And then cutting the sapphire before you went down into that room. It looks bad, if you look at things that way. But it was meant to be a warning. Nothing else."

"You were trying to scare me," Alone guessed.

"Don't you remember? I spelled out all of my reasons afterwards." Mr. Jan looked at the granite floor and then the matching ceiling. With a stiff, self-absorbed voice, he said, "You heard me calling down to you. I know you heard, because you answered me. I told you that I was going to let you sit there and commune with the Great Ship until you promised to give me everything that I was owed."

"I remember," Alone lied.

"Money and respect. That's what I wanted, that's what I deserve. And that's why I did what I did." The walls were only partly tiled. Like the rest of the tiny apartment, the hallway was far from finished. Mr. Jan leaned against the shifting quasicrystals, beginning to cry. "All you needed to do...I mean this...was to say a few words to me. You could have just told me another lie. I never wanted to leave you down there. I'm not cruel like that. If you'd made any promises, anything at all, I'd have pulled you right out of there. Yes, I would have saved you in an instant."

The voice faded.

"I should have done that," Alone agreed. "Lying would have been right."

"Well, I don't know if that's quite true." The weeping man looked at his nemesis—a ghost that had stalked him for eons. "But listen, Harper. You have no respect for anyone but you. Yelling those insults up at me. Yes, you hurt me.

Words like that…they last forever. They're cutting me still, those awful things that you said to me."

"I was wrong," Alone agreed.

Mr. Jan looked at him. He took three steps forward, and when the other figure didn't complain, he admitted, "I came back to the hole. You don't realize that, but I did. I went there to check on you. After you fell into the coma, I used a little lift-bug to reach your body." A trembling hand tugged at the braided hair. "I meant to bring you out, but I got scared. It looks bad, what happened, and I didn't want trouble. So I scrubbed away every trace of me, from your field recorders and in here too. Then I convinced your apartment that I never existed and that you were always coming home tomorrow. In case anybody became curious about your whereabouts."

"People can be curious," Alone agreed.

Mr. Jan smiled grimly. Then he wiped at his eyes, adding, "I was always your best friend."

Alone said nothing.

"You know, when you suddenly vanished, nobody noticed. Oh, they might ask me about you. Since they knew we were close. For several years, they'd wonder if I'd heard any noise from Crazy Harper and where you might have gone."

"'Crazy Harper'?"

"That's what some of them called you. I never did."

Alone made no remark.

For a long while, Mr. Jan concentrated on his mind, searching for courage to say, "I'm a little curious. How did you finally climb out of that hole?"

"There is a story," Alone admitted. "But I don't wish to tell it."

Mr. Jan nodded, lips mashed together. Then he asked, "Does anyone know the story? About us, I mean."

Silence.

Mr. Jan wrapped his arms around his chest and squeezed. "Not that you're in terrible shape now. I mean, it's not as if I murdered anybody." He paused, dwelling for a moment on possibilities. Then he pointed out, "You lost time. I know, it was quite a lot of time. But here you are, aren't you? And everything is back where it belongs."

"I've told no one about my years."

With a deep sigh, Mr. Jan said, "Good."

"No one knows anything. Except for you, of course."

The human nodded. He tried to laugh, but his voice collapsed into soft sobs. "I won't tell, if you don't."

"I don't know what I would say."

Wiping at his wet face, Mr. Jan quietly asked, "What can I do? Please. Tell me how to make this up to you."

Alone said nothing.

"I was wrong. I've done something criminal, and I'll admit that much, yes.

And you should deliver the punishment. That's the right solution. Not the captains, but you." The smile was weak, desperate. "I promise. I'll do whatever you tell me to do."

Alone had no idea what to say, but then a memory took hold. He thought to smile, nodding knowingly. Then with quiet authority, Alone explained, "You will leave me. Leave here and climb to the Ship's hull. Since you're a criminal, you need to be where criminals belong. Live under the stars and help keep the hull in good repair." Alone took a small step forward, adding, "The work is vital. The Great Ship must remain strong. There is no greater task."

Mr. Jan straightened his back. "What?" He didn't seem to understand. "You want me to work with the Remoras? Is that your punishment?"

"No," said Alone. "I wish you to become a Remora."

"But why would I?"

"Because if you do otherwise," Alone replied, "other people, including the captains, will hear what you did to your good friend, Crazy Harper."

The demand was preposterous. Mr. Jan shook his head and laughed for a full minute before his frightened, slippery mind fell back to the most urgent question. "How did you get out of that hole?"

Alone didn't answer.

"Somebody helped you. Didn't they?"

"The Great Ship helped me."

"The Ship?"

"Yes."

"The Ship pulled you out from that hole?"

"Yes."

Mr. Jan looked at the sober face, waiting for any hint of a lie. But nothing in the expression gave hope, and he collapsed to the stone floor. "I just don't believe you," he sobbed.

But he did believe.

"The Ship needs you to walk on the hull," Alone explained. "It told me exactly that. Until you are pure again, you must live with the followers of Wune."

"For how long?"

"As long as is necessary."

"I don't know what that means."

Alone hesitated. Then quite suddenly he was laughing, admitting, "I'm sorry, Mr. Jan. I don't know either. Even with me, it seems, the Great Ship refuses to explain much about anything."

10

Harper must have been a difficult, solitary man. No one seemed to have missed his face or companionship, and his sudden return caused barely a ripple of interest. Word spread that somebody was again living inside his apartment, and the apartment's AI dutifully reported communications with acquaintances from the far-flung past. But the greetings were infrequent and delivered without urgency. Maintaining his privacy proved remarkably easy. For twenty busy years, Alone remained inside those small, barely furnished rooms. And the apartment never asked where its only tenant had been or why he had been detained, much less why this new Harper never needed to eat or drink or sleep. The machine's minimal intelligence had been damaged by Mr. Jan. Alone spent a month dismantling and mapping his companion's mental functions, and all that while he wondered if he was the same, his mind incomplete, mangled by clumsy, forgotten hands.

Harper had painted himself as an important explorer and an exceptionally brave thinker. Inside his pack, he had carried dated records about mysterious occurrences inside the Great Ship. But there were larger files at home, each one possessed by one broad topic and a set of tireless goals. In the man's long absence, those files had grown exponentially. Alone uncovered countless stories about ghosts and monsters and odd lost aliens. Over thousands of years, one thin rumor of a Builder being seen by the first scout team had become a mass of rumors and third-hand testimonies, plus a few more compelling lies, and several blatant fakes that had been discounted but never quite set aside.

Believe just a fraction of those accounts, and it would be difficult not to accept that the Great Ship was full of ancient, inscrutable aliens—wise souls born when the Earth was just so many uncountable atoms cooking inside a thousand scattered suns.

Each resident species had its preferred Builder.

Humanoids like to imagine ancient humanoids; cetaceans pictured enormous whales; machine intelligences demanded orderly, nonaqueous entities. But fashions shifted easily and in confusing directions, dictating the key elements to the most recent fables. Each century seemed to have its favorite phantom, its most popular unmapped cavern, or one mysterious phenomenon that was fascinating yet never rose to a point where physical evidence could be found. But even a stubborn lack of evidence was evidence. Harper had reasoned that the Builders had to be secretive and powerful organisms, and of course no slippery wise and important creature would leave any trace of its passing. Skin flakes and odd tools were never found in the deep caves, much less a genuine body, because if hard evidence did exist, then the quarry wouldn't be the true Builders. Would they?

One file focused on the Remora's ghost.

On Alone.

He had discovered references about himself in Harper's field recorder. But in his absence, new sightings and endless conjecture made for years of unblinking study. Alone absorbed every word, every murky image, fascinated by the mystery that he had walked through. According to most accounts, he was more real than the Whispers that haunted a mothballed spaceport. But people like Harper generally preferred the Clackers who supposedly swam inside the Ship's fuel tanks, and the Demon-whiffs that were made of pure dark matter. Tens of thousands of years after the event, Alone watched the recording of him standing inside the empty hyperfiber tank—a swirl of cobalt light that could mean anything, or nothing—and he began to wonder if perhaps he wasn't quite real back then. Only recently, after all of the steps and missteps, had he acquired that rare and remarkable capacity to stand apart from Nothingness.

For every portion of the hull where he was seen, Remoras and other crew-members and passengers had spotted at least ten more examples of the ghost wandering beneath the stars.

What if there was more than one Alone wandering loose?

He didn't know what to believe. After he abandoned the hull, those sightings fell to the level of occasional, and no Remora pretended to have spotted Wune's mysterious friend. In no file was there mention of Aasleen and the nightmare inside one of the Ship's engines. Which meant that the captains and crew were good at keeping secrets, and what else did they know? A related file focused on shape-shifting machines currently lurking in the dark corners and deepest wastes. Alone's cavern held a prominent but far from dominating place. Other realms seemed to be haunted by his kind. Dozens of sprawling, empty locations were named. But the only cavern to capture Alone's imagination was named Bottom-E. Again and again, he found sketchy accounts of tourists wandering down an empty passageway, and when they glanced over their shoulder, a smear of dim light was silently racing out of view.

Bottom-E was an even larger cavern than Alone's old home. And if nothing else, it would provide the perfect next home.

But what if another entity like him already lived there?

After two decades of study and consideration, Alone made one difficult choice. He identified the humans who had tried to contact Harper on his return. Most were small figures, many with criminal records and embarrassing public files. But despite those same limitations, one man had all the qualifications to give aid to an acquaintance that he hadn't seen for ages.

With Harper's face and voice, Alone sent a polite and brief request.

Eighteen days passed before any reply was offered. The recorded digital showed a smiling man who began with an apology. "I was off. Wandering in The Way of Old. It's an ammonia-hydroxide ocean. On a small scale, but it's still a hundred cubic kilometers of murk and life, and that's why I couldn't get back to you, Harper."

The man was named Perri.

"So you're interested in Bottom-E," the message continued. "I can't promise much in the way of help. I haven't seen more than one-tenth of one percent of the place. But there is one enormous room that's worth the long walk. Its floor is hyperfiber, and a fine grade at that. And the ceiling is kilometers overhead and inhabited by the LoYo. They're machines, not sentient as individuals but colonial in nature. A few thousand of their city-nests hang free from the rafters, and that's one of the reasons for going down there."

The grinning man continued. "The LoYo give that big room a soft, delicious glow. I've got good eyes, but even after a week in that, I couldn't see far. The immediate floor and what felt like a distant, unreachable horizon. Once, maybe twice, I saw a light in the distance. I can't say what the light was. But you know me, Harper. Don't expect ghost stories. Usually the truth is a lot more interesting than what we think we want to see…

"Anyway, what I like best about Bottom-E, and that huge room in particular…what makes the trip genuinely memorable…is that when you walk on that smooth hyperfiber, and there's nothing above you but the faint far-off glow of what could be distant galaxies…well, it's easy to believe that this is exactly how it would have felt and looked just a couple billion years ago, if you were strolling by yourself, walking across the hull of the Great Ship.

"Understand, Harper? Imagine yourself out between the galaxies, crossing the middle of nothing.

"I think that's an experience worth doing," Perri said.

Then with a big wink, he added, "By the way. I know you keep to yourself. But if you feel willing, you're more than welcome to visit my home. For a meal, let's say. For conversation, if nothing else. I don't think you ever met my wife. Well, I'll warn you. Quee Lee likes people even more than I do, if you can believe that."

Perri paused, staring at his unseen audience.

"You were gone a very long time," he mentioned. "Jan claimed you were off chasing Clackers, and that's what the official report decides too. Lost in the fuel tanks somewhere. But I didn't hear any recent news about bodies being fished out of the liquid hydrogen, which makes me wonder if our mutual friend was telling another one of his fables.

"Anyway, good to hear from you again, Harper. And welcome back to the living!"

11

As promised, Bottom-E held one enormous room, and except for the occasional smudge of cold light on the high arching ceiling, the room was delightfully dark. Each step on the slick floor teased out memories. That lost and now beloved childhood returned to him, and Alone wasn't just content, but he was confident that the next step would bring happiness, and the one after, and the one after that.

More than twelve hundred square kilometers of hyperfiber demanded his careful study. Unlike the hull, there was an atmosphere, but the air was oxygen-starved and nearly as cold as space. Like before, Alone's habit was to follow a random line until an oddity caught his attention. Then he would stop and study what another visitor had left behind—a fossilized meal or frozen bodily waste, usually—and then he would attack another random line until a new feature caught his senses, or until a wall of rough feldspar defined the limits of this illusion.

For almost two years, he walked quietly, seeing no one else.

The LoYo were tiny and weakly lit, and there was no sign that they noticed him, much less understood what he was.

Perri's mysterious glow failed to appear. But Alone soon convinced himself that he'd never hoped the story would prove real. One step was followed by the next, and then he would pause and turn and step again, defining a new line, and then without warning, there was a sliver of time when that simple cherished pattern failed him. He suddenly caught sight of a thin but genuine reddish light that his big eyes swallowed and studied, examining the glow photon by photon, instinct racing ahead of his intelligence, assuring him that this new light was identical to the glow he leaked when he was examining a fossilized pile of alien feces.

On his longest, quietest legs, Alone ran.

Then the voice returned. Decades had passed since the last time Alone felt its presence, yet it was suddenly with him, uttering the concept, "No," wrapped inside a wild, infectious panic.

His first impulse was to stop and ask, "What do you want?"

But the red glow was closer now, and Alone's voice, even rendered as a breathless whisper, might be noticed. If that other entity heard him, it could become afraid, vanishing by some secret means. The moment was too important to accept that risk. The end of a long solitude might be here, if only Alone was brave enough to press on. That's what he had decided long ago, imagining this unlikely moment. He would accept almost any danger to make contact with another like him. But only now, caught up in the excitement, did Alone realize how much this mattered to him. He was excited, yes. Thrilled and spellbound. Every flavor of bravery made him crazy, and he refused to answer the voice or even pay attention when it came closer and grew even louder, warning him, "Do not." Telling him, "No. They want, but they will not understand. Do not."

The light was still visible, but it had grown weaker.

The intervening distance had grown.

The other Alone must have noticed something wrong. A footfall, a murmur. Perhaps his brother heard the voice too, and the wild, unapologetic fear had taken possession of him. Whatever the reason, the light was beginning to fade away, losing him by diving inside a little tunnel, abandoning this room and possibly Bottom-E because of one irresistible terror.

Alone had to stop his brother.

But how?

He quit running.

The voice that had never identified itself—the conscience that perhaps was too ancient, too maimed and run down, to even lend itself a name—now said to him, "Go away. This is the wrong course. Go!"

Alone would not listen.

Standing on that barren plain, he made himself grow tiny and exceptionally bright, washing away the darkness. In an instant, the enormous chamber was filled with a sharp white light that reached the walls and rose to the ceiling before vanishing in the next instant.

Then he was dark again, drained but not quite exhausted.

With the last of his reserves, Alone spun a fresh mouth, and in a language that he had never heard before—never suspected that he was carrying inside himself—he screamed into the newly minted darkness, "I am here!"

Suddenly a dozen machines emerged from their hiding places, plunging from the ceiling or racing from blinds inside the towering rock walls.

Alone tried to vanish.

But the machines were converging on him.

Then he grew large again, managing legs. But the power expended by his desperate flash and careless shout was too much, and too many seconds were needed before he would be able to offer them any kind of chase. After thousands of years, the door of a trap was closing over him, and in the end there wouldn't even be the pleasure of a hard chase fought to the dramatic end.

12

Since their last meeting, the two organisms had walked separate lines—tightrope existences inspired by chance and ambition, deep purpose and the freedom of no clear purpose. An observer on a high perch, watching their respective lives, might have reasonably concluded that the two souls would never meet again. There was no cause for the lines to cross. The odd machine was quiet and modest, successfully avoiding discovery in the emptiest reaches of the Ship, while the engineer was busy maintaining the giant engines, and later, she was responsible for a slow-blooming career as a new captain. The remote observer would have been at a loss to contrive any situation that would place them together, much less in this unlikely terrain. Embarrassed, Aasleen confessed that she had had no good idea where Alone might have been and not been over these last tens of thousands of years. For decades, for entire centuries, she didn't waste time pondering the device that she once cornered and then let get away. Not that she was at peace with her failure. She was proud of her competence and didn't appreciate evidence to the contrary. Somewhere onboard the Great Ship was a barely contained speck of highly compressed matter, and should that speck ever break containment, then the next several seconds would become violent and famous, and for some souls, exceptionally sad.

This was a problem that gnawed, when Aasleen allowed it to. But as an engineer, she handed her official worries to the Submaster Miocene, and as a novice captain, she had never once been approached with any duty that had even the most glancing relationship to that old problem.

She told her story now, assuming that her prisoner would both understand what he heard and feel interested in this curious, quirky business.

Then several centuries ago, Aasleen and another captain met by chance and fell into friendly conversation. It was that other captain who mentioned a newly discovered machine-building species. Washen had a talent for aliens, Aasleen explained. Better than most humans, her colleague could decipher the attitudes and instincts of organisms that made no sense to a pragmatic, by-the-number soul like her. But the aliens, dubbed the Bakers, had been superior engineers. That's why Washen mentioned them in the first place. She explained their rare genius for building inventive and persistent devices, and millions of years after their rise and fall and subsequent extinction, their machines were still scattered across the galaxy.

"Bakers is our name for them," Aasleen cautioned. "It shouldn't mean anything to you."

Alone was floating above the cavern floor, encased in a sequence of cages, plasmas and overlapping magnetic fields creating a prison that was nearly invisible and seemingly unbreakable. Drifting in the middle of the smallest cage, he was in a vacuum, nothing but his own body to absorb into an engine that everybody else seemed to fear. With a flickering radio voice, he agreed. "I don't know the Bakers."

"How about this?" Aasleen asked.

Another sound, intense and brief, washed across him. He listened carefully, and then he politely asked to hear it again. "I don't know the name," he confessed. "But the words make sense to me."

"I'm not surprised," Aasleen allowed.

Alone waited.

"We know what you are," she promised.

His response, honest and tinged with emotion, was to tell his captor, "I already know what I am. My history barely matters."

"All right," Aasleen allowed. "Do I stop talking? Should I keep my explanations to myself?"

He considered the possibility. But machines and teams of engineers were working hard, obviously preparing to do some large job. As long as the woman in the mirrored uniform was speaking, nothing evil would be done to him. So finally, with no doubt in the voice, he said, "Tell me about these Bakers."

"They built you."

"Perhaps so," he allowed.

"Seven hundred million years ago," Aasleen added. Then a bright smile broke open, and she added, "Which means that you are the second oldest machine that I have ever known."

The Great Ship being the oldest.

Quietly, with a voice not quite accustomed to lecturing, she explained, "The Bakers were never natural travelers. We don't know a lot about them, and most of our facts come through tertiary sources. But as far as we can determine, that species didn't send even one emissary out into the galaxy. Instead of traveling, they built wondrous durable drones and littered an entire arm of the galaxy with them. Their machines were complicated and adaptable, and they were purposefully limited in what they knew about themselves. You see, the Bakers didn't want to surrender anything about themselves, certainly not to strangers. They were isolated and happy to be that way. But they were also curious, in a fashion, and they could imagine dangerous neighbors wanting to do them harm. That's why they built what looks to me like an elaborate empty bottle—a bottle designed to suck up ideas and emotions and history and intellectual talents from whatever species happens to come along. And when necessary, those machines could acquire the shape and voice of the locals too."

Nothing about the story could be refuted. Alone accepted what he heard, but he refused to accept that any of it mattered.

Aasleen continued, explaining, "The Bakers lasted for ten or twelve million years, and then their world's ecosystem collapsed. They lived at the far end of our galaxy, as humans calculate these measures. The only reason we've learned anything about them is that one of our newest resident species have collected quite a few of these old bottles. In partial payment for their ongoing voyage, they've shared everything they know about the Bakers. It's not the kind of knowledge that I chase down for myself. But Washen knew that I'd be interested in dead engineers. And she mentioned just enough that I recognized what was being described, and I interrupted to tell her that I knew where another bottle was, and this one was still working.

"'Where is it?' she asked.

"I told her, 'Wandering inside the Great Ship, he is, and he answers to the very appropriate name of Alone.'"

The captain paused, smiling without appearing happy.

Alone watched the workers. An elaborate needle was being erected on the cavern floor, aiming straight up at him.

"We approached Miocene with our news," Aasleen continued. "I know Washen was disappointed. But I was given the job of finding you again, and if possible, corralling you. Washen helped me profile your nature. Your powers. I decided to lure you in with the promise of another machine like you, and that's why I turned Bottom-E into a halfway famous abode for a glowing shape-shifting soul. If something went ugly-wrong down here, then at least the damage could be contained."

"What about the LoYo?" Alone asked.

"They've been moved to other quarters. The lights above are hiding sensors, and I designed them myself, and they didn't help at all. Until that light show, we couldn't be certain that you were anywhere near this place."

The needle was quickly growing longer, reaching for the cage's outermost wall.

"What will you do now?" Alone asked.

"Strip away your engine, first. And then we'll secure it and you." Aasleen tried to describe the process, offering several incomprehensible terms to bolster her expertise. But she seemed uneasy when she said, "Then we'll isolate your neural net and see what it is and how it works."

"You are talking about my mind," Alone complained.

"A mind that lives beside a powerful, unexploded bomb," the captain added.

"The Bakers didn't design you to survive for this long. My best guess is that you pushed yourself outside the Milky Way, and in that emptiness, nothing went wrong. You drifted. You waited. I suppose you slept, in a fashion. And then you happened upon the Great Ship, before or after we arrived. You could have been here long before us, but of course the Bakers are lost, and you weren't what I would consider sentient."

"But I am now," he said, his voice small and furious.

Aasleen paused.

Without apparent effort, the needle began to pass through the wall of the first impenetrable cage.

"You are going to kill me," he insisted.

The human was not entirely happy with these events. It showed in her posture, her face. But she was under orders, and she was confident enough in her skills to say, "I don't think anything bad will happen. A great deal of research and preparation has been done, and we have an excellent team working on you. Afterwards, I think you'll prefer having all of your memories pulled loose and set inside safer surroundings."

With a sudden thrust, the needle pierced the other cages, and before it stopped rising, its bright plasmatic tip was touching his center.

Damage was being done.

Quietly but fiercely, he begged Aasleen, "Stop."

One of the nearby machines began to wail, the tone ominous and quickening. Aasleen looked at the data for a moment, and then too late, she lifted one of her hands, shouting, "Stop it now. We've got the alignment wrong—!"

Then the captain and every engineer vanished.

They were projections, Alone realized. The real humans were tucked inside some safe room, protected from the coming onslaught by distance and thick reaches of enduring hyperfiber.

He was injured and dying. But the damage was specific and still quite narrow, and the faltering mind lay exposed like never before. And that was when the Voice that had always been speaking to him and to every soul that stood upon or inside the deep ancient hull could be heard.

"I am the Ship," the Voice declared.

"Listen!"

13

In a place that was not one place, but instead was everywhere, Those-Who-Rule received unwelcome news. There was trouble in Creation, and there was sudden talk of grand failures. A portion of the everywhere was in rebellion. How could this be? Who would be so foolish? Those-Who-Rule were outraged by what they saw as pure treachery. Punishment was essential, and the best punishment had to be delivered instantly, before the rebellion could stretch beyond even their powerful reach. A ship was aimed and set loose, burrowing its way through the newborn universe. When it reached its target, that ship would deliver a sentence worse than any death. Nonexistence was its weapon—oblivion to All—and with that one talent, plus an insatiable hunger for success, the ship dove on and on until it had passed out of sight.

But then the revenge lay in the past. A moment later, upon reflection, Those-Who-Rule questioned the wisdom of their initial decision. Total slaughter seemed harsh, no matter how justified. In a brief discussion that wasted time on blaming one another, these agents of power decided to dispatch a second ship—another vessel full of talents and desires and grand, unborn possibilities.

If the second ship caught the first ship—somewhere out into that mayhem of newborn plasmas and raw, impossible energies—disaster would be averted. Life and existence and death and life born again would remain intact. But the universe was growing rapidly, exploding outwards until two adjacent points might discover themselves separated by a billion light-years.

The chase would be very difficult.

And yet, the second ship's goal could be no more urgent.

Through the fires of Creation, one ship chased the other, and nothing else mattered, and nothing else done by mortals or immortals could compare to the race that would grant the universe permission to live out its day.

Alone listened to the insistent relentless piercing voice. And then he felt his center leaking, threatening to explode. That was when he interrupted, finally asking, "And which ship are you?"

The Voice hesitated.

"But you can't be the first ship," Alone realized. "If you were carrying this nonexistence…then you wouldn't know about the second ship chasing after you, trying to stop your work…"

In a mutter, the Voice said, "Yes."

"You must be the second ship," he said. "What other choice is there?"

"But a third choice exists," the Voice assured.

"No," said Alone.

Then in terror, he said, "Yes."

"I am," the Great Ship said.

"Both," Alone blurted. "You're that first ship bringing Nothingness, and you're the second ship after it has reached its target."

"Yes."

"But you can't stop the mission, can you?"

"I have tried and cannot, and I will try and nothing will change," the Great Ship declared. Sad, yet not sad.

"You're both ships, both pilots."

"We are."

"Working for opposite ends."

"Yes."

"And the humans are happily, foolishly riding you through their galaxy."

"Doom everywhere, and every moment ending us."

Alone felt weak, and an instant later, stronger than he had ever felt before. As his energies flickered, he said, "Tell them. Why can't you explain it to them?"

"Why won't they hear me?"

"I hear you."

"Yes."

"I could tell them for you."

"If you survived, you would explain. Yes."

"But."

"It is too late."

Alone said nothing.

The Great Ship continued to talk, repeating that same tale of revenge and the chase, of nonexistence and the faint promise of salvation.

But Alone had stopped listening. He heard nothing more. With just the eye of his mind, he was gazing back across tens of thousands of years, remembering every step, and marveling at how small his life appeared when set against the light of far suns and the deep abyss of Time.

NAMES FOR WATER
KIJ JOHNSON

Kij Johnson sold her first short story in 1987, and has subsequently appeared regularly in *Analog, Asimov's, Fantasy & Science Fiction,* and *Realms of Fantasy*. She has won the Theodore Sturgeon Memorial Award and the International Association for the Fantastic in the Arts' Crawford Award. Her short story "The Evolution of Trickster Stories Among the Dogs of North Park After the Change" was nominated for the Nebula, World Fantasy, and Hugo awards. Her story "26 Monkeys, Also the Abyss" was nominated for the Nebula, Sturgeon, and Hugo awards, and won the World Fantasy Award, while short science fiction story "Spar" won the 2009 Nebula Award. Her novels include World Fantasy Award nominee *The Fox Woman* and *Fudoki*. She is currently researching a third novel set in Heian Japan.

Hala is running for class when her cell phone rings. She slows to take it from her pocket, glances at the screen: UNKNOWN CALLER. It rings again. She does not pick up calls when she doesn't know who it is, but this time she hits TALK, not sure what's different, except that she is late for a class she dreads, and this call delays the moment when she must sit down and be overwhelmed.

"Hello," she says.

No one speaks. There is only the white noise that is always in the background of her cell phone calls. It could be the result of a flaw in the tiny cheap speaker but is probably microwaves, though she likes to imagine sometimes that it is the whisper of air molecules across all the thousands of miles between two people.

The hiss in her ear: she walks across the commons of the Engineering building, a high-ceilinged room crowded with students shaking water from their jackets and umbrellas on their way to class. Some look as overwhelmed as she feels. It is nearly finals and they are probably not sleeping any more than she is.

Beyond the glass wall it is raining. Cars pass on Loughlin Street, across the wet lawn. Water sprays from their wheels.

Her schoolwork is not going well. It is her third year toward an engineering degree, but just now that seems an unreachable goal. The science is simple enough, but the mathematics has been hard, and she is losing herself in the tricky mazes of Complex Variables. She thinks of dropping the class and switching her major to something simpler, but if she doesn't become an engineer what will she do instead?

"This is Hala," she says, her voice sharper. "Who is this?" This is the last thing she needs right now: a forgotten phone in a backpack, crushed against a text book and accidentally speed-dialing her; or worse, someone's idea of a prank. She listens for breathing but hears only the constant hiss. No, it is not quite steady, or perhaps she has never before listened carefully. It changes, grows louder and softer like traffic passing, as though someone has dropped a phone onto the sidewalk of a busy street.

She wonders about the street, if it is a real street—where in the city it is, what cars and buses and bicycles travel it. Or it might be in another city, somewhere distant and fabulous. Mumbai. Tokyo. Wellington. Santiago. The names are like charms that summon unknown places, unfamiliar smells, the tastes of new foods.

Class time. Students pool in the classroom doorways and push through. She should join them, find a seat, turn on her laptop; but she is reluctant to let go of this strange moment for something so prosaic. She puts down her bag and holds the phone closer.

The sound in her ear ebbs and flows. No, it is not a street. The cell phone is a shell held to her ear, and she knows with the logic of dreams or exhaustion that it is *water* she hears: surf rolling against a beach, an ocean perhaps. No one speaks or breathes into the phone because it is the water itself that talks to her.

She says to it, "The Pacific Ocean." It is the ocean closest to her, the one she knows best. It pounds against the coast an hour from the university. On weekends back when school was not so hard, she walked through the thick-leaved plants that grew on its cliffs. The waves threw themselves against the rocks, and burst into spray that made the air taste of salt and ozone. Looking west at dusk, the Pacific seemed endless; but it was not: six thousand miles to the nearest land; ninety million miles to the sun as it dropped below the horizon; and beyond that, to the first star, a vast—but measurable—distance.

Hala likes the sudden idea that if she calls the water by its right name, it will speak in more than this hiss. "The Atlantic Ocean," she says. She imagines waters deep with fish, floored with eyeless crabs and abandoned telecommunication cables. "The Arctic. The Indian Ocean." Ice blue as turquoise; water like sapphires.

The waves keep their counsel. She has not named them properly.

She speaks the names of seas: the Mediterranean, the Baltic, the Great Bight of Australia, the Red and Black and Dead seas. They are an incantation filled with the rumble of great ships and the silence of corals and anemones.

When these do not work, she speaks the words for such lakes as she remembers. "Superior. Victoria. Titicaca." They have waves, as well. Water brushes their shores pushed by winds more than the moon's inconstant face. Birds rise at dusk from the rushes along shoreline marshes and return at dawn; eagles ride the thermals above basalt cliffs and watch for fish. "Baikal. The Great Bear. Malawi."

The halls are empty now. Perhaps she is wrong about what sort of water it is, and so she tries other words. Streams, brooks, kills, runs, rills: water summoned by gravity, coaxed or seduced or forced from one place to the next. An estuary. Ponds and pools. Snow and steam. "Cumulus," she says, and thinks of the clouds mounding over Kansas on summer afternoons. "Stratus. Altostratus." Typhoons, waterspouts. There is so much water, so many possibilities, but even if she knew the names of each raindrop, and every word in every language for ice, she would be wrong. It is not these things.

She remembers the sleet that cakes on her car's windshield when she visits her parents in Wisconsin in winter. A stream she remembers from when she was a child, minnows shining uncatchable just under the surface. The Mississippi: broad as a lake where it passes St. Louis; in August, it is the color of *café au lait* and smells of mud and diesel exhaust. Hoarfrost coats a century-old farmhouse window in starbursts. Bathtubs fill with blue-tinted bubbles that smell of lavender. These are real things, but they are wrong. They are not names but memories.

It is not the water of the world, she thinks. It is perhaps the water of dreams. "Memory," she says, naming a hidden ocean of the heart. "Longing, death, joy." The sound in her ear changes a little, as though the wind in that distant place has grown stronger or the tide has turned, but it is still not enough. "The womb. Love. Hope." She repeats, "Hope, hope," until it becomes a sound without meaning.

It is not the water of this *world*, she thinks.

This is the truth. It is water rolling against an ocean's sandy shore; but it is alien sand on another world, impossibly distant. It is unknown, unknowable, a riddle she will never answer in a foreign tongue she will never hear.

It is also an illusion brought on by exhaustion. She knows the sound is just white noise; she's known that all along. But she wanted it to mean something— enough that she was willing to pretend to herself, because just now she needs a charm against the sense that she is drowning in schoolwork and uncertainty about her future.

Tears burn her eyes, a ridiculous response. "Fine," she says, like a hurt child; "You're not even there." She presses END and the phone goes silent, a shell of dead plastic filled with circuit boards. It is empty.

Complex Variables. She'll never understand today's lesson after coming in ten minutes late. She shoulders her bag to leave the building. She forgot her umbrella, so she'll be soaked before she gets to the bus. She leans forward hoping her hair will shield her face, and steps out into the rain.

The bus she just misses drives through a puddle and the splash is an elegant complex shape, a high-order Bézier curve. The rain whispers on the lawn; chatters in the gutters and drains.

The oceans of the heart.

She finds UNKNOWN CALLER in her call history and presses TALK. The phone rings once, twice. Someone—something—picks up.

"Hala," she says to the hiss of cosmic microwaves, of space. "Your name is Hala."

"Hala," a voice says very loud and close. It is the unsuppressed echo common to local calls. She knows this. But she also knows it is real, a voice from a place unimaginably distant, but attainable. It is the future.

She will pass Complex Variables with a C+. She will change her major to physics, graduate, and go to grad school to study astrophysics. Seven years from now, as part of her dissertation, she will write a program that searches the data that will come from the Webb telescope, which will have been launched in 2014. Eleven years and six months from now, her team of five will discover water's fingerprint splashed across the results matrix from a planet circling Beta Leonis, fifty light years away: a star ignored for decades because of its type. The presence of phyllosilicates will indicate that the water is liquid. Eighteen months later, their results will be verified.

One hundred and forty-six years from now, the first men and women will stand on the planet circling Beta Leonis, and they will name the ocean Hala.

Hala doesn't know this. But she snaps the phone shut and runs for class.

FAIR LADIES
THEODORA GOSS

Theodora Goss was born in Hungary and spent her childhood in various European countries before her family moved to the United States. Although she grew up on the classics of English literature, her writing has been influenced by an Eastern European literary tradition in which the boundaries between realism and the fantastic are often ambiguous. Her publications include the short story collection *In the Forest of Forgetting* (2006); *Interfictions* (2007), a short story anthology coedited with Delia Sherman; and *Voices from Fairyland* (2008), a poetry anthology with critical essays and a selection of her own poems. She has been a finalist for the Nebula, Crawford, and Mythopoeic Awards, as well as on the Tiptree Award Honor List, and has won the World Fantasy and Rhysling Awards.

When Rudolf Arnheim heard what his father had done, he kicked the leg of a table that his mother had brought to Malo as part of her dowery. It had been in her family for two hundred years, and had once stood in the palace of King Radomir IV of Sylvania. The leg broke and the tabletop fell, scattering bits of inlaid wood and ivory over the stone floor.

"Damn!" he said. And then, "Damn him!" as though trying to assign blame elsewhere, although he knew well enough what his mother would say, both about her table and about his father's decision.

"What are you going to do?" asked Karl, when the three of them were sitting in leather armchairs in the Café Kroner.

Rudolf, who was almost but not quite drunk, said, "I'll refuse to see her."

"You'll refuse your father?" said Gustav.

They had been at the university together. Gustav Malev had come to the city from the forests near Gretz. His father's father had been a farmer who, by hoarding his wealth, had purchased enough land to marry the daughter of a local brewer and send his son to the university. The brewing operation had flourished; glasses of dark, bitter Malev beer were drunk from the Caucasus to the Adriatic. Gustav, two generations removed from tilling the soil, still looked like the farmer his grandfather had been. He was large and slow, with red hair that stood up on his head like a boar-bristle brush. In contrast, Karl Reiner was small, thin, with black hair that hung down to his shoulders in the latest Aesthetic fashion. He knew the best places to drink absinthe in Karelstad. His father was a government official, like his father and his father's father before him. Most likely, Karl would be a government official as well.

Rudolf looked at his friends affectionately. How he liked Karl and Gustav! Of course, he would not want to be either of them. *I may not have Karl's brains,* he thought, *but I would not be such a weasely-looking fellow for all the prizes and honors of the university,* none of which, incidentally, had come to Rudolf. *And while Gustav is as rich as Croesus, and a very good sort of fellow to boot, what was his grandfather?* And he remembered with pride that his grandfather had been a baron, as his father was a baron. His father, the Baron. He could not understand his father's preposterous—preposterous—he could not remember the word. Yes, Gustav and Karl were his best friends.

He stood up and stumbled, almost falling on Karl. "Really, you know, I think I'm going to throw up."

Karl paid the bill, while Gustav held him under the arms as they wound their way around the small tables to the front entrance.

"The Pearl," said Karl later, when they were sitting in their rooms. They shared an apartment near the university, on Ordony Street. "I wonder what she's like, after all these years. No one has seen her since before the war. She must be forty, at least."

Rudolf put his head in his hands. He had thrown up twice on his way home, and his head ached.

"Surely your father won't expect you to—take her as a mistress," said Gustav, with the delicacy of a country boy. He still blushed when the women on the street corners called and whistled to him.

"I don't know what he expects," said Rudolf, although his father had made it relatively clear.

"As far as I can tell, Rudi, your entire university education has been a waste of money," his father had said. Rudolf hated to be called Rudi. His father was sitting behind a large mahogany desk and he was standing in front of it, which put him, he felt, in a particularly disadvantageous position. "You have shown absolutely no intellectual aptitude, and no preference for any profession other than that of drunkard. You have made no valuable connections. And now I hear that you have formed a liaison with a young woman who works in a hat shop. You will argue that you are only acting like the men with whom you associate," although Rudolf had been about to do nothing of the sort. "Well, they can afford to waste their time drinking and forming inappropriate alliances. Karl Reiner has already been promised a position at the Ministry of Justice, and Gustav Malev will return home to work in his family's business. But we are not rich, although our family is as old as Sylvania, and on your mother's side descended from King Radomir IV himself." Rudolf thought of all the things he would rather do than listen once again to the history of his family, including being branded with a hot iron and drowned in a horse pond. "I have paid for what has proven to be a very expensive university education, in part because of the dissolute life you have led with your friends. You sicken me—you and your generation. You don't understand the sacrifices we made. When I was in the trenches, all I could think of was Malo, how I was fighting for her and for Sylvania. However, now that you have completed your studies, I expect you to take your place in society. Your future, and the future of Malo, depends on the position you obtain, and on whom you marry. You will immediately give up any relationship you have with this young woman." And then his father had told him about The Pearl.

"I will pay for her apartment and expenses. It will be a heavy burden on my purse, but you must be taken in hand. You must be made to attend to your responsibilities. I would do it myself, but I cannot leave Malo until I know how the wheat is performing. If you paid any attention, you would know how precarious a position we are in, how important it is that you begin to consider more than yourself. You would know how precarious a position we are in, how important it is that you begin to consider more than yourself. She will introduce you to the men you need to know to advance your career, and keep you from forming any unfortunate ties."

The Pearl. She had been one of what a Sylvanian writer of the previous generation had referred to as the *grandes coquettes*, mistresses of great men who had moved through society almost as easily as respectable women because of their beauty and wit. She had been called The Pearl because she had shone so brightly, first in the theater and then in the social world of Karelstad, when Rudolf was still learning to toddle on his nurse's strings. She had been famous for her luminescent beauty, adored by the leading noblemen and government officials of her day and tolerated by their wives. Until, one day, she had disappeared.

Rudolf's relationship with Kati, who did indeed work in a hat shop, was less serious than his father suspected. She had allowed him to go so far and no further, in the hope that someday she would be offered a more legitimate role, and become a baroness. He would have been eager, if somewhat apprehensive, at the thought of having an official, paid mistress. But not one who must be at least twice his age, and certainly not one chosen by his father.

"How in the world did your father find her?" asked Gustav, but Rudolf had no idea.

They had been walking for at least an hour, farther and farther away from what Rudolf called civilization, meaning Dobromir, the town closest to Malo, the estate that had been in his father's family for generations. When the roads had ended, they had walked on paths marked by cartwheels, and finally over fields where there were no paths. Now they had stopped at the edge of a wood. Rudolf looked down with distaste at the mud on his boots.

"There," said his father.

Rudolf looked up and saw a cottage built of stone, like the cottages of farm laborers but without their neat orderliness or the geraniums that always seemed to grow in pots on their windowsills. This cottage seemed almost deserted, with moss growing on the stones and over the thatched roof. It was surrounded by what was probably supposed to be a garden, but was overrun by weeds, and although it was late summer, the apples on the two ancient apple trees by the fence were small and hard. In the garden, a woman was working with a spade. As they approached, she stood up and looked at them. She had a straw hat on her head.

"Wait here," said his father. He opened a gate that was leaning on its hinges and walked into the garden. When he reached the woman, he bowed. Rudolf was astonished. Who, in this godforsaken place, would his father bow to?

Rudolf heard them speaking in low voices. To pass the time, he tried to wipe the mud off his boots on the grass.

His father and the woman both turned and looked at him. Then, his father walked back to where Rudolf stood waiting. "Come," he said, "and keep your mouth shut. I don't want her to think that my son is a fool."

She looked thin, almost malnourished, in a dress that was too large for her and had faded from too many washings. When she lifted her head to look at him and Rudolf could see under the brim of her hat, he saw that her skin was freckled by the sun, with lines at the corners of the eyes and mouth. Her eyes were a strange, light green, almost gray, and they stared at him until he felt compelled to look down. Despite the sunlight in the clearing, he shivered.

"This is your son," she said. "He looks like you, twenty years ago."

"It would, as I have said, be a great favor to me, and I would of course make certain that you had only the finest…"

"I have no wish to return to Karelstad, Morek. If I do as you ask, it will not be because I want to live in a fine apartment or wear costly jewels. It will be because once, long ago, when I needed kindness, you were kind. Kinder than you knew."

"And the boy is acceptable?"

"He could be lame and a hunchback, and it would make no difference."

Rudolf felt his face grow hot. He opened his mouth.

"Excellent," said his father. "The keys to the apartment will be waiting for you. Send for him when you're ready."

The woman nodded, then turned back to her weeding.

Rudolf trudged over the fields and along the country roads behind his father, wondering what had just happened.

The summons came two weeks later. *Meet me at 2:00 p.m. at Agneta's,* said the note. It was written on thick paper, soft, heavy, the color of cream, scented with something not even Karl, who considered himself a connoisseur of women's perfumes, could identify. "It's not jasmine," he said. "Sort of like jasmine mixed with lily, but with something else…"

"What do you think she wants?" asked Gustav.

"She's his mistress," said Karl. "What do *you* think she wants?"

"I don't know," said Rudolf. What would he say to her? He imagined her in a straw hat and a faded dress in the middle of Agneta's, with its small tables at which students, artists, and women in the latest fashions from Paris sipped from cups of Turkish coffee or ate Hungarian pastries. Suddenly, he felt sorry for her. Karelstad had changed so much since she had last seen it. It had been impoverished but not damaged during the war, and since the divisions of Trianon it had become one of the most fashionable capitals in Europe. She would look, would be, so out of place. He would be kind to her, would not mind his own embarrassment. Perhaps they could come to some sort of agreement. She could live in her apartment and do, well, whatever she wanted, and he would be free of any obligations to her.

He looked at himself in the mirror. He looked rather fine, if he did say so himself. He practiced an expression of sympathy and solicitousness.

By the time he was sitting at one of the small tables, he was feeling less sympathetic. How like his father, to embarrass him in front of all these people. He did not know most of them, of course, but sitting next to the door—surely that was General Schrader, whom he had seen once in a parade commemorating Sylvanian liberation from the Turks, and he was almost certain that the woman with the ridiculously long feathers in her hat was the wife of someone important. Hadn't he seen her sitting on the platform at his graduation?

General Schrader had risen. There was a woman joining him, a woman so striking that Rudolf could not help staring at her. She was wearing a green dress, a dress of almost poisonous green. A green cowl of the same material framed her face, a pale face with a bright red mouth, so vivid that Rudolf thought, *I've never seen anything so alive.*

But she did not stop at the general's table. Instead, she walked across the room in his direction. At every second or third table she stopped. Men rose and bowed, women either turned their heads, refusing to look at her, or kissed her on both cheeks. In her wake, she left whispers, until the café sounded like a forest of falling leaves.

"So nice to see you again, Countess," Rudolf heard her say, and the woman with the feathered hat responded, "Good God! Can it really be you, come back from the dead to steal our husbands? Where did I leave mine? Oh my, I'm going to have a heart attack any minute. My dear, where have you been?"

A long, lean man sitting in a corner rose, kissed her hands, and said, "You'll sit to me again, won't you?"

"That's Friedrich, the painter," said Karl. "I've never seen him talk to anyone since I started coming here four years ago. I'll bet you four kroners that she's a film actress from Germany."

"I don't think so," said Gustav. "I think—"

And then she was at their table.

"You must be Rudolf's friends," she said. "It was so nice to meet you. Must you be leaving so soon?"

"Yes, I'm afraid so," said Gustav, hastily rising. "Come on, Karl. I'm sure Rudolf wants some privacy."

And then he was alone with her, or as alone as one can be in Agneta's, with a roomful of people trying, surreptitious, to see whom she was speaking with.

"Hello, Rudolf," she said. "Thank you for being prompt. Could you order me some coffee? And light me a cigarette. I haven't had a cigarette in—it must be twenty years now. I've made a list of the people you'll need to meet. You can tell me which ones you've met already." She waited, looking at him from beneath long black lashes. Her eyes were still green, but somehow they had acquired depth, like a forest pool. "My coffee?"

"Yes, of course," said Rudolf. He gestured for the waiter and suddenly realized that his palms were damp.

The party had lasted long past midnight. The Crown Prince himself had been there. The guest list had also included the Prime Minister; General Schrader; the countess of the feathered hat, this time in a tiara; the painter Friedrich; the French ambassador, Anita Dak, the principal dancer from the Ballet Russes, which was staging *Copélia* in Karelstad; a professor of mathematics in a shabby coat, invited because he had just been inducted into the National Academy; young men in the government who talked about the situation in Germany between dances; young men in finance who talked about whether the kroner was going up or down, seeming not to care which as long as they were buying or selling at the right times; mothers dragging girls who danced with the young men, awkwardly aware of their newly upswept hair and bare shoulders, then went back to giggling in corners of the ballroom. At first Rudolf had felt out of place, intimidated, although as the future Baron Arnheim he certainly had a right to be there, should probably have been there all along rather than smoking in cafés with Karl and Gustav. But it did not matter. He was escorting The Pearl.

She walked beside him down the darkened street, her white furs clasped around her. She had not wanted to take a cab. "It's not far," she had said. "I want to see the night, and the moon." It shone above the housetops, swimming among the clouds.

"Here it is," she said. It had been three weeks since he had met her at Agneta's, and he had never yet seen where she lived, the apartment that his father was paying for. He had wanted to, but had not, somehow, wanted to ask. He still did not know, exactly, how to talk to her.

"Could I—could I come up?" he asked.

For a moment, she did not answer. Then, "All right," she said.

Her apartment was larger than the one he shared with Karl and Gustav, and luxuriously furnished. He recognized a table, a sofa, even some paintings from Malo, and suddenly realized that his mother must have sent them. His father might have paid for an apartment, but he could never have furnished one.

She turned on a lamp, but the corners of the room remained in shadow. She shone in the darkness like a pale moon.

"You made me dance with every girl at the party, but you wouldn't dance with me," he said.

"That wasn't the point," she said. "How did you like the French ambassador's daughter? Charlotte De Grasse—she's nineteen, charming, and an heiress."

"I want to dance with you," he said.

She looked at him for a moment. He could not tell what she was thinking. Then she went to the gramophone and put on a record: a waltz.

Nervously, he took her in his arms. She was wearing something gray, like cobwebs, and her eyes had become gray as well. A scent enveloped him, the perfume that Karl had been unable to place.

"You're exquisite," he said, then realized how stupid that had sounded.

"Don't fall for me," she said. And then, almost as though he did not know what he was doing, he started to dance with her in his arms, around and around and around.

She sat on the edge of the bed. In the morning light coming through the windows, her robe was the color of milk. She had washed her face. Once again she looked like the woman that Rudolf had seen near Malo: thin, but now paler and more tired, with blue shadows under her eyes. Older than she had looked last night. It was just after dawn; the birds in the park had been singing for an hour.

"This is who I am, Rudolf," she said. "Beneath the evening gowns and cosmetics. Do you understand?"

He pulled her to him by the lapel of her robe, then slipped it off her shoulder. He kissed her skin there, then on her collarbone and her neck. The scent still clung around her, as though it were not a perfume but an exhalation of her flesh. "I don't care," he said.

"No," she said, sounding sad. "I didn't think you would."

Last night, he had touched her carefully, hungrily. At times he had thought, *She is delicate, I must be very gentle.* At times he had thought, *I would like to devour her.* Her fingers had traveled over him, and he had thought they were like feathers, so soft. At times he had shuddered, thinking, *They are like spiders. She is the one who will devour me.* He had looked down into her eyes and wondered if he would drown, and wanted to drown, and had at times felt, with terror and ecstasy, as though he were drowning and could no longer breathe. Finally, when he lay spent and she kissed him on the mouth, he had thought, *It is like being kissed by a flower.*

He pulled her down beside him and kissed her, insistently.

"Rudolf," she said. "The French ambassador's daughter—"

"Can go to hell," he said. And a part of him noticed, gratified, that this time she touched him as hungrily as he had touched her. Afterward, he lay with his head just beneath her breasts, moving as she breathed, his fingers stroking the skin of her stomach.

"I can't stay," she said. "Soon, I'll have to return to Dobromir. Once you have a position and are engaged, you won't need me anymore, and then I'll go."

He raised himself up on his elbow. "Don't be ridiculous. Why would you want to go back to there, to that hovel? And why should I marry anyone? I want to be with you."

"I told you not to fall for me." She sighed. "The first time I came to Karelstad, all I wanted was to dress in silk, wear high heels, smoke cigarettes. Motorcars! Champagne! The lights of the city at night, so much more exciting than the moon and stars. The theater, playing a part. It allowed me to be something other than myself. And then the men bringing me flowers, white fox furs, diamonds to wear around my neck, like drops of water turned to stone. Many, many men, Rudolf."

Frowning, he turned his head. "I don't want to hear about them."

She stroked his hair. "But I became sick. Very, very sick. I had to go back, live among the trees, drink water from the stream. If I stay here much longer, I'll become sick again."

"How can you know that?" he said.

He turned to look at her, and saw a tear slide from the corner of her eye. He pulled himself up until he lay beside her and kissed it away. "All right then, I'll come to Malo. I'll live in that hovel of yours, or if you don't want me to, I'll visit every day. At least we can see each other."

She smiled, although her eyes still had the brightness of unshed tears. "Now you're being ridiculous. Don't you realize what Malo is? It's been there, the forest and the fields, for a thousand years. The barons of Malo have cared for that land, and you must care for it, as your son must care for it after you. If I thought you would abandon Malo, I would leave today, knowing that my time here in Karelstad, with you, had served no purpose. Tell me now, Rudolf. Will you abandon Malo?"

Her smile frightened him. She seemed, suddenly, kind and sad and implacable. "If I don't, how long do we have?"

"I promised your father that I would stay until your wedding day. But you must not delay it, you must not put off taking the position I've found for you. You must not try for more than I can give."

"Damn my father," he said. "All right, then. I'll do as I'm told, like a good boy. And if I'm good, what do I get, now? Today?"

She wrapped her arms around him, and suddenly he felt a constriction in his chest, a sudden stopping of the heart he had felt only when seeing a serpent in his path or listening to Brahms. He could not breathe again. He wondered why anyone had thought breathing was important.

"You know," said Karl, "I would probably kill you if it would make her look at me."

They were sitting in the park. Karl and Rudolf were smoking cigarettes. Gustav was smoking a pipe.

"How you can stand that foul stench…" said Rudolf.

"It's no worse than Karl's French cigarettes," said Gustav. "Good Turkish tobacco, that's what this is."

Rudolf knocked ash off the tip of his cigarette. "Well, it smells like you're smoking manure."

"He doesn't want to stink for The Pearl," said Karl. "Rudolf, I hope you enjoyed my announcement of your probable demise."

"*If* she would look at you, but she won't," said Rudolf. He had spent the night with her. He spent every night with her now, knowing and yet refusing to believe that his time with her was coming to an end. Several months ago, he had shared with Karl and Gustav every detail of his frustratingly slow and not at all certain conquest of Kati. But he had told them nothing about the nights he had spent with The Pearl. Karl had hinted several times that he would like to know more. Gustav had stayed silent.

"Why is that, do you think?" asked Karl. "While your face is pleasant enough, you're not exactly the Crown Prince, and my uncle is a minister. Hell, I may even be a minister myself someday."

"Because she's a Fair Lady," said Gustav.

"A what?" asked Karl.

"My grandmother told me about them, once when I had the measles and had to stay home from school. You really don't know about the Fair Ladies?"

Karl blew cigarette smoke through his nose in a contemptuous sort of way. "Why should I?"

"Because they're dangerous," said Gustav. "They live in the forest, inside trees or at the bottoms of pools, and when they see a woodsman or a hunter, maybe, they beckon to him, and he goes to dance with them. He dances with the Fair Ladies until he's skin and bone, or maybe a hundred years have passed and all his friends and relatives are dead, or he promises to give the Fair Ladies anything they want, even the heart out of his chest or his first male child. I tell you, Fair Ladies are dangerous."

"And imaginary," said Karl.

"Ask my grandmother. One of her nephews was taken away by a Fair Lady. She had him for three days, and when she returned him, there were things missing from his house. All of his mother's clothes, some jewelry that had been sitting on her dresser, phonograph records. He said that had been the price of his return—he had promised them to the Fair Lady."

"Sounds like a thief, not a fairy," said Karl.

"Fairies are imaginary. Fair Ladies are real. How else do you explain the fact that when she comes into the room, you actually, unbelievably, shut up?" Gustav put his pipe into his mouth, inhaled, and blew out a smoke ring. "I think she's getting ready to steal our Rudi away. What do you think she'll want, Rudi? The heart out of your chest?"

"Well, Rudi, what do you think? Is she a Fair Lady?" asked Karl. "You haven't said anything for a while."

"She's found me a job," said Rudolf. "I'm going to be secretary to the Prime Minister."

"Hell!" said Karl. And then, "Bloody hell!"

"And I'm supposed to marry someone named Charlotte. She's the French ambassador's daughter. As soon as I'm married, she says, she's going to go back to Malo." He threw his cigarette on the path and ground it out, savagely, with his boot heel.

He wasn't going to do it. He wasn't going to marry Charlotte.

He had to tell her. Go to her and say, "Come away with me. If you don't want to stay in Karelstad, we'll go to Berlin or Vienna. I'll work to support us, and if you do get sick—why should you get sick when you're with me? but if you do—I'll find the best doctors to treat you. At Vienna they have the best medical school in Europe. Don't you see that I can't live without you?"

What had Gustav said? That Fair Ladies were dangerous. Well, she had taken the heart out of his chest, all right.

"Be happy, Rudolf," she had said to him. And, "Tomorrow is your wedding day. I will not see you again, after tonight." He had made love to her fiercely, angrily. And when he stood for the last time in the hallway, she had cupped his cheek with her hand, kissed him as tenderly as a mother kisses a child, and said "Goodbye." Then, she had closed the door.

But here he was, standing in the street across from her apartment building. He would cross the street, go up the stairs to her apartment, knock on her door, bang on it if she refused to open, and tell her that he wasn't going to go through with it.

"What are you doing here, young Arnheim?" He felt a hand on his shoulder, and turned to see the painter Friedrich standing beside him. "I passed Szent Benedek's on my way here and saw the wedding guests going in. You don't want to disappoint them, do you? If you run, you can be there in ten minutes. So go already." He waved his hand, as though shooing a fly.

"I can't," said Rudolf. "I have to see her, talk to her."

"To say what, exactly? That you're in love with her, that you want to spend the rest of your life with her? Don't you think she's heard it all before?"

"I don't care. This is different. She loves me too, I know she does."

The painter put his hands in his pockets. He looked down at the pavement, then spoke slowly. "It's possible. She's capable of love, although you wouldn't know it from the stories people tell, sitting around their fires in the winter, in places like Lilafurod and Gretz. I'm going to tell you a story of my own. It will take five minutes, which will give you ten minutes to get there, just in time for the wedding.

"Once upon a time, there were three young men as stupid, if that is possible, as you and your friends. Their names were Péter Andrassyi, Morek Arnheim, and Herman Schrader. Andrassyi was a count, and he was rich enough to buy himself a mistress, the fabulous Pearl of great price, who had just finished a successful run as Juliet at the National Theater. The famously irascible theater critic Mor Benjamin wrote that no other actress could die as convincingly as she could. She had been sitting for me—I had painted the posters for the play, and I asked her to sit for another project of mine, a small painting of a sylph standing naked by a stream, reflected in the water. Twice a week she would come to my studio, and I would paint her—naked, as I said. Have you ever seen a case of tuberculosis? No? Well, that's what it was like. She just started wasting away. I asked her what was wrong, what she was eating. She said she was well enough, that she didn't want to talk about it. But when she started coughing up blood, or whatever she has in those veins of hers, she told me. Her kind—they don't belong here, and if they stay too long, they sicken and then die. I went to Andrassyi's apartment. I told him about her condition, about what I had seen and what he must have noticed himself. Do you know what he said to me? That I shouldn't stick my nose into what was not my business, that I had always been jealous of him and simply wanted her for my own. He would not let her go, and as long as he wanted her, as long as he told her that he could not live without her, she would not leave Karelstad. I argued with her! How I argued. But she said, "He loves me. You know what I am, Friedrich. My nature binds me to him, more strongly than any of your legal ties. It isn't in the stories, is it, that we can be so caught?"

"I thought Gustav was joking," said Rudolf. "Do you mean that she's really—"

"Quiet, pup," said Friedrich. "I only have three more minutes to finish my story. So, I challenged him to a duel. It was stupid—he was an excellent shot and I was a poor one, but I was young and in love with her myself, although in a different way than he was. Artists aren't quite human either, you know. They also love differently. Schrader was his second. Arnheim, your father, was mine. I had no friend of my own to second me, and I knew that your father was an honorable, if intolerably boring, man. We met in the park at dawn, when there would be no observers. Andrassyi should have shot me—I should have died that day, but the luck that rewards all fools was with me, and he missed. I, who had never before hit a target, shot him dead. I was brought before a judge, but what could he do? There were two witnesses to swear that we had agreed on the place, the time, the weapons—Andrassyi had even shot first.

"When I told her, she screamed at me and beat me with her fists. Then, she wept for a long time. And then she went back to Malo. I asked your father to take her—there was no train back then, they went in a carriage and the journey took two days. She wrote to me, once. The letter said only, *Thank you. I am better now.* And there I thought she would stay, until your father decided that his ambitions for you were more important than her life. Why she would agree to come back for a pup like you—"

"Not for me," said Rudolf. "For Malo. She cares about Malo—" He felt as though he had been hit, by something he could neither understand nor name. The street seemed to be reeling around him.

"Why do you think I'm here?" asked Friedrich. "To take her back. I don't know if she feels about you as she felt about Andrassyi, but I'm fairly certain that if you walk into that apartment, if you tell her that you want her, she will not leave. She values her life, and knows that staying will kill her. But that's what it means, to be what she is—she would stay for you and die."

"I—I love her. I would never hurt her."

"Then let her go. Do you know what love is, young Arnheim? Ordinary, human love. It's when you see another person—see her as she is, not as you would like her to be. Have you seen her?"

Her pallor, these last few days. The dark circles under her eyes. The sharpness of her rib cage under his hands. Rudolf looked up at her window. What was she doing now? Packing, no doubt. She had accomplished what she came for. He thought, *I hope she weeps for me, a little.*

Then, he turned in the direction of Szent Benedek's and began to run.

Gustav caught him just as he was about to step through the door to the courtyard.

"Where are you going, so early?"

"Hunting," he said, as though the answer were obvious. He wore his flannel hunting coat and carried a rifle.

"I think I'll go with you," said Gustav.

"You'll ruin your shoes."

"They're more appropriate than boots, for a funeral."

The grass was still wet from the night's rains. They walked over the lawn, away from the house that had stood there for fifteen generations, looking, with its battlements and turrets, like a miniature medieval fortress. They passed the privet maze and rose garden, then the herb garden where bees were already at work among the lavender, and followed the road that led to the old chapel.

"Once," said Gustav, "this forest used to stretch across Sylvania. That's why the Romans called it Sylvania—The Forest. There was plenty of room, then."

"For what?" asked Rudolf.

"For whatever you're hunting."

They walked in silence. The sky was growing brighter, and the birds in the trees were filling the air with a cacophony of song.

"Mary, mother of God!" said Gustav suddenly. He surveyed one of his shoes, which was covered with mud. He had stepped into a puddle.

"I told you," said Rudolf.

"You know what that reminds me of?" asked Gustav. "Karl. He always insisted on wearing his city clothes in the country. You should have seen him when he visited me last year, at Gretz! But I knew that if I stopped to change, you would leave without me. Have you talked to him lately?"

"Karl? We don't talk anymore. He believes in the Reich. He thinks it will unite all of Europe. There will be no more war, he says, when Europe is united. He says we must all be international—under a German flag, of course. I don't believe in peace at that price."

"Well, perhaps he is a realist and we are the romantics, clinging to our old ways, our country houses and the lands our parents have farmed for generations. Perhaps in his new world order there will be no place for us."

"Speak for yourself," said Rudolf. "Any German who comes to Malo will get a bullet through the head, until I run out of bullets. And then they can shoot me. There are worse things than dying as a Sylvanian. My father said that to me before he died. He could barely speak after the stroke—but he was right."

"What about Lotta and the baby?"

"They leave for France next week. My mother will take them. If there's going to be a war, I want them out of it."

They stopped. They had come to the chapel. It had been built of the same gray stone as the house, but was now covered with ivy that was starting to obscure even some of the windows, with their pictures of saints and martyrs. It was surrounded by a graveyard.

"We used to come here on Sunday mornings," said Rudolf. "The family and all the laborers on the estate, worshiping together. Karl would call it positively feudal. But now everyone goes to the church in Dobromir. No one comes here anymore."

Nevertheless, among the gravestones stood a priest, beside a fresh grave, reading the burial rites. Around him stood the mourners, their heads bowed.

"So she died," said Gustav.

"She died," said Rudolf. "I would have taken her to a doctor, but she sent me away. And when I heard that she was sick, here at Malo—I wrote to her twice, but she never answered. I could not go to her without her permission—she would not have wanted that."

"What could a doctor have done?" asked Gustav. "Given her medicine? Who knows what it would have done—to her. Or cut her open, and found—what? Would she have had a heart, like a woman? Or would she have had—what a tree has?"

"He could have done something," said Rudolf.

"I doubt it. How do you save a fairy tale?"

"And so we commit her body to the ground, as ashes return to ashes and dust to dust. The Lord bless her and keep her, the Lord make his face to shine upon her, the Lord give her peace. *Amen*," said the priest. The funeral was over.

The mourners lifted their heads and looked at the two men. Later, when Gustav described it to his wife, sitting by their fire at home in Gretz, he shivered. "It was as though someone had thrown cold water at me. A shock, and then a sensation like water trickling down my back, as long as they continued to look at me. So many of them at once." Girls from the cafés and dance halls of Karelstad, some in silk stockings and fur stoles and hats that perched on their heads like birds that had landed at rakish angles, some in mended gloves and threadbare coats. Girls who acted in films, or modeled for artists, or waited tables until a gentleman friend came along. Slim, pale, glamorous, with dark circles under their eyes.

They walked out of the graveyard, passing the two men. Several nodded at Rudolf as they passed and one of them stopped for a moment, put her hand on his lapel, and said, "You were good to her." Then they walked away along the muddy road in their high heels, whispering together like leaves in a forest.

"Good morning, Baron," said the priest. "Would you like to see the stone? It's exactly as you ordered." They walked over and looked. There was no name on the stone, only the word

Fairest

"I'm surprised, Father," said Gustav.

"Why, because she lies in holy ground? God created the forests before He created Adam. She is His creature, just as you are, my son."

"Then you believe she had a soul?" asked Gustav.

"I wouldn't say that. But I've worked with these—young ladies for many years. We have a mission for them in the city. They go there, like moths to a flame. They can't help themselves. It's something in their nature. The priest that served here before me—your father knew him, Baron, old Father Dominik—told me that once, when the forest was larger than it is now and the cities were smaller, it was not so dangerous for them. A farmer would come upon them and they would force him to dance all night. He would find his way home the next morning, with his shoes worn out and no great harm done, although his wife or sweetheart might be angry. But now the forest is logged by the timber companies, and the cities glow all night like gems. They go to Karelstad and the theater managers hire them, or the film directors, and eventually they become sick. It's as though a cancer eats them up inside, draws the life, the brightness, out of them. They die young."

"Did I kill her?" asked Rudolf. It was the first thing he had said since he entered the graveyard. "Did going back a second time make her sick again?"

"I can't tell you that," said the priest.

"But I loved her," he said, as though to himself. "I wonder if that matters."

"It mattered to her," said the priest.

"Father," said Gustav, "what will happen to those girls, if the war comes?"

The priest looked at the gravestone for a moment. "I don't know. But you must remember that they've survived. The Romans write of the *Puellae Alba* who lived in the forests of Sylvania. A thousand years ago, they were here. We're no good for them, with our motor cars, phonographs, electric lights. Tanks won't be any better. But as long as the forest remains, they'll be here. Or so I prefer to believe. And as long as they're here, Sylvania will be here, in some fashion."

The two men walked back along the path, without speaking. Then, "What will you do now?" asked Gustav.

"Have breakfast. Send my wife and son to France. Fight the Germans."

"Sausage and eggs?"

"Do you ever think of anything other than immediate pleasures?"

"Frequently, and I always regret it."

Rudolf Arnheim laughed. A flock of wood doves, startled, flew up into the air, their wings flashing in the light of the risen sun.

PLUS OR MINUS
JAMES PATRICK KELLY

James Patrick Kelly has had an eclectic writing career. He has written novels, short stories, essays, reviews, poetry, plays, and planetarium shows. His most recent book is a collection of stories entitled *The Wreck of the Godspeed*. His short novel *Burn* won the Nebula Award in 2007. He has won the Hugo Award twice: in 1996, for his novelette "Think Like a Dinosaur," and in 2000, for his novelette "Ten to the Sixteenth to One." His fiction has been translated into eighteen languages. With John Kessel he is co-editor of *The Secret History of Science Fiction*, *Feeling Very Strange: The Slipstream Anthology,* and *Rewired: The Post-Cyberpunk Anthology*. He writes a column on the internet for *Asimov's* and is on the faculty of the Stonecoast Creative Writing MFA Program at the University of Southern Maine and on the Board of Directors of the Clarion Foundation. He produces two podcasts: James Patrick Kelly's StoryPod on Audible and the Free Reads Podcast.

Everything changed once Beep found out that Mariska's mother was the famous Natalya Volochkova. Mariska's life aboard the *Shining Legend* went immediately from bad to awful. Even before he singled her out, she had decided that there was no way she'd be spending the rest of her teen years crewing on an asteroid bucket. Once Beep started persecuting her, she began counting down the remaining days of the run as if she were a prisoner. She tried explaining that she had no use for Natalya Volochkova, who had never been much of a mother to her, but Beep wouldn't hear it. He didn't care that Mariska had only signed on to the *Shining Legend* to get back at her mother for ruining her life.

Somehow that hadn't worked out quite the way she had planned.

For example, there was crud duty. With a twisting push Mariska sailed into the command module, caught herself on a handrail, and launched toward the starboard wall. The racks of instrument screens chirped and beeped and buzzed; command was one of the loudest mods on the ship. She stuck her landing in front of the navigation rack and her slippers caught on the deck burrs, anchoring her in the ship's .0006 gravity. Sure enough, she could see new smears of mold growing from the crack where the nav screen fit into the wall. This was Beep's fault, although he would never admit it. He kept the humidity jacked up in Command, said that dry air gave him nosebleeds. Richard FiveFord claimed they came from all the drugs Beep sniffed but Mariska didn't want to believe that. Also Beep liked to sip his coffee from a cup instead sucking it out of a bag, even though he slopped all the time. Fungi loved the sugary spatters. She sniffed one particularly vile looking smear of mold. It smelled faintly like the worms she used to grow back home on the Moon. She wiped her nose with the sleeve of her jersey and reached to the holster on her belt for her sponge. As she scrubbed, the bitter vinegar tang of disinfectant gel filled the mod. Not for the first time, she told herself that this job stunk.

She felt the tingle of Richard FiveFord offering a mindfeed and opened her head. =*What*?=

His feed made a pleasant fizz behind her eyes, distracting her. =*You done any time soon?*= Distraction was Richard's specialty.

=*No.*=

=*Didit is making a dream for us.*=

She slapped her sponge at the wall in frustration. =*This sucks.*= Mariska couldn't remember the last time Didit or Richard FiveFord had pulled crud duty.

=*Should we wait for you?*=

=*If you want.*= But she knew they wouldn't. =*Might be another hour.*=

"You're working, Volochkova." Beep's voice crackled over the loudspeaker. One of his quirks was snooping their private feeds and then yelling at them over the ship's com.

"Yes, sir," she said. Beep liked to be called sir. It made him feel like the captain of the *Shining Legend* instead of senior monkey of its maintenance crew.

"She's working, FiveFord. Leave our sweet young thing alone."

She felt Richard's feed pop like a bubble. He was more afraid of Beep than she was even though the old crank hardly ever bullied Richard. Mariska hated being called *sweet young thing*. She wasn't sweet and she wasn't all that young. She was already fifteen in conscious years, eighteen if you counted the time she had hibernated.

When Mariska finished wiping the wall down, she paused at the navigation rack. She let her gaze blur until all she saw was meaningless shimmer of green and blue light. Not that she understood the rack much better once she focused again. She had been job shadowing Beep for 410 million kilometers and eleven months now. They had traveled all the way to SinoStar's *Rising Dragon* station and were passing Mars orbit on the way back to the Moon and she had mastered less than two-thirds of the nav rack's screens. If she had used a feed to learn the readouts, she would have been nav qualified by now, but Beep wouldn't allow feed learning. He insisted that she shadow him. Another quirk. He was such a fossil.

"Close astrometry," she ordered. The shipbrain cleared the readouts of the astrometry cluster from the screen. "Time?" A new cluster appeared. It was 14:03:34 on 5 July 2163. The mission was in its three hundred and ninth standard day.

Enough water ice aboard for two hundred and eleven days of oxygen renewal. Mid-course switchover from acceleration to deceleration would take place in three days, two hours, and fifty-nine minutes. The ship's reaction mass reserves of hydrogen would permit braking for one hundred and seventy-three days. More than they needed. Acquisition of the approach signal for *Sweetspot* station would occur in one just hundred and fifteen days, three hours, forty-seven minutes.

Mariska bit her lip. Even if by some miracle she could get home the day after tomorrow, it wouldn't be soon enough for her. She glanced up at the tangle of cables that Beep had strung from nav's access port to its backup rack. They swayed weightlessly in the currents of the air recycling system. Were those blue-black splotches on that cable sheath? They were. With a groan, Mariska peeled her slippers from the deck and launched herself toward the ceiling, sponge at the ready.

It took almost two hours to finish—although crud duty was never-ending. In another week it would be back; crud had been climbing the walls of spaceships for two hundred years now. The stuff offended Mariska's lunar sensibilities. There had been none of it on the Moon, or if there had been, she had never seen any. But Haworth, the crater city where she had grown up, was a huge environment. Compared to it, the *Shining Legend* was a drop in the Muoi swimming pool.

By the time she flew back to Wardroom C, Glint, Didit and Richard were already lost in the dream. Each had tethered themselves to the wall and drifted aimlessly, occasionally nudging into one another. They weren't asleep exactly. It was just that linking feeds to create a communal dream took concentration. Reality just got in the way. But Richard noticed when Mariska came through the hatchway and roused himself.

"Mariska." His voice drowsed. "Hey monkeys, it's Mariska."

Glint blinked as if she were a mirage. "Mariska." To Glint she probably was. "'S not too late."

She knew it was, but she opened her head a crack to take in their common feed. Didit had created a circus framework; she was good at dream narratives. She had raised a striped tent and a rusting iron pyramid from a grassy field. A parade of outsized animals trudged down a dirt road: cows and polar bears and elephants and a whale with squat legs. Glint's contribution was sensory. She was an amateur artist and had painted the feed with moist summer heat, the smell of popcorn and barns and sweat, the tootling of a pipe organ and delicate taste of dust from the road. But what Mariska liked most was her sky. It was the deep blue of the oceans as seen from space and had a kind of delicious weight, as if it had been filled with more air than any sky had ever been. Richard supplied the details. He was the only one of them who had actually lived on Earth and had seen an elephant or had walked on living grass.

If Mariska had spotted any of her bunkmates in the dream, she might have tried to catch up to them, even though they had created the feed without her and were already deep into its mysteries. She gave up looking when she heard laughter and applause coming from the tent. She was alone again. So what was new? She closed her head and left them to their fun.

Mariska was the youngest of the five-person crew assigned to the *Shining Legend*. There were three other maintenance monkeys job shadowing Beep. This was her first—and last—asteroid run. Being the rookie shadow meant getting stuck with the worst chores, having no say about anything and getting left out half the time. She stripped off her coverall and underwear, wadded the lot into a ball and crammed it into the clothes processor. She didn't know which she hated more, the mindless work or the smothering boredom when there was no work to do. She heaved herself into the cleanser, zipped the seal shut and slipped the spray wand from its slot. On the Moon, she could have let the cleanser fill with steam. Warm mist would bead on her skin and trickle deliciously down her body. But in space, there was no down. The wand's vacuum nozzle sucked the water off her before she had a chance to savor it. She came out of the cleanser free of mold spores but chilled. She snatched a fresh coverall from the processor's drawer.

As she dressed she tried to convince herself that getting left out didn't matter, that she didn't even like the other monkeys. Of course, this wasn't true. She would have done almost anything to get them to accept her as an equal. She jammed her arm into a sleeve. She was irked that Richard hadn't made the others wait for her. She knew he wanted to have sex with her and recently she had been surprised to find herself warming to him, despite his nightmarish body. Even though he had lived in space for four of his nineteen years, Richard had been warped by Earth's freakish gravity. He was tall and his head was way too big and all those grotesque muscles scared her. If she was a monkey, then he was a gorilla.

Mariska had made out a couple of times with Glint, but it wasn't very good for either of them. Glint and Didit were sister clones of a woman named Xu Jingchu, a big name at SinoStar Ltd. Glint was eighteen and Didit was fifteen. Genetically tweaked for weightlessness, they were as dainty as Richard was gross. They had slender limbs and beautifully defined ribcages and were so tiny that they might have been mistaken for elves or fourth graders. Their delicate bones were continually reinforced by some kind of superpowered osteoblasts or something. They had thick pubic hair and small breasts but no wasteful reproductive systems. People living on the Moon or Mars or in space didn't make babies by having sex. Their kids would have two heads or no lungs because of the cosmic radiation. At the start of the run Mariska had hoped that she and the Jingchu sisters might be friends. But it never really happened, despite all her efforts to reach out. Didit and Glint treated her like the rookie she was.

Mariska was a clone too, but Natalya Volochkova had had her daughter tweaked to go to the stars. Mariska hadn't asked for the genes that made it possible for her to hibernate and she didn't want to crew on a starship. But her mother had made those decisions for her—or thought she had until Mariska had run away to crew on an asteroid bucket. She had hoped to keep her past a secret from the little crew of the *Shining Legend*. But Beep had found her out and told everyone and now she was sure they resented her for throwing away a chance they all would have jumped at.

When Didit's arm brushed her sister's face, she murmured something that Mariska didn't catch. She studied the two sisters and wondered if maybe her body unnerved them as much as Richard's unnerved her.

"Moo," said Glint. "*Moooo.*"

Mariska had an impulse to yank on her tether, pull the little monkey down and tell her to start the dream over. Include her this time. "Moo yourself," said Mariska. She flipped out of the wardroom and angrily pulled herself upspine toward Galley.

Mariska shook a sippy cup of borscht until it was hot. She bungeed herself to a dining stand and woke up the screen beside it. Lately she had been looking at the news. Even though it was boring, it made her feel grownup. Today was all about Mars. Construction of the last phase of the Martinez space elevator had finally been funded. Maybe a job there for her? Vids of genetically tweaked Martians picketing the domes of Earth-standard Martians. Never mind—she was never going to Mars. They were taking applications again for emigration to the colony on Delta Pavonis 5, the terrestrial planet that the *Gorshkov* had just discovered. Natalya Volochkova had been chief medical officer on that mission. Mariska didn't get why the *Gorshkov* crew hadn't given it a real name. Who would want to move to a planet called 5?

She sipped some of the borscht and sighed. Another thing that she hated about space was everything tasted bland, like oatmeal or crackers.

She checked her inbox and as usual there was a message from her mother. *Golubushka, nothing, nothing, nothing, can't wait to see you again, love, Mama.* She deleted it, as usual. Once again, nothing from Jak. Back on the Moon they had been all but engaged to be married and become deep spacers and go to the stars together. But she was over him now. Still it would be nice to hear something, seeing as how she would have gladly had sex with *him* if only *he* had waited for her. Maybe he was applying to emigrate to Planet 4. Maybe he was already there. Good riddance.

She missed him.

"Mind if I join you?"

She hadn't heard Beep slip into the stand beside her. With its clatter of fans, pumps and compressors, Galley was almost as noisy as Command. The creak of the hull expanding and contracting was particularly bad here. "No sir," she said, and wiped the screen.

Beep was maybe forty, maybe eighty. She couldn't tell. Living in space faded different people at different rates. The stubble on his head and his chin had gone gray and there was a dimpled scar on his cheek where the cancer had been carved out. He had the slouch that all bucket monkeys got from spending too much time weightless. There was nothing special about his coveralls, but one of the *Shining Legend*'s two override cards hung from his neck on a green lanyard.

"I had a message today from your mother." He scanned the galley menu. "I was given instruction." His eyes were watery and vague.

"Really?" She felt her cheeks flush. "What did she say?"

"To take good care of you." He pointed at the menu. "Ha-ha-*ha*." Seconds passed and then the oven stuck its tongue out at him. On it was a steaming tart. He swiped it into the air, caught it before it could fly across the room, then juggled it from hand to hand until it floated, cooling, in front of him. "We go way back, Natalya and I," he said at last. "A thick stick now, isn't she?"

There was nothing safe she could say about that.

"Your mother doesn't understand you, young Volochkova. She wants you to be a deep spacer, not a bucket monkey."

"She's never bothered to understand me."

"You had the tweak. You can hibernate, sleep your way to the stars. So why are you dancing on one foot?"

She snorted in derision. "Only losers hibernate. You wake up and nothing is the same. You lose everything."

He shook his head as if he didn't believe her. "You know, I was supposed to be a spacer. Zoom through the wormhole to the stars." He sailed a flat hand back and forth imitating a spaceship. "Your mother Natalya pronounced me unfit." He caught his tart and bit into it. "Thinner than water, I was back then." Mariska watched crumbs fly out of his mouth. More crud duty.

"That has nothing to do with me...sir." She realized that she had been forgetting to say it.

"One generation plants the tree, the next gets the shade." His laugh was like a grunt. "I met her when she wasn't much older than you."

Mariska jacked her guess about his age way, way up.

He stuffed the rest of the tart into his mouth and took his time chewing. "I'd say that you remind me of her, but then you *are* her." He held a finger to his lips, cutting off her objection. "What's my name, young Volochkova? No, not Beep."

"Lincoln Larrabee, sir." This was the longest conversation they'd had in months. She wished she knew how to end it.

"Good of you to know that." He considered the back of his hand for a moment. "So if we have to share the same sky, we should help each other. I'm worried about FiveFord."

She hadn't noticed anything odd about Richard, other than that he wouldn't take no for an answer. "Why?"

"Space blues. Apathy. Burn out. Maybe you've missed the signs, but he won't be worth a mushroom in another couple of weeks."

"But he's only nineteen."

"Do us a favor, would you? I mean, for the good of the ship and all." He poked his forefinger to her shoulder, as if she hadn't been paying attention. "Give

FiveFord that ride he's been waiting for."

"*What?*"

"Go knee to knee with him. You're patched, aren't you? You can't get pregnant."

She couldn't believe he was saying this to her until she realized that he must have been sniffing. "Are you high?"

"Why?" When he winked at her, his eyelid fluttered. "Aren't you?"

"No."

"Then let's fix that." He fumbled at the breast pocket of his coverall, withdrew a sniffer and offered it to her.

She resisted the impulse to bat the thing out of his hand. "You're crazy." She wasn't about to *sir* him when he was twisted.

"What, it's just some harmless wizard. You get high. I've watched you."

"That's different." His lopsided grin infuriated her. She had accepted his bullying because she thought he was in control of things. "You're supposed to be responsible. You're wearing the override."

He peeled the card from his coverall and twirled it on its lanyard. "But I'm not on duty." He tucked it into the pocket where the sniffer had been.

"You're always on duty." She could hear her voice tremble. "What if something goes wrong?"

He waved the sniffer absently under his nose but did not squeeze off a dose. "You know why they call us monkeys?"

She closed her eyes, wishing this was just a nightmare she was having.

"It comes from first days," he said, "back in astronaut time. Everything was automatic then. The engineers didn't trust the old guys to do anything, not even think. Test animals don't make decisions and that's all the astronauts were. They used to say they were men sent to do monkeys' work."

She snapped the bungee against her wrist to keep from screaming. Beep was always saying things like that. She didn't know what he was talking about half the time.

"We're just along for the ride. Look here." He held up three fingers on his left hand. "Three wardrooms." He showed her all five fingers of his right. "Five of us. Crews used to need all that bunk space, but there was nothing for them to do. So they cut back. Everything is automatic now."

"But I'm shadowing you on the nav rack." Her voice was so small that she almost couldn't hear herself over Galley noise.

"Sure, so you can read it. But if we get a course wobble, can you calculate a new trajectory home?" He waited for her reply but there was nothing she could say. "You want Didit tweaking the magnetic containment field in the reactor?"

"I'd tell the computers to…."

"The computers are automatic. They don't need monkeys to override a busted routine."

"Then why are we here?"

"Crud duty? Fix lights? Fetch the ice?" He scratched under his arm and shrieked *hoo-hoo-hoo.*

When Mariska motioned for the sniffer, Beep grinned. She brought it to her face, cupped hands over it and squeezed off a dose, which sparkled up her nose. The wizard sank to her lungs and streamed into her blood. Seconds later her brain was twinkling.

"Feel better?" said Beep.

For the moment, the wizard was more important than her fear and confusion. "We're not monkeys," she said. "We're remoras."

He cupped the sniffer to his nose. "Say again?" He pressed the trigger.

"Remoras. The fish that stick onto sharks and clean parasites off them."

When Beep burst out laughing, his sniffer shot across Galley and out into the spine. She chuckled too but it was only because she was seriously twisted.

"Yes, loosen your cheeks." He patted the packet where he'd put the override, as if to make sure he hadn't lost it too. "Why don't you think I like you?"

This also struck her as funny. "Because you don't." She giggled. "Sir."

"Look here." He pointed and the screen next to her woke up. She saw a grainy vid, obviously transcribed from a feed. On it was Mariska, except not. She was wearing a dress that was black and shiny and barely covered the crotch. The shoulders were bare except for the two skinny ribbons which kept the dress from falling off. She was wearing black strappy shoes with heels six centimeters long. The eyeshadow was purple.

She would never wear such ridiculous shoes. Or eyeshadow. "What is this?"

The Mariska on the screen tugged the dress up so that black lace panties peeked from beneath the hem. One of the ribbons slipped. The face's hungry expression stunned her.

"Stop it."

The scene shifted and another Mariska was perched in a golden cage. She was nearly naked this time. The arms fitted into outspread white wings like the ones they used in aviariums on the Moon. Feathers dangled from a golden chain around the waist but didn't conceal much. The chest horrified her. Although she was fifteen, she was still pathetically flat-chested—her mother's fault. But the figure on the screen would have needed at least a C-cup bra to cover the bare breasts. Someone—*something* opened the door to the golden cage, but all she could see was a hand with long, pointed fingernails.

Beep froze the vid. "They go on from there," he said. "Much further on."

"They?" Mariska couldn't find her voice. "Where... *who?*"

"FiveFord has been making fake feeds where you do whatever he can imagine. It started on the outbound, but he didn't start to obsess until a couple of weeks ago. He makes one almost every day now. Sometimes he'll steal from his sleep time. I've seen this with shadows before." He gestured at the screen. "They make all kinds of deranged dream feeds, design inventions that could never work, study eight languages and learn none. I've got nothing against it in general, but sometimes they turn inward and swallow themselves. Then we have a problem."

Mariska was outraged. "You're as bad as he is." She reached past him and wiped the screen. "You're snooping this?"

"Fifteen-year-olds aren't exactly my favorite flavor, young Volochkova. I don't like this any more than you do." He fixed her with an accusing stare. "But tell me you've never created a fake feed before."

Of course she had. Not a lot, but more than a couple. She and her friend Grieg used to fake Mr. Holmgren, their ag teacher. They had him diddling Librarian Jane, the star from *Crosswhen,* and President Kwa and Godzilla. But that had been funny. Somehow she didn't think Richard FiveFord was doing fakes of her for laughs.

"Make him stop. Right now."

Beep showed her his hands, palms up. "Feeds are thought, young Volochkova. You can't stop thoughts. And it's not as if he's sharing with anyone. He can't know that I've snooped his kink. Or that I gave you a sneak preview." Beep released the bungee from his dining stand. "Anyway, I just thought you might be interested." He pushed toward the spine. "You can make him stop any time you want to. Reality trumps fantasy."

"I'm not sleeping with that pervert."

He waved without looking back. "Your decision." He flew through the hatch.

Her borscht was cold and she had lost her appetite. She shoved the cup into the disposal chute and flew back to Wardroom C. She hesitated at the hatch. Didit, Glint and Richard were still linked into their common dream. Now she wondered exactly what they were sharing. After all, this was a feed that they had deliberately kept her from. What kinks might be happening under that imaginary striped tent? She shook her head. No, that was paranoid thinking. Glint had invited her to join them, after all. Still, she braced against the hatchway and then threw herself at her sleep closet before any of them noticed her.

She sealed herself in but didn't turn on the lights. Her mind was churning as she floated in the darkness. Why had Natalya Volochkova contacted Beep? Did her mother know how he had been tormenting her? Would whatever she told him make any difference? Mariska doubted it. She decided to resent her mother's interference, even if things did somehow get better. The whole point of signing on for an asteroid run was to escape the controlling bitch. Then Mariska got stuck thinking about what Beep had said. How could he ever have believed she'd let Richard touch her after she'd seen those fakes?

All the grownups in her life were out of control.

The longer she spent in the dark, the lonelier she felt. She had no friends on the *Shining Legend.* The only friends she did have were back on the Moon, forty million kilometers away.

And Jak had left her.

She woke up the screen and drilled down through the menus until she came to her feed editor. She linked it to the encrypted partition where she kept her secret shrine to Jak. She didn't give a damn if Beep was snooping. There was a specific feed she had created of things she remembered about the Muoi pool. She and Jak used to swim laps there together; she found a sequence where they were sitting on the edge, their feet dangling in the water. In real life she had been wearing her aquablade swimsuit but now she changed it to the two piece that she never liked because it made her look like a little girl. In real life, they had talked about sharing a closet on a starship, maybe even the famous *Gorshkov*, assuming that her mother wouldn't be aboard. In her fake, there was no talk of the future. She scripted him to play with the waistband of her suit, which she had let him do sometimes. She brushed a kiss across his shoulder, licking the beads of water which clung to his bare skin. The shouts of kids playing in the shallow end bounced off the low ceiling of the pool's cave. Jak slipped his three middle fingers slowly down the bumps of her spine and then just inside her suit, which she had never let him do. The fake Mariska closed her eyes. The real Mariska sucked in a ragged breath. She could see her imaginary Jak getting hard under his swimsuit. But suddenly she was sad. Too sad. She knew there would be tears if she pushed the fake any further. And none of them, not Jak or Beep or Richard or the Jingchus or her mother, was worth crying over.

The *Shining Legend* was possibly the ugliest spaceship in SinoStar's fleet. At the back end of its long spine was a heavily shielded antimatter drive. Forward of the reactor was a skirt of battered cargo buckets. Outbound, these had carried agro and manufactured goods destined for *Rising Dragon* station. Inbound, they contained unprocessed nickel-iron ore and dirty chunks of ice from SinoStar's asteroid mines. Next to the buckets were storage mods. Further upspine, a hodgepodge of crew mods had accreted over the years: Command, Galley, Service, Health, Rec and Wardrooms A, B and C. Three crawlerbots, nicknamed Apple, Banana and Cherry wandered the various hulls of the ship checking for micrometeor damage. A watchbot named Eye flew alongside, held by a magnetic tether. Their asteroid bucket looked to Mariska like a pile of junk that had fallen out of a closet.

The ship ran on antimatter and water. Electrolytic cells dissociated hydrogen and oxygen from ice that had been treated back on *Sweetspot*. The hydrogen was used by the positron reactor for thrust, the oxygen refreshed the atmosphere in the crew's quarters. Unlike the starship *Gorshkov*, the *Shining Legend* was not a closed system. Scrubbers removed carbon dioxide from the atmosphere and vented it to space. The cells replaced the oxygen lost in this process and therefore required a constant supply of water. When reserves ran low, the crew fetched blocks of the treated ice, stored on loading porches outside the storage mods.

Qualifying in cargo was the last step before a shadow could advance to senior crew; it was the one job where the computers needed human help. Both Richard and Glint were shadowing cargo on this run. Glint had failed cargo once already but she'd been doing better this time. They used the crawlerbots to load, store and offload material at either end of the run and bring in the ice while the ship was in transit. In the old days, cargo monkeys used to suit up and actually drive the bots, but now everything was handled remotely from Command.

Throughout the run, Richard, Glint and Beep would gather at the cargo rack in Command to divert the bots from their normal rounds. But having people look over her shoulder made Glint nervous, especially after she had failed cargo. Back at *Rising Dragon* station she had put several new dents in the buckets while loading ore. Her problem was that when she got flustered, she lost track of where the edges of her bots were. She was fine as long as she didn't actually see anyone, so Richard and Beep had taken to monitoring her from a distance when she took her turn on the rack.

So Mariska was surprised when Richard flew into the Rec mod.

"Isn't Glint on ice duty today?" She was working out on the treadmill.

"She is." Richard maneuvered himself into the weight machine and buckled in.

"Aren't you supposed to be watching her?"

"I am."

"But you're not."

"No." He smiled at no one in particular as he adjusted the arms of the machine. "I'd rather be here with you." He set the resistance to four kilograms for curls.

"*Richard.*"

He laughed. "Beep told me to take a break. He's watching her but she hasn't messed up since *Dragon*. Ninety-seven days and counting. She's so good now that she's boring."

Mariska had logged just three kilometers and had seven more to go. At least a half-hour before she finished her workout and could escape him. She pulled her towel from its clip and wiped her face. Sweat was another thing she hated about space. She missed swimming.

How was she supposed to act around Richard anyway? She couldn't help but wonder what was going on behind those wide brown eyes when he looked at her. Probably imagining new kinks. But with more than a hundred days left in the run, she couldn't afford to confront him. Feuds in space tended to take up a lot of room. On a ship the size of the *Shining Legend,* that would be trouble. But she wasn't about to pretend that she was comfortable being alone with him.

After he finished the curls, he did shoulder squats. The weight machine clanked and wheezed and its gyros hummed. The more reps he did, the more the veins stood out at his temples. Richard was proud of his foolish muscles and worked hard to keep them. Now he was grunting from the effort. It was kind of disgusting. He told her once when they were high on wizard that he'd be like some kind of superhero if he ever visited the Moon. She'd tried not to laugh at his ignorance. There was hardly any crime at Haworth. The Moon had no need of another Lord Danger.

"You haven't been very nice to me lately." He was smiling, his cheeks flushed from his workout. "What did I do wrong?"

"Nothing." She wasn't going to think feathers and golden chains.

"Somehow you make nothing sound an awful lot like something." He waited for her to answer; she let him wait. "Okay." He reconfigured the weight machine for squat thrusts. "*One. Two.*" The count exploded out of him when he kicked his legs back. "*Three. Four. Five.*" He was so strong that he overpowered the gyro. When the apparatus banged against the wall, she could feel the entire mod shake. It was a point of pride with Richard that he could do this. "*Thirteen. Fourteen. Fifteen.*" No one else aboard could. Sometimes she could feel him working out as far away as Galley.

Richard stopped at twenty, sucking air in huge gulps. Mariska felt a familiar tingle; since he was out of breath and couldn't speak, he was offering her his feed.

"No thanks," she said. She woke up the screen in front of them, picked a 3D channel at random. It was old sci-fi from the previous century: a space captain in a ridiculously tight uniform was sitting on a shiny chair on the bridge of some fairy-tale spaceship. The camera pulled back. Everyone on the screen was sitting on chairs.

There were no chairs on the *Shining Legend*.

"Artificial gravity." Richard climbed on the stationary bike and started peddling. "I could use some of that just now."

Mariska ignored him and pretended interest in the 3D.

Now the people on the bridge were staring at a viewscreen showing another silly spaceship. In an external shot, one ship veered sharply away from the other, narrowly avoiding a collision. Back on the bridge, the crew were all leaning to their left.

"Sorry," said Richard, "but they'd all be puddles of jelly on the wall." He shook his head. "People on Earth still watch this stuff."

The counter on the treadmill clicked over to ten kilometers. "Really?" Mariska slowed her pace to a walk. Her legs felt pleasantly heavy.

"People on Earth are stupid. They don't know anything about living about space. That's why I left."

"There are stupid people everywhere." She unbungeed herself. "The trick is not to let them do anything stupid to you."

Richard shot her a quizzical look. "Meaning?

"Meaning have a nice workout, Richard." She said, and kicked out of Rec.

Mariska had never had a feed from her mother before. At first she wasn't sure that she should accept it. Natalya Volochkova was a fossil like Beep. Her generation used feeds only for the most intimate sort of contact, which was the last thing Mariska wanted. But this feed had been the only message from her mother for several days now. Mariska was curious to know why she had stopped.

=*Moya radost, you know this isn't what I wanted for us.*= Natalya Volochkova was seated in a plastic chair in a spare room that was clearly not at their home in Haworth. The focus was tight, the light harsh. Mariska tried to zoom out but the feed refused her command. There was a stale papery smell to the room that made Mariska think that she might be looking at a museum or a library. Some kind of storage area. =*You think you are doing what is right. Maybe, but where you are now is not where you will be when you grow up.*=

"I am grown up!" Of course, her mother couldn't hear her.

=*I know you have been suffering, but things will get better.*= There was a weight to her voice that Mariska had never heard before. =*I promise.*=

"Just stop your interfering, bitch."

=*I'm on Mars just now, but I won't be staying. I don't know if you've heard but we're commissioning a new starship, the Natividad.*=

Mariska felt her throat tightening.

=*It's been more than a year since I've heard anything from you. I write, you are silent. At least I know that you are safe. I'm sorry if you're unhappy.*= She was shocked to see her mother's eyes shine with tears. =*I wish I knew what you're thinking just now. But if you really want me out of your life, then I must accept that. I've been offered a place on the Natividad. I had hoped to bring you with me but....*=

"Go then." Mariska closed her mind. The bare room and her sad mother disappeared. "*Leave.*" She deleted the feed.

Mariska tried to relax into the delicate embrace of her closet's sleep net but her thoughts kept tumbling over one another. Mariska wondered at how little she understood herself. After all, this was exactly what she wanted. Natalya Volochkova was finally leaving her alone.

So why did she feel betrayed?

Glint's scream shook the walls of Galley fifteen meters away. Mariska choked on a mouthful of butterscotch pudding. When she poked her head out of the hatch Beep almost tore it off as he shot upspine toward Command. She followed at a distance. Ahead she saw Richard desperately trying to pull Glint downspine. Glint flailed at him like a drowning swimmer.

"What?" Beep shouted over her shrieking.

"Seda...tive," said Richard. Glint spun in his grasp and they crashed against the deck of the spine. "Ooof. Glint, no."

"*What?*" said Beep.

"Something about the ice."

It was a measure of Glint's panic that she gave musclebound Richard all he could handle. But when he finally yanked her arms behind her back, she slumped forward. Her screams melted into sobs.

"You." Beep pushed Mariska at them. "Help." He flew into Command.

They wrangled her downspine to Health and strapped her to an examining table. Richard tried to comfort her while Mariska tapped at the med rack and charged a face mask with somapal. When Richard pressed it to Glint's nose and mouth, she groaned and went limp.

They stared at each other across the table. Richard was breathing hard enough for three people.

"What about the ice?" said Mariska.

"Don't know." He shook his head. "There wasn't time."

"Let's find out." He followed her out.

"Where?" Beep muttered to himself as his fingers danced over screens on the cargo rack. "Where, where, where?" He was barefoot and held himself still by curling his toes into the deck burrs. His hair was mussed. He looked like he had just woken up; she thought he might be twisted. "Damn it, where?" Mariska had never noticed how long Beep's toes were. There was fine black hair on the joints.

He stabbed at the rack. The screens that had been showing crawlerbot Banana's view switched to Eye flying next to the *Shining Legend*. He panned up and down the ship. Mariska gasped when Eye looked past the porch on Storage D, where their reserves of treated ice were supposed to be.

It was empty. Behind her, Richard made a strangled noise.

"Come on. Where?" Now Beep turned the eye away from the ship to scan the nearby space.

Mariska tore herself away from cargo to access the nav rack. "Time cluster," she said.

It was 04:33:04 on 15 July 2163. The mission was in its three hundred and nineteenth standard day. The ship had completed its mid-course switchover from acceleration and was now seven days, two hours, and eleven minutes into deceleration toward home. Acquisition of the approach signal for *Sweetspot* station would occur in one hundred and five days, eighteen hours, and twenty-one minutes.

"There."

The ship's reaction mass reserves of hydrogen would permit braking for just sixty-eight more days. The inventory of ice finished updating. It would be sufficient for forty-seven days of oxygen renewal. The screen began to flash red.

Eyes wide with terror, Mariska glanced across Command at Eye's view. Two blue-white blocks the size of lunar rovers were tumbling sedately away from them toward the blaze of stars.

"The problem isn't fuel," said Mariska. "If they start a ship soon enough, it can match trajectories with us. Then we offload some replacement ice and finish our deceleration."

"Except there won't be any *we*." Glint looked hollow. "We'll suffocate by then."

"Not necessarily." Richard was trying to convince himself. "Not at all."

"We've got tons of ice back in the buckets," said Didit. "Asteroid ice. Tons."

The four of them had gathered in Wardroom C while Beep was in Command talking to experts at *Sweetspot* station. No one wanted to be alone, but being together and seeing how scared they all were made waiting for Beep an agony. There were long silences, punctuated either by hopeful declarations or sniffles. They all cried some, Glint the most. Mariska was surprised at how little she cried. She was sure she was going to die.

"Such an idiot." Glint rubbed the heels of her hands against her temples. "The stupidest damn stupidhead in all of space."

Didit poked her listlessly. "Shut up, Glint."

"It's my fault too," said Richard, not for the first time. "Should've been watching you. That's what backup is for. More eyes, no surprise."

Twenty hours before, while retrieving a block of treated ice, Glint had bumped the Cherry crawler against the side of the open airlock. The ship's computers had interpreted this as a potential failure and had triggered lockdown protocol. Glint hadn't wanted yet another screwup on her record, so she had gunned Cherry into the airlock just before the doors slid shut. Once it was safely inside, she had cancelled the lockdown. It was, after all, a false alarm. The shipbrain would still record the incident, but an anomaly without consequences wouldn't get Glint in any trouble.

Only now the consequences were dire. Normally, Glint would have instructed Cherry just to drop the ice and leave the airlock. Then, after checking that the primary ice restraints on the storage porch had re-engaged, it would have resumed its automated search for micrometeorite damage. But the crawler was on the wrong side of the doors and its restraint routine had been interrupted by the lockdown. This wouldn't have been a problem had not the secondary restraint, a sheet of nanofabric that covered the ice reserves, failed. The two remaining blocks had somehow nudged out from underneath and taken off. Simulations showed that some kind of vibration could have set the ice in motion. On a ship as old as the *Shining Legend,* shakes and rattles were to be expected.

Mariska guessed that the ice had come loose when Richard banged the weight machine against the wall of Rec. From the way he avoided her gaze, she guessed he thought so too. Was that why he kept apologizing for leaving Glint to fetch the ice?

What everyone was wondering, although no one dared say it aloud yet, was how Beep could have let Glint trash the safety protocols so totally. He'd told Richard that he'd watch her. Had he had his nose in a sniffer?

"Here it is," said Mariska. "That data feed I was looking for."

=*Untreated water is a poor conductor of electricity, impeding the reaction in electrolytic cells so that the dissociation of hydrogen and oxygen occurs very slowly. Typically the addition of salt electrolytes will increase the conductivity of water as much as a millionfold. Using water treated for enhanced conductivity enables Sino-Star's advanced electrolytic cells to achieve efficiencies of between 50% and 70%=*

"So salt." Didit brightened. "We get ice from the buckets and just add salt."

"We don't have that kind of salt," Glint said wearily. "And we sure as hell don't have enough of it."

"Hey, all the feed said was that the cells would be slow." Didit wasn't giving up. "Slow is better than nothing." She looked to Mariska for confirmation.

"Plus raw asteroid ice is full of dust and crap. It'll just clog the cells." Glint's chin quivered but she held the tears back. "Face it, we're slagged."

"Shut up, Glint."

"There's a way," said Richard. "There has got to be a way."

Nobody bothered to agree or disagree. The silence stretched.

"Buck up, monkeys." Beep appeared at the hatchway. "We haven't fallen out of our tree yet. Everyone up to Command and I'll tell you the plan."

The word *plan* seemed to lift the four teenagers. Didit reached over and gave Glint's hair a sisterly pull. "Told you." As they followed him upspine, Mariska caught herself grinning with relief. The brains at *Sweetspot* must have seen something she hadn't.

Beep waited until they had settled themselves around the cargo rack. One of the screens showed Banana crawler parked in front of Storage D. "So we use the crawlers to fetch raw ice from the buckets. We chip off chunks and boil all the impurities out."

Mariska knew that couldn't be right. "How do we do that?" said Mariska. "We have no way to capture…."

"Volochkova, did I ask you to speak?"

"No."

"No, *what?*" His voice was cutting.

"No, sir." She noticed that the skin of his face seemed stretched too tight.

"Leave your ignorance in your pockets. All of you." He let rebuke hang in the air for a long moment. "Next we start collecting leftover salts from the electrolytic cells and stop dumping the stuff into space. We add it to the purified water we're going to make. They're telling me that using fresh water slows down the electrolytic cells. It's like watching toenails grow."

"We know that," said Didit. "Mariska found a feed."

"We've got enough treated ice…" He glanced over at the nav rack. "…for forty-seven days. Let's see how much salt we can save by then. Okay, monkeys? Trouble is knocking but we're not letting it in. I'll suit up and ride Banana back to the buckets."

"While the reactor is at cruising power?" Too late, Mariska realized that she had spoken without permission. This time Beep was more forgiving.

"I've damped it down." He nodded at the energy rack. "Besides, how else am I going to sort ice from ore?" His grin was bleak. "But thanks for your concern, young Volochkova. I do realize that radiation isn't my friend." Didit laughed nervously. The others glared at Mariska as if she were trying to kill them: They were fine with letting Beep risk the exposure. After all, he was senior monkey.

"So, FiveFord and Glint, get Apple and Cherry started for the porch. Didit, lower the air pressure in the airlock to four-tenths of a bar." He pushed off and floated over them. "Young Volochkova, you come with me to Service and help prep the suit. That way you can wash all those worries about my safety."

On their way downspine, Beep caught himself at the hatch to Wardroom A. "I need my coolwear." He waved her on. "Power my suit up and start the checklist. I'll be down in two kicks."

There were a dozen spacesuits bungeed to the walls of Service. Most of them hadn't been touched in years. As part of their cargo chores, however, Glint and Richard had powered five of them up regularly during the run to make sure they still worked. They were all low pressure, which meant Beep needed to prebreathe oxygen before the spacewalk to keep from getting the bends. Since Beep had been aboard the *Shining Legend* for more than a decade, he had a custom-fitted suit. Mariska opened it, plugged its battery cord into the fastcharge outlet and started its power on self-test. She was moving through the rest of the checklist when Beep flew in.

He had the hood of his coolwear pulled back, but otherwise it covered his entire body. The white of the fabric made the deep flush on Beep's face stand out. When Richard exerted himself, he just turned red. Beep was practically purple and was sucking in huge gulps of air

Mariska could see beads of sweat at his hairline. "Beep," she said, "tell me you're not high."

"Borrowing some courage is all." He landed in front of the oxygen bar. "And don't be warming my ears about it." He clapped the mask over his face, and glared at her.

Back in Command, she had suspected that something was wrong with him. Now she was certain of it. But there was nothing she could do, so she went back to the checklist. After fifteen minutes, he pulled the mask away and thrust the override card at her. "Hold this while I suit up."

She took it and he raised his arms. Mariska grasped his waist. She could feel the pulse of the coolant in his coolwear, which was designed to keep the spacesuit from overheating. She raised him over her head and jiggled him through the suit's opening

He fit his arms into the sleeves but then paused. "How many oxygen bottles do I have?"

"Two," she said. "Checklist calls for two, primary and backup." She didn't understand why he was asking. Two four-thousand-cubic-centimeter bottles had been the standard design spec since before she was born.

"How many are left?"

She shrugged.

"Go look."

Mystified, she opened the locker, counted thirty-seven filled and fourteen empty bottles. She reported this.

"Worth knowing." He finished sealing himself into the suit. "Worth remembering. So, let's dance."

She handed him his helmet to carry, unbungeed him from the wall and tugged on the suit's tether. He bobbed behind her like a man-sized balloon as she pulled him downspine to Storage D.

The air was already thinning in the airlock and it felt colder than it actually was. Beep turned on his boot magnets, enabling him to stand upright in front of her. She was expecting him to fit the helmet onto the suit's collar so she could lock it down. He surprised her.

"Not yet, young Volochkova. Time for a quick chat. You have the override?"

She offered it to him. He shook his head.

"I'm leaving it with you for now. That means you're in charge in case anything spills. I am thinking that you can make the hard decisions. At least, Natalya could."

Mariska wasn't her mother; for some reason Beep still wouldn't accept that. "But Richard is senior to me. And Glint…"

He snorted. "FiveFord could drown in a glass of water. He should go back to Earth and dig holes with all those muscles. Only he'd probably fall in. And Glint… poor Glint is broken." He pointed at the override. "You show them the override and tell them I said."

"What is this, Beep?" She tucked it into the pocket of her coverall.

"This?" He smirked. "Just a little walk. *La-la-la.* But before I go… Remember the fakes I showed you? Ah, I thought you might. So that was just a little joke. The fakes never existed, or at least, you saw all there was of them. All that I made."

"*You?*"

"I like to stir the soup, Natalya." His laugh had a chemical edge. "The runs are so damn long, too damn boring. Hard to stay interested. So we play tricks. It's tradition, how bucket monkeys keep from going crazy."

Mariska felt suddenly dizzy in the thin air, afraid to say what she was thinking. "Why tell me this now?"

"I'd say it was conscience, if I had one." His mouth tightened. He raised the helmet over his head and stared into it. "Time to go."

"Wait." She caught at the front of his suit. "That was a lie about the raw ice, wasn't it? And the leftover salt—that can't possibly work. And you—you're going to get a crazy dose of radiation…."

"One less mouth to breathe." Beep stuck his chin out at her. "You'll know what to do when the time comes." He lowered the helmet onto his head. She wanted to hammer on it, get him to stop, make all of this go away. Instead she locked it to his suit.

By the time she got back to Command, Beep had already turned Banana downspine and was accelerating toward the buckets. The others watched the screen that showed the crawler's camera, but Mariska was fixed on the overview that the Eye saw.

"He's going kind of fast." Richard was beginning to suspect what Mariska already knew.

"Then tell him to slow down," said Didit.

Beep must have turned his boot magnets off. On the Eye, she saw that they had come off the racing crawler and his only contact was the joystick which he grasped with both hands. His legs swung upward relative to the surface of the ship until he was upside down. He looked like a gymnast doing a handstand as the crawler hurtled toward the buckets.

"Call him," said Richard. "Glint?"

"Doesn't work."

"It's dead. He must have disabled it."

Glint's hand trembled as she pointed at the Eye's screen. Didit was sobbing.

"Override it."

"With what?"

"*Stop him.*"

At the exact moment the crawler crashed into the bucket, Beep released his hold. His momentum flung him clear of the *Shining Legend*, tumbling helmet over boot.

They watched as he applied gas thrusters to correct his wild rotation.

They watched him spread his arms to embrace the darkness as he shot away from the ship.

They watched in shock as he faded to a speck of space debris and was gone.

"Still, you could have stopped him," said Richard.

"How?" Mariska was tired of their accusations. The weight of what she had done—and not done—was crushing her.

"You could have."

Glint was no help. She had kicked her slippers free of the deck burrs and was floating aimlessly around Command. She seemed not to notice when she bumped into things.

"But we still have ice," said Didit. "Who's going to fetch the ice?"

"Nobody." Glint's head lolled backwards. "It's just like Mariska said. A fairy tale."

"What does she know?" Didit's hands curled into fists; she was ready to punch someone. "Maybe she made Beep do it."

"He gave her the override."

The four of them considered this fact in silence. Richard ran a finger down the edge of the cargo rack. It came away with a smudge of ugly blue. "The crud is back," he said to no one in particular

"It's her first run," said Didit. "Why her?"

Glint cackled. "Because he hated her?"

"We should contact *Sweetspot*. Tell them what's happening here." Richard nodded at the override hanging around Mariska's neck. "Maybe we should enable comm now?"

Mariska brought up the comm cluster and flashed the override at the nav rack. Then she paused, considering. "Close communication," she said. "Time?"

"Sure," said Glint. "Let's check the doomsday clock."

Didit turned on her and shouted. "Shut the fuck up, Glint."

The screen still flashed red. It was 08:14:56 on 17 July 2163. The mission was in its three hundred and eleventh standard day. They were eight days, twenty-two hours, and six minutes into deceleration. Acquisition of the approach signal for *Sweetspot* station would occur in one hundred days, twenty-three hours, and fifty-one minutes.

"There," said Mariska. "See?"

The ship's reaction mass reserves of hydrogen would permit braking for eighty-nine more days. The ice inventory would supply be sufficient for seventy-three days of oxygen renewal.

"See what?" said Richard.

"We gained twenty-six days." Mariska felt as if she were rising out of herself and looking down at them from the Eye. "Beep gave us twenty-six more days."

"So what?" Now Glint shouted. "Seventy-three from one hundred. A month of no air."

"Right," said Mariska. "But if we decrease demand again, we buy even more time."

"Decrease demand?" Fear filled Richard's voice.

"And the rescue ship—they don't have to wait until we get all the way to *Sweetspot*. They can come out to meet us…"

"Someone else sacrifices?" said Didit. "That's your plan?"

"Nobody has to sacrifice." She pushed herself over to the environment rack. "Somebody just has to stop breathing."

"Oh, great," said Glint.

"Who?" said Richard.

Mariska's mind was racing as she brought up the crew's med files. It could work. It had to work.

It was just above freezing in the mod; Mariska was pleased. The inner shell of the *Shining Legend* was fitted with heating strips to keep the bitter cold of space from penetrating crew areas. But Mariska had disabled the shell heaters in Service as part of her plan. She faced Richard as he gripped her waist in his strong hands and lifted her. The Jingchu sisters stood together to one side, wisps of their breath curling into the chill. They were holding hands, which was a good sign. Mariska was worried about Glint's mood swings. Sometimes it seemed as if she resented getting this chance to survive. She just wanted to have the dying over with. But Didit kept pulling her back from despair.

Richard was concentrating so hard on lowering Mariska into the suit that she couldn't help herself. She touched his neck. He glanced up, about to apologize, but she winked at him. "Permission to nap?" She tugged the lanyard of the override around his neck. "*Sir?*"

He grinned. "Permission granted."

She shivered as he sealed her into the suit. Was this the last time anyone would ever touch her? Bad thought. No bad thoughts. "Ninety-six days," she said. "We can do this, right?"

Richard and Didit answered, "Right." Glint just glared; she still thought that Mariska was abandoning them.

"No chores, understand? Let the crud run wild. And sleep as much as you can."

"We will," said Didit.

"Just remember to wake up when it's time to swap my bottles."

Richard handed her the helmet. "Don't worry."

She tried to think of what else she could say to keep from saying goodbye. "This is it, then." Mariska could feel her throat closing; she didn't want them to see how scared she was. "Okay monkeys, out of here before you freeze to death." She lowered the helmet to the collar and Richard locked it to the spacesuit. She felt a tear pool at the corner of her eye, but the helmet's tinted faceplate hid it nicely.

So, how was she going to do this? She didn't really know how to trigger the hibernation response. The one time she had done it had been five years ago. That had been the first time she had tried to escape from her mother, by running away three years into the future. She had been furious at Natalya Volochkova then. Had that had anything to do with it? She was still mad at her, but not as much as she had been. She tried working up some hate for Beep but all she could think about were his two bottles of oxygen. Six hours, and then? Maybe she should get mad at herself for signing on to crew on the *Shining Legend*. Bucket monkey—the worst job in space. And now she might die a bucket monkey. Bad thought. No bad thoughts. She did the math again while she waited for something to happen. She had thirty-seven bottles. Each could provide three hours of oxygen, plus or minus ninety seconds. Altogether, a hundred and eleven hours. *Sweetspot* claimed the soonest the rescue ship could rendezvous was ninety-five days, plus or minus maybe half a day. Altogether, two thousand, two hundred, and eighty hours. Plus or minus. But if she hibernated she might reduce her oxygen intake to as low as four percent of normal. Four percent of two thousand, two hundred, and eighty hours was ninety-one hours. That meant she only needed ninety-one hours of oxygen and had a hundred and eleven hours bottled. Plus or minus. Was four percent possible? She didn't know. The first and only time she had hibernated it hadn't been in a hibernation pod with the proper euthermic arousal protocols. She had induced it by sheer willpower in her bed on Haworth. And at room temperature. They said afterward that she was crazy to try it, lucky to survive. But this time she had the cold on her side. Four percent. Ninety-one hours.

And if five percent was the best she could do? Bad thought. No bad thoughts.

Mariska wasn't as big as Beep, and subtracting her consumption from the load on the electrolytic cells only gained the crew another twenty-four days. But twenty-four and seventy-two would stretch the oxygen resupply reserve to ninety-six days. Which was exactly when they would rendezvous with the rescue ship from Mars.

Plus or minus.

Mariska felt good. Cold, but good. The numbers added up. They could do this. All she had to do was close her eyes and stop breathing so much.

Mariska's blood was pounding. Her fingers throbbed and it felt as if someone kept clapping hands over her ears. She thought her heart might explode. Time to open her eyes.

Storage. She knew this was Storage. But where was Storage? Someplace full of floating bottles. And Richard. His name was FiveFord and he could drown in a glass of water. She could see that he wasn't very smart, sleeping in Storage when he was supposed to be doing something. Something. She was gasping and her throat was sandpaper. She thought she should go back to sleep. Or die. But then there were other people in Storage. People in spacesuits. One of them pushed Richard aside and he crashed into a wall. Mariska wished he would wake up. She blinked because her eyes were filling with smoke. Then Spacesuit Person was in front of her. Shaking her. This must be the rescue. *Yay!* She couldn't tell who it was at first because the helmet had a mirror face. Then she saw the name. Black letters below the collar. *Volochkova.* That was her name. Mariska giggled. Was she rescuing herself? Why didn't Richard FiveFord get up? This was what they had been waiting for.

Xu Jingchu didn't look much like Didit or Glint to Mariska. She was old and her life had tugged at her. She was Earthborn, a head taller than Mariska, and her loose muscles and spindly posture made her look as if she were suffering from some wasting sickness.

And she was grieving.

"When Glint said that she wanted to make one more run, I swear I fought her," said Xu Jingchu. "I wanted her to learn the business, not qualify as senior crew." The old woman had Mariska's hand in hers. "I'd already arranged for her to work at *Sweetspot*, move on to the materials processing division. But she insisted on one more chance at cargo. Why?" She kept rubbing her finger across Mariska's palm. "I don't even shop for myself anymore, so why should she be fetching ice and loading ore into buckets?"

Mariska was exhausted and just wanted Xu Jingchu to go away. The old woman was no longer talking to her—she had been arguing with her dead daughter for the last few minutes. Mariska let her head fall back on the pillow of the hospital bed, hoping that her mother would pick up on the signal.

"She was proud," said Natalya Volochkova. "She wanted to do her best."

"Proud." Jingchu's expression was bitter. "Of dying for nothing?"

"Glint and Didit were very brave." Natalya Volochkova stood up. "They fought right to the end. They just ran out of time."

"Yes." Xu Jingchu squeezed Mariska's hand and let go. "Yes, they were good girls." She stood too. "I appreciate everything you did, Dr. Volochkova. I know you took extraordinary measures to save them."

"I couldn't have done anything without you."

She bowed in acknowledgement. "As you say, time ran out. Thank you, Mariska, for seeing me. I hope we can meet again under more pleasant circumstances." She gathered herself to leave.

"Excuse me," said Mariska. "But did Glint ever visit Earth?"

Xu Jingchu looked puzzled. "No, not really. Of course the clinic was in Chicago so they were born there. But they were tweaked for space. Staying in Earth gravity would've been agony." Her expression darkened. "Why?"

"I just wondered if she had ever seen the sky."

"The sky?"

"Mariska is still not herself." Her mother rested a hand on Xu Jingchu's arm. "We came close to losing her too."

She nodded and a wisp of white hair fell across her forehead. "Of course." She let herself be led away.

Natalya Volochkova had been right. It had been a mistake to see Xu Jingchu so soon. And now her mother had rescued her from the sad old woman. Mariska was still getting used to the idea that Natalya Volochkova might not be the enemy. Had she come back into the room then, Mariska would have tried to thank her. But her mother was still trying not to push herself on Mariska.

Mariska had learned meditation as part of her spacer training, and her doctors kept urging her to try it now, find a silence in herself that would give her peace. But what had happened still roared through her mind. The *Shining Legend's* shipbrain had captured the crew's last moments. Glint and Didit had died in each other's arms in the wardroom, but Richard, the strongest of them, had muscled his way to her even as the oxygen levels in his blood crashed. He had died changing her last bottle. She couldn't imagine being that brave. She knew she hadn't earned that kind of devotion.

To escape these dark thoughts, she called up a feed she had been working on.

A dusty dirt road cut across a grassy field. The sky above was the deep blue of the oceans as seen from space. It had a delicious weight, as if it had been filled with more air than any sky had ever been. Mariska stood on the side of the road as a parade of animals passed: cows and polar bears and elephants and two zebras wearing top hats and a whale with squat legs. Didit, Glint and Richard drove up in a bathtub filled with water. Didit waved.

=We set up a tent.=

Mariska looked up. =Nice sky.=

Glint smiled. =Not too blue?=

=Perfect.=

Richard leaned out of the bathtub reaching for Mariska. She stepped back. =Coming?=

She shook her head. =Not yet.=

=Want us to wait?=

She shook her head again. Richard pulled his arm back into the bathtub and tapped Didit on the shoulder.

Mariska watched them go. In the distance she could hear the tootle of a pipe organ.

THE MAN WITH THE KNIVES
ELLEN KUSHNER

Ellen Kushner was born in Washington, DC, and raised in Cleveland, Ohio. She attended Bryn Mawr College and graduated from Barnard College. Her first novel, *Swordspoint: A Melodrama of Manners*, introduced the fantasy world to Riverside, to which she has since returned in *The Fall of the Kings* (written with Delia Sherman), *The Privilege of the Sword*, and several short stories, including the one that follows. Her second novel, *Thomas the Rhymer*, won the Mythopoeic Award and the World Fantasy Award. Kushner is also the editor of *Basilisk* and *The Horns of Elfland* (co-edited with Don Keller and Delia Sherman), and has taught writing at the Clarion and Odyssey workshops. Upcoming is anthology *Welcome to Bordertown* (co-edited with Holly Black) and the audio drama *The Witches of Lublin* (co-written with Yale Strom and Elizabeth Schwartz). Kushner lives in Manhattan, on Riverside Drive, with her partner, the author and editor Delia Sherman.

Her father had told her a story about a sailor who fell out of love with the sea, so he put his oar up on his shoulder and walked inland far and far, until he finally met someone who looked at the oar and said, "What's that thing you're carrying, friend?" and there he stayed. Her father told her he had done much the same thing himself: crossed from the mainland to the island, and then walked inland through the hills and forests until he found a place where no one could read a book, and settled there with his little daughter. He gave the villagers what he could in the way of physick, and taught Sofia to read and to do the same. Her father was gone, now, and here she was, alone with them all, with her goats and her garden at the edge of a village full of people who had never read a book.

And so she remained, not getting any younger, until the man with the knives appeared.

He was going to die here, he was going to cough up his lungs and shiver away to nothingness in a place where no one knew his name. When he fled the house by the sea he had taken his rings with him. They told the story of who he was, but here they were a book no one could read. He kept them in a pouch inside his shirt, along with his surgical knives and two books on anatomy, plus a hunk of dry cheese he was too weak to chew. He was going to die here in the forest of someone else's land, like an old crow or an abandoned dog. Then he saw the light and thought, "Under a roof, at least."

The man on the doorstep could barely breathe, let alone talk. She was used to sick villagers turning up at odd hours, but this one she didn't recognize. He was not young. His face was gray, and he was soaked and shivering. He couldn't hurt her.

"Come in," she said.

For a moment he took his hands away from his mouth and his chest, held them open to her in an odd gesture that seemed to say, "I have nothing." Then he doubled over onto his knees, hacking and gasping for breath. She practically dragged him to the fire, where water was always boiling. "Take your clothes off," she said, and he laughed, pounding his chest for air. She handed him a dry blanket and turned pointedly away from him, rummaging for syrups and compounds. What she gave him to drink made him fall asleep right there by the hearth, clutching her old gray wool blanket, the one Eudoxa had given her for saving her baby, who was now a mother herself.

He was in the earth he was in the earth someone was trying to bury him and pouring earth strange earth into his lungs he couldn't breathe and Shhh, said the sea washing over him, Shushh, it's all right, sleep now…. It was only sleep, not death.

She touched his head. His hair grew thick , but was all patchy and uneven on his head. She checked to see if he had mange, but that wasn't it. Someone had cut chunks of it off, with a knife, maybe?

They brought his lover up from the sea, from the rocks under their window. He had heard nothing, would never know if he had cried out as he slipped from the rocks. The sea roared too loudly there. It had been their bedtime music for years, the sea at night, and by day, the bees in the wild red thyme in the mountains above the house.

They told him, He's dead, lord, and he said, No, never. He is not friend to death. Death fears him. They told him he could look, and he moved through the colonnaded porch and suddenly Marina, the housekeeper, stood in the way saying, Lord, don't look, but he looked past her and saw, no blood, no blood no blood, just something very very broken, and no blood at all so he took the nearest sharp thing and ran it down his arm, and they bound his arm saying it was too much, too much too soon, time enough for that at the burial and he started shouting, What? What? Are you insane? but he was using the wrong words; their faces showed they did not understand him.

Usually she touched her patients only enough to diagnose and treat them, leaving the nursing to the women of the family. But here, alone, she was all there was. And so she bathed his body, like a mother, or a wife. He was modest; he'd tried to stop her. But he stank, and she wasn't having that. She told him he'd like being clean, and she put wild red thyme in the hot water for him, to help clear his chest. He wept as the scent rose.

Everyone let out their few drops of blood, and clipped a bit of hair to lay on— to lay on the— He'd let his blood already; he took the knife and hacked at his hair, the hair that had lain across his lover's breast, tangled in his hands and covered his eyes—

"Do you like it?" he'd asked, when they came in sight of the island for the very first time.

"I can see colors, some. It's beautiful."

"Where do you come from?" she asked the sleeping man, who coughed as he slept. To her alarm, he turned his head to her, opened his eyes, and said clearly: "I have knives." But that was all; he'd been dreaming her and her question. His eyes closed again, his head turned away.

The knives were not to sever him from his past, or even to separate him from other people They were to go deeper, see more, know more. He didn't want to hurt anyone, not even himself, anymore. Not here. Not on an island where honey ran sweet in the comb, where the bees sang one kind of song in sweet-smelling thyme, and the sea sang another against black rocks below the white house they made together, a long porch to shade them from the sun, and windows open at night for the crash and hiss of the waves, to remind them that they were on an island, that it would take a ship with sails to find them, or to take them away.

It was strange to find she did not ask his name. She thought he would not willingly give it to her. Maybe she simply didn't need it, since there were only two of them, alone there in her house away from the village. It was a quiet month, with no babies born, no sudden fevers or falls from rocks. After his storm, the weather was benign.

If he could have torn out his own eyes to stop the visions coming, he would have done it. But he saw more sharply with his eyes closed: his lover under the earth, in it, part of it, defenseless and undefended. With nothing else to see, that's what he saw.

She saw: The day he breathed most deeply. The night he slept without waking. The night he slept without screaming. The morning he hauled himself up onto his feet, the blanket wrapped around himself, and silently took the bucket from her hand. The night he moved his bedding out to the shed, by the goats.

The day he found the soup was burning, and cleaned out the pot, and made soup fresh.

No one else knew that she actually burned soup, though she was sure they all suspected it.

He staggered away from the place where the vision was the sharpest, stumbling over rocks, through the brush that grew along the sea and away from it, up into hills with forests where no one would find him, through villages where no one knew his name. He ate what they gave him. His useless body he gave to the wind and the rain. But they spat it back at him. And so he took it along to the next farmstead, the next village, where people asked who he was and what he wanted, and he had no words for them.

The night she touched his chest, to see if the lungs were clear, and touched his brow to see if the fever was gone, and touched his throat to see if the breath was strong.

It had been night. Night, and the wind. He had not heard his lover leave the bed, had not even felt his weight shift away. His lover often went for walks at night; it was not much darker to him than day. He liked to fight the wind along the cliffs above the waves.

The night she touched his brow to see if the skin was cool, and touched his lips to see if he felt her there, and touched his face to see how he held her gaze.

The waves stopped roaring when she touched him. The world grew very small. There was nothing inside him but what she was looking for.
When she gazed at him, she saw no one he knew.

Already she knew his body well, and so she was not astonished, when she lay in his arms at last, at the whiteness of his skin where the sun had never been. She was barely astonished to be there at all; it was as if his body had been calling her from the start, glowing like candleflame even beneath his rags, and she the moth drawn to the heat of his skin, his white, fine-grained skin, his long and supple hands, his sharp and delicate bones, his harsh and fallen face with its green eyes, a green like nothing else she'd ever seen in a living being.

He let her explore him, let her discover herself through him. It was as if she was reading a book, soaking up learning, following letters with her finger, spelling out new words with her mouth.

She said, "What is your name?"
He was silent. He didn't want to hear those sounds again.

"Your name?" she asked gently, again. "Can you tell me?"

He shook his head.

"What shall I call you, then?"

He made the sound "*Camp*-ee-un."

"*Campione*? Is that good?"

He laughed and shook his head again. "No. Not good. Me."

"My name is Sofia."

"*So*-fya."

"Yes. I'm a physician. I can read. Can you read, Campione?"

"Yes. I have reading things."

"Reading things? You mean, you have read things?"

"No, no!" Again the shaking of the head, and this time he used his hands as well, spreading the fingers as if he'd dropped something he couldn't find. "Reading—to read—small-from-trees—what word?"

"'Small-from-trees'—do you mean books? You have *books* to read?"

He nodded. "I show you." So that was what was in the bundle tied up with rags, the bundle he brought that she had left alone, partly to honor his privacy, and partly, though she hated to admit it, because it was so disgusting. Inside was cleaner cloth, and then… the books.

Anatomy. Drawings of the insides of people—truths she'd glimpsed the ragged, colorful facts of more than once as she worked to save someone, but here they were, laid out in black and white like a map. Dispassionate and true. And also in black and white, patterned unrecognizable, were letters making words she did not know. His language, his words.

She could barely speak. "Who made these? Where did you get them?"

He shook his head.

She spoke. He listened. He found words at need. When he was alone, he thought only in the words that she would understand. To look, to feel, needed no words. What she wanted, and what she gave. What he could give her now.

"I am not young," he would murmur regretfully into her hair. His speech was broken, oddly accented and missing words, but that phrase he knew. "Sorry. I am not beautiful now."

She wanted to tell him men were not supposed to be beautiful, but "You are to me," she'd say, speaking the truth.

He spread his hands open, lacking the words to argue, just laughing ruefully, as though that were refutation enough.

"You see me," she explained doggedly, wanting to convince him. "And I see you."

He stiffened against her embrace, as though she'd angered or insulted him; but she waited, and he relaxed again, melting against her bones.

"You not know me," he muttered.

"True. It's funny that you make me happy."

"Funny laughing?"

"No." She chuckled. "Well, a little. Funny—" She tickled him, and delighted to feel him squirm like a child— "Funny like strange."

"I am stranger."

"Yes," she said; "you are that."

He knew that she had brought him back to life. When he felt the sun on his arms, when he smelt sage and lavender and rosemary as he turned the earth in her garden, when he smiled because she called to him across the yard, he knew he owed her everything. She remade the world.

When he gave her joy, sometimes in his own release he'd howl like a woman in childbirth. She had witnessed that sort of pain enough that it scared her. But she learned that it was over a moment later. Herself, in joy, she sang: long, loud summer and midwinter carols she hadn't known her throat was capable of.

"Why don't you sing?" she asked him bravely once, her face buried in the fold between his armpit and his chest. It took him a long time to understand her—and then he answered, "Most men don't."

Once, though, he shouted out a word—screamed it, pleading with his body and the night before he fell down onto her, dense and heavy as clay. She tried to hold him, but he rolled away from her, shielding himself with palms outturned, warding off something only he could see.

She said, "My love?" and he gasped, "Yes, words—words to me, please—" and, baffled, she started to sing, a silly children's song about a goat on a hillside. He drew in deep breaths, asked her a question about what a line meant, and was himself again.

The word he'd kept shouting out was his own language. Was it a name, perhaps? As sometimes she cried out his in her pleasure?

The next day, while she swept out the cottage and pounded herbs into paste at her workbench, she thought about the fact that there had been others. Others before her. Did she mind that she was not his first love, though he was hers? Did she care? She cared a little, she decided. She did not like to think of him loving someone else. But it was entirely unreasonable to *mind*.

"My hair, so white—"

"I like it. Was it darker once?"

"Yes. More darker, yes. Old, now. Bad."

"You are not bad. The goats like you. You take very good care of them."

"Goats…."

"Say it. Say, 'I am good.'"

"I am goat."

"No, *good*."

"You. Are. Good."

It couldn't last, and she knew it couldn't last. It was her life, after all, to be woken at all hours, to be summoned urgently to human horrors and discomforts; even he couldn't change that. When the knocking and shouting outside the door began, smashing their bubble of dark and cozy sleep, she rolled over, untangled and pushed him away, fumbling for her nightgown and a blanket to go to the door.

"Come quick!" Markos, his face flushed in the lantern light. "Oh come quick, please come, we've found him—"

She hadn't even known a man was missing. No one had told her, or asked her to join the search.

Sofia dressed in a blur, by the light of a lamp her lover must have lit. She found her bag of bandages and salves by rote, and was out the door with Markos. A second man came behind them, the tall stranger. He followed them to a house, where old Stephan was laid out on the floor, moaning like the wind.

Sofia knelt. They brought her light. They kept trying to tell her what had happened. She shut out the sounds and only looked and felt. It was the leg, the left leg. Around the knee was horribly swollen. Broken? Stephan shouted when she tried to move it.

Sofia closed her eyes. Behind them she saw, clear and black and white, the diagram in Campione's books. The knee, and the threads that connected the joints under the muscles. And then she knew.

When it was finished, the last bandage neatly tied, and Stephan nearly drowned in wine and snoring happily, dawn was breaking. By the gray light she saw Campione accepting a cup of hot tea. But he didn't drink it; he gave it to her. The whole house watched while she drank it, and then the women kissed her and rubbed her hands with cloths dipped in lemon water.

"Who's this, then?" Old Marya nodded at the tall stranger.

"My servant," Sofia said quickly, before she could think. "He helps me with my goats. And carries my things. He came to me in the rains, looking for work." Was she talking too much? "He sleeps in the goatshed. I let him sleep there."

"Is he mute?"

"Sometimes," Campione answered.

Marya laughed, displaying all that was left of her teeth. "You should mend the healer's roof. Just stand on a goat; you're tall enough you don't even need a ladder!"

Campione smiled thinly and ducked his head. Sofia could tell he'd barely understood one word.

The language was a mask that he put on, like those masks they had for the crazy torchlit parties on the streets of his old city, hiding his true face. Weirdly, masks transformed not only faces. When they tied theirs on, his graceful friends became tottering old men or prancing beasts, mincing maidens or loping fools. The mask went deep.

Not deep enough. He wanted true transformation: to lose the memory of torches, friends and streets—to forget there ever was a mask at all. To become the thing he mimed. To lose what he had been.

"When I was a girl, after my father died, I found a bird dead in the wood. I opened it with my knife, then and there, to see what was inside."

"Yes?"

"I've never told anyone this."

"Tell me."

She did know other stories. The one about the girl whose lover came to her every night, strong and lovely in the dark. Her sisters scared her into burning him with light—and then began the girl's sorrows, and her wanderings.

The girl in that story was a young thing, though, with friends and family she thought that she could trust. Sofia was a woman, and kept her own counsel.

The villagers asked him: How are you? and he said: Well. They asked him, Where is your lady? and he said: Garden.

They asked him, Where do you come from? and he said: I don't understand.

"Where do you come from?"

It trembled on her tongue a hundred times a day, but she never let it take shape in the air between them, even in the dark when her tongue was velvet night on the star-spangled sky of his skin. Instead she said, "I am happy. I am so happy with you. I never thought I could be happy like this."

He didn't really have the words to argue, and finally he stopped trying.

On the other side of the world, on the other side of sleep, was a city he had loved with his whole heart. There came a time when his shadow began to stretch across it more and more, taking up too much room, until it wasn't his city anymore. His city was one where he and his lover lurked, notorious and indecipherable.

They'd needed a place where they could be unknown again, the peerless swordsman and the mad aristocrat. A place that didn't need them, didn't care how they had held men's lives in their hand; the swordsman, flawed, turned recluse, the nobleman, overreaching, turned rogue. They needed a place where they could matter only to each other. An island, with a house above the sea.

It had been sweet, so sweet. He thought he'd gotten it right, this time. He thought they could be happy, alone. Hadn't they both been happy? Hadn't they?

They brought him up from the sea, no blood no blood. The dead eyes would not look at him.

During the daylight, they were careful not to touch too much. Her cottage was isolated, but not remote. Anyone could come running up at any time—and that is what happened, on a bright, clear afternoon. Sofia was trying to mend a basket with reeds, so that she didn't have to ask someone in the village to do it for her again, and Campione was indicating they might need to be soaked in water first, when they heard a rustle, and a cry, and it was young Antiope, wailing that her husband had fallen, fallen from a tree nearby, gone high in a tree to pick lemons that she fancied in her condition god help her, while everyone else was picking olives, and now—and now—

His friends brought Illyrian, staggering between them, gasping for air. Sofia got his shirt off, laid him down, felt his ribs. His chest moved in and out as it should—but he was choking. It was something inside him, something she couldn't feel, something she couldn't see. Illy's lips began to turn blue. Unable to breathe he was drowning on dry land.

Campione was beside her, holding something. A book? Couldn't he see it was too late for drawings and diagrams? He opened it. It was a case, a case full of exquisite knives.

"Please," Campione said. "Hold." He didn't mean the knives; he meant Illyrian. Sofia took the boy's shoulders. She watched in horror as Campione drove the little knife between the boy's ribs.

Antiope screamed and screamed. Campione shoved a reed into the wound, and blood gushed out of it. But before anyone could attack the man, Illyrian breathed. A great *whoosh* of air into his lungs, and the color returned to his face, while the blood poured out the reed.

Campione shrugged. "Please," he said again; "hold."

He meant the reed, this time. Sofia took it from him, careful to keep it in place, watching, fascinated, as the young man breathed steadily and the blood drained out of his chest.

Illy's young wife covered his face in kisses. Their friends stood a respectful distance from Campione, who took his knife to clean.

His hands shook, putting the knives away. He had his back to them all; they couldn't see. They'd think that he had done all this before.

They moved Illyrian into her house to watch all night, watching his breath for when the blood returned, to unstopper the reed and let it out again. A rib had broken inside, and pierced a vein, it seemed. She fed him wine mixed with poppy, and as the dawn came, Illy's color deepened, rosy, like the sky, his breath quiet as dawn wind, and the bleeding ended.

Campione sewed up the wound his knife had made. She felt sick, sick with love for him and sick with wanting to know all that he knew.

He'd taken up something new to study, now that he had time. How amusing, here on this island, to be the one who wielded the steel! The little instruments, sharp and precise. You needed sure eyes and a steady hand. He hardly dared to use them, but he read the books and tried. He wasted paper tracing the diagrams, slicing them with a scalpel taken from its velvet case, small and fine as a pen. He modeled chests and legs and stomachs out of wet clay, made his incisions and excisions, grumbling at how hard it was to clean the knives afterwards, while his lover laughed at him:

"You should have let me teach you the sword, back home, after all. It's so much easier to clean."

"For your man," they said now, when they brought her a chicken, or some cheese, or a bottle of red wine. "Be sure you share it with the man with the knives."

She did not ask to look at the knives again. He never took them out when she was there. But she knew the knives came out when she was gone. He would show her when he was ready, she thought. She could look at his books, and study them, and wait.

He cried, so, in his sleep.

His lover often went for walks at night; it was not much darker to him than day, and there were fewer people about. He liked to fight the wind.

Night, and the wind. He had not heard him leave the bed, had not felt his weight shift away.

Hadn't they both been happy? Hadn't they?

In his sleep, she learned his language from his dreams. She learned the words for *No*, and *Stop*. She heard him speak in tones she never heard him use by day, dry and acerbic, like powdered lime without any honey.

His lover was a swordsman, with nothing to fight now but the wind.
His lover could see nothing in the dark, and not much more by day.
Had he seen where the rocks ended and the night sky began?
Had the wind caught him, challenged him, and won?

She did not mean to spy on him. It was a hot day. She had been weeding; he'd been washing clothes. He'd hung them out all over the big bushes of rosemary and thyme to dry sweetly in the sun, and he'd gone inside her thick-walled house to rest, she thought. After a while, she went herself, to get out of the heat.

She opened the door, and stopped.

Her love was sitting at her long table, the case of knives open before him.

She watched him pick up each knife in turn, hold it up to the light, and touch himself lightly with it, as if deciding which one should know him more deeply.

She watched him place the tip of one to his arm, and gently press, and watch the blood run down.

"Campione," she said from the doorway.

He spoke some words she didn't understand. He cut himself in yet another place.

"Bad?" she asked.

He answered her again in that other tongue. But at least he laid the knife aside as the words came pouring out of him, thick and fast and liquid.

"I understand," she said; "I understand."

"You don't." He looked at her. "You cannot."

"You're hurt," she said. He shrugged, and ran his thumb over the shallow cuts he'd made, as if to erase them. "No, hurt inside. You see what is not bearable to see. I know."

"I see it in my mind," he muttered. "So clear—so clear—clear and bad, I see."

She came behind him, now, and touched his arms. "Is there no medicine for your grief?"

He folded his face between her breasts, hearing her living heartbeat.

"Can I cure you, Campione?"

And he said, "No."

"Can I try?" she asked.

And he said, "Try."

They brought his lover up from the sea, from the rocks under their window. He hadn't heard him fall, would never know if he had cried out in surprise, or silently let himself slip from the rocks and into the sea that surrounded them.

The man with the knives married her on midsummer's day. There were bonfires, and feasting and dancing. He got pretty drunk, and danced with everyone. Everyone seemed happy in her happiness. They jumped over the dying fire, and into their new life together.

And, carefully, he placed the feel of her warm, living flesh over the dread of what he had left, buried, for the earth to touch, on the other side of the island; what he'd left, buried, for the earth to take of what he once had; for the earth to take away the beauty that had been taken away from him by a foot that had slipped, sure as it was always sure, out into the space that would divide them forever.

THE JAMMIE DODGERS AND THE ADVENTURE OF THE LEICESTER SQUARE SCREENING
CORY DOCTOROW

Cory Doctorow is the co-editor of the popular *Boing Boing* website (boingboing.net), a co-founder of the internet search-engine company OpenCola.com, and until recently was the outreach coordinator for the Electronic Frontier Foundation (www.eff.org). In 2001, he won the John W. Campbell Award as the year's Best New Writer. His stories have appeared in *Asimov's, Science Fiction Age, The Infinite Matrix, On Spec, Salon,* and elsewhere, and were collected in *A Place So Foreign and Eight More* and *Overclocked*. His well-received first novel, *Down and Out in the Magic Kingdom,* won the Locus Award as Best First Novel, and was followed shortly by a second novel, *Eastern Standard Tribe,* then by *Someone Comes to Town, Someone Leaves Town, Little Brother,* and *Makers.* Doctorow's other books include *The Complete Idiot's Guide to Publishing Science Fiction,* written with Karl Schroeder, a guide to *Essential Blogging,* written with Shelley Powers, and, most recently, *Content: Selected Essays of Technology, Creativity, Copyright, and the Future of the Future.* His most recent book is novel *For the Win.*

There is a phone, there is a phone, there is a phone like no phone that was ever hatched by the feverish imaginations of the world's phone manufacturers, a phone so small and so featureful and so *perfect* for my needs that it couldn't possibly have lasted. And it didn't. And so now I hunt the phone, and now I have

found

the

phone!

I saw it sitting in the window of the Cash Converters in the Kentish Town High Street. This little pawn-shop was once a tube-station, believe it or not, used as a bomb-shelter during the Blitz, and you can still find photos of the brave Sons and Daughters of England sleeping in ranks on the platform rolled up in blankets like subterranean grubs waiting to hatch, sheltering from Hitler's bombers as they screamed overhead. Now the top of the station is a pawn-broker's, and around the back there's a "massage parlour" that offers discreet services for the discerning gentleman.

I am no gentleman, but I *am* discerning. And what I was discerning right *now* is a HTC Screenparty Mark I phone, circa 2014, running some ancient and crumbly version of Google's Android operating system and there, right *there*, on the back panel, is a pair of fisheye lenses: one is the camera. The other is the *projector*.

That's the business, that projector. The Screenparty I was the first-ever phone ever delivered with a little high-powered projector built into it, and the only Android phone that had one, because ten minutes after it shipped, Apple dusted off some old patent on putting projectors in handheld devices and used the patent to beat the Screenparty I to death. And yes, there were projectors in the iPhones that followed, but you couldn't do what I planned on doing with an iPhone, not with all the spyware and copyright rubbish that Apple's evil wizards have crammed into their pocket-sized jailers.

I had to have that Screenparty. So I squared up my shoulders and pulled my scarf tighter around my neck, and I thought, *You are a respectable fellow, you are a respectable fellow. You did not eat garbage this morning. You did not sleep in an abandoned building. You did not grow up on a council estate. You are a bloody toff.* A deep breath—fog in the cold air—and I was through the door, winking back at the CCTV that peered down at me from the ceiling, then smiling my best smile at the lad behind the counter, who looks like any kid from my estate, skinny and jug-eared with too many spots that are the color that spots go when you pick at them.

"Hello there, my son," I said, putting on the voice that a toff would use if he wanted to sound like he was being matey and not at all superior.

The lad grinned. "You like the phone, mister? Saw you lookin' at it. Just got it in, that one."

"It's a funny little thing. I remember when they first came out. Never worked very well. But they were good fun, when they did."

The lad reached into the window—the shop was that small, he didn't even have to get off his chair—and plucked out the phone. I saw that it was absolutely cherry—mint condition, the plastic film still covering the screen. Which meant that the battery was almost certainly in good nick, too. That was good—no one made batteries for the Screenparty anymore. He handed it to me and fished behind the counter for a mains-cable, then passed that over, too. I plugged one into the other and hit the power button. The phone chimed, began to play its animation and then the projector lit up, splashing its startup routine on the ceiling's grimy acoustic tiles, a montage of happy people all over the world watching movies that were being projected from their happy little phones and played against nearby walls.

I waited for it to finish booting up its ancient operating system with something like nostalgia, seeing old icons and chrome I hadn't seen since I was a boy. Then I tapped around and finally said, "You won't be wanting much for this, I suppose. A fiver?" It was worth more than five pounds, but I was betting that the lad didn't really know *what* it was worth, and by starting the bidding very low, I reckoned I could keep the final price from going too high. (Well, it couldn't go *too* high, since all I had in my pocket was ten pounds plus some change).

The boy shook his head and made to put the phone away. "You're having a laugh. Something like this, worth a lot more than five quid."

I shrugged. "If that's how you feel." I sprinkled a little wave at him and turned for the door.

"Wait!" he said. "What about twenty?"

I snorted. "Son," I said. "That phone was obsolete four years ago. It's a miracle that it even works. If it breaks, no one'll be able to mend it. Can't even buy a battery for it. Five pounds is a good price for a little fun, a gizmo that you can amuse the boys with at the pub."

He took the phone out of the window. "I got all the packaging and whatnot, too. Came in from a storage locker that went into arrears, the company sold off the contents for the back-rent. Will you go ten?"

I shook my head. "Five is my offer." I had noticed something when I came into the shop, a little ace in the hole, and so now I fished it out. "Five, and a bit of information."

The boy rolled his eyes. I upped my mental estimate of him a little. Pawnbrokers must get every chancer and twit in the world coming over their threshold with some baroque hustle or other.

"I'll give you the information and you can decide if you think it's worth it, how about that?"

The boy narrowed his eyes, nodded a fraction of an inch.

"That game back there, that old DSi cartridge in its box, just there?" I pointed, then quickly put my hand back down. I forgot about the new cuts there, a little run-in with some barbed wire, not the sort of thing a toff would have. The boy reached into his case and pulled it out: *Star Wars Cantina Dance Off*, he said, setting it down on the glass. The box was a little scuffed, but still presentable.

"Google it," I said. He snorted and turned around to get his phone. In one smooth motion, I dropped the Screenparty in my pocket with one hand and opened the door with the other. One step backwards took me over the threshold, and I pivoted on my back foot so I was facing forward and did a runner, lighting off up the Kentish Town High Street toward the back streets, down the canal embankment, and off along the towpath. As I ran, I thumbed my panic button in my coat pocket and the infra-red LEDs sewn into my jacket all went to max intensity, blinding ever CCTV I passed.

Yes, I stole the bloody phone. But that lad got the best of the deal, have no fear: *Cantina Dance Off* had a secret mode that let you make Jabba get up to all kinds of disgusting sexy things with slave-girl Leia, not to mention what you could get Chewbacca to do to R2D2. It was pulled off the shelves in 48 hours and is the rarest video-game ever sold. As of today, copies are changing hands for upwards of 15,000 quid. So yeah, I stole the phone. But I *could* have bought *Dance Off* for three pounds and flogged it for 15 grand. The lad got the best of the deal. I'm an honest thief.

Cecil was at his edit suite when I came back to the squat, a pub in Bow that some previous owner had driven into bankruptcy and ruin, but not before covering its ancient brickwork in horrible pebble-dashing, covering its crazed hand-painted signs up with big laser-printed vinyl banners swirling with JPEG artifacts, and covering up the worn wooden floors with cheap linoleum. The bank—or whoever owned the derelict building—had never got round to turning off the electricity which powered the boiler that kept the damp from eating the building alive.

Cecil sat cross-legged on a banquette, scowling at his screens, hands flying over his mouse and trackball, scrubbing the video on his screens back and forth. He didn't look up when I came down the stairs, having chinned myself to the upper floor by the moulding around back of the pub, through the window with the loose board. But he *did* look up when I sat the phone down in front of him, with a precise *click* as it touched the table before his keyboard. He looked at me, at the phone. Rubbed his eyes. Looked back at me.

"Oh, Fingo, you shouldn't have," he said, and smiled like a million watts at me, scratching at his stubbly chin and neck with his chewed-down fingernails. He picked up the phone in his nimble hands and turned it over and over. "Been ages since we had one of these. What'd you pay for it?"

I smiled. "15,000 pounds."

He nodded. "They're getting more expensive."

There's about eight of us in the Jammie Dodgers, which is what Cecil calls his gang. "About eight" because some come and go as their relationships with their families wax and wane. Cecil's 17 and he isn't the oldest of us—Sal is 20, and I once heard Amir admit to 22—but Cecil's got all the ideas.

Cecil and I grew up on the same estate, in a part of east London where rows of Victorian paupers' cottages had been taken over by rich children who turned the local pubs into "hotspots" where you wouldn't find anyone over 25, where the fashion designers came to spy on the club-kids for next year's "street wear" line. Pubs where you could get a pint for a couple pounds turned into places that sold "real ale" for a fiver and eye-wateringly expensive Scotch over perfectly formed ice-spheres.

We weren't mates back then, not until both our families got dragged into the mandatory "safe network use" counselling sessions. He'd been downloading his obscure Keith Kennenson videos for his Great Work, whereas I'd just been looking to fill my phone up with music. We were both kids, dumb enough to do our wicked deeds without a proxy, and so we got the infamous red disconnection notice through the door, both our families were added to the blacklist of house-holds that could not be legally connected to the net for a full year. We all got dragged down to the day-long seminars where a patronizing woman from the BPI explained how our flagrant piracy would destroy the very fabric of British society.

Between the videos where posh movie-stars and rockers explained how bad we were, and videos where the blokes that held the cameras and built the sets explained how hard they worked, Cecil and I began to pass files back and forth. He touched his phone to mine and I tapped the "allow" button and got a titanic wad of video in return. I picked out a few dozen of my favorite songs to pass back, then snuck off to the bathroom to watch, screwing in a headphone and turning the volume down.

It was about ten minutes' worth of video, and it was of Keith Kennenson, of course. I knew him because he'd just played a hard-fighting cop who fought the mob in a flooded coastal California town, but this was from much earlier. *Much* earlier. It had scenes of Kennenson as a ten-year-old, talking with his dad (a character actor I recognized, but couldn't place), then as a teenager, mouthing off to his teachers, then back to his dad—pretty sure that the character actor was in another role, but it was a very tight edit—then forward to the latest Kennenson cop role, and it became clear that this was all a flashback during a tense moment while Kennenson was hiding out from gangsters under a pier, his breath rasping in the wet dark.

"What the hell was that?" I whispered to him when I got back to my seat.

He grinned and rubbed his hands. "The Great Work," he said, pronouncing the capital letters. "You know Keith Kennenson, yeah? Well, I'm making a movie that tells the story of all the lives he's ever played, as though it were one, long life—from the kid he played on *Two Sugars, Please* to the Navy frogman in *Drums of War* to the President of the United States in *Mr President, Please!* to the supercop in *Indefatigable*—all cut together to make one incredible biopic!" He mimed a cackle and rubbed his hands together, earning us dirty looks from the BPI lady who'd been lecturing us about how poor Sir Keith Richards couldn't afford to keep up his fleet of Bentleys and Rollers if we didn't stop with our evil downloading. He ignored it. "The music you sent me looks pretty cool, too."

I felt inadequate. But I also felt like he was a certified nutter.

At the tea-break, he grabbed me by the arm and hustled me outside of the leisure centre. We hid under the climbing frame in the playground and he sparked up a gigantic spliff—"it's just something we grow in an abandoned building site, hardly gets you off," he croaked—and passed it over. Then, as the munchies overtook him, he produced an entire packet of Jammie Dodgers—shortbread cookies with raspberry jam in the middles—from under his shirt, lifted from the snacks table.

"Jammie Dodgers! It's so bloody Dickensian," he said, giggling around a mouthful of cookie crumbs and fragrant smoke.

I laughed too. "We should start a gang!" I said.

And three months later, when my mum lost her benefits because she couldn't go online to renew them and couldn't get down to the Jobcentre to queue up for them, not with her legs; when his dad lost his job because he wasn't able to put in the extra hours on email that everyone else was doing, that's exactly what we did. We'd caused our families enough trouble—it was time to hit the road.

I put the new OS onto the Screenparty while I was recharging it. It was finicky work—the phone was so old that I had to update it three times before I could get it to the stage where it would even accept the latest bootleg Android flavour, the one with all the video codecs, even the patented ones. I was worried I'd end up bricking it, but I managed it. Thank Spaghetti Monster for HOWTOs!

But the battery wouldn't take the charge. Age or a manufacturing defect had turned it into a dud. That sent me on another net-trawl, looking for a recipe to convert another battery for use. Turned out that HTC had followed Nokia's lead in putting in a bunch of crypto on a little chip on the battery that it used to authenticate to the phone, to prove that it was a real, licensed battery—so I had to get a similar HTC battery and transfer the auth chip to it, which was even more finicky. It took the rest of the day, but when Cecil put one caffeine-shaky hand on my shoulder around 10PM, I was able to turn and beam at him and show him the phone in full glory. He beamed back at me and I knew I'd done right by him.

"You're a true maestro," he said, hefting the phone. Some of our fellow Jammie Dodgers had drifted in and out through my works that day, and now they filed in behind Cecil and giggled and poked each other like naughty children. Cecil rubbed the phone against a thumb drive and transferred his cut, then walked to the window, slid away the board, aligned the projector's eye with the crack and then used his laser-pointer to find the mirror he'd set into the wall of the tall council high-rise opposite the pub. He was trying to get the pointer to bounce off the mirror and then show up on the large, blank wall of the adjacent high-rise.

Once he had the shot lined up, he fitted a little monocle to the projector's eye and tapped at the phone's screen. A moment later, the phone's speaker started to play the familiar sting music he used for his Great Work, and I rushed to the next window to see the result. At first, it was just a big, fuzzy blur on the blank wall, a watery light-show. My heart sank—it wasn't going to work after all.

But as Cecil turned the monocle's focus dial, the image sharpened, and sharpened again, and then it was as if I was watching a film at a big, open air cinema—like one of those American drive-in theatres. There was no sound, but that was all right: there was Keith Kennenson, in his role as an angry priest struggling with alcoholism in inner-city Boston in *Whiskey and the Drum*, tearing off his dog-collar as he lost his faith, storming out the door, and now he was walking down a street that wasn't Boston at all—it was the moon base from

Skyjacked!, and the cut was so smooth that you'd swear they were one movie, and Kennenson bounded down the ramp toward the main door where the bomber had hidden his charge, Kennenson's face a grim mask—

He clicked the phone off. The Jammie Dodgers lost our minds. "It worked, it worked!" We danced ring-a-rosie like toddlers and collapsed in each other's arms.

"Right, all good," he said. "Tomorrow night we move."

It's amazing what a lot of respect high-viz vest and a couple of traffic pylons will get you, even in Leicester Square. We started work at 8AM, when the only people in the square were a long queue of tourists waiting for cheap theatre tickets and a few straights clicking over the pavement in their work shoes as they rushed for offices in Soho. Between me and Sal and Amir, we got nine little "security mirrors" placed on the walls of strategic buildings in less than an hour. At one point, a Community Support Officer—one of those fake coppers who sign up for the sheer thrill of the authority—even directed traffic around our ladder. I was glad of all the little IR LEDs I'd strung unobtrusively around my helmet then, for they surely blew out the cameras in his hat and epaulettes.

It was Cecil that hired the hotel room overlooking the square, using a pre-paid debit card from a newsagent's. They asked for his national ID card and he claimed in a funny mid-Atlantic drawl that he'd emigrated to the States ten years before and never been issued one, and said that his passport was at the Russian embassy getting a business-traveller's visa glued into it. They accepted a California "driver's license" that I made up at the squat, decorating it with a wide variety of impressive security holograms that I printed from a little specialist ID printer I found at an industrial surplus store. I was worried I'd overdone it—one of the holos was almost certainly a Masonic symbol—but the desk clerk just put it down on the photocopier and took a copy. The holograms did a great job of blocking Cecil's face on the copy.

From then, it was just a waiting game. Waiting for the sun to set. Waiting for the crowds to fill the square. Waiting for the first film showings to let in, the huge queues snaking around the square as each attendee had his phone and electronics taken off and put into storage during the movie. Then the second screening. Finally, at 11:30, the square was well-roaring: everyone who'd been at the second show, everyone queued up for the third show, everyone spilling out of the pubs—a heaving mass of humanity.

You can fit eight Jammie Dodgers into a single-occupancy Leicester Square hotel room. Provided that they don't all try to breathe in at once. We breathe in shifts.

Cecil knelt at the window, phone on the sill, careful marks he'd made with a sharp pencil and his laser-pointer showing the precise angles to each mirror. He looked around at us all, his eyes shining. "This is it," he said. "My Leicester Square premier."

The monocle is already glued to the phone's back over the projector's eye. The phone's been fitted to a little movable tripod. And now, with a trembling fingertip, Cecil prods the screen. Then, quickly, nimbly, spinning the focus knob on the monocle. Then the hiss of air sucked over teeth and we all rush to the window to see, peering around the drapes. He was much better on the focus this time, faster despite his trembling hand. There, on the marquee of the Odeon, Keith Kennenson as an eight-year-old, begging his mother to let him have a puppy, then a montage of shots of Kennenson with his different dogs, a mix of reality TV, feature films, dramas, comedies, the story of a life with dogs, the same character actors moving in and out of shot.

Below, the crowd boiled over. People were pointing, laughing, screeching, aiming their phones at the Odeon, and coppers were rushing about, shouting into their lapels, and—He moved the phone, swiveling it to line up with the next mark and BAM, there was Kennenson again, a series of love scenes this time, writ large on the huge marquee of the Virgin Megatheatre, and the crowd looked this way and that, trying to see where the magic pictures made of light and ingenuity had went and they found it, and the police rushed around again and BAM—

It was now screening on the Empire, and now it was an extended battle, Kennenson fighting a shark, a ninja, terrorists, Romans, Nazis and BAM, it was in the gardens in the middle of the square. The crowd was going wild, moving like a great wave from side to side, phones held high, getting in the cops' way.

"Time to go," I said, watching more cops trying to push their way into the square, then more. "Time to *go*, Cec," I said again, tugging his arm. The other Dodgers were already stealing out the door, padding their way to the fire-stairs and the lifts, led by tall Sal with a pad of post-it notes that she carefully stuck over the eye of each CCTV as she passed it, her infrared LEDs having temporarily blinded it already.

Cecil let me lead him away. He was trembling all over, and there were tears rolling down his cheeks, though he didn't seem aware of them. We peeled off our gloves and stuck them in our pockets, pulled off our hairnets, and removed the disposable booties from our shoes. We made our way down the lift in silence, Cecil visibly pulling himself together, so that he was able to calmly nod at the night clerk, tossing a twangy, "Guh-night!" over his shoulder as we stepped out into bedlam.

And that is how I will always picture Cecil B DeVil, standing there on the edges of Leicester Square, face turned up to the flashing lights, cheeks wet with new tears, as the disposable phone abandoned in the hotel window played out another 18 minutes and 12 seconds of the Great Work before the law found it and shut it down, provoking howls from the crowd.

But the howls didn't turn ugly, didn't turn into a riot. Instead, what we got was—an ovation.

Somewhere in the crowd, someone began to clap. And then someone else clapped, and then hundreds were clapping, and whistling and catcalling, and Cecil and I looked at each other and he was crying so hard the snot was running down his face. I thought of my family on the estate and damned if I didn't start to cry, too.

For a pair of hardened gangsters, we were a bloody soppy pair.

THE MAIDEN FLIGHT OF MCCAULEY'S *BELLEROPHON*
ELIZABETH HAND

Elizabeth Hand published her first story in 1988 and her first novel, *Winterlong*, in 1990. The author of nine novels and three collections of short fiction, Hand has established herself as one of the finest and most respected writers of outsider fantasy and science fiction working today. Her work has won the Nebula, World Fantasy, James Tiptree, Jr., International Horror Guild, and Mythopoeic awards. Her most recent books are novel *Generation Loss* and short novel *Illyria*. She is currently working on a new novel, *Wonderwall*.

Being assigned to The Head for eight hours was the worst security shift you could pull at the museum. Even now, thirty years later, Robbie had dreams in which he wandered from the Early Flight gallery to Balloons & Airships to Cosmic Soup, where he once again found himself alone in the dark, staring into the bland gaze of the famous scientist as he intoned his endless lecture about the nature of the universe.

"Remember when we thought nothing could be worse than that?" Robbie stared wistfully into his empty glass, then signaled the waiter for another bourbon and Coke. Across the table, his old friend Emery sipped a beer.

"I liked The Head," said Emery. He cleared his throat and began to recite in the same portentous tone the famous scientist had employed. "Trillions and trillions of galaxies in which our own is but a mote of cosmic dust. It made you think."

"It made you think about killing yourself," said Robbie. "Do you want to know how many times I heard that?"

"A trillion?"

"Five thousand." The waiter handed Robbie a drink, his fourth. "Twenty-five times an hour, times eight hours a day, times five days a week, times five months."

"Five thousand, that's not so much. Especially when you think of all those trillions of galleries. I mean galaxies. Only five months? I thought you worked there longer."

"Just that summer. It only seemed like forever."

Emery knocked back his beer. "A long time ago, in a gallery far, far away," he intoned, not for the first time.

Thirty years before, the Museum of American Aviation and Aerospace had just opened. Robbie was nineteen that summer, a recent dropout from the University of Maryland, living in a group house in Mount Rainier. Employment opportunities were scarce; making $3.40 an hour as a security aide at the Smithsonian's newest museum seemed preferable to bagging groceries at Giant Food. Every morning he'd punch his time card in the guards' locker room and change into his uniform. Then he'd duck outside to smoke a joint before trudging downstairs for morning meeting and that day's assignments.

Most of the security guards were older than Robbie, with backgrounds in the military and an eye on future careers with the DC Police Department or FBI. Still, they tolerated him with mostly good-natured ribbing about his longish hair and bloodshot eyes. All except for Hedge, the security chief. He was an enormous man with a shaved head who sat, knitting, behind a bank of closed-circuit video monitors, observing tourists and guards with an expression of amused contempt.

"What are you making?" Robbie once asked. Hedge raised his hands to display an intricately patterned baby blanket. "Hey, that's cool. Where'd you learn to knit?"

"Prison." Hedge's eyes narrowed. "You stoned again, Opie? That's it. Gallery Seven. Relieve Jones."

Robbie's skin went cold, then hot with relief when he realized Hedge wasn't going to fire him. "Seven? Uh, yeah, sure, sure. For how long?"

"Forever," said Hedge.

"Oh, man, you got The Head." Jones clapped his hands gleefully when Robbie arrived. "Better watch your ass, kids'll throw shit at you," he said, and sauntered off.

Two projectors at opposite ends of the dark room beamed twin shafts of silvery light onto a head-shaped Styrofoam form. Robbie could never figure out if they'd filmed the famous scientist just once, or if they'd gone to the trouble to shoot him from two different angles.

However they'd done it, the sight of the disembodied Head was surprisingly effective: it looked like a hologram floating amid the hundreds of back-projected twinkly stars that covered the walls and ceiling. The creep factor was intensified by the stilted, slightly puzzled manner in which the Head blinked as it droned on, as though the famous scientist had just realized his body was gone, and was hoping no one else would notice. Once, when he was really stoned, Robbie swore that the Head deviated from its script.

"What'd it say?" asked Emery. At the time he was working in the General Aviation Gallery, operating a flight simulator that tourists clambered into for three-minute rides.

"Something about peaches," said Robbie. "I couldn't understand, it sort of mumbled."

Every morning, Robbie stood outside the entrance to Cosmic Soup and watched as tourists streamed through the main entrance and into the Hall of Flight. Overhead, legendary aircraft hung from the ceiling. The 1903 Wright Flyer with its Orville mannequin; a Lilienthal glider; the Bell X-1 in which Chuck Yeager broke the sound barrier. From a huge pit in the center of the hall rose a Minuteman III ICBM, rust-colored stains still visible where a protester had tossed a bucket of pig's blood on it a few months earlier. Directly above the entrance to Robbie's gallery dangled the *Spirit of St. Louis*. The aides who worked upstairs in the planetarium amused themselves by shooting paperclips onto its wings.

Robbie winced at the memory. He gulped what was left of his bourbon and sighed. "That was a long time ago."

"*Tempus fugit*, baby. Thinking of which—" Emery dug into his pocket for a Blackberry. "Check this out. From Leonard."

Robbie rubbed his eyes blearily, then read.

> From: l.scopes@MAAA.SI.edu
> Subject: Tragic Illness
> Date: April 6, 7:58:22 PM EDT
> To: emeryubergeek@gmail.com
>
> Dear Emery,
> I just learned that our Maggie Blevin is very ill. I wrote her at Christmas but never heard back. Fuad El-Hajj says she was diagnosed with advanced breast cancer last fall. Prognosis is not good. She is still in the Fayetteville area, and I gather is in a hospice. I want to make a visit though not sure how that will go over. I have something I want to give her but need to talk to you about it.
>
> L.

"Ahhh." Robbie sighed. "God, that's terrible."

"Yeah. I'm sorry. But I figured you'd want to know."

Robbie pinched the bridge of his nose. Four years earlier, his wife, Anna, had died of breast cancer, leaving him adrift in a grief so profound it was as though he'd been poisoned, as though his veins had been pumped with the same chemicals that had failed to save her. Anna had been an oncology nurse, a fact that at first afforded some meager black humor, but in the end deprived them of even the faintest of false hopes borne of denial or faith in alternative therapies.

There was no time for any of that. Zach, their son, had just turned twelve. Between his own grief and Zach's subsequent acting-out, Robbie got so depressed that he started pouring his first bourbon and coke before the boy left for school.

Two years later, he got fired from his job with the County Parks Commission.

He now worked in the shipping department at Small's, an off-price store in a desolate shopping mall that resembled the ruins of a regional airport. Robbie found it oddly consoling. It reminded him of the museum. The same generic atriums and industrial carpeting; the same bleak sunlight filtered through clouded glass; the same vacant-faced people trudging from Dollar Store to SunGlass Hut, the way they'd wandered from the General Aviation Gallery to Cosmic Soup.

"Poor Maggie." Robbie returned the Blackberry. "I haven't thought of her in years."

"I'm going to see Leonard."

"When? Maybe I'll go with you."

"Now." Emery shoved a twenty under his beer bottle and stood. "You're coming with me."

"What?"

"You can't drive—you're snackered. Get popped again, you lose your license."

"Popped? Who's getting popped? And I'm not snackered, I'm—" Robbie thought. "Snockered. You pronounced it wrong."

"Whatever." Emery grabbed Robbie's shoulder and pushed him to the door. "Let's go."

Emery drove an expensive hybrid that could get from Rockville to Utica, New York, on a single tank of gas. The vanity plate read MARVO and was flanked by bumper stickers with messages like GUNS DON'T KILL PEOPLE: TYPE 2 PHASERS KILL PEOPLE and FRAK OFF! as well as several slogans that Emery said were in Klingon.

Emery was the only person Robbie knew who was somewhat famous. Back in the early 1980s, he'd created a local-access cable TV show called *Captain Marvo's Secret Spacetime,* taped in his parents' basement and featuring Emery in an aluminum foil costume behind the console of a cardboard spaceship. Captain Marvo watched videotaped episodes of low-budget 1950s science fiction serials with titles like *Payload: Moondust* while bantering with his co-pilot, a homemade puppet made by Leonard, named Mungbean.

The show was pretty funny if you were stoned. Captain Marvo became a cult hit, and then a real hit when a major network picked it up as a late-night offering. Emery quit his day job at the museum and rented studio time in Baltimore. He sold the rights after a few years, and was immediately replaced by a flashy actor in Lurex and a glittering robot sidekick. The show limped along for a season, then died. Emery's fans claimed this was because their slacker hero had been sidelined.

But maybe it was just that people weren't as stoned as they used to be. These days the program had a surprising afterlife on the internet, where Robbie's son Zach watched it with his friends, and Emery did a brisk business selling memorabilia through his official Captain Marvo website.

It took them nearly an hour to get into DC and find a parking space near the Mall, by which time Robbie had sobered up enough to wish he'd stayed at the bar.

"Here." Emery gave him a sugarless breath mint, then plucked at the collar of Robbie's shirt, acid-green with SMALLS embroidered in purple. "Christ, Robbie, you're a freaking mess."

He reached into the back seat, retrieved a black t-shirt from his gym bag. "Here, put this on."

Robbie changed into it and stumbled out onto the sidewalk. It was mid-April but already steamy; the air shimmered above the pavement and smelled sweetly of apple blossom and coolant from innumerable air conditioners. Only as he approached the museum entrance and caught his reflection in a glass wall did Robbie see that his t-shirt was emblazoned with Emery's youthful face and foil helmet above the words O CAPTAIN MY CAPTAIN.

"You wear your own t-shirt?" he asked as he followed Emery through the door.

"Only at the gym. Nothing else was clean."

They waited at the security desk while a guard checked their IDs, called upstairs to Leonard's office, signed them in and took their pictures before finally issuing each a Visitor's Pass.

"You'll have to wait for Leonard to escort you upstairs," the guard said.

"Not like the old days, huh, Robbie?" Emery draped an arm around Robbie and steered him into the Hall of Flight. "Not a lot of retinal scanning on your watch."

The museum hadn't changed much. The same aircraft and space capsules gleamed overhead. Tourists clustered around the lucite pyramid that held slivers of moon rock. Sunburned guys sporting military haircuts and tattoos peered at a mockup of an F-15 flight deck. Everything had that old museum smell: soiled carpeting, machine oil, the wet-laundry odor wafting from steam tables in the public cafeteria.

But The Head was long gone. Robbie wondered if anyone even remembered the famous scientist, dead for many years. The General Aviation Gallery, where Emery and Leonard had operated the flight simulators and first met Maggie Blevin, was now devoted to Personal Flight, with models of jetpacks worn by alarmingly lifelike mannequins.

"Leonard designed those." Emery paused to stare at a child-sized figure who seemed to float above a solar-powered skateboard. "He could have gone to Hollywood."

"It's not too late."

Robbie and Emery turned to see their old colleague behind them.

"Leonard," said Emery.

The two men embraced. Leonard stepped back and tilted his head. "Robbie.

I wasn't expecting you."

"Surprise," said Robbie. They shook hands awkwardly. "Good to see you, man."

Leonard forced a smile. "And you."

They headed toward the staff elevator. Back in the day, Leonard's hair had been long and luxuriantly blond. It fell unbound down the back of the dogshit-yellow uniform jacket, designed to evoke an airline pilot's, that he and Emery and the other General Aviation aides wore as they gave their spiel to tourists eager to yank on the controls of their Link Trainers. With his patrician good looks and stern gray eyes, Leonard was the only aide who actually resembled a real pilot.

Now he looked like a cross between Obi-Wan Kenobi and Willie Nelson. His hair was white, and hung in two braids that reached almost to his waist. Instead of the crappy polyester uniform, he wore a white linen tunic, a necklace of unpolished turquoise and coral, loose black trousers tucked into scuffed cowboy boots, and a skull earring the size of Robbie's thumb. On his collar gleamed the cheap knock-off pilot's wings that had once adorned his museum uniform jacket. Leonard had always taken his duties very seriously, especially after Margaret Blevin arrived as the museum's first Curator of Proto-Flight. Robbie's refusal to do the same, even long after he'd left the museum himself, had resulted in considerable friction between them over the intervening years.

Robbie cleared his throat. "So, uh. What are you working on these days?" He wished he wasn't wearing Emery's idiotic t-shirt.

"I'll show you," said Leonard.

Upstairs, they headed for the old photo lab, now an imaging center filled with banks of computers, digital cameras, scanners.

"We still process film there," Leonard said as they walked down a corridor hung with production photos from *The Day the Earth Stood Still* and *Frau im Mond*. "Negatives, old motion picture stock—people still send us things."

"Any of it interesting?" asked Emery.

Leonard shrugged. "Sometimes. You never know what you might find. That's part of Maggie's legacy—we're always open to the possibility of discovering something new."

Robbie shut his eyes. Leonard's voice made his teeth ache. "Remember how she used to keep a bottle of Scotch in that side drawer, underneath her purse?" he said.

Leonard frowned, but Emery laughed. "Yeah! And it was good stuff, too."

"Maggie had a great deal of class," said Leonard in a somber tone.

You pompous asshole, thought Robbie.

Leonard punched a code into a door and opened it. "You might remember when this was a storage cupboard."

They stepped inside. Robbie did remember this place—he'd once had sex here with a General Aviation aide whose name he'd long forgotten. It had been a good-sized supply room then, with an odd, sweetish scent from the rolls of film stacked along the shelves.

Now it was a very crowded office. The shelves were crammed with books and curatorial reports dating back to 1981, and archival boxes holding god knows what—Leonard's original government job application, maybe. A coat had been tossed onto the floor in one corner. There was a large metal desk covered with bottles of nail polish, an ancient swivel chair that Robbie vaguely remembered having been deployed during his lunch hour tryst.

Mostly, though, the room held Leonard's stuff: tiny cardboard dioramas, mockups of space capsules and dirigibles. It smelled overpoweringly of nail polish. It was also extremely cold.

"Man, you must freeze your ass off." Robbie rubbed his arms.

Emery picked up one of the little bottles. "You getting a manicurist's license?"

Leonard gestured at the desk. "I'm painting with nail polish now. You get some very unusual effects."

"I bet," said Robbie. "You're, like huffing nail polish." He peered at the shelves, impressed despite himself. "Jeez, Leonard. You made all these?"

"Damn right I did."

When Robbie first met Leonard, they were both lowly GS-1s. In those days, Leonard collected paper clips and rode an old Schwinn bicycle to work. He entertained tourists by making balloon animals. In his spare time, he created Mungbean, Captain Marvo's robot friend, out of a busted lamp and some spark plugs.

He also made strange ink drawings, hundreds of them. Montgolfier balloons with sinister faces; B-52s carrying payloads of soap bubbles; caricatures of the museum director and senior curators as greyhounds sniffing each other's nether quarters.

It was this last, drawn on a scrap of legal paper, which Margaret Blevin picked up on her first tour of the General Aviation Gallery. The sketch had fallen out of Leonard's jacket: he watched in horror as the museum's deputy director stooped to retrieve the crumpled page.

"Allow me," said the woman at the director's side. She was slight, forty-ish, with frizzy red hair and enormous hoop earrings, wearing an indian-print tunic over tight, sky-blue trousers and leather clogs. She snatched up the drawing, stuffed it in her pocket and continued her tour of the gallery. After the deputy director left, the woman walked to where Leonard stood beside his flight simulator, sweating in his polyester jacket as he supervised an overweight kid in a Chewbacca t-shirt. When the kid climbed down, the woman held up the crumpled sheet.

"Who did this?"

The other two aides—one was Emery—shook their heads.

"I did," said Leonard.

The woman crooked her finger. "Come with me."

"Am I fired?" asked Leonard as he followed her out of the gallery.

"Nope. I'm Maggie Blevin. We're shutting down those Link Trainers and making this into a new gallery. I'm in charge. I need someone to start cataloging stuff for me and maybe do some preliminary sketches. You want the job?"

"Yes," stammered Leonard. "I mean, sure."

"Great." She balled up the sketch and tossed it into a wastebasket. "Your talents were being wasted. That looks just like the director's butt."

"If he was a dog," said Leonard.

"He's a son of a bitch, and that's close enough," said Maggie. "Let's go see Personnel."

Leonard's current job description read Museum Effects Specialist, Grade 9, Step 10. For the last two decades, he'd created figurines and models for the museum's exhibits. Not fighter planes or commercial aircraft—there was an entire division of modelers who handled that.

Leonard's work was more rarefied, as evidenced by the dozens of flying machines perched wherever there was space in the tiny room. Rocket ships, bat-winged aerodromes, biplanes and triplanes and saucers, many of them striped and polka-dotted and glazed with, yes, nail polish in circus colors, so that they appeared to be made of ribbon candy.

His specialty was aircraft that had never actually flown; in many instances, aircraft that had never been intended to fly. Crypto-aviation, as some disgruntled curator dubbed it. He worked from plans and photographs, drawings and uncategorizable materials he'd found in the archives Maggie Blevin had been hired to organize. These were housed in a set of oak filing cabinets dating to the 1920s. Officially, the archive was known as the Pre-Langley Collection. But everyone in the museum, including Maggie Blevin, called it the Nut Files.

After Leonard's fateful promotion, Robbie and Emery would sometimes punch out for the day, go upstairs and stroll to his corner of the library. You could do that then—wander around workrooms and storage areas, the library and archives, without having to check in or get a special pass or security clearance. Robbie just went along for the ride, but Emery was fascinated by the things Leonard found in the Nut Files. Grainy black-and-white photos of purported UFOs; typescripts of encounters with deceased Russian cosmonauts in the Nevada desert; an account of a Raelian wedding ceremony attended by a glowing crimson orb. There was also a large carton donated by the widow of a legendary rocket scientist, which turned out to be filled with 1950s foot fetish pornography, and 16-millimeter film footage of several Pioneers of Flight doing something unseemly with a spotted pig.

"Whatever happened to that pig movie?" asked Robbie as he admired a biplane with violet-striped ailerons.

"It's been de-accessioned," said Leonard.

He cleared the swivel chair and motioned for Emery to sit, then perched on the edge of his desk. Robbie looked in vain for another chair, finally settled on the floor beside a wastebasket filled with empty nail polish bottles.

"So I have a plan," announced Leonard. He stared fixedly at Emery, as though they were alone in the room. "To help Maggie. Do you remember the *Bellerophon*?"

Emery frowned. "Vaguely. That old film loop of a plane crash?"

"*Presumed* crash. They never found any wreckage, everyone just assumes it crashed. But yes, that was the *Bellerophon*—it was the clip that played in our gallery. Maggie's gallery."

"Right—the movie that burned up!" broke in Robbie. "Yeah, I remember, the film got caught in a sprocket or something. Smoke detectors went off and they evacuated the whole museum. They got all on Maggie's case about it, they thought she installed it wrong."

"She didn't." Leonard said angrily. "One of the tech guys screwed up the installation—he told me a few years ago. He didn't vent it properly, the projector bulb overheated and the film caught on fire. He said he always felt bad she got canned."

"But they didn't fire her for that." Robbie gave Leonard a sideways look. "It was the UFO—"

Emery cut him off. "They were gunning for her," he said. "C'mon, Rob, everyone knew—all those old military guys running this place, they couldn't stand a woman getting in their way. Not if she wasn't Air Force or some shit. Took 'em a few years, that's all. Fucking assholes. I even got a letter-writing campaign going on the show. Didn't help."

"Nothing would have helped." Leonard sighed. "She was a visionary. She *is* a visionary," he added hastily. "Which is why I want to do this—"

He hopped from the desk, rooted around in a corner and pulled out a large cardboard box.

"Move," he ordered.

Robbie scrambled to his feet. Leonard began to remove things from the carton and set them carefully on his desk. Emery got up to make more room, angling himself beside Robbie. They watched as Leonard arranged piles of paper, curling 8x10s, faded blueprints and an old 35mm film viewer, along with several large manila envelopes closed with red string. Finally he knelt beside the box and very gingerly reached inside.

"I think the Lindbergh baby's in there," whispered Emery.

Leonard stood, cradling something in his hands, turned and placed it in the middle of the desk.

"Holy shit." Emery whistled. "Leonard, you've outdone yourself."

Robbie crouched so he could view it at eye level: a model of some sort of flying machine, though it seemed impossible that anyone, even Leonard or Maggie Blevin, could ever have dreamed it might fly. It had a zeppelin-shaped body, with a sharp nose like that of a Lockheed Starfighter, slightly uptilted.

Suspended beneath this was a basket filled with tiny gears and chains, and beneath that was a contraption with three wheels, like a velocipede, only the wheels were fitted with dozens of stiff flaps, each no bigger than a fingernail, and even tinier propellers.

And everywhere, there were wings, sprouting from every inch of the craft's body in an explosion of canvas and balsa and paper and gauze. Bird-shaped wings, bat-shaped wings; square wings like those of a box-kite, elevators and hollow cones of wire; long tubes that, when Robbie peered inside them, were filled with baffles and flaps. Ailerons and struts ran between them to form a dizzying grid, held together with fine gold thread and monofilament and what looked like human hair. Every bit of it was painted in brilliant shades of violet and emerald, scarlet and fuchsia and gold, and here and there shining objects were set into the glossy surface: minute shards of mirror or colored glass; a beetle carapace; flecks of mica.

Above it all, springing from the fuselage like the cap of an immense toadstool, was a feathery parasol made of curved bamboo and multicolored silk.

It was like gazing at the Wright Flyer through a kaleidoscope.

"That's incredible!" Robbie exclaimed. "How'd you do that?"

"Now we just have to see if it flies," said Leonard.

Robbie straightened. "How the hell can that thing fly?"

"The original flew." Leonard leaned against the wall. "My theory is, if we can replicate the same conditions—the *exact same* conditions—it will work."

"But." Robbie glanced at Emery. "The original didn't fly. It crashed. I mean, presumably."

Emery nodded. "Plus there was a guy in it. McCartney—"

"McCauley," said Leonard.

"Right, McCauley. And you know, Leonard, no one's gonna fit in that, right?" Emery shot him an alarmed look. "You're not thinking of making a full-scale model, are you? Because that would be completely insane."

"No." Leonard fingered the skull plug in his earlobe. "I'm going to make another film—I'm going to replicate the original, and I'm going to do it so perfectly that Maggie won't even realize it's *not* the original. I've got it all worked out." He looked at Emery. "I can shoot it on digital, if you'll lend me a camera. That way I can edit it on my laptop. And then I'm going to bring it down to Fayetteville so she can see it."

Robbie and Emery glanced at each other.

"Well, it's not completely insane, " said Robbie.

"But Maggie knows the original was destroyed," said Emery. "I mean, I was there, I remember—she saw it. We all saw it. She has cancer, right? Not Alzheimer's or dementia or, I dunno, amnesia."

"Why don't you just Photoshop something?" asked Robbie. "You could tell her it was an homage. That way—"

Leonard's glare grew icy. "It is not an homage. I am going to Cowana Island, just like McCauley did, and I am going to re-create the maiden flight of the *Bellerophon*. I am going to film it, I am going to edit it. And when it's completed, I'm going to tell Maggie that I found a dupe in the archives. Her heart broke when that footage burned up. I'm going to give it back to her."

Robbie stared at his shoe, so Leonard wouldn't see his expression. After a moment he said, "When Anna was sick, I wanted to do that. Go back to this place by Mount Washington where we stayed before Zach was born. We had all these great photos of us canoeing there, it was so beautiful. But it was winter, and I said we should wait and go in the summer."

"I'm not waiting." Leonard sifted through the papers on his desk. "I have these—"

He opened a manila envelope and withdrew several glassine sleeves. He examined one, then handed it to Emery.

"This is what survived of the original footage, which in fact was *not* the original footage—the original was shot in 1901, on cellulose nitrate film. That's what Maggie and I found when we first started going through the Nut Files. Only of course nitrate stock is like a ticking time bomb. So the Photo Lab duped it onto safety film, which is what you're looking at."

Emery held the film to the light. Robbie stood beside him, squinting. Five frames, in shades of amber and tortoiseshell, with blurred images that might have been bushes or clouds or smoke damage, for all Robbie could see.

Emery asked, "How many frames do you have?"

"Total? Seventy-two."

Emery shook his head. "Not much, is it? What was it, fifteen seconds?"

"Seventeen seconds."

"Times twenty-four frames per second—so, out of about 400 frames, that's all that's left."

"No. There was actually less than that, because it was silent film, which runs at more like 18 frames per second, and they corrected the speed. So, about 300 frames, which means we have about a quarter of the original stock." Leonard hesitated. He glanced up. "Lock that door, would you, Robbie?"

Robbie did, looked back to see Leonard crouched in the corner, moving aside his coat to reveal a metal strongbox. He prised the lid from the top.

The box was filled with water—Robbie *hoped* it was water. "Is that an aquarium?"

Leonard ignored him, tugged up his sleeves, then dipped both hands below the surface. Very, very carefully he removed another metal box. He set it on the floor, grabbed his coat and meticulously dried the lid, then turned to Robbie.

"You know, maybe you should unlock the door. In case we need to get out fast."

"Jesus Christ, Leonard, what is it?" exclaimed Emery. "Snakes?"

"Nope." Leonard plucked something from the box, and Emery flinched as a serpentine ribbon unfurled in the air. "It's what's left of the original footage—

the 1901 film."

"That's nitrate?" Emery stared at him, incredulous. "You *are* insane! How the hell'd you get it?"

"I clipped it before they destroyed the stock. I think it's okay—I take it out every day, so the gases don't build up. And it doesn't seem to interact with the nail polish fumes. It's the part where you can actually see McCauley, where you get the best view of the plane. See?"

He dangled it in front of Emery, who backed toward the door. "Put it away, put it away!"

"Can I see?" asked Robbie.

Leonard gave him a measuring look, then nodded. "Hold it by this edge—"

It took a few seconds for Robbie's eyes to focus properly. "You're right," he said. "You can see him—you can see someone, anyway. And you can definitely tell it's an airplane."

He handed it back to Leonard, who fastidiously replaced it, first in its canister and then the water-filled safe.

"They could really pop you for that." Emery whistled in disbelief. "If that stuff blew? This whole place could go up in flames."

"You say that like it's a bad thing." Leonard draped his coat over the strongbox, then started to laugh. "Anyway, I'm done with it. I went into the Photo Lab one night and duped it myself. So I've got that copy at home. And this one—"

He inclined his head at the corner. "I'm going to take the nitrate home and give it a Viking funeral in the back yard. You can come if you want."

"Tonight?" asked Robbie.

"No. I've got to work late tonight, catch up on some stuff before I leave town."

Emery leaned against the door. "Where you going?"

"South Carolina. I told you. I'm going to Cowana Island, and..." Robbie caught a whiff of acetone as Leonard picked up the *Bellerophon*. "I am going to make this thing fly."

"He really is nuts. I mean, when was the last time he even saw Maggie?" Robbie asked as Emery drove him back to the mall. "I still don't know what really happened, except for the UFO stuff."

"She found out he was screwing around with someone else. It was a bad scene. She tried to get him fired; he went to Boynton and told him Maggie was diverting all this time and money to studying UFOs. Which unfortunately was true. They did an audit, she had some kind of nervous breakdown even before they could fire her."

"What a prick."

Emery sighed. "It was horrible. Leonard doesn't talk about it. I don't think he ever got over it. Over her."

"Yeah, but..." Robbie shook his head. "She must be, what, twenty years older than us? They never would have stayed together. If he feels so bad, he should just go see her. This other stuff is insane."

"I think maybe those fumes did something to him. Nitrocellulose, it's in nail polish, too. It might have done something to his brain."

"Is that possible?"

"It's a theory," said Emery broodingly.

Robbie's house was in a scruffy subdivision on the outskirts of Rockville. The place was small, a bungalow with masonite siding, cracked cinderblock foundation and the remains of a garden that Anna had planted. A green GMC pickup with expired registration was parked in the drive. Robbie peered into the cab. It was filled with empty Bud Light bottles.

Inside, Zach was hunched at a desk beside his friend Tyler, owner of the pickup. The two of them stared intently into a computer screen.

"What's up?" said Zach without looking away.

"Not much," said Robbie. "Eye contact."

Zach glanced up. He was slight, with Anna's thick blonde curls reduced to a buzzcut that Robbie hated. Tyler was tall and gangly, with long black hair and wire-rimmed sunglasses. Both favored tie-dyed t-shirts and madras shorts that made them look as though they were perpetually on vacation.

Robbie went into the kitchen and got a beer. "You guys eat?"

"We got something on the way home."

Robbie drank his beer and watched them. The house had a smell that Emery once described as Failed Bachelor. Unwashed clothes, spilled beer, marijuana smoke. Robbie hadn't smoked in years, but Zach and Tyler had taken up the slack. Robbie used to yell at them but eventually gave up. If his own depressing example wasn't enough to straighten them out, what was?

After a minute, Zach looked up again. "Nice shirt, Dad."

"Thanks, son." Robbie sank into a beanbag chair. "Me and Emery dropped by the museum and saw Leonard."

"Leonard!" Tyler burst out laughing. "Leonard is so fucking sweet! He's, like, the craziest guy ever."

"All Dad's friends are crazy," said Zach.

"Yeah, but Emery, he's cool. Whereas that guy Leonard is just wack."

Robbie nodded somberly and finished his beer. "Leonard is indeed wack. He's making a movie."

"A real movie?" asked Zach.

"More like a home movie. Or, I dunno—he wants to reproduce another movie, one that was already made, do it all the same again. Shot by shot."

Tyler nodded. "Like *The Ring* and *Ringu*. What's the movie?"

"Seventeen seconds of a 1901 plane crash. The original footage was destroyed, so he's going to re-stage the whole thing."

"A plane crash?" Zach glanced at Tyler. "Can we watch?"

"Not a real crash—he's doing it with a model. I mean, I think he is."

238 — ELIZABETH HAND

"Did they even have planes then?" said Tyler.

"He should put it on YouTube," said Zach, and turned back to the computer.

"Okay, get out of there." Robbie rubbed his head wearily. "I need to go online."

The boys argued but gave up quickly. Tyler left. Zach grabbed his cellphone and slouched upstairs to his room. Robbie got another beer, sat at the computer and logged out of whatever they'd been playing, then typed in MCCAULEY BELLEROPHON.

Only a dozen results popped up. He scanned them, then clicked the Wikipedia entry for Ernesto McCauley.

> McCauley, Ernesto (18??–1901) American inventor whose eccentric aircraft, the *Bellerophon,* allegedly flew for seventeen seconds before it crashed during a 1901 test flight on Cowana Island, South Carolina, killing McCauley. In the 1980s, claims that this flight was successful and predated that of the Wright Brothers by two years were made by a Smithsonian expert, based upon archival film footage. The claims have since been disproved and the film record unfortunately lost in a fire. Curiously, no other record of either McCauley or his aircraft has ever been found.

Robbie took a long pull at his beer, then typed in MARGARET BLEVIN.

> Blevin, Margaret (1938–) Influential cultural historian whose groundbreaking work on early flight earned her the nickname "The Magnificent Blevin." During her tenure at the Smithsonian's Museum of American Aeronautics and Aerospace, Blevin redesigned the General Aviation Gallery to feature lesser-known pioneers of flight, including Charles Dellschau and Ernesto McCauley, as well as…

"'The Magnificent Blevin'?" Robbie snorted. He grabbed another beer and continued reading.

> But Blevin's most lasting impact upon the history of aviation was her 1986 bestseller *Wings for Humanity!,* in which she presents a dramatic and visionary account of the mystical aspects of flight, from Icarus to the Wright Brothers and beyond. Its central premise is that millennia ago a benevolent race seeded the Earth, leaving isolated locations with the ability to engender human-powered flight. "We dream of flight because flight is our birthright," wrote Blevin, and since its publication *Wings for Humanity!* has never gone out of print.

"Leonard wrote this frigging thing!"

"What?" Zach came downstairs, yawning.

"This Wikipedia entry!" Robbie jabbed at the screen. "That book was never a bestseller—she snuck it into the museum gift shop and no one bought it. The only reason it's still in print is that she published it herself."

Zach read the entry over his father's shoulder. "It sounds cool."

Robbie shook his head adamantly. "She was completely nuts. Obsessed with all this New Age crap, aliens and crop circles. She thought that planes could only fly from certain places, and that's why all the early flights crashed. Not because there was something wrong with the aircraft design, but because they were taking off from the wrong spot."

"Then how come there's airports everywhere?"

"She never worked out that part."

"'We must embrace our galactic heritage, the spiritual dimension of human flight, lest we forever chain ourselves to earth,'" Zach read from the screen. "Was she in that plane crash?"

"No, she's still alive. That was just something she had a wild hair about. She thought the guy who invented that plane flew it a few years before the Wright Brothers made their flight, but she could never prove it."

"But it says there was a movie," said Zach. "So someone saw it happen."

"This is Wikipedia." Robbie stared at the screen in disgust. "You can say any fucking thing you want and people will believe it. Leonard wrote that entry, guarantee you. Probably she faked that whole film loop. That's what Leonard's planning to do now—replicate the footage then pass it off to Maggie as the real thing."

Zach collapsed into the bean bag chair. "Why?"

"Because he's crazy, too. He and Maggie had a thing together."

Zach grimaced. "Ugh."

"What, you think we were born old? We were your age, practically. And Maggie was about twenty years older—"

"A cougar!" Zach burst out laughing. "Why didn't she go for you?"

"Ha ha ha." Robbie pushed his empty beer bottle against the wall. "Women liked Leonard. Go figure. Even your mom went out with him for a while. Before she and I got involved, I mean."

Zach's glassy eyes threatened to roll back in his head. "Stop."

"We thought it was pretty strange," admitted Robbie. "But Maggie was good-looking for an old hippie." He glanced at the Wikipedia entry and did the math. "I guess she's in her seventies now. Leonard's in touch with her. She has cancer. Breast cancer."

"I heard you," said Zach. He rolled out of the beanbag chair, flipped open his phone and began texting. "I'm going to bed."

Robbie sat and stared at the computer screen. After a while he shut it down. He shuffled into the kitchen and opened the cabinet where he kept a quart of

Jim Beam, hidden behind bottles of vinegar and vegetable oil. He rinsed out the glass he'd used the night before, poured a jolt and downed it; then carried the bourbon with him to bed.

The next day after work, he was on his second drink at the bar when Emery showed up.

"Hey." Robbie gestured at the stool beside him. "Have a set."

"You okay to drive?"

"Sure." Robbie scowled. "What, you keeping an eye on me?"

"No. But I want you to see something. At my house. Leonard's coming over, we're going to meet there at six-thirty. I tried calling you but your phone's off."

"Oh. Right. Sorry." Robbie signaled the bartender for his tab. "Yeah, sure. What, is he gonna give us manicures?"

"Nope. I have an idea. I'll tell you when I get there, I'm going to Royal Delhi first to get some takeout. See you—"

Emery lived in a big townhouse condo that smelled of Moderately Successful Bachelor. The walls held framed photos of Captain Marvo and Mungbean alongside a lifesized painting of Leslie Nielsen as Commander J. J. Adams.

But there was also a climate-controlled basement filled with Captain Marvo merchandise and packing material, with another large room stacked with electronics equipment—sound system, video monitors and decks, shelves and files devoted to old Captain Marvo episodes and dupes of the Grade Z movies featured on the show.

This was where Robbie found Leonard, bent over a refurbished Steenbeck editing table.

"Robbie." Leonard waved, then returned to threading film onto a spindle. "Emery back with dinner?"

"Uh uh." Robbie pulled a chair alongside him. "What are you doing?"

"Loading up that nitrate I showed you yesterday."

"It's not going to explode, is it?"

"No, Robbie, it's not going to explode." Leonard's mouth tightened. "Did Emery talk to you yet?"

"He just said something about a plan. So what's up?"

"I'll let him tell you."

Robbie flushed angrily, but before he could retort there was a knock behind them.

"Chow time, campers." Emery held up two steaming paper bags. "Can you leave that for a few minutes, Leonard?"

They ate on the couch in the next room. Emery talked about a pitch he'd made to revive Captain Marvo in cellphone format. "It'd be freaking perfect, if I could figure out a way to make any money from it."

Leonard said nothing. Robbie noted the cuffs of his white tunic were stained with flecks of orange pigment, as were his fingernails. He looked tired, his face lined and his eyes sunken.

"You getting enough sleep?" Emery asked.

Leonard smiled wanly. "Enough."

Finally the food was gone, and the beer. Emery clapped his hands on his knees, pushed aside the empty plates, then leaned forward.

"Okay. So here's the plan. I rented a house on Cowana for a week, starting this Saturday. I mapped it online and it's about ten hours. If we leave right after you guys get off work on Friday and drive all night, we'll get there early Saturday morning. Leonard, you said you've got everything pretty much assembled, so all you need to do is pack it up. I've got everything else here. Be a tight fit in the Prius, though, so we'll have to take two cars. We'll bring everything we need with us, we'll have a week to shoot and edit or whatever, then on the way back we swing through Fayetteville and show the finished product to Maggie. What do you think?"

"That's not a lot of time," said Leonard. "But we could do it."

Emery turned to Robbie. "Is you car road-worthy? It's about twelve hundred miles roundtrip."

Robbie stared at him. "What the hell are you talking about?"

"The *Bellerophon*. Leonard's got storyboards and all kinds of drawings and still frames, enough to work from. The realtor's in Charleston; she said there wouldn't be many people this early in the season. Plus there was a hurricane a couple years ago, I gather the island got hammered and no one's had money to rebuild. So we'll have it all to ourselves, pretty much."

"Are you high?" Robbie laughed. "I can't just take off. I have a job."

"You get vacation time, right? You can take a week. It'll be great, man. The realtor says it's already in the 80s down there. Warm water, a beach—what more you want?"

"Uh, maybe a beach with people besides you and Leonard?" Robbie searched in vain for another beer. "I couldn't go anyway—next week's Zach's spring break."

"Yeah?" Emery shook his head. "So, you're going to be at the store all day, and he'll be home getting stoned. Bring him. We'll put him to work."

Leonard frowned, but Robbie looked thoughtful. "Yeah, you're right. I hadn't thought of that. I can't really leave him alone. I guess I'll think about it."

"Don't think, just do it. It's Wednesday, tell 'em you're taking off next week. They gonna fire you?"

"Maybe."

"I'm not babysitting some—" Leonard started.

Emery cut him off. "You got that nitrate loaded? Let's see it."

They filed into the workroom. Leonard sat at the Steenbeck. The others watched as he adjusted the film on its sprockets. He turned to Robbie, then indicated the black projection box in the center of the deck.

"Emery knows all this, so I'm just telling you. That's a quartz halogen lamp. I haven't turned it on yet, because if the frame was just sitting there it might incinerate the film, and us. But there's only about four seconds of footage, so we're going to take our chances and watch it, once. Maybe you remember it from the gallery?"

Robbie nodded. "Yeah, I saw it a bunch of times. Not as much as The Head, but enough."

"Good. Hit that light, would you, Emery? Everyone ready? Blink and you'll miss it."

Robbie craned his neck, staring at a blank white screen. There was a whir, the stutter of film running through a projector.

At the bottom of the frame the horizon lurched, bright flickers that might be an expanse of water. Then a blurred image, faded sepia and amber, etched with blotches and something resembling a beetle leg: the absurd contraption Robbie recognized as the original *Bellerophon*. Only it was moving—it was flying—its countless gears and propellers and wings spinning and whirring and flapping all at once, so it seemed the entire thing would vibrate into a thousand pieces. Beneath the fuselage, a dark figure perched precariously atop the velocipede, legs like black scissors slicing at the air. From the left corner of the frame leaped a flare of light, like a shooting star or burning firecracker tossed at the pedaling figure. The pilot listed to one side, and—

Nothing. The film ended as abruptly as it had begun. Leonard quickly reached to turn off the lamp, and immediately removed the film from the take-up drive.

Robbie felt his neck prickle—he'd forgotten how weird, uncanny even, the footage was.

"Jesus, that's some bizarre shit," said Emery.

"It doesn't even look real." Robbie watched as Leonard coiled the film and slid it in a canister. "I mean, the guy, he looks fake."

Emery nodded. "Yeah, I know. It looks like one of those old silents, *The Lost World* or something. But it's not. I used to watch it back when it ran a hundred times a day in our gallery, the way you used to watch The Head. And it's definitely real. At least the pilot, McCauley—that's a real guy. I got a big magnifier once and just stood there and watched it over and over again. He was breathing, I could see it. And the plane, it's real too, far as I could tell. The thing I can't figure is, who the hell shot that footage? And what was the angle?"

Robbie stared at the empty screen, then shut his eyes. He tried to recall the rest of the film from when it played in the General Aviation gallery: the swift, jerky trajectory of that eerie little vehicle with its bizarre pilot, a man in a black suit and bowler hat; then the flash from the corner of the screen, and the man toppling from his perch into the white and empty air. The last thing you saw was a tiny hand at the bottom of the frame, then some blank leader, followed by the words THE MAIDEN FLIGHT OF MCCAULEY'S "*BELLEROPHON*"

(1901). And the whole thing began again.

"It was like someone was in the air next to him," said Robbie. "Unless he only got six feet off the ground. I always assumed it was faked."

"It wasn't faked," said Leonard. "The cameraman was on the beach filming. It was a windy day, they were hoping that would help give the plane some lift but there must have been a sudden gust. When the *Bellerophon* went into the ocean, the cameraman dove in to save McCauley. They both drowned. They never found the bodies, or the wreckage. Only the camera with the film."

"Who found it?" asked Robbie.

"We don't know." Leonard sighed, his shoulders slumping. "We don't know anything. Not the name of the cameraman, nothing. When Maggie and I ran the original footage, the leader said 'Maiden Flight of McCauley's *Bellerophon.*' The can had the date and 'Cowana Island' written on it. So Maggie and I went down there to research it. A weird place. Hardly any people, and this was in the summer. There's a tiny historical society on the island, but we couldn't find anything about McCauley or the aircraft. No newspaper accounts, no grave-stones. The only thing we did find was in a diary kept by the guy who delivered the mail back then. On May 13, 1901, he wrote that it was a very windy day and two men had drowned while attempting to launch a flying machine on the beach. Someone must have found the camera afterward. Somebody processed the film, and somehow it found its way to the museum."

Robbie followed Leonard into the next room. "What was that weird flash of light?"

"I don't know." Leonard stared out a glass door into the parking lot. "But it's not overexposure or lens flare or anything like that. It's something the camera-man actually filmed. Water, maybe—if it was a windy day, a big wave might have come up onto the beach or something."

"I always thought it was fire. Like a rocket or some kind of flare."

Leonard nodded. "That's what Maggie thought, too. The mailman—mostly all he wrote about was the weather. Which if you were relying on a horse-drawn cart makes sense. About two weeks before he mentioned the flying machine, he described something that sounds like a major meteor shower."

"And Maggie thought it was hit by a meteor?"

"No." Leonard sighed. "She thought it was something else. The weird thing is, a few years ago I checked online, and it turns out there was an unusual amount of meteor activity in 1901."

Robbie raised an eyebrow. "Meaning?"

Leonard said nothing. Finally he opened the door and walked outside. The others trailed after him.

They reached the edge of the parking lot, where cracked tarmac gave way to stony ground. Leonard glanced back, then stooped. He brushed away a few stray leaves and tufts of dead grass, set the film canister down and unscrewed the metal lid. He picked up one end of the coil of film, gently tugging until it trailed a few inches across the ground. Then he withdrew a lighter, flicked it and held the flame to the tail of film.

"What the—" began Robbie.

There was a dull *whoosh*, like the sound of a gas burner igniting. A plume of crimson and gold leaped from the canister, writhing in the air within a ball of black smoke. Leonard staggered to his feet, covering his head as he backed away.

"Leonard!" Emery grabbed him roughly, then turned and raced to the house.

Before Robbie could move, a strong chemical stink surrounded him. The flames shrank to a shining thread that lashed at the smoke, then faded into flecks of ash. Robbie ducked his head, coughing. He grasped Leonard's arm and tried to drag him away, glanced up to see Emery running toward them with a fire extinguisher.

"Sorry," gasped Leonard. He made a slashing motion through the smoke, which dispersed. The flames were gone. Leonard's face was black with ash. Robbie touched his own cheek gingerly, looked at his fingers and saw they were coated with something dark and oily.

Emery halted, panting, and stared at the twisted remains of the film can. On the ground beside it, a glowing thread wormed toward a dead leaf, then expired in a gray wisp. Emery raised the fire extinguisher threateningly, set it down and stomped on the canister.

"Good thing you didn't do that in the museum," said Robbie. He let go of Leonard's arm.

"Don't think it didn't cross my mind," said Leonard, and walked back inside.

They left Friday evening. Robbie got the week off, after giving his dubious boss a long story about a dying relative down south. Zach shouted and broke a lamp when informed he would be accompanying his father on a trip during his spring vacation.

"With Emery and *Leonard?* Are you fucking *insane?*"

Robbie was too exhausted to fight: he quickly offered to let Tyler come with them. Tyler, surprisingly, agreed, and even showed up on Friday afternoon to help load the car. Robbie made a pointed effort not to inspect the various backpacks and duffel bags the boys threw into the trunk of the battered Taurus. Alcohol, drugs, firearms: he no longer cared.

Instead he focused on the online weather report for Cowana Island: 80 degrees and sunshine, photographs of blue water, white sand, a skein of pelicans skimming above the waves. Ten hours, that wasn't so bad. In another weak moment, he told Zach he could drive part of the way, so Robbie could sleep.

"What about me?" asked Tyler. "Can I drive?"

"Only if I never wake up," said Robbie.

Around six Emery pulled into the driveway, honking. The boys were already slumped in Robbie's Taurus, Zach in front with earbuds dangling around his face and a knit cap pulled down over his eyes, Tyler in the back, staring blankly as though they were already on I-95.

"You ready?" Emery rolled down his window. He wore a blue flannel shirt and a gimme cap that read STARFLEET ACADEMY. In the hybrid's passenger seat, Leonard perused a road atlas. He looked up and shot Robbie a smile.

"Hey, a road trip."

"Yeah." Robbie smiled back and patted the hybrid's roof. "See you."

It took almost two hours just to get beyond the gravitational pull of the Washington Beltway. Farms and forest had long ago disappeared beneath an endless grid of malls and housing developments, many of them vacant. Every time Robbie turned up the radio for a song he liked, the boys complained that they could hear it through their earphones.

Only as the sky darkened and Virginia gave way to North Carolina did the world take on a faint fairy glow, distant green and yellow lights reflecting the first stars and a shining cusp of moon. Sprawl gave way to pine forest. The boys had been asleep for hours, in that amazing, self-willed hibernation they summoned whenever in the presence of adults for more than fifteen minutes. Robbie put the radio on, low, searched until he caught the echo of a melody he knew, and then another. He thought of driving with Anna beside him, a restive Zach behind them in his car seat; the aimless trips they'd make until the toddler fell asleep and they could talk or, once, park in a vacant lot and make out.

How long had it been since he'd remembered that? Years, maybe. He fought against thinking of Anna; sometimes it felt as though he fought Anna herself, her hands pummeling him as he poured another drink or staggered up to bed.

Now, though, the darkness soothed him the way those long-ago drives had lulled Zach to sleep. He felt an ache lift from his breast, as though a splinter had been dislodged; blinked and in the rearview mirror glimpsed Anna's face, slightly turned from him as she gazed out at the passing sky.

He started, realized he'd begun to nod off. On the dashboard his fuel indicator glowed red. He called Emery, and at the next exit pulled off 95, the Prius behind him.

After a few minutes they found a gas station set back from the road in a pine grove, with an old-fashioned pump out front and yellow light streaming through a screen door. The boys blinked awake.

"Where are we?" asked Zach.

"No idea." Robbie got out of the car. "North Carolina."

It was like stepping into a twilight garden, or some hidden biosphere at the zoo. Warmth flowed around him, violet and rustling green, scented overpoweringly of honeysuckle and wet stone. He could hear rushing water, the stirring of wind in the leaves and countless small things—frogs peeping, insects he couldn't identify. A nightbird that made a burbling song. In the shadows behind the building, fireflies floated between kudzu-choked trees like tiny glowing fish.

For an instant he felt himself suspended in that enveloping darkness. The warm air moved through him, sweetly fragrant, pulsing with life he could neither see nor touch. He tasted something honeyed and faintly astringent in the back of his throat, and drew his breath in sharply.

"What?" demanded Zach.

"Nothing." Robbie shook his head and turned to the pump. "Just—isn't this great?"

He filled the tank. Zach and Tyler went in search of food, and Emery strolled over.

"How you holding up?"

"I'm good. Probably let Zach drive for a while so I can catch some Zs."

He moved the car, then went inside to pay. He found Leonard buying a pack of cigarettes as the boys headed out, laden with energy drinks and bags of chips. Robbie slid his credit card across the counter to a woman wearing a tank top that set off a tattoo that looked like the face of Marilyn Manson, or maybe it was Jesus.

"Do you have a restroom?"

The woman handed him a key. "Round back."

"Bathroom's here," Robbie yelled at the boys. "We're not stopping again."

They trailed him into a dank room with gray walls. A fluorescent light buzzed overhead. After Tyler left, Robbie and Zach stood side by side at the sink, trying to coax water from a rusted spigot to wash their hands.

"The hell with it," said Robbie. "Let's hit the road. You want to drive?"

"Dad." Zach pointed at the ceiling. "Dad, look."

Robbie glanced up. A screen bulged from a small window above the sink. Something had blown against the wire mesh, a leaf or scrap of paper.

But then the leaf moved, and he saw that it wasn't a leaf at all but a butterfly.

No, not a butterfly—a moth. The biggest he'd ever seen, bigger than his hand. Its fan-shaped upper wings opened, revealing vivid golden eyespots; its trailing lower wings formed two perfect arabesques, all a milky, luminous green.

"A luna moth," breathed Robbie. "I've never seen one."

Zach clambered onto the sink. "It wants to get out—"

"Hang on." Robbie boosted him, bracing himself so the boy's weight wouldn't yank the sink from the wall. "Be careful! Don't hurt it—"

The moth remained where it was. Robbie grunted—Zach weighed as much as he did—felt his legs trembling as the boy prised the screen from the wall, then struggled to pull it free.

"It's stuck," he said. "I can't get it—"

The moth fluttered weakly. One wing-tip looked ragged, as though it had been singed.

"Tear it!" Robbie cried. "Just tear the screen."

Zach wedged his fingers beneath a corner of the window frame and yanked, hard enough that he fell. Robbie caught him as the screen tore away to dangle above the sink. The luna moth crawled onto the sill.

"Go!" Zach banged on the wall. "Go on, fly!"

Like a kite catching the wind, the moth lifted. Its trailing lower wings quivered and the eyespots seemed to blink, a pallid face gazing at them from the darkness. Then it was gone.

"That was cool." For an instant, Zach's arm draped across his father's shoulder, so fleetingly Robbie might have imagined it. "I'm going to the car."

When the boy was gone, Robbie tried to push the screen back into place. He returned the key and went to join Leonard, smoking a cigarette at the edge of the woods. Behind them a car horn blared.

"Come on!" shouted Zach. "I'm leaving!"

"Happy trails," said Leonard.

Robbie slept fitfully in back as Zach drove, the two boys arguing about music and a girl named Eileen. After an hour he took over again.

The night ground on. The boys fell back asleep. Robbie drank one of their Red Bulls and thought of the glimmering wonder that had been the luna moth. A thin rind of emerald appeared on the horizon, deepening to copper, then gold as it overtook the sky. He began to see palmettos among the loblolly pines and pin oaks, and spiky plants he didn't recognize. When he opened the window, the air smelled of roses, and the sea.

"Hey." He poked Zach, breathing heavily in the seat beside him. "Hey, we're almost there."

He glanced at the directions, looked up to see the hybrid passing him and Emery gesturing at a sandy track that veered to the left. It was bounded by barbed wire fences and clumps of cactus thick with blossoms the color of lemon cream. The pines surrendered to palmettos and prehistoric-looking trees with gnarled roots that thrust up from pools where egrets and herons stabbed at frogs.

"Look," said Robbie.

Ahead of them the road narrowed to a path barely wide enough for a single vehicle, built up with shells and chunks of concrete. On one side stretched a blur of cypress and long-legged birds; on the other, an aquamarine estuary that gave way to the sea and rolling white dunes.

Robbie slowed the car to a crawl, humping across mounds of shells and doing his best to avoid sinkholes. After a quarter-mile, the makeshift causeway ended. An old metal gate lay in a twisted heap on the ground, covered by creeping vines. Above it a weathered sign clung to a cypress.

WELCOME TO COWANA ISLAND
NO DUNE BUGGIES

They drove past the ruins of a mobile home. Emery's car was out of sight. Robbie looked at his cellphone and saw there was no signal. In the back,

Tyler stirred.

"Hey Rob, where are we?"

"We're here. Wherever here is. The island."

"Sweet." Tyler leaned over the seat to jostle Zach awake. "Hey, get up. "

Robbie peered through the overgrown greenery, looking for something resembling a beach house. He tried to remember which hurricane had pounded this part of the coast, and how long ago. Two years? Five?

The place looked as though it had been abandoned for decades. Fallen palmettos were everywhere, their leaves stiff and reddish-brown, like rusted blades. Some remained upright, their crowns lopped off. Acid-green lizards sunned themselves in driveways where ferns poked through the blacktop. The remains of carports and decks dangled above piles of timber and mold-blackened sheetrock. Now and then an intact house appeared within the jungle of flowering vines.

But no people, no cars except for an SUV crushed beneath a toppled utility pole. The only store was a modest grocery with a brick facade and shattered windows, through which the ghostly outlines of aisles and displays could still be glimpsed.

"It's like *28 Days*," said Zach, and shot a baleful look at his father.

Robbie shrugged. "Talk to the man from the Starfleet Academy."

He pulled down a rutted drive to where the hybrid sat beneath a thriving palmetto. Driftwood edged a path that led to an old wood-frame house raised on stiltlike pilings. Stands of blooming cactus surrounded it, and trees choked with honeysuckle. The patchy lawn was covered with hundreds of conch shells arranged in concentric circles and spirals. On the deck a tattered red whirligig spun in the breeze, and rope hammocks hung like flaccid cocoons.

"I'm sleeping there," said Tyler.

Leonard gazed at the house with an unreadable expression. Emery had already sprinted up the uneven steps to what Robbie assumed was the front door. When he reached the top, he bent to pick up a square of coconut matting, retrieved something from beneath it then straightened, grinning.

"Come on!" he shouted, turning to unlock the door; and the others raced to join him.

The house had linoleum floors, sifted with a fine layer of sand, and mismatched furniture—rattan chairs, couches covered with faded barkcloth cushions, a canvas seat that hung from the ceiling by a chain and groaned alarmingly whenever the boys sat in it. The sea breeze stirred dusty white curtains at the windows. Anoles skittered across the floor, and Tyler fled shouting from the outdoor shower, where he'd seen a black widow spider. The electricity worked, but there was no air conditioning and no television; no internet.

"This is what you get for three hundred bucks in the off season," said Emery when Tyler complained.

"I don't get it." Robbie stood on the deck, staring across the empty road to where the dunes stretched, tufted with thorny greenery. "Even if there was a hurricane—this is practically oceanfront, all of it. Where is everybody?"

"Who can afford to build anything?" said Leonard. "Come on, I want to get my stuff inside before it heats up."

Leonard commandeered the master bedroom. He installed his laptop, Emery's camera equipment, piles of storyboards, the box that contained the miniature *Bellerophon*. This formidable array took up every inch of floor space, as well as the surface of a ping-pong table.

"Why is there a ping-pong table in the bedroom?" asked Robbie as he set down a tripod.

Emery shrugged. "You might ask, why is there not a ping-pong table in all bedrooms?"

"We're going to the beach," announced Zach.

Robbie kicked off his shoes and followed them, across the deserted road and down a path that wound through a miniature wilderness of cactus and bristly vines. He felt lightheaded from lack of sleep, and also from the beer he'd snagged from one of the cases Emery had brought. The sand was already hot; twice he had to stop and pluck sharp spurs from his bare feet. A horned toad darted across the path, and a skink with a blue tongue. His son's voice came to him, laughing, and the sound of waves on the shore.

Atop the last dune small yellow roses grew in a thick carpet, their soapy fragrance mingling with the salt breeze. Robbie bent to pluck a handful of petals and tossed them into the air.

"It's not a bad place to fly, is it?"

He turned and saw Emery, shirtless. He handed Robbie a bottle of Tecate with a slice of lime jammed in its neck, raised his own beer and took a sip.

"It's beautiful." Robbie squeezed the lime into his beer, then drank. "But that model. It won't fly."

"I know." Emery stared to where Zach and Tyler leaped in the shallow water, sending up rainbow spray as they splashed each other. "But it's a good excuse for a vacation, isn't it?"

"It is," replied Robbie, and slid down the dune to join the boys.

Over the next few days, they fell into an odd, almost sleepless rhythm, staying up till two or three A.M., drinking and talking. The adults pretended not to notice when the boys slipped a Tecate from the fridge, and ignored the incense-scented smoke that drifted from the deck after they stumbled off to bed. Everyone woke shortly after dawn, even the boys. Blinding sunlight slanted through the worn curtains. On the deck where Zack and Tyler huddled inside their hammocks, a treefrog made a sound like rusty hinges. No one slept enough, everyone drank too much.

For once it didn't matter. Robbie's hangovers dissolved as he waded into water warm as blood, then floated on his back and watched pelicans skim above him. Afterward he'd carry equipment from the house to the dunes, where Emery had created a shelter from old canvas deck chairs and bedsheets. The boys helped, the three of them lugging tripods and digital cameras, the box that contained Leonard's model of the *Bellerophon*, a cooler filled with beer and Red Bull.

That left Emery in charge of household duties. He'd found an ancient red wagon half-buried in the dunes, and used this to transport bags of tortilla chips and a cooler filled with Tecate and limes. There was no store on the island save the abandoned wreck they'd passed when they first arrived. No gas station, and the historical society building appeared to be long gone.

But while driving around, Emery discovered a roadside stand that sold home-made salsa in mason jars and sage-green eggs in recycled cardboard cartons. The drive beside it was blocked with a barbed-wire fence and a sign that said BEWARE OF TWO-HEADED DOG.

"You ever see it?" asked Tyler.

"Nope. I never saw anyone except an alligator." Emery opened a beer. "And it was big enough to eat a two-headed dog."

By Thursday morning, they'd carted everything from one end of the island to the other, waiting with increasing impatience as Leonard climbed up and down dunes and stared broodingly at the blue horizon.

"How will you know which is the right one?" asked Robbie.

Leonard shook his head. "I don't know. Maggie said she thought it would be around here—"

He swept his arm out, encompassing a high ridge of sand that crested above the beach like a frozen wave. Below, Tyler and Zach argued over whose turn it was to haul everything uphill again. Robbie shoved his sunglasses against his nose.

"This beach has probably been washed away a hundred times since McCauley was here. Maybe we should just choose a place at random. Pick the highest dune or something."

"Yeah, I know." Leonard sighed. "This is probably our best choice, here."

He stood and for a long time gazed at the sky. Finally he turned and walked down to join the boys.

"We'll do it here," he said brusquely, and headed back to the house.

Late that afternoon they made a bonfire on the beach. The day had ended gray and much cooler than it had been, the sun swallowed in a haze of bruise-tinged cloud. Robbie waded into the shallow water, feeling with his toes for conch shells. Beside the fire, Zach came across a shark's tooth the size of a guitar pick.

"That's probably a million years old," said Tyler enviously.

"Almost as old as Dad," said Zach.

Robbie flopped down beside Leonard. "It's so weird," he said, shaking sand from a conch. "There's a whole string of these islands, but I haven't seen a boat the whole time we've been here."

"Are you complaining?" said Leonard.

"No. Just, don't you think it's weird?"

"Maybe." Leonard tossed his cigarette into the fire.

"I want to stay." Zack rolled onto his back and watched as sparks flew among the first stars. "Dad? Why can't we just stay here?"

Robbie took a long pull from his beer. "I have to get back to work. And you guys have school."

"Fuck school," said Zach and Tyler.

"Listen." The boys fell silent as Leonard glared at them. "Tomorrow morning I want to set everything up. We'll shoot before the wind picks up too much. I'll have the rest of the day to edit. Then we pack and head to Fayetteville on Saturday. We'll find some cheap place to stay, and drive home on Sunday."

The boys groaned. Emery sighed. "Back to the salt mines. I gotta call that guy about the show."

"I want to have a few hours with Maggie." Leonard pulled at the silver skull in his ear. "I told the nurse I'd be there Saturday before noon."

"We'll have to leave pretty early," said Emery.

For a few minutes nobody spoke. Wind rattled brush in the dunes behind them. The bonfire leaped, then subsided, and Zach fed it a knot of driftwood. An unseen bird gave a piping cry that was joined by another, then another, until their plaintive voices momentarily drowned out the soft rush of waves.

Robbie gazed into the darkening water. In his hand, the conch shell felt warm and silken as skin.

"Look, Dad," said Zach. "Bats."

Robbie leaned back to see black shapes dodging sparks above their heads.

"Nice," he said, his voice thick from drink.

"Well." Leonard stood and lit another cigarette. "I'm going to bed."

"Me too," said Zach.

Robbie watched with mild surprise as the boys clambered to their feet, yawning. Emery removed a beer from the cooler, handed it to Robbie.

"Keep an eye on the fire, compadre," he said, and followed the others.

Robbie turned to study the dying blaze. Ghostly runnels of green and blue ran along the driftwood branch. Salt, Leonard had explained to the boys, though Robbie wondered if that was true. How did Leonard know all this stuff? He frowned, picked up a handful of sand and tossed it at the feeble blaze, which promptly sank into sullen embers.

Robbie swore under his breath. He finished his beer, stood and walked unsteadily toward the water. The clouds obscured the moon, though there was a faint umber glow reflected in the distant waves. He stared at the horizon, searching in vain for some sign of life, lights from a cruiseship or plane; turned and gazed up and down the length of the beach.

Nothing. Even the bonfire had died. He stood on tiptoe and tried to peer past the high dune, to where the beach house stood within the grove of palmettos.

Night swallowed everything,

He turned back to the waves licking at his bare feet. Something stung his face, blown sand or maybe a gnat. He waved to disperse it, then froze.

In the water, plumes of light coiled and unfolded, dazzling him. Deepest violet, a fiery emerald that stabbed his eyes; cobalt and a pure blaze of scarlet. He shook his head, edging backward; caught himself and looked around.

He was alone. He turned back, and the lights were still there, just below the surface, furling and unfurling to some secret rhythm.

Like a machine, he thought; some kind of underwater windfarm. A wave-farm?

But no, that was crazy. He rubbed his cheeks, trying to sober up. He'd seen something like this in Ocean City late one night—it was something alive, Leonard had explained, plankton or jellyfish, one of those things that glowed. They'd gotten high and raced into the Atlantic to watch pale-green streamers trail them as they body-surfed.

Now he took a deep breath and waded in, kicking at the waves, then halted to see if he'd churned up a luminous cloud.

Darkness lapped almost to his knees: there was no telltale glow where he'd stirred the water. But a few yards away, the lights continued to turn in upon themselves beneath the surface: scores of fist-sized nebulae, soundless and steady as his own pulse.

He stared until his head ached, trying to get a fix on them. The lights weren't diffuse, like phosphorescence. And they didn't float like jellyfish. They seemed to be rooted in place, near enough for him to touch.

Yet his eyes couldn't focus: the harder he tried, the more the lights seemed to shift, like an optical illusion or some dizzying computer game.

He stood there for five minutes, maybe longer. Nothing changed. He started to back away, slowly, finally turned and stumbled across the sand, stopping every few steps to glance over his shoulder. The lights were still there, though now he saw them only as a soft yellowish glow.

He ran the rest of the way to the house. There were no lights on, no music or laughter.

But he could smell cigarette smoke, and traced it to the deck where Leonard stood beside the rail.

"Leonard!" Robbie drew alongside him, then glanced around for the boys.

"They slept inside," said Leonard. "Too cold."

"Listen, you have to see something. On the beach—these lights. Not on the beach, in the water." He grabbed Leonard's arm. "Like—just come on."

Leonard shook him off angrily. "You're drunk."

"I'm not drunk! Or, okay, maybe I am, a little. But I'm not kidding. Look—"

He pointed past the sea of palmettos, past the dunes, toward the dark line of waves. The yellow glow was now spangled with silver. It spread across the water, narrowing as it faded toward the horizon, like a wavering path.

Leonard stared, then turned to Robbie in disbelief. "You idiot. It's the fuck-ing moon."

Robbie looked up. And yes, there was the quarter-moon, a blaze of gold between gaps in the cloud.

"That's not it." He knew he sounded not just drunk but desperate. "It was *in* the water—"

"Bioluminescence." Leonard sighed and tossed his cigarette, then headed for the door. "Go to bed, Robbie."

Robbie started to yell after him, but caught himself and leaned against the rail. His head throbbed. Phantom blots of light swam across his vision. He felt dizzy, and on the verge of tears.

He closed his eyes; forced himself to breathe slowly, to channel the pulsing in his head into the memory of spectral whirlpools, a miniature galaxy blossoming beneath the water. After a minute he looked out again, but saw nothing save the blades of palmetto leaves etched against the moonlit sky.

He woke several hours later on the couch, feeling as though an axe were embedded in his forehead. Gray light washed across the floor. It was cold; he reached fruitlessly for a blanket, groaned and sat up.

Emery was in the open kitchen, washing something in the sink. He glanced at Robbie, then hefted a coffee pot. "Ready for this?"

Robbie nodded, and Emery handed him a steaming mug. "What time is it?'

"Eight, a little after. The boys are with Leonard—they went out about an hour ago. It looks like rain, which kind of throws a monkey wrench into everything. Maybe it'll hold off long enough to get that thing off the ground."

Robbie sipped his coffee. "Seventeen seconds. He could just throw it into the air."

"Yeah, I thought of that too. So what happened to you last night?"

"Nothing. Too much Tecate."

"Leonard said you were raving drunk."

"Leonard sets the bar pretty low. I was—relaxed."

"Well, time to unrelax. I told him I'd get you up and we'd be at the beach by eight."

"I don't even know what I'm doing. Am I a cameraman?"

"Uh uh. That's me. You don't know how to work it, plus it's my camera. The boys are in charge of the windbreak and, I dunno, props. They hand things to Leonard."

"Things? What things?" Robbie scowled. "It's a fucking model airplane. It doesn't have a remote, does it? Because that would have been a *good* idea."

Emery picked up his camera bag. "Come on. You can carry the tripod, how's that? Maybe the boys will hand you things, and you can hand them to Leon-ard."

"I'll be there in a minute. Tell Leonard he can start without me."

After Emery left he finished his coffee and went into his room. He rummaged through his clothes until he found a bottle of Ibuprofen, downed six, then pulled on a hooded sweatshirt and sat on the edge of his bed, staring at the wall.

He'd obviously had some kind of blackout, the first since he'd been fired from the Parks Commission. Somewhere between his seventh beer and this morning's hangover was the blurred image of Crayola-colored pinwheels turning beneath dark water, his stumbling flight from the beach and Leonard's disgusted voice: *You idiot, it's the fucking moon.*

Robbie grimaced. He *had* seen something, he knew that.

But he could no longer recall it clearly, and what he could remember made no sense. It was like a movie he'd watched half-awake, or an accident he'd glimpsed from the corner of his eye in a moving car. Maybe it had been the moonlight, or some kind of fluorescent seaweed.

Or maybe he'd just been totally wasted.

Robbie sighed. He put on his sneakers, grabbed Emery's tripod and headed out.

A scattering of cold rain met him as he hit the beach. It was windy. The sea glinted gray and silver, like crumpled tinfoil. Clumps of seaweed covered the sand, and small round discs that resembled pieces of clouded glass: jellyfish, hundreds of them. Robbie prodded one with his foot, then continued down the shore.

The dune was on the north side of the island, where it rose steeply a good fifteen feet above the sand. Now, a few hours before low tide, the water was about thirty feet away. It was exactly the kind of place you might choose to launch a human-powered craft, if you knew little about aerodynamics. Robbie didn't know much, but he was fairly certain you needed to be higher to get any kind of lift.

Still, that would be for a full-sized craft. For a scale model you could hold in your two cupped hands, maybe it would be high enough. He saw Emery pacing along the water's edge, vidcam slung around his neck. The only sign of the others was a trail of footsteps leading to the dune. Robbie clambered up, using the tripod to keep from slipping on sand the color and texture of damp cornmeal. He was panting when he reached the top.

"Hey Dad. Where were you?"

Robbie smiled weakly as Zach peered out from the windbreak. "I have a sinus infection."

Zach motioned him inside. "Come on, I can't leave this open."

Robbie set down the tripod, then crouched to enter the makeshift tent. Inside, bedsheet walls billowed in the wind, straining at an elaborate scaffold of broom handles, driftwood, the remains of wooden deck chairs. Tyler and Zach sat crosslegged on a blanket and stared at their cellphones.

"You can get a strong signal here," said Tyler. "Nope, it's gone again."

Next to them, Leonard knelt beside a cardboard box. Instead of his customary white tunic, he wore one that was sky-blue, embroidered with yellow birds. He glanced at Robbie, his gray eyes cold and dismissive. "There's only room for three people in here."

"That's okay—I'm going out," said Zach, and crawled through the gap in the sheets. Tyler followed him. Robbie jammed his hands into his pockets and forced a smile.

"So," he said. "Did you see all those jellyfish?"

Leonard nodded without looking at him. Very carefully he removed the *Bellerophon* and set it on a neatly folded towel. He reached into the box again, and withdrew something else. A doll no bigger than his hand, dressed in black frockcoat and trousers, with a bowler hat so small that Robbie could have swallowed it.

"*Voila,*" said Leonard.

"Jesus, Leonard." Robbie hesitated, then asked, "Can I look at it?"

To his surprise, Leonard nodded. Robbie picked it up. The little figure was so light he wondered if there was anything inside the tiny suit.

But as he turned it gently, he could feel slender joints under its clothing, a miniature torso. Tiny hands protruded from the sleeves, and it wore minute, highly polished shoes that appeared to be made of black leather. Under the frock coat was a waistcoat, with a watch-chain of gold thread that dangled from a nearly invisible pocket. From beneath the bowler hat peeked a fringe of red hair fine as milkweed down. The cameo-sized face that stared up at Robbie was Maggie Blevin's, painted in hairline strokes so that he could see every eyelash, every freckle on her rounded cheeks.

He looked at Leonard in amazement. "How did you do this?"

"It took a long time." He held out his hand, and Robbie returned the doll. "The hardest part was making sure the *Bellerophon* could carry her weight. And that she fit into the bicycle seat and could pedal it. You wouldn't think that would be difficult, but it was."

"It—it looks just like her." Robbie glanced at the doll again, then said, "I thought you wanted to make everything look like the original film. You know, with McCauley—I thought that was the point."

"The point is for it to fly."

"But—"

"You don't need to understand," said Leonard. "Maggie will."

He bent over the little aircraft, its multi-colored wings and silken parasol bright as a toy carousel, and tenderly began to fit the doll-sized pilot into its seat.

Robbie shivered. He'd seen Leonard's handiwork before, mannequins so realistic that tourists constantly poked them to see if they were alive.

But those were life-sized, and they weren't designed to resemble someone he *knew.* The sight of Leonard holding a tiny Maggie Blevin tenderly, as though she were a captive bird, made Robbie feel lightheaded and slightly sick. He turned toward the tent opening. "I'll see if I can help Emery set up."

Leonard's gaze remained fixed on the tiny figure. "I'll be right there," he said at last.

At the foot of the dune, the boys were trying to talk Emery into letting them use the camera.

"No way." He waved as Robbie scrambled down. "See, I'm not even letting your dad do it."

"That's because Dad would suck," Zach said as Emery grabbed Robbie and steered him toward the water. "Come on, just for a minute."

"Trouble with the crew?" asked Robbie.

"Nah. They're just getting bored."

"Did you see that doll?"

"The Incredible Shrinking Maggie?" Emery stopped to stare at the dune. "The thing about Leonard is, I can never figure out if he's brilliant or potentially dangerous. The fact that he'll be able to retire with a full government pension suggests he's normal. The Maggie voodoo doll, though…"

He shook his head and began to pace again. Robbie walked beside him, kicking at wet sand and staring curiously at the sky. The air smelled odd, of ozone or hot metal. But it felt too chilly for a thunderstorm, and the dark ridge that hung above the palmettos and live oaks looked more like encroaching fog than cumulus clouds.

"Well, at least the wind's from the right direction," said Robbie.

Emery nodded. "Yeah. I was starting to think we'd have to throw it from the roof."

A few minutes later, Leonard's voice rang out above the wind. "Okay, everyone over here."

They gathered at the base of the dune and stared up at him, his tunic an azure rent in the ominous sky. Between Leonard's feet was a cardboard box. He glanced at it and went on.

"I'm going to wait till the wind seems right, and then I'll yell '*Now!*' Emery, you'll just have to watch me and see where she goes, then do your best. Zach and Tyler—you guys fan out and be ready to catch her if she starts to fall. Catch her *gently*," he added.

"What about me?" called Robbie.

"You stay with Emery in case he needs backup."

"Backup?" Robbie frowned.

"You know," said Emery in a low voice. "In case I need help getting Leonard back to the rubber room."

The boys began to walk toward the water. Tyler had his cellphone out. He looked at Zach, who dug his phone from his pocket.

"Are they *texting* each other?" asked Emery in disbelief. "They're ten feet apart."

"Ready?" Leonard shouted.

"Ready," the boys yelled back.

Robbie turned to Emery. "What about you, Captain Marvo?"

Emery grinned and held up the camera. "I have never been readier."

Atop the dune, Leonard stooped to retrieve the *Bellerophon* from its box. As he straightened, its propellers began turning madly. Candy-striped rotators spun like pinwheels as he cradled it against his chest, his long white braids threatening to tangle with the parasol.

The wind gusted suddenly: Robbie's throat tightened; as he watched, the tiny black figure beneath the fuselage swung wildly back and forth, like an accelerated pendulum. Leonard slipped in the sand and fought to regain his balance.

"Uh oh," said Emery.

The wind died, and Leonard righted himself. Even from the beach, Robbie could see how his face had gone white.

"Are you okay?" yelled Zach.

"I'm okay," Leonard yelled back.

He gave them a shaky smile, then stared intently at the horizon. After a minute his head tilted, as though listening to something. Abruptly he straightened and raised the *Bellerophon* in both hands. Behind him, palmettos thrashed as the wind gusted.

"*Now!*" he shouted.

Leonard opened his hands. As though it were a butterfly, the *Bellerophon* lifted into the air. Its feathery parasol billowed. Fan-shaped wings rose and fell; ailerons flapped and gears whirled like pinwheels. There was a sound like a train rushing through a tunnel, and Robbie stared open-mouthed as the *Bellerophon* skimmed the air above his head, its pilot pedaling furiously as it headed toward the sea.

Robbie gasped. The boys raced after it, yelling. Emery followed, camera clamped to his face and Robbie at his heels.

"This is fucking incredible!' Emery shouted. "Look at that thing go!"

They drew up a few yards from the water. The *Bellerophon* whirred past, barely an arm's-length above them. Robbie's eyes blurred as he stared after that brilliant whirl of color and motion, a child's dream of flight soaring just out of reach. Emery waded into the shallows with his camera. The boys followed, splashing and waving at the little plane. From the dune behind them echoed Leonard's voice.

"*Godspeed.*"

Robbie gazed silently at the horizon as the *Bellerophon* continued on, its pilot silhouetted black against the sky, wings opened like sails. Its sound grew fainter, a soft whirring that might have been a flock of birds. Soon it would be gone. Robbie stepped to the water's edge and craned his neck to keep it in sight.

Without warning a green flare erupted from the waves and streamed toward the little aircraft. Like a meteor shooting *upward*, emerald blossomed into a blinding radiance that engulfed the *Bellerophon*. For an instant Robbie saw the flying machine, a golden wheel spinning within a comet's heart.

Then the blazing light was gone, and with it the *Bellerophon*.

Robbie gazed, stunned, at the empty air. After an endless moment he became aware of something—someone—near him. He turned to see Emery stagger from the water, soaking wet, the camera held uselessly at his side.

"I dropped it," he gasped. "When that—whatever the fuck it was, when it came, I dropped the camera."

Robbie helped him onto the sand.

"I felt it." Emery shuddered, his hand tight around Robbie's arm. "Like a riptide. I thought I'd go under."

Robbie pulled away from him. "Zach?" he shouted, panicked. "Tyler, Zach, are you—"

Emery pointed at the water, and Robbie saw them, heron-stepping through the waves and whooping in triumph as they hurried back to shore.

"What happened?" Leonard ran up alongside Robbie and grabbed him. "Did you see that?"

Robbie nodded. Leonard turned to Emery, his eyes wild. "Did you get it? The *Bellerophon*? And that flare? Like the original film! The same thing, the exact same thing!"

Emery reached for Robbie's sweatshirt. "Give me that, I'll see if I can dry the camera."

Leonard stared blankly at Emery's soaked clothes, the water dripping from the vidcam.

"Oh no." He covered his face with his hands. "Oh no…"

"We got it!" Zach pushed between the grownups. "We got it, we got it!" Tyler ran up beside him, waving his cellphone. "Look!"

Everyone crowded together, the boys tilting their phones until the screens showed black.

"Okay," said Tyler. "Watch this."

Robbie shaded his eyes, squinting.

And there it was, a bright mote bobbing across a formless gray field, growing bigger and bigger until he could see it clearly—the whirl of wings and gears, the ballooning peacock-feather parasol and steadfast pilot on the velocipede; the swift silent flare that lashed from the water, then disappeared in an eyeblink.

"Now watch mine," said Zach, and the same scene played again from a different angle. "Eighteen seconds."

"Mine says twenty," said Tyler. Robbie glanced uneasily at the water.

"Maybe we should head back to the house," he said.

Leonard seized Zach's shoulder. "Can you get me that? Both of you? Email it or something?"

"Sure. But we'll need to go where we can get a signal."

"I'll drive you," said Emery. "Let me get into some dry clothes."

He turned and trudged up the beach, the boys laughing and running behind him.

Leonard walked the last few steps to the water's edge, spray staining the tip of one cowboy boot. He stared at the horizon, his expression puzzled yet oddly expectant.

Robbie hesitated, then joined him. The sea appeared calm, green-glass waves rolling in long swells beneath parchment-colored sky. Through a gap in the clouds he could make out a glint of blue, like a noonday star. He gazed at it in silence, and after a minute asked, "Did you know that was going to happen?"

Leonard shook his head. "No. How could I?"

"Then—what was it?" Robbie looked at him helplessly. "Do you have any idea?"

Leonard said nothing. Finally he turned to Robbie. Unexpectedly, he smiled.

"I have no clue. But you saw it, right?" Robbie nodded. "And you saw her fly. The *Bellerophon*."

Leonard took another step, heedless of waves at his feet. "She flew." His voice was barely a whisper. "She really flew."

That night nobody slept. Emery drove Zach, Tyler and Leonard to a Dunkin' Donuts where the boys got a cellphone signal and sent their movie footage to Leonard's laptop. Back at the house, he disappeared while the others sat on the deck and discussed, over and over again, what they had seen. The boys wanted to return to the beach, but Robbie refused to let them go. As a peace offering, he gave them each a beer. By the time Leonard emerged from his room with the laptop, it was after three A.M.

He set the computer on a table in the living room. "See what you think." When the others had assembled, he hit Play.

Blotched letters filled the screen: THE MAIDEN FLIGHT OF MCCAULEY'S *BELLEROPHON*. The familiar tipsy horizon appeared, sepia and amber, silvery flashes from the sea below. Robbie held his breath.

And there was the *Bellerophon* with its flickering wheels and wings propelled by a steadfast pilot, until the brilliant light struck from below and the clip abruptly ended, at exactly seventeen seconds. Nothing betrayed the figure as Maggie rather than McCauley; nothing seemed any different at all, no matter how many times Leonard played it back.

"So that's it," he said at last, and closed his laptop.

"Are you going to put it on YouTube?" asked Zach.

"No," he replied wearily. The boys exchanged a look, but for once remained silent.

"Well." Emery stood and stretched his arms, yawning. "Time to pack."

Two hours later they were on the road.

The hospice was a few miles outside town, a rambling old white house surrounded by neatly kept azaleas and rhododendrons. The boys were turned loose to wander the neighborhood. The others walked up to the veranda, Leonard carrying his laptop. He looked terrible, his gray eyes bloodshot and his face unshaved. Emery put an arm over his shoulder and Leonard nodded stiffly.

A nurse met them at the door, a trim blonde woman in chinos and a yellow blouse.

"I told her you were coming," she said as she showed them into a sunlit room with wicker furniture and a low table covered with books and magazines. "She's the only one here now, though we expect someone tomorrow."

"How is she?" asked Leonard.

"She sleeps most of the time. And she's on morphine for the pain, so she's not very lucid. Her body's shutting down. But she's conscious."

"Has she had many visitors?" asked Emery.

"Not since she's been here. In the hospital a few neighbors dropped by. I gather there's no family. It's a shame." She shook her head sadly. "She's a lovely woman."

"Can I see her?" Leonard glanced at a closed door at the end of the bright room.

"Of course."

Robbie and Emery watched them go, then settled into the wicker chairs.

"God, this is depressing," said Emery.

"It's better than a hospital," said Robbie. "Anna was going to go into a hospice, but she died before she could."

Emery winced. "Sorry. Of course, I wasn't thinking."

"It's okay."

Robbie leaned back and shut his eyes. He saw Anna sitting on the grass with azaleas all around her, bees in the flowers and Zach laughing as he opened his hands to release a green moth that lit momentarily upon her head, then drifted into the sky.

"Robbie." He started awake. Emery sat beside him, shaking him gently. "Hey—I'm going in now. Go back to sleep if you want, I'll wake you when I come out."

Robbie looked around blearily. "Where's Leonard?"

"He went for a walk. He's pretty broken up. He wanted to be alone for a while."

"Sure, sure." Robbie rubbed his eyes. "I'll just wait."

When Emery was gone he stood and paced the room. After a few minutes he sighed and sank back into his chair, then idly flipped through the magazines and books on the table. *Tricycle*, *Newsweek*, the *Utne Reader*; some pamphlets on end-of-life issues, works by Viktor Frankl and Elisabeth Kübler-Ross.

And, underneath yesterday's newspaper, a familiar sky-blue dustjacket emblazoned with the garish image of a naked man and woman, hands linked as they floated above a vast abyss, surrounded by a glowing purple sphere. Beneath them the title appeared in embossed green letters.

Wings for Humanity!
The Next Step is OURS!

by Margaret S. Blevin, Ph.D.

Robbie picked it up. On the back was a photograph of the younger Maggie in a white embroidered tunic, her hair a bright corona around her piquant face. She stood in the Hall of Flight beside a mockup of the Apollo Lunar Module, the Wright Flyer high above her head. She was laughing, her hands raised in welcome. He opened it to a random page.

> …that time has come: With the dawn of the Golden Millennium we will welcome their return, meeting them at last as equals to share in the glory that is the birthright of our species.

He glanced at the frontispiece and title page, and then the dedication.

> *For Leonard, who never doubted*

"Isn't that an amazing book?"

Robbie looked up to see the nurse smiling down at him.

"Uh, yeah," he said, and set it on the table.

"It's incredible she predicted so much stuff." The nurse shook her head. "Like the Hubble Telescope, and that caveman they found in the glacier, the guy with the lens? And those turbines that can make energy in the jet stream? I never even heard of that, but my husband said they're real. Everything she says, it's all so hopeful. You know?"

Robbie stared at her, then quickly nodded. Behind her the door opened. Emery stepped out.

"She's kind of drifting," he said.

"Morning's her good time. She usually fades around now." The nurse glanced at her watch, then at Robbie. "You go ahead. Don't be surprised if she nods off."

He stood. "Sure. Thanks."

The room was small, its walls painted a soft lavender-gray. The bed faced a large window overlooking a garden. Goldfinches and tiny green wrens darted between a bird feeder and a small pool lined with flat white stones. For a moment Robbie thought the bed was empty. Then he saw an emaciated figure had slipped down between the white sheets, dwarfed by pillows and a bolster.

"Maggie?"

The figure turned its head. Hairless, skin white as paper, mottled with bruises like spilled ink. Her lips and fingernails were violet; her face so pale and lined it was like gazing at a cracked egg. Only the eyes were recognizably Maggie's, huge, the deep slatey blue of an infant's. As she stared at him, she drew her wizened arms up, slowly, until her fingers grazed her shoulders. She reminded Robbie disturbingly of a praying mantis.

"I don't know if you remember me." He sat in a chair beside the bed. "I'm Robbie. I worked with Leonard. At the museum."

"He told me." Her voice was so soft he had to lean close to hear her. "I'm glad they got here. I expected them yesterday, when it was still snowing."

Robbie recalled Anna in her hospital bed, doped to the gills and talking to herself. "Sure," he said.

Maggie shot him a glance that might have held annoyance, then gazed past him into the garden. Her eyes widened as she struggled to lift her hand, fingers twitching. Robbie realized she was waving. He turned to stare out the window, but there was no one there. Maggie looked at him, then gestured at the door.

"You can go now," she said. "I have guests."

"Oh. Yeah, sorry."

He stood awkwardly, then leaned down to kiss the top of her head. Her skin was smooth and cold as metal. "Bye, Maggie."

At the door he looked back, and saw her gazing with a rapt expression at the window, head cocked slightly and her hands open, as though to catch the sunlight.

Two days after they got home, Robbie received an email from Leonard.

> Dear Robbie,
> Maggie died this morning. The nurse said she became unconscious early yesterday, seemed to be in pain but at least it didn't last long. She had arranged to be cremated. No memorial service or anything like that. I will do something, probably not till the fall, and let you know.
>
> Yours, Leonard

Robbie sighed. Already the week on Cowana seemed long ago and faintly dreamlike, like the memory of a childhood vacation. He wrote Leonard a note of condolence, then left for work.

Weeks passed. Zach and Tyler posted their clips of the *Bellerophon* online. Robbie met Emery for drinks ever week or two, and saw Leonard once, at Emery's Fourth of July barbecue. By the end of summer, Tyler's footage had been viewed 347,623 times, and Zach's 347,401. Both provided a link to the Captain Marvo site, where Emery had a free download of the entire text of *Wings for Humanity!* There were now over a thousand Google hits for Margaret Blevin, and Emery added a *Bellerophon* t-shirt to his merchandise: organic cotton with a silk-screen image of the baroque aircraft and its bowler-hatted pilot.

Early in September, Leonard called Robbie.

"Can you meet me at the museum tomorrow, around eight-thirty? I'm having a memorial for Maggie, just you and me and Emery. After hours, I'll sign you in."

"Sure," said Robbie. "Can I bring something?"

"Just yourself. See you then."

He drove in with Emery. They walked across the twilit Mall, the museum a white cube that glowed against a sky swiftly darkening to indigo. Leonard waited for them by the side door. He wore an embroidered tunic, sky-blue, his white hair loose upon his shoulders, and held a cardboard box with a small printed label.

"Come on," he said. The museum had been closed since five, but a guard opened the door for them. "We don't have a lot of time."

Hedges sat at the security desk, bald and even more imposing than when Robbie last saw him, decades ago. He signed them in, eying Robbie curiously, then grinning when he read his signature.

"I remember you—Opie, right?"

Robbie winced at the nickname, then nodded. Hedges handed Leonard a slip of paper. "Be quick."

"Thanks. I will."

They walked to the staff elevator, the empty museum eerie and blue-lit. High above them the silent aircraft seemed smaller than they had been in the past, battered and oddly toylike. Robbie noticed a crack in the *Gemini VII* space capsule, and strands of dust clinging to the Wright Flyer. When they reached the third floor, Leonard led them down the corridor, past the Photo Lab, past the staff cafeteria, past the library where the Nut Files used to be. Finally he stopped at a door near some open ductwork. He looked at the slip of paper Hedges had given him, punched a series of numbers into the lock, opened it, then reached in to switch on the light. Inside was a narrow room with a metal ladder fixed to one wall.

"Where are we going?" asked Robbie.

"The roof," said Leonard. "If we get caught, Hedges and I are screwed. Actually, we're all screwed. So we have to make this fast."

He tucked the cardboard box against his chest, then began to climb the ladder. Emery and Robbie followed him, to a small metal platform and another door. Leonard punched in another code and pushed it open. They stepped out into the night.

It was like being atop an ocean liner. The museum's roof was flat, nearly a block long. Hot air blasted from huge exhaust vents, and Leonard motioned the others to move away, toward the far end of the building.

The air was cooler here, a breeze that smelled sweet and rainwashed, despite the cloudless sky. Beneath them stretched the Mall, a vast green gameboard, with the other museums and monuments huge gamepieces, ivory and onyx and glass. The spire of the Washington Monument rose in the distance, and beyond that the glittering reaches of Roslyn and Crystal City

"I've never been here," said Robbie, stepping beside Leonard.

Emery shook his head. "Me neither."

"I have," said Leonard, and smiled. "Just once, with Maggie."

Above the Capitol's dome hung the full moon, so bright against the starless sky that Robbie could read what was printed on Leonard's box.

MARGARET BLEVIN

"These are her ashes." Leonard set the box down and removed the top, revealing a ziplocked bag. He opened the bag, picked up the box again and stood. "She wanted me to scatter them here. I wanted both of you to be with me."

He dipped his hand into the bag and withdrew a clenched fist; held the box out to Emery, who nodded silently and did the same; then turned to Robbie.

"You too," he said.

Robbie hesitated, then put his hand into the box. What was inside felt gritty, more like sand than ash. When he looked up, he saw that Leonard had stepped forward, head thrown back so that he gazed at the moon. He drew his arm back, flung the ashes into the sky and stooped to grab more.

Emery glanced at Robbie, and the two of them opened their hands.

Robbie watched the ashes stream from between his fingers, like a flight of tiny moths. Then he turned and gathered more, the three of them tossing handful after handful into the sky.

When the box was finally empty Robbie straightened, breathing hard, and ran a hand across his eyes. He didn't know if it was some trick of the moonlight or the freshening wind, but everywhere around them, everywhere he looked, the air was filled with wings.

THE MIRACLE AQUILINA
MARGO LANAGAN

Margo Lanagan has published three collections of short stories, *White Time*, *Black Juice*, and *Red Spikes*, and a novel, *Tender Morsels*. She is a four-time World Fantasy Award winner (for best novel, novella, short story, and collection), has also won four Aurealis and four Ditmar awards, and two of her books were Printz Honor Books. Her work has also been nominated for Hugo, Nebula, International Horror Guild, Bram Stoker, and Theodore Sturgeon awards, the Los Angeles Times Book Prize, and the Commonwealth Writers' Prize, and twice been placed on the James Tiptree, Jr. Award honor list. She attended the Clarion West Writers Workshop in 1999, has taught at Clarion South three times, and will teach at Clarion West in 2011. Margo lives in Sydney. She is currently working on her fourth collection, *Yellowcake*, and on a novel about selkies based on her World Fantasy Award-winning novella "Sea-Hearts."

You'd have thought the bread-dough was the Captain's head, the way I went at it, squashing any mouth or eye that opened. *Bringing shame upon us*—smush, I smeared that mouth shut. *No daughter of mine*—punch, that one too. Daughter of his? I was my own self; he did not own me. If I was anyone else's I was Klepper's; he owned more parts of me than Father did, than Father wanted to *know* about. I was *married* to Klepper in all but name; part of him floated in me, growing slowly into a bigger shame—

Thump, squash—I shook the thought out of my head. Reddy was spinning one of her stories—of a fisher-girl and a kingmaker, this one—to keep Amber and Roper quiet at their needlework, and I began to listen too, to stop from thinking more, from caring, from fearing. And I was almost lost in the poor girl's story—how insolent she was to the king, and how lucky he did not have her hanged for it!—when the Captain strode in, all leathered-plate and rage. He had his helmet on, even; he was only indoors for a moment.

"Here," he said. "I'll show you." He came for me, and so swiftly I didn't even flinch away. He grasped my arm; he tore me off the dough and pushed me to the door, my hands all floury claws. "I'll show you how girls end up, that don't do as they're told."

Reddy was half up, and Amber and Roper turned in their seats, a matched pair, but they would do nothing, only gape there. They would never defy him, or question; they would never save me. Then we were out on the bright street, and me all aproned and floury. I shook him off, but he caught my elbow again, hard, that everyone should see he was in command of me.

"This woman." He muttered it as if woman-ness itself were an evil. "She worships wooden saints—you've seen them. She prostrates herself before those foolish things. Which would be bad enough."

There was a law, that those people be left at peace in their beliefs. Even if our Aquilin gods were richer and more clearly seen—for their stories and families were all written down strand for strand, and painted on walls for those of us who couldn't read, and taught in church and school—still we were to indulge the saint-followers, allow them their shrines and mutterings, only jeer among ourselves.

"She was one of ours, from a faithful family, but her nurse impressed her to the saints-belief, corrupted her." Ah, that was the cause of his bitterness, was it?

"She's to be punished for that?" I said, because I was not sure what the law was, for our people gone over to the saints' ways, but I did not think we could call it exactly a *crime*.

"No!" He pushed me to the right, through the council portico, along the colonnade there, people glancing at us but too important about their own business to accost us. "She refused the King himself, is her offence!"

"Refused him what?" I struggled as much as I could without making a scene. "Let go of me! I will walk with you!"

"You will," he said, "you will." And did not let go. "Refused him herself. Her hand, or failing that her body. Wife or concubine he offered her. Wife! Out in the fields with her sheep, she was! Who knows what vermin were on her; who knows what lads had been at her willy-nilly? And our King says *I will have you, I will save you, you are beautiful enough to be queen or mistress to me!* And *No!*, she says! She would rather turn to leather out there on the hillside, making her signs on herself, chattering to her pixies. A madwoman, or at the least imprudent! You will see, though." He shook me, and I staggered. "You will see how imprudence is dealt with, and wilfulness."

We were going down the backs now, where it was unpaved, and smelt, and was narrow. He pushed me ahead of him. There was the barracks, with soldiers smoking at the upper windows, grinning down, and the woman-houses, the crones at the doors watching us shrewdly as we passed. Then we turned the corner, and there was the prison, blind of windows, its wall-tops all spikes and potsherds.

The guard at the entry-way saluted my father, staring hard at nothing. For a moment I felt the bitterness of belonging to a Captain. This guard's respect was for my father's rank only; the Captain the man was as nothing to him. *I* was as nothing, a parcel or a document the Captain brought with him to his place of work.

In we went, and along in the blind stony darkness, farther in and along again, until we were deep in the place. He was imprisoning me? He was placing me in a cell, to teach me this lesson? I would not learn it, no matter what weight of stone and military he put about me, no matter how long he kept me from the world.

Finally we came to a door that stood open; here the guard gave me a look of alarm, even as he sharpened his stance for my father. From inside came the sound of a whip through the air, like a little outraged shout, and a slap on something wet.

The chamber was vast, yet not airy. Evils were done here, it was easy to tell; their equipments reared and languished in the shadows, away from the men grouped torchlit in the middle of the room.

The woman was in a cleared space at their centre, as straight as if she stood on a hilltop stretching to glimpse a distant beacon. Her back was to us; her dress-cloth was shredded into her flesh from the whipping; her blood ran freely down.

"Her legs," said the King. You could tell him by his seatedness and stillness; if a gathering can have two centres, he was the other.

Two soldiers hoisted up her skirts, from bare dirty heels, from white calves. The backs of her knees made my insides shrink, the vulnerable creases of them, the fine skin.

"Her buttocks, too," said His Majesty.

Something gave, in the crowd of men—a kind of relief, or excitement. The soldiers pulled the skirts up above her thighs and buttocks—all I could think was how soft, how that flesh would sting to the whip. My own buttocks clenched at the sight, my own thighs expected that sting. But the woman herself, she stood straight and trembled not at all, as if there were no indignity in what they did, let alone any pain to come.

They made her hold her own skirts aside; the first strokes striped, then diamonded her flesh. She did not wince, or cry out. Her back glittered crimson in the torches' light, and black with the wet threads; now the stripes on her thighs and calves began to join together red; now the first gleam of blood showed there.

"The arrogance of her!" growled the Captain to himself, and this seemed to remind him that he had a voice, and he took my arm harder, and shook it. "You see? This is what's done to girls who will not be bid!"

He met my eye and he was all hot rage, that this demonstrating to me was even necessary. He could not turn me by the power of his words. He could raise his voice as loud and long as he liked, but he could not control me by the raising, as once he'd used to. *I will see whom I please,* I'd said. *I will marry whom I please. It is Klepper I want, not some rock-headed legionnaire you owe a favor to.*

"Cease," said the King's cold voice onto the congested air, and there was no sound but the breathing of the soldiers who had been taking turns to beat the woman. "Let me see her," he said.

She did not wait for them to turn her, but dropped her skirts, and spun on the wetness of her own spilt blood, to face him. The soldiers moved to take her arms, much as the Captain had mine, but the King waved them aside, a casual movement, but involving many weighty rings, from which red light flashed, and a shard of kingfisher blue.

They stepped back from her; she stood, tall and full of joy, and truly my breath stopped in my throat for several moments, for it was clear what drove the King to want to marry her. She was the model of an Aquilina: broad-browed, straight-nosed, full-lipped, strong-jawed, all strength and delicacy combined. Her eyes were clear, green, open; they gazed down at the King, almost in amusement, I thought. I loved her in an instant myself, for what they had done to her, and for why. But he is the *King!* I thought. What does she have, that she can dismiss the King's wishes? That she is not dazzled by him, that she holds her own ground? I wanted to know, and I wanted it for myself.

"What have you to say, shepherdess?" There was steel in the King's voice, for he saw, as all of us could see, that she had defeated him with her carriage and beauty.

"I have nothing to say, sir," she said happily.

"Are you mad, girl?" said a courtier at the King's side. I had seen that man before. I didn't like him; he was all bones and brains. "Have your pains driven you mad, that you affect such cheer, such insolence?"

She glanced at him bemused, then returned her gaze to His Majesty. "I assure you, I have all my senses at my own command."

"You will marry me, then," he said, his voice momentarily softer, fuller, with something in it that would have been pleading, had this not been the Aquilin king, who pled with no one, not prelate nor general nor sultan nor sent prince from foreign parts of anywhere in the world.

"I will not," she said. "As I have told you, I belong body and soul—"

"To your lord," said Mr Bones-and-brains disgustedly. "Yes, girl, we have heard all that." He waved her to turn her back on us again. "Bite deeper, lads! Scatter the floor with her flesh!"

Willingly she turned. But a gasp went up, from me and from all around me. For though her blood had stained all the back of her skirt, though she stood in a puddle and her feet were red with it, her flesh within the torn dress-back was white, was clean, as if no whip had touched it. And when they lifted her skirts, her calves there, and then her thighs and buttocks, were unwelted and unbled, restored entirely to wholeness, to perfection.

Astonishment stilled them all, the soldiers agape, the nobles hands to mouths. Then gradually all turned from the marvel of the woman's recovery to His Majesty. He gazed on her grimly, up and down, his eyes a-glisten with moving thought. What would he do? What power was being shown him, that undid this work of his upon her body? Whom did she have behind her, and how would he conquer them?

"Put her in the pot," he said very softly—you see, Father, how much power a *soft* voice can carry? "We will make a soup of her."

There, again, the air changed; the excitement pitched itself a little higher, into a kind of gaiety. All was business and haste to obey him, our King our church our god and saints. I had never seen it so direct, how his will drove us, how he sat at the centre and played us all like game-pieces, or as a spinner's foot sets the pedal, then the wheel, in motion.

Pale-faced, the Captain pulled me back against the wall. "She is some kind of monster!" He watched the summoned servants run for kindling.

"She is one of us," I said. Her Aquilin hair gleamed motionless, smooth black around her head, caught away forward over one shoulder so as not to snarl with the blood-wetted whip. "And she is a miracle. If truly it is her Lord—"

He slapped my cheek, hard.

I regarded him, half my face burning from the blow, my eyes drinking back the tears that had sprung from the shock of it. His fear and weakness were written strong as his rage in his face. *Don't think I cannot force you,* he had said to me. But I did think it; I knew it. My sisters would bow their heads and do what he told them, but I—he had this weakness in him, when it came to me. He had this softness. I would have my way.

"We should worship her as a miracle," I said evenly, coldly, straight into his eyes.

"We should kill her, and smartly! She is a demon! The longer she lives, the longer she dazzles such fools as you! You will see," he hissed close to my face, "how pretty she is, all red-boiled and bursting. You will see what insolence will bring you, and thinking you can please yourself!"

It took some while to ready the pot, though boiling water was brought down from the council-house kitchens. It was a large pot, big enough to boil several people at once, I would have thought. They built the fire so high that the walk-way around the top of the pot began to scorch, and a man was sent up there, to keep it wetted, and not catch fire himself. Every face about me, except for the King's and the more important of the courtiers' imitating him, was alive with surprise and curiosity, or with a kind of greed—whether for more suffering by the Aquilina or more embarrassment of the King I could not tell—and some with suppressed mirth. Whatever his state of mind, every man here, at this moment, contained very little more than the vitality of his interest in what would befall them next, this woman and this king, what damage would be done by each upon the other. I was glad the maid had her back to us still and did not see any of this, how eagerly men wished her ill, and the lengths they were going to, to see her harmed and to have that harm endure.

They led the woman to a spread net of rope, such as is used to tangle and tie a mad bull in, and subdue it. They made her stand in the middle of it; they threw the corner-ties over a ceiling-beam and the net rose around her and lifted her, and up it carried her to the railing of the pot-platform, where a hook held it aside from the rising steam. Up went the King and his nearest; one of these turned and beckoned for more to climb the wooden steps, and my father was high-ranked enough that he could bustle me up there, and press me to the front of the crowd, where a second railing kept us from pitching forward ourselves into the bubbles, into the cauldron full of torch-flash and darkness.

"You see what fate awaits you, girl," said the King, stilling the murmur around him that the sight of the water had started.

Silence from the net.

"Answer His Majesty!" snapped some official.

"His Majesty did not ask a question," she said coolly; I could not see her face for stripes of rope-shadow. But her voice was clear enough, fine and light among these rumblers and roarers. "Yes," she said, "I see my fate there in that water, in that fire—is that the answer you wish for?" A green eye, only, looking sharpish out.

"You know the answer I want, girl," said the King, and truly he did look most handsome and noble, regarding her fiercely and gently both, as if he could not quite believe what he had come to, as if he might take pity on her at any moment, did she show any sign of distress, or of indecision. "Marry me and you live. Refuse me and I lower you to boiling."

"Then lower me, Your Majesty, if those are my only choices. For my body and soul are not mine to give to you." And her fingers, strong and lean and sun-browned, sprang through the netting and grasped it in preparation.

Soldiers unhooked her, and let her out to swing in the steam, in the silence but for the fire-noise, but for the water bursting and rolling. Within the ropes, she looked up and listened, as if she were a child hiding, waiting for the seeker to find her, for her amusement to begin.

The King gave a sign. Some other behind him passed it on, and the men below began to let out the rope.

It would have been most unsatisfactory for His Majesty, for the drowning woman let out not a whimper, let alone a scream or a begging for mercy, but went down into the water silent as a turnip or herbouquet, and the water closed over her head, and her dark hair lifted and snaked on the bubbled water a moment among the ropes. Then, only the weighted corner ropes stood stiff out of the turmoiling water, and the steam buffeted all our faces, without cease.

"There," said the King. His be-ringed hand gestured for the bringing up of her body. Little sighs of accomplishment sounded around us, murmurs of excitement at the prospect of seeing what had been done on her, but my father the Captain only leaned, with his wrists on the rail and his hands fisted, looking down, watching the woman boil.

Up they hoisted her, but we could not see her immediately for the steam pouring up and the water pouring down, and then she was only a slumped thing in the net there. The man with the hook-stick caught and pulled the net towards the platform, and a space was made, several people having to move down the steps to make room.

But not us; we were only one layer of watchers from where she was brought to land. Her small foot hung white below.

"You said she would be boiled red," I whispered to the Captain.

The foot touched the wooden platform and dragged as if it were dead—but then the touch woke it, and it braced itself against the boards, and in the moment that the net was loosed from above and fell open about her, up rose the shepherdess, the miracle girl, to standing. The steam of the boiled rope, of her boiled self, rushed up, rushed out. "Praise my Lord and Lady and all the Saints for their works and wonders!" came her clear, happy voice out of the cloud, and there she was, not a mark upon her, no worse for her wetting, or for being wrapped in boiling-wet cloth and cloaked in boiling-wet hair.

All fell back from her—in horror, in wonder, in both—and the Captain pulled me back too, so it should appear I did the right thing, instead of standing forward and laughing and clapping my hands with delight, as I was tempted to do.

The King? I saw a flash in his eyes, just a moment there and then gone, of the rage I had seen in the Captain's face, hissing and pressed close to mine. Then the handsome man was stony-faced again.

"Bring my robe and mask," he said, and on the word *mask* his voice broke to a growl. "Bring me a flask of spirit. Bring reeds, bring knives—you know what I need." He did not look at those he commanded; his gaze was fixed on the steaming, smiling woman.

The courtiers looked to Bones-and-brains, who was a little forward of them, startled-faced and on the point of speaking. But the King was motionless, watching the shepherdess like a hunter keeping a faun in sight as he fits an arrow to the string. Mr Bones stepped back into the servants' doubtful silence, not taking his eyes from his master. "You heard His Majesty," he said sharply over his shoulder.

The whole platform about us was glances like knives or darts thrown hither and thither, the very air dangerous with them. The Captain kept his grim face so steady that I could watch in his eyes the last of the steam rising off the lady, but the rest of the court and chamber were too nervous to speak or stay still. "Where should we be?" hissed someone. "Is it safe for us?"

The King stepped towards the outer railing, men scattering like shooed flies before him. He looked down on the great room; there was standing-room for many watchers around the rack, and the wheel, and on either side of the cat-pit. "Along the wall there," he said with a large gesture.

"All along, sir?" said Mr Bones, with doubt in his voice, then, "Very well," he added most obediently.

"What is he doing? What is he planning?" I hissed under the turn and shuffle of people around us, the quiet exclamations around the King's iron silence.

"He does it in battle," said the Captain, his voice dead of opinion or feeling. "Only a King has this power; the priests awaken it when they invest him."

"Power to what?" I knew a dozen outlandish stories: that the King could fly, or call down thunderbolts, or conjure great winds to flatten the enemy like a field of grain stalks.

The Captain only watched. No one seemed ready to climb down from our platform here. Men ran about below, and castle-servants came with arms full of *reeds*, of all things, green harmless reeds, and were told where and how to lay them on the flags. Mr Bones directed them very quietly and calmly, perhaps hoping to be halted in this work by his king, and not wanting to miss hearing that command.

They laid out a wide shape with the reeds lengthwise up and down it, something like a very fat, very flattened scorpion, legged and tailed. Then bags and bags, they brought, of tiny knives with nubby handles smooth as finger-bones, and the blades also short like fish-fins, with one vicious edge. I had seen someone draw the shape in the dust somewhere, whispering, and sweep the shape away when I asked what it was. Dozens of these knife-lets they laid out in a kind of crown around the shape's head, and in a double line fanning inward down its middle, then flaring outward and edging its tail. All while they worked the King watched closed-mouthed from the platform, and the shepherdess behind him at the centre of her net and her strangeness stood sodden and proud-backed, clasping her hands before her, her face neither raised in arrogance nor lowered in humiliation. She met no one's gaze and spoke not a word, but only was fully engaged with her own thoughts and her own will. Around her grew a fear and a thickening silence, pricked by knife-clinks on the flagstones, underlined by Bones-and-brains's soft voice.

The shape was complete upon the floor; now a priest approached the platform, a pile of darkness in his arms. He was an older priest, not frail—no Aquilin priest lacks bodily strength—but honed almost to a skeleton by his life of privations and the cruel torchlight.

"Wait, I will come down," said the King, and a sigh of terror and doubt sounded around my father and me, a tiny wind, quick-suppressed. The King turned at the top of the stairs: "Bring her!" he cried, and with a shock I thought he meant bring *me*, but of course he spoke of the woman there. "Come, men." He glanced at the assembly, and I took care to put my face behind a man's shoulder, so that he would not see and dismiss me. "Stand like men behind your god and king."

The Captain held me back, while others with many doubtful glances at one another shuffled stairwards and down. Soldiers took the woman in hand. She came awake at their touch, but did not resist it, and allowed herself to be taken as if this were a favor being done her, not a punishment being administered. And as the guard passed with her, she saw me, unshielded now by any man but only in my floury apron, with still my sleeves rolled up for the baking and my hands half-wiped of the makings, and the strings of my house-cap dangling down.

I stifled a curtsey; she saw that. She saw, I was sure, all my thoughts and words caught in my throat, too many of them to say. It surprised her greatly to see me here so domestic, so unbelonging—she paused, and the guard allowed it, and she held her mouth on the point of its blossoming into a smile. Her gaze touched my Captain's hand upon my arm, the tightness of his grip. She gave the tiniest, tiniest tilt of her head and a nod to me, in the fleet moment in which we met, and she went on, her wet skirt drawing a train of water across the boards of the platform. I felt myself to have been blessed. Every moment rang and swelled with meanings now, death had been so close, and the wonders so great by which she had evaded it.

"We stay here," said the Captain. He drew me to the corner of the platform and penned me there, standing behind me. I felt very vulnerable, with my clear view, vulnerable to dismissal, vulnerable to whatever evil might happen below. I shielded my own father, who had called himself my protector once, who had stood to my defense in tiny battles I had had, against my sisters, my mother, my fellows. Now he had sworn himself my enemy over this matter with Klepper; he wanted me to feel the full brunt of the world, as punishment for having gone against him.

All eyes were on the priest. His face was haughty as only a priest's can be and not be laughed at. He accepted the empty spirit-flask from the King, and laid it in a wooden box made perfectly to its size. He unravelled the dark stuff from his arms and draped it upon His Majesty with great care. What was it made from? It seemed not more than shadow or gauze, but sometimes great clots and knots came out of the pile, to be loosened or left in their mass, like the clothing of beggars, or indeed of whipped people's garments, cut to threads and then re-matted by the beatings. Was it black, was it purple?

Then out of the last armful of cloth-stuff, a head-dress of uncertain design but suggesting once having been plumed, and a ragged mask, skull-like and dog-like and altogether repellent—these emerged and finally covered our king's handsomeness, so that all I could recognise him by was his bearing within the threads and tatters, by his stillness when all about were leaning to each other, and whispering, and shifting from foot to foot. His stillness seemed to me an actual substance, like a smoke or smell, that spread out among his followers and froze them too in their places, turned the guard to stone who had just ushered the house servants out of the chamber.

It had no need to still the Captain and me, for we were already motionless, all but unbreathing above the gathering. My eyes took in the last tiniest movements: the settling of reeds on the flags, the wagging shaft of light from a knife-blade as it rocked to a halt. The woman herself, positioned at the scorpion's head where the knives were laid densest, moved not a hair or a finger, but against the King's fearsome stillness—I felt it, I almost *saw* it—she poured out her own, which was of a different make, radiant and graceful, and careless of all the fear that infected the air around.

Several moments of perfect stillness passed. Then His Majesty drew a mighty breath; it whistled in through the mask's apertures; it swelled the chest of his webbed and ragged drapery.

When he spoke, it was with a voice not his own. Monstrously deep, was this voice, and breathy with the breath of different lungs, not a king's, not any kind of man's. Vast hollows full of smoke and stone were these caves of lungs, and the chamber rang enlarged with the breath and voice of them, and the air stung with the burning, with the danger introduced to the place.

The woman regarded him, uncowed by the wordless noise spilling from the mask, or by the force with which its sounding filled and tested the limits of the room.

And then I did not see what she did, or how the king-monster next moved, for the reeds on the floor began to hiss together and to rattle and to rise, and the knives to glint and stand, some on their handles, some on the tips of their blades.

Then they leaped up, and I gasped—but they did not come at us. At the scorpion's head they fitted their blades together, and grew and worked against each other; along its spine they danced up in an arch and bobbed there, winking. The reeds flew out, to make a fine weaving, to indicate an outline: a long sketchy crocodile-head, muscled shoulders, strong haunches, between them a bulky belly flattened as yet to the floor. The tail went from wisps to cable at the foot of the platform, and the knifelets busied and tinkled along its length, then firmed in their places, and even the reedy parts began to smoothen out, and their green-ness to gleam, and when I looked up to the rest it was bulked there clearly alive, trembling with a pulse from some big magicked heart inside it, swelling and shrinking and swelling with its ongoing breath. And eager, it was, restrained—only just—by the King's voice pouring through the mask.

Completed, the creature described a great hunched curve, nearly to my eye-level on the high platform; all men were dolls beside it, and the shepherdess was the smallest doll of all. Spiked head to tail-tip, was the beast, with knife-blades become spines, and its claws were of the same sharpness. Its mouth could not contain all its mass of teeth, but two of them must needle upward and another two down, outside its lips of glinting mail. From its nostrils puffed an air choking in its heat and smell, and the thing did not care that we could not breathe it, we courtiers, we watchers. All its attention, as a cat's is with a sparrow, was directed from the limits of its poised body, its bunched muscles, through its dazzle-yellow eyes, upon the woman before it, standing in my view like a priest between candles, between the two gleaming uprights of its projecting teeth.

As the King spoke, it huffed a breath at her. She blinked, but no more than that; her clothing sizzled dry at the front, and a lock of her hair glowed and fell to white ash on her bodice. She gazed at the teeth massed before her—we all did, for they were like lanterns in the dark chamber—at the tongue, golden, curved and crackled on the surface, and within the cracks red, bright as blown-upon coals.

The King ceased his awful ventriloquy. The great lizard grinned, or perhaps only prepared its mouth. It did not pounce like a cat, or like a cat toy with its prey; in a bite it had taken the woman in down to the thighs; in a second one, she was gone, and the thing was reared-headed, tossing her back into its throat as a bird must do a beakful of water, swallowing her down a neck that it stretched out as if purposely to show her traveling down its length and narrowness. The fire-tongue flailed against the scaly lips and the skin stretched and winked, and I will never forget the sound of the lizard gulping—relishless, only mechanical, the kiss and slide of searing flesh within its throat.

The Captain hissed so hard, I felt his spittle on my cheek. "Is what happens when you do not marry as you are told!"

He shook with fear, though, and I did not. Nonsense, I thought. As if the King himself would go through such a business for only me, a captain's daughter of his vast military. Still it did speak to me, this horror before me and my father's spittle cool on my skin. It told me the size of his rage; it showed me the enormity of refusing a king's, or a father's, demands. I could not deny that it impressed itself upon me as a lesson: however enraged the Captain was with my refusal of that foolish soldier, his wrath when he learned the rest of it would be something else again to witness.

Then there was no more space or time or breath for learning, for the creature sprang and bucked as if speared. Flame spouted from its mouth, shrivelling the flesh and igniting the clothing of a guard, and throwing him back so that he fell, and rolled, and tumbled into the cat-pit. Forgotten, he was, immediately, by me and all the company, because the lizard folded, flopped open again and contorted, hugely, dangerously above and below us. It leaped and whipped, growling gasps in its throat, fire and fumes sputtering at its lips. It flung itself to the floor, coiled and writhed there; its tail broke the wheel in a single swipe, and set the pieces burning; it coughed forth a fire-ball that flew against a wall and burst, leaving a vast black star-shape on the stone.

And then, the belly-skin of the beast opened, like a dreadful flower, like a house-fire bursting up through thatch and timbers. Think of any bird you have gutted, any fish or four-legged thing; add fire and magic and stupendous size to the wonders of those internals, and then picture from the glare, from the garden of flame, from the welter of dragon-juices, through the smoke of its dying gasps, a small, cool woman climbing towards you.

The sight of her froze the Captain faster in his fear than had any of the lizard's cavorting. "No!" he whispered at my ear, as I leaned out elated, all but cheering.

She stepped down free of the dying ruin of the creature, to stand on a dagger-shape of flayed skin like some weird cindered carpet, the beast's last breaths heaving behind her. "Sir!" she said, to the King and to the power within and beyond him. "You see you are matched and bettered! I tell you!" She laughed, which in that chamber full of fear, the courtiers piled wide-eyed on the steps where they had scrambled to escape the monster's flailing, was the clearest, refreshingest sound, like water filling a cup when you are thirsty. "I tell you, sir: my Lord's and my Lady's powers are greater than myself, and longer than my life. To kill me, foolish man, makes no mark upon Them. And should you succeed, further I tell you this: Does anyone tell my life, or pen it onto skin, or rush-paper, or read it off again, or even only hear it said, at nurse's knee or among the gossips in the marketplace, they will be blessed, and the women of their family kept strong and fruitful and safe in childbed. My faith is pure and powerful, here and beyond the grave; it is only the very hem of the mantle of the King and Queen who work the world, from the depths of the seas to the heights of the stars, and every continent and creature in between."

The Captain was gone from behind me; others had taken his place, pressing forward, staring down, marvelling at the beast's remains, the straight-backed woman defying the King, the smouldering rack, the flaming wheel, the burnt guard dead in the pit.

And then there he was, my father at the foot of the steps, pushing free of the crowd, drawing his sword.

"I will rid you of her, Your Majesty!" he cried.

He strode to her; she watched him come, unmoved, unafraid, a woman indulging a child. I so strongly expected his humiliation, his defeat, her continuing, that I waited in utter calm as he slashed her throat through to the spine-bones, as she fell, as she bled, her heart living on, unaware that the head was gone, flinging and spreading the bright blood on the charred dragon-skin, slowing, slowing, stopping. My father stood over her the while; we all stood over her, attentive, as closely as the dragon had attended in the moments before it ate her.

But she only died, the shepherdess, and was dead; there were no more miracles to her.

I cried out, loud and high in the huge room under the smoking roof-beams. They held me back from clambering over the railing, from crawling underneath it and smashing my own life away on the flags before my father. "She is maddened," someone said. "She should never have been allowed to see—it has unhinged her." But I was clear in my own mind, afflicted indeed by a terrible sanity, a terrible seeing of this moment as it truly was, with the miracle woman gone from the world and me still prisoned in it, with my lover and my baby and my punishments awaiting, with my angry father—while she was free, dissolved into her faith, glorifying her gods among all the saints there. Such a stab of jealousy I suffered! Such rage did I try to loose, at her and my father both, such grief that a soul so freshly known, so marvellous, was so quickly snatched from my sight.

They tried to help me down; I would not be helped. They had to bind and carry me, and quickly, for the roof was fully afire now, and the King and his closest had been hurried away. My father met us at the foot of the stairs, took me up and slung me like a carcass over his shoulder. I banged away my tears against his back, and strained, as we passed the swollen smouldering corse of the dragon, its juices running out black, to see the body and the skewed head of the saint who had burst him open with her holiness. She lay there uncovered; she would not even be buried with her own rites and customs, but roof slates would rain upon her as she stewed and shrank in the lizard-blood. Beams would crush her bones; fire would consume them.

My father carried me out, through the long halls of the prison and into the day. The courtiers and councillors and soldiers flowed out with us, exclaiming, into the crowd, into the clamour of the town; my noise went unheard among them, and the tears ran unnoticed through my eyebrows, down my forehead, and onto the leather of the Captain's back-plate, drawing long dark lines there.

THE TASTE OF NIGHT
PAT CADIGAN

Pat Cadigan is the author of about a hundred short stories and fourteen books, two of which, *Synners* and *Fools*, won the Arthur C. Clarke Award. She was born in New York, grew up in Massachusetts, and spent most of her adult life in the Kansas City area. She now lives in London with her husband, the Original Chris Fowler, her son, musician and composer Robert M. Fenner, the Supreme Being, Miss Kitty Calgary, and co-conspirator, writer, and raconteuse Amanda Hemingway. She is pretty sure there isn't a more entertaining household.

The taste of night rather than the falling temperature woke her. Nell curled up a little more and continued to doze. It would be a while before the damp chill coming up from the ground could get through the layers of heavy cardboard to penetrate the sleeping bag and blanket cocooning her. She was fully dressed and her spare clothes were in the sleeping bag, too—not much but enough to make good insulation. Sometime in the next twenty-four hours, though, she would have to visit a laundromat because *phew*.

Phew was one of those things that didn't change; well, not so far, anyway. She hoped it would stay that way. By contrast, the taste of night was one of her secret great pleasures although she still had no idea what it was supposed to mean. Now and then something *almost* came to her, *almost*. But when she reached for it either in her mind or by actually touching something, there was nothing at all.

Sight. Hearing. Smell. Taste. Touch. _____.

Memory sprang up in her mind with the feel of pale blue stretched long and tight between her hands.

The blind discover that their other senses, particularly hearing, intensify to compensate for the lack. The deaf can be sharp-eyed but also extra sensitive to vibration, which is what sound is to the rest of us.

However, those who lose their sense of smell find they have lost their sense of taste as well because the two are so close. To lose feeling is usually a symptom of a greater problem. A small number of people feel no pain but this puts them at risk for serious injury and life-threatening illnesses.

That doctor had been such a patient woman. Better yet, she had had no deep well of stored-up suspicion like every other doctor Marcus had taken her to.

279

Nell had been able to examine what the doctor was telling her, touching it all over, feeling the texture. Even with Marcus's impatience splashing her like an incoming tide, she had been able to ask a question.

A sixth sense? Like telepathy or clairvoyance?

The doctor's question had been as honest as her own and Nell did her best to make herself clear.

If there were some kind of extra sense, even a person who had it would have a hard time explaining it. Like you or me trying to explain sight to someone born blind.

Nell had agreed and asked the doctor to consider how the other five senses might try to compensate for the lack.

That was where the memory ended, leaving an aftertaste similar to night, only colder and with a bit of sour.

Nell sighed, feeling comfortable and irrationally safe. Feeling safe was irrational if you slept rough. Go around feeling safe and you wouldn't last too long. It was just that the indented area she had found at the back of this building—cinema? auditorium?—turned out to be as cozy as it had looked. It seemed to have no purpose except as a place where someone could sleep unnoticed for a night or two. More than two would have been pushing it, but that meant nothing to some rough sleepers. They'd camp in a place like this till they wore off all the hidden. Then they'd get seen and kicked out. Next thing you knew, the spot would be fenced off or filled in so no one could ever use it again. One less place to go when there was nowhere to stay.

Nell hated loss, hated the taste: dried-out bitter crossed with salty that could hang on for days, weeks, even longer. Worse, it could come back without warning and for no reason except that, perhaps like rough sleepers, it had nowhere else to go. There were other things that tasted just as bad to her but nothing worse, and nothing that lingered for anywhere nearly as long, not even the moldy-metal tang of disappointment.

After a bit, she realized the pools of color she'd been watching behind her closed eyes weren't the remnants of a slow-to-fade dream but real voices of real humans, not too far away, made out of the same stuff she was; either they hadn't noticed her or they didn't care.

Nell uncurled slowly—never make any sudden moves was another good rule for rough sleepers—and opened her eyes. An intense blue-white light blinded her with the sound of a cool voice in her right ear:

Blue-white stars don't last long enough for any planets orbiting them to develop intelligent life. Maybe not any life, even the most rudimentary. Unless there is a civilization advanced enough to seed those worlds with organisms modified to evolve at a faster rate. That might beg the question of why an advanced civilization would do that. But the motives of a civilization that advanced would/could/might seem illogical if not incomprehensible to any not equally developed.

Blue-white memory stretched farther this time: a serious-faced young woman in a coffee shop, watching a film clip on a notebook screen. Nell had sneaked a look at it on her way to wash up in the women's restroom. It took her a little while to realize that she had had a glimpse of something to do with what had been happening to her, or more precisely, *why* it was happening, what it was supposed to mean. On the heels of that realization had come a new one, probably the most important: *they* were communicating with her.

Understanding always came to her at oblique angles. The concept of that missing sixth sense, for instance—when she finally became aware of it, she realized that it had been lurking somewhere in the back of her mind for a very, very long time, years and years, a passing notion or a ragged fragment of a mostly forgotten dream. It had developed so slowly that she might have lived her whole life without noticing it, instead burying it under more mundane concerns and worries and fears.

Somehow it had snagged her attention—a mental pop-up window. Marcus had said everyone had an occasional stray thought about something odd. Unless she was going to write a weird story or draw a weird picture, there was no point in obsessing about it.

Was it the next doctor who had suggested she do exactly that—write a weird story or draw a weird picture, or both? Even if she had really wanted to, she couldn't. She knew for certain by then that she was short a sense, just as if she were blind or deaf.

Marcus had said he didn't understand why that meant she had to leave home and sleep on the street. She didn't either, at the time. But even if she had understood enough to tell him that *the motives of a civilization that advanced would/could/might seem illogical if not incomprehensible to any not equally developed,* all it would have meant to him was that she was, indeed, crazy as a bedbug, unquote.

The social worker he had sent after her hadn't tried to talk her into a hospital or a shelter right away but the intent was deafening. Every time she found Nell it drowned everything else out. Nell finally had to make her say it just to get some peace. For a few days after that, everything was extra scrambled. She was too disoriented to understand anything. All she knew was that *they* were bombarding her with their communication and her senses were working overtime, trying to make up for her inadequacy.

The blinding blue-white light dissolved and her vision cleared. Twenty feet away was an opening in the back of the building the size of a double-garage door. Seven or eight men were hanging around just outside, some of them sitting on wooden crates, smoking cigarettes, drinking from bottles or large soft-drink cups. The pools of color from their voices changed to widening circular ripples, like those spreading out from raindrops falling into still water. The colors crossed each other to make new colors, some she had never seen anywhere but in her mind.

The ripples kept expanding until they reached the backs of her eyes and swept through them with a sensation of a wind ruffling feathery flowers. She saw twinkling lights and then a red-hot spike went through her right temple. There was just enough time for her to inhale before an ice-pick went through her eye to cross the spike at right angles.

Something can be a million lightyears away and in your eye at the same time.

"Are you all right?"

The man bent over her, hands just above his knees. Most of his long hair was tied back except for a few long strands that hung forward in a way that suggested punctuation to Nell. Round face, round eyes with hard lines under them.

See. Hear. Smell. Taste. Touch. _____.

Hand over her right eye, she blinked up at him. He repeated the question and the words were little green balls falling from his mouth to bounce away into the night. Nell caught her lower lip between her teeth to keep herself from laughing. He reached down and pulled the hand over her eye to one side. Then he straightened up and pulled a cell phone out of his pocket. "I need an ambulance," he said to it.

She opened her mouth to protest but her voice wouldn't work. Another man was coming over, saying something in thin, tight silver wires.

And then it was all thin, tight silver wires everywhere. Some of the wires turned to needles and they seemed to fight each other for dominance. The pain in her eye flared more intensely and a voice from somewhere far in the past tried to ask a question without morphing into something else but it just wasn't loud enough for her to hear.

Nell rolled over onto her back. Something that was equal parts anxiety and anticipation shuddered through her. Music, she realized; very loud, played live, blaring out of the opening where the men were hanging around. Chords rattled her blood, pulled at her arms and legs. The pain flared again but so did the taste of night. She let herself fall into it. The sense of falling became the desire to sleep but just as she was about to give in, she would slip back to wakefulness, back and forth like a pendulum. Or like she was swooping from the peak of one giant wave, down into the trough and up to the peak of another.

Her right eye was forced open with a sound like a gunshot and bright light filled her mouth with the taste of icicles.

"Welcome back. Don't take this the wrong way but I'm very sorry to see you here."

Nell discovered only her left eye would open but one eye was enough. Ms. Dunwoody, Call-Me-Anne, the social worker. Not the original social worker Marcus had sent after her. That had been Ms. Petersen, Call-Me-Joan, who had been replaced after a while by Mr. Carney, Call-Me-Dwayne. Nell had seen him only twice and the second time he had been one big white knuckle, as if he were holding something back—tears? hysteria? Whatever it was leaked from him in twisted shapes of shifting colors that left bad tastes in her mouth. Looking away from him didn't help—the tastes were there whether she saw the colors or not.

It was the best they could do for her, lacking as she was in that sense. At the time, she hadn't understood. All she had known was that the tastes turned her stomach and the colors gave her headaches. Eventually, she had thrown up on the social worker's shoes and he had fled without apology or even so much as a surprised curse, let alone a good-bye. Nell hadn't minded.

Ms. Dunwoody, Call-Me-Anne, was his replacement and she had managed to find Nell more quickly than she had expected. Ms. Dunwoody, Call-Me-Anne, had none of the same kind of tension in her but once in a while she exuded a musty, stale odor of resignation that was very close to total surrender.

Surrender. It took root in Nell's mind but she was slow to understand because she only associated it with Ms. Dunwoody, Call-Me-Anne's unspoken (even to herself) desire to give up. If she'd just had that missing sense, it would have been so obvious right away.

Of course, if she'd had that extra sense, she'd have understood the whole thing right away and everything would be different. Maybe not a whole lot easier, since she would still have had a hard time explaining sight to all the blind people, so to speak, but at least she wouldn't have been floundering around in confusion.

"Nell?" Ms. Dunwoody, Call-Me-Anne, was leaning forward, peering anxiously into her face. "I *said*, do you know why you're here?"

Nell hesitated. "Here, as in…" Her voice failed in her dry throat. The social worker poured her a glass of water from a pitcher on the bedside table and held it up, slipping the straw between her dry lips so she could drink. Nell finished three glasses and Ms. Dunwoody, Call-Me-Anne, made a business of adjusting her pillows before she lay back against the raised mattress.

"Better?" she asked Nell brightly.

Nell made a slight, non-committal dip with her head. "What was the question?" she asked, her voice still faint.

"Do you know where you are?" Ms. Dunwoody, Call-Me-Anne, said.

Nell smiled inwardly at the change and resisted the temptation to say, *Same place you are—here.* There were deep lines under the social worker's eyes, her clothes were wrinkled, and lots of little hairs had escaped from her tied-back hair. No doubt she'd had less rest in the last twenty-four hours than Nell. She looked around with her one good eye at the curtains surrounding them and at the bed. "Hospital. Tri-County General."

She could see that her specifying which hospital had reassured the social worker. That was hardly a major feat of cognition, though; Tri-County General was where all the homeless as well as the uninsured ended up.

"You had a convulsion," Call-Me-Anne told her, speaking slowly and carefully now as if to a child. "A man found you behind the concert hall and called an ambulance."

Nell lifted her right hand and pointed at her face.

Call-Me-Anne hesitated, looking uncertain. "You seem to have hurt your eye."

She remembered the sensation of the spike and the needle so vividly that she winced.

"Does it hurt?" Call-Me-Anne asked, full of concern. "Should I see if they can give you something for the pain?"

Nell shook her head no; a twinge from somewhere deep in her right eye socket warned her not to do that again or to make any sudden movements, period.

"Is there anyone you'd like me to call for you?" the social worker asked.

Frowning a little, Nell crossed her hands and uncrossed them in an absolutely-not gesture. Call-Me-Anne pressed her lips together but it didn't stop a long pink ribbon from floating weightless out from her mouth. Too late—she had already called Marcus, believing that by the time he got here, Nell actually would want to see him. And if not, she would claim that Marcus had insisted on seeing *her,* regardless of Nell's wishes, because he was her husband and loyalty and blah-blah-blah-social-worker-blather.

All at once there was a picture in her mind of a younger and not-so-tired Ms. Dunwoody, Call-Me-Anne, and just as suddenly, it came to life.

I feel that if we can re-unite families, then we've done the best job we can. Sometimes that isn't possible, of course, so the next best thing we can do is provide families for those who need them.

Call-Me-Anne's employment interview, she realized. What *they* were trying to tell her with that wasn't at all clear. That missing sense. Or maybe because *they* had the sense, they were misinterpreting the situation.

"Nell? *Nell?*"

She tried to pull her arm out of the social worker's grip and couldn't. The pressure was a mouthful of walnut shells, tasteless and sharp. "What do you want?"

"I *said*, are you *sure?*"

Nell sighed. "There's a story that the first people in the New World to see Columbus's ships couldn't actually *see* them because such things were too far outside their experience. You think that's true?"

Call-Me-Anne, her expression a mix of confusion and anxiety. Nell knew what that look meant—she was afraid the situation was starting to get away from her. "Are you groggy? Or just tired?"

"I don't," she went on, a bit wistful. "I think they didn't know what they were seeing and maybe had a hard time with the perspective but I'm sure they saw them. After all, they *were* made by other humans. But something coming from another world, all bets are off."

Call-Me-Anne's face was very sad now.

"I sound crazy to you?" Nell gave a short laugh. "*Scientists* talk about this stuff."

"You're not a scientist, Nell. You were a librarian. With proper treatment and medication, you could—"

Nell laughed again. "If a librarian starts thinking about the possibility of life somewhere else in the universe, it's a sign she's going crazy?" She turned her head away and closed her eyes. Correction, eye. She couldn't feel very much behind the bandage, just enough to know that her right eyelid wasn't opening or closing. When she heard the social worker walk away, she opened her eye to see the silver wires had come back. They bloomed like flowers, opening and then flying apart where they met others and connected, making new blooms that flew apart and found new connections. The world in front of Nell began to look like a cage, although she had no idea which side she was on.

Abruptly, she felt one of the wires go through her temple with that same white-hot pain. A moment later, a second one went through the bandage over her right eye as easily as if it wasn't there, going all the way through her head and out, pinning her to the pillow.

Her left eye was watering badly but she could see Call-Me-Anne rushing back with a nurse. Their mouths opened and closed as they called her name. She saw them reaching for her but she was much too far away.

And that was how it would be. No, that was how it was always, but the five senses worked so hard to compensate for the one missing that people took the illusion of contact for the real thing. The power of suggestion—where would the human race be without it?

Sight. Hearing. Smell. Taste. Touch. _____.

Contact.

The word was a poor approximation but the concept was becoming clearer in her mind now. Clearer than the sight in her left eye, which was dimming. But still good enough to let her see Call-Me-Anne was on the verge of panic.

A man in a white uniform pushed her aside and she became vaguely aware of him touching her. But there was still no *contact*.

Nell labored toward wakefulness as if she were climbing a rock wall with half a dozen sandbags dangling on long ropes tied around her waist. Her mouth was full of steel wool and sand. She knew that taste—medication. It would probably take most of a day to spit that out.

She had tried medication in the beginning because Marcus had begged her to. Anti-depressants, anti-anxiety capsules, and finally anti-psychotics—they had all tasted the same because she hadn't been depressed, anxious, or psychotic. Meanwhile, Marcus had gotten farther and farther away, which, unlike the dry mouth, the weight gain, or the tremors in her hands, was not reversible.

Call-Me-Anne had no idea about that. She kept trying to get Nell to see Marcus, unaware they could barely perceive each other anymore. Marcus didn't realize it either, not the way she did. Marcus thought that was reversible, too.

Pools of color began to appear behind her heavy eyelids, strange colors that shifted and changed, green to gold, purple to red, blue to aqua, and somewhere between one color and another was a hue she had never found anywhere else and never would.

Sight. Hearing. Smell. Taste. Touch. _____.

C-c-c-contact...

The word was a boulder trying to fit a space made for a pebble smoothed over the course of eons and a distance of lightyears into a precise and elegant thing.

Something can be a million lightyears away and in your eye at the same time.

Sight. Hearing. Smell. Taste. Touch. _____.

C-c-c-con...nect.

C-c-c-commmmune.

C-c-c-c-c-communnnnnnnnicate.

She had a sudden image of herself running around the base of a pyramid, searching for a way to get to the top. While she watched, it was replaced by a new image, of herself running around an elephant and several blind men; she was still looking for a way to get to the top of the pyramid.

The image dissolved and she became aware of how heavy the overhead lights were on her closed eyes. Eye. She sighed; even if she did finally reach understanding—or it reached her—how would she ever be able to explain what blind men, an elephant, and a pyramid combined with Columbus's ships meant?

The musty smell of surrender broke in on her thoughts. It was very strong; Call-Me-Anne was still there. After a bit, she heard the sound of a wooden spoon banging on the bottom of a pot. Frustration, but not just any frustration: Marcus's.

She had never felt him so clearly without actually seeing him. Perhaps Call-Me-Anne's surrender worked as an amplifier.

The shifting colors resolved themselves into a new female voice. "...much do either of you know about the brain?"

"Not much," Call-Me-Anne said. Marcus grunted, a stone rolling along a dirt path.

"Generally, synesthesia can be a side effect of medication or a symptom."

"What about mental illness?" Marcus asked sharply, the spoon banging louder on the pot.

"Sometimes mentally ill people experience it but it's not a specific symptom of mental illness. In your wife's case, it was a symptom of the tumors."

"Tumors?" Call-Me-Anne was genuinely upset. Guilt was a soft scratching noise, little mouse claws on a hard surface.

"Two, although there could be three. We're not sure about the larger one. The smaller one is an acoustic neuroma, which—"

"Is that why she hears things?" Marcus interrupted.

The doctor hesitated. "Probably not, although some people complain of tinnitus. It's non-cancerous, doesn't spread, and normally very slow-growing. Your wife's seems to be growing faster than normal. But then there's the other one." Pause. "I've only been a neurosurgeon for ten years so I can't say I've seen everything but this really is quite, uh…unusual. She must have complained of headaches."

A silence, then Call-Me-Anne cleared her throat. "They seemed to be cluster headaches. Painful but not exactly rare. I have them myself. I gave her some of my medication but I don't know if she took it."

Another small pause. "Sometimes she said she had a headache but that's all," Marcus said finally. "We've been legally separated for a little over two years, so I'm not exactly up-to-date. She sleeps on the street."

"Well, there's no telling when it started until we can do some detailed scans."

"How much do those cost?" Marcus asked. Then after a long moment: "Hey, *she* left *me* to sleep on the *street* after I'd already spent a fortune on shrinks and prescriptions and hospitalizations. Then they tell me you can't force a person to get treated for anything unless they're a danger to the community, blah, blah, blah. Now she's got brain tumors and I'm gonna get hit for the bill. Dammit, I shoulda divorced her but it felt too—" The spoon scraped against the iron pot. "Cruel."

"You were hoping she'd snap out of it?" said the doctor. "Plenty of people feel that way. It's normal to hope for a miracle." Call-Me-Anne added some comforting noises, and said something about benefits and being in the system.

"Yeah, okay," Marcus said. "But you still didn't answer my question. How much do these scans cost?"

"Sorry, I couldn't tell you, I don't have anything to do with billing," the doctor said smoothly. "But we can't do any surgery without them."

"I thought you already did some," Marcus said.

"We were going to. Until I saw what was behind her eye."

"It's that big?" asked Marcus.

"It's not just that. It's—not your average tumor."

Marcus gave a humorless laugh. "Tumors are standardized, are they?"

"To a certain extent, just like the human body. This one, however, isn't behaving quite the way tumors usually do." Pause. "There seems to be some gray matter incorporated into it."

"What do you mean, like it's tangled up in her brain? Isn't that what a tumor does, get all tangled up in a person's brain? That's why it's hard to take out, right?"

"This is different," the doctor said. "Look, I've been debating with myself whether I should tell you about this—"

"If you're gonna bill me, you goddam better tell me," Marcus growled. "What's going on with her?"

"Just from what I could see, the tumor has either co-opted part of your wife's brain—stolen it, complete with blood supply—or there's a second brain growing in your wife's skull."

There was a long pause. Then Marcus said, "You know how crazy that sounds? You got any pictures of this?"

"No. Even if I did, you're not a neurosurgeon, you wouldn't know what you were looking at."

"No? I can't help thinking I'd know if I were looking at two brains in one head or not."

"The most likely explanation for this would be a parasitic twin," the doctor went on. "It happens more often than you'd think. The only thing is, parasitic twins don't suddenly take to growing. And if it had always been so large, you'd have seen signs of it long before now.

"Unfortunately, I couldn't even take a sample to biopsy. Your wife's vitals took a nosedive and we had to withdraw immediately. She's fine now—under the circumstances. But we need to do those scans as soon as possible. Her right eye was so damaged by this tumor that we couldn't save it. If we don't move quickly enough, it's going to cause additional damage to her face."

Nell took a deep breath, and let it out slowly. She hadn't thought they would hear her but they had; all three stopped talking and Call-Me-Anne and Marcus scurried over to the side of her bed, saying her name in soft, careful whispers, as if they thought it might break. She kept her eyes closed and her body limp, even when Call-Me-Anne took her hand in both of hers and squeezed it tight. After a while, she heard them go.

How had they done that, she marveled. How had they done it from so far away?

Something can be a million lightyears away and in your eye at the same time.

Her mind's eye showed her a picture of two vines entangled with each other. Columbus's ships, just coming into view. The sense she had been missing was not yet fully developed, not enough to reconcile the vine and the ships. But judging from what the doctor said, it wouldn't be long now.

THE EXTERMINATOR'S WANT-AD
BRUCE STERLING

Bruce Sterling published his first novel, *Involution Ocean*, in 1977. The author of ten novels and four short story collections, he is still perhaps best known in science fiction as the Godfather of Cyberpunk. He edited the cyberpunk anthology *Mirrorshades*, and his early novels, *The Artificial Kid* and *Schismatrix,* are perhaps the closest things he wrote to cyberpunk. After closing the 'zine *Cheap Truth* and leaving cyberpunk to others in November 1986, he went on to write major science fiction novels like *Holy Fire, Distraction,* and *The Zenith Angle*. He is the author of a large and influential body of short fiction, much of which has been collected in *Crystal Express, Globalhead, A Good Old-Fashioned Future,* and *Visionary in Residence*. His most recent books are new novel *The Caryatids* and major career retrospective *Ascendancies: The Best of Bruce Sterling*.

So, I'm required to write this want-ad in order to get any help with my business. Only I have, like, a very bad trust rating on this system. I have rotten karma and an awful reputation. "Don't even go there, don't listen to a word he says: because this guy is pure poison."

So, if that kind of crap is enough for you, then you should stop reading this right now.

However, somebody is gonna read this, no matter what. So let me just put it all out on the table. Yes, I'm a public enemy. Yes, I'm an ex-con. Yes, I'm mad, bad, and dangerous to link to.

But my life wasn't always like this. Back in the good old days, when the world was still solid and not all termite-eaten like this, I used to be a well-to-do, well-respected guy.

Let me explain what went on in prison, because you're probably pretty worried about that part.

First, I was a nonviolent offender. That's important. Second, I turned myself in to face "justice." That shows that I knew resistance was useless. Also a big point on my side.

So, you would think that the maestros of the new order would cut me some slack in the karma ratings: but no. I'm never trusted. I was on the losing side of a socialist revolution. They didn't call me a "political prisoner" of their "revolution," but that's sure what went on. If you don't believe that, you won't believe anything else I say, so I might as well say it flat-out.

So, this moldy jail I was in was this old dot-com McMansion, out in the Permanent Foreclosure Zone in the dead suburbs. That's where they cooped us up. This gated community was built for some vanished rich people. That was their low-intensity prison for us rehab detainees.

As their rehab population, we were a so-called "resiliency commune." This meant we were penniless, and we had to grow our own food, and also repair our own jail. Our clothes were unisex plastic orange jumpsuits. They had salvaged those somewhere. They always had plenty of those.

So, we persisted out there as best we could, under videocam surveillance, with parole cuffs on our ankles. See, that was our life. Every week, our itchy, dirty column of detainees got to march thirteen miles into town, where our captors lived. We did hard-labor "community service" there with our brooms, shovels, picks, and hoes. We got shown off in public as a warning to the others.

This place outside was a Beltway suburb before Washington was abandoned. The big hurricane ran right over it, and crushed it down pretty good, so now it was a big green hippie jungle. Our prison McMansion had termites, roaches, mold, and fleas, but once it was a nice house. This rambling wreck of a town was half storm-debris. All the lawns were replaced with wet, weedy, towering patches of bamboo, or marijuana—or hops, or kenaf, whatever (I never could tell those farm crops apart).

The same goes for the "garden roofs," which were dirt piled on top of the dirty houses. There were smelly goats running loose, chickens cackling. Salvaged umbrellas and chairs toppled in the empty streets. No traffic signs, because there were no cars.

Sustainable Utopia here is a densely crowded settlement full of people in poorly washed clothing who are hanging out making nice. Constant gossip—they call that "social interaction." No sign of that one percent of the population that once owned half of America. The rich elite just blew it totally. They dropped their globalized ball. They panicked. So they're in jail, like I was. Or they're in exile somewhere, or else they jumped out of penthouses screaming when the hyperinflation ate them alive.

And boy, do I ever miss them. No more billboards, no more chain stores, no big-box Chinese depots and no neon fried-food shacks. It's become another world, as in "another world is possible," and we're stuck in there. It's very possible, very real, and it's very smelly. There are constant power blackouts.

Every once in a while, some armed platoon of "resilient nation-builder" militia types would come by on their rusty bicycles. Sometimes they brought shot-up victims on stretchers. The Liberated Socialist Masses were plucking their homemade banjos on their rickety porches. Lots of liberty, equality, fraternity, solidarity, compost dirt, unshaved legs, and dense crowding.

Otherwise, the crickets chirp.

Those were, like, the lucky people who were outside our prison. Those cooperative people are the networked future.

So, my cellmate Claire was this forty-something career lobbyist who used to be my boss inside the Beltway. Claire was full of horror stories about the cruelty of the socialist regime. Because, in the old days before we got ourselves arrested, alarmist tales of this kind were Claire's day-job. Claire peddled political spin to the LameStream Media to make sure that corporations stayed in command, so that situations like our present world stayed impossible.

Obviously Claire was not that great at this strategy. Me, I was more of the geek technician in our effort. My job was to methodically spam and troll the sharing-networks. I would hack around with them, undermine them, and make their daily lives difficult. Threaten IP lawsuits. Spread some Fear Uncertainty and Doubt. Game their reputation systems. Gold-farm their alternative economies. Engage in DDOS attacks. Harass the activist ringleaders with blistering personal insults. The usual.

Claire and I had lots of co-workers all up and down K-Street. Both seaboards, too, and all over Texas. Lavishly supported by rich-guy think-tanks, we were the covert operatives in support of an ailing system. We did that work because it paid great.

Personally, I loved to buy stuff: I admired a consumer society. I sincerely liked to carry out a clean, crisp, commercial transaction: the kind where you simply pay some money for goods and services. I liked driving my SUV to the mall, whipping out my alligator wallet, and buying myself some hard liquor, a steak dinner, and maybe a stripper. All that awful stuff at the Pottery Barn and Banana Republic, when you never knew "Who the hell was buying that?" That guy was me.

Claire and I hated the sharing networks, because we were paid to hate them. We hated all social networks, like Facebook, because they destroyed the media that we owned. We certainly hated free software, because it was like some ever-growing anti-commercial fungus. We hated search engines and network aggregators, people like Google—not because Google was evil, but because they weren't. We really hated "file-sharers"—the swarming pirates who were chewing up the wealth of our commercial sponsors.

We hated all networks on principle: we even hated power networks. Wind and solar only sorta worked, and were very expensive. We despised green power networks because climate change was a myth. Until the climate actually changed. Then the honchos who paid us started drinking themselves to death.

If you want to see a truly changed world, then a brown sky really makes a great start. Back in the day, we could tell the public, "Hey, the sky up there is still blue, who do you believe, me or your lying eyes?" And we tried that, but we ran out of time for it. After that tipping-point, our bottom-line economy was not "reality" at all. That was the myth.

My former life in mythland had suited me just great. Then I had no air conditioning. My world was wet, dirty, smelly, moldy, swarming with fleas, chiggers, bedbugs, and mosquitoes. Also, I was in prison. When myths implode, that's what happens to good people.

So, Claire and I discussed our revenge, whenever we were out of earshot and oversight of the solar-powered prison webcams. Claire and I spent a lot of time on revenge fantasies, because that kept our morale up.

"Look, Bobby," she told me, as she scratched graffiti in the wall with a ten-penny nail, "this rehab isn't a proper 'prison' at all! This is a bullshit psychological operation intended to brainwash us. Leftists in power always do that! If they give you a fair trial, you can at least get a sentence and do time. If they claim you are crazy, they can sit on your neck forever!"

"Maybe we really are crazy now," I said. "Having the sky change color can do that to people."

"There's only one way out of this Kumbaya nuthouse," she said. "We gotta learn to talk the way they want to hear! So that's our game plan from now on. We act very contrite, we do their bongo dance, whatever. Then they let us out of this gulag. After that, we can take some steps."

Claire was big on emigrating from the USA. Claire somehow imagined that there was some country in the world that didn't have weather. The inconvenient laws of physics had never much appealed to Claire. We'd donated the laws of physics to our opponents by pretending that air wasn't air. Now the long run of that tactic was splattered all around us. We had nothing left but worthless paper money and some Red State churches half-full of Creationists.

We had gone bust. We had suffered a vast, Confederate-style defeat. The economy was Gone with the Wind, and everybody was gonna stay poor, angry, and dirt-stupid for the next century.

So: when we weren't planting beans in the former backyard, or digging mold out of the attic insulation, we had to do rehab therapy. This was our prisoner consciousness-building encounter scheme. The regime made us play social games. We weren't allowed computer games in prison: just dice, graph paper, and some charcoal sticks that we made ourselves.

So, we played this elaborate paper game called "Dungeons and Decency." Three times a week. The lady warden was our Dungeon Master.

This prison game was diabolical. It was very entertaining, and compulsively playable. This game had been designed by left-wing interaction designers, the kind of creeps who built not-for-profit empires like Wikipedia. Except they'd designed it for losers like us.

Everybody in rehab had to role-play. We had to build ourselves another identity, because this new pretend-identity was supposed to help us escape the stifling spiritual limits of our previous, unliberated, greedy individualist identities.

In this game, I played an evil dwarf. With an axe. Which would have been okay, because that identity was pretty much me all along. Except that the game's reward system had been jiggered to reward elaborate acts of social collaboration. Of course we wanted to do raids and looting and cool fantasy fighting, but that wasn't on. We were very firmly judged on the way we played this rehab game. It was never about grabbing the gold. It was all about forming trust coalitions so as to collectively readjust our fantasy infrastructure.

This effort went on endlessly. We played for ages. We kept demanding to be let out, they kept claiming we didn't get it yet. The prison food got a little better. The weather continued pretty bad. We started getting charity packages. Once some folk singers came by, and played us some old Johnny Cash songs. Otherwise, the gaming was pretty much it.

A whole lot was resting on this interactive Dungeons game. If you did great, they gave you some meat and maybe a parole hearing. If you blew it off, you were required to donate blood into the socialized health-care system. Believe you me, when they tap you more than a couple of times, on a diet of homegrown cabbage? You start feeling mighty peaked.

Yeah, it got worse. Because we had to cooperate with other teams of fantasy game players in other prisons. These other convicts rated our game performance, while we were required to rate them. We got to see the highlights of their interaction on webcams—(we prisoners were always on webcams).

We were supposed to rate these convicts on how well they were sloughing off their selfish ways, and learning to integrate themselves into a spiritualized, share-centric, enlightened society. Pretty much like Alcoholics Anonymous, but without the God or the booze.

Worse yet, this scheme was functioning. Some of our cellmates, especially the meek, dorky, geeky ones, were quickly released. The wretches strung out on dope were pretty likely to manage in the new order, too. They'd given up jailing people for that.

This degeneration had to be stopped somehow. Since I had been a professional troll, I was great at gaming. I kept inventing ways to hack the gaming system and get people to fight. This was the one thing I could do inside the prison that recalled the power I'd once held in my old life.

So, I threw myself into that therapy heart and soul. I worked my way up to fifteenth level Evil Dwarf. I was the envy of the whole prison system, a living legend. I got myself some prison tattoos, made a shiv…. Maybe I had a bleak future, stuck inside the joint, but I still had integrity! I had defied their system! I could vote down the stool-pigeons and boost the stand-up guys who were holding out against the screws!

I was doing great at that, really into it, indomitable—until Claire told me that my success was queering her chances of release. They didn't care what I did inside the fantasy game. All that time, I was really being judged on my abuse of the ratings system. Because they knew what I was up to. It was all a psychological trap! The whole scheme was their anti-hacker honeypot. I had fallen into it like the veriest newbie schmo!

You see, they were scanning us all the time. Nobody ever gets it about the tremendous power of network surveillance. That's how they ruled the world, though: by valuing every interaction, by counting every click. Every time one termite touched the feelers of another termite, they were adding that up. In a database.

Everybody was broke: extremely poor, like preindustrial hard-scrabble poor, very modest, very "green." But still surviving. The one reason we weren't all chewing each other's cannibal thigh bones (like the people on certain more disadvantaged continents) was because they'd stapled together this survival regime out of socialist software. It was very social. Ultra-social. No "privatization," no "private sector," and no "privacy."

They pretended that it was all about happiness and kindliness and free-spirited cooperation and gay rainbow banners and all that. It was really a system that was firmly based on "social capital." Everything social was your only wealth. In a real "gift economy," you were the gift. You were living by your karma. Instead of a good old hundred-dollar bill, you just had a virtual facebooky thing with your own smiling picture on it, and that picture meant "Please Invest in the Bank of Me!"

That was their New Deal. One big game of socially approved activities. For instance: reading Henry David Thoreau. I did that. I kinda had to. I had this yellow, crumbly, prison edition of a public-domain version of *Walden*.

Man, I hated that Thoreau guy. I wanted to smack Mr. Nonviolent Moral Resistance right across his chops. I did learn something valuable from him, though. This communard Transcendental thing that had us by the neck? The homemade beans, the funky shacks, the passive-aggressive peacenik dropout thing? That was not something that had invaded America from Mars. That was part of us. It had been there all along. Their New Age spiritual practice was America's dark freaky undercurrent. It was like witchcraft in the Catholic Church.

Now these organized network freaks had taken over the hurricane wreck of the church. They were sacrificing goats in there, and having group sex under their hammer and sickle while witches read Tarot cards to the beat of techno music.

These Lifestyle of Health and Sustainability geeks were maybe seven percent of America's population. But the termite people had seized power. They were the Last Best Hope of a society on the skids. They owned all the hope because they had always been the ones who knew our civilization was hopeless.

So, I was in their prison until I got my head around that new reality. Until I realized that this was inevitable. That it was the way forward. That I loved Little Brother. After that, I could go walkies.

That was the secret. All the rest of it: the natural turmoil of the period…the swarms of IEDs, and the little flying bomb drones, and the wiretaps, and the lynch mobs, and the incinerators and the "regrettable excesses," as they liked to call them—those were not the big story. That was like the exciting sci-fi post-apocalypse part that basically meant nothing that mattered.

Everybody wants the cool post-disaster story—the awesome part where you take over whole abandoned towns, and have sex with cool punk girls in leather

THE EXTERMINATOR'S WANT-AD — 295

rags who have sawed-off shotguns. Boy, I could only wish. In Sustainable-Land, did we have a cool, wild, survivalist lifestyle like that? No way. We had, like, night-soil buckets and vegetarian okra casseroles.

The big story was all about a huge, doomed society that had wrecked itself so thoroughly that its junkyard was inherited by hippies. The epic tale of the Soviet Union, basically. Same thing, different verse. Only more so.

Well, I could survive in that world. I could make it through that. People can survive a Reconstruction: if they keep their noses clean and don't drink themselves to death. The compost heap had turned over. All the magic mushrooms came out of the dark. So they were on top, for a while. So what?

So I learned to sit still and read a lot. Because that looks like innocent behavior. When all the hippie grannies are watching you over their HAL 9000 monitors, poring over your every activity like Vegas croupiers with their zoom and slo-mo, then quietly reading paper books looks great. That's the major consolation of philosophy.

So, in prison, I read, like, Jean-Paul Sartre (who was still under copyright, so I reckon they stole his work). I learned some things from him. That changed me. "Hell is other people." That is the sinister side of a social-software shared society: that people suck, that hell is other people. Sharing with people is hell. When you share, then no matter how much money you have, they just won't leave you alone.

I quoted Jean-Paul Sartre to the parole board. A very serious left-wing philosopher: lots of girlfriends (even feminists), he ate speed all the time, he hung out with Maoists. Except for the Maoist part, Jean-Paul Sartre is my guru.

My life today is all about my Existential authenticity. Because I'm a dissident in this society. Maybe I'm getting old-fashioned, but I'll never go away. I'll never believe what the majority says it believes. And I won't do you the favor of dying young, either.

Because the inconvenient truth is that, authentically, about fifteen percent of everybody is no good. We are the nogoodniks. That's the one thing the Right knows, that the Left never understands: that, although fifteen percent of people are saintly and liberal bleeding hearts, and you could play poker with them blindfolded, another fifteen are like me. I'm a troll. I'm a griefer. I'm in it for me, folks. I need to "collaborate" or "share" the way I need to eat a bale of hay and moo.

Well, like I said to the parole board: "So what are you going to do to me? Ideally, you keep me tied up and you preach at me. Then I become your hypocrite. I'm still a dropout. You don't convince me."

I can tell you what finally happened to me. I got off. I never expected that, couldn't predict it, it came out of nowhere. Yet another world was possible, I guess. It's always like that.

There was a nasty piece of work up in the hills with some "social bandits." Robin Hood is a cool guy for the peace and justice contingent, until he starts robbing the social networks, instead of the Sheriff of Nottingham. Robin goes where the money is—until there's no money. Then Robin goes where the food is.

So, Robin and his Merry Band had a face-off with my captors. That got pretty ugly, because social networks versus bandit mafias is like Ninjas Versus Pirates: it's a counterculture fight to the finish.

However, my geeks had the technology, while redneck Robin just had his terrorist bows and arrows and the suits of Lincoln green. So, he fought the law and the law won. Eventually.

That fight was always a much bigger deal than I was. As dangerous criminals go, a keyboard-tapping troll like me was small potatoes compared to the redneck hillbilly mujihadeen.

So the European Red Cross happened to show up during that episode (because they like gunfire). The Europeans are all prissy about the situation, of course. They are like: "What's with these illegal detainees in orange jumpsuits, and how come they don't have proper medical care?"

So, I finally get paroled. I get amnestied. Not my pal Claire, unfortunately for her. Claire and our female warden had some kind of personal difficulty, because they'd been college roommates or something—like, maybe some stolen boyfriend trouble. Something very girly and tenderly personal, all like that—but in a network society, the power is *all* personal. "The personal is political." You mess with the tender feelings of a network maven, and she's not an objective bureaucrat following the rule of law. She's more like: "To the Bastille with this subhuman irritation!"

Claire was all super-upset to see that I got my walking papers while she was heading for the gulag's deepest darkest inner circles. Claire was like: "Bobby, wait, I thought you and I were gonna watch each other's backs!" And I'm like, "Girlfriend, if it were only a matter of money, I would go bail for you. But I got no money. Nobody does. So, *hasta luego*. I'm on my own."

So at last, I was out of the nest. And I needed a job. In a social network society, they don't have any jobs. Instead, you have to invent public-spirited network-y things to do in public. If people really like what you do for "the commons," then you get all kinds of respect and juice. They make nice to you. They suck up to you all the time, with potluck suppers, and they redecorate your loft. And I really hated that. I still hate it. I'll always hate it.

I'm not a make-nice, live-in-the-hive kind of guy. However, even in a very densely networked society, there are some useful guys that you don't want to see very much. They're very convenient members of society, crucial people even, but they're just not sociable. You don't want to hang around with them, you don't want to give them backrubs, follow their lifestream, none of that. Society's antisocial guys.

There's the hangman. No matter how much justice he dishes out, the hangman is never a popular guy. There's the gravedigger. The locals sure had plenty of work for him, so that job was already taken.

Then there was the exterminator. The man who kills bugs. Me. In a messed-up climate, there are a whole lotta bugs. Zillions of them. You get those big empty suburbs, the burnt-out skyscrapers, lotta wreckage, junk, constant storms, and no air conditioning? Smorgasbord for roaches and silverfish.

Tear up the lawns and grow survival gardens, and you are gonna get a whole lot of the nastiness that lefties call "biodiversity." Vast swarming mobs of six-legged vermin. An endless, fertile, booming supply.

Mosquitoes carry malaria, fleas carry typhus. Malaria and typhus are never popular, even in the greenest, most tree-huggy societies.

So I found myself a career. A good career. Killing bugs. Megatons of them.

My major challenge is the termites. Because they are the best-organized. Termites are fascinating. Termites are not just pale little white-ants that you can crush with your thumb. The individual termites, sure they are, but a nest of termites is a network society. They share everything. They bore a zillion silent holes through seemingly solid wood. They have nurses, engineers, soldiers, a whole social system. They run off fungus inside their guts. It's amazing how sophisticated they are. I learn something new about them every day.

And, I kill them. I'm on call all the time, to kill termites. I got all the termite business I can possibly handle. I figure I can combat those swarmy little pests until I get old and gray. I stink of poison constantly, and I wear mostly plastic, and I'm in a breathing mask like Darth Vader, but I am gonna be a very useful, highly esteemed member of this society.

There will still be some people like me when this whole society goes kaput. And, someday, it surely will. Because no Utopia ever lasts. Except for the termites, who've been at it since the Triassic period.

So, that is my story. This is my want-ad. It's all done now, except for the last part. That's your part: the important part where you yourself can contribute.

I need a termite intern. It's steady work and lots of it. And now, because I wrote all this for you, you know what kind of guy you are pitching in with.

I know that you're out there somewhere. Because I'm not the only guy around like me. If you got this far, you're gonna send me email and a personal profile.

It would help a lot if you were a single female, twenty-five to thirty-five, shapely, and a brunette.

MAP OF SEVENTEEN
CHRISTOPHER BARZAK

Christopher Barzak grew up in rural Ohio, went to a university in a decaying post-industrial city in Ohio, and has lived in a Southern California beach town, the capital of Michigan, and in the suburbs of Tokyo, Japan, where he taught English in rural junior high and elementary schools. His stories have appeared in many venues, including *Strange Horizons*, *Salon Fantastique*, *Interfictions*, *Asimov's*, and *Lady Churchill's Rosebud Wristlet*. His first novel, *One for Sorrow*, was published in 2007, and won the Crawford Award that year. His second book, *The Love We Share Without Knowing*, is a novel in stories set in Japan, and was chosen for the James Tiptree, Jr. Award Honor List and was a Nebula nominee for Best Novel. He is the co-editor (with Delia Sherman) of anthology *Interfictions 2*. Currently he lives in Youngstown, Ohio, where he teaches creative writing at Youngstown State University in the Northeast Ohio MFA program.

Everyone has secrets. Even me. We carry them with us like contraband, always swaddled in some sort of camouflage we've concocted to hide the parts of ourselves the rest of the world is better off not knowing. I'd write what I'm thinking in a diary if I could believe others would stay out of those pages, but in a house like this there's no such thing as privacy. If you're going to keep secrets, you have to learn to write them down inside your own heart. And then be sure not to give that away to anyone either. At least not to just anyone at all.

Which is what bothers me about *him*, the guy my brother is apparently going to marry. Talk about secrets. Off Tommy goes to New York City for college, begging my parents to help him with money for four straight years, then after graduating at the top of his class—in studio art, of all things (not even a degree that will get him a job to help pay off the loans our parents took out for his education)—he comes home to tell us he's gay, and before we can say anything, good or bad, runs off again and won't return our calls. And when he did start talking to Mom and Dad again, it was just short phone conversations and emails, asking for help, for more money.

Five years of off-and-on silence and here he is, bringing home some guy named Tristan who plays the piano better than my mother and has never seen a cow except on TV. We're supposed to treat this casually and not bring up the fact that he ran away without letting us say anything at all four years ago, and to try not to embarrass him. That's Tommy Terlecki, my big brother, the gay surrealist Americana artist who got semi-famous not for the magical creatures and visions he paints, but for his horrifically exaggerated family portraits of us dressed up in ridiculous roles: *American Gothic*, Dad holding a pitchfork, Mom presenting her knitting needles and a ball of yarn to the viewer as if she's coaxing you to give them a try, me with my arms folded under my breasts, my face angry within the frame of my bonnet, scowling at Tommy, who's sitting on the ground beside my legs in the portrait, pulling off the Amish-like clothes. What I don't like about these paintings is that he's lied about us in them. The Tommy in the portrait is constrained by his family's way of life, but it's Tommy who's put us in those clothes to begin with. They're how he sees us, not the way we are, but he gets to dramatize a conflict with us in the paintings anyway, even though it's a conflict he himself has imagined.

Still, I could be practical and say the *American Gothic* series made Tommy's name, which is more than I can say for the new stuff he's working on: *The Sons of Melusine*. They're like his paintings of magical creatures, which the critic who picked his work out of his first group show found too precious in comparison to the "promise of the self-aware, absurdist family portraits this precocious young man from the wilderness of Ohio has also created." Thank you, Google, for keeping me informed on my brother's activities. *The Sons of Melusine* are all bare-chested men with curvy muscles who have serpentine tails and faces like Tristan's, all of them extremely attractive and extremely in pain: out of water mostly, gasping for air in the back alleys of cities, parched and bleeding on beaches, strung on fishermen's line, the hook caught in the flesh of a cheek. A new Christ, Tommy described them when he showed them to us, and Mom and Dad said, "Hmm, I see."

He wants to hang an *American Gothic* in the living room, he told us, after we'd been sitting around talking for a while, all of us together for the first time in years, his boyfriend Tristan smiling politely as we tried to catch up with Tommy's doings while trying to be polite and ask Tristan about himself as well. "My life is terribly boring, I'm afraid," Tristan said when I asked what he does in the city. "My family's well off, you see, so what I do is mostly whatever seems like fun at any particular moment."

Well off. Terribly boring. Whatever seems like fun at any particular moment. I couldn't believe my brother was dating this guy, let alone planning to marry him. This is Tommy, I reminded myself, and right then was when he said, "If it's okay with you, Mom and Dad, I'd like to hang one of the *American Gothic* paintings in here. Seeing how Tristan and I will be staying with you for a while, it'd be nice to add some touches of our own."

Tommy smiled. Tristan smiled and gave Mom a little shrug of his shoulders. I glowered at them from across the room, arms folded across my chest on purpose.

Tommy noticed and, with a concerned face, asked me if something was wrong. "Just letting life imitate art," I told him, but he only kept on looking puzzled. Faker, I thought. He knows exactly what I mean.

Halfway through that first evening, I realized this was how it was going to be as long as Tommy and Tristan were with us, while they waited for their own house to be built next to Mom and Dad's: Tommy conducting us all like the head of an orchestra, waving his magic wand. He had Mom and Tristan sit on the piano bench together and tap out some "Heart and Soul." He sang along behind them for a moment, before looking over his shoulder and waving Dad over to join in. When he tried to pull me in with that charming squinty-eyed devil grin that always gets anyone—our parents, teachers, the local police officers who used to catch him speeding down back roads—to do his bidding, I shook my head, said nothing, and left the room. "Meg?" he said behind me. Then the piano stopped and I could hear them whispering, wondering what had set me off this time.

I'm not known for being easy to live with. Between Tommy's flare for making people live life like a painting when he's around, and my stubborn, immovable will, I'm sure our parents must have thought at some time or other that their real children had been swapped in the night with changelings. It would explain the way Tommy could make anyone like him, even out in the country, where people don't always think well of gay people. It would explain the creatures he paints that people always look nervous about after viewing them, the half-animal beings that roam the streets of cities and back roads of villages in his first paintings. It would explain how I can look at any math problem or scientific equation my teachers put before me and figure them out without breaking a sweat. And my aforementioned will. My will, this thing that's so strong I sometimes feel like it's another person inside me.

Our mother is a mousy figure here in the Middle of Nowhere, Ohio. The central square is not even really a square but an intersection of two highways where town hall, a general store, beauty salon and Presbyterian church all face each other like lost old women casting glances over the asphalt, hoping one of the others knows where they are and where they're going, for surely why would anyone stop here? My mother works in the library, which used to be a one-room schoolhouse a hundred years ago, where they still use a stamp card to keep track of the books checked out. My father is one of the township trustees and he also runs our farm. We raise beef cattle, Herefords mostly, though a few Hereford and Angus mixes are in our herd, so you sometimes get black cows with polka-dotted white faces. I never liked the mixed calves, I'm not sure why, but Tommy always said they were his favorites. Mutts are always smarter than streamlined gene pools, he said. Me? I always thought they looked like heartbroken mimes with dark, dewy eyes.

From upstairs in my room I could hear the piano start again, this time a clas-sical song. It had to be Tristan. Mom only knows songs like "Heart and Soul" and just about any song in a hymn book. They attend, I don't. Tommy and I gave up church ages ago. I still consider myself a Christian, just not the church-going kind. We're lucky to have parents who asked us why we didn't want to go, instead of forcing us like tyrants. When I told them I didn't feel I was learning what I needed to live in the world there, instead of getting mad, they just nodded and Mom said, "If that's the case, perhaps it's best that you walk your own way for a while, Meg."

They're so *good*. That's the problem with my parents. They're so good, it's like they're children or something, innocent and naïve. Definitely not stupid, but way too easy on other people. They never fuss with Tommy. They let him treat them like they're these horrible people who ruined his life and they never say a word. They hug him and calm him down instead, treat him like a child. I don't get it. Tommy's the oldest. Isn't he the one who's supposed to be mature and put together well?

I listened to Tristan's notes drift up through the ceiling from the living room below, and lay on my bed, staring at a tiny speck on the ceiling, a stain or odd flaw in the plaster that has served as my focal point for anger for many years. Since I can remember, whenever I got angry, I'd come up here and lie in this bed and stare at that speck, pouring all of my frustrations into it, as if it were a black hole that could suck up all the bad. I've given that speck so much of my worst self over the years, I'm surprised it hasn't grown darker and wider, big enough to cast a whole person into its depths. When I looked at it now, I found I didn't have as much anger to give it as I'd thought. But no, that wasn't it either. I realized all of my anger was floating around the room instead, buoyed up by the notes of the piano, by Tristan's playing. I thought I could even see those notes shimmer into being for a brief moment, electrified by my frustration. When I blinked, though, the air looked normal again, and Tristan had brought his melody to a close.

There was silence for a minute, some muffled voices, then Mom started up "Amazing Grace." I felt immediately better and breathed a sigh of relief. Then someone knocked on my door and it swung open a few inches, enough for Tommy to peek inside. "Hey, Sis. Can I come in?"

"It's a free country."

"Well," said Tommy. "Sort of."

We laughed. We could laugh about things we agreed on.

"Sooo," said Tommy, "what's a guy gotta do around here to get a hug from his little sister?"

"Aren't you a little old for hugs?"

"Ouch. I must have done something really bad this time."

"Not bad. Something. I don't know what."

"Want to talk about it?"

"Maybe."

Tommy sat down on the corner of my bed and craned his neck to scan the room. "What happened to all the unicorns and horses?"

"They died," I said. "Peacefully, in their sleep, in the middle of the night. Thank God."

He laughed, which made me smirk without wanting to. This was the other thing Tommy had always been able to do: make it hard for people to stay mad at him. "So you're graduating in another month?" he said. I nodded, turned my pillow over so I could brace it under my arm to hold me up more comfortably. "Are you scared?"

"About what?" I said. "Is there something I should be scared of?"

"You know. The future. The rest of your life. You won't be a little girl anymore."

"I haven't been a little girl for a while, Tommy."

"You know what I mean," he said, standing up, tucking his hands into his pockets like he does whenever he's being Big Brother. "You're going to have to begin making big choices," he said. "What you want out of life. You know it's not a diploma you receive when you cross the graduation stage. It's really a ceremony where your training wheels are taken off. The cap everyone wants to throw in the air is a symbol of what you've been so far in life: a student. That's right, everyone wants to cast it off so quickly, eager to get out into the world. Then they realize they've got only a couple of choices for what to do next. The armed service, college or working at a gas station. It's too bad we don't have a better way to recognize what the meaning of graduation really is. Right now, I think it leaves you kids a little clueless."

"Tommy," I said, "yes, you're eleven years older than me. You know more than I do. But really, you need to learn when to shut the hell up and stop sounding pompous."

We laughed again. I'm lucky that, no matter what makes me mad about my brother, we can laugh at ourselves together.

"So what are you upset about then?" he asked after we settled down.

"Them," I said, trying to get serious again. "Mom and Dad. Tommy, have you thought about what this is going to do to them?"

"What do you mean?"

"I mean, what the town's going to say? Tommy, do you know in their church newsletter they have a prayer list and our family is on it?"

"What for?" he asked, beginning to sound alarmed.

"Because you're gay!" I said. It didn't come out how I wanted, though. By the way his face, always alert and showing some kind of emotion, receded and locked its door behind it, I could tell I'd hurt his feelings. "It's not like that," I said. "They didn't ask to be put on the prayer list. Fern Baker put them on it."

"Fern Baker?" Tommy said. "What business has that woman got still being alive?"

"I'm serious, Tommy. I just want to know if you understand the position you've put them in."

He nodded. "I do," he said. "I talked with them about Tristan and me coming out here to live three months ago. They said what they'll always say to me or you when we want or need to come home."

"What's that?"

"Come home, darling. You and your Tristan have a home here too." When I looked down at my comforter and studied its threads for a while, Tommy added, "They'll say the come home part to you, of course. Not anything about bringing your Tristan with you. Oh, and if it's Dad, he might call you sweetie the way Mom calls me darling."

"Tommy," I said, "if there was a market for men who can make their sisters laugh, I'd say you're in the wrong field."

"Maybe we can make that a market."

"You need lots of people for that," I said.

"Mass culture. Hmm. Been there, done that. It's why I'm back. *You* should give it a try, though. It's an interesting experience. It might actually suit you, Meg. Have you thought about where you want to go to college?"

"It's already decided. Kent State in the fall."

"Kent, huh? That's a decent school. You wouldn't rather go to New York or Boston?"

"Tommy, even if you hadn't broken the bank around here already, I don't have patience for legions of people running up and down the streets of Manhattan or Cambridge like ants in a hive."

"And a major?"

"Psychology."

"Ah, I see, you must think there's something wrong with you and want to figure out how to fix it."

"No," I said. "I just want to be able to break people's brains open to understand why they act like such fools."

"That's pretty harsh," said Tommy.

"Well," I said, "I'm a pretty harsh girl."

After Tommy left, I fell asleep without even changing out of my clothes. In the morning when I woke, I was tangled up in a light blanket someone—Mom, probably—threw over me before going to bed the night before. I sat up and looked out the window. It was already late morning. I could tell by the way the light winked off the pond in the woods, which you can see a tiny sliver of, like a crescent moon, when the sun hits at just the right angle towards noon. Tommy and I used to spend our summers on the dock our father built out there. Reading books, swatting away flies, the soles of our dusty feet in the air behind us. He was so much older than me but never treated me like a little kid. The day he left for New York City, I hugged him on the front porch before Dad drove him to the airport, but burst out crying and ran around back of the house, beyond the fields, into the woods, until I reached the dock. I thought Tommy would follow, but he was the last person I wanted to see right then, so I thought out with my mind in the direction of the house, pushing him away. I turned him around in his tracks and made him tell our parents he couldn't find me. When he didn't come, I knew that I had used something inside me to stop him. Tommy wouldn't have ever let me run away crying like that without chasing after me if I'd let him make that choice on his own. I lay on the dock for an hour, looking at my reflection in the water, saying, "What are you? God damn it, you know the answer. Tell me. What *are* you?"

If Mom had come back and seen me like that, heard me speak in such a way, I think she probably would have had a breakdown. Mom can handle a gay son mostly. What I'm sure she couldn't handle would be if one of her kids talked to themselves like this at age seven. Worse would be if she knew why I asked myself that question. It was the first time my will had made something happen. And it had made Tommy go away without another word between us.

Sometimes I think the rest of my life is going to be a little more difficult everyday.

When I was dressed and had a bowl of granola and bananas in me, I grabbed the novel I was reading off the kitchen counter and opened the back door to head back to the pond. Thinking of the summer days Tommy and I spent back there together made me think I should probably honor my childhood one last summer by keeping up tradition before I had to go away. I was halfway out the door, twisting around to close it, when Tristan came into the kitchen and said, "Good morning, Meg. Where are you off to?"

"The pond," I said.

"Oh the pond!" Tristan said, as if it were a tourist site he'd been wanting to visit. "Would you mind if I tagged along?"

"It's a free country," I said, thinking I should probably have been nicer, but I turned to carry on my way anyway.

"Well, sort of," Tristan said, which stopped me in my tracks.

I turned around and looked at him. He did that same little shrug he did the night before when Tommy asked Mom and Dad if he could hang the *American Gothic* portrait in the living room, then smiled, as if something couldn't be helped. "Are you just going to stand there, or are you coming?" I said.

Quickly Tristan followed me out, and then we were off through the back field and into the woods, until we came to the clearing where the pond reflected the sky, like an open blue eye staring up at God.

I made myself comfortable on the deck, spread out my towel and opened my book. I was halfway done. Someone's heart had already been broken and no amount of mixed CDS left in her mailbox and school locker were ever going to set things right. Why did I read these things? I should take the bike to the library and check out something Classic instead, I thought. Probably there's something I should be reading right now that everyone else in college will have read. I worried about things like that. Neither of our parents went to college. I remember Tommy used to worry the summer before he went to New York that he'd get there and never be able to fit in. "Growing up out here is going to be a black mark," he'd said. "I'm not going to know how to act around anyone there because of this place."

I find it ironic that it's this place—us—that helped Tommy start his career.

"This place is amazing," said Tristan. He stretched out on his stomach beside me, dangling the upper half of his torso over the edge so he could pull his fingers through the water just inches below us. "I can't believe you have all of this to yourself. You're so lucky."

"I guess," I said, pursing my lips. I still didn't know Tristan well enough to feel I could trust his motivations or be more than civil to him. Pretty. Harsh. Girl. I know.

"Wow," said Tristan, pulling his lower half back up onto the deck with me. He looked across the water, blinking. "You really don't like me," he said.

"That's not true," I said immediately, but even I knew that was mostly a lie. So I tried to revise. "I mean, it's not that I don't like you. I just don't know you so well, that's all."

"Don't trust me, eh?"

"Really," I said, "why should I?"

"Your brother's trust in me doesn't give you a reason?"

"Tommy's never been known around here for his good judgment," I said.

Tristan whistled. "Wow," he said again, this time elongating it. "You're tough as nails, aren't you?"

I shrugged. Tristan nodded. I thought this was a sign we'd come to an understanding, so I went back to reading. Not two minutes passed, though, before he interrupted again.

"What are you hiding, Meg?"

"What are you talking about?" I said, looking up from my book.

"Well obviously if you don't trust people to this extreme, you must have something to hide. That's what distrustful people often have. Something to hide. Either that or they've been hurt an awful lot by people they loved."

"You do know you guys can't get married in Ohio, right? The people decided in the election a couple of years ago."

"Ohhhh," said Tristan. "The people. The people the people the people. Oh, my dear, it's always the people! Always leaping to defend their own rights but always ready to deny someone else theirs. Wake up, baby. That's history. Did that stop other people from living how they wanted? Well, I suppose sometimes. Screw the people anyhow. Your brother and I will be married, whether or not the people make some silly law that prohibits it. The people, my dear, only matter if you let them."

"So you'll be married like I'm a Christian even though I don't go to church."

"Really, Meg, you do realize that even if you consider yourself a Christian, those other people don't, right?"

"What do you mean?"

Tristan turned over on his side so he could face me, and propped his head in his hand. His eyes are green. Tommy's are blue. If they could have children, they'd be so beautiful, like sea creatures or fairies. My eyes are blue too, but they're like Dad's, dull and flat, like a blind old woman's eyes rather than the shallow-ocean-with-dancing-lights-on-it blue that Mom and Tommy have. "I mean," said Tristan, "those people only believe you're a real Christian if you attend church. It's the body of Christ rule and all that. You *have* read the Bible, haven't you?"

"Parts," I said, squinting a little. "But anyway," I said, "it doesn't matter what they think of me. I know what's true in my heart."

"Well precisely," said Tristan.

I stopped squinting and held his stare. He didn't flinch, just kept staring back. "Okay," I said. "You've made your point."

Tristan stood and lifted his shirt above his head, kicked off his sandals, and dove into the pond. The blue rippled and rippled, the rings flowing out to the edges, then silence and stillness returned, but Tristan didn't. I waited a few moments, then stood halfway up on one knee. "Tristan?" I said, and waited a few moments more. "Tristan," I said, louder this time. But he still didn't come to the surface. "Tristan, stop it!" I shouted, and immediately his head burst out of the water at the center of the pond.

"Oh this is lovely," he said, shaking his wet, brown hair out of his eyes. "It's like having Central Park in your back yard!"

I picked my book up and left, furious with him for frightening me. What did he think? It was funny? I didn't stay to find out. I didn't turn around or say anything in response to Tristan either, when he began calling for me to come back.

Tommy was in the kitchen making lunch for everyone when I burst through the back door and slammed it shut behind me like a small tornado had blown through. "What's wrong now?" he said, looking up from the tomato soup and grilled cheese sandwiches he was making. "Boy trouble?"

He laughed, but this time I didn't laugh with him. Tommy knew I wasn't much of a dater, that I didn't have a huge interest in going somewhere with a guy from school and watching a movie or eating fast food while they practiced on me to become better at making girls think they've found a guy who's incredible. I don't get that stuff, really. I mean, I like guys. I had a boyfriend once. I mean a real one, not the kind some girls call boyfriends but really aren't anything but the guy they dated that month. That's not a boyfriend. That's a candidate. Some people can't tell the difference. Anyway, I'm sure my parents have probably thought I'm the same way as Tommy, since I don't bring boys home, but I don't bring boys home because it all seems like something to save for later. Right now, I like just thinking about me, *my* future. I'm not so good at thinking in the first person plural yet.

I glared at Tommy before saying, "Your boyfriend sucks. He just tricked me into thinking he'd drowned."

Tommy grinned. "He's a bad boy, I know," he said. "But Meg, he didn't mean anything by it. You take life too seriously. You should really relax a little. Tristan is playful. That's part of his charm. He was trying to make you his friend, that's all."

"By freaking me out? Wonderful friendship maneuver. It amazes me how smart you and your city friends are. Did Tristan go to NYU, too?"

"No," Tommy said flatly. And on that one word, with that one shift of tone in his voice, I could tell I'd pushed him into the sort of self I wear most of the time: the armor, the defensive position. I'd crossed one of his lines and felt small and little and mean. "Tristan's family is wealthy," said Tommy. "He's a bit of the black sheep, though. They're not on good terms. He could have gone to college anywhere he wanted, but I think he's avoided doing that because it would make them proud of him for being more like them instead of himself. They're different people, even though they're from the same family. Like how you and I are different from Mom and Dad about church. Anyway, they threatened to cut him off if he didn't come home to let them groom him to be more like them."

"Heterosexual, married to a well-off woman from one of their circle and ruthless in a board room?" I offered.

"Well, no," said Tommy. "Actually they're quite okay with Tristan being gay. He's different from them in another way."

"What way?" I asked.

Tommy rolled his eyes a little, weighing whether or not he should tell me anymore. "I shouldn't talk about it," he said, sighing, exasperated.

"Tommy, tell me!" I said. "How bad could it be?"

"Not bad so much as strange. Maybe even unbelievable for you, Meg." I frowned, but he went on. "The ironic thing is, the thing they can't stand about Tristan is something they gave him. A curse, you would have called it years ago. Today I think the word we use is gene. In any case, it runs in Tristan's family, skipping generations mostly, but every once in a while one of the boys are born...well, different."

"Different but not in the gay way?" I said, confused.

"No, not in the gay way," said Tommy, smiling, shaking his head. "Different in the way that he has two lives, sort of. The one here on land with you and me, and another one in, well, in the water."

"He's a rebellious swimmer?"

Tommy laughed, bursting the air. "I guess you could say that," he said. "But no. Listen, if you want to know, I'll tell you, but you have to promise not to tell Mom and Dad. They think we're here because Tommy's family disowned him for being gay. I told them his parents were Pentecostal, so it all works out in their minds.

"Okay," I said. "I promise."

"What would you say," Tristan began, his eyes shifting up as if he were searching for the right words in the air above him. "What would you say, Meg, if I told you the real reason is because Tristan's not completely human. I mean, not in the sense that we understand it."

I narrowed my eyes, pursed my lips, and said, "Tommy, are you on drugs?"

"I wish!" he said. "God, those'll be harder to find around here," he laughed. "No, really, I'm telling the truth. Tristan is something…something else. A water person? You know, with a tail and all?" Tommy flapped his hand in the air when he said this. I smirked, waiting for the punch line. But when one didn't come, it hit me.

"This has something to do with *The Sons of Melusine*, doesn't it?"

Tommy nodded. "Yes, those paintings are inspired by Tristan."

"But Tommy," I said, "why are you going back to this type of painting? Sure it's an interesting gimmick, saying your boyfriend's a merman. But the critics didn't like your fantasy paintings. They liked the *American Gothic* stuff. Why would they change their minds now?"

"Two things," Tommy said, frustrated with me. "One: a good critic doesn't dismiss entire genres. They look at technique and composition of elements and the relationship the painting establishes with this world. Two: it's not a gimmick. It's the truth, Meg. Listen to me. I'm not laughing anymore. Tristan made his parents an offer. He said he'd move somewhere unimportant and out of the way, and they could make up whatever stories about him for their friends to explain his absence if they gave him part of his inheritance now. They accepted. It's why we're here."

I didn't know what to say, so I just stood there. Tommy ladled soup into bowls for the four of us. Dad would be coming in from the barn soon, Tristan back from the pond. Mom was still at the library and wouldn't be home till evening. This was a regular summer day. It made me feel safe, that regularity. I didn't want it to ever go away.

I saw Tristan then, trotting through the field out back, drying his hair with his pink shirt as he came. When I turned back to Tommy, he was looking out the window over the sink, watching Tristan too, his eyes watering. "You really love him, don't you?" I said.

Tommy nodded, wiping his tears away with the backs of his hands. "I do," he said. "He's so special, like something I used to see a long time ago. Something I forgot how to see for a while."

"Have you finished *The Sons of Melusine* series then?" I asked, trying to change the subject. I didn't feel sure of how to talk to Tommy right then.

"I haven't," said Tommy. "There's one more I want to do. I was waiting for the right setting. Now we have it."

"What do you mean?"

"I want to paint Tristan by the pond."

"Why the pond?"

"Because," said Tommy, returning to gaze out the window, "it's going to be a place he can be himself at totally now. He's never had that before."

"When will you paint him?"

"Soon," said Tommy. "But I'm going to have to ask you and Mom and Dad a favor."

"What?"

"Not to come down to the pond while we're working."

"Why?"

"He doesn't want anyone to know about him. I haven't told Mom and Dad. Just you. So you have to promise me two things. Don't come down to the pond, and don't tell Tristan I told you about him."

Tristan opened the back door then. He had his shirt back on and his hair was almost dry. Pearls of water still clung to his legs. I couldn't imagine those being a tail, his feet a flipper. Surely Tommy had gone insane. "Am I late for lunch?" Tristan asked, smiling at me.

Tommy turned and beamed him a smile back. "Right on time, love," he said, and I knew our conversation had come to an end.

I went down the lane to the barn where Dad was working, taking his lunch with me when he didn't show up to eat with us. God, I wished I could tell him how weird Tommy was being, but I'd promised not to say anything, and even if my brother was going crazy, I wouldn't go back on my word. I found Dad coming out of the barn with a pitchfork of cow manure, which he threw onto the spreader parked outside the barn. He'd take that to the back field and spread it later probably, and then I'd have to watch where I stepped for a week whenever I cut through the field to go to the pond. When I gave him his soup and sandwich, he thanked me and asked what the boys were doing. I told him they were sitting in the living room under the *American Gothic* portrait fiercely making out. He almost spit out his sandwich, he laughed so hard. I like making my dad laugh because he doesn't do it nearly enough. Mom's too nice, which sometimes is what kills a sense of humor in people, and Tommy always was too testing of Dad to ever get to a joking relationship with him. Me, though, I can always figure out something to shock him into a laugh.

"You're bad, Meg," he said, after settling down. Then: "Were they really?"

I shook my head. "Nope. You were right the first time, Dad. That was a joke." I didn't want to tell him his son had gone mad, though.

"Well I thought so, but still," he said, taking a bite of his sandwich. "All sorts of new things to get used to these days."

I nodded. "Are you okay with that?" I asked.

"Can't not be," he said. "Not an option."

"Who says?"

"I need no authority figure on that," said Dad. "You have a child and, no matter what, you love them. That's just how it is."

"That's not how it is for everyone, Dad."

"Well thank the dear Lord I'm not everyone," he said. "Why would you want to live like that, with all those conditions on love?"

I didn't know what to say. He'd shocked me into silence the way I could always shock him into laughter. We had that effect on each other, like yin and yang. My dad's a good guy, likes the simpler life, seems pretty normal. He wears Allis Chalmers tractor hats and flannel shirts and jeans. He likes oatmeal and meatloaf and macaroni and cheese. Then he opens his mouth and turns into the Buddha. I swear to God, he'll do it when you're least expecting it. I don't know sometimes whether he's like me and Tommy, hiding something different about himself but just has all these years of experience to make himself blend in. Like maybe he's an angel beneath that sun-browned, beginning-to-wrinkle human skin. "Do you really feel that way?" I asked. "It's one thing to say that, but is it that easy to truly feel that way?"

"Well it's not what you'd call easy, Meg. But it's what's right. Most of the time doing what's right is more difficult than doing what's wrong."

He handed me his bowl and plate after he finished, and asked if I'd take a look at Buttercup. Apparently she'd been looking pretty down. So I set the dishes on the seat of the tractor and went into the barn to visit my old girl, my cow Buttercup, who I've had since I was a little girl. She was my present on my fourth birthday. I'd found her with her mother in a patch of buttercups and spent the summer with her, sleeping with her in the fields, playing with her, training her as if she were a dog. By the time she was a year old, she'd even let me ride her like a horse. We were the talk of the town, and Dad even had me ride her into the ring at the county fair's Best of Show. Normally she would have been butchered by now—no cow lasted as long as Buttercup had on Dad's farm—but I had saved her each time it ever came into Dad's head to let her go. He never had to say anything. I could see his thoughts as clear as if they were stones beneath a clear stream of water, I could take them and break them or change them if I needed. The way I'd changed Tommy's mind the day he left for New York, making him turn back and leave me alone by the pond. It was a stupid thing, really, whatever it was, this thing I could do with my will. Here I could change people's minds, but I used it to make people I loved go away with hard feelings and to prolong the life of a cow.

Dad was right. She wasn't looking good, the old girl. She was thirteen and had had a calf every summer for a good ten years. I looked at her now and saw how selfish I'd been to make him keep her. She was down on the ground in her stall, legs folded under her, like a queen stretched out on a litter, her eyes half-closed, her lashes long and pretty as a woman's. "Old girl," I said. "How you doing?" She looked up at me, chewing her cud, and smiled. Yes, cows can smile. I can't stand it that people can't see this. Cats can smile, dogs can smile, cows can too. It just takes time and you have to really pay attention to notice. You can't look for a human smile; it's not the same. You have to be able to see an animal for itself before it'll let you see its smile. Buttercup's smile was warm, but fleeting. She looked exhausted from the effort of greeting me.

I patted her down and brushed her a bit and gave her some ground molasses to lick out of my hand. I liked the feel of the rough stubble on her tongue as it swept across my palm. Sometimes I thought if not psychology, maybe veterinary medicine would be the thing for me. I'd have to get used to death, though. I'd have to be okay with helping an animal die. Looking at Buttercup, I knew I didn't have that in me. If only I could use my will on myself as well as it worked on others.

When I left the barn, Dad was up on the seat of the tractor, holding his dishes, which he handed me again. "Off to spread this load," he said, starting the tractor after he spoke. He didn't have to say anymore about Buttercup. He knew I'd seen what he meant. I'd have to let her go someday, I knew. I'd have to work on that, though. I just wasn't ready.

The next day I went back to the pond only to find Tristan and Tommy already there. Tommy had a radio playing classical music on the dock beside him while he sketched something in his notebook. Tristan swam towards him, then pulled his torso up and out by holding onto the dock so he could lean in and kiss Tommy before letting go and sinking back down. I tried to see if there were scales at his waistline, but he was too quick. "Hey!" Tommy shouted. "You dripped all over my sketch you wretched whale! What do you think this is? Sea World?"

I laughed, but Tommy and Tristan both looked over at me, eyes wide, mouths open, shocked to see me there. "Meg!" Tristan said from the pond, waving his hand. "How long have you been there? We didn't hear you."

"Only a minute," I said, stepping onto the dock, moving Tommy's radio over before spreading out my towel to lie next to him. "You should really know not to mess with him when he's working," I added. "Tommy is a perfectionist, you know."

"Which is why I do it," Tristan laughed. "Someone needs to keep him honest. Nothing can be perfect, right Tommy?"

"Close to perfect, though," Tommy said.

"What are you working on?" I asked, and immediately he flipped the page over and started sketching something new.

"Doesn't matter," he said, his pencil pulling gray and black lines into existence on the page. "Tristan ruined it."

"I *had* to kiss you," Tristan said, swimming closer to us.

"You always have to kiss me," Tommy said.

"Well, yes," said Tristan. "Can you blame me?"

I rolled my eyes and opened my book.

"Meg," Tommy said a few minutes later, after Tristan had swum away, disappearing into the depths of the pond and appearing on the other side, smiling brilliantly. "Remember how I said I'd need you and Mom and Dad to do me that favor?"

"Yeah."

"I'm going to start work tomorrow, so no more coming up on us without warning like that, okay?"

I put my book down and looked at him. He was serious. No joke was going to follow this gravely intoned request. "Okay," I said, feeling a little stung. I didn't like it when Tommy took that tone with me and meant it.

I finished my book within the hour and got up to leave. Tommy looked up as I bent to pick up my towel and I could see his mouth opening to say something, a reminder, or worse: a plea for me to believe what he'd said about Tristan the day before. So I locked eyes with him and took hold of that thought before it became speech. It wriggled fiercely, trying to escape the grasp of my will, flipping back and forth like a fish pulled out of its stream. But I won. I squeezed it between my will's fingers, and Tommy turned back to sketching without another word.

The things that are wrong with me are many. I try not to let them be the things people see in me, though. I try to make them invisible, or to make them seem natural, or else I stuff them up in that dark spot on my ceiling and will them into non-existence. This doesn't usually work for very long. They come back, they always come back, whatever they are, if it's something really a part of me and not just a passing mood. No amount of willing can change those things. Like my inability to let go of Buttercup, my anger with the people of this town, my frustration with my parents' kindness to a world that doesn't deserve them, my annoyance with my brother's light-stepped movement through life. I hate that everything we love has to die, I despise narrow thinking, I resent the unfairness of the world and the unfairness that I can't feel at home in it like it seems others can. All I have is my will, this sharp piece of material inside me, stronger than metal, that everything I encounter breaks itself upon.

Mom once told me it was my gift, not to discount it. I'd had a fit of anger with the school board and the town that day. They'd fired one of my teachers for not teaching creationism alongside evolution, and somehow thought this was completely legal. And no one seemed outraged but me. I wrote a letter to the newspaper declaring the whole affair an obstruction to teacher's freedoms, but it seemed that everyone—kids at school and their parents—just accepted it until a year later the courts told us it was unacceptable.

I cried and tore apart my room one day that year. I hated being in school after they did that to Mr. Turney. When Mom heard me tearing my posters off the walls, smashing my unicorns and horses, she burst into my room and threw her arms around me and held me until my will quieted again. Later, when we were sitting on my bed, me leaning against her while she combed her fingers through my hair, she said, "Meg, don't be afraid of what you can do. That letter you wrote, it was wonderful. Don't feel bad because no one else said anything. You made a strong statement. People were talking about it at church last week. They think people can't hear, or perhaps they mean for them to hear. Anyway, I'm proud of you for speaking out against what your heart tells you isn't right. That's your gift, sweetie. If you hadn't noticed, not everyone is blessed with such a strong, beautiful will."

It made me feel a little better, hearing that, but I couldn't also tell her how I'd used it for wrong things too: to make Tommy leave for New York without knowing I was okay, to make Dad keep Buttercup beyond the time he should have, to keep people far away so I wouldn't have to like or love them. I'd used my will to keep the world at bay, and that was my secret: that I didn't really care for this life I'd been given, that I couldn't stop myself from being angry at the whole fact of it, life, that the more things I loved, the worse it would be because I'd lose all those things in the end. So Buttercup sits in the barn, her legs barely strong enough for her to stand on, because of me not being able to let go. So Tommy turned back and left because I couldn't bear to say goodbye. So I didn't have any close friends because I didn't want to have to lose anymore than I already had to lose in my family.

My will was my gift, she said. So why did it feel like such a curse to me?

When Mom came home later that evening, I sat in the kitchen and had a cup of tea with her. She always wanted tea straight away after she came home. She said it calmed her, helped her ease out of her day at the library and back into life at home. "How are Tommy and Tristan adjusting?" she asked me after a few sips, and I shrugged.

"They seem to be doing fine, but Tommy's being weird and a little mean."

"How so?" Mom wanted to know.

"Just telling me to leave them alone while he works and he told me some weird things about Tristan and his family too. I don't know. It all seems so impossible."

"Don't underestimate people's ability to do harm to each other," Mom interrupted. "Even those that say they love you."

I knew she was making this reference based on the story Tommy had told her and Dad about Tristan's family disowning him because he was gay, so I shook my head. "I understand that, Mom," I said. "There's something else too." I didn't know how to tell her what Tommy had told me, though. I'd promised to keep it between him and me. So I settled for saying, "Tristan doesn't seem the type who would want to live out here away from all the things he could enjoy in the city."

"Perhaps that's all grown old for him," Mom said. "People change. Look at you, off to school in a month or so. Between the time you leave and the first time you come home again, you'll have become someone different, and I won't have had a chance to watch you change." She started tearing up. "All your changes all these years, the Lord's let me share them all with you and now I'm going to have to let you go and change into someone without me around to make sure you're safe."

"Oh Mom," I said. "Don't cry."

"No, no," she said. "I want to cry." She wiped her cheeks with the backs of her hands, smiling. "I just want to say, Meg, don't be so hard on other people. Or yourself. It's hard enough as it is, being in this world. Don't judge so harshly. Don't stop yourself from seeing other people's humanity because they don't fit into your scheme of the world."

I blinked a lot, then picked up my mug of tea and sipped it. I didn't know how to respond. Mom usually never says anything critical of us, and though she said it nicely, I knew she was worried for me. For her to say something like that, I knew I needed to put down my shield and sword and take a look around instead of fighting. But wasn't fighting the thing I was good at?

"I'm sorry, Mom," I said.

"Don't be sorry, dear. Be happy. Find the thing that makes you happy and enjoy it, like your brother is doing."

"You mean his painting?" I said.

"No," said Mom. "I mean Tristan."

One day towards the end of my senior year, our English teacher Miss Portwood told us that many of our lives were about to become much wider. That we'd soon have to begin mapping a world for ourselves outside of the first seventeen years of our lives. It struck me, hearing her say that, comparing the years of our lives to a map of the world. If I had a map of seventeen, of the years I'd lived so far, it would be small and plain, outlining the contours of my town with a few landmarks on it like Marrow's Ravine and town square, the schools, the pond, our fields and the barn and the home we live in. It would be on crisp, fresh paper, because I haven't traveled very far, and stuck to the routes I know best. There would be nothing but waves and waves of ocean surrounding my map of my hometown. In the ocean I'd draw those sea beasts you find on old maps of the world, and above them I'd write the words "There Be Dragons."

What else is out there, beyond this edge of the world I live on? Who else is out there? Are there real reasons to be as afraid of the world as I've been?

I was thinking all this when I woke up the next morning and stared at the black spot on my ceiling. That could be a map of seventeen, too. Nothing but white around it, and nothing to show for hiding myself away. Mom was right. Though I was jealous of Tommy's ability to live life so freely, he was following a path all his own, a difficult one, and needed as many people who loved him to help him do it. I could help him and Tristan both probably just by being more friendly and supportive than suspicious and untrusting. I could start by putting aside Tommy's weirdness about Tristan being a cursed son of Melusine and do like Mom and Dad: just humor him. He's an artist after all.

So I got up and got dressed and left the house without even having breakfast. I didn't want to let another day go by and not make things okay with Tommy for going away all those years ago. Through the back field I went, into the woods, picking up speed as I went, as the urgency to see him took over me. By the time I reached the edge of the pond's clearing, I had a thousand things I wanted to say. When I stepped out of the woods and into the clearing, though, I froze in place, my mouth open but no words coming out because of what I saw there.

Tommy was on the dock with his easel and palette, sitting in a chair, painting Tristan. And Tristan—I don't know how to describe him, how to make his being something possible, but these words came into mind: tail, scales, beast and beauty. At first I couldn't tell which he was, but I knew immediately that Tommy hadn't gone insane. Or else we both had.

Tristan lay on the dock in front of Tommy, his upper body strong and muscular and naked, his lower half long and sinuous as a snake. His tail swept back and forth, occasionally dipping into the water for a moment before returning to the position Tommy wanted. I almost screamed, but somehow willed myself not to. I hadn't left home yet, but a creature from the uncharted world had traveled onto my map where I'd lived the past seventeen years. How could this be?

I thought of that group show we'd all flown to New York to see, the one where Tommy had hung his first in the series of *American Gothic* alongside those odd, magical creatures he painted back when he was just graduated. The critic who'd picked him out of that group show said that Tommy had technique and talent, was by turns fascinating and annoying, but that he'd wait to see if Tommy would develop a more mature vision. I think when I read that back then, I had agreed.

I'd forgotten the favor I'd promised: not to come back while they were working. Tommy hadn't really lied when he told me moving here was for Tristan's benefit, to get away from his family and the people who wanted him to be something other than what he is. I wondered how long he'd been trying to hide this part of himself before he met Tommy, who was able to love him because of who and what he is. What a gift and curse that is, to be both of them, to be what Tristan is and for Tommy to see him so clearly. My problems were starting to shrivel the longer I looked at them. And the longer I looked, the more I realized the dangers they faced, how easily their lives and love could be shattered by the people in the world who would fire them from life the way the school board fired Mr. Turney for actually teaching us what we can know about the world.

I turned and quietly went back through the woods, but as I left the trail and came into the back field, I began running. I ran from the field and past the house, out into the dusty back road we live on, and stood there looking up and down the road at the horizon, where the borders of this town waited for me to cross them at the end of summer. Whether there were dragons waiting for me after I journeyed off the map of my first seventeen years didn't matter. I'd love them when it called for loving them, and I'd fight the ones that needed fighting. That was my gift, like Mom had told me, what I could do with my will. Maybe instead of psychology I'd study law, learn how to defend it, how to make it better, so that someday Tommy and Tristan could have what everyone else has.

It's a free country after all. Well, sort of. And one day, if I had anything to say about it, that would no longer be a joke between Tommy and me.

THE NATURALIST
MAUREEN MCHUGH

Maureen McHugh was born in Loveland, Ohio, and received a B.A. from Ohio University in 1981, where she took a creative writing course from Daniel Keyes in her senior year. After several years as a part-time college instructor, she spent a year teaching in Shijiazhuang, China. It was during this period she sold her first story, "All in a Day's Work," which appeared in *The Twilight Zone Magazine*. She has written four novels, including James Tiptree, Jr. Award winner and Hugo and Nebula Award nominee *China Mountain Zhang*, *Half the Day Is Night*, *Mission Child*, and *Nekropolis*. Her short fiction, including Hugo Award winner "The Lincoln Train," was collected in *Mothers and Other Monsters*, which was a finalist for the Story Prize. She is currently a partner at No Mimes Media, an Alternate Reality Game company, and was a writer and/or managing editor for numerous projects, including *Year Zero* and *I Love Bees*.

Cahill lived in the Flats with about twenty other guys in a place that used to be an Irish bar called Fado. At the back of the bar was the Cuyahoga River, good for protection since zombies didn't cross the river. They didn't crumble into dust, they were just stupid as bricks and they never built a boat or a bridge or built anything. Zombies were the ultimate trash. Worse than the guys who cooked meth in trailers. Worse than the fat women on WIC. Zombies were just useless dumbfucks.

"They're too dumb to find enough food to keep a stray cat going," Duck said.

Cahill was talking to a guy called Duck. Well, really, Duck was talking and Cahill was mostly listening. Duck had been speculating on the biology of zombies. He thought that the whole zombie thing was a virus, like Mad Cow Disease. A lot of the guys thought that. A lot of them mentioned that movie, *28 Days*, where everybody but a few people had been driven crazy by a virus.

"But they gotta find something," Duck said. Duck had a prison tattoo of a mallard on his arm. Cahill wouldn't have known it was a mallard if Duck hadn't told him. He could just about tell it was a bird. Duck was over six feet tall and Cahill would have hated to have been the guy who gave Duck such a shitty tattoo cause Duck probably beat him senseless when he finally got a look at the thing. "Maybe," Duck mused, "maybe they're solar powered. And eating us is just a bonus."

"I think they go dormant when they don't smell us around," Cahill said.

Cahill didn't really like talking to Duck, but Duck often found Cahill and started talking to him. Cahill didn't know why. Most of the guys gave Duck a wide berth. Cahill figured it was probably easier to just talk to Duck when Duck wanted to talk.

Almost all of the guys at Fado were white. There was a Filipino guy, but he pretty much counted as white. As far as Cahill could tell there were two kinds of black guys, regular black guys and Nation of Islam. The Nation of Islam had gotten organized and turned a place across the street—a club called Heaven—into their headquarters. Most of the regular black guys lived below Heaven and in the building next door.

This whole area of the Flats had been bars and restaurants and clubs. Now it was a kind of compound with a wall of rubbish and dead cars forming a perimeter. Duck said that during the winter they had regular patrols organized by Whittaker and the Nation. Cold as shit standing behind a junked car on its side, watching for zombies. But they had killed off most of the zombies in this area and now they didn't bother keeping watch. Occasionally a zombie wandered across the bridge and they had to take care of it, but in the time Cahill had been in Cleveland, he had seen exactly four zombies. One had been a woman.

Life in the zombie preserve really wasn't as bad as Cahill had expected. He'd been dumped off the bus and then spent a day skulking around expecting zombies to come boiling out of the floor like rats and eat him alive. He'd heard that the life expectancy of a guy in a preserve was something like two and a half days. But he'd only been here about a day and a half when he found a cache of liquor in the trunk of a car and then some guys scavenging. He'd shown them where the liquor was and they'd taken him back to the Flats.

Whittaker was a white guy who was sort of in charge. He'd had made a big speech about how they were all more free here in the preserve than they'd ever been in a society that had no place for them, about how there used to be spaces for men with big appetites like the Wild West and Alaska—and how that was all gone now but they were making a great space for themselves here in Cleveland where they could live true to their own nature.

Cahill didn't think it was so great, and glancing around he was pretty sure that he wasn't the only one who wouldn't chuck the whole thing for a chance to sit and watch the Sox on TV. Bullshitting was what the Whittakers of the world did. It was part of running other people's lives. Cahill had dragged in a futon and made himself a little room. It had no windows and only one way in, which was good in case of attack. But he found most of the time he couldn't sleep there. A lot of time he slept outside on a picnic table someone had dragged out into the middle of the street.

What he really missed was carpet. He wanted to take a shower and then walk on carpet in a bedroom and get dressed in clean clothes.

A guy named Riley walked over to Cahill and Duck and said, "Hey, Cahill. Whittaker wants you to go scavenge."

Cahill hated to scavenge. It was nerve-wracking. It wasn't hard; there was a surprising amount left in the city, even after the groceries had been looted. He shrugged and thought about it and decided it was better not to say no to Whittaker. And it gave him an excuse to stop talking to Duck about zombies. He followed Riley and left Duck sitting looking at the water, enjoying the May sun.

"I think it's a government thing," Riley said. Riley was black but just regular black, not Nation of Islam. "I think it's a mutation of the AIDs virus."

Jesus Christ. "Yeah," Cahill said, hoping Riley would drop it.

"You know the whole AIDs thing was from the CIA, don't you? It was supposed to wipe out black people," Riley said.

"Then how come fags got it first?" Cahill asked.

He thought that might piss Riley off but Riley seemed pleased to be able to explain how gay guys were the perfect way to introduce the disease because nobody cared fuckall what happened to them. But that really, fags getting it was an accident because it was supposed to wipe out all the black people in Africa and then the whites could just move into a whole new continent. Some queer stewardess got it in Africa and then brought it back here. It would kill white people but it killed black people faster. And now if you were rich they could cure you or at least give you drugs for your whole life so you wouldn't get sick and die, which was the same thing, but they were still letting black people and Africans die.

Cahill tuned Riley out. They collected two other guys. Riley was in charge. Cahill didn't know the names of the two other guys—a scrawny, white-trash-looking guy and a light-skinned black guy.

Riley quit talking once they had crossed the bridge and were in Cleveland.

On the blind, windowless side of a warehouse the wall had been painted white, and in huge letters it said:

Hell from beneath is moved for thee to meet thee at thy coming.
Isaiah (ch. XIV, v. 9)

This same quote was painted at the gate where the bus had dumped Cahill off.

There were crows gathering at Euclid and, Riley guessed, maybe around East Ninth, so they headed north towards the lake. Zombies stank and the crows tended to hang around them. Behind them the burned ruins of the Renaissance hotel were still black and wet from the rain a couple of days ago.

When they saw the zombie there were no crows but that may have been because there was only one. Crows often meant a number of zombies. She fixed on them, turning her face towards them despite the blank whiteness of her eyes. She was black and her hair had once been in cornrows, though now half of it was loose and tangled. They all stopped and stood stock still. No one knew how zombies "saw" people. Maybe infrared like pit vipers. Maybe smell. Cahill could not tell from this far if she was sniffing. Or listening. Or maybe even tasting the air. Taste was one of the most primitive senses. Primitive as smell. Smelling with the tongue.

She went from standing there to loping towards them. That was one of the things about zombies. They didn't lean. They didn't anticipate. One minute they were standing there, the next minute they were running towards you. They didn't lead with their eyes or their chins. They were never surprised. They just were. As inexorable as rain. She didn't look as she ran, even though she was running through debris and rubble, placing her feet and sometimes barely leaping.

"Fuck," someone said.

"Pipes! Who's got pipes!" Riley shouted.

They all had pipes and they all got them ready. Cahill wished he had a gun but Whittaker confiscated guns. Hell, he wished he had an MK 19, a grenade launcher. And a humvee and some support, maybe with mortars while he was at it.

Then she was on them and they were all swinging like mad because if she got her teeth into any of them, it was all over for that guy. The best thing to do was to keep up a goddamn flurry of swinging pipes so she couldn't get to anyone. Cahill hit other pipe mostly, the impact clanging through his wrist bones, but sometimes when he hit the zombie he felt the melon thunk. She made no noise. No moaning, no hissing, no movie zombie noises, but even as they crushed her head and knocked her down (her eye socket gone soft and one eye a loose silken white sack) she kept moving and reaching. She didn't try to grab the pipes, she just reached for them until they had pounded her into broken bits.

She stank like old meat.

No blood. Which was strangely creepy. Cahill knew from experience that people had a lot more blood in them than you ever would have thought based on TV shows. Blood and blood and more blood. But this zombie didn't seem to have any blood.

Finally Riley yelled, "Get back, get back!" and they all stepped back.

All the bones in her arms and legs were broken and her head was smashed to nothing. It was hard to tell she had ever looked like a person. The torso hitched its hips, raising its belly, trying to inchworm towards them, its broken limbs moving and shuddering like a seizure.

Riley shook his head and then said to them. "Anybody got any marks? Everybody strip."

Everybody stood there for a moment, ignoring him, watching the thing on the broken sidewalk.

Riley snarled, "I said strip, motherfuckers. Or nobody goes back to the compound."

"Fuck," one of the guys said, but they all did and, balls shriveled in the spring cold, paired off and checked each other for marks. When they each announced the other was clear, they all put their clothes back on and piled rubble on top of the twitching thing until they'd made a mound, while Riley kept an eye out for any others.

After that, everyone was pretty tense. They broke into an apartment complex above a storefront. The storefront had been looted and the windows looked empty as the socket of a pulled tooth, but the door to the apartments above was still locked which meant that they might find stuff untouched. Cahill wondered: if zombies did go dormant without food, what if someone had gotten bit and went back to this place, to their apartment? Could they be waiting for someone to enter the dark foyer, for the warmth and smell and the low steady big drum beat of the human heart to bring them back?

They went up the dark stairwell and busted open the door of the first apartment. It smelled closed, cold and dank. The furniture looked like it had been furnished from the curb, but it had a huge honking television. Which said everything about the guy who had lived here.

They ignored the TV. What they were looking for was canned goods. Chef Boy-ar-dee. Cans of beef stew. Beer. They all headed for the kitchen and guys started flipping open cabinets.

Then, like a dumbshit, Cahill opened the refrigerator door. Even as he did it, he thought, "Dumbass."

The refrigerator had been full of food, and then had sat, sealed and without power, while that food all rotted into a seething, shit-stinking mess. The smell was like a bomb. The inside was greenish black.

"Fuck!" someone said and then they all got out of the kitchen. Cahill opened a window and stepped out onto the fire escape. It was closest and everyone else was headed out into the living room where someone would probably take a swing at him for being an asshole. The fire escape was in an alley and he figured that he could probably get to the street and meet them in front, although he wasn't exactly sure how fire escapes worked.

Instead he froze. Below him, in the alley, there was one of those big dumpsters, painted green. The top was off the dumpster and inside it, curled up, was a zombie. Because it was curled up, he couldn't tell much about it—whether it was male or female, black or white. It looked small and it was wearing a striped shirt.

The weird thing was that the entire inside of the dumpster had been covered in aluminum foil. There wasn't any sun yet in the alley but the dumpster was still a dull and crinkly mirror. As best he could tell, every bit was covered.

What the fuck was that about?

He waited for the zombie to sense him and raise its sightless face but it didn't move. It was in one corner, like a gerbil or something in an aquarium. And all that freaking tinfoil. Had it gone into apartments and searched for aluminum foil? What for? To trap sunlight? Maybe Duck was right, they *were* solar powered. Or maybe it just liked shiny stuff.

The window had been hard to open and it had been loud. He could still smell the reek of the kitchen. The sound and the stink should have alerted the zombie.

Maybe it was dead. Whatever that meant to a zombie.

He heard a distant whump. And then a couple more, with a dull rumble of explosion. It sounded like an air strike. The zombie stirred a little, not even raising its head. More like an animal disturbed in its sleep.

The hair was standing up on the back of Cahill's neck. From the zombie or the air strike, he couldn't tell. He didn't hear helicopters. He didn't hear anything. He stamped on the metal fire escape. It rang dully. The zombie didn't move.

He went back inside, through the kitchen and the now empty apartment, down the dark stairwell. The other guys were standing around in the street, talking about the sounds they'd heard. Cahill didn't say anything, didn't say they were probably Hellfire missiles although they sure as hell sounded like them, and he didn't say there was a zombie in the alley. Nobody said anything to him about opening the refrigerator, which was fine by him.

Riley ordered them to head back to see what was up in the Flats.

While they were walking, the skinny little guy said, "Maybe one of those big cranes fell. You know, those big fuckers by the lake that they use for ore ships and shit."

Nobody answered.

"It could happen," the little guy insisted.

"Shut up," Riley said.

Cahill glanced behind them, unable to keep from checking his back. He'd been watching since they started moving, but the little zombie didn't seem to have woken up and followed them.

When they got to Public Square they could see the smoke rising, black and ugly, from the Flats.

"Fuck," Cahill said.

"What is that?" Riley said.

"Is that the camp?" "Fuck is right." "One of the buildings is on fire?" Cahill wished they would shut the fuck up because he was listening for helicopters.

They headed for Main Avenue. By the time they got to West 10th, there was a lot more smoke and they could see some of it was rising from what used to be Shooters. They had to pick their way across debris. Fado and Heaven were gutted, the buildings blown out. Maybe someone was still alive. There were bodies. Cahill could see one in what looked like Whittaker's usual uniform of orange football jersey and black athletic shorts. Most of the head was missing.

"What the fuck?" Riley said.

"Air strike," Cahill said.

"Fuck that," Riley said. "Why would anyone do that?"

Because we weren't dying, Cahill thought. We weren't supposed to figure out how to stay alive. We certainly weren't supposed to establish some sort of base. Hell, the rats might get out of the cage.

The little guy who thought it might have been a crane walked up behind Riley and swung his pipe into the back of Riley's head. Riley staggered and the little guy swung again, and Riley's skull cracked audibly. The little guy hit a third time as Riley went down.

The little guy was breathing heavy. "Fucking bastard," he said, holding the pipe, glaring at them. "Whittaker's bitch."

Cahill glanced at the fourth guy with them. He looked as surprised as Cahill. "You got a problem with this?" the little guy said.

Cahill wondered if the little guy had gotten scratched by the first zombie and they had missed it. Or if he was just bugfuck. Didn't matter. Cahill took a careful step back, holding his own pipe. And then another. The little guy didn't try to stop him.

He thought about waiting for a moment to see what the fourth guy would do. Two people would probably have a better chance than one. Someone to watch while the other slept. But the fourth guy was staring at the little guy and at Riley, who was laid out on the road, and he didn't seem to be able to wrap his head around the idea that their base was destroyed and Riley was dead.

Too stupid to live, and probably a liability. Cahill decided he was better off alone. Besides, Cahill had never really liked other people much anyway.

He found an expensive loft with a big white leather couch and a kitchen full of granite and stainless steel and a bed the size of a football field and he stayed there for a couple of days, eating pouches of tuna he found next door but it was too big and in a couple of days, the liquor cabinet was empty. By that time he had developed a deep and abiding hatred for the couple who had lived here. He had found pictures of them. A dark-haired forty-ish guy with a kayak and a shit-eating grin. He had owned some kind of construction business. She was a toothy blonde with a big forehead who he mentally fucked every night in the big bed. It only made him crazy horny for actual sex.

He imagined they'd been evacuated. People like them didn't get killed, even when the zombies came. Even in the first panicked days when they were in dozens of cities and it seemed like the end of the world, before they'd gotten them under control. Somewhere they were sitting around in their new, lovely loft with working plumbing, telling their friends about how horrible it had been.

Finally, he dragged the big mattress to the freight elevator and then to the middle of the street out front. Long before he got it to the freight elevator, he had completely lost the righteous anger that had possessed him when he thought of the plan, but by then he was just pissed at everything. He considered torching the building but in the end he got the mattress down to the street, along with some pillows and cushions and magazines and kitchen chairs and set fire to the pile, then retreated to the third floor of the building across the way. Word was that zombies came for fire. Cahill was buzzing with a kind of suicidal craziness by this point, simultaneously terrified and elated. He settled in with a bottle of cranberry vodka, the last of the liquor from the loft, and a fancy martini glass, and waited. The vodka was not as awful as it sounded. The fire burned, almost transparent at first, and then orange and smoky.

After an hour he was bored and antsy. He jacked off with the picture of the toothy blonde. He drank more of the cranberry vodka. He glanced down at the fire and they were there.

There were three of them, one standing by a light pole at the end of the street, one standing in the middle of the street, one almost directly below him. He grabbed his length of pipe and the baseball bat he'd found. He had been looking for a gun but hadn't found one. He wasn't sure that a gun would make much difference anyway. They were all unnaturally still. None of them had turned their blind faces towards him. They didn't seem to look at anything—not him, not the fire, not each other. They just stood there.

All of the shortcomings of this presented themselves. He had only one way out of the building, as far as he knew, and that was the door to the street where the zombies were. There was a back door but someone had driven a UPS truck into it and it was impassable. He didn't have any food. He didn't have much in the way of defense—he could have made traps. Found bedsprings and rigged up spikes so that if a zombie came in the hall and tripped it, it would slam the thing against the wall and shred it. Not that he had ever been particularly mechanical. He didn't really know how such a thing would work.

Lighter fluid. He could douse an area in lighter fluid or gasoline or something, and if a zombie came towards him, set fire to the fucker. Hell, even an idiot could make a Molotov cocktail.

All three of the zombies had once been men. One of them was so short he thought it was a child. Then he thought maybe it was a dwarf. One of them was wearing what might have once been a suit, which was a nice thing. Zombie businessmen struck Cahill as appropriate. The problem was that he didn't dare leave until they did, and the mattress looked ready to smolder for a good long time.

It did smolder for a good long time. The zombies just stood there, not looking at the fire, not looking at each other, not looking at anything. The zombie girl, the one they'd killed with Riley, she had turned her face in their direction. That was so far the most human thing he had seen a zombie do. He tried to see if their noses twitched or if they sniffed but they were too far away. He added binoculars to his mental list of shit he hoped to find.

Eventually he went and explored some of the building he was in. It was offices and the candy machine had been turned over and emptied. He worried when he prowled the darkened halls that the zombies had somehow sensed him, so he could only bring himself to explore for a few minutes at a time before he went back to his original window and checked. But they were just standing there. When it got dark, he wondered if they would lie down, maybe sleep like the one in the dumpster but they didn't.

The night was horrible. There was no light in the city, of course. The street was dark enough that he couldn't see the short zombie. Where it was standing was a shadow and a pretty much impenetrable one. The smoldering fire cast no real light at all. It was just an ashen heap that sometimes glowed red when a breeze picked up. Cahill nodded off and jerked awake, counting the zombies, wondering if the little one had moved in on him. If the short one sensed him, wouldn't they all sense him? Didn't the fact that two of them were still there mean that it was still there, too? It was hard to make out any of them, and sometimes he thought maybe they had all moved.

At dawn they were all three still there. All three still standing. Crows had gathered on the edge of the roof of a building down the street, probably drawn by the smell.

It sucked.

They stood there for that whole day, the night, and part of the next day before one of them turned and loped away, smooth as glass. The other two stood there for a while longer—an hour? He had no sense of time anymore. Then they moved off at the same time, not exactly together but apparently triggered by the same strange signal. He watched them lope off.

He made himself count slowly to one thousand. Then he did it again. Then finally he left the building.

For days the city was alive with zombies for him although he didn't see any. He saw crows and avoided wherever he saw them. He headed for the lake and found a place not far from the Flats, an apartment over shops, with windows that opened. It wasn't near as swanky as the loft. He rigged up an alarm system that involved a bunch of thread crossing the open doorway to the stairwell and a bunch of wind chimes. Anything hit the thread and it would release the wind chimes which would fall and make enough noise to wake the fucking dead.

For the first time since he left the loft, he slept that night.

The next day he sat at the little kitchen table by the open window and wrote down everything he knew about zombies.

1.they stink
2.they can sense people
3.they didn't sense me because I was up above them? they couldn't smell me? they couldn't see me?
4.sometimes they sleep or something sick? worn down? used up charge?
5.they like fire
6.they don't necessarily sleep
7.they like tinfoil ???

Things he didn't know but wanted to:

1.do they eat animals
2.how do they sense people
3.how many are there

4.do they eventually die? fall apart? Use up their energy?

It was somehow satisfying to have a list.

He decided to check out the zombie he had seen in the dumpster. He had a back pack now with water, a couple of cans of Campbell's Chunky soups—including his favorite, chicken and sausage gumbo, because if he got stuck somewhere like the last time, he figured he'd need something to look forward to—a tub of Duncan Hines Creamy Home-Style Chocolate Buttercream frosting for dessert, a can opener, a flashlight with batteries that worked, and his prize find, binoculars. Besides his length of pipe, he carried a Molotov cocktail; a wine bottle three-fourths filled with gasoline mixed with sugar, corked, with a gasoline-soaked rag rubber-banded to the top and covered with a sandwich bag so it wouldn't dry out.

He thought about cars as he walked. The trip he was making would take him an hour and it would have been five minutes in a car. People in cars had no fucking appreciation for how big places were. Nobody would be fat if there weren't any cars. Far down the street, someone came out of a looted store carrying a cardboard box.

Cahill stopped and then dropped behind a pile of debris from a sandwich shop. If it was a zombie, he wasn't sure hiding would make any difference, and he pulled his lighter out of his pocket, ready to throw the bottle. But it wasn't a zombie. Zombies, as far as he knew, didn't carry boxes of loot around. The guy with the box must have seen Cahill moving because he dropped the box and ran.

Cahill occasionally saw other convicts, but he avoided them, and so far, they avoided him. There was one dude who Cahill was pretty sure lived somewhere around the wreckage of the Renaissance Hotel. He didn't seem to want any company, either. Cahill followed to where this new guy had disappeared around a corner. The guy was watching and when he saw Cahill, he jogged away, watching over his shoulder to see if Cahill would follow. Cahill stood until the guy had turned the corner.

By the time Cahill got to the apartment where he'd seen the zombie in the dumpster, he was pretty sure that the other guy had gotten behind him and was following him. It irritated him. Dickweed. He thought about not going upstairs, but decided that since the guy wasn't in sight at the moment, it would give Cahill a chance to disappear. Besides, they hadn't actually checked out the apartment and there might be something worth scavenging. In Cahill's months of scavenging, he had never seen a zombie in an apartment, or even any evidence of one, but he always checked carefully. The place was empty, still stinking a little of the contents of the fridge, but the smell was no worse than a lot of places and a lot better than some. Rain had come in where he'd left the kitchen window open, warping the linoleum. He climbed out onto the fire escape and looked down. The dumpster was empty, although still lined with some tattered aluminum foil. He pulled out his binoculars and checked carefully, but he couldn't really see anything.

He stood for a long time. Truthfully he couldn't be a hundred percent sure it was a zombie. Maybe it had been a child, some sort of refugee? Hard to imagine any child surviving in the city. No, it had to be a zombie. He considered lighting and tossing the Molotov cocktail and seeing if the zombie came to the alley, but didn't want to wait it out in this apartment building. Something about this place made him feel vulnerable.

Eventually he rummaged through the apartment. The bedside table held neither handgun nor D batteries, two things high on his scavenger list. He went back down the dark stairwell and stopped well back from the doorway. Out in the middle of the street, in front of the building to his left but visible from where he stood, was an offering. A box with a bottle of whiskey set on it. Like some kind of perverse lemonade stand.

Fucking dickweed.

If the guy had found a handgun, he could be waiting in ambush. Cahill figured there was a good chance he could outlast the guy but he hated waiting in the stairwell. There were no apartments on the first level, just a hallway between two storefronts. Cahill headed back upstairs. The apartment he'd been in before didn't look out the front of the building. The one that did was locked.

Fuck.

Breaking open the lock would undoubtedly make a hell of a lot of racket. He went back to the first apartment, checked one more time for the zombie, and peed in the empty toilet. He grabbed a pillow from the bed.

Cahill went back downstairs and sat down on the bottom step and wedged the pillow in behind his back. He set up his bottle and his lighter beside him on the step, and his pipe on the other side and settled in to watch. He could at least wait until dark although it wasn't even mid-morning yet. After a while he ate his soup—the can opener sounded louder than it probably was.

It was warm midday and Cahill was drowsy warm when the guy finally, nervously, walked out to the box and picked up the whiskey. Cahill sat still in the shadow of the stairwell with his hand on his pipe. As best as he could tell, he was unnoticed. The guy was a tall, skinny black man wearing a brown Cleveland football jersey and a pair of expensive-looking, olive-green suit pants. Cahill looked out and watched the guy walk back up the street. After a minute, Cahill followed.

When Cahill got out to the main drag, the guy was walking up Superior towards the center of downtown. Cahill took a firm hold of his pipe.

"Hey," he said. His voice carried well in the silence.

The guy started and whirled around.

"What the fuck you want?" Cahill asked.

"Bro," the man said. "Hey, were you hiding back there?" He laughed nervously and held up the bottle. "Peace offering, bro. Just looking to make some peace."

"What do you want?" Cahill asked.

"Just, you know, wanna talk. Talk to someone who knows the ropes, you know? I just got here and I don't know what the fuck is going on, bro."

"This is a fucking penal colony," Cahill said.

"Yeah," the guy laughed. "A fucking zombie preserve. I been watching out for them zombies. You look like you been here awhile."

Cahill hadn't bothered to shave and last time he'd glanced in a mirror he'd looked like Charles Manson, only bearded and taller. "Lie down with your hands away from your body," Cahill said.

The black guy squinted at Cahill. "You shittin' me."

"How do I know you don't have a gun?" Cahill asked.

"Bro, I don't got no gun. I don't got nothin' but what you see."

Cahill waited.

"Listen, I'm just trying to be friendly," the guy said. "I swear to God, I don't have anything. How do I know *you're* not going to do something to me? You're a freaky dude—you know that?"

The guy talked for about five minutes, finally talking himself into lying down on his stomach with his arms out. Cahill moved fast, patting him down. The guy wasn't lying, he didn't have anything on him.

"Fuck man," the guy said. "I told you that." Once he was sure Cahill wasn't going to do anything to him he talked even more. His name was LaJon Watson and his lawyer had told him there was no way they were going to drop him in the Cleveland Zombie Preserve because the Supreme Court was going to declare it unconstitutional. His lawyer had been saying that right up until the day they put LaJon on the bus, which was when LaJon realized that his lawyer knew shit. LaJon wanted to know if Cahill had seen any zombies and what they were like and how Cahill had stayed alive.

Cahill found it hard to talk. He hadn't talked to anyone in weeks. Usually someone like LaJon Watson would have driven him nuts, but it was nice to let the tide of talk wash over him while they walked. He wasn't sure that he wouldn't regret it, but he took LaJon back to his place. LaJon admired his alarm system. "You gotta show me how to unhook it and hook it back up. Don't they see it? I mean, has one of them ever hit it?"

"No," Cahill said. "I don't think they can see."

There were scientists studying zombies and sometimes there was zombie stuff on Fox News, but LaJon said he hadn't paid much attention to all that. He really hadn't expected to need to know about zombies. In fact, he hadn't been sure at first that Cahill wasn't a zombie. Cahill opened cans of Campbell's Chunky Chicken and Dumplings. LaJon asked if Cahill warmed them over a fire or what. Cahill handed him a can and a spoon.

LaJon wolfed down the soup. LaJon wouldn't shut up, even while eating. He told Cahill how he'd looked in a bunch of shops, but most of them had been pretty thoroughly looted. He'd looked in an apartment, but the only thing on the shelves in a can was tomato paste and evaporated milk. Although now that he thought about it, maybe he could have made some sort of tomato soup or something. He hadn't slept in the two days he'd been here and he was going crazy and it was a great fucking thing to have found somebody who could show him the ropes.

LaJon was from Cincinnati. Did Cahill know anybody from Cincinnati? Where had Cahill been doing time? (Auburn.) LaJon didn't know anybody at Auburn, wasn't that New York? LaJon had been at Lebanon Correctional. Cahill was a nice dude, if quiet. Who else was around, and was there anyone LaJon could score from? (Cahill said he didn't know.) What did people use for money here anyway?

"I been thinking," LaJon said, "about the zombies. I think it's pollution that's mutating them like the Teenage Mutant Ninja Turtles."

Cahill decided it had been a mistake to bring LaJon. He picked up the bottle of whiskey and opened it. He didn't usually use glasses but got two out of the cupboard and poured them each some whiskey.

LaJon apologized, "I don't usually talk this much," he said. "I guess I just fucking figured I was dead when they dropped me here." He took a big drink of whiskey. "It's like my mouth can't stop."

Cahill poured LaJon more to drink and nursed his own whiskey. Exhaustion and nerves were telling, LaJon was finally slowing down. "You want some frosting?" Cahill asked.

Frosting and whiskey was a better combination than it had any right to be. Particularly for a man who'd thought himself dead. LaJon nodded off.

"Come on," Cahill said. "It's going to get stuffy in here." He got the sleepy drunk up on his feet.

"What?" LaJon said.

"I sleep outside, where it's cooler." It was true that the apartment got hot during the day.

"Bro, there's zombies out there," LaJon mumbled.

"It's okay, I've got a system," Cahill said. "I'll get you downstairs and then I'll bring down something to sleep on."

LaJon wanted to sleep where he was and, for a moment, his eyes narrowed to slits and something scary was in his face.

"I'm going to be there, too," Cahill said. "I wouldn't do anything to put myself in danger."

LaJon allowed himself to be half-carried downstairs. Cahill was worried when he had to unhook the alarm system. He propped LaJon up against the wall and told him 'Just a moment.' If LaJon slid down the wall and passed out, he'd be hell to get downstairs. But the lanky black guy stood there long enough for Cahill to get the alarm stuff out of the way. He was starting to sober up a little. Cahill got him down to the street.

"I'll get the rest of the whiskey," Cahill said.

"What the fuck you playing at?" LaJon muttered.

Cahill took the stairs two at a time in the dark. He grabbed pillows, blankets, and the whiskey bottle and went back down to the sidewalk. He handed LaJon the whiskey bottle. "It's not so hot out here," he said, although it was on the sidewalk with the sunlight.

LaJon eyed him drunkenly.

Cahill went back upstairs and came down with a bunch of couch cushions. He made a kind of bed and got LaJon to sit on it. "We're okay in the day," he said. "Zombies don't like the light. I sleep in the day. I'll get us upstairs before night."

LaJon shook his head, took another slug of whiskey, and lay back on the cushions. "I feel sick," he said.

Cahill thought the motherfucker was going to throw up, but instead LaJon was snoring.

Cahill sat for a bit, planning and watching the street. After a bit, he went back to his apartment. When he found something good scavenging, he squirreled it away. He came downstairs with duct tape. He taped LaJon's ankles together. Then his wrists. Then he sat LaJon up. LaJon opened his eyes, said, "What the fuck?" drunkenly. Cahill taped LaJon's arms to his sides, right at his elbows, running the tape all the way around his torso. LaJon started to struggle, but Cahill was methodical and patient, and he used the whole roll of tape to secure LaJon's arms. From shoulders to waist, LaJon was a duct tape mummy.

LaJon swore at him, colorfully then monotonously.

Cahill left him there and went looking. He found an upright dolly at a bar, and brought it back. It didn't do so well where the pavement was uneven, but he didn't think he could carry LaJon far and if he was going to build a fire, he didn't want it to be close to his place, where zombies could pin him in his apartment. LaJon was still where he left him, although when he saw Cahill, he went into a frenzy of struggling. Cahill let him struggle. He lay the dolly down and rolled LaJon onto it. LaJon fought like anything, so in the end, Cahill went back upstairs and got another roll of duck tape and duck taped LaJon to the dolly. That was harder than duct taping LaJon the first time, because LaJon was scared and pissed now. When Cahill finally pulled the dolly up LaJon struggled so hard that the dolly was unmanageable, which pissed Cahill off so much he just let go.

LaJon went over, and without hands to stop himself, face planted on the sidewalk. That stilled him. Cahill pulled the dolly upright then. LaJon's face was a bloody mess and it looked like he might have broken a couple of teeth. He was conscious, but stunned. Cahill started pushing the dolly and LaJon threw up.

It took a couple of hours to get six blocks. LaJon was sober and silent by the time Cahill decided he'd gone far enough.

Cahill sat down, sweating, and used his t-shirt to wipe his face.

"You a bug," LaJon said.

Bug was prison slang for someone crazy. LaJon said it with certainty.

"Just my fucking luck. Kind of luck I had all my life. I find one guy alive in this fucking place and he a bug." LaJon spat. "What are you gonna do to me?"

Cahill was so tired of LaJon that he considered going back to his place and leaving LaJon here. Instead, he found a door and pried it open with a tire iron. It had been an office building and the second floor was fronted with glass. He had a hell of a time finding a set of service stairs that opened from the outside on the first floor. He found some chairs and dragged them downstairs. Then he emptied file cabinets, piling the papers around the chairs. LaJon watched him, getting more anxious.

When it looked like he'd get a decent fire going, he put LaJon next to it. The blood had dried on LaJon's face and he'd bruised up a bit. It was evening.

Cahill set fire to the papers and stood, waiting for them to catch. Burnt paper drifted up, raised by the fire.

LaJon squinted at the fire, then at Cahill. "You gonna burn me?"

Cahill went in the building and settled upstairs where he could watch.

LaJon must have figured that Cahill wasn't going to burn him. Then he began to worry about zombies. Cahill watched him start twisting around, trying to look around. The dolly rocked and LaJon realized that if he wasn't careful, the dolly would go over again and he'd faceplant and not be able to see.

Cahill gambled that the zombies wouldn't be there right away, and found a soda machine in the hallway. He broke it open with his tire iron and got himself a couple of Cokes and then went back to watch it get dark. The zombies weren't there yet. He opened a warm Coke and settled in a desk chair from one of the offices—much more comfortable than the cubicle chairs. He opened a jar of peanut butter and ate it with a spoon.

It came so fast that he didn't see it until it was at the fire. LaJon saw it before he did and went rigid with fear. The fire was between LaJon and the zombie.

It just stood there, not watching the fire, but standing there. Not "looking" at LaJon, either. Cahill leaned forward. He tried to read its body language. It had been a man, overweight, maybe middle-aged, but now it was predatory and gracile. It didn't seem to do any normal things. It was moving and it stopped. Once stopped, it was still. An object rather than an animal. Like the ones that had come to the mattress fire, it didn't seem to need to shift its weight. After a few minutes, another one came from the same direction and stopped, looking at the fire. It had once been a man, too. It still wore glasses. Would there be a third? Did they come in threes? Cahill imagined a zombie family. Little triplets of zombies, all apparently oblivious of each other. Maybe the zombie he'd seen was still in the zombie den? He had never figured out where the zombies stayed.

LaJon was still and silent with terror, but the zombies didn't seem to know or care that he was there. They just stood, slightly askew and indifferent. Was it the fire? Would they notice LaJon when the fire died down?

Then there was a third one, but it came from the other side of the fire, the same side LaJon was on so there was no fire between it and LaJon. Cahill saw it before LaJon did, and from its directed lope he was sure it was aware of LaJon.

LaJon saw it just before it got to him. His mouth opened wide and it was on him, hands and teeth. LaJon was clearly screaming, although behind the glass of the office building, Cahill couldn't hear him.

Cahill was watching the other zombies. They didn't react to the noise at all. Even when there was blood all over, they didn't seem to sense anything. Cahill reflected, not for the first time, that it actually took people a lot longer to die than it did on television or in the movies. He noted that the one that had mauled and eventually killed LaJon did not seem to prefer brains. Sometime in the night, the fire died down enough that the zombies on the wrong side of the fire seemed to sense the body of LaJon, and in an instant, they were feeding. The first one, apparently sated, just stood, indifferent. Two more showed up in the hours before dawn and fed in the dim red of the embers of the fire. When they finally left, almost two days later, there was nothing but broken bones and scattered teeth.

Cahill lay low for a while after that, feeling exhausted. It was hot during the day and the empty city baked. But after a few days, he went out and found another perch and lit another fire. Four zombies came to that fire, despite the fact it was smaller than his first two. They had all been women. He still had his picture of the toothy blonde from the loft, and after masturbating, he looked out at the zombie women, blank-white eyes and indifferent bodies, and wondered if the toothy blonde had been evacuated or if she might show up at one of his fires. None of the women at the fire appeared to be her, although it wasn't always easy to tell. One was clearly wearing the remnants of office clothes, but the other three were blue jean types and all four had such rats' nests of hair that he wasn't sure if their hair was short or long.

A couple of times he encountered zombies while scavenging. Both times his Molotov cocktails worked, catching fire. He didn't set the zombies on fire, just threw the bottle so that the fire was between him and the zombie. He watched them stop, then he backed away, fast. He set up another blind in an apartment and, over the course of a week, built a scaffolding and a kind of block and tackle arrangement. Then he started hanging around where the bus dropped people off, far enough back that the guys patrolling the gate didn't start shooting or something. He'd scoured up some bottles of water and used them to shave and clean up a bit.

When they dropped a new guy off, Cahill trailed him for half a day, and then called out and introduced himself. The new guy was an Aryan Nation asshole named Jordan Schmidtzinsky who was distrustful, but willing to be led back to Cahill's blind. He wouldn't get drunk, though, and in the end, Cahill had to brain him with a pipe. Still, it was easier to tape up the unconscious Schmidtzinsky than it had been the conscious LaJon. Cahill hoisted him into the air, put a chair underneath him so a zombie could reach him, and then set the fire.

Zombies did not look up. Schmidtzinsky dangled above the zombies for two whole days. Sometime in there he died. They left without ever noticing him. Cahill cut him down and lit another fire and discovered that zombies were willing to eat the dead, although they had to practically fall over the body to find it.

Cahill changed his rig so he could lower the bait. The third guy was almost Cahill's undoing. Cahill let him wander for two days in the early autumn chill before appearing and offering to help. This guy, a black city kid from Nashville who for some reason wouldn't say his name, evidently didn't like the scaffolding outside. He wouldn't take any of Cahill's whiskey, and when Cahill pretended to sleep, the guy made the first move. Cahill was lucky not to get killed, managing again to brain the guy with his pipe.

But it was worth it, because when he suspended the guy and lit the fire, one of the four zombies that showed up was the skinny guy who'd killed Riley back the day the air strike had wiped out the camp.

He was white-eyed like the other zombies, but still recognizable. It made Cahill feel even more that the toothy blonde might be out there, unlikely as that actually was. Cahill watched for a couple of hours before he lowered Nashville. The semiconscious Nashville started thrashing and making weird coughing choking noises as soon as Cahill pulled on the rope, but the zombies were oblivious. Cahill was gratified to see that once the semiconscious Nashville got so his shoes were about four feet above the ground, three of four zombies around the fire (the ones for whom the fire was not between them and Nashville) turned as one and swarmed up the chair.

He was a little nervous that they would look up—he had a whole plan for how he would get out of the building—but he didn't have to use it.

The three zombies ate, indifferent to each other and the fourth zombie, and then stood.

Cahill entertained himself with thoughts of the toothy blonde and then dozed. The air was crisp, but Cahill was warm in an overcoat. The fire smelled good. He was going to have to think about how he was going to get through the winter without a fire—unless he could figure out a way to keep a fire going well above the street and above zombie attention but right now things were going okay.

He opened his eyes and saw one of the zombies bob its head.

He'd never seen that before. Jesus, did that mean it was aware? That it might come upstairs? He had his length of pipe in one hand and a Molotov in the other. The zombies were all still. A long five minutes later, the zombie did it again, a quick, birdlike head bob. Then, bob-bob, twice more, and on the second bob, the other two that had fed did it too. They were still standing there, faces turned just slightly different directions as if they were unaware of each other, but he had seen it.

Bob-bob-bob. They all three did it. All at the same time.

Every couple of minutes they'd do it again. It was—communal. Animal-like. They did it for a couple of hours and then they stopped. The one on the other side of the fire never did it at all. The fire burned low enough that the fourth one came over and worked on the remnants of the corpse and the first three just stood there.

Cahill didn't know what the fuck they were doing, but it made him strangely happy.

When they came to evacuate him, Cahill thought at first it was another air strike operation—a mopping up. He'd been sick for a few days, throwing up, something he ate, he figured. He was scavenging in a looted drug store, hoping for something to take—although everything was gone or ruined—when he heard the patrol coming. They weren't loud, but in the silent city noise was exaggerated. He had looked out of the shop, seen the patrol of soldiers and tried to hide in the dark ruins of the pharmacy.

"Come on out," the patrol leader said. "We're here to get you out of this place."

Bullshit, Cahill thought. He stayed put.

"I don't want to smoke you out, and I don't want to send guys in there after you," the patrol leader said. "I've got tear gas but I really don't want to use it."

Cahill weighed his options. He was fucked either way. He tried to go out the back of the pharmacy, but they had already sent someone around and he was met by two scared nineteen-year-olds with guns. He figured the writing was on the wall and put his hands up.

But the weird twist was that they *were* evacuating him. There'd been some big government scandal. The Supreme Court had closed the reserves, the President had been impeached, elections were coming. He wouldn't find that out for days. What he found out right then was that they hustled him back to the gate and he walked out past rows of soldiers into a wall of noise and light. Television cameras showed him lost and blinking in the glare.

"What's your name?"

"Gerrold Cahill," he said.

"Hey Gerrold! Look over here!" a hundred voices called.

It was overwhelming. They all called out at the same time, and it was mostly just noise to him, but if he could understand a question, he tried to answer it. "How's it feel to be out of there?"

"Loud," he said. "And bright."

"What do you want to do?"

"Take a hot shower and eat some hot food."

There was a row of sawhorses and the cameras and lights were all behind them. A guy with corporal's stripes was trying to urge him towards a trailer, but Cahill was like someone knocked down by a wave who tries to get to their feet only to be knocked down again.

"Where are you from?" "Tell us what it was like!"

"What was it like?" Cahill said. Dumbshit question. What was he supposed to say to that? But his response had had the marvelous effect of quieting them for a moment which allowed him to maybe get his bearings a little. "It wasn't so bad."

The barrage started again but he picked out "Were you alone?"

"Except for the zombies."

They liked that and the surge was almost animalistic. Had he seen zombies? How had he survived? He shrugged and grinned.

"Are you glad to be going back to prison?"

He had an answer for that, one he didn't even know was in him. He would repeat it in the interview he gave to the *Today Show* and again in the interview for *20/20*. "Cleveland was better than prison," he said. "No alliances, no gangs, just zombies."

Someone called, "Are you glad they're going to eradicate the zombies?"

"They're going to what?" he asked.

The barrage started again, but he said, "What are they going to do to the zombies?"

"They're going to eradicate them, like they did everywhere else."

"Why?" he asked.

This puzzled the mob. "Don't you think they should be?"

He shook his head.

"Gerrold! Why not?"

Why not indeed? "Because," he said, slowly, and the silence came down, except for the clicking of cameras and the hum of the news vans idling, "because they're just...like animals. They're just doing what's in their nature to be doing." He shrugged. Then the barrage started again. Gerrold! Gerrold! Do you think people are evil? But by then he was on his way to a military trailer, an examination by an army doctor, a cup of hot coffee and a meal and a long hot shower.

Behind him the city was dark. At the moment, it felt cold behind him, but safe, too, in its quiet. He didn't really want to go back there. Not yet.

He wished he'd had time to set them one last fire before he'd left.

SINS OF THE FATHER
SARA GENGE

In addition to working as a doctor in Madrid, Sara Genge writes speculative fiction for the sleepless mind. Her work has appeared in *Strange Horizons*, *Cosmos*, *Weird Tales*, and *Shimmer Magazine*, among others, including translations into Greek, Czech, and Spanish. "Sins of the Father" is her sixth story for *Asimov's*.

Mother, I received your letter a year ago. The men brought it up to town from the nest of brambles where the tide had left it. Luckily for you, they've learned to recognize the sheen of the bone-white logs where you write your messages and bring them uphill for me to read.

If it were up to me, I'd leave your letters on the shore to rot. But the men think your messages are important, maybe contain a sign that the merfolk are relenting on the technological restrictions you've imposed on humans. They wouldn't believe me if I told them that the message is not for them, not even really for me, even though it is to me that you address your concerned words. The sea is free and your message can be read. What better propaganda than your constant chiding, your denunciation of my treason and your resolve never to allow me back into the sea?

I chirped at the log and your words bounced back at me like a slap. After all these years, you are still so restrained, so proper! I shouted at the men who'd brought me the message as they stood sweaty on my doorstep. With Spanish patience, they left me alone. Why is it that your letters always elicit the same reaction? A merman should be capable of getting over his mother, even if he isn't capable of getting over losing his place in the sea.

Do you know what it's like living here? Dry comes to mind, and poor. You made it so, but you only know what they tell you.

No matter, I can fix that. Propaganda works both ways: our kinsman, mermaids and mermen, will read and repeat my words. You must know what you've done, all of you, and then maybe your heart will soften and you will listen to my plea.

Like so many love stories, mine started at a party.
The town was decked in paper flags and light bulbs. The old generators were

dragged out to cough up light along with smoke and the children ran around round-eyed at the small miracle. The merfolk allow a yearly festival. They reckon their world can deal with this small ecological disaster.

Even the women drank, and the men taught the younger children to tip the *bota* up over their heads and catch the red liquid in their mouths without splashing their best clothes.

By midnight, despite the food, everyone was tipsy and girls started asking me to dance. I'm sure it was a dare, but I wasn't complaining.

Rosita, normally a timid creature, kept coming back for more.

"Pobrecito," she whispered, daintily probing the dry scales on my neck. "Does it hurt very much?"

"It mostly just itches," I told her. "It's much worse in winter. Sometimes one of them gets infected." I cursed myself; she didn't need to know that. But she didn't seem to care and looked up earnestly into my face.

"I know of a remedy that might help. But don't tell anyone I told you about it, eh? It's embarrassing," she said.

I promised to keep it a secret.

"You have to take your," she blushed and lowered her voice, "*pee*. Put it on the dry parts every morning. It helps."

I stopped dancing and pulled away from her. Couples swerved to avoid us. Did she really think I'd fall for that prank? They'd nicknamed me lizard. Would they call me peeman next?

"Sorry, *Señorita*. Was this your friends' idea? Shame on them, for suggesting it, and shame on you, for carrying it out."

She looked confused for a minute, then lifted her eyebrows in surprise and started giggling into her hand.

"Oh no, it wasn't a joke. I would never joke about someone else's discomfort. Oh, I'm really sorry that you thought that, oh, you poor thing. No, no! The remedy really works and I meant it in earnest. The women use it all the time in winter." She fixed her eyes on mine, willing me to understand.

I didn't.

"In winter?" I asked.

"Yes, because of the skirts." She squirmed.

I shook my head and she sighed and leaned in to whisper into my ear, putting her hand on my shoulder to bring me closer. She didn't seem repulsed by my skin.

"Because we don't wear pants and our legs rub together. *Down there*." I could hardly hear her, she was whispering so soft, and her wine breath tickled my ear. "In winter the cold chaps the skin and it hurts like the devil." She let go of my shoulder but kept her voice lowered. "Remember Manuela? Trinidad's grandma? They said she died of that, her legs rubbed raw and then one day she woke up with them puffed and swollen and the next week she was dead."

The song wound to an end. I assured her I believed her and grabbed her by the waist. She didn't move away. Instead, she placed her left hand on my shoulder and her right in my hand. We stood still for a whole minute until the band started playing again and we were free to dance.

My town hangs from a cliff over a ravine, in the Archipelago that was once the Iberian Peninsula, in the middle of the Great Sea.

What little land we have, we need for planting, so the villagers carve houses from stone, using the silt as base for whitewash and walling themselves into the earth with brick and plaster. I love them: houses like wombs. No fear of escape. Sometimes, when the sea calls out to me so loud and deep that I falter, I dig into my house and feel as surrounded as if I were floating underwater. Nothing reaches me inside my cave, except the pull of moon on blood that never leaves a merman. And if that fails, there's always wine.

A week after the festival, I took my place in Severino's tavern. All the men were here, fleeing their women and their religion for wine and tapas. I drank and peeled scales from my face, dropping them on the floor while the men looked away politely.

I looked around at sun-scared men, the visible heat, the card games. This is a fragment of Spain that exists outside of History. It was never like this, not even in the period that it supposedly imitates, the late nineteenth and early twentieth century. It was never this sad. My scales piled up, slight and luminescent, among the olive pits and cigarette butts. I was part of the cliché, but you, Mother, made it this way.

You suffer humans to live so you can laugh and point. The merfolk could wish humans away with a flick from their collective tail, but instead they leave them these islands of dirt and inbreeding, make museums out of them, examples for the younger generations of mer who are eager to exploit resources that they can't put back. Of course, there can be no industry in these prisons and the humans get extra points for going for the whole historical hogwash and keeping their old customs, their clothes and their beliefs. For every seven years of continuity, the merfolk desalt a few crates of silt and throw it on the shore. Allow me to say, with my acquired Spanish irony, that by my calculations, you will have reconstructed the whole of the peninsula in another two thousand years.

The Preserves are put to other uses. Where else could you send people like me? The sea is free; there are no prisons to send traitors. I was given a choice between my tail and my life and I chose my life. My tail was ripped down the middle, joints turned around and flippers lifted at a right angle to serve as feet. You may not agree with me, Mother. I know, for you, this is the ultimate embarrassment. But it was my choice to make.

"Say something to me in mermaid," Rosita whispered from behind the barred window of her house. To dance during the village festival was one thing, but addressing a man walking down her street was quite another, and she didn't want her mother to hear her.

"*For one, we call ourselves merfolk. We aren't all female,*" I blurted. The old language sounded strange in the air. Without the blending power of water, the clicks were isolated, individual.

Rosita giggled. "How shrill! Not like a man at all." She blushed behind her fan, probably aware that she might have offended me. I smiled back; *no hard feelings, Rosita.*

"Rosita, who are you talking to?" Rosa's mother was nearing forty and sounded like an old woman.

"Just talking to the *vecina,*" she said, and winked at me. I inched away: she'd told her mother she was talking to a neighbor *girl*, and it wouldn't do for me to be caught in front of her house. Rosita fluttered her fan at me. I knew there was a fan language used by women to communicate with men behind their elder's backs, but I didn't know it. I never thought I'd have any use for it.

Rosita shook her head at my ignorance: "Day after tomorrow at three o'clock beneath the big olive tree in Vicente's plot," she whispered, "I'll bring my younger sister as chaperone."

I walked away, bewildered. Just like that, she'd decided that I would be courting her. I wasn't sure how this had happened. I was twice Rosita's age, although I doubted she realized it. To her, I must have looked no older than thirty: still marriageable for a man. Still, I was hardly her best choice. She was pretty; she could take her pick from the dozen men her age scattered in the surrounding villages. These girls don't date lightly; every boyfriend a girl has before marriage lowers her reputation. No decent woman dates more than two men before settling down.

Rosita was throwing a card away, and she wouldn't have done it if she hadn't thought I was worth it.

That evening, I saw her again. She was standing in front of Severino's tavern, looking uncomfortable. Her face lit up when she saw me approach.

"Ah, thank God! I thought I was going to have to wait all day. Could you tell Don Severino that my father wants a measure of wine?"

I nodded and stood there for a second, wanting to talk to her but not quite daring. The sun was setting and the evening was taking the worst out of the heat. No wonder she was reluctant to enter the tavern, women don't do these things in the village and all the grandmothers had brought a chair out to their doorways, the better to chat and spy on the neighbors.

The beads tinkled behind me, enclosing me in the male enclave of the tavern.

"Pedro's daughter, Rosita, wants some wine," I informed Severino.

The men smiled into their glasses. They had seen us dancing. I could pretend all I wanted, but they knew Rosita wasn't just a casual acquaintance.

"What do you want?" I heard Severino asking outside.

Rosita answered in a whisper. Obviously, she knew all eyes were on her. I thought it was indelicate of her father to ask her to fetch him wine in these circumstances. Everyone's eyes were on her, examining her behavior and trying to find fault. There's little entertainment in a small village.

"I'm not sure about this," Severino said. Through the bead curtains, I saw him looking around at the square. His voice lowered: "I don't want it said I give women alcohol."

"But my father asked me…" Rosita mumbled. If she didn't come back home with the wine, the townsfolk would think she'd been asking for it for herself and that Severino, honest man that he was, had refused for her own good. The two of them were making me uncomfortable.

I *could've* gone out and offered to accompany her home with the wine. Severino wouldn't have been able to argue with that arrangement, but it would be a public signal of a relationship and possibly humiliate Rosita further.

"Aw, Severino, give the girl that wine," said an old man sitting next to me.

"The *comadres* are out!" Severino whispered. I felt for him: all those older women, watching to see what he did. Rosita stared at the ground.

"You afraid of a bunch of old women?" the old man asked.

That settled it. Severino puffed up his chest and went to fetch the wine. Gallantly, he helped Rosita hoist the amphora on her shoulder and ducked inside the tavern as she headed back home.

Rosita had chosen a sandy day for our first date. The Sahara dropped its load on us and I stomped my way to the olive tree, burying my face in my arm and trying to see through the dust. The sky was red and it was even hotter than usual. I had an image of myself veering off the road, blinded by the dirt, and falling into the gorge. After that, I dragged my feet and ignored the sand that got under my scales and scraped my skin.

She was only twenty minutes late. When I first saw her, I feared there had been a death in the family. She was dressed in black, a sinister Madonna with a shawl draped around her head. Then I noticed the red chrysanthemum on her lapel and realized she was just wearing her winter coat, which looked black in this red light. If someone had died, color would have been banished from her attire and she wouldn't have been allowed even that simple flower.

Rosa nodded to me when she reached me under the tree. Two eyes, black olives, stared up at me through the grit.

"Did you try my remedy?" she asked. She glanced at the little bundle beside her and I understood we couldn't speak freely. I was surprised that the little girl didn't complain about going out in the dust. But she took her job seriously, knowing that her sister's honor depended on her credibility as a witness and on her ability to keep her mouth shut.

I nodded, my scales had gotten better, although I doubted anything could

heal my skin's thirst for salt water. We stood in silence for a minute, not knowing what to say.

"Let's walk," Rosa suggested.

We roamed the dry fields with the little girl in tow.

After half an hour, Rosa asked me to turn back towards the tree. Her sister
skipped ahead and Rosa used the opportunity to squeeze my hand through the
cloth of her shawl. Then she nodded to me and they left. The little girl bolted
home, but Rosita walked sedately and I watched her go, wondering if her hips
were swinging more than usual. The road, cliff and gorge were invisible in the
dust and Rosita, in her black clothes, seemed like a wobbling ghost.

A week later, she was back at Severino's door, fidgeting. Once Rosita's father
discovered he could send his daughter for wine, he didn't see any reason to stop
doing so.

This time, however, we were dating publicly, so I hoisted the jar on my own
shoulders and walked her back home.

"Thank *Virgencita* you where there," she said. She seemed upset. She'd probably been anticipating another fight with Severino.

I mumbled something comforting. I had trouble understanding why they
made such a fuss about young women and wine. I had a feeling there was a conspiracy to make a girl's life so difficult that she wouldn't be tempted to remain
a spinster. Judging by the way Rosita clung to my arm, I guessed the message
had sunk in.

"Is it like this in the sea? Do the old women also say mean things about people,
about girls?" Like everyone in town, Rosita blamed the old women for gossiping.
I felt the widows were only the enforcers of a system that everyone supported.

"No. Women do pretty much what they want. My mother, for example, is a
dictator."

"What's a dictator?"

"It's someone who has defeated all her political enemies and rules unchallenged.
It's a very hard position to attain because so many enemies have to be dealt with.
Most politicians never aspire to anything higher than a democratically elected
position." I noticed her baffled look. "That means that their enemies agree not
to attack them for a certain number of years and in exchange they'll step down
from power after their term is up."

Rosita nodded wisely. "The priest said something in school, about how the
mer treat women better."

I laughed. The priest doubled as a schoolteacher and he was something of a
Christian revolutionary.

Rosita covered her mouth, noticing her slip. I calmed her down and told her
she could be a dictator for all I cared. She assured me all she wanted was to dress
up in colorful clothes from time to time. And for the old women to stop talking.
I left the jar in front of her house and walked away.

Our courtship lasted a reasonable time, neither more nor less. We were married in spring and we danced to torch-light until dawn.

"When are we visiting your parents?" Rosita asked.

I tumbled her back onto the bed. Those days, everything was for fun.

"My mother would rip my heart out if she ever saw me again." I answered, truthfully, but with a twinkle in my eye. With Rosita, I could laugh at the saddest things.

After we'd finished making love, Rosita nestled against me and whispered in my ear:

"Won't she forgive you? After all, you're married now."

I laughed. I knew the answer well, but I found her assumption revealing. In the culture she'd been raised, the most anyone could aspire to was marriage. Rosita believed my mother would forgive whatever offence I'd committed once I brought home a wife. How could she not want to meet her daughter-in-law? Not to speak of the children we'd surely have. I was married now, and hence a man. Nothing I'd done before was more than a childhood prank.

I was foolish. I laughed and didn't explain to her how different my people are. Maybe her culture had finally gotten to me and it didn't cross my mind to open my heart to my wife. You can't spend your life in a misogynist society and not have it catch a little.

Or maybe, I simply didn't want to dwell on what I'd lost, but I thought about you, Mother, and wondered what you would have thought of Rosita.

Our marriage would not go down in history as the longest, but I doubt there was ever a happier couple of newlyweds. Rosita got pregnant almost immediately and it looked as though the harvest would be good.

Then, just like that, hail came.

You, people from the deep, do not understand weather. For you, bad weather is a slight annoyance, a disruptor of parties, a disperser of plankton. You swim deep, where the currents are constant and change is slow. Weather doesn't threaten your survival. It doesn't threaten the issue of your womb.

Mother, these humans live hand-to-mouth. This is how *you* make them live. Losing one crop means hunger. Having a baby at the same time is a disaster. Her parents had four other unmarried daughters to feed: they could not help us out.

Oddly enough, Rosita didn't seem too worried. It went beyond the silly happiness of pregnancy. When we finally realized we had nothing, a busy hope overtook her. She put her marriage chest together and repacked her doilies. I asked her what was going on.

"Your mother will have to take us in now. We're family and we need help. I'm looking forward to living in the sea."

I'm not sure what she expected the sea to be like. I bet all she aspired to was a world in which she could go and buy wine without being stared at. When she saw my face, she laughed. The beauty had been sucked out of her, but the pretty still shone in her dainty bones, clearly visible after the famine.

"Oh, come on! She won't let her grandson starve, will she?"

What was I to do? Tell her that there was no hope? Tell her that my own mother wouldn't help me, would kill me if I dared wade into the sea?

I completed my act of treason and told Rosita our secrets. I told her she could be changed to swim free in the sea. I told her she'd feel no more discomfort than I did above land. Our mouths were green from eating grass and the dust had crept into the house while Rosita was weak from hunger and pregnancy. It wasn't a difficult decision to make. I didn't, however, tell her all the truth.

This is the story I want you to tell my child.

I know you won't like talking to him about dry land. I know you'll hate me with each breath that delivers my story, but I also know you'll say the words with feeling and conviction. You'll follow my wishes to the letter, Mother, because this is the mer way. Even a traitor has rights and even a traitor's story deserves to be heard. The condemned man has a right to a last meal; the merman has a right to his last words. I, being both and neither, go to my death on an empty stomach.

Believe me, Mother, when I say that I don't do this to punish you. You did what you had to do, just as I did what I was forced to do. You exiled me long ago. The reason has largely become a question of semantics. I'll make this easier for you and reaffirm my heresy:

You deny merfolk evolved from humans. I have proved you wrong. Merfolk were artificially geneered from humans to survive the climate cataclysm. The merfolk then devised a way to enhance the climate change, causing the water to rise, not six meters, as had been predicted, but over twenty, hence turning over control of the planet to the new species and killing thousands in the process. It's not my fault the younger generation of merfolk agrees with me and is willing to make amends with Humanity.

There. This confession should make things easier for you. The father for the son; that's the deal. Please forgive me this last cruelty from the grave.

"What do we do now?" Rosita asks when we reach the beach.

"We wade into the water," I tell her. "They'll come out to meet us."

She has no fear of drowning. Truck with merfolk is men's domain and women don't go near the sea. I teach her to float and paddle. If you take poorly to her, I want to give her a shot at swimming back to shore.

She's so trusting, she learns fast.

"You go ahead; I want you to be the first one my mother sees. If something happens just swim back. I might disappear suddenly, but don't worry about me. There are guards at the border and they might take me down for questioning," I lie.

I realize I've frightened her. "Don't worry, it'll only be a few minutes. If anything happens, just paddle back and wait for me on the shore."

She nods. For a second, I resent her for trusting me, even though I am the one who is lying to her.

There she goes. I chirp at her as she swims, engraving our story into her bones. The mer will tear me apart as soon as my scent spreads into the water. My body isn't a good vehicle for this message, so I'm placing it in Rosita.

The story of how we met goes into Rosa's left foot. The story of how I'm leaving her, into her right. I've tried to do the tale justice, nipping the bone at a microscopic level. The bones in her toes, in particular, I find endearing, and I pay them special attention, weaving the story into filigrees which I'm certain you'll appreciate. Think of me when you chirp at my bride and her bones sing back to you.

So, this is my wife, Mother. Truth be told, I don't know what I'm doing, sending her to you like this. Is this song in her bones like the sealed letters from the stories, telling you to kill the bearer? I think not. The merfolk have always been exacting, but never cruel. My bride is not what is wrong with her species and you know that genes do not determine behavior. Look at you; look at me. Who would think we were related?

Come now, Mother, find it in you to like this girl. She bears my child and I have kept my chirps away from her abdomen. You are threatening two innocents, for the crimes of your son, and that is not the mer way.

Do not make the child pay for the sins of the father.

THE SULTAN OF THE CLOUDS
GEOFFREY A. LANDIS

Geoffrey A. Landis is the author of one novel, *Mars Crossing*, and one collection of short stories, *Impact Parameter and Other Quantum Realities*. He has also written more than eighty short stories, which have appeared in publications such as *Analog*, *Asimov's* and *Fantasy & Science Fiction*, as well as in anthologies. He is the winner of the Nebula Award, two Hugo Awards, and the Locus Award for his fiction, as well as two Rhysling awards for SF poetry. Outside of science fiction, Dr. Landis is a physicist who works for NASA at the John Glenn Research Center in Cleveland, Ohio. He was on the science team of the Mars Pathfinder and Mars Exploration Rover missions, and has published 400 scientific papers and been awarded seven patents. He currently works on developing new technology for future planetary missions, including missions to explore Venus. He lives in Berea, Ohio, with his wife, writer Mary A. Turzillo, and four cats.

When Leah Hamakawa and I arrived at Riemann orbital, there was a surprise waiting for Leah: a message. Not an electronic message on a link-pad, but an actual physical envelope, with Doctor Leah Hamakawa lettered on the outside in flowing handwriting.

Leah slid the note from the envelope. The message was etched on a stiff sheet of some hard crystal that gleamed a brilliant translucent crimson. She looked at it, flexed it, ran a fingernail over it, and then held it to the light, turning it slightly. The edges caught the light and scattered it across the room in droplets of fire. "Diamond," she said. "Chromium impurities give it the red color; probably nitrogen for the blue. Charming." She handed it to me. "Careful of the edges, Tinkerman; I don't doubt it might cut."

I ran a finger carefully over one edge, but found that Leah's warning was unnecessary; some sort of passivation treatment had been done to blunt the edge to keep it from cutting. The letters were limned in blue, so sharply chiseled on the sheet that they seemed to rise from the card. The title read, "Invitation from Carlos Fernando Delacroix Ortega de la Jolla y Nordwald-Gruenbaum." In smaller letters, it continued, "We find your researches on the ecology of Mars to be of some interest. We would like to invite you to visit our residences at Hypatia at your convenience and talk."

I didn't know the name Carlos Fernando, but the family Nordwald-Gruen-baum needed no introduction. The invitation had come from someone within the intimate family of the Satrap of Venus.

Transportation, the letter continued, would be provided.

The Satrap of Venus. One of the twenty old men, the lords and owners of the solar system. A man so rich that human standards of wealth no longer had any meaning. What could he want with Leah?

I tried to remember what I knew about the Sultan of the clouds, satrap of the fabled floating cities. It seemed very far away from everything I knew. The society, I thought I remembered, was said to be decadent and perverse, but I knew little more. The inhabitants of Venus kept to themselves.

Riemann station was ugly and functional, the interior made of a dark anodized aluminum with a pebbled surface finish. There was a viewport in the lounge, and Leah had walked over to look out. She stood with her back to me, framed in darkness. Even in her rumpled ship's suit, she was beautiful, and I wondered if I would ever find the clue to understanding her.

As the orbital station rotated, the blue bubble of Earth slowly rose in front of her, a fragile and intricate sculpture of snow and cobalt, outlining her in a sapphire light. "There's nothing for me down there," she said.

I stood in silence, not sure if she even remembered I was there.

In a voice barely louder than the silence, she said, "I have no past."

The silence was uncomfortable. I knew I should say something, but I was not sure what. "I've never been to Venus," I said at last.

"I don't know anybody who has." Leah turned. "I suppose the letter doesn't specifically say that I should come alone." Her tone was matter of fact, neither discouraging nor inviting.

It was hardly enthusiastic, but it was better than no. I wondered if she actually liked me, or just tolerated my presence. I decided it might be best not to ask. No use pressing on my luck.

The transportation provided turned out to be the *Sulieman*, a fusion yacht.

Sulieman was more than merely first-class, it was excessively extravagant. It was larger than many ore transports, huge enough that any ordinary yacht could have easily fit within the most capacious of its recreation spheres. Each of its private cabins—and it had seven—was larger than an ordinary habitat module. Big ships commonly were slow ships, but *Sulieman* was an exception, equipped with an impressive amount of delta-V, and the transfer orbit to Venus was scheduled for a transit time well under that of any commercial transport ship.

We were the only passengers.

Despite its size, the ship had a crew of just three: captain, and first and second pilot. The captain, with the shaven head and saffron robe of a Buddhist novice, greeted us on entry, and politely but firmly informed us that the crew were not answerable to orders of the passengers. We were to keep to the passenger section, and we would be delivered to Venus. Crew accommodations were separate from the passenger accommodations, and we should expect not to see or hear from the crew during the voyage.

"Fine," was the only comment Leah had.

When the ship had received us and boosted into a fast Venus transfer orbit, Leah found the smallest of the private cabins and locked herself in it.

Leah Hamakawa had been with the Pleiades Institute for twenty years. She had joined young, when she was still a teenager—long before I'd ever met her—and I knew little of her life before then, other than that she had been an orphan. The institute was the only family that she had.

It seems to me sometimes that there are two Leahs. One Leah is shy and child-like, begging to be loved. The other Leah is cool and professional, who can hardly bear being touched, who hates—or perhaps disdains—people.

Sometimes I wonder if she had been terribly hurt as a child. She never talks about growing up, never mentions her parents. I had asked her, once, and the only thing she said was that that is all behind her, long ago and far away.

I never knew my position with her. Sometimes I almost think that she must love me, but cannot bring herself to say anything. Other times she is so casually thoughtless that I believe she never thinks of me as more than a technical assistant, indistinguishable from any other tech. Sometimes I wonder why she even bothers to allow me to hang around.

I damn myself silently for being too cowardly to ask.

While Leah had locked herself away, I explored the ship. Each cabin was spherical, with a single double-glassed octagonal viewport on the outer cabin wall. The cabins had every luxury imaginable, even hygiene facilities set in smaller adjoining spheres, with booths that sprayed actual water through nozzles onto the occupant's body.

Ten hours after boost, Leah had still not come out. I found another cabin and went to sleep.

In two days I was bored. I had taken apart everything that could be taken apart, examined how it worked, and put it back together. Everything was in perfect condition; there was nothing for me to fix.

But, although I had not brought much with me, I'd brought a portable office. I called up a librarian agent, and asked for history.

In the beginning of the human expansion outward, transport into space had been ruinously expensive, and only governments and obscenely rich corporations could afford to do business in space. When the governments dropped out, a handful of rich men bought their assets. Most of them sold out again, or went bankrupt. A few of them didn't. Some stayed on due to sheer stubbornness, some with the fervor of an ideological belief in human expansion, and some out of a cold-hearted calculation that there would be uncountable wealth in space, if only it could be tapped. When the technology was finally ready, the twenty families owned it all.

Slowly, the frontier opened, and then the exodus began. First by the thousands: Baha'i, fleeing religious persecution; deposed dictators and their sycophants, looking to escape with looted treasuries; drug lords and their retinues, looking to take their profits beyond the reach of governments or rivals. Then, the exodus began by the millions, all colors of humanity scattering from the Earth to start a new life in space. Splinter groups from the Church of John the Avenger left the unforgiving mother church seeking their prophesied destiny; dissidents from the People's Republic of Malawi, seeking freedom; vegetarian communes from Alaska, seeking a new frontier; Mayans, seeking to reestablish a Maya homeland; libertarians, seeking their free-market paradise; communists, seeking a place outside of history to mold the new communist man. Some of them died quickly, some slowly, but always there were more, a never-ending flood of dissidents, malcontents and rebels, people willing to sign away anything for the promise of a new start. A few of them survived. A few of them thrived. A few of them grew.

And every one of them had mortgaged their very balls to the twenty families for passage.

Not one habitat in a hundred managed to buy its way out of debt—but the heirs of the twenty became richer than nations, richer than empires.

The legendary war between the Nordwald industrial empire and the Gruenbaum family over solar-system resources had ended when Patricia Gruenbaum sold out her controlling interest in the family business. Udo Nordwald, tyrant and patriarch of the Nordwald industrial empire—now Nordwald-Gruenbaum—had no such plans to discard or even dilute his hard-battled wealth. He continued his consolidation of power with a merger-by-marriage of his only son, a boy not even out of his teens, with the shrewd and calculating heiress of la Jolla. His closest competitors gone, Udo retreated from the outer solar system, leaving the long expansion outward to others. He established corporate headquarters, a living quarters for workers, and his own personal dwelling in a place which was both central to the inner system, and also a spot that nobody had ever before thought possible to colonize. He made his reputation by colonizing the planet casually called the solar system's Hell planet.

Venus.

The planet below grew from a point of light into a gibbous white pearl, too bright to look at. The arriving interplanetary yacht shed its hyperbolic excess in a low pass through Venus' atmosphere, rebounded leisurely into high elliptical orbit, and then circularized into a two-hour parking orbit.

Sulieman had an extravagant viewport, a single transparent pane four meters in diameter, and I floated in front of it, watching the transport barque glide up to meet us. I had thought *Sulieman* a large ship; the barque made it look like a miniature. A flattened cone with a rounded nose and absurdly tiny rocket engines at the base, it was shaped in the form of a typical planetary-descent lifting body, but one that must have been over a kilometer long, and at least as wide. It glided up to the *Sulieman* and docked with her like a pumpkin mating with a pea.

The size, I knew, was deceiving. The barque was no more than a thin skin over a hollow shell made of vacuum-foamed titanium surrounding a vast empty chamber. It was designed not to land, but to float in the atmosphere, and to float it required a huge volume and almost no weight. No ships ever landed on the surface of Venus; the epithet "hell" was well chosen. The transfer barque, then, was more like a space-going dirigible than a spaceship, a vehicle as much at home floating in the clouds as floating in orbit.

Even knowing that the vast bulk of the barque was little more substantial than vacuum, though, I found the effect intimidating.

It didn't seem to make any impression on Leah. She had come out from her silent solitude when we approached Venus, but she barely glanced out the viewport in passing. It was often hard for me to guess what would attract her attention. Sometimes I had seen her spend an hour staring at a rock, apparently fascinated by a chunk of ordinary asteroidal chondrite, turning it over and examining it carefully from every possible angle. Other things, like a spaceship nearly as big as a city, she ignored as if they had no more importance than dirt.

Bulky cargos were carried in compartments in the hollow interior of the barque, but since there were just two of us descending to Venus, we were invited to sit up in the pilot's compartment, a transparent blister almost invisible at the front.

The pilot was another yellow-robed Buddhist. Was this a common sect for Venus pilots, I wondered? But this pilot was as talkative as *Sulieman*'s pilot had been reclusive. As the barque undocked, a tether line stretched out between it and the station. The station lowered the barque toward the planet. While we were being lowered down the tether, the pilot pointed out every possible sight—tiny communications satellites crawling across the sky like turbocharged ants; the pinkish flashes of lightning on the night hemisphere of the planet far below; the golden spider's web of a microwave power relay. At thirty kilometers, still talking, the pilot severed the tether, allowing the barque to drop free. The Earth and moon, twin stars of blue and white, rose over the pearl of the horizon. Factory complexes were distantly visible in orbit, easy to spot by their flashing navigation beacons and the transport barques docked to them, so far away that even the immense barques were shrunken to insignificance.

We were starting to brush atmosphere now, and a feeling of weight returned, and increased. Suddenly we were pulling half a gravity of overgee. Without ever stopping talking, the pilot-monk deftly rolled the barque inverted, and Venus was now over our heads, a featureless white ceiling to the universe. "Nice view there, is it not?" the pilot said. "You get a great feel for the planet in this attitude. Not doing it for the view, though, nice as it is; I'm just getting that old hypersonic lift working for us, holding us down. These barques are rather a bit fragile; can't take them in too fast, have to play the atmosphere like a big bass fiddle. Wouldn't want us to bounce off the atmosphere, now, would you?" He didn't pause for answers to his questions, and I wondered if he would have continued his travelogue even if we had not been there.

The gee level increased to about a standard, then steadied.

The huge beast swept inverted through the atmosphere, trailing an ionized cloud behind it. The pilot slowed toward subsonic, and then rolled the barque over again, skipping upward slightly into the exosphere to cool the glowing skin, then letting it dip back downward. The air thickened around us as we descended into the thin, featureless haze. And then we broke through the bottom of the haze into the clear air below it, and abruptly we were soaring above the endless sea of clouds.

Clouds.

A hundred and fifty million square kilometers of clouds, a billion cubic kilometers of clouds. In the ocean of clouds the floating cities of Venus are not limited, like terrestrial cities, to two dimensions only, but can float up and down at the whim of the city masters, higher into the bright cold sunlight, downward to the edges of the hot murky depths.

Clouds. The barque sailed over cloud-cathedrals and over cloud-mountains, edges recomplicated with cauliflower fractals. We sailed past lairs filled with cloud-monsters a kilometer tall, with arched necks of cloud stretching forward, threatening and blustering with cloud-teeth, cloud-muscled bodies with clawed feet of flickering lightning.

The barque was floating now, drifting downward at subsonic speed, trailing its own cloud-contrail, which twisted behind us like a scrawl of illegible handwriting. Even the pilot, if not actually fallen silent, had at least slowed down his chatter, letting us soak in the glory of it. "Quite something, isn't it?" he said. "The kingdom of the clouds. Drives some people batty with the immensity of it, or so they say—cloud-happy, they call it here. Never get tired of it, myself. No view like the view from a barque to see the clouds." And to prove it, he banked the barque over into a slow turn, circling a cloud pillar that rose from deep down in the haze to tower thousands of meters above our heads. "Quite a sight."

"Quite a sight," I repeated.

The pilot-monk rolled the barque back, and then pointed, forward and slightly to the right. "There. See it?"

I didn't know what to see. "What?"

"There."

I saw it now, a tiny point glistening in the distance. "What is it?"

"Hypatia. The jewel of the clouds."

As we coasted closer, the city grew. It was an odd sight. The city was a dome, or rather, a dozen glistening domes melted haphazardly together, each one faceted with a million panels of glass. The domes were huge; the smallest nearly a kilometer across, and as the barque glided across the sky the facets caught the sunlight and sparkled with reflected light. Below the domes, a slender pencil of rough black stretched down toward the cloudbase like taffy, delicate as spun glass, terminating in an absurdly tiny bulb of rock that seemed far too small to counterbalance the domes.

"Beautiful, you think, yes? Like the wonderful jellyfishes of your blue planet's oceans. Can you believe that half a million people live there?"

The pilot brought us around the city in a grand sweep, showing off, not even bothering to talk. Inside the transparent domes, chains of lakes glittered in green ribbons between boulevards and delicate pavilions. At last he slowed to a stop, and then slowly leaked atmosphere into the vacuum vessel that provided the buoyancy. The barque settled down gradually, wallowing from side to side now that the stability given by its forward momentum was gone. Now it floated slightly lower than the counterweight. The counterweight no longer looked small, but loomed above us, a rock the size of Gibraltar. Tiny fliers affixed towropes to hardpoints on the surface of the barque, and slowly we were winched into a hard-dock.

"Welcome to Venus," said the monk.

The surface of Venus is a place of crushing pressure and hellish temperature. Rise above it, though, and the pressure eases, the temperature cools. Fifty kilometers above the surface, at the base of the clouds, the temperature is tropical, and the pressure the same as Earth normal. Twenty kilometers above that, the air is thin and polar cold.

Drifting between these two levels are the ten thousand floating cities of Venus.

A balloon filled with oxygen and nitrogen will float in the heavy air of Venus, and balloons were exactly what the fabled domed cities were. Geodetic structures with struts of sintered graphite and skin of transparent polycarbonate synthesized from the atmosphere of Venus itself, each kilometer-diameter dome easily lifted a hundred thousand tons of city.

Even the clouds cooperated. The thin haze of the upper cloud deck served to filter the sunlight so that the intensity of the sun here was little more than the Earth's solar constant.

Hypatia was not the largest of the floating cities, but it was certainly the richest, a city of helical buildings and golden domes, with huge open areas and elaborate gardens. Inside the dome of Hypatia, the architects played every possible trick to make us forget that we were inside an enclosed volume.

But we didn't see this part, the gardens and waterfalls, not at first. Leaving the barque, we entered a disembarking lounge below the city. For all that it featured plush chaise lounges, floors covered with genetically engineered pink grass, and priceless sculptures of iron and of jade, it was functional: a place to wait.

It was large enough to hold a thousand people, but there was only one person in the lounge, a boy who was barely old enough to have entered his teens, wearing a bathrobe and elaborately pleated yellow silk pants. He was slightly pudgy, with an agreeable, but undistinguished, round face.

After the expense of our transport, I was surprised at finding only one person sent to await our arrival.

The kid looked at Leah. "Doctor Hamakawa. I'm pleased to meet you." Then he turned to me. "Who the hell are you?" he said.

"Who are you?" I said. "Where's our reception?"

The boy was chewing on something. He seemed about to spit it out, and then thought better of it. He looked over at Leah. "This guy is with you, Dr. Hamakawa? What's he do?"

"This is David Tinkerman," Leah said. "Technician. And, when need be, pilot. Yes, he's with me."

"Tell him he might wish to learn some manners," the boy said.

"And who are you?" I shot back. "I don't think you answered the question."

The not-quite-teenager looked at me with disdain, as if he wasn't sure if he would even bother to talk to me. Then he said, in a slow voice as if talking to an idiot, "I am Carlos Fernando Delacroix Ortega de la Jolla y Nordwald-Gruenbaum. I own this station and everything on it."

He had an annoying high voice, on the edge of changing, but not yet there.

Leah, however, didn't seem to notice his voice. "Ah," she said. "You are the scion of Nordwald-Gruenbaum. The ruler of Hypatia."

The kid shook his head and frowned. "No," he said. "Not the scion, not exactly. I am Nordwald-Gruenbaum." The smile made him look like a child again; it make him look likable. When he bowed, he was utterly charming. "I," he said, "am the sultan of the clouds."

Carlos Fernando, as it turned out, had numerous servants indeed. Once we had been greeted, he made a gesture and an honor guard of twenty women in silken doublets came forward to escort us up.

Before we entered the elevator, the guards circled around. At a word from Carlos Fernando, a package was brought forward. Carlos took it, and, as the guards watched, handed it to Leah. "A gift," he said, "to welcome you to my city."

The box was simple and unadorned. Leah opened it. Inside the package was a large folio. She took it out. The book was bound in cracked, dark red leather, with no lettering. She flipped to the front. "Giordano Bruno," she read. "On the Infinite Universe and Worlds." She smiled, and riffled through the pages. "A facsimile of the first English edition?"

"I thought perhaps you might enjoy it."

"Charming." She placed it back in the box, and tucked it under her arm. "Thank you," she said.

The elevator rose so smoothly it was difficult to believe it traversed two kilometers in a little under three minutes. The doors opened to brilliant noon sunlight. We were in the bubble city.

The city was a fantasy of foam and air. Although it was enclosed in a dome, the bubble was so large that the walls nearly vanished into the air, and it seemed unencumbered. With the guards beside us, we walked through the city. Everywhere there were parks, some just a tiny patch of green surrounding a tree, some forests perched on the wide tops of elongated stalks, with elegantly sculpted waterfalls cascading down to be caught in wide fountain basins. White pathways led upward through the air, suspended by cables from impossibly narrow beams, and all around us were sounds of rustling water and birdsong.

At the end of the welcoming tour, I realized I had been imperceptibly but effectively separated from Leah. "Hey," I said. "What happened to Dr. Hamakawa?"

The honor guard of women still surrounded me, but Leah, and the kid who was the heir of Nordwald-Gruenbaum, had vanished.

"We're sorry," one of the woman answered, one slightly taller, perhaps, than the others. "I believe that she has been taken to her suite to rest for a bit, since in a few hours she is to be greeted at the level of society."

"I should be with her."

The woman looked at me calmly. "We had no instructions to bring you. I don't believe you were invited."

"Excuse me," I said. "I'd better find them."

The woman stood back, and gestured to the city. Walkways meandered in all directions, a three-dimensional maze. "By all means, if you like. We were instructed that you were to have free run of the city."

I nodded. Clearly, plans had been made with no room for me. "How will I get in touch?" I asked. "What if I want to talk to Leah—to Doctor Hamakawa?"

"They'll be able to find you. Don't worry." After a pause, she said, "Shall we show you to your place to domicile?"

The building to which I was shown was one of a cluster that seemed suspended in the air by crisscrossed cables. It was larger than many houses. I was used to living in the cubbyholes of habitat modules, and the spaciousness of the accommodations startled me.

"Good evening, Mr. Tinkerman." The person greeting me was a tall Chinese man perhaps fifty years of age. The woman next to him, I surmised, was his wife. She was quite a bit younger, in her early twenties. She was slightly overweight by the standards I was used to, but I had noticed that was common here. Behind her hid two children, their faces peeking out from behind her and then darting back again to safety. The man introduced himself as Truman Singh, and his wife as Epiphany. "The rest of the family will be about to meet you in a few hours, Mr. Tinkerman," he said, smiling. "They are mostly working."

"We both work for His Excellency," Epiphany added. "Carlos Fernando has asked our braid to house you. Don't hesitate to ask for anything you need. The cost will go against the Nordwald-Gruenbaum credit, which is," she smiled, "quite unlimited here. As you might imagine."

"Do you do this often?" I asked. "House guests?"

Epiphany looked up at her husband. "Not too often," she said, "not for His Excellency, anyway. It's not uncommon in the cities, though; there's a lot of visiting back and forth as one city or another drifts nearby, and everyone will put up visitors from time to time."

"You don't have hotels?"

She shook her head. "We don't get many visitors from outplanet."

"You said 'His Excellency,'" I said. "That's Carlos Fernando? Tell me about him."

"Of course. What would you like to know?"

"Does he really—" I gestured at the city—"own all of this? The whole planet?"

"Yes, certainly, the city, yes. And also, no."

"How is that?"

"He will own the city, yes—this one, and five thousand others—but the planet? Maybe, maybe not. The Nordwald-Gruenbaum family does claim to own the planet, but in truth that claim means little. The claim may apply to the surface of the planet, but nobody owns the sky. The cities, though, yes. But, of course, he doesn't actually control them all personally."

"Well, of course not. I mean, hey, he's just a kid— He must have trustees, or proxies or something, right?"

"Indeed. Until he reaches his majority."

"And then?"

Truman Singh shrugged. "It is the Nordwald-Gruenbaum tradition—written into the first Nordwald's will. When he reaches his majority, it is personal property."

There were, as I discovered, eleven thousand, seven hundred, and eight cities floating in the atmosphere of Venus. "Probably a few more," Truman Singh told me. "Nobody keeps track, exactly. There are myths of cities that float low down, never rising above the lower cloud decks, forever hidden. You can't live that deep—it's too hot—but the stories say that the renegade cities have a technology that allows them to reject heat." He shrugged. "Who knows?" In any case, of the known cities, the estate to which Carlos Fernando was heir owned or held shares or partial ownership of more than half.

"The Nordwald-Gruenbaum entity have been a good owners," Truman said. "I should say, they know that their employees could leave, to another city, if they had to, but they don't."

"And there's no friction?"

"Oh, the independent cities, they all think that the Nordwald-Gruenbaums have too much power!" He laughed. "But there's not much they can do about it, eh?"

"They could fight."

Truman Singh reached out and tapped me lightly on the center of my forehead with his middle finger. "That would not be wise." He paused, and then said more slowly, "We are an interconnected ecology here, the independents and the sultanate. We rely on each other. The independents could declare war, yes, but in the end nobody would win."

"Yes," I said. "Yes, I see that. Of course, the floating cities are so fragile—a single break in the gas envelope—"

"We are perhaps not as fragile as you think," Truman Singh replied. "I should say, you are used to the built worlds, but they are vacuum habitats, where a single blow-out would be catastrophic. Here, you know, there is no pressure difference between the atmosphere outside and the lifesphere inside; if there is a break, the gas equilibrates through the gap only very slowly. Even if we had a thousand broken panels, it would take weeks for the city to sink to the irrecoverable depths. And, of course, we do have safeguards, many safeguards." He paused, and then said, "but if there were a war... we are safe against ordinary hazards, you can have no fear of that... but against metastable bombs... well, that would not be good. No, I should say that would not be good at all."

The next day I set out to find where Leah had been taken, but although everyone I met was unfailingly polite, I had little success in reaching her. At least I was beginning to learn my way around.

The first thing I noticed about the city was the light. I was used to living in orbital habitats, where soft, indirect light was provided by panels of white-light diodes. In Hypatia City, brilliant Venus sunlight suffused throughout the interior. The next thing I noticed were the birds.

Hypatia was filled with birds. Birds were common in orbital habitats, since parrots and cockatiels adapt well to the freefall environment of space, but the volume of Hypatia was crowded with bright tropical birds, parrots and cockatoos and lorikeets, cardinals and chickadees and quetzals, more birds than I had names for, more birds than I had ever seen, a raucous orchestra of color and sound.

The floating city had twelve main chambers, separated from one another by thin, transparent membranes with a multiplicity of passages, each chamber well-lit and cheerful, each with a slightly different style.

The quarters I had been assigned were in sector Carbon, where individual living habitats were strung on cables like strings of iridescent pearls above a broad fenway of forest and grass. Within sector Carbon, cable-cars swung like pendulums on long strands, taking a traveler from platform to platform across the sector in giddy arcs. Carlos Fernando's chambers were in the highest, centermost bubble—upcity, as it was called—a bubble dappled with colored light and shadow, where the architecture was fluted minarets and oriental domes. But I wasn't, as it seemed, allowed into this elite sphere. I didn't even learn where Leah had been given quarters.

I found a balcony on a tower that looked out through the transparent canopy over the clouds. The cloudscape was just as magnificent as it had been the previous day; towering and slowly changing. The light was a rich golden color, and the sun, masked by a skein of feathery clouds like a tracery of lace, was surrounded by a bronze halo. From the angle of the sun it was early afternoon, but there would be no sunset that day; the great winds circling the planet would not blow the city into the night side of Venus for another day.

Of the eleven thousand other cities, I could detect no trace—looking outward, there was no indication that we were not alone in the vast cloudscape that stretched to infinity. But then, I thought, if the cities were scattered randomly, there would be little chance one would be nearby at any given time. Venus was a small planet, as planets go, but large enough to swallow ten thousand cities—or even a hundred times that—without any visible crowding of the skies.

I wished I knew what Leah thought of it.

I missed Leah. For all that she sometimes didn't seem to even notice I was there... our sojourn on Mars, brief as it had been... we had shared the same cubby. Perhaps that meant nothing to her. But it had been the very center of my life.

I thought of her body, lithe and golden-skinned. Where was she? What was she doing?

The park was a platform overgrown with cymbidian orchids, braced in the air by the great cables that transected the dome from the stanchion trusswork. This seemed a common architecture here, where even the ground beneath was suspended from the buoyancy of the air dome. I bounced my weight back and forth, testing the resonant frequency, and felt the platform move infinitesimally under me. Children here must be taught from an early age not to do that; a deliberate effort could build up destructive oscillation. I stopped bouncing, and let the motion damp.

When I returned near the middle of the day, neither Truman nor Epiphany were there, and Truman's other wife, a woman named Triolet, met me. She was a woman perhaps in her sixties, with dark skin and deep gray eyes. She had been introduced to me the previous day, but in the confusion of meeting numerous people in what seemed to be a large extended family, I had not had a chance to really meet her yet. There were always a number of people around the Singh household, and I was confused as to how, or even if, they were related to my hosts. Now, talking to her, I realized that she, in fact, was the one who had control of the Singh household finances.

The Singh family were farmers, I discovered. Or farm managers. The flora in Hypatia was decorative, or served to keep the air in the dome refreshed, but the real agriculture was in separate domes, floating at an altitude that was optimized for plant growth, and had no inhabitants. Automated equipment did the work of sowing and irrigation and harvest. Truman and Epiphany Singh were operational engineers, making those decisions that required a human input, watching that the robots kept on track and were doing the right things at the right times.

And, there was a message waiting for me, inviting me in the evening to attend a dinner with His Excellency, Carlos Fernando Delacroix Ortega de la Jolla y

Nordwald-Gruenbaum.

Triolet helped me with my wardrobe, along with Epiphany, who had returned by the time I was ready to prepare. They both told me emphatically that my serviceable but well-worn jumpsuit was not appropriate attire. The gown Triolet selected was far gaudier than anything I would have chosen for myself, an electric shade of indigo accented with a wide midnight-black sash. "Trust us, it will be suitable," Epiphany told me. Despite its bulk, it was light as a breath of air.

"All clothes here are light," Epiphany told me. "Spider's silk."

"Ah, I see" I said. "Synthetic spider silk. Strong and light; very practical."

"Synthetic?" Epiphany asked, and giggled. "No, not synthetic. It's real."

"The silk is actually woven by spiders?"

"No, the whole garment is." At my puzzled look, she said, "Teams of spiders. They work together."

"Spiders."

"Well, they're natural weavers, you know. And easy to transport."

I arrived at the banquet hall at the appointed time and found that the plasma-arc blue gown that Epiphany had selected for me was the most conservative dress there. There were perhaps thirty people present, but Leah was clearly the center. She seemed happy with the attention, more animated than I'd recalled seeing her before.

"They're treating you well?" I asked, when I'd finally made it through the crowd to her.

"Oh, indeed."

I discovered I had nothing to say. I waited for her to ask about me, but she didn't. "Where have they given you to stay?"

"A habitat next section over," she said. "Sector Carbon. It's amazing—I've never seen so many birds."

"That's the sector I'm in," I said, "but they didn't tell me where you were."

"Really? That's odd." She tapped up a map of the residential sector on a screen built into the diamond tabletop, and a three-dimensional image appeared to float inside the table. She rotated it and highlighted her habitat, and I realized that she was indeed adjacent, in a large habitat that was almost directly next to the complex I was staying in. "It's a pretty amazing place. But mostly I've been here in the upcity. Have you talked to Carli much yet? He's a very clever kid. Interested in everything—botany, physics, even engineering."

"Really?" I said. "I don't think they'll let me into the upcity."

"You're kidding; I'm sure they'll let you in. Hey—" she called over one of the guards. "Say, is there any reason Tinkerman can't come up to the centrum?"

"No, madam, if you want it, of course not."

"Great. See, no problem."

And then the waiters directed me to my place at the far end of the table.

The table was a thick slab of diamond, the faceted edges collecting and refracting rainbows of color. The top was as smooth and slippery as a sheet of ice. Concealed inside were small computer screens so that any of the diners who wished could call up graphics or data as needed during a conversation. The table was both art and engineering, practical and beautiful at the same time.

Carlos Fernando sat at the end of the table. He seemed awkward and out of place in a chair slightly too large for him. Leah sat at his right, and an older woman—perhaps his mother?—on his left. He was bouncing around in his chair, alternating between playing with the computer system in his table and sneaking glances over at Leah when he thought she wasn't paying attention to him. If she looked in his direction, he would go still for a moment, and then his eyes would quickly dart away and he went back to staring at the graphics screen in front of him and fidgeting.

The server brought a silver tray to Carlos Fernando. On it was something the size of a fist, hidden under a canopy of red silk. Carlos Fernando looked up, accepted it with a nod, and removed the cloth. There was a moment of silence as people looked over, curious. I strained to see it.

It was a sparkling egg.

The egg was cunningly wrought of diamond fibers of many colors, braided into intricate lacework resembling entwined Celtic knots. The twelve-year-old satrap of Venus picked it up and ran one finger over it, delicately, barely brushing the surface, feeling the corrugations and relief of the surface.

He held it for a moment, as if not quite sure what he should do with it, and then his hand darted over and put the egg on the plate in front of Leah. She looked up, puzzled.

"This is for you," he said.

The faintest hint of surprise passed through the other diners, almost subvocal, too soft to be heard.

A moment later the servers set an egg in front of each of us. Our eggs, although decorated with an intricate filigree of finely painted lines of gold and pale verdigris, were ordinary eggs—goose eggs, perhaps.

Carlos Fernando was fidgeting in his chair, half grinning, half biting his lip, looking down, looking around, looking everywhere except at the egg or at Leah.

"What am I to do with this?" Leah asked.

"Why," he said, "perhaps you should open it up and eat it."

Leah picked up the diamond-laced egg and examined it, turned it over and rubbed one finger across the surface. Then, having found what she was looking for, she held it in two fingers and twisted. The diamond eggshell opened, and inside it was a second egg, an ordinary one.

The kid smiled again and looked down at the egg in front of him. He picked up his spoon and cracked the shell, then spooned out the interior.

At this signal, the others cracked their own eggs and began to eat. After a moment, Leah laid the decorative shell to one side and did the same. I watched her for a moment, and then cracked my own egg.

It was, of course, excellent.

Later, when I was back with the Singh family, I was still puzzled. There had been some secret significance there that everybody else had seen, but I had missed. Mr. Singh was sitting with his older wife, Triolet, talking about accounts.

"I must ask a question," I said.

Truman Singh turned to me. "Ask," he said, "and I shall answer."

"Is there any particular significance," I said, "to an egg?"

"An egg?" Singh seemed puzzled. "Much significance, I would say. In the old days, the days of the asteroid miners, an egg was a symbol of luxury. Ducks were brought into the bigger habitats, and their eggs were, for some miners, the only food they would ever eat that was not a form of algae or soybean."

"A symbol of luxury," I said, musing. "I see. But I still don't understand it." I thought for a moment, and then asked, "is there any significance to a gift of an egg?

"Well, no," he said, slowly, "not exactly. An egg? Nothing, in and of itself."

His wife Triolet, asked, "You are sure it's just an egg? Nothing else?"

"A very elaborate egg."

"Hmmm," she said, with a speculative look in her eye. "Not, maybe, an egg, a book, and a rock?"

That startled me a little. "A book and a rock?" The Bruno book—the very first thing Carlos Fernando had done on meeting Leah was to give her a book. But a rock? I hadn't see anything like that. "Why that?"

"Ah," she said. "I suppose you wouldn't know. I don't believe that our customs here in the sky cities are well known out there in the outer reaches."

Her mention of the outer reaches—Saturn and the Beyond—confused me for a moment, until I realized that, viewed from Venus, perhaps even Earth and the built worlds of the orbital clouds would be considered "outer."

"Here," she continued, "as in most of the ten thousand cities, an egg, a book, and a rock is a special gift. The egg is symbolic of life, you see; a book symbolic of knowledge; and a rock is the basis of all wealth, the minerals from the asteroid belt that built our society and bought our freedom."

"Yes? And all three together?"

"They are the traditional gesture of the beginning of courtship," she said.

"I still don't understand."

"If a young man gives a woman an egg, a book, and a rock," Truman said, "I should say this is his official sign that he is interested in courting her. If she accepts them, then she accepts his courtship."

"What? That's it, just like that, they're married?"

"No, no, no," he said. "It only means that she accepts the courtship—that she takes him seriously and, when it comes, she will listen to his proposal. Often a woman may have rocks and eggs from many young men. She doesn't have to accept, only take him seriously."

"Oh," I said.

But it still made no sense. How old was Carlos Fernando, twenty Venus years? What was that, twelve Earth years or so? He was far too young to be proposing.

"No one can terraform Venus," Carlos Fernando said.

Carlos Fernando had been uninterested in having me join in Leah's discussion, but Leah, oblivious to her host's displeasure (or perhaps simply not caring), had insisted that if he wanted to talk about terraforming, I should be there.

It was one room of Carlos Fernando's extensive palaces, a rounded room, an enormous cavernous space that had numerous alcoves. I'd found them sitting in one of the alcoves, an indentation that was cozy but still open. The ubiquitous female guards were still there, but they were at the distant ends of the room, within command if Carlos Fernando chose to shout, but far enough to give them the illusion of privacy.

The furniture they were sitting on was odd. The chairs seemed sculpted of sapphire smoke, yet were solid to the touch. I picked one up and discovered that it weighed almost nothing at all. "Diamond aerogel," Carlos Fernando said. "Do you like it?"

"It's amazing," I said. I had never before seen so much made out of diamond. And yet it made sense here, I thought; with carbon dioxide an inexhaustible resource surrounding the floating cities, it was logical that the floating cities would make as much as they could out of carbon. But still, I didn't know you could make an aerogel of diamond. "How do you make it?"

"A new process we've developed," Carlos Fernando said. "You don't mind if I don't go into the details. It's actually an adaptation of an old idea, something that was invented back on Earth decades ago, called a molecular still."

When Carlos Fernando mentioned the molecular still, I thought I saw a sharp flicker of attention from Leah. This was a subject she knew something about, I thought. But instead of following up, she went back to his earlier comment on terraforming.

"You keep asking questions about the ecology of Mars," she said. "Why so many detailed questions about Martian ecopoiesis? You say you're not interested in terraforming, but are you really? You aren't thinking of the old idea of using photosynthetic algae in the atmosphere to reduce the carbon dioxide, are you? Surely you know that that can't work."

"Of course." Carlos Fernando waved the question away. "Theoretical," he said. "Nobody could terraform Venus, I know, I know."

His pronouncement would have been more dignified if his voice had finished changing, but as it was, it wavered between squeaking an octave up and then going back down again, ruining the effect. "We simply have too much atmosphere," he said. "Down at the surface, the pressure is over ninety bars—even if the carbon dioxide of the atmosphere could be converted to oxygen, the surface atmosphere would still be seventy times higher than the Earth's atmospheric pressure."

"I realize that," Leah said. "We're not actually ignorant, you know. So high a pressure of oxygen would be deadly—you'd burst into flames."

"And the leftover carbon," he said, smiling. "Hundreds of tons per square meter."

"So what are you thinking?" she asked.

But in response, he only smiled. "Okay, I can't terraform Venus," he said. "So tell me more about Mars."

I could see that there was something that he was keeping back. Carlos Fernando had some idea that he wasn't telling.

But Leah did not press him, and instead took the invitation to tell him about her studies of the ecology on Mars, as it had been transformed long ago by the vanished engineers of the long-gone Freehold Toynbee colony. The Toynbee's engineers had designed life to thicken the atmosphere of Mars, to increase the greenhouse effect, to melt the frozen oceans of Mars.

"But it's not working," Leah concluded. "The anaerobic life is being out-competed by the photosynthetic oxygen-producers. It's pulling too much carbon dioxide out of the atmosphere."

"But what about the Gaia effect? Doesn't it compensate?"

"No," Leah said. "I found no trace of a Lovelock self-aware planet. Either that's a myth, or else the ecology on Mars is just too young to stabilize."

"Of course on Venus, we would have no problem with photosynthesis removing carbon dioxide."

"I thought you weren't interested in terraforming Venus," I said.

Carlos Fernando waved my objection away. "A hypothetical case, of course," he said. "A thought exercise." He turned to Leah. "Tomorrow," he said, "would you like to go kayaking?"

"Sure," she said.

Kayaking, on Venus, did not involve water.

Carlos Fernando instructed Leah, and Epiphany helped me.

The "kayak" was a ten-meter-long gas envelope, a transparent cylinder of plastic curved into an ogive at both ends, with a tiny bubble at the bottom where the kayaker sat. One end of the kayak held a huge, gossamer-bladed propeller that turned lazily as the kayaker pedaled, while the kayaker rowed with flimsy wings, transparent and iridescent like the wings of a dragonfly.

The wings, I discovered, had complicated linkages; each one could be pulled, twisted, and lifted, allowing each wing to separately beat, rotate, and camber.

"Keep up a steady motion with the propeller," Epiphany told me. "You'll lose all your maneuverability if you let yourself float to a stop. You can scull with the wings to put on a burst of speed if you need to. Once you're comfortable, use the wings to rise up or swoop down, and to maneuver. You'll have fun."

We were in a launching bay, a balcony protruding from the side of the city. Four of the human-powered dirigibles that they called kayaks were docked against the blister, the bulge of the cockpits neatly inserted into docking rings so that the pilots could enter the dirigible without exposure to the outside atmosphere. Looking out across the cloudscape, I could see dozens of kayaks dancing around the city like transparent squid with stubby wings, playing tag with each other and racing across the sky. So small and transparent compared to the magnificent clouds, they had been invisible until I'd known how to look.

"What about altitude?" I asked.

"You're about neutrally buoyant," she said. "As long as you have airspeed, you can use the wings to make fine adjustments up or down."

"What happens if I get too low?"

"You can't get too low. The envelope has a reservoir of methanol; as you get lower, the temperature rises and your reservoir releases vapor, so the envelope inflates. If you gain too much altitude, vapor condenses out. So you'll find you're regulated to stay pretty close to the altitude you're set for, which right now is," she checked a meter, "fifty-two kilometers above local ground level. We're blowing west at a hundred meters per second, so local ground level will change as the terrain below varies; check your meters for altimetry."

Looking downward, nothing was visible at all, only clouds, and below the clouds, an infinity of haze. It felt odd to think of the surface, over fifty kilometers straight down, and even odder to think that the city we were inside was speeding across that invisible landscape at hundreds of kilometers an hour. There was only the laziest feeling of motion, as the city drifted slowly through the ever-changing canyons of clouds

"Watch out for wind shear," she said. "It can take you out of sight of the city pretty quickly, if you let it. Ride the conveyor back if you get tired."

"The conveyor?"

"Horizontal-axis vortices. They roll from west to east, and east to west. Choose the right altitude, and they'll take you wherever you want to go."

Now that she'd told me, I could see the kayakers surfing the wind-shear, rising upward and skimming across the sky on invisible wheels of air.

"Have fun," she said. She helped me into the gondola, tightened my straps, looked at the gas pressure meter, checked the purge valve on the emergency oxygen supply, and verified that the radio, backup radio, and emergency locator beacons worked.

Across the kayak launch bay, Leah and Carlos Fernando had already pushed off. Carlos was sculling his wings alternatingly with a practiced swishing motion, building up a pendulum-like oscillation from side to side. Even as I watched, his little craft rolled over until for a moment it hesitated, inverted, and then rolled completely around.

"Showing off," Epiphany said, disdainfully. "You're not supposed to do that.

Not that anybody would dare correct him."

She turned back to me. "Ready?" she asked.

"Ready as I'm going to be," I said. I'd been given a complete safety briefing that explained the backup systems and the backups to the backups, but still, floating in the sky above a fifty-two-kilometer drop into the landscape of hell seemed an odd diversion.

"Go!" she said. She checked the seal on the cockpit, and then with one hand she released the docking clamp.

Freed from its mooring, the kayak sprang upward into the sky. As I'd been instructed, I banked the kayak away from the city. The roll made me feel suddenly giddy. The kayak skittered, sliding around until it was moving sideways to the air, the nose dipping down so that I was hanging against my straps. Coordinate the turn, I thought, but every slight motion I made with the wings seemed amplified drunkenly, and the kayak wove around erratically.

The radio blinked at me, and Epiphany's voice said, "You're doing great. Give it some airspeed."

I wasn't doing great; I was staring straight down at lemon-tinted haze and spinning slowly around like a falling leaf. Airspeed? I realize that I had entirely forgotten to pedal. I pedaled now, and the nose lifted. The sideways spin damped out, and as I straightened out, the wings bit into the air. "Great," Epiphany's voice told me. "Keep it steady."

The gas envelope seemed too fragile to hold me, but I was flying now, suspended below a golden sky. It was far too complicated, but I realized that as long as I kept the nose level, I could keep it under control. I was still oscillating slightly—it was difficult to avoid overcontroling—but on the average, I was keeping the nose pointed where I aimed it.

Where were Leah and Carlos Fernando?

I looked around. Each of the kayaks had different markings—mine was marked with gray stripes like a tabby cat—and I tried to spot theirs.

A gaggle of kayaks was flying together, rounding the pylon of the city. As they moved around the pylon they all turned at once, flashing in the sunlight like a school of fish suddenly startled.

Suddenly I spotted them, not far above me, close to the looming wall of the city; the royal purple envelope of Carlos Fernando's kayak and the blue and yellow stripes of Leah's. Leah was circling in a steady climb, and Carlos Fernando was darting around her, now coming in fast and bumping envelopes, now darting away and pulling up, hovering for a moment with his nose pointed at the sky, then skewing around and sliding back downward.

Their motions looked like the courtship dance of birds.

The purple kayak banked around and swooped out and away from the city; and an instant later, Leah's blue and yellow kayak banked and followed. They both soared upward, catching a current of air invisible to me. I could see a few of the other fliers surfing on the same updraft. I yawed my nose around to follow them, but made no progress; I was too inexperienced with the kayak to be able to guess the air currents, and the wind differential was blowing me around the city in exactly the opposite of the direction I wanted to go. I pulled out and away from the city, seeking a different wind, and for an instant I caught a glimpse of something in the clouds below me, dark and fast moving.

Then I caught the updraft. I could feel it, the wings caught the air and it felt like an invisible giant's hand picking me up and carrying me—

Then there was a sudden noise, a stuttering and ripping, followed by a sound like a snare drum. My left wing and propeller ripped away, the fragments spraying into the sky. My little craft banked hard to the left. My radio came to life, but I couldn't hear anything as the cabin disintegrated around me. I was falling.

Falling.

For a moment I felt like I was back in zero-gee. I clutched uselessly to the remains of the control surfaces, connected by loose cords to fluttering pieces of debris. Pieces of my canopy floated away and were caught by the wind and spun upward and out of sight. The atmosphere rushed in, and my eyes started to burn. I made the mistake of taking a breath, and the effect was like getting kicked in the head. Flickering purple dots, the colors of a bruise, closed in from all directions. My vision narrowed to a single bright tunnel. The air was liquid fire in my lungs. I reached around, desperately, trying to remember the emergency instructions before I blacked out, and my hands found the emergency air-mask between my legs. I was still strapped into my seat, although the seat was no longer attached to a vehicle, and I slapped the breathing mask against my face and sucked hard to start the airflow from the emergency oxygen. I was lucky; the oxygen cylinder was still attached to the bottom of the seat, as the seat, with me in it, tumbled through the sky. Through blurred eyes, I could see the city spinning above me. I tried to think of what the emergency procedure could be and what I should do next, but I could only think of what had gone wrong. What had I done? For the life of me I couldn't think of anything that I could have done that would have ripped the craft apart.

The city dwindled to the size of an acorn, and then I fell into the cloud layer and everything disappeared into a pearly white haze. My skin began to itch all over. I squeezed my eyes shut against the acid fog. The temperature was rising. How long would it take to fall fifty kilometers to the surface?

Something enormous and metallic swooped down from above me, and I blacked out.

Minutes or hours or days later I awoke in a dimly lit cubicle. I was lying on the ground, and two men wearing masks were spraying me with jets of a foaming white liquid that looked like milk but tasted bitter. My flight suit was in shreds around me.

I sat up, and began to cough uncontrollably. My arms and my face itched like blazes, but when I started to scratch, one of the men reached out and slapped my hands away.

"Don't scratch."

I turned to look at him, and the one behind me grabbed me by the hair and smeared a handful of goo into my face, rubbing it hard into my eyes.

Then he picked up a patch of cloth and tossed it to me. "Rub this where it itches. It should help."

I was still blinking, my face dripping, my vision fuzzy. The patch of cloth was wet with some gelatinous slime. I grabbed it from him, and dabbed it on my arms and then rubbed it in. It did help, some.

"Thanks," I said. "What the hell—"

The two men in face masks looked at each other. "Acid burn," the taller man said. "You're not too bad. A minute or two of exposure won't leave scars."

"What?"

"Acid. You were exposed to the clouds."

"Right."

Now that I wasn't quite so distracted, I looked around. I was in the cargo hold of some sort of aircraft. There were two small round portholes on either side. Although nothing was visible through them but a blank white, I could feel that the vehicle was in motion. I looked at the two men. They were both rough characters. Unlike the brightly colored spider-silk gowns of the citizens of Hypatia, they were dressed in clothes that were functional but not fancy, jumpsuits of a dark gray color with no visible insignia. Both of them were fit and well-muscled. I couldn't see their faces, since they were wearing breathing masks and lightweight helmets, but under their masks I could see that they both wore short beards, another fashion that had been missing among the citizens of Hypatia. Their eyes were covered with amber-tinted goggles, made in a crazy style that cupped each eye with a piece that was rounded like half an eggshell, apparently stuck to their faces by some invisible glue. It gave them a strange, bug-eyed look. They looked at me, but behind their face masks and google-eyes I was completely unable to read their expression.

"Thanks," I said. "So, who are you? Some sort of emergency rescue force?"

"I think you know who we are," the taller one said. "The question is, who the hell are you?"

I stood up and reached out a hand, thinking to introduce myself, but both of the men took a step back. Without seeming to move his hand, the taller one now had a gun, a tiny omniblaster of some kind. Suddenly a lot of things were clear.

"You're pirates," I said.

"We're the Venus underground," he said. "We don't like the word pirates very much. Now, if you don't mind, I have a question, and I really would like an answer. Who the hell are you?"

So I told him.

The first man started to take off his helmet, but the taller pirate stopped him. "We'll keep the masks on, for now. Until we decide he's safe." The taller pirate said he was named Esteban Jaramillo; the shorter one Esteban Francisco. That was too many Estebans, I thought, and decided to tag the one Jaramillo and the other Francisco.

I discovered from them that not everybody in the floating cities thought of Venus as a paradise. Some of the independent cities considered the clan of Nordwald-Gruenbaum to be well on its way to becoming a dictatorship. "They own half of Venus outright, but that's not good enough for them, no, oh no," Jaramillo told me. "They're stinking rich, but not stinking rich enough, and the very idea that there are free cities floating in the sky, cities that don't swear fealty to them and pay their goddamned taxes, that pisses them off. They'll do anything that they can to crush us. Us? We're just fighting back."

I would have been more inclined to see his point if I didn't have the uncomfortable feeling that I'd just been abducted. It had been a tremendous stroke of luck for me that their ship had been there to catch me when my kayak broke apart and fell. I didn't much believe in luck. And they didn't bother to answer when I asked about being returned to Hypatia. It was pretty clear that the direction we were headed was not back toward the city.

I had given them my word that I wouldn't fight, or try to escape—where would I escape to?—and they accepted it. Once they realized that I wasn't who they had expected to capture, they pressed me for news of the outside. "We don't hear a lot of outside news."

There were three of them in the small craft, the two Estebans, and the pilot, who was never introduced. He did not bother to turn around to greet me, and all I ever saw of him was the back of his helmet. The craft itself they called a manta; an odd thing that was partly an airplane, partly dirigible, and partly a submarine. Once I'd given my word that I wouldn't escape, I was allowed to look out, but there was nothing to see but a luminous golden haze.

"We keep the manta flying under the cloud decks," Jaramillo said. "Keeps us invisible."

"Invisible from whom?" I asked, but neither one of them bothered to answer. It was a dumb question anyway; I could very well guess who they wanted to keep out of sight of. "What about radar?" I said.

Esteban looked at Esteban, and then at me. "We have means to deal with radar," he said. "Just leave it at that and stop it with the questions you should know enough not to ask."

They seemed to be going somewhere, and eventually the manta exited the cloudbank into the clear air above. I pressed toward the porthole, trying to see out. The cloudscapes of Venus were still fascinating to me. We were skimming the surface of the cloud deck—ready to duck under if there were any sign of watchers, I surmised. From the cloudscape it was impossible to tell how far we'd come, whether it was just a few leagues, or halfway around the planet. None of the floating cities were visible, but in the distance I spotted the fat torpedo shape of a dirigible. The pilot saw it as well, for we banked toward it and sailed slowly up, slowing down as we approached, until it disappeared over our heads, and then the hull resonated with a sudden impact, and then a ratcheting clang.

"Soft dock," Jaramillo commented, and then a moment later another clang, and the nose of the craft was suddenly jerked up. "Hard dock," he said. The two Estebans seemed to relax a little, and a whine and a rumble filled the little cabin. We were being winched up into the dirigible.

After ten minutes or so, we came to rest in a vast interior space. The manta had been taken inside the envelope of the gas chamber, I realized. Half a dozen people met us.

"Sorry," Jaramillo said, "but I'm afraid we're going to have to blind you. Nothing personal."

"Blind?" I said, but actually, that was good news. If they'd had no intention to release me, they wouldn't care what I saw.

Jaramillo held my head steady while Francisco placed a set of the google-eyed glasses over my eyes. They were surprisingly comfortable. Whatever held them in place, they were so light that I could scarcely feel that they were there. The amber tint was barely noticeable. After checking that they fit, Francisco tapped the side of the goggles with his fingertip, once, twice, three times, four times. Each time he touched the goggles, the world grew darker, and with a fifth tap, all I could see was inky black. Why would sunglasses have a setting for complete darkness, I thought? And then I answered my own question: the last setting must be for e-beam welding. Pretty convenient, I thought. I wondered if I dared to ask them if I could keep the set of goggles when they were done.

"I am sure you won't be so foolish as to adjust the transparency," one of the Estebans said.

I was guided out the manta's hatch and across the hanger, and then to a seat.

"This the prisoner?" a voice asked.

"Yeah," Jaramillo said. "But the wrong one. No way to tell, but we guessed wrong, got the wrong flyer."

"Shit. So who is he?"

"Technician," Jaramillo said. "From the up and out."

"Really? So does he know anything about the Nordwald-Gruenbaum plan?"

I spread my hands out flat, trying to look harmless. "Look, I only met the kid twice, or I guess three times, if you—"

That caused some consternation; I could hear sudden buzz of voices, in a language I didn't recognize. I wasn't sure how many of them there were, but it seemed like at least half a dozen. I desperately wished I could see them, but that would very likely be a fatal move. After a moment, Jaramillo said, his voice now flat and expressionless, "You know the heir of Nordwald-Gruenbaum? You met Carlos Fernando in person?"

"I met him. I don't know him. Not really."

"Who did you say you were again?"

I went through my story, this time starting at the very beginning, explaining how we had been studying the ecology of Mars, how we had been summoned to Venus to meet the mysterious Carlos Fernando. From time to time I was interrupted to answer questions—what was my relationship with Leah Hamakawa? (I wished I knew.) Were we married? Engaged? (No. No.) What was Carlos Fernando's relationship with Dr. Hamakawa? (I wished I knew.) Had Carlos Fernando ever mentioned his feelings about the independent cities? (No.) His plans? (No.) Why was Carlos Fernando interested in terraforming (I don't know.) What was Carlos Fernando planning? (I don't know.) Why did Carlos Fernando bring Hamakawa to Venus? (I wished I knew.) What was he planning? What was he planning? (I don't know. I don't know.)

The more I talked, the more sketchy it seemed, even to me.

There was silence when I had finished talking. Then, the first voice said, take him back to the manta.

I was led back inside and put into a tiny space, and a door clanged shut behind me. After a while, when nobody answered my call, I reached up to the goggles. They popped free with no more than a light touch, and, looking at them, I was still unable to see how they attached. I was in a storage hold of some sort. The door was locked.

I contemplated my situation, but I couldn't see that I knew any more now than I had before, except that I now knew that not all of the Venus cities were content with the status quo, and some of them were willing to go to some lengths to change it. They had deliberately shot me down, apparently thinking that I was Leah—or possibly even hoping for Carlos Fernando? It was hard to think that he would have been out of the protection of his bodyguards. Most likely, I decided, the bodyguards had been there, never letting him out of sight, ready to swoop in if needed, but while Carlos Fernando and Leah had soared up and around the city, I had left the sphere covered by the guards, and that was the opportunity the pirates in the manta had taken. They had seen the air kayak flying alone and shot it out of the sky, betting my life on their skill, that they could swoop in and snatch the falling pilot out of midair.

They could have killed me, I realized.

And all because they thought I knew something—or rather, that Leah Hamakawa knew something—about Carlos Fernando's mysterious plan.

What plan? He was a twelve-year-old kid, not even a teenager, barely more than an overgrown child! What kind of plan could a kid have?

I examined the chamber I was in, this time looking more seriously at how it was constructed. All the joints were welded, with no obvious gaps, but the metal was light, probably an aluminum-lithium alloy. Possibly malleable, if I had the time, if I could find a place to pry at, if I could find something to pry with.

If I did manage to escape, would I be able pilot the manta out of its hanger in the dirigible? Maybe. I had no experience with lighter-than-air vehicles, though, and it would be a bad time to learn, especially if they decided that they wanted to shoot at me. And then I would be—where? A thousand miles from anywhere. Fifty million miles from anywhere I knew.

I was still mulling this over when Esteban and Esteban returned.

"Strap in," Esteban Jaramillo told me. "Looks like we're taking you home."

The trip back was more complicated than the trip out. It involved two or more transfers from vehicle to vehicle, during some of which I was again "requested" to wear the opaque goggles.

We were alone in the embarking station of some sort of public transportation. For a moment, the two Estebans had allowed me to leave the goggles transparent. Wherever we were, it was unadorned, drab compared to the florid excess of Hypatia, where even the bus stations—did they have bus stations?—would have been covered with flourishes and artwork.

Jaramillo turned to me and, for the first time, pulled off his goggles so he could look me directly in the eye. His eyes were dark, almost black, and very serious,

"Look," he said, "I know you don't have any reason to like us. We've got our reasons, you have to believe that. We're desperate. We know that his father had some secret projects going. We don't know what they were, but we know he didn't have any use for the free cities. We think the young Gruenbaum has something planned. If you can get through to Carlos Fernando, we want to talk to him."

"If you get him," Esteban Francisco said, "push him out a window. We'll catch him. Easy." He was grinning with a broad smile, showing all his teeth, as if to say he wasn't serious, but I wasn't at all sure he was joking.

"We don't want to kill him. We just want to talk," Esteban Jaramillo said. "Call us. Please. Call us."

And with that, he reached up and put his goggles back on. Then Francisco reached over and tapped my goggles into opacity, and everything was dark, and, with one on either side of me, we boarded the transport—bus? zeppelin? rocket?

Finally I was led into a chamber and was told to wait for two full minutes before removing the goggles, and after that I was free to do as I liked.

It was only after the footsteps had disappeared that it occurred to me to wonder how I was supposed to contact them, if I did have a reason to. It was too late to ask, though; I was alone, or seemed to be alone.

Was I being watched to see if I would follow orders, I wondered? Two full minutes. I counted, trying not to rush the count. When I got to a hundred and twenty, I took a deep breath, and finger-tapped the goggles to transparency.

When my eyes focused, I saw I was in a large disembarking lounge with genetically engineered pink grass and sculptures of iron and of jade. I recognized it. It was the very same lounge at which we had arrived at Venus three days ago—was it only three? Or had another day gone by?

I was back in Hypatia City.

Once again I was surrounded and questioned. As with the rest of Carlos Fernando's domain, the questioning room was lushly decorated with silk-covered chairs and elegant teak carvings, but it was clearly a holding chamber.

The questioning was by four women, Carlos Fernando's guards, and I had the feeling that they would not hesitate to tear me apart if they thought I was being less than candid with them. I told them what had happened, and at every step they asked questions, making suggestions as to what I could have done differently. Why had I taken my kayak so far away from any of the other fliers and out away from the city? Why had I allowed myself to be captured, without fighting? Why didn't I demand to be returned and refuse to answer any questions? Why could I describe none of the rebels I'd met, except for two men who had—as far as they could tell from my descriptions—no distinctive features?

At the end of their questioning, when I asked to see Carlos Fernando, they told me that this would not be possible.

"You think I allowed myself to be shot down deliberately?" I said, addressing myself to the chief among the guards, a lean woman in scarlet silk.

"We don't know what to think, Mr. Tinkerman," she said. "We don't like to take chances."

"What now, then?"

"We can arrange transport to the built worlds," she said. "Or even to the Earth."

"I don't plan to leave without Doctor Hamakawa," I said.

She shrugged. "At the moment, that's still your option, yes," she said. "At the moment."

"How can I get in contact with Doctor Hamakawa?"

She shrugged. "If Doctor Hamakawa wishes, I'm sure she will be able to contact you."

"And if I want to speak to her?"

She shrugged. "You're free to go now. If we need to talk to you, we can find you."

I had been wearing one of the gray jumpsuits of the pirates when I'd been returned to Hypatia; the guard women had taken that away. Now they gave me a suit of spider-silk in a lavender brighter than the garb an expensive courtesan would wear in the built worlds surrounding Earth, more of an evening gown than a suit. It was nevertheless subdued compared to the day-to-day attire of Hypatia citizens, and I attracted no attention. I discovered that the google-eyed sunglasses had been neatly placed in a pocket at the knees of the garment. Apparently people on Venus keep their sunglasses at their knees. Convenient when you're sitting, I supposed. They hadn't been recognized as a parting gift from the pirates, or, more likely, had been considered so trivial as to not be worth confiscating. I was unreasonably pleased; I liked those glasses.

I found the Singh habitat with no difficulty, and when I arrived, Epiphany and Truman Singh were there to welcome me and to give me the news.

My kidnapping was already old news. More recent news was being discussed everywhere.

Carlos Fernando Delacroix Ortega de la Jolla y Nordwald-Gruenbaum had given a visitor from the outer solar system, Doctor Leah Hamakawa—a person who (they had heard) had actually been born on Earth—a rock.

And she had not handed it back to him.

My head was swimming.

"You're saying that Carlos Fernando is proposing marriage? To Leah? That doesn't make any sense. He's a kid, for Jove's sake. He's not old enough."

Truman and Epiphany Singh looked at one another and smiled. "How old were you when we got married?" Truman asked her. "Twenty?"

"I was almost twenty-one before you accepted my book and my rock," she said.

"So, in Earth years, what's that?" he said. "Thirteen?"

"A little over twelve," she said. "About time I was married up, I'd say."

"Wait," I said. "You said you were twelve years old when you got married?"

"Earth years," she said. "Yes, that's about right."

"You married at twelve? And you had—" I suddenly didn't want to ask, and said, "Do all women on Venus marry so young?"

"There are a lot of independent cities" Truman said. "Some of them must have different customs, I suppose. But it's the custom more or less everywhere I know."

"But that's—" I started to say, but couldn't think of how to finish. Sick? Perverted? But then, there were once a lot of cultures on Earth that had child marriages.

"We know the outer reaches have different customs," Epiphany said. "Other regions do things differently. The way we do it works for us."

"A man typically marries up at age twenty-one or so," Truman explained. "Say, twelve, thirteen years old, in Earth years. Maybe eleven. His wife will be about fifty or sixty—she'll be his instructor, then, as he grows up. What's that in Earth years—thirty? I know that in old Earth custom, both sides of a marriage are supposed to be the same age, but that's completely silly, is it not? Who's going to be the teacher, I should say?

"And then, when he grows up, by the time he reaches sixty or so he'll marry down, find a girl who's about twenty or twenty-one, and he'll serve as a teacher to her, I should say. And, in time, she'll marry down when she's sixty, and so on."

It seemed like a form of ritualized child abuse to me, but I thought it would be better not to say that aloud. Or, I thought, maybe I was reading too much into what he was saying. It was something like the medieval apprentice system. When he said teaching, maybe I was jumping to conclusions to think that he was talking about sex. Maybe they held off on the sex until the child grew up some. I thought I might be happier not knowing.

"A marriage is braided like a rope," Epiphany said. "Each element holds the next."

I looked from Truman to Epiphany and back. "You, too?" I asked Truman. "You were married when you were twelve?"

"In Earth years, I was thirteen, when I married up Triolet," he said. "Old. Best thing that ever happened to me. God, I needed somebody like her to straighten me out back then. And I needed somebody to teach me about sex, I should say, although I didn't know it back then."

"And Triolet—"

"Oh, yes, and her husband before her, and before that. Our marriage goes back a hundred and ninety years, to when Raj Singh founded our family; we're a long braid, I should say."

I could picture it now. Every male in the braid would have two wives, one twenty years older; one twenty years younger. And every female would have an older and a younger husband. The whole assembly would indeed be something you could think of as a braid, alternating down generations. The interpersonal dynamics must be terribly complicated. And then I suddenly remembered why we were having this discussion. "My god," I said. "You're serious about this. So you're saying that Carlos Fernando isn't just playing a game. He actually plans to marry Leah."

"Of course," Epiphany said. "It's a surprise, but then, I'm not at all surprised. It's obviously what His Excellency was planning right from the beginning. He's a devious one, he is."

"He wants to have sex with her."

She looked surprised. "Well, yes, of course. Wouldn't you? If you were twenty— I mean, twelve years old? Sure you're interested in sex. Weren't you? It's about time His Excellency had a teacher." She paused a moment. "I wonder if she's any good? Earth people—she probably never had a good teacher of her own."

That was a subject I didn't want to pick up on. Our little fling on Mars seemed a long way away, and my whole body ached just thinking of it.

"Sex, it's all that young kids think of," Truman cut in. "Sure. But for all that, I should say that sex is the least important part of a braid. A braid is a business, Mr. Tinkerman, you should know that. His Excellency Carlos Fernando is required to marry up into a good braid. The tradition, and the explicit terms of the inheritance, are both very clear. There are only about five braids on Venus that meet the standards of the trust, and he's too closely related to half of them to be able to marry in. Everybody has been assuming he would marry the wife of the Telios Delacroix braid; she's old enough to marry down now, and she's not related to him closely enough to matter. His proposition to Doctor Hamakawa—yes, that has everybody talking."

I was willing to grasp at any chance. "You mean, his marriage needs to be approved? He can't just marry anybody he likes?"

Truman Singh shook his head. "Of course he can't! I just told you. This is business as well as propagating the genes for the next thousand years. Most certainly he can't marry just anybody."

"But I think he just outmaneuvered them all," Epiphany added. "They thought they had him boxed in, didn't they? But they never thought that he'd go find an outworlder."

"They?" I said. "Who's they?"

"They never thought to guard against that," Epiphany continued.

"But he can't marry her, right?" I said. "For sure, she's not of the right family. She's not of any family. She's an orphan, she told me that. The institute is her only family."

Truman shook his head. "I think Epiphany's right," he said. "He just may have outfoxed them, I should say. If she's not of a family, doesn't have the dozens or hundreds of braided connections that everybody here must have, that means they can't find anything against her."

"Her scientific credentials—I bet they won't be able to find a flaw there." Epiphany said. "And, an orphan? That's brilliant. Just brilliant. No family ties at all. I bet he knew that. He worked hard to find just the right candidate, you can bet." She shook her head, smiling. "And we all thought he'd be another layabout, like his father."

"This is awful," I said. "I've got to do something."

"You? You're far too old for Dr. Hayakawa." Epiphany looked at me apprais-ingly. "A good looking man, though—if I were ten, fifteen years younger, I'd give you another look. I have cousins with girls the right age. You're not married, you say?"

Outside the Singh quarters in sector Carbon, the sun was breaking the horizon as the city blew into the daylit hemisphere.

I hadn't been sure whether Epiphany's offer to find me a young girl had been genuine, but it was not what I needed, and I'd refused as politely as I could manage.

I had gone outside to think, or as close to "outside" as the floating city allowed, where all the breathable gas was inside the myriad bubbles. But what could I do? If it was a technical problem, I would be able to solve it, but this was a human problem, and that had always been my weakness.

From where I stood, I could walk to the edge of the world, the transparent gas envelope that held the breathable air in, and kept the carbon dioxide of the Venus atmosphere out. The sun was surrounded by a gauzy haze of thin high cloud, and encircled by a luminous golden halo, with mock suns flying in formation to the left and the right. The morning sunlight slanted across the cloudtops. My eyes hurt from the direct sun. I remembered the sun goggles in my knee pocket, and pulled them out. I pressed them onto my eyes, and tapped on the right side until the world was a comfortable dim.

Floating in the air, in capital letters barely darker than the background, were the words LINK: READY.

I turned my head, and the words shifted with my field of view, changing from dark letters to light depending on the background.

A communications link was open? Certainly not a satellite relay; the glasses couldn't have enough power to punch through to orbit. Did it mean the manta was hovering in the clouds below?

"Hello, hello," I said, talking to the air. "Testing. Testing?"

Nothing.

Perhaps it wasn't audio. I tapped the right lens: dimmer, dimmer, dark; then back to full transparency. Maybe the other side? I tried tapping the left eye of the goggle, and a cursor appeared in my field of view.

With a little experimentation, I found that tapping allowed input in the form of Gandy-encoded text. It seemed to be a low bit-rate text only; the link power must be miniscule. But Gandy was a standard encoding, and I tapped out "CQ CQ."

Seek you, seek you.

The LINK: READY message changed to a light green, and in a moment the words changed to HERE.

WHO, I tapped.

MANTA 7, was the reply. NEWS?

CF PROPOSED LH, I tapped. !

KNOWN, came the reply. MORE?

NO

OK. SIGNING OUT.

The LINK: READY message returned.

A com link, if I needed one. But I couldn't see how it helped me any.

I returned to examining the gas envelope. Where I stood was an enormous transparent pane, a square perhaps ten meters on an edge. I was standing near the bottom of the pane, where it abutted to the adjacent sheet with a joint of very thin carbon. I pressed on it, and felt it flex slightly. It couldn't be more than a millimeter thick; it would make sense to make the envelope no heavier than necessary. I tapped it with the heel of my hand, and could feel it vibrate; a resonant frequency of a few Hertz, I estimated. The engineering weak point would be the joint between panels: if the pane flexed enough, it would pop out from its mounting at the join.

Satisfied that I had solved at least one technical conundrum, I began to contemplate what Epiphany had said. Carlos Fernando was to have married the wife of the Telios Delacroix braid. Whoever she was, she might be relieved at discovering Carlos Fernando making other plans; she could well think the arranged marriage as much a trap as he apparently did. But still. Who was she, and what did she think of Carlos Fernando's new plan?

The guards had made it clear that I was not to communicate with Carlos Fernando or Leah, but had no instructions forbidding access to Braid Telios Delacroix.

The household seemed to be a carefully orchestrated chaos of children and adults of all ages, but now that I understood the Venus societal system a little, it made more sense. The wife of Telios Delacroix—once the wife-apparent of His Excellency Carlos Fernando—turned out to be a woman only a few years older than I was, with closely cropped gray hair. I realized I'd seen her before. At the banquet, she had been the woman sitting next to Carlos Fernando. She introduced herself as Miranda Telios Delacroix and introduced me to her up-husband, a stocky man perhaps sixty years old.

"We could use a young husband in this family," he told me. "Getting old, we are, and you can't count on children—they just go off and get married themselves."

There were two girls there, who Miranda Delacroix introduced as their two children. They were quiet, attempting to disappear into the background, smiling brightly but with their heads bowed to the ground, looking up at me through lowered eyelashes when they were brought out to be introduced. After the adults' attention had turned away from them, I noticed both of them surreptitiously studying me. A day ago I wouldn't even have noticed.

"Now, either come and sit nicely and talk, or else go do your chores," Miranda told them. "I'm sure the outworlder is quite bored with your buzzing in and out."

They both giggled and shook their heads and then disappeared into another room, although from time to time one or the other head would silently pop out to look at me, disappearing instantly if I turned my head to look

We sat down at a low table that seemed to be made out of oak. Her husband brought in some coffee and then left us alone. The coffee was made in the Thai style, in a clear cup, in layers with thick sweet milk.

"So you are Doctor Hamakawa's friend," she said. "I've heard a lot about you. Do you mind my asking, what exactly is your relationship with Doctor Hamakawa?"

"I would like to see her," I said.

She frowned. "So?"

"And I can't."

She raised an eyebrow.

"He has these woman, these bodyguards—"

Miranda Delacroix laughed. "Ah, I see! Oh, my little Carli is just too precious for words. I can't believe he's jealous. I do think that this time he's really infatuated." She tapped on the tabletop with her fingers for a moment, and I realized that the oak tabletop was another one of the embedded computer systems. "Goodness, Carli is not yet the owner of everything, and I don't see why you shouldn't see whomever you like. I've sent a message to Doctor Hamakawa that you would like to see her."

"Thank you."

She waved her hand.

It occurred to me that Carlos Fernando was about the same age as her daughters, perhaps even a classmate of theirs. She must have known him since he was a baby. It did seem a little unfair to him—if they were married, she would have all the advantage, and for a moment I understood his dilemma. Then something she had said struck me.

"He's not yet owner of everything, you said," I said. "I don't understand your customs, Mrs. Delacroix. Please enlighten me. What do you mean, yet?"

"Well, you know that he doesn't come into his majority until he's married," she said.

The picture was beginning to make sense. Carlos Fernando desperately wanted to control things, I thought. And he needed to be married to do it. "And once he's married?"

"Then he comes into his inheritance, of course," she said. "But since he'll be married, the braid will be in control of the fortune. You wouldn't want a twenty-one-year-old kid in charge of the entire Nordwald-Gruenbaum holdings? That would be ruinous. The first Nordwald knew that. That's why he married his son into the la Jolla braid. That's the way it's always been done."

"I see," I said. If Miranda Delacroix married Carlos Fernando, she—not he—would control the Nordwald-Gruenbaum fortune. She had the years of experience, she knew the politics, how the system worked. He would be the child in the relationship. He would always be the child in the relationship.

Miranda Delacroix had every reason to want to make sure that Leah Hamakawa didn't marry Carlos Fernando. She was my natural ally.

And also, she—and her husband—had every reason to want to kill Leah Hamakawa.

Suddenly the guards that followed Carlos Fernando seemed somewhat less of an affectation. Just how good were the bodyguards? And then I had another thought. Had she, or her husband, hired the pirates to shoot down my kayak? The pirates clearly had been after Leah, not me. They had known that Leah was flying a kayak; somebody must have been feeding them information. If it hadn't been her, then who?

I looked at her with new suspicions. She was looking back at me with a steady gaze. "Of course, if your Doctor Leah Hamakawa intends to accept the proposal, the two of them will be starting a new braid. She would nominally be the senior, of course, but I wonder—"

"But would she be allowed to?" I interrupted. "If she decided to marry Carlos Fernando, wouldn't somebody stop her?"

She laughed. "No, I'm afraid that little Carli made his plan well. He's the child of a Gruenbaum, all right. There's no legal grounds for the families to object; she may be an outworlder, but he's made an end run around all the possible objections."

"And you?"

"Do you think I have choices? If he decides to ask me for advice, I'll tell him it's not a good idea. But I'm halfway tempted to just see what he does."

And give up her chance to be the richest woman in the known universe? I had my doubts.

"Do you think you can talk her out of it?" she said. "Do you think you have something to offer her? As I understand it, you don't own anything. You're hired help, a gypsy of the solar system. Is there a single thing that Carli is offering her that you can match?"

"Companionship," I said. It sounded feeble, even to me.

"Companionship?" she echoed, sarcastically. "Is that all? I would have thought most outworlder men would have promised love. You are honest, at least, I'll give you that,"

"Yes, love," I said, miserable. "I'd offer her love."

"Love," she said. "Well, how about that. Yes, that's what outworlders marry for; I've read about it. You don't seem to know, do you? This isn't about love. It's not even about sex, although there will be plenty of that, I can assure you, more than enough to turn my little Carlos inside out and make him think he's learning something about love.

"This is about business, Mr. Tinkerman. You don't seem to have noticed that. Not love, not sex, not family. It's business."

Miranda Telios Delacroix's message had gotten through to Leah, and she called me up to her quarters. The women guards did not seem happy about this, but they had apparently been instructed to obey her direct orders, and two red-clad guardswomen led me to her quarters.

"What happened to you? What happened to your face?" she said, when she saw me.

I reached up and touched my face. It didn't hurt, but the acid burns had left behind red splotches and patches of peeling skin. I filled her in on the wreck of the kayak and the rescue, or kidnapping, by pirates. And then I told her about Carlos. "Take another look at that book he gave you. I don't know where he got it, and I don't want to guess what it cost, but I'll say it's a sure bet it's no facsimile."

"Yes, of course." she said. "He did tell me, eventually."

"Don't you know it's a proposition?"

"Yes; the egg, the book, and the rock," she said. "Very traditional here. I know you like to think I have my head in the air all the time, but I do pay some attention to what's going on around me. Carli is a sweet kid."

"He's serious, Leah. You can't ignore him."

She waved me off. "I can make my own decisions, but thanks for the warnings."

"It's worse than that," I told her. "Have you met Miranda Telios Delacroix?"

"Of course," she said.

"I think she's trying to kill you." I told her about my experience with kayaks, and my suspicion that the pirates had been hired to shoot me down, thinking I was her.

"I believe you may be reading too much into things, Tinkerman," she said. "Carli told me about the pirates. They're a small group, disaffected; they bother shipping and such, from time to time, but he says that they're nothing to worry about. When he gets his inheritance, he says he will take care of them."

"Take care of them? How?"

She shrugged. "He didn't say."

But that was exactly what the pirates—rebels—had told me: that Carlos had a plan, and they didn't know what it was. "So he has some plans he isn't telling," I said.

"He's been asking me about terraforming," Leah said, thinking. "But it doesn't make sense to do that on Venus. I don't understand what he's thinking. He could split the carbon dioxide atmosphere into oxygen and carbon; I know he has the technology to do that."

"He does?"

"Yes, I think you were there when he mentioned it. The molecular still. It's solar-powered micromachines. But what would be the point?"

"So he's serious?"

"Seriously thinking about it, anyway. But it doesn't make any sense. Nearly pure oxygen at the surface, at sixty or seventy bars? That atmosphere would be even more deadly than the carbon dioxide. And it wouldn't even solve the greenhouse effect; with that thick an atmosphere, even oxygen is a greenhouse gas."

"You explained that to him?"

"He already knew it. And the floating cities wouldn't float any more. They rely on the gas inside—breathing air—being lighter than the Venusian air. Turn the Venus carbon dioxide to pure O_2, the cities fall out of the sky."

"But?"

"But he didn't seem to care."

"So terraforming would make Venus uninhabitable, and he knows it. So what's he planning?"

She shrugged. "I don't know."

"I do," I said. "And I think we'd better see your friend Carlos Fernando."

Carlos Fernando was in his playroom.

The room was immense. His family's quarters were built on the edge of the upcity, right against the bubble-wall, and one whole side of his playroom looked out across the cloudscape. The room was littered with stuff: sets of interlocking toy blocks with electronic modules inside that could be put together into elaborate buildings, models of spacecraft and various lighter-than-air aircraft, no doubt vehicles used on Venus, a contraption of transparent vessels connected by tubes that seemed to be a half-completed science project, a unicycle that sat in a corner, silently balancing on its gyros. Between the toys were pieces of light, transparent furniture. I picked up a chair, and it was no heavier than a feather, barely there at all. I knew what it was now, diamond fibers that had been engineered into a foamed, fractal structure. Diamond was their chief working material; it was something that they could make directly out of the carbon dioxide atmosphere, with no imported raw materials. They were experts in diamond, and it frightened me.

When the guards brought us to the playroom, Carlos Fernando was at the end of the room farthest from the enormous window, his back to the window and to us. He'd known we were coming, of course, but when the guards announced our arrival he didn't turn around, but called behind him "It's okay—I'll be with them in a second."

The two guards left us.

He was gyrating and waving his hands in front of a large screen. On the screen, colorful spaceships flew in three-dimensional projection through the complicated maze of a city that had apparently been designed by Escher, with towers connected by bridges and buttresses. The viewpoint swooped around, chasing some of the spaceships, hiding from others. From time to time bursts of red dots shot forward, blowing the ships out of the sky with colorful explosions as Carlos Fernando shouted "Gotcha!" and "In your eye, dog."

He was dancing with his whole body; apparently the game had some kind of full-body input. As far as I could tell, he seemed to have forgotten entirely that we were there.

I looked around.

Sitting on a padded platform no more than two meters from where we had entered, a lion looked back at me with golden eyes. He was bigger than I was. Next to him, with her head resting on her paws, lay a lioness, and she was watching me as well, her eyes half-open. Her tail twitched once; twice. The lion's mane was so huge that it must have been shampooed and blow-dried.

He opened his mouth and yawned, then rolled onto his side, still watching me.

"They're harmless," Leah said. "Bad-Boy and Knickers. Pets."

Knickers—the female, I assumed—stretched over and grabbed the male lion by the neck. Then she put one paw on the back of his head and began to groom his fur with her tongue.

I was beginning to get a feel for just how different Carlos Fernando's life was from anything I knew.

On the walls closer to where Carlos Fernando was playing his game were several other screens. The one to my left looked like it had a homework problem partially worked out. Calculus, I noted. He was doing a chain-rule differentiation and had left it half-completed where he'd gotten stuck, or bored. Next to it was a visualization of the structure of the atmosphere of Venus. Homework? I looked at it more carefully. If it was homework, he was much more interested in atmospheric science than in math; the map was covered with notes and had half a dozen open windows with details. I stepped forward to read it more closely.

The screen went black.

I turned around, and Carlos Fernando was there, a petulant expression on his face. "That's my stuff," he said. His voice squeaked on the word "stuff." "I don't want you looking at my stuff unless I ask you to, okay?"

He turned to Leah, and his expression changed to something I couldn't quite read. He wanted to kick me out of his room, I thought, but didn't want to make Leah angry; he wanted to keep her approval. "What's he doing here?" he asked her.

She looked at me, and raised her eyebrows.

I wish I knew myself, I thought, but I was in it far enough, I had better say something.

I walked over to the enormous window, and looked out across the clouds. I could see another city, blue with distance, a toy balloon against the golden horizon.

"The environment of Venus is unique," I said. "And to think, your ancestor Udo Nordwald put all this together."

"Thanks," he said. "I mean, I guess I mean thanks. I'm glad you like our city."

"All of the cities," I said. "It's a staggering accomplishment. The genius it must have taken to envision it all, to put together the first floating city; to think of this planet as a haven, a place where millions can live. Or billions—the skies are nowhere near full. Someday even trillions, maybe."

"Yeah," he said. "Really something, I guess."

"Spectacular." I turned around and looked him directly in the eye. "So why do you want to destroy it?"

"What?" Leah said.

Carlos Fernando had his mouth open, and started to say something, but then closed his mouth again. He looked down, and then off to his left, and then to the right. He said, "I... I..." but then broke off.

"I know your plan," I said. "Your micromachines—they'll convert the carbon dioxide to oxygen. And when the atmosphere changes, the cities will be grounded. They won't be lighter than air, won't be able to float any more. You know that, don't you? You want to do it deliberately."

"He can't," Leah said, "it won't work. The carbon would—" and then she broke off. "Diamond," she said. "He's going to turn the excess carbon into diamond."

I reached over and picked up a piece of furniture, one of the foamed-diamond tables. It weighted almost nothing.

"Nanomachinery," I said. "The molecular still you mentioned. You know, somebody once said that the problem with Venus isn't that the surface is too hot. It's just fine up here where the air's as thin as Earth's air. The problem is, the surface is just too darn far below sea level.

"But every ton of atmosphere your molecular machines convert to oxygen, you get a quarter-ton of pure carbon. And the atmosphere is a thousand tons per square meter."

I turned to Carlos Fernando, who still hadn't managed to say anything. His silence was as damning as any confession. "Your machines turn that carbon into diamond fibers, and build upward from the surface. You're going to build a new surface, aren't you—a completely artificial surface. A platform up to the sweet spot, fifty kilometers above the old rock surface. And the air there will be breathable."

At last Carlos found his voice. "Yeah," he said. "Dad came up with the machines, but the idea of using them to build a shell around the whole planet—that idea was mine. It's all mine. It's pretty smart, isn't it? Don't you think it's smart?"

"You can't own the sky," I said, "but you can own the land, can't you? You will have built the land. And all the cities are going to crash. There won't be any dissident cities, because there won't be any cities. You'll own it all. Everybody will have to come to you."

"Yeah," Carlos said. He was smiling now, a big goofy grin. "Sweet, isn't it?" He must have seen my expression, because he said, "Hey, come on. It's not like they were contributing. Those dissident cities are full of nothing but malcontents and pirates."

Leah's eyes were wide. He turned to her and said, "Hey, why shouldn't I? Give me one reason. They shouldn't even be here. It was all my ancestor's idea, the floating city, and they shoved in. They stole his idea, so now I'm going to shut them down. It'll be better my way."

He turned back to me. "Okay, look. You figured out my plan. That's fine, that's great, no problem, okay? You're smarter than I thought you were, I admit it. Now, just, I need you to promise not to tell anybody, okay?"

I shook my head.

"Oh, go away," he said. He turned back to Leah. "Doctor Hamakawa," he said. He got down on one knee, and, staring at the ground, said, "I want you to marry me. Please?"

Leah shook her head, but he was staring at the ground, and couldn't see her. "I'm sorry, Carlos," she said. "I'm sorry."

He was just a kid, in a room surrounded by his toys, trying to talk the adults into seeing things the way he wanted to see them. He finally looked up, his eyes filling with tears. "Please," he said. "I want you to. I'll give you anything. I'll give you whatever you want. You can have everything I own, all of it, the whole planet, everything."

"I'm sorry," Leah repeated. "I'm sorry."

He reached out and picked up something off the floor—a model of a space-ship—and looked at it, pretending to be suddenly interested in it. Then he put it carefully down on a table, picked up another one, and stood up, not looking at us. He sniffled, and wiped his eyes with the back of his hand—apparently forgetting he had the ship model in it—trying to do it casually, as if we wouldn't have noticed that he had been crying.

"Ok," he said. "You can't leave, you know. This guy guessed too much. The plan only works if it's secret, so that the malcontents don't know it's coming, don't prepare for it. You have to stay here. I'll keep you here, I'll—I don't know. Something."

"No," I said. "It's dangerous for Leah here. Miranda already tried to hire pirates to shoot her down once, when she was out in the sky kayak. We have to leave."

Carlos looked up at me, and with sudden sarcasm, said, "Miranda? You're joking. That was me who tipped off the pirates. Me. I thought they'd take you away and keep you. I wish they had."

And then he turned back to Leah. "Please? You'll be the richest person on Venus. You'll be the richest person in the solar system. I'll give it all to you. You'll be able to do anything you want."

"I'm sorry," Leah repeated. "It's a great offer. But no."

At the other end of the room, Carlos' bodyguards were quietly entering. He apparently had some way to summon them silently. The room was filling with them, and their guns were drawn, but not yet pointed.

I backed toward the window, and Leah came with me.

The city had rotated a little, and sunlight was now slanting in through the window. I put my sun goggles on.

"Do you trust me?" I said quietly.

"Of course," Leah said. "I always have."

"Come here."

LINK: READY blinked in the corner of my field of view.

I reached up, casually, and tapped on the side of the left lens. CQ MANTA, I tapped. CQ.

I put my other hand behind me and, hoping I could disguise what I was doing as long as I could, I pushed on the pane, feeling it flex out.

HERE, was the reply.

Push. Push. It was a matter of rhythm. When I found the resonant frequency of the pane, it felt right, it built up, like oscillating a rocking chair, like sex.

I reached out my left hand to hold Leah's hand, and pumped harder on the glass with my right. I was putting my weight into it now, and the panel was bowing visibly with my motion. The window was making a noise now, an infrasonic thrum too deep to hear, but you could feel it. On each swing the pane of the window bowed further outward.

"What are you doing?" Carlos shouted. "Are you crazy?"

The bottom bowed out, and the edge of the pane separated from its frame.

There was a smell of acid and sulfur. The bodyguards ran toward us, but—as I'd hoped—they were hesitant to use their guns, worried that the damaged panel might blow completely out.

The window screeched and jerked, but held, fixed in place by the other joints. The way it was stuck in place left a narrow vertical slit between the window and its frame. I pulled Leah close to me, and shoved myself backwards, against the glass, sliding along against the bowed pane, pushing it outward to widen the opening as much as I could.

As I fell, I kissed her lightly on the edge of the neck.

She could have broken my grip, could have torn herself free.

But she didn't.

"Hold your breath and squeeze your eyes shut," I whispered, as we fell through the opening and into the void, and then with my last breath of air, I said, "I love you."

She said nothing in return. She was always practical, and knew enough not to try to talk when her next breath would be acid. "I love you too," I imagined her saying.

With my free hand, I tapped, MANTA

NEED PICKUP. FAST.

And we fell.

"It wasn't about sex at all," I said. "That's what I failed to understand." We were in the manta, covered with slime, but basically unhurt. The pirates had accomplished their miracle, snatched us out of midair. We had information they needed; and in exchange, they would give us a ride off the planet, back where we belonged, back to the cool and the dark and the emptiness between planets. "It was all about finance. Keeping control of assets."

"Sure it's about sex," Leah said. "Don't fool yourself. We're humans. It's always about sex. Always. You think that's not a temptation? Molding a kid into just exactly what you want? Of course it's sex. Sex and control. Money? That's just the excuse they tell themselves."

"But you weren't tempted," I said.

She looked at me long and hard. "Of course I was." She sighed, and her expression was once again distant, unreadable. "More than you'll ever know."

ITERATION
JOHN KESSEL

John Kessel lives in Raleigh, North Carolina, where he is professor of American literature and creative writing at North Carolina State University. A writer of erudite short fiction that often makes reference to or pastiches popular culture, Kessel received the Nebula Award for the novella "Another Orphan" and for the novelette "Pride and Prometheus." He has published a range of impressive short fiction, including a series of time travel stories featuring character Detlev Gruber (the most recent of which is "It's All True"), and a series of science fiction stories set in the same world as James Tiptree, Jr. Award winner "Stories for Men." Kessel's short fiction has been collected in three volumes, *Meeting in Infinity*, *The Pure Product*, and *The Baum Plan for Financial Independence*, and he has published three novels: *Freedom Beach* (with James Patrick Kelly), *Good News from Outer Space*, and *Corrupting Dr. Nice*. He and Kelly also co-edited the anthology *The Secret History of Science Fiction*, that makes the case for the rapprochement, over the last forty years, of literary and science fiction.

Enzo worked at the checkout in Tyler's Superstore. Tyler's had started life as a grocery but now offered a farmer's market, a bakery, a deli, a butcher shop, aisles of housewares, appliances, tableware, crockery, a pharmacy, a huge wine section, CDs and DVDs, photo reprints, small furniture, an optometrist, and a section for TVs and electronics. The ambient lights were low and soothing, the music bland, the employees, like Enzo, treading water. Enzo would be stuck at Tyler's until the place was driven out of business by some still-more-gargantuan sensorium that sold everything from new spouses to plastic surgery.

Until then he worked checkout.

"Where is the bottled water?" asked a harried woman trailing a crying toddler.

"Over there, ma'am, aisle six, under that big blue sign that says Bottled Water."

She glared at him. "Don't be smart."

When she turned her back, Enzo flipped her off.

Kwasniewski, the assistant manager, saw him, stalked over, and gave him a five-minute tongue-lashing.

The store was filled with worn-out people 24/7. Like Enzo, they were spending money they didn't have. The global economy, the news told them, was booming. So why was everybody he knew working two jobs and living from one paycheck to the next? Why did everybody buy lottery tickets? Why did they try out for *Become Megarich!* and *You Can't Be Too Thin!* then watch those shows or a dozen like them nightly on various screens in astonishing lifelike splendor?

The magazines at the checkout counter were plastered with bright images of celebrities—beautiful people getting married, getting pregnant, getting divorced, getting arrested, going into rehab, getting out of rehab, having affairs, gaining weight and then losing it again. Everybody wanted to be a celebrity. If you weren't a celebrity, you might as well kill yourself.

At night he went home and surfed the web.

At home that night Enzo received an anonymous email headlined "Re-invent the world." No text—just a link.

The link took him to a black screen with the single word, Iteration, in purple. Enzo clicked on it, and was led through a series of images and instructions. On the screen came up a simulation of the city. Using keyboard commands or mouse clicks or touchscreen gestures, you could zoom in on a neighborhood, a street, a single building—home or business—or even an individual person. Or you could back off to see the state, the country, the continent, even the globe itself.

You could alter any element of the simulation. The function page read:

1) You may change one small thing per session.

2) One session per 24-hour period

Just a fancy MUD, with superior graphics. Still, it was interesting. Some major code writing had gone into this.

Enzo typed in his first change: good coffee.

The next morning Enzo could barely keep his eyes open. He had stayed up too late. After two hours working checkout Enzo saw Kwasniewski coming for him. He was carrying a cup of coffee.

"Take a load off your feet, Enzo." Kwasniewski handed him the cup. "Ten minutes."

The coffee was just the way he liked it, sweet and hot. Astonished, Enzo sat in the break room and watched Kwasniewski work the register.

The sofa in the room did not reek of mildew like it usually did.

When he came back to the register, Kwasniewski moved down to spell Cindy in the next slot.

Enzo looked it up: iteration was a mathematical process whereby one arrives at the correct answer for an equation by substituting an approximate value for X—a guess, in effect—then running it through the equation. You then put the new answer in place of X and run it through again. Each repetition produces a more exact answer.

"Clean water," Enzo typed in that night.

The next day Enzo's battered junker wasn't in the slot outside his apartment. Instead of a car key on his key ring he had a key to a bike lock that released a shining new streetbike with cargo carrier on back. Enzo rode the bike to work. It seemed like half of the employees arriving that morning came on bikes. The traffic in the streets was less. Little electric vans dropped people off at their work and stores.

Tyler's seemed subtly different.

Among the celebrity magazines, one bore the photo of a homely kid with big ears who scored the highest on the national merit scholarship test.

Enzo changed one thing every night. But the next morning he could never remember what he'd chosen. Every day he inspected the world and vaguely speculated about what had been altered. Small things.

But of course, everything was tied to everything else, and whatever you changed, changed things around it, connected to it, or even distant things, tied by a long thread of associations.

How many hits was the Iteration site getting? How many people, Enzo wondered, were entering their own changes into Iteration every day?

By the end of the week the store seemed much smaller, and less busy. The people who came in looked more rested. They knew Enzo by name. They joked about politics, but there was no edge of anger in their voices.

The woman from last week came in. Enzo was surprised to realize that he now knew her name—Mrs. Carmello. She looked a little dazed. "Where is the bottled water?" she asked.

Instinctively, Enzo looked over to Aisle 6. A big blue sign said Fruit Juice. "Bottled water?" He smiled. "Why would anyone bottle water, Mrs. C? You might as well try to sell air."

There are data sets in iteration that converge to single points, called attractive fixed points. Enzo wondered what point his series was converging toward? But it wasn't just his series. It was everybody's.

And what if somebody was making bad changes? Not everyone agreed what was bad or good. Bullies. Risk takers. Sociopaths. Did they have their own versions of Iteration? Were they at work in Enzo's world?

On the cover of the magazines was the team of volunteers who were working in the Paraguay economic miracle. Or Mrs. Shanks, a New York City librarian. Or some programming geek. He wasn't sure this was an improvement. Who wanted to read about librarians?

Infant mortality was at a historic low. People were calling it the best TV season since 1981. Psychiatrists were switching to internal medicine. The Buffalo Bills won the Super Bowl. Glaciers were returning to western Greenland.

The blizzard hit in early March and paralyzed the city. Enzo was riding the streetcar up Summer Street through a cloud of white when an electric van skidded through a stoplight and broadsided them. Enzo was thrown onto a thin elderly man with a green muffler wrapped around his neck. As Enzo helped the old man up, amid the shaken passengers, he saw that the woman driving the van had gotten out, looking dazed, her hand to her head. As he watched, a pickup truck followed the van through the stoplight and slid sideways into the van, pinning the woman between the vehicles. The jolt to the streetcar knocked the old man's head against a seat rail and drove Enzo to his knees.

The woman's screams tore through the swirling snow. People called 911 but the rescue vehicles were slow to respond. The old man, unconscious, bled profusely from a cut on his scalp. A number of passengers tried to help free the screaming woman from the van wreck while Enzo cradled the old man's head in his lap, holding the green muffler against his scalp to stop the bleeding. The air was bitterly cold and snow blew so thick outside the streetcar that Enzo could not see the building facades thirty feet away. Whose idea was this blizzard? The accident?

Was it anyone's idea? An unintended consequence?

The people on the streetcar and scattered passersby worked to free the woman. They kept her alive until the ambulance finally arrived. "She'll lose that leg," Enzo heard one of the EMTs, whose face was blanched white from the cold, say. The old man watched Enzo with patient eyes. When the medics finally came to take over from Enzo, the old man smiled weakly at him. "Thank you," he said.

If he should make a small mistake it would get corrected automatically, and might even speed up the approach to the final result.

No one on the streetcar, Enzo realized, could have prevented the accident. There was really nobody to blame. But the people had dealt with it, in small ways, as best they could. People, when they had to, behaved remarkably well.

Enzo's next change: better prosthetics.

Iterates may be categorized into stable and unstable sets depending on whether a neighborhood under iteration converges or diverges. Some move toward stability, others away.

Enzo told himself the changes he made were for everyone's good. And people would like them. Or at least they would act like they did.

As best he could tell, life got better. Some things still went wrong. For instance, one morning when Enzo awoke there was a woman in the bed beside him. She was very beautiful. The previous night had been glorious.

She slid out from beneath the covers. He touched her arm, and she faced him. "I have to go now," she said. Her eyes were dark brown, almost black.

"Please don't."

"This is supposed to be an improvement," she said.

"It is."

"Not for me." She gathered up her clothes and left.

Enzo did not have to be at work for two hours. He got out of bed and put on some clothes. He made a cup of coffee. It was hot and sweet. He sat at his kitchen table and wrote a poem.

A lovely woman
Left her scent on my pillow.
There are no small things.

THE CARE AND FEEDING OF YOUR BABY KILLER UNICORN
DIANA PETERFREUND

Diana Peterfreund grew up in Florida and graduated from Yale University with degrees in Geology and Literature. She has been a costume designer, a cover model, and a food critic, and her travels have taken her from the cloud forests of Costa Rica to the underground caverns of New Zealand. She is the author of the four books in the "Secret Society Girl" series, as well as young adult novel *Rampant*, a contemporary fantasy about killer unicorns, and its sequel, *Ascendant*. She has also written film novelization *Morning Glory*, several short stories set in the killer unicorn world, and critical essays about popular young adult and children's fiction. Diana lives in Washington, DC, with her husband and daughter, and is hard at work on her next young adult novel, a post-apocalyptic retelling of the Jane Austen classic, *Persuasion*.

"Cool. It's a freak show," says Aidan. "I didn't know they had those anymore."

I don't think we're supposed to call them freak shows. Though I know my parents would freak if they knew I was anywhere near one. Too much nudity, too many pathways into the occult.

The tent is near the back of the carnival, decorated with garishly painted plywood signs and lit by a string of lights at the entrance flap that does little more than cast long shadows, obscuring most of the ads.

So far, the carnival has been pretty lame. There's a Ferris wheel, but it costs four dollars to go around a single time—Yves says they must have to pay a fortune for insurance. The hot dogs look ancient and shriveled, and taste more like jerky. The cotton candy is deflated, the funnel cake soggy, and they aren't selling anything cool like deep-fried Twinkies. I had to beg my parents to let me come too. You see, the fairgrounds back up to the woods, and I'm not allowed anywhere near the woods anymore.

Maybe if we played some games on the midway it would have been fun, but Aidan pronounced them childlike and insipid, suitable only for jocks and their sheeplike followers, and we all agreed. Except for Yves, in a move clearly designed to recall my collection of bobble-headed monkeys that we'd amassed over several summers spent being childish and insipid at the Skee-Ball range down the shore.

Yves loves telling cringe-worthy stories about the dumb stuff we used to do, especially since last fall. Most especially whenever he catches me flirting with Aidan.

"Ewww," says Marissa, insinuating herself and her bare-midriff top between Aidan and me. "A two-headed cow? Is it, like, alive?"

"Probably not," says Yves from behind us. "I bet it's pickled."

I look over my shoulder and wrinkle up my nose at him. Yves's eyes are dark, framed by even darker lashes that were always too long and full for a boy. His hands are balled up in his jacket pockets and he's giving me one of those long piercing looks that have been another one of his specialties since last fall.

Summer refuses to go inside the freak show, citing how inhumane it is to put people with deformities up on display. But a quick glance at the signs out front reveals only one sideshow performer whose "qualities" don't seem self-inflicted: the wolf-boy. The others are a tattooed man, a sword swallower, and some guy called the human hanger who looks like his claim to carnival fame is dangling stuff from his body piercings. Gross. Maybe my parents have a point. I move down to examine the next sign, and freeze.

VENOM

THE WORLD'S ONLY LIVE CAPTIVE UNICORN

They said it couldn't be done, but we have one!

Be one of the few to see this monster . . . and SURVIVE!

There's a bad drawing beneath the words, nothing like the blurry photos on the news, or the pictures you've seen of the corpses. The unicorn on the sign looks like one from the old fairy books, white, rearing, its mane flying out behind it in artful spirals. Just like a fairy tale, except for the fangs and the blood-red eyes.

I stumble back and almost trip over Marissa. "A unicorn?" she says. "But it can't be a real one."

"Of course it's not," says Aidan. "They'd never be allowed to put it on display. Way too dangerous. It's probably pickled too."

Marissa points at the sign. "But it says it's alive."

"Maybe a fake one," says Katey, clinging to her boyfriend, Noah. "They have this patented process where they graft the horns of a baby goat together, and it grows up with one horn. Like a bonsai tree. We learned about it in Bio class."

I shudder and move away from the tent. Before unicorns came back, people used to do that and pretend it was this gentle, magical creature. No one realized the old stories were lies.

"Well, that's totally worth five bucks," says Aidan. "I want to check it out. A killer unicorn! You know they never caught the one that killed those kids in the woods last fall."

"They can't," says Noah. "They say no one can catch one, and no one can tame one either. This one has got to be a fake."

My arms tangle up, hugging myself to keep out the cold. But it's a warm spring evening. Nothing like last fall, with its cold gray skies, crisp leaves, bloodcurdling screams.

Summer shakes her head vehemently. "Yeah, I'm definitely not going in now."

"Come on," says Katey. "It isn't a real one. If it were, it would be on TV, not stuck in some sideshow tent."

"Fine," Aidan says to Summer. "Be lame." He cocks his head at me, grinning. "Let's go."

If my folks disapproved of body piercings and the occult, then a unicorn was definitely off-limits. Especially for me.

"Wen?" Yves's voice comes from way too close. He's the only one outside my family who knows. "You don't have to."

I turn to him. He's offering me his hand like we're still six years old. Like holding his hand will be as simple as it was when we were kids. Like holding *him* can be as natural as it was last fall. But like I told him then, it was an accident. A mistake.

I stare at him. He's holding out his hand like things can ever be the same between us again.

"Hey!" I call to Aidan and the others. "Wait up."

It isn't a fake.

I can tell the instant I'm inside the tent, though I can't even see it yet. But it smells like last fall in here, the weird scent that at the time I thought was someone burning leaves, or plant matter rotting after the October rains.

The interior of the tent looks like a museum gallery, with a dark, winding path snaking past individual exhibits that stand out like islands of amber red light in the gloom. Noah has already pulled Katey into a dark corner behind the sea serpent bones to make out. I can see them even better inside the blackened tent than I could in the glare of the midway.

It's the unicorn that does this to me. Its evil tingles along my nerve endings, waking them, tuning them like a drug so that everything is clearer, stronger, slower.

The two-headed calf is, in fact, pickled; a fetal calf mutation preserved in a giant tank that glows green to heighten the creep factor. Aidan and Marissa gape at it, then skip over to watch the sword swallower do his thing. I close my eyes and try to push the unicorn out. I'm hot all over, like that time my cousins Rebecca and John and I got into the brandy at Christmas.

The sword swallower licks the sword from end to end, grinning at us, then leans his head back and lifts the rapier into the air, poising it carefully over his mouth. I watch each inch of it descend into the man's gullet, see every movement of his neck muscles, every twitch as he fights to suppress his gag reflex.

The suppressed magic breaks free, loosing within me a painful clarity, every moment of time stretched out to encompass unbearable detail. I can hear Marissa's heartbeat, quickened because of the sight before her, quickening more when she shivers in disgust and leans against Aidan. Blood pounds in my ears, like that time my cousins Rebecca and John and I bet to see who could hold their breath longest at the bottom of their pool.

I can even feel the soil beneath my soles, and I let myself be pulled along in my steps like I'm a train car on a track, tugged inexorably toward something that lies in the darkness beyond.

Like the time my cousins Rebecca and John and I went out to the woods near their house last fall and I watched them die.

I never should have come in here. It was wrong; I knew that, but I'd wanted to show off for Aidan.

There's a woman seated on a metal folding chair in front of a curtain partitioning off the back of the tent. Over the flap is another drawing of a unicorn, rampant red against a black field. She stamps out her cigarette. "You here to see Venom?" she asks. She's dressed in flowing skirts and a corset, but looks more like a biker babe than a fairy-tale princess.

"Yes," says Aidan, behind me.

"I have to go with you," says the woman, pulling herself to her feet. "For safety."

Marissa stands back. "So it is real?"

Aidan rolls his eyes. "Part of the show. Like the sword swallower popping those balloons to show it was sharp."

I take a deep breath. And like the sword swallower, this is real. They have a real unicorn back there. Poisonous. Man-eating. We should run. Now.

The woman holds open the flap and ushers us inside, and the others jostle around me, but I can't take another step. In my head I hear my cousins screaming. No one here knows, and Yves is still outside. They were two years older than me, seniors at another school. No one knows those kids who were killed by a unicorn were my cousins. No one knows I was there.

My parents said not to tell. Fewer questions, then, about how I'd survived. Less temptation, then, to explore the evil that dwells in my blood.

"Coming, Wen?" Aidan asks, and grabs my hand. Something like an electric shock breaks through my thoughts, and I follow him beyond the curtain. There's a small observation space in front of a sturdy-looking metal grate. Beyond the grate: darkness and a tiny pool of yellow light.

The woman lifts a whistle on a chain hanging around her neck and blows a low, warbling note. Beyond the bars the unicorn steps into the light. Or actually, it hobbles. It's a small one, not like the kind that killed Rebecca and John. Each of its cloven hooves is encircled with heavy metal clamps, and they are chained, left to right, front to back, so the unicorn can take only tiny steps. The front leg irons connect to a Y-shaped metal pole ending in another metal clamp securing the beast's neck. Thus chained, it can only hold its head out straight, the better for us to admire its goatlike face and long corkscrew horn.

The unicorn is enormously fat. Underneath a coat of sparse, wiry white hair, its belly distends almost to its knobby knees. Patches of its coat are bare, and in the bald spots I can see scabs and even open sores, like it's been chewing itself.

The unicorn's watery blue eyes glare at each of my friends in turn. Its mouth opens in a snarl, revealing pointed yellow fangs and unhealthy-looking gums. It growls a low, bleating growl at Noah and Katey, at Marissa and Aidan. And then it turns to me.

Its pupils dilate, its mouth closes, and then it moves toward the bars.

We all jump back.

"Venom!" yells the woman. The unicorn's horn scrapes the bars. It bends its knees now, struggling to lower its head in the confines of the irons, bleating as the edges of the neck brace scrape against its skin.

"Venom!" the woman screams. "Get back. Now!" The unicorn does not obey.

My friends take another big step back toward the curtains. "Lady…" Aidan says. I can hear their heartbeats pounding away. But I can't take my eyes off the unicorn.

The monster limps and stumbles, trying to put one knee on the ground and then the other, constrained by its bonds, never breaking eye contact with me, never letting go of the pleading look in its eyes.

The woman snaps to and turns to me. "You."

I blink as she grabs my arm. The unicorn stops what it's doing and begins growling again.

"You're one of us," she hisses at me.

Oh, no.

"Lady, get your monster under control," Aidan says. The unicorn bangs against the grate, and the bars *bend* under its weight.

Under *her* weight, I realize at once. It's a female.

"Who are you?" the unicorn wrangler asks, and her grip tightens. She's so strong. Insanely strong.

But so am I. I yank my arm loose, then fly back through the curtains, mindless of her shouts or my friends' shock or the soundless pleas of the unicorn. I run with speed I haven't felt since last fall. Speed that meant I was the only one who got away when that unicorn attacked my cousins and me on the trail. Speed that those people from the Italian nunnery mentioned when they came to my parents' house to explain to us that I'm something special when it comes to unicorns. I draw them in like unicorn catnip. I'm immune to their deadly venom. I'm capable of hearing their thoughts. When I'm around them, I'm blindingly fast and scarily strong. And I, unlike most of the people on the planet, have the ability to capture and kill them, if properly trained.

They said they had a place to train girls with powers like mine. They called us unicorn hunters. My parents kicked them out. My father said they were papists at best and exploiters and magicians at worst, and there was no way he was letting me get anywhere near a unicorn. After all, we'd already seen what those monsters had done to Rebecca and John.

I flee with this inhuman speed through the twisting paths of the sideshow tent and break through the flaps into the benign neon night. And the first thing I see, when the moon stops spinning in the sky and the sense of unicorn fades, is that Yves and Summer are sitting on a bench in the shadows, and they're kissing.

Yves gives Summer a ride home, which means I'm sitting in the back. He turned sixteen last summer, which makes him almost a year older than the rest of our crowd. I choose the seat behind the driver's side, so I can't see Yves in the mirror, even if I wanted to. Summer chatters the whole way, splitting her monologue between the two of us, and I wonder what she thinks of me, and of the rumors about me and Yves. When we arrive at Summer's house, Yves gets out of the car and walks her to her front door, and I stare as hard as I can at the moon. It seems to take a really long time for him to get back. He doesn't move to put the car in gear.

"You staying back there? Am I your chauffeur?"

I kick the back of his seat.

"What was the unicorn like?"

"Real." I say, and then, to keep him from asking anything else, "What was Summer's tongue like?"

Yves peels out.

As soon as Yves pulls into his driveway, I open my door and tumble out, unsteady because the car is still moving. I sprint across his lawn, jump over Biscuit, old Mrs. Schaffer's annoying yellow cat, and am halfway up my front walk before I hear the engine die, before he shouts at me.

"Wen! Wait, Wen, we should talk about this!"

And then I'm inside my house, and I can't hear him yelling anymore, and I can't see the moon, and most of all, I can't feel that unicorn calling out to me from all the way across town.

That's the part I still don't get, after I've knocked on my folks' door to say good night and changed into my pajamas and said my prayers and gotten into bed. Because if I'd done like those Italian nuns had asked, if I'd gone off with them, I'd have trained to be a unicorn hunter. A unicorn killer.

But there was no mistaking that unicorn. She wanted my help. Did she want me to kill her? I could easily believe that living in captivity, confined day and night by all those chains, might be unbearable. Was that what she wanted? A mercy killing?

I punch my pillow down and pull the covers over my head to protect my eyes from the moonlight, which seems so much brighter now than it did at the carnival. *Just stop thinking about the unicorn. Just stop.*

For six months I lived in fear of waking up one morning and finding a whole herd of monsters in my backyard, such was my power to draw their evil down on me. But now that I've met another unicorn, now that I know what it is to have one near, I understand. I recognize what it feels like now. I just have to overcome it. The trick is to think of something else. Something pleasant.

So I imagine I'm kissing Aidan, that he is touching my back the way he touched my hand in the tent tonight. It's probably not the right image, though, because the only experience I have kissing anyone is with Yves, last fall. And instead of feeling Aidan's long blond hair between my fingers, I am feeling Yves's dark, wiry curls; I'm feeling Yves's full lips against mine; I'm hearing Yves whisper my name, just like he did last fall, like instead of grabbing him by the shoulders and kissing him I'd waved my arms and conjured lightning out of a blue sky.

I'm glad for Summer. I really am. I want Yves to find a girlfriend and forget about trying to go out with me. I want him to forget about kissing me, even if it was his first kiss as well. And I want to forget too.

I want to forget it all.

Yves isn't waiting for me at my locker on Monday morning. He and Summer spend lunch canoodling at the far end of the table. Which is fine by me. Less fine is that Marissa hangs off Aidan all through the food line and arranges the seating so he's nearest her and farthest from me at lunch. Plus, they only want to talk about their current events class. Apparently the government napalmed some unicorn-infested prairie out West somewhere to try to control the spread of the monsters. It didn't work.

"The pictures on the news didn't look anything like that thing we saw at the sideshow," says Aidan. "Maybe it was a fake."

I keep my mouth filled with coleslaw. Least fine of all is that the unicorn has been calling to me all weekend. Even in church on Sunday. I almost told my parents, but I was too scared by what they'd say. Like maybe if I still feel it, it's because I haven't been trying hard enough to banish this evil from my heart.

I can feel it tugging on me now.

"Of course it was a fake," says Marissa. "Everyone knows that unicorns can't be captured."

"*Everyone* knows a lot of things," Noah points out. "Like how you can't kill them with napalm. But then they also show unicorn corpses on the news. Who killed them, and how?"

I dare to look up then, and I notice that Yves is focusing on me. Only we know who is really killing unicorns, and I swore Yves to secrecy last fall.

Right before I kissed him.

Katey shudders and pulls the crusts off her sandwich. "Fake or not, it was scary. Unicorns are awful—the ones on the news, the little fat one at the fair—doesn't matter. I hope whoever is killing them gets that one in the woods. The one that killed those kids last fall."

"Don't you think there are better things to do than just wipe them out?" Summer asks. "They're an endangered species."

"They're *dangerous*," Noah corrects, slipping his arm around Katey. "I bet you'd drop your whole animal rights act if you had seen that thing try to break through the bars and eat Wen last weekend."

"It tried to eat you?" Yves asks abruptly.

You'd know that if you weren't so busy macking with Summer, I almost snap at him. But the truth is, I don't think it was trying to eat me. Get to me, certainly. But eat me?

I wonder what else they say about unicorns that isn't true. I wonder, if I'd gone with those guys from Italy last fall, would I know now?

After school I head straight to the library, because if not, Yves might think I want a ride home, which would probably complicate whatever after school plans he has with Summer. In the library I do a little bit of homework and a lot of thinking, and eventually I go over to the computers and look up the city bus routes online.

It takes me three different buses to get out to the fairgrounds, and I almost turn around and go home at each change. I probably shouldn't be doing this, but at the same time, I have to know. Maybe I'm imagining it, letting the fear of last fall put all sort of ideas in my head.

The sun's already low in the sky by the time I reach the entrance gate, and once inside the fairgrounds, I lose my nerve. I buy and drink a soda. Then I play ten straight rounds of Skee-Ball and win so many tickets that the carnie manning the machines starts giving me the stink eye, so I finish up and trade my tickets for the first thing my eyes land on: a unicorn doll.

"Not a common choice," the carnie says, digging it out of the pile of teddy bears and puppy dogs. "Not these days, anyway. Kids are too scared by the news stories."

He hands me the doll, and its gilt horn sags over one eye. I focus on it and say nothing, worried for a second that he's calling me a sicko for picking up such a macabre doll.

"You know we have one here, in the sideshow?" says the carnie, who apparently never learned when to leave well enough alone. "At least, that's the pitch. They keep it locked up real tight, though, so maybe it is real."

I nod.

"But they weren't showing it today." He shrugs. "Said it's sick."

And then, over the din of bells and alarms on the midway, over the screams of the people on the rides and the raucous music emanating from every speaker on the fairgrounds, I hear her. The unicorn. She is sick. And she needs help.

And before I know it I've taken off, backpack flouncing hard against my spine, unicorn doll grasped firmly in my fist. The same speed that carried me far away from the unicorn last Saturday now takes me back to the sideshow tent, but I know—somehow I know—she's not inside. It never occurs to me to stop, to push this unicorn sense away, to pray for God's protection from this evil. Instead, I just go.

I wave at the guy manning the entrance, and as soon as his attention's elsewhere, I sidle toward the side, pretending to read the garish posters advertising the acts within, then skitter around the corner. The side wall of the tent comes flush with the fences surrounding the fairgrounds, but I can see that the tent actually extends a ways beyond that. I press against the canvas walls, but they're pulled snug, with little room to maneuver around, and massive bungee cords secure the sides to the fence so no one can sneak inside the fairgrounds—or, apparently, sneak out.

I'm ready to go back to the entrance of the fairgrounds and walk all the way around the outside, when I hear the unicorn cry out again. And this time it's not in my head but a shrieking roar of anguish so loud that I can see the people on the midway pause in surprise.

And then my foot is on the lowest bungee cord and I'm pulling myself over the top of the fence with one hand. I drop to the ground on the other side, soft as a cat. The sun has dipped below the horizon, and twilight blurs the edges of the trailers, caravans, and Porta Potties that fan out haphazardly over the dirt. Still, I know exactly where she is, and I beeline toward her.

What I'm going to do once I get there, I don't know. Even if the unicorn wants to die, I have no clue how to kill her.

The unicorn wrangler's trailer is dented and in need of a new paint job. I plaster myself to its rusted sides as I hear a voice coming from a tentlike patio spilling out the back. I recognize the voice as the woman who grabbed my arm last weekend, and she's saying words my father would wash my mouth out for.

The unicorn is alternating pitiful little bleats with full-on growls, and I edge closer, trying to peek between the trailer and the canvas flaps and see what's going on. The canvas lean-to is secured to the top of the trailer with ropes and staked into the bare ground like a picnic cover on a camper. Is the woman beating the poor thing? Or maybe punishing it for eating a fellow carnie?

"Don't you dare—" the woman puffs, out of breath. "Not until I come back, do you hear?"

The unicorn moans again, and I hear a screen door smack against the aluminum siding. I drop to my stomach and peek through the gap between the ground and the canvas tent flap. The unicorn is staring at me. It's shifting from foot to foot, lowing, and as it struggles to turn, I can see that there's something weird sticking out of its butt. It looks like two sticks or something, but then I peer closer and realize they are legs. Two tiny legs ending in cloven hooves.

The unicorn's not fat. She's in labor.

She struggles to lie down on the hay coating the ground, pulling against her chains so she can lick her backside. I hear the screen door open again, and my view is blocked by the women's feet and the dirty hem of her skirt.

"I said wait," the woman snaps at the monster, who merely growls in response. "I don't have it ready yet." She sets down a large bucket, and cold water sloshes over the top and splashes me.

That's weird. I've heard of people boiling hot water before births—though I'm not sure why—but a bucket of cold water?

The unicorn pauses in her labor pains and lays her head against the ground. One big blue eye bores right into mine.

"You better pray this one is stillborn, Venom," the woman says, and her foot taps the earth near my face. "I hate doing this."

The unicorn stares at me, her bloodshot eye wide with terror. And with a shudder that goes from the top of my head into the tip of my toes, I get it.

The unicorn bleats and moans and licks and pushes, and slowly I can see the baby's head pushing out to meet those spindly legs. The head is mottled white and red, and its eyes bulge out from either side of its oblong cranium. Between the baby's eyes is nothing—no horn. Maybe it grows in later, like antlers on a deer. Some sort of glossy membrane encases the baby's body, and it's turning translucent in the air, or maybe because it's being stretched. I can't tell.

I'm scared someone will come round the corner and catch me peeping underneath the tent. I'm terrified the wrangler will lean down and see me. I can't believe I'm watching the birth of a unicorn. How many people alive have ever seen anything so extraordinary?

The unicorn wrangler is clearly one of them, as I can hear her hissing with impatience, and her foot hasn't stopped its restive tapping. The unicorn turns to lick at the baby, and the membrane splits wide. For the first time I see the baby unicorn move. It blinks and wiggles and slides even farther out of its mother.

The wrangler hurries over to the unicorn, grabs the baby by its slimy two front legs, and yanks it the rest of the way out. Venom screams in pain, and then the ground is covered with some sort of foul-smelling liquid.

"Jesus, Venom!" cries the woman, dangling the baby just out of my sight range. "You reek." She takes a single step back toward the bucket, and the unicorn pauses in its anguish to lock gazes with me.

My hand shoots out beneath the flap and tips the bucket over.

Cold water floods the hay inside the tent and spills outside to soak the front of my shirt and pants. I bite back a gasp, but I needn't bother, since the wrangler is screaming bloody murder. She drops the baby unicorn, who tumbles into the wet hay in a heap. Then the woman snatches up the bucket and vanishes into the trailer.

The baby shifts feebly on the ground, bits of membrane and hay sticking to its wet hide as it tries to slither back toward its mother's warmth. But there's something wrong with Venom. She keeps trying to raise herself and move toward her child, but can't. She looks at me again, pain and pleading shooting at me like an arrow.

"No," I say. "I can't."

From inside the trailer I hear water running. She's refilling the bucket. She's going to come out here any minute, and then she's going to drown that baby. That poor, innocent little unicorn baby who never killed anyone's cousins. Who never did anything but get dropped moments after it was born. How can it be evil?

Venom pulls herself over to the foal, licks the rest of the membrane away, and rubs it all over with her snout. The baby's crying high-pitched, pitiful little bleats and trying to crawl under its mother's fur. The unicorn glares at me and growls.

I say that word the wrangler used, stuff the doll into my backpack, and pull myself beneath the tent flaps, smearing mud, wet hay, and much nastier stuff all over my clothes. As soon as I'm inside, Venom nudges the baby at me with her nose.

"I can't," I repeat, but then why am I here?

The pitch of water hitting bucket grows higher. Soon the bucket will be filled. Venom bleats again and, with much effort, shoves herself to her feet to face me.

I stumble backward as Venom bends her knees and bows, touching her long corkscrew horn to the ground. She looks up at me from her supine position, and her desperate supplication hits me with the force of a blow.

The sound of running water dies.

I snatch up the baby and run, not looking back when I hear the screen door slam, not stopping when the wrangler screams, not noticing until I'm miles away how fast I'm going. Or how I don't even feel out of breath.

When I finally do arrive home, it's black out. I sneak around the side of the house into the garage and unwrap the foal from my gym uniform, which is now every bit as streaked with afterbirth and mud as my clothes. I don't know how I'm going to explain the mess to my mother.

I don't know how I'm going to explain the unicorn, either.

The baby unicorn hasn't shivered since I wrapped it up in my clothes, and its skin is dry and crusty now. I'm pretty sure its mother would have licked it clean, but I'm not about to do that. Still, I know I need to keep the baby warm. And find it something to eat.

Our garage is too stuffed with junk to fit the car anymore, but that makes it a perfect hiding place for the foal. I shove aside boxes of picture albums and Christmas ornaments and pull down a ratty old quilt we sometimes use for picnics. If I can make a nest of the blanket, maybe I can put it behind the storage freezer. The heat from the motor will probably be enough to keep the baby warm overnight. I look back to where I left the unicorn on the pile of my dirty gym clothes. The foal is pushing itself up on wobbly feet and taking a few tentative steps.

Uh-oh.

Near the door there's an old plastic laundry basket filled with gardening tools that I dump out onto the concrete. I arrange the blanket inside, hoping the tall sides of the basket will be enough to keep the unicorn from getting out. And the sides and lid have enough holes in them that I won't worry about the baby suffocating. I wedge the basket in the space I've made behind the freezer and put the unicorn inside. As an afterthought I pull out the unicorn doll I won on the midway and put it in there with the baby.

It's bleating again, but you can't hear it above the sound of the freezer. Bet it's hungry. I wonder what I can feed it, since unicorn milk isn't an option. I grab my book bag and head inside, making a beeline for the stairs.

"Wen!" my mother calls from the kitchen, but I don't stop. "Wendy Elizabeth, you get down here!"

I grimace at the use of my full name. "Can't," I call from the top of the darkened stairwell. "My, um…"

Mom starts up the stairs, so I duck into my bedroom and pull off my clothes, stuffing the dirty stuff into the back of my closet. I'm in my underwear when she tries the door and I push against it.

"Mom!" I cry. "I'm not dressed!"

"You're late for dinner! Why didn't you call?"

I lower my voice, and then I tell my mother a lie. "My, uh, my period started at Katey's house and it made a mess and I was too embarrassed so I walked home."

"Oh, honey." My mom's voice is softer now. "Well, wash up and come downstairs. Make sure you get your pants in the laundry tonight, though, so it doesn't stick. There's stain remover by the washer downstairs."

"Thanks," I say. If the blood does stain, how will I explain getting my period all over my *shirt?* But that's the least of my problems. After washing the blood off my arms and face—which grosses me out more than I can say—I pull on fresh clothes and log on to the Internet. I look up both how to care for orphaned deer fawns and how to care for orphaned lions, figuring that if anything, a unicorn is a mix of the two.

This is going to be harder than I thought. Apparently it's not as simple as just giving them milk. Fawns drink something called "deer colostrum," and lions take special high-protein baby formulas. Neither of which I have any ability to get my hands on.

What am I doing? I can't take care of a baby unicorn. Even if I could figure out how to feed it, it can't be legal! And it can't be right.

Back downstairs Mom and Dad are waiting at the table. I slide into my seat, and Dad says grace. Dinner takes forever, and I can barely eat a bite. Dad doesn't eat much either, because Mom is trying out a Moroccan recipe she got from Yves's mother, and Dad thinks anything more exotic than spaghetti is too weird to count as food.

But it does give me an idea. Yves's mom sometimes cooks with goat's milk. Maybe that's closer to unicorn than cow. After the endless dinner and the even more endless washing up, I turn to Mom. "Can I run over to Yves's house really quickly? I need to get his notes from history class." Lie number two.

"Be quick," my mother warns.

Yves answers at the kitchen door. "Hey," he says, leaning against the frame. "What's up?"

"I need to borrow some goat's milk."

"Borrow?" He raises his eyebrows. "Like you're going to bring it back?"

"No. I mean I would like you to give me some goat's milk. Please."

Yves shrugs and heads toward the fridge. "Just so you know," he says, retrieving the slim carton from a shelf on the door, "it's pretty nasty all by itself. What do you need it for?"

So I lie again. "My mom has this new recipe she's trying out and she, uh, remembered you'd have some…"

"At nine o'clock at night?" Yves's big, dark eyes are staring right through me. It's not fair. It's hard enough lying to my parents, but Yves?

"Yeah. It needs to… marinate overnight or something. I don't know. She just sent me over here." I look away. "So, in case we ever need to get more, where does your mom buy this stuff?"

"There's a Caribbean grocer downtown," Yves says, handing me the carton. "Hey, Wen, you okay?"

I step off the stoop into the darkness so he can't see my eyes. Biscuit the cat is off on another of his nocturnal strolls. He's shredding Yves's mom's flower bed. Mrs. Schaffer really needs to get that beast under control. "I'm fine."

I'm not fine. I haven't been this not-fine in months. And we both know what happened then.

Part of me expects him to come forward and touch my arm the way he's been doing since last fall, but he doesn't. He stays on the stoop, and there's a space the size of Summer between us.

"Well, see you at school," he says.

I return to my own yard and approach the garage with trepidation. I hope this works. I hope I'm not too late. How soon after birth should a baby unicorn eat?

What if it's already dead? I catch my breath, freezing with my hand on the door. What if I went through all this and the unicorn died while I was eating dinner? All that effort, all that terror, and it might just croak in my garage, alone, without its mother nearby.

And maybe that would be all right. Maybe the wrangler knew what she was doing when she tried to drown it. After all, these things are deadly. Dangerous. Evil. Maybe she had the right idea, to never let it grow up. But then I remember the look in Venom's eyes, and I rush inside.

Behind the storage freezer the laundry basket is still and silent. I open the lid, and the unicorn is curled up inside, nestled up against the plush unicorn doll on the blanket. I reach inside and touch its flank. A heartbeat flutters through its velvety skin. It starts from its sleep and turns its head toward my hand, noses my palm and wraps its lips around my finger. Something inside me lets go. Yes, it's a tiny little man-eating monster. But it needs me.

I grab an empty water bottle, a rubber band, and a pair of my mother's rubber-tipped gardening gloves. I cut a finger off the gloves and poke a hole in the tip. Then I fill the bottle with the goat's milk and secure the glove finger onto the opening with the rubber band. A few moments against the back of the freezer, and the milk loses its refrigerator chill. That's going to have to be enough.

"Come here, baby," I say to the unicorn, lifting it out of the nest and cradling it against me. I try to get the bottle into its mouth, but the unicorn is having none of that, and struggles while goat's milk streams out of the hole in the glove and smears over us both.

Gross. The unicorn begins to cry, soft little bleats, and tries to burrow into my torso. I bite my lip, knowing just how it feels. What do I think I'm doing? Goat milk. What a dumb idea.

I pull off the rubber and stick my finger into the bottle. "Here," I say again, pushing my milk-coated finger past its lips. This time the baby unicorn suckles, its tongue surprisingly firm. I plunge my finger into the bottle again and again, and slowly, painstakingly, we make it through about a sixth of the bottle. This is going to take a while. There has to be a better way.

I put the glove finger back on the bottle, then squeeze my finger over it, covering both the bottle opening and the pinprick hole in the glove tip. Milk dribbles out and down my finger, but slowly, controlled by the pressure of my finger on the rubber. I place my finger back into the baby's mouth and let it eat.

Its eyes are closed as it suckles, its spindly legs drawn up against its body for warmth. Its skin is mostly white, covered with a soft, velvety down. It doesn't look dangerous at all. I guess this early, without its venomous horn, it's not. Just soft and fragile and dainty. I run a finger down its delicate snout. Between its eyes is a reddish mark, like a starburst or a flower.

"Flower," I say, and it opens its eyes for a moment and looks at me.

Oh, no. Now I've named it.

I can't sleep. Down the hall, my parents' room has been dark for hours, but I'm tossing and turning, trying to imagine what it's like for the little unicorn, alone in the garage. Is it awake? Hungry? Suffocating? Dying of carbon monoxide poisoning from the fumes off the freezer?

Finally I toss a jacket on, slip into my flats, and tiptoe down the hall. Outside, the moon is bright on the lawn, and I realize I should have brought a flashlight. If my parents wake up and see the light on in the garage, they'll freak out.

But once I'm inside the garage, I find I can see just fine. Maybe it's the moonlight. Maybe it's the unicorn. I peek into the laundry basket. Flower is curled up next to the doll again, and I can see its chest move as it breathes. I hope it's a girl. Flower would be a pretty funny name for a boy.

Except, wasn't the skunk in *Bambi* a boy? His name was Flower, and that turned out okay. Bambi, also, was a boy with a girl's name.

I lay my head against the side of the freezer. I can't name this thing Flower. I can't keep it either. It's so dangerous, not only to my parents, who might have to come into the garage for the lawn mower and end up eaten—but also for me. It's magic, and it's all around me, and that's just not right.

Did God place this unicorn in my path as a temptation meant to be overcome? I stare down at the tiny creature curled up in the basket. It's so fragile, like a lamb. How is it to blame for its lot in life? I rest my hand on the unicorn's back, just to feel it breathe. I watch its eyelids flutter, its tiny tail swish slightly against the blanket.

When I wake the next morning, my neck is killing me from sleeping hunched over, and I can't feel anything below my elbow, since the rim of the laundry basket has cut off my circulation. The sun is peeking into the windows of the garage, and the air is stained with the scent of sour milk. The unicorn stirs, yawns adorably, then proceeds to have diarrhea all over the picnic blanket.

No goat milk. Check.

As I'm cleaning up—Flower is now cuddled on a red and white Christmas tree apron—I realize that I'm going to be gone at school all day. I'll have no chance to feed the baby before I go, and what if my mom comes in here and wonders where her gardening stuff has gone and why the freezer is pulled away from the wall?

Flower starts bleating again as I leave the garage and make my way into the house. In the kitchen my dad is eating oatmeal and grousing about how Biscuit peed on the newspaper again. The funny pages survived; the business section did not. He takes in my pajama pants and jacket.

"Where were you?"

"You weren't in the woods, were you?" Mom's eyes are wide with fright.

"No!" I'm so tired of lying. "I was looking for something in the garage."

This, of course, sets off another round of lying, as I try to make up a non-unicorn-based object that I was looking for, and my mother offers to scour the garage for it later, and I tell yet more lies in order to convince her to keep out of there.

Here's a question for Sunday school: Can one lie to one's parents in order to save a life?

I hop in the shower, throw on clean clothes, say a quick prayer that Flower survives and goes undetected until this afternoon, and head to school. School consists of the following: English, math, and history classes, where I fail to pay attention while I fret about Flower; lunchtime, where I brainstorm ideas about what to feed the unicorn and try to avoid glancing at the end of the table, where Summer is sitting on Yves's lap; study hall, where I think about how if I were the kind of girl who knew how to skip and sneak out of school, this would have been an excellent time to slip home and check up on the unicorn; gym, where we play kick ball; and then bio class, where the teacher says our new unit is going to be on endangered species and extinction, and how there are all kinds of animals that we once thought were extinct (like these tree frogs in South America) or imaginary (like giant squids and unicorns) and it turns out that they were just really endangered, and how changes in the environment can either bring the population back or else put the animal in danger.

"So we might have all these unicorns around this past year because we destroyed their natural habitat?" asks Summer, sitting in the front row with Yves.

"They've got the woods all to themselves now," grumbles Noah. After what happened to Rebecca and John, the government closed all the local parks and the state forest that backs up to so many of our housing developments until they could determine the risk to the public. The deer hunters and the Boy Scouts are still pretty livid about it. As for me, even if they ever do open the woods again, I won't be allowed to go back. Not until the unicorns are gone.

"Not anymore," says Aidan. "Didn't you hear? They caught that unicorn, the one that killed the kids. It's dead."

My head whips around. "What?"

Aidan is sprawled out behind his desk, and as usual, he's gotten half the class's attention. "Was on the news last night. They showed the corpse and everything."

My knuckles grow white, my breath grows shallow, and it's funny but I can feel Yves's gaze on the back of my head as easily as I could feel Venom calling to me from across the fairgrounds. Class devolves into a discussion of what they are not showing us on TV, until the teacher manages to regain control.

They caught it. A chorus of angels are singing somewhere in the vicinity of my sternum. They caught it. I don't care what my folks said about the special unicorn hunters. Maybe they use magic, but they answered my prayers. Someone avenged my cousins' deaths. We're all safe.

And then I remember Flower.

When school lets out, Aidan invites me to go with him and the others to the mall, but I need to tend to the unicorn in my parents' garage. I head to the grocery store, where I buy a real baby bottle, some formula, and some hamburger meat. I'm terrified of what the lady at the checkout counter will think of my purchases, but she says nothing, just takes my money and watches me stuff everything into my backpack.

Yves honks at me as I hit the street. "Need a ride?"

"Stalker," I say, and climb in. "Aren't you going to the mall?"

"Nah." He shrugs. "Summer has yearbook, and I don't need an Orange Julius." He pulls out onto the road and casts me a sidelong glance. "So, they caught that unicorn."

"Yeah." I look out the window.

"How do you feel?"

"Better." And as soon as I say it, I realize it's the truth. Who knew I had such viciousness inside me? I wonder if that's what comes of spending the night communing with a killer unicorn. Even a newborn one. I'm sure my parents would agree.

Then again, they are probably also thrilled to hear that my cousins' killer is dead.

We ride the rest of the way home in silence, and my heart plummets as I see my mom on our front yard wielding hedge clippers.

"Hey, Mrs. G," Yves says as we get out of his car.

I clutch my backpack to my chest and try very hard not to look at the garage. Does she know? Even from here I can tell Flower is scared, starving, alone. Is it possible my mom didn't see it? Or doesn't know what it is she saw? After all, Flower has no horn.

My mom brushes her hair out of her eyes and waves, and I can breathe again.

"How did that marinade work out for you?" Yves asks Mom.

She cocks her head to the side. "I'm sorry, dear?"

Yves fixes me with a look. "Never mind. I must have been confused."

I beeline for the house, hoping Mom will stay outside long enough for me to snag the blender without notice.

"*Thanks for the ride, Yves!*" Yves calls after me. "*You're my knight in shining armor!*"

My knight has another damsel. Not that I care.

I dump my textbooks on the kitchen table, grab the blender off the counter, and shove it into my backpack.

Back outside, Yves is nowhere to be seen and my mom looks like she's packing it in. She stretches and rolls out her neck muscles.

"I can take those clippers back to the garage for you," I say quickly.

"Thank you, sweetie." My mom brushes dirt off her knees. "I need to get better at keeping my gardening stuff in one place. You know I had these clippers under the porch all winter?"

Well, that was a close call. I go to take the clippers from her, but she doesn't let go.

"I'm . . . glad to see you going out with your friends again, sweetie."

I tug on the clippers and keep my eyes down.

"I know the past few months have been hard on you, with all our restrictions." She places her other hand over mine. "But it's for your own safety—your life *and* your eternal soul. Those monsters—they're demons."

"They're animals," I reply, and pull the clippers away. "We learned in bio class that they're back because of environmental degradation of their habitat."

Mom smiles at me and nods. I half-expect her to pat me on the head. "That's the science, my dear. But what happened to Rebecca and John—that was the work of the Devil. And what happens to you when you are near the creatures? It's sorcery. The snake in the Garden of Eden was an animal as well. Remember that. Don't let that evil into your heart."

She leaves me on the porch, blinking back tears. I want to run inside and climb into her lap and have her sing me lullabies or hymns or whatever it takes to drown out Flower's cries of fear and hunger. The unicorn has been calling to me since the second I got out of Yves's car.

What if I just left it there? It won't be able to survive alone much longer. If Flower dies, I won't be able to hear it cry, won't feel its pain. I won't be caring for a demon, like Mom says. No matter how innocent the baby unicorn looks, I know what lurks within. It was foolish of me to obey Venom yesterday, foolish of me to defy my parents and everything I knew was right.

Maybe after it's dead I can go and bury it. Or drag it into the woods. Or...

Except how could I save it from drowning, from the quick death the wrangler offered—only to subject it to a day and night of terror and hunger and loneliness? What right do I have to torture it so?

Ignoring the garage and my backpack filled with groceries, I head to my bedroom. I do my homework, I surf the Internet, and I pray to God to deafen me to the baby unicorn that screams inside my head.

I resist it for two hours, and then I find myself on my way to the garage, backpack in hand. All my life I have learned that my God is a God of love, and that above all He wishes me to be compassionate. And then He places in my path a monster. If this is a test, then surely I am failing.

Inside the garage the unicorn is standing and pushing its face against the lid of the laundry basket. It has made a mess inside again. I sigh and empty out the basket. While I get its formula ready, the unicorn takes a few tottering steps on the concrete floor, unsteady on its matchstick legs, then wipes out and starts crying. I do my best to ignore it while I blend the formula according to directions, then add a few handfuls of raw hamburger and set the blender to puree. The resulting mixture looks and smells like something you'd see on a reality television show, and I wonder if this will be any more palatable to the unicorn. Baby birds eat regurgitated bits of bugs or other meat from their mothers, though. Maybe unicorns work the same way.

Flower seems to like it, sucking from the bottle like a pro and pawing at me for more. After eating, it settles down pretty quickly into the cardboard box nest I've made for it. It drifts off to sleep as I'm rinsing out the blender, but when I cross the garage to return Mom's gardening tools to the laundry basket, the unicorn wakes up and starts crying at me.

I swallow until I can speak. "Stop."

Bleat, bleat. Bleeeeeaaaaaaaaaat.

"Stop, please!" Why couldn't I kill it? Why couldn't I let it die? I clap my hands over my ears and squeeze my eyes shut.

Bleeeeaaaaaat. I hear Flower throwing itself against the sides of the box.

"No!" I say sharply. "Stop it. Settle down."

And, amazingly, the unicorn listens.

By the end of the following week, I've fallen into a routine. My life circles around Flower—when to feed the unicorn, when to clean out his box, when to sneak out of the house, how quickly I need to run home from school to take care of the little monster. In the middle of the night, I can tell when he stirs from his sleep, when he needs me. Oh, yes, it's a boy. I made that little discovery the other day when I got a good look at his backside.

Flower thrives on the burger-formula solution and begins growing by leaps and bounds. Wooly white hair sprouts all over his body, and I worry less about whether or not he will be too cold at night. I've taken to sneaking out of the house to walk the unicorn around the backyard, hoping to tire him out enough that he won't go wandering around the garage the next day. Luckily, he seems to be a nocturnal creature, happy to snooze the day away. I'm not so lucky, and I walk around school half in a daze, doze off in class, and suffer long, concerned looks from Yves at his place at the other end of the lunch table. He hasn't spoken to me since the goat milk incident.

If I weren't so tired, I'd wonder about that, and also about the damage this behavior is doing to my eternal soul. Every night I pray to God to send me strength, but it's never been enough to kill Flower, nor even to leave him alone long enough to let him die. Apparently my parents had nothing to worry about. Even if they had let me go with those people, I'd never have been able to bring myself to hunt unicorns.

Saturday afternoon our crowd has a picnic at the newly reopened park. All around, families are walking the trails, playing Frisbee in the fields, or barbecuing in the pavilions.

"I think it's premature," says Katey, unpacking sandwiches and bags of potato chips from a cooler. "They caught one unicorn. Doesn't mean there aren't more."

"If you're so scared, why did you come?" asks Marissa, pulling out a six-pack of sodas. Today she's in a pair of shorts cut almost to the crotch.

Katey gives Marissa a smile that is more like a growl. "Noah will protect me. Won't you, sweetie?"

Noah is standing next to Marissa, but moves really quickly. Yves is sitting on the picnic table, and Summer is on the bench propped up against his knee. Aidan is stealing carrots from the plate where I'm setting out vegetables. He grins at me, his mouth a row of baby carrots laid end to end.

"Hey," he says through the veggies, "did you see the corpse they put on the news yet?"

I have not. My parents deemed it unnecessarily macabre, and not only forbade me from watching the news, but also hid the metro section of the newspaper the following day. Aidan has brought the video, downloaded from YouTube, on his cell phone. We cluster around to watch. The audio is terrible, and the first minute is all the mayor shaking hands with the wildlife control people, none of whom, I note with interest, look like they could be unicorn hunters. To start with, there's not a single girl in the bunch.

There's a ticker running across the bottom of the screen that explains what neighborhood watch group found the corpse. Apparently the wildlife control folks aren't the ones who killed the unicorn after all. Then the video cuts to another scene, where photographers and people with cameras cluster around a small table in the police station. The camera zooms in on the corpse.

It's Venom.

I reel back from the group, a gasp lodged in my throat. How I recognize the remains of Flower's mother on a two-inch screen, I don't know. But it's her. The unicorn from the carnival. The one that bowed before me and begged me to save her child. *Dead.*

When? How? Did the wrangler kill her when I escaped with the baby? Venom wasn't looking too good that night, was having trouble standing after the wrangler ripped Flower out of her. Did she somehow injure herself then?

But what I know for certain is it's not the unicorn that killed Rebecca and John. It's not even the same kind. That one was big, and dark, with a horn that curved instead of twisted.

And then I realize something else. If the unicorn they "caught" was Venom, it means the one terrorizing these woods is still out there. Which means that all my friends, all these people in the park—they're in terrible danger.

Even more because they are here with me.

I turn and sprint away as my friends start calling my name. I run into the parking lot, breathing hard and wondering how I can get the city to close the parks down again. I hear feet pounding behind me, then feel a hand on my arm.

"Wen!" It's Yves, and Summer and Aidan are right behind him. They each stop a few feet away, giving me space, but not enough. I back up again.

"Get away," I tell Yves. "Don't come near me." I breathe the air, tasting it for any trace of unicorn. We're safe, so far.

"It's okay, Wen," he says.

"What's wrong?" asks Aidan.

"It's the unicorn," Summer explains. "Those kids it killed—they were her cousins."

I rip my arm out of Yves's grip and glare at him so hard he stumbles backward. *"You told her?"*

"Wen," says Aidan, coming forward. "I'm so sorry. I didn't know. Man, I'm such a moron. I—"

"That's not it. That unicorn, in the video. That's the one from the fair. They have the wrong one. The one that killed Rebec—it's still out there." I'm crying now, words choking me, breath stinging my throat.

"What do you mean?" Yves says.

Oh, no. This burning, this clarity, this smell of rot and forest fire. I know it. It's coming.

"Get away!" I scream at him. "Get away from me right now!"

And then I start to run.

They say on the news that no one died in the attack. Yves calls from the hospital, reporting that the unicorn knocked Aidan down and broke his arm, then ran right by them.

Of course. It was trying to get to me.

I huddle under an old afghan on the couch while Mom makes me hot chocolate and smoothes my hair. I can hear the helicopters overhead, watch as their searchlights scour the woods behind our house. The parks and forests have been closed again, and the whole town is on lockdown. I wonder if the unicorn is waiting out there for me, or if it has enough sense to go back into hiding.

"You did the right thing," Mom says. "Running away from a populated area. It was stupid to reopen the parks, to think there was only one of them out there…."

I sip my hot chocolate and don't correct her. After all, it's true that there *was* more than one unicorn in our town. And even if they do kill this one, there's still Flower, tucked away safe and sound in the garage.

Sometime late that night they report that the unicorn has been eliminated, but that the wilderness shutdown remains in full effect, for public safety. Yeah, right. They couldn't have gotten hunters over here from Italy so fast. My parents, now seated on either side of me, praise God for his protection and mercy, but I just sob into their hugs and reassurances and promises that they can keep me safe. My parents are so much older and wiser than I am. How can they be so wrong about this? How can any of us be safe when I'm raising the instrument of our destruction in our own garage? How can we guard ourselves against unicorns when I'm spending half my nights feeding one from a bottle?

I excuse myself, claiming I need some alone time. This is, miraculously, not a lie. Then I head to the garage.

In my father's toolbox is a small hand axe. I'm doing this for the right reasons. The wrangler was correct all along. Maybe she was in the same situation I'm in. Tricked into caring for a unicorn that became increasingly dangerous, that created little monsters of its own. Maybe she was right to try to drown Venom's offspring, to let Venom die—or even kill the unicorn herself at last. Maybe the wrangler possessed the grace that I could not muster on my own.

I approach Flower's box. I can tell he's happy I've come, but something's wrong. There's a hole chewed in the side of the box. The box is empty.

"Flower?" I say, spinning. He's still in the garage, hiding. He thinks this is a game. Flower's joy is palpable. He's so proud of himself. Clever beast, escaping. Freedom. Showing off for me when I come home. Each emotion is clearer than the last, and I realize that every moment I spend with the unicorn is giving it more access to my mind, to my soul.

I tighten my grip on the handle of the axe. I *must* cast it out. "Come here, Flower."

The unicorn usually obeys my every command, but he's hesitant now. Perhaps he's even smarter than I thought. Perhaps since I can read his thoughts, he can read mine and knows I mean him harm. I try to project my usual tenderness.

"Flower," I coax, following my senses through the garage, behind the saw table, under the disused weight bench, over to the old camping equipment. There are holes in the bag where we keep our cooking supplies, and utensils are strewn all over the floor. "Come here, baby."

I hear rustling from the darkness. Flower is unsure of my motives, confused by my tone.

"Flower," I try again, my voice wavering over more sobs. How do soldiers do it? How do the real unicorn hunters? The trained ones? "Don't you get it? I have to! I *have* to…"

The unicorn steps out of the shadows, his blue eyes trained on me. His mouth is open, panting slightly, so that he almost looks like he's smiling. I can see brand-new white teeth breaking through the gums. Teeth that helped him chew through the cardboard. Teeth he might use on my parents, or my friends.

I have to, I cry to the unicorn inside my head. Flower's matchstick legs wobble a few steps closer, and he watches me, eyes full of trust. This is the creature I've held and fed every night and every morning.

The flower in the center of his forehead is red now, glistening, enflamed and engorged like a massive, starburst-shaped boil. The horn is coming. The horn, and the poison, and all of the danger that marks this monster's—this demon's—entire species. I can't let him survive. I can't.

This is the animal I caressed until he fell asleep, who I crooned to while he cried, who I dreamed of every night, who I've run through the yard by moonlight, who I rushed home to day after day. I watched him be born; I held him in my arms, still wet from his mother; and I crushed him to my chest so he wouldn't freeze. I've hidden him and protected him and given up everything to keep him safe.

Flower bends his forelegs and lowers his head to the floor. He bows before me, just like his mother, and stretches out his neck as if for sacrifice. I could do it now; it would be so easy.

I drop the axe and fall to my knees.

Under cover of twilight I take Flower out to the woods. The deadly woods. The forbidden woods. With an old rubber-coated bicycle chain for a collar and a leash made from steel cable that Dad uses to tie his boat to his truck, I secure the unicorn to a tree, then create a makeshift shelter in the brush right next to it. From a few feet away you can hardly tell there's anything unnatural there. And at least he's out of our yard. No one will go into the woods—not after this new attack.

Flower is quiet while I work, and still, as if he knows how close he came to death. He trots obediently into the shelter and settles down on a pile of leaves. I leave the unicorn a package of ground turkey for dinner. Now that his teeth are in, I don't even need to bother with the blender anymore, but I figure that the food should still be soft. Baby food, for a predator.

The woods are still now. No helicopters, no searchlights. No sounds of birds or insects, either, as if they also recognize the presence of my monster. Beyond Flower, I can sense no unicorn. I stretch out my awareness to its limit, searching for the other one I know must still be alive, and I find nothing. It feels incredible, but then I recoil from the magic.

After all, haven't I sinned enough for one day?

In Sunday school the next morning, we talk about the Book of Daniel. When we get to the part about the one-horned goat, everyone goes quiet. It's bad timing on the teacher's part.

"Ms. Guzman?" A boy raises his hand. "Do you think that's a unicorn? That one they put on the news the other day—it kind of looked like a goat."

"It's possible," Ms. Guzman says. "In fact, there are older translations of the Bible that call it a unicorn. When this translation was made, however, we didn't know there were unicorns, so they called it a goat instead. If Daniel did see a unicorn in his prophetic vision, what do you think it meant?"

"That whatever was coming would be much more vicious and dangerous than if it was a goat," says one of the girls. "If it really was a unicorn in his vision, that makes it a much scarier one."

"And it makes more sense if it is a unicorn," says another girl, "because it goes on to say that neither the ram nor anyone else was strong enough to withstand the goat's power. And that's what they say about unicorns, that no one can cure the poison, that no one can catch or kill them."

"Someone can catch them," I find myself saying. "And maybe the goat kind of unicorn—Well, maybe they aren't vicious. So maybe the vision meant that Daniel should—"

"What?" asks the boy. "Hang out with the man-eating monster?"

"He hung out with man-eating lions," I snap.

"I think we're getting a little off topic," says Ms. Guzman. "The point is, no matter how powerful this unicorn might be—and the angel Gabriel explains to Daniel that the unicorn in the vision represents the pagan king Alexander the Great—all these kingdoms, the ram, the unicorn, all of it, are destined to fall because they are man's kingdoms, human kingdoms, and not the kingdom of God."

Ms. Guzman talks about God a little more, but I can't pay attention. I've been praying to God about Flower for weeks, hoping He'll forgive me for lying to my parents, hoping He'll forgive me for betraying Rebecca's and John's memories by taking care of a unicorn. I've been waiting for a single sign of violence from Flower, a clear sign that he is as dangerous as all the others so I can kill him with a clear conscience—but I've not seen anything. Is it because Flower isn't a killer? Or is it because I'm like Daniel in the lion's den? Is God protecting me?

And if so, why didn't He protect Rebecca and John?

Weeks pass, and Flower remains my secret. The unicorn is eating real food now—chicken thighs and kidneys and pork shoulders and anything else I can find on sale at the supermarket. I'm burning through my savings at an alarming rate, but I know my mom would notice if I started stealing meat from our fridge. Flower must be deadly bored, hanging out in the makeshift shelter all day, but he's out of sight of my parents and out of reach of any danger, so that's all that matters. With the woods off-limits to everyone in the neighborhood, the only thing that could hurt him is one of his elders, and I haven't sensed any during our nightly runs through the forest. The unicorn likes when I run alongside him, I've learned, and I admit, I love how fast we can go together. Branches and roots are never in my way when I'm flying through the forest with the unicorn at my side. If only he weren't illegal, I'd keep Flower around and stay on the track team.

But if I tried that, the unicorn might try to eat the spectators. Plus, Aidan would totally call me out on being a jock. Not that it matters. Even if Aidan did decide he liked me, I could never go out with him. Every time I see his cast, I'm reminded that it's only through God's grace that I avoided being the cause of his death. I could have killed them all, and yet I persist in this defiant path through my own weakness.

School is torture now. Since finding out about my cousins, Summer writes my odd behavior off as post-traumatic stress when it comes to unicorns. Yves doesn't correct her, and I don't enlighten any of them. They know unicorns are deadly, my parents tell me that they are evil, and I know everyone is right.

But I still love mine.

Flower is already half as tall as his mother, and his silver-white coat turns long and wavy. I draw the line at brushing it, but I'm pretty sure that if I bothered to, Flower would look as pretty as any unicorn in a fairy story. Even his dangerous horn is pretty—a smooth, creamy gray that twists like a corkscrew and seems to grow longer by the day. You can hardly see the remnants of the flower-shaped marking that gave my Flower his name.

One night, as I sneak into the woods for our usual evening romp, I catch a strange scent in the air. The reek of unicorn is as strong as ever, but there's something else carried aloft on the summer breeze. Something horrible. Flower rustles in the shelter as I approach, and the unicorn's elation stings like a cramp. What kind of life have I consigned this animal to? Alone all day, chained to a tree, never allowed to run except for a short half-hour each night when I should be in bed?

From my pocket I retrieve the bits of ham I secreted away from dinner and hurry toward the clearing. The smell grows stronger, and as I round the last tree, I put my foot down in something slick and sprawl onto the forest floor.

At eye level is a rabbit. Or what used to be a rabbit. The remains—mostly skin—are almost unrecognizable, except for a pair of floppy ears.

A few feet farther on is the half-digested skin of a chipmunk. Then a squirrel, and a scattering of sparrows.

I raise myself on my elbows and try not to gag.

In the center of the carnage sits Flower, with what looks like leftover raccoon all over his snout, and his chain lying in crumpled chewed-up chunks at his hooves. Flower looks at me, proud as punch, and thumps his tail against the earth.

Flower? Try *Flayer*.

My killer unicorn is finally living up to the name.

I fix the restraints, but the unicorn gnaws through them again. I spend the last of my savings on the heaviest chain the local hardware store supplies. Flayer, as I've taken to calling him, takes four days to chew up this one and then, in retaliation, procures a feast. I find the unicorn on his back in the shelter, four hooves in the air, drunk with the blood of small woodland creatures.

Oddly enough, this new evidence of the unicorn's deadly abilities only confuses me further. I wonder if killer unicorns are really the work of the Devil. I've seen Flayer in his natural element, covered in gore, tearing apart flesh and bone, and loving every minute—and though he's not exactly a candidate for a petting farm, neither does he seem like an evil demon. Dogs and cats and great white sharks do that too. Biscuit likes leaving mice and frogs and crickets as gifts on old Mrs. Schaffer's porch. I eat cows and chickens and pigs and fish. Flayer is a predator. That's not against God's plan.

But then I remember what that other unicorn did to my cousins, and I'm not so sure. Perhaps my ability to accept these acts of violence in my unicorn is nothing more than a sign of my own corrupted soul. I defied my parents, indulged the magic, raised a killer unicorn by hand. Maybe I'm past all redemption.

As if to prove the point, on our run this evening Flayer decides to snatch bats out of thin air for an evening snack. I hear him crunch their little bones, listen to them squeak their last, and shut my eyes to the sight of him tearing through their leathery wings. An animal that eats bats must be a creature of darkness, right?

We return to the shelter and I get Flayer settled down for the night, encouraging him to lie quietly and remain here, and above all, not to destroy the final length of chain. Thankfully, even when he has escaped his bonds, the unicorn hasn't wandered too far on his own yet. With the woods being off-limits, I can only hope that whatever slim precautions I can take will be enough to protect him from people, and enough to protect people from *him*. I've read stuff online about how baby fawns will wait in the brush for their mother to forage, but Flayer's obviously not going to be a baby much longer. He'll graduate from bats to people. Then what will I do?

I think about this on my much slower walk back to my yard and as I edge around the moonlight on my lawn, sticking to shadows in case my parents are randomly looking out the window.

They aren't. But someone else is. As I am rounding the back porch, I catch movement out of the corner of my eye. Yves is standing at his bedroom window, and he's staring down at me.

I successfully avoid him the entire next day at school, and volunteer to accompany Mom on a shopping trip on Saturday, so I miss both of his phone calls and the time he drops by the house for a chat. My parents raised me to return calls, but I find that disobeying them concerning the unicorn is indeed a slippery slope, and I avoid calling him all evening. He's waiting for me on the porch after church on Sunday, though, and since my parents are there, I can hardly run past him and into the house—or worse, up to the woods.

"Hey there, Wen," he says. "Long time, no see."

If I were any good at lying, I'd have explained to my folks that I was mad at Yves. If I were any good at lying, I'd tell Yves he was imagining things in his bedroom that night.

But I'm not, and Yves knows it. And as soon as the screen door closes after my parents, the smile fades from his face.

"What's going on with you?" The spring sun suddenly feels more like the glow of an interrogation lamp. I can feel my church skirt sticking to the back of my knees.

"Nothing."

"Don't give me that. You're hiding from everyone in school, and you're sneaking into the woods."

I look away. Old Mrs. Schaffer is shuffling down the street, pausing at telephone poles and mailboxes and peering into open garage doors.

At church today I prayed that God would show me a way out of this mess. I can't let Flayer go, but I can't keep him either. I can't tell my parents what I've been up to. I can't figure out what to do. I know now why the lady at the carnival was so upset. Like me, she was trapped.

And Venom ended up dead. My throat closes up if I try to picture a future like that for my unicorn.

"Do you have a death wish?" Yves's voice cuts through my reverie.

"What?" I turn back to him.

"Are you out there looking for—for unicorns? You think you can kill them or something, because of what those people said to you?"

I laugh. "Trust me, Yves. If there's one thing I'm positive I can't do, it's kill a unicorn." Spoil it rotten with hamburger meat? Teach it to come when called? Treat it like a jogging partner? Sure. But kill one? Forget it.

Yves's collar is open, and there's a dab of moisture in the hollow at his throat. I wonder how long he's been waiting out here for me. And if it's this hot for him,

Flayer must really be sweltering in his shelter—if the unicorn is even there, and not out on a rampage.

I shut my eyes for a moment. If I don't stop dwelling on Flayer, Yves will be able to read the truth on my face. If I don't stop staring at him, things will get even weirder.

"Wen, I *saw* you." He takes two steps, and suddenly he's on top of me, speaking in a voice that's so low I almost need my unicorn senses to hear him. He puts his hand over mine on the porch railing, and it practically sears my skin. "Tell me. You know you can tell me anything."

"Hello, children." Mrs. Schaffer's standing on the walk. "You haven't seen my Biscuit around anywhere, have you?"

"No, ma'am," Yves mumbles. Beside him, I stiffen. He glances at our joined hands, and when I try to pull away, he clamps down. He knows me so well.

"I haven't seen the poor thing since Friday morning."

I can't swallow. I certainly can't speak. Yves squeezes my hand in his, and it's not hard enough to bring tears, but somehow they're welling up in my eyes.

"I'm just so worried about him," Mrs. Schaffer goes on.

I hate that mangy old cat. It pees on our newspaper. It rips up our flower beds. It tears down the wind catchers Mom hangs on our porch.

And it's totally toast.

"I'm sorry, Mrs. Schaffer," I choke out. "I—"

"—hope you find him soon," Yves finishes, and tugs my hand. "We have to go."

I stumble, blind with tears, into the backyard. I've hated Biscuit for years, but that doesn't make him food. Random, nameless rabbits and raccoons are one thing. But Biscuit? Mrs. Schaffer loved him like I love Flayer. What have I done?

Yves pulls me into the shade behind the kitchen door and makes me look at him. We used to make mud pies back here. We used to make dandelion crowns and willow swords.

"It's a unicorn, isn't it?" he asks. "A unicorn ate Biscuit."

I nod, miserably.

"Oh, no. Wen, I'm so sorry." He pulls me into a hug. "I know it was just a stupid cat, but it must remind you of—"

"No." I shove the word out as I push him away. "You don't understand. It's my fault."

"Stop saying that," he cries. "This is exactly what I'm talking about. You have to stop blaming yourself for this. Stop punishing yourself. Stop going into the woods and endangering yourself. I don't care if you think you're irresistible to unicorns or whatever stupid stuff those people told you."

"Invincible," I say with a sniff. "*And* irresistible, I guess."

"Listen to me," he says, and tilts his head close to mine. "Look at me."

I do. I see a hundred Sunday afternoons and a thousand after-school playdates and one very black night last fall. Yves's eyes are dark and clear. "Rebecca and John weren't your fault, and Biscuit isn't either."

"It is. This one is." I take a deep breath, but I don't look away. "Yves."

"Wen." It's a whisper.

"I have to show you something. You're the only one who'll understand."

He doesn't hesitate, not even for a moment. I'm the girl who beats him at Skee-Ball; he's the first boy I ever kissed. Yves takes my hand, and I lead him into the forbidden woods.

I can feel the unicorn, sleeping through the afternoon heat. We'll just have to keep our distance, like with Venom at the sideshow. Flayer is chained, so Yves will be safe.

As we reach the shelter, Flayer rouses and bounds out, tail wagging, silver hair shining in the sunlight, horn still streaked with the blood of his latest kill. The beast pauses as he sees Yves, then bares his teeth in a growl.

And in the slowness and clarity that comes with my powers, I can see my fatal mistake. It took Flayer four days to chew through this chain the last time, and that was Thursday night. It's Sunday afternoon. I've cut it too close. The chain dangles at the unicorn's throat, mangled beyond hope of repair.

I hold fast to Yves's hand as the monster lunges.

"No!"

My sharp tone stops the unicorn short. Yves gasps.

"Sit."

Flayer parks his behind on the earth and looks at me in frustration.

"Wen?" Yves's voice trembles.

"Down," I order. The unicorn grumbles, and lowers himself to the ground, tilting his deadly horn up and away. I grab the broken end of the chain, hold on tight, and turn back to my friend. "This is Flayer."

Yves looks as though he might faint.

"Remember that night at the carnival?" I crouch next the unicorn and rub his stomach. "The unicorn there—Venom—she was pregnant."

"Pregnant," Yves repeats flatly.

"And I went back a few days later and found her giving birth. And… I can't explain it, but it was like she asked me to take care of the baby. So I took it."

Flayer lifts his hind leg in the air and bleats. I intensify my massage.

"I've been caring for him ever since." The unicorn's mouth opens, and his bloodstained tongue lolls between fanged jaws. "And, aside from Biscuit—well, and I guess some squirrels and stuff—"

I babble on. I don't know for how long. It feels so good, to confess all this to Yves. I tell him about the goat's milk, and the laundry basket. I tell him about the hamburger and the bicycle chains. I tell him about the moonlight runs through the forest. I tell him about the time with the axe, and the way Flayer can call to me from half a mile away.

Yves listens to everything, and then he says, "Do you have any idea what you've done?"

I nod, staring down at my pet. "Yeah. Broke the law. Endangered our entire neighborhood. Lied to everyone."

He shakes his head. "Wen, you *trained* a killer unicorn. No one can do that. No one can catch one, no one can kill one, no one can tame one! But you did!"

"I—"

"Even the one at the carnival was covered in chains. They're wild, vicious, but this one…" Yves gestures to Flayer, who wags his tail like Yves is about to throw him a ham hock. "He listens to you! He stays where you want him to. It's a miracle."

I stare down at the unicorn. *A miracle.*

I've been praying to God to deliver me from my unwelcome powers, the curse of my dangerous and unholy magic. I've been praying for Him to direct my hand, to give me strength to destroy the demon unicorn He placed in my path. And all this time, I thought He'd refused because of my own sins—my defiance of the law, my disobedience toward my parents. I thought I'd failed Him.

But what if… God *wanted* me to care for this unicorn? What if He sent it to me to discover a way to prevent what happened to my cousins from ever occurring again?

What if my powers aren't a curse at all? What if they're… a gift?

"We have to tell the world," Yves finishes.

I snuggle the unicorn close to my chest. "No way. If I come out of the woods with Flayer by my side, he'll be taken from me, experimented on, destroyed. What chance does this little guy have against helicopters and searchlights? Against napalm?"

Yves says, "There has to be something. Maybe your parents—"

"My parents think unicorns are demons and my powers are witchcraft."

It'll never work. Too many lives have been destroyed by unicorns. Even Yves looks uncertain as I continue to cuddle the killer unicorn in my lap.

If only they could feel what it's like to run through the woods by Flayer's side. If only they knew how much Flayer loves me, and I him. I never feel so free, so right as I do when I'm alone in the forest with the unicorn. If only God would reveal His plan to them as well.

"Okay," says Yves. "What about those people in Italy? The unicorn hunters? They understand your powers, right?"

Yeah, but even they wanted to use my powers to help them *kill* unicorns. Maybe I could show them how to use our gifts for this instead, but first I'd have to persuade them to spare my unicorn. I scratch the base of Flayer's horn, where the tiny flower marking is barely visible. Protecting Flayer is what matters most. The world can wait.

"Stay," I say to the unicorn as I join Yves again. "What if I left?"

"You mean, like, run away?" Yves looks stricken. "Wen, you can't—"

"Flayer and me, we're safe in the forest. And I can keep an eye on him, make sure he eats only wild animals. And me… I used to be a really good camper."

"But what about school? What about food? What about the other unicorns?" Yves shakes his head. "No, there's got to be another way."

"A way where I can save Flayer?" I ask. "What way is that? Everyone in the world wants him dead but me!"

"We could—" Yves casts about desperately for an alternative. "We could ask Summer. She's involved in the Sierra Club, she knows people at the World Wildlife Fund…"

Right. Her.

"Yves." I bite my lip, but it's too late and the words pour out. "I know you and Summer—"

He kisses me then. Full on, noses smashing. Our arms go around each other, and Flayer bleats in surprise, but I don't care. Last fall may have been a mistake, but this isn't. I just wish I had figured it out before. Before Summer. Before Flayer. Before I feared I'd never see him again.

We're still kissing when Mom and Dad come up over the hill. I feel Flayer's alarm, hear him start to growl, and I pull away from Yves. My parents' faces are dark with fury, dim with shock. Their daughter, their little Wen. Lying. Woods. Magic. *Kissing*.

I move to stand beside my killer unicorn.

THE NIGHT TRAIN
LAVIE TIDHAR

Lavie Tidhar grew up on a kibbutz in Israel and has since lived in South Africa, the UK, Vanuatu, and Laos. He is the author of novel *The Bookman,* linked story collection *HebrewPunk*, novellas "Cloud Permutations" and "An Occupation of Angels," and the novel *The Tel Aviv Dossier* (with Nir Yaniv). He also edited anthology *The Apex Book of World SF*, and runs the World SF Blog. Forthcoming works include novels *Osama* and *Martian Sands*, and second in the Bookman Chronicles, *Camera Obscura*, all due later this year.

Her name wasn't Molly and she didn't wear shades, reflective or otherwise.

She was watching the length of the platform.

Hua Lamphong at dusk: a warm wind blowing through the open platforms where the giant beasts puffed smoke and steam into the humid air, the roof of the train station arching high overhead.

Her name wasn't Noi, either, in case you asked, though it's a common enough name. It wasn't Porn, or Ping. It wasn't even Friday.

She was watching the platform, scanning passengers climbing aboard, porters shifting wares, uniformed police patrolling at leisure. She was there to watch out for the Old Man.

She wasn't even a girl. Not exactly. And as for why the Old Man was called the Old Man…

He was otherwise known as Boss Gui: head and *bigfala bos* of the Kunming Toads. She got the job when she'd killed Gui's Toad bodyguards—by default, as it were.

But that had happened back in Kunming. This was Bangkok, Bangkok at dusk—this was Hua Lamphong, greatest of train stations, where the great slugs breathed steam and were rubbed and scrubbed by the slug-boys whose job it was to nurture them before departure. And the Old Man wasn't exactly an old man, either.

Scanning, waiting for the Old Man to arrive: Yankee tourists with in-built cams flashing as they posed beside the great beasts, these neo-nagas of reconstituted DNA, primitive nervous system, and prodigious appetite. Scanning: a group of Martian-Chinese from Tong Yun City walking cautiously—unused to the heavier gravity of this home/planet. Scanning: three Malay businessmen—Earth-Belt Corp. standardized reinforced skeletons—they moved gracefully, like dancers—wired through and through, hooked up twenty-four Earth-hours an Earth-day, seven Earth-days a week to the money-form engines, the great pulsating web of commerce and data, that singing, Sol-system-wide, von Neumann-machine expanded network of networks of networks....

Wired with hidden weaponry, too: she made a note of that.

An assassin can take many shapes. It could be the sweet old lady carrying two perfectly balanced baskets of woven bamboo over her shoulders, each basket filled with sweet addictive fried Vietnamese bananas. It could be the dapper K-pop starlet with her entourage, ostensibly here to rough it a bit for the hovering cameras. It could be the couple of French backpackers—he with long, thinning silver hair and a cigarette between his lips, she with a new face courtesy of Soi Cowboy's front-and-back street cosmetic surgeries—baby-doll face, but the hands never lie and the hands showed her true age, in the lines etched there, the drying of the skin, the quick-bitten nails polished a cheap red—

An assassin could be anyone. A Yankee rich kid on a retro-trip across Asia, reading *Air America* or *Neuromancer* in a genuine reproduction 1984 POD-paperback; it could be the courteous policeman helping a pretty young Lao girl with her luggage; it could be the girl herself—an Issan farmer's daughter exported to Bangkok in a century-long tradition, body augmented with vibratory vaginal inserts, perfect audio/visual-to-export, always-on record, a carefully tended Louis Wu habit and an as-carefully-tended retirement plan—make enough money, get back home to Issan *wan bigfala mama*, open up a bar/hotel/bookshop and spend your days on the Mekong, waxing lyrical about the good old days, listening to Thai pop and K-pop and Nuevo Kwasa-Kwasa, growing misty-eyed nostalgic....

Could be anyone. She waited for the Old Man to arrive. The trains in Hua Lamphong never left on time.

Her name before, or after, doesn't matter. They used to call her Mulan Rouge, which was a silly name, but the *farangs* loved it. Mulan Rouge, when she was still working Soi Cowboy, on the stage, on her knees or hands-and-knees, but seldom on her back—earning the money for the operation that would rescue her from that boy's body and make her what she truly was, which was *kathoey*.

They call it the third sex, in Thailand. But she always considered herself, simply, a woman.

She ran a perimeter check. Up front, she was awed as always by the slug. It was tied up to the front of the train, a beast fifty meters long and thirty wide. It glistened and farted as the slug-boys murmured soothing words to it and rubbed its flesh, thirty or forty of them swarming like flies over the corpulent flesh of the slug. She checked out the driver—the woman was short, dark-skinned—a highlander from Laos, maybe. The driver sat in her harness high above the beast, her helmet entirely covering her head—the only thing she wore. Pipes came out of her flesh and into the slug's. They were one—her mind driving the beast forward, a peaceful run, the Bangkok to Nong Khai night ride, and she was the night rider. She was the train.

There were stories about joined minds like this in the Up There. Up There, beyond the atmosphere, where the universe truly began. Where the Exodus ships lumbered slowly out of the solar system, in search of better futures far away. They said there were ships driven by minds, human/Other interfaces, holding sleepers inside them like wombs. They told stories of ships who had gone mad, of sleepers destined never to awake, slow silent ships drifting forever in galactic space… or, worse, ships where the sleepers *were* awakened, where the ship-mind became a dark god, demanding worship…. Mulan didn't know who *they* were, or how they knew. These were stories, and stories were a currency in and of itself. Darwin's Choice used to tell her stories….

She met him/her flesh-riding an older kathoey body, at a club on Soi Cowboy. Darwin's Choice—not the most imaginative name (he told her, laughing)—but he liked it. He had watched her dance and, later, signalled for her to join him.

She thought of him as a *he*, though Others had no sex, and most had little interest in flesh-riding. He had evolved in the Breeding Grounds, post-Cohen, billions of generations after that first evolutionary cycle in Jerusalem, and she only thought of him as *him* because the bodies he surfed always had a penis. He used to hold the penis in his hand and marvel at it. He always chose pre-op bodies, with breasts but no female genitalia. He always dressed as a woman. Surgery was expensive, and a lot of kathoey worked it off in stages. Taking on a passenger helped pay the bills—it wasn't just a matter of cutting off cock-and-balls and refashioning sex, there was the matter of cheekbones to sand down and an Adam's apple to reduce, bum to pad—if you *really* had the money you got new hands. The hands usually gave it away—that is, if you wanted to pass for a woman.

Which many kathoey didn't. Darwin's Choice always surfed older kathoey who never had the basic equipment removed. "I am neither male, nor female," he once told her. "I am not even an *I*, as such. No more than a human—a network of billions of neurons firing together—is truly an *I*. In assuming kathoey, I feel closer to humanity, in many ways. I feel—divided, and yet whole."

Like most of what he said, it didn't make a lot of sense to her. He was one of the few Others who tried to understand humanity. Most Others existed within their networks, using rudimentary robots when they needed to interact with the physical world. But Darwin's Choice liked to body-surf.

With him, she earned enough for the full body package.

And more than that.

Through him, she discovered in herself a taste for controlled violence.

Boss Gui finally came gliding down the platform—fat-boy Gui, the Old Man, *olfala bigfala bos* in the pidgin of the asteroids. His Toads surrounded him—human/toad hybrids with Qi-engines running through them: able to inflate themselves at will, to jump higher and farther, to kill with the hiss of a poisoned, forked tongue—people moved away from them like water from a hot skillet.

Boss Gui came and stood before her. "Well?" he demanded.

He looked old. Wrinkles covered his hands and face like scars. He looked tired, and cranky—which was understandable, under the circumstances.

She had recommended delaying the trip. The Old Man had refused to listen. And that was that.

She said, "I cannot identify an obvious perp—"

He smiled in satisfaction—

"But that is not to say there isn't one."

"I am Boss Gui!" he said. Toad-like, he inflated as he spoke. "Who dares try to kill me?"

"I did," she said, and he chuckled—and deflated, just a little.

"But you didn't, my little sparrow."

They had reached an understanding, the two of them. She didn't kill him—having to return the client's fee had been a bitch—and he, in turn, gave her a job. It had security attached—a pension plan, full medical, housing, and salary, calculated against inflation. There were even stock options.

She had never regretted her decision—until now.

"It's still too dangerous," she said now. "You're too close—"

"Silence!" he regarded her through rheumy eyes. "I am Boss Gui, boss of the Kunming Toads!"

"We are a long way from Kunming."

His eyes narrowed. "I am seventy-nine years old and still alive. How old are *you?*"

"You know how old," she said, and he laughed. "Sensitive about your age," he said. "How like a woman." He hawked up phlegm and spat on the ground. It hissed, burning a small, localised hole in the concrete.

She shrugged. "Your cabin is ready," she said; then: "Sir."

He nodded. "Very good," he said. "Tell the driver we are ready to depart."

A taste for controlled violence...

Darwin's Choice used his human hosts hard. He strove to understand humanity. For that purpose he visited ping-pong shows, kickboxing exhibits, Louis Wu emporiums, freak shows, the Bangkok Opera House, shopping malls, temples, churches, mosques, synagogues, slums, high-rises, and train stations.

"Life," he once told her, "is a train station."

She didn't know what to make of that. What she did know: to understand humanity he tried what they did. His discarded bodies were left with heroin addiction, genital sores, hangovers, and custom-made viruses that were supposed to self-destruct but sometimes didn't. Sometimes, either to apologise or for his own incomprehensible reasons, he would go into the cosmetic surgeries on Soi Cowboy and come out with a full physical sex-transfer—seemingly unaware that his hosts might have preferred to remain non-op. Sometimes he would wire them up in strange ways—for a month, at one point, he became a tentacle-junkie and would return from the clinics with a quivering mass of additional, aquatic limbs.

But it was his taste for danger—even while he experienced none, even while his true self kept running independently in the background, in a secure location somewhere on Earth or in orbit—that awakened her own.

The first time she killed a man…

They had gone looking for opium and found an ambush. The leader said, "Kill the flesh-rider and keep the kathoey. We'll sell her in—"

She had acted instinctively. She didn't know what she was doing until it was done. Her knife—

The blade flashing in the neon light—

A scream, cut short—a gurgle—

Blood ruined her second-best blouse—

The sound of something breaking—the pain only came later. They had smashed in her nose—

Darwin's Choice *watching*—

She killed the second one with her bare hands, thumbs pressing on his windpipe until he stopped struggling—

She laid him down on the ground almost tenderly—

Pain, making her scream, but her lungs wouldn't work—

They hit her with a taser, but somehow she didn't pass out—

She fell, but forward—hugging the man with the taser, sharing the current until there was only darkness.

"You were clinically dead," he told her, later. He sounded impressed. "What was it like?"

"Like nothing," she told him. "There was nothing there."

"You were switched off?"

She had to laugh. "You could say that."

They made love the night she was released from hospital. She licked his nipples, slowly, and felt him harden in her hand. She stroked him, burying her face in his full breasts. He reached down, touched her, and it was like electricity. She kept thinking of the dead men….

When she came, he said, "You would do it again—"

It wasn't a question.

She was tuning in to people's nodes, picking up network traffic to and from—the Malay business guys were high-encryption/high-bandwidth clouds, impossible to hack through, but here and there—

Kid with vintage paperback was on a suitably retro playlist with a random shuffle—she caught the Doors singing "The End," which was replaced with Thaitanium's "Tom Yum Samurai," only to segue into Drunken Tiger's "Great Rebirth." Issan-girl was plugged in—a humming battery was sending a low current into her brain. She would be out for the journey…. The K-pop princess was playing *Guilds of Ashkelon*. So were her entourage. The French backpackers were stoned on one thing or another. Others were chatting, stretching, reading, farting, tidying away bags and ordering drinks—life on board the night train to Nong Khai was always the same.

The train was coming alive, the slug belching steam—the whole train shuddered as it began to crawl along the smooth tracks, slug-boys falling off it like fleas.

Tuning, scanning—someone two cars down watching the feed from a reality-porn channel, naked bodies woven together like a tapestry, a beach somewhere—Koh Samui or an off-Earth habitat, it was impossible to say.

Boss Gui: "I'm hungry!"

Mulan Rouge: "Food's coming—" In the dining car they were getting ready, a wok already going, rice cooker steaming, crates of beer waiting—

"I want kimchi!"

"I'll see if they have any—" though she knew they didn't.

"No need." A long, slow, drawn-out hum from one of the Toads. "I keep for boss."

Limited vocabulary—you didn't breed Toads for their brains.

She watched the toad reach into what the Australians called an *esky*. There was a jar of kimchi in there, and… other stuff.

Like a jar of living flies, for the Toads. Like what appeared to be a foetal sac, preserved in dry ice….

Other things.

She left them to it, returned to watching—waiting.

"You would do it again," Darwin's Choice had said. And he—she—it—was right. Mulan had liked it—a sense of overwhelming *power* came with violence, and if it could be controlled, it could be used. Power depended on how you used it.

She counted the succeeding years in augmentations and bodies. Three in Vientiane—she had followed Darwin's Choice there to buy up a stash of primitive communist VR art—the deal went wrong and she had to execute two men and a woman before they got away. She'd had snake eyes installed after that. A man and a kathoey in Chiang Mai—DC was buying a genuine *Guilds of Ashkelon* virtual artefact that had turned out to be a fake. She'd had her skeleton strengthened following that….

With each kill, new parts of her. With each, more power—but never over him.

Gradually, Darwin's Choice appeared less and less in the flesh. She had to cast around for work, hiring out as bodyguard, enforcer—hired killer, sometimes, only sometimes. Finally DC never reappeared. He had tried to explain it to her, once:

"We are I-loops but, unlike humans, we are *self-aware* I-loops. Not self-aware in the sense of consciousness, or what humans call consciousness. Self-aware in the sense that we are—we *can*—know every loop, every routine and subroutine. Digital, not neurological. And as we are aware so do we change, mutating code, merging code, sharing...."

"Is that how you make love?"

"Love is a physical thing," he said. "It's hormone-driven."

"You can only feel love when you're body-surfing?"

He only shrugged.

"How do you..." she searched for the word, settled on—"mate?"

Imagine two or more Others. Endless lines of code meeting in digital space—*if*s and *and*s and *or*s branching into probabilities, cycling through endless branches of logic at close to the speed of light—

"Is that what you're like?"

"No. Shh..."

...and *meeting*, merging, mixing, mutating—"And dying; to be an Other is to die, again and again, to *evolve* with every cycle, to cull and select and grow, achieve new, unexpected forms—"

...not so much *mating* as *joining*, and splitting, and joining again—"A bit like that old story about humans replacing every single atom in their bodies every seven years—how the body wears out and regenerates and changes but the entity still retains the illusion of person, remains an I-loop—"

...but for Others, it meant becoming something new—"Giving birth to one's self, in essence."

The body he was surfing had been stoned, then, when he told her all this. When he was gone, she hired out. She enjoyed the work, but freelancing was hard. When the contract on Boss Gui came, she took it—and upgraded to corporate.

"We are never alone," DC had told her, just before he left forever. "There are always... us. So many of us..."

"Can't you all join?" she asked. "Join into one?"

"Too much code slows you down," he said. "We have... limits. Though we share, too—share the way humans can't."

"We can share in ways *you* can't," she said. Her finger dug into his anus when she spoke. DC squirmed under her, then gave a small moan. His breasts were freckled, his penis circumcised. "True," he said—whispered—and drew her to him with an urgency they were sharing only rarely, by then.

That had been the last time....

She wondered which species' sharing was better—figured she would never know.

They said sex was overrated....

Yankee boy blue was no longer listening to the Doors—she couldn't sense his node any more at all. She blinked, feeling panic rise. How had he slipped past her? Scanning for him—his vintage sci-fi paperback was still on his bunk.

Shit.

She glanced back into the cabin—Boss Gui glared up at her, then clutched his bloated stomach and gave a groan. The two Toads jumped—too hard, and hit the ceiling.

Double shit—she said, "What's wrong?" but knew.

He said, "It's starting."

She shook her head. "It can't. It's too soon."

"It's *time*."

"Shit!"—a third time, and it was counterproductive and she knew it.

Boss Gui's face was twisted in pain. "It's coming!"

And suddenly she picked up the North American's node.

"Sh—"

They were going to Nong Khai, from there to cross into Laos. Boss Gui wanted to expand the business, and business was booming in a place called Vang Vieng, a tawdry little mini-Macau at the foothills of the mountains, four hours from Vientiane—a place of carefully regulated lawlessness, of cheap opium and cheaper synths, of games-worlds cowboys and body hackers, of tentacle-junkies and doll emporiums and government taxes that Boss Gui wanted a part of.

A *large* part of.

There were families running Vang Vieng but he was the Old Man, *olfala bigfala bos blong ol man tod blong Kunming*, and the Chinese had anyway bought up most of Laos back in the early privatisation days. He would cut deals with some, terminate the others, and slice himself a piece of the Vang Vieng dumpling—that was the plan.

She had advised him against it. She told him it was too soon to travel. She asked him to wait.

He wouldn't.

She sort of had an inkling as to the why....

She was picking up the kid's node right next to the driver's.

Which was not good at all.

The driver's, first: an incomprehensible jumble of emotion, in turns horny, soothing, driven, paused—the driver and the slug as one, their minds pulsating in union—hunger and lust made it go faster. Snatches of Beethoven—for some reason it calmed down the slugs. The driver not aware of the extra passenger—yet.

The kid wasn't really a kid....

His node blocked to her—black impenetrable walls, an emptiness not even returning pings. He was alone in his own head—which must have been terrifying.

She had to get to the front of the train. She had to get on the slug. And Boss Gui was convulsing.

"Why are you just standing there, *girl?*"

She tried to keep her voice even. "I found the assassin. He is planning to kill the slug—destroy the entire train, and you with it."

Boss Gui took that calmly. "Clever," he said, then grimaced. His naked belly glistened, a dark shape moving beneath the membrane of skin. The Toads looked helpless, standing there. She flashed them a grin. "I'll be right back," she said. Then she left, hearing Boss Gui's howl of rage behind her.

Running down the length of the train—through the dining car, past toilets already beginning to smell, past *farang* backpackers and Lao families and Thais returning to Udon from the capital—past babies and backpacks and bemused conductors in too-tight trousers that showed their butts off to advantage—warm wind came in through the open windows and she blocked out the public nodes broadcasting news in Thai and Belt Pidgin. The end of the train was a dead end, a smooth wall with no windows. She kicked it—again and again, augmented muscles expending too much energy, but it began to break, rusting old metal giving way, and fading sunlight seeped through.

How had the kid gotten through? He must have had gecko-hands—climbed out the window and crawled his way along the side of the train, below the window line, all the way to the slug....

She reached out—sensed the driver's confusion as another entity somehow wormed its way into the two-way mahout/slug interface. *Stop!*

Confusion from the slug. The signals rushing through, too fast—horny/hungry/faster—faster!

He was going to crash the train. The driver: *Who is this? You can't—*

She kept kicking. The wall gave way—behind it was the slug's wide back, the driver sitting cross-legged on the beast, the intruder behind it, a hand on the driver's shoulder—the hand grew roots that penetrated the woman and the beast both.

Hostile mahout interface initiated.

The driver was fighting it, and losing badly. No one hijacked slug trains.

On her private channel—Boss Gui, screaming. "Get back here!"

"Get your own fucking midwife!"

But she could sense his pain, confusion. How many times had he gone through it in the past? she wondered.

The hijacker had kept the driver alive. Had to—the whole thing had to look like an accident, the driver's body found in the wreckage, unmolested—no doubt he planned to jump before impact.

Could he?

She crept behind him. Neither hijacker nor driver paid her any attention. And what could she do? Killing the hijacker would kill the interface—he was already in too deep.

Unless...

From Boss Gui, far away—"Hurry!"

Sometimes she wondered what would have happened if Darwin's Choice had stayed behind. It was possible for kathoey to give birth, these days... could an Other foster a child? Would he want to?

Or he could have flesh-ridden a host... she would have kept the male parts just for that. If he'd asked her.

But he never did.

The hijacker must have had an emergency eject. She had to find the trigger for it—

Wind was rushing at her, too fast. It was hard to maintain balance on the soft spongy flesh of the slug. It was accelerating—too fast.

She was behind the hijacker now—she reached out, put her hand on the back of his head. A black box...

She punched through with a data-spike while her other hand—

Darkness. The smell of rotting leaves. The smell of bodies in motion, sweat—hunger, a terrible hunger—

"Who the fuck are you? How did you *get* in here?"

Panic was good. She sent through images—her standing behind him, the data-spike in his head—and what else she was doing.

"You can't do that...."

She had pushed a second data-spike through his clothes and through the sphincter muscle, into the bowels themselves—detached a highly illegal replicator probe inside.

She felt the slug slow down, just a fraction. The hijacker trying to understand—

She said, "I am being nice."

She was.

He had a choice.

The probe inside him was already working. It was the equivalent of graffiti artists at work. It replicated a message, over every cell, every blood vessel, every muscle and tendon. It would be impossible to scrub—you'd need to reach a good clinic and by then it'd be too late.

The message said, *I killed the slug train to Nong Khai.*

It was marking him. He wasn't harmed. She couldn't risk killing him, killing the interface. But this way, whether he got off the train or not, he was a dead man.

"I'll count to five."

He let go at three.

Light, blinding her. The wind rushed past—the driver sat as motionless as ever, but the train had slowed down. The hijacker was gone—she followed him back through the hole in the wall.

He was lying on his bunk, still reading his book. He wasn't listening to music any more. Their eyes met. She grinned. He turned his gaze. She had given him a choice and she'd abide by it—but if the Toads happened to find out, she didn't rate his chances....

Well, the next stop was in an hour. She'd give him an extra half-hour after that—a running start.

She went back to the boss.

"It's coming!" Boss Gui said. She knelt beside him. His belly-sac was moving, writhing, the thing inside trying to get out. She helped—a fingernail slicing through the membrane, gently. A sour smell—she reached in where it was sticky, gooey, warm—found two small arms, a belly—pulled.

"You sorted out the problem?"

"Keep breathing."

"Yes?"

"Yes, of course I did! Now push!"

Boss Gui pushed, breathing heavily. "I'm getting too old for this..." he said.

Then he heaved, one final time, and the small body *detached* itself from him and came into her hands. She held it, staring at the tiny body, the bald head, the small penis, the five-fingered hands—a tiny Boss Gui, not yet fat but just as wrinkled.

It was hooked up with a cord to its progenitor. With the same flick of a nail, she cut it cleanly.

The baby cried. She rocked it, said, "There, there."

"Drink," Boss Gui said—weakly. One of the Toads came forward. Boss Gui fastened lips on the man/toad's flesh and sucked—a vampire feasting. He had Toad genes—so did the baby, who burped and suddenly ballooned in her hands before shrinking again.

"A true Gui!" the Old Man said.

She stared at the little creature in her hands.... "Which makes how many, now?" she said.

The boss shrugged, pushing the Toad away, buttoning up his own shirt. "Five, six? Not many."

"You would install him at Vang Vieng?"

"An assurance of my goodwill—and an assurance of Gui control there, too, naturally. Yes. An heir is only useful when he is put to use."

She thought of Darwin's Choice. "Evolution is everything," he would have told her. "We evolve constantly, with every cycle. Whereas you..."

She stared at the baby clone. It burped happily and closed its little eyes. Gui's way was not unpopular with the more powerful families... but sooner or later someone would come to challenge succession and then it wouldn't matter how many Guis there were.

Suddenly she missed DC, badly.

She rocked the baby to sleep, hugging it close to her chest. The train's thoughts came filtering through in the distance—comfort, and warmth, food and safety—the slow rhythmic motion was soothing. After a while, when the baby was asleep, she handed him to the Old Man, no words exchanged, and went to the dining car in search of a cup of tea.

STILL LIFE
(A SEXAGESIMAL FAIRY TALE)
IAN TREGILLIS

Ian Tregillis is a 2005 graduate of the Clarion Writers Workshop. His first novel, *Bitter Seeds*, debuted in April 2010. The second and third volumes of the Milkweed trilogy (*The Coldest War* and *Necessary Evil*, respectively) are forthcoming from Tor in October 2011 and 2012. He is also a contributor to several Wild Cards shared-world superhero anthologies. He holds a doctorate in physics from the University of Minnesota for research on radio galaxies, but lives in New Mexico, where he consorts with scientists, writers, and other unsavory types. His website is www.iantregillis.com.

Every evening was a *fin de siècle* in the great sprawling castle-city of Nycthemeron. But, of course, to say it was evening meant no more than to say it was morning, or midnight, or yesterday, or six days hence, or nineteen years ago. For it was every inch a timeless place, from the fig trees high in the Palazzo's Spire-top cloud gardens all the way down to the sinuous river Gnomon encircling the city.

Nycthemeron had tumbled from the calendar. It had slipped into the chasm between tick and tock, to land in its own instantaneous eternity. And so its residents occupied their endless moment with pageants and festivals and reveled in century-long masques, filled forever with decadent delights. They picnicked in the botanical gardens, made love in scented boudoirs, danced through their eternal twilight. And they disregarded the fog that shrouded their city with soft gray light.

As for time? Time was content to leave them there. It felt no pity, no compassion, for the people stuck in that endless *now*. This wasn't because time was cold, or cruel, or heartless. But it had no concern for that glistening place, no interest in the people who existed there.

Except one. Her name was Tink.

And it was said (among the people who said such things) that if you sought something truly special for your sweetheart, or if you yearned for that rarest of experiences—something novel, something new—you could find it at Tink's shop in the Briardowns. For Tink was something quite peculiar: she was a clockmaker.

Indeed, so great were her talents that normally staid and proper clock hands fluttered with delight at her approach. Time reveled in her horological handiwork. If it had to be measured, quantified, divvied up and parceled out, it would do so only on a timepiece of Tink's design.

How could this be? She was a clockwork girl, they said. And indeed, if you were to stand near Tink, to wait for a quiet moment and then bend your ear in her direction, you might just hear the phantom *tickticktickticktickticktick* serenading every moment of her life. Who but a clockwork girl would make such a noise, they said. And others would nod, and agree, and consider the matter settled.

But they were wrong. Tink was a flesh and blood woman, as real as anybody who danced on the battlements or made love in the gardens. She was no mere clockwork.

Tink was the object of time's affection. It attended her so closely, revered and adored her so completely, that it couldn't bear to part from her, even for an instant. But time's devotion carried a price. Tink *aged*.

She was, in short, a living clock. Her body was the truest timepiece Nycthemeron could ever know; her thumping heart, the metronome of the world.

But the perfectly powdered and carefully coifed lovelies who visited her shop knew nothing of this. They made their way to the Briardowns, in the shadow of an ancient aqueduct, seeking the lane where hung a wooden sign adorned with a faceless clock. Midway down, between an algebraist's clinic and a cartographer's studio, Tink's storefront huddled beneath an awning of pink alabaster.

Now, on this particular afternoon (let us pretend for the moment that such distinctions were meaningful in Nycthemeron) the chime over Tink's door announced a steady trickle of customers. The Festival of the Leaping Second was close, and if ever there was an occasion to ply one's darling with wonderments, it was this. Soon revelers would congregate on the highest balconies of the Spire. There they would grasp the hands of an effigy clock and click the idol forward one second. Afterward, they would trade gifts and kisses, burn the effigy, then seek out new lovers and new debaucheries.

If you were to ask the good people of Nycthemeron just how frequently they celebrated the Festival of the Leaping Second, they would smile and shrug and tell you: *When the mood descends upon us.* But Tink knew differently. The Festival came every twenty years, as measured by her tick-tock heartbeat. She felt this, knew it, as a fish feels water and knows how to swim.

To a marchioness with a fringe of peacock feathers on her mask, Tink gave an empty, pentagonal hourglass. "Turn this after your favorite dance, and you'll live that moment five times over," she said.

To a courtier in a scarlet cravat, Tink gave a paper packet of wildflower seeds. "Spread these in your hair," she said. "They'll blossom the moment you kiss your honey love, and you will be the posy she takes home."

Tink requested only token payments for these trinkets, expecting neither obligation nor gratitude in return. Some, like the marchioness, paid handsomely;

others, such as the tatterdemalion scholar, gave what they could (in his case, a leather bookmark). And sometimes she traded her wares for good will, as she did with the stonemason and gardener.

Though she was young and strong and did not ache, Tink spent what her body considered a long day rummaging through her shop for creative ways to brighten static lives. Her mind was tired, her stomach empty.

Unlike the rest of Nycthemeron's populace, Tink had to sleep. She announced her shop closed for the remainder of the day. Cries of dismay arose from the people queued outside (though of course they had long ago forgotten the meaning of "day").

"The Festival!" they cried; a chorus of painted, feathered, and sequined masks. Everyone wore a mask, as demanded by the calculus of glamour.

"Come back tomorrow," she said (though of course they had forgotten the meaning of this, too). But a tall fellow in a cormorant mask came jogging up the lane.

"Wait! Timesmith, wait!"

Nobody had ever called her that, but the phrase amused her. Few people dared to let the word "time" touch their lips. The rest of Tink's petitioners grumbled at the bold fellow's approach. They dispersed, shaking their heads and bemoaning their bad luck.

"Sorry, pretties. Sorry, lovelies," said Tink. "You'll get your goodies tomorrow."

The newcomer laid a hand upon the door, panting slightly. His breeches, she noticed, displayed shapely calves. "Are you Tink?"

"I am."

"Fabled maker of clocks and wonderments, I hear."

"Let me guess," said Tink. "You're seeking something for the Festival. Something with which to impress your lady love. You want me to win her heart for you, is that so?"

His shrug ruffled the long silk ribbons looped around the sleeves of his shirt. Some were vermilion, and others cerulean, like his eyes. "It's true, I confess."

"The others wanted the same," she said. "I told them I could do no more today. Why should I become a liar?"

"Do it for my flaxen-haired beauty."

Tink thought she recognized this fellow. And so she asked, knowing the answer, "Will you love her forever?"

"Forever? That is all we have. Yes, I will love her forever, and she me. Until the Festival ends."

Aha. "You are Valentine."

He bowed, with a flourish. The ribbons fluttered on his arms again. "You know me?"

"Everybody knows you."

Valentine: the legendary swain of Nycthemeron. Valentine, who could spend centuries on a single seduction. Valentine, famed for his millennial waltz. Charmer, lothario, friend of everyman, consort of the queen.

Though it was against her better judgment, Tink beckoned him inside. Valentine's eyes twinkled as he examined her space. The shelves were stacked with odds and ends culled from every corner of Nycthemeron: strange objects floating in yellow pickle jars; workbenches strewn with gears and mainsprings, loupes and screws and a disassembled astrolabe; the smell of oil and peppermint.

He said, "Your sign says 'Timepieces.'"

"Is that somehow strange?"

"But you gave that fellow with the scarlet cravat just a packet of wildflowers."

"You know this how?"

"I stopped him and asked. I knew he'd come from your shop because he looked happy." He crossed his arms. "Flowers are nice, but they're no timepiece."

"Everything is a clock," said Tink. "Even the buckles on your shoes and the boards beneath your feet. But this place," she said, with a gesture that implied all of Nycthemeron, "has forgotten that."

"The stories are true. You are a peculiar one." And then he cocked his head, as if listening to something. "They say you are a clockwork, you know. "

His gaze was a stickpin and Tink a butterfly. She shrugged, and blushed, and turned away.

Which was odd. Time had never seen her fall shy.

"As for your lady love," said Tink, changing the subject, "I know what to do. Come with me."

She led him to shelves stacked with clocks of sand, and candle wax, and other things. (Time frequently sprawled here, like a cat in sunlight.) She stopped at a grandfather clock carved in the guise of a fig tree. Tink set it to one minute before midnight.

"Hold out your hand," Tink said. She gave the clock a nod of encouragement, and it began to tock-tick-tock its way toward midnight. Valentine watched with fascination. But, of course, he had never seen a working clock.

A miniscule hatch opened above the twelve and a seed *plinked* into Valentine's hand. Tink repeated the process.

"What are these?" he asked.

"Intercalary seeds. At the Festival, put one under your tongue. Have your lady do the same. The seeds will release one minute that belongs solely to the pair of you."

Valentine tucked the seeds into the tasseled sash at his waist. He took her hand. His touch, she noticed with a shudder, was warm and gentle. With his other hand he removed his mask, saying, "I am in your debt."

He winked and kissed her hand. Now, Tink was prepared for this, for Valentine was nothing if not notorious for his charms. But when she saw the laugh lines around his eyes, and felt his breath tickle the back of her hand, and felt his soft lips brush against her skin, her metronome heart—

   ...diners in a sidewalk café marveled at a turtledove hanging motionless overhead, just for an instant...

—skipped—

   ...the candles in a Cistercian chapel, all 419 of them, stopped flickering, just for an instant...

   —a—

   ...all the noises of life and love and revelry and sorrow, the voice of Nycthemeron, fell silent, just for an instant...

   —beat.

Tink did not sleep that night. Lying on a downy mattress just wide enough for one—she had never needed anything more, having never known loneliness—she replayed those few minutes with Valentine in her head, again and again. She smelled the back of her hand, imagined it was his breath tickling her skin.

Tink could win his heart. All she needed was time.

She awoke with a plan.

In order to win Valentine's heart, she had to know him, and he had to know her. In order to know him, she had to be near him. To be near him, she had to get into the Palazzo. She could get into the Palazzo if she brought a birthday gift for Queen Perjumbellatrix.

Of course, birthdays held no meaning in a place exiled from the calendar. But the eternal queen was fond of gifts, and so she held masques and received tributes once per year (measured, as always, by the ticking of Tink's heart). And Valentine, her consort, attended each. Even so, Tink would be fortunate to get more than a few moments with him.

Thus, after the Festival, Tink went to work on a special series of clocks. Each was designed to delight the revelers in Her Majesty's grand ballroom.

And each was designed to steal one minute from Her Majesty. Each clock would swaddle Tink and Valentine in sixty purloined seconds. Nor was that all.

For Valentine—pretty, perfect Valentine—minutes held no meaning. One was much the same as another. Thus, it would be nothing odd for him to experience a conversation strung across the decades, one minute per year.

But Tink—mortal, metronome Tink—had to *live* her way from one stolen minute to the next. So she designed the clocks to string those moments together like pearls on a necklace, forming one continuous assignation with Valentine.

The first clock was a simple thing: a wind-up circus. But Her Majesty disappointed courtiers throughout the Palazzo when she declared it her favorite tribute.

Tink curtsied, feeling like a dandelion in a rose garden. The braids in her silvery hair had unraveled, and her gown—the finest from the secondhand shop in the Briardowns—was not fine at all in this company.

She retreated to a corner of the ballroom. Tink had never learned to dance.

Valentine danced with every lady in the hall, always returning to Perjumbel-latrix in the interim. He hadn't changed one tock from the way he'd appeared at Tink's shop. The ribbons on his sleeves traced spirals in the air when he twirled his partners so, the feathers of his cormorant mask fluttered when he tipped his ladies thus. Tink fidgeted with her embroidery, waiting until the clockwork elephants on the queen's gift trumpeted midnight.

Everything stopped. The ballroom became a sculpture garden, an expressionist swirl of skin and feathers and jewels and silks. Beads of wine from a tipped goblet sparkled like rubies suspended in midair; plucked harp strings hung poised to fling notes like arrows.

"Well done, Timesmith." Tink turned. Valentine bowed at her. "It is a wonder," he said, marveling at the motionless dancers. "But I think your wonderment has missed its mark, no?" He pointed: Tink's clock had made a statue of the statuesque monarch.

Tink swallowed, twice. She found her voice: "The clock is for her. But this," she said, "is for you." *And me.*

Valentine smiled. "I've never seen its equal." He took her hand. Her skin tingled beneath his fingertips. "Thank you." Her metronome heart skipped another beat when he touched his lips to the back of her hand. But the world had stopped, so nobody noticed.

He asked, "How long will they stay like this?"

"That's complicated," said Tink. "But they're safe."

The room blurred about them. Merrymakers blinked into new positions around the ballroom. The eternally tipping wine goblet became an ice sculpture of the queen. And her gift, the clockwork circus, became an orrery.

A year had passed.

"I see! I see, I see!" Valentine clapped. He understood, for every moment was the same to him.

"Do you like it?" she asked.

"It's marvelous," he said. "Now let *me* show *you* something you've never known. Dance with me."

She wanted to waltz with him, but feared to try. She had impressed him. But could that be undone by a single awkward step? Valentine was a graceful creature, accustomed to graceful partners.

"I don't, that is, I've never—"

"Trust me," he said.

Valentine pulled her to the center of the ballroom. His hand warmed the small of her back. He smelled like clean salt, like the distant sea. Dancing, she discovered, came naturally. It was, after all, a form of rhythm. And what was rhythm but a means of marking time?

The room blurred around them. The orrery became an hourglass. They wove and whirled amongst the motionless dancers. Tink laughed. It was working.

"Look," said Valentine. "Look at their eyes."

Masks hid their faces, but not their eyes. She looked upon a man who wore the burgundy cummerbund of a baronet. His eyes glistened with hidden tears. They pirouetted past a countess with a diadem on her brow, butterfly wings affixed to her cheeks, and soul-deep weariness in her eyes.

Valentine asked, "What do you see?"

"Sorrow," said Tink.

"They've lost something. We all have."

"Three things," said Tink. For suddenly she knew what Valentine wanted and needed. He didn't know it himself.

Yet still they danced. It was wonderful; it was magical. But his eyes returned again and again to Perjumbellatrix. He danced with Tink—and what a dancer he was—but his heart and mind were elsewhere.

The final timepiece expended its stolen minute. The bubble of intimacy popped under the assault of music, laughter, and voices raised in tribute to the queen.

"Truly marvelous," said Valentine. "Thank you for this dance, Timesmith." With a wink, a bow, and a kiss, he returned to his place beside the queen.

Tink's feet ached. Her lungs pumped like bellows. Her skin wasn't quite as smooth as it had been when their dance began. She had aged twenty years in twenty minutes. But it was a small price for the key to somebody's heart.

She returned to her shop, deep in thought. And so she did not notice how the hands of every clock bowed low to her, like a bashful admirer requesting a dance. Time had seen how she had laughed with joy in Valentine's arms. It yearned, desperately, to dance with her.

Tink spent months (measured, as always, by the thumping of her heart) holed up in her shop. She labored continuously, pausing only for food and rest. And, on several occasions, to climb a staircase of carved peridot and dip a chalice in the waters atop the aqueduct.

Far above the city, craftsmen and courtiers built an effigy clock atop the Spire. Valentine, Tink knew, was there. She wondered if he ever gazed from that aerie upon the Briardowns, wondered if his thoughts ever turned from queen to clockmaker.

When the Festival of the Leaping Second returned to Nycthemeron, and a crowd again milled outside Tink's shop, they found it locked and the storefront dark. Her neighbors, the algebraist and the cartographer, told of her forays along the aqueduct and of strange sounds from her workshop: splashing, gurgling, the creak of wooden gears.

By now, of course, the queen had grown quite fond of Tink's wonderments. And when she heard that the clockmaker had arrived, promising something particularly special for the Festival, she ordered a new riser built for Tink's work.

There, Tink built a miniature Nycthemeron: nine feet tall at the Spire, six feet wide, encircled by a flowing replica of the river Gnomon, complete with aqueducts, waterwheels, sluices, gates, and even a tiny clockmaker's shop in a tiny Briardowns. There, a model clockmaker gazed lovelorn at the Spire, where a model Valentine gazed down.

When the revelry culminated in the advance of the effigy, Tink filled the copper reservoir on her water clock. And everybody, including the queen and lovely Valentine at her side, marveled at Tink's work.

The water flowed backward. It sprang from the waterwheels to leap upon the aqueducts and gush uphill, where special pumps pulled it down to begin again.

It was a wonder, they said. An amazement. A delight.

Only time, and time alone, understood what she had done. Tink had given the people of Nycthemeron something they had lost.

She had given them their past.

Tink went home feeling pleased. Just a few more clocks, just a few more stolen moments, and Valentine would express adoration. But she couldn't work as many hours at a stretch as she had in her youth. She had to unlock his heart before time rendered her an unlovable crone.

But there were interruptions. People peppered her with strange requests: vague notions they couldn't express and that Tink couldn't deliver. The fellow in the scarlet cravat returned, seeking a means of visiting "that place."

"What place?" Tink asked.

"That—" he waved his hands in frustration, indicating some vague and distant land "—place." He shrugged. "I see it in my head. I've been there, but I don't know how to return. It's here, and yet it's not here, too."

Tink could not help him. Nor could she help the baroness who requested a clockwork key that would open a door to "that other Nycthemeron." At first they came in a slow trickle, these odd requests. But the trickle became a torrent. Tink closed her shop so that she could finish the next sequence of birthday clocks for Queen Perjumbellatrix.

Valentine invited Tink for another spin around a ballroom filled with motionless revelers. He was, of course, as handsome as ever. But when he doffed his mask, Tink saw the crease of a frown perched between his cerulean eyes. Her metronome heart did a little jig of concern.

"You look troubled," she said as he took her hand.

Valentine said, "Troubled? I suppose I am."

"Perhaps I can help," said Tink. "After all, my skills are not inconsiderable." She added what she hoped was a coquettish lilt to these words.

Valentine wrapped his arm around Tink's waist. They waltzed past a duchess and her lissome lover. "I find my thoughts drifting to a new place. A different Nycthemeron."

Tink faltered. The dancers blurred into a new configuration. Another precious year had passed.

Valentine danced mechanically. His movements were flawless, but devoid of the grace that had made Tink swoon when first they had danced together. And for her part, her whirring mind couldn't concentrate on one thing or the other; she stepped awkwardly, without poise or balance.

It wasn't supposed to be like this. Her gift was meant to impress Valentine, not confuse and distract him. But she had her pilfered minutes and intended to use them.

She rested her head on his shoulder, enjoying his scent and the fluid play of muscles in his arm. "What sort of place?" she asked.

"I don't know," he said. "It's a place I've been, someplace close, even, but I don't know how to get there."

The revelers snapped into new arrangements; another year lost. Valentine led her in a swooping two-step around the ballroom. There was, it seemed, more room to move.

"Is it here in Nycthemeron? A forgotten courtyard? A secluded cloister?"

"I can't say. I feel like it may be. . . everywhere. Strange, isn't it?" He shook his head and smiled. "No matter. Once again you have done a magnificent thing."

But Tink barely heard his praise. She had given the people of Nycthemeron their past. But what did that mean to timeless people in a timeless city? Nothing. They were afflicted with strange thoughts they couldn't comprehend: memories of times past. To them, the past was a foreign place they couldn't visit.

They waltzed. Tink's feet ached, twinges of betrayal from her aging body. Blur. They danced a sarabande. Her back ached. Blur. Her lungs burned. Blur.

Tink *saw* the thinning of the ballroom crowd.

"Valentine, have you noticed there are fewer people in this ballroom every year?"

"Yes."

"Where are they going?"

"They're trying to leave Nycthemeron," he said.

"Oh, no," she said, and crashed to the floor.

"Timesmith!" Valentine leapt to her side, cradled her head in his hands. "Please forgive me. Are you hurt?"

The ballroom floor was hard and her body less resilient than it had been minutes and years ago. But she disregarded her bruises, because Valentine was sopping wet. His slippery hands had lost their grip on her. He smelled of river grass and mud.

"What happened?" she asked.

"The queen sent me to stop her half-brother from trying to swim his way out of Nycthemeron. That's where they're going. To the river."

But, of course, nobody could leave Nycthemeron. Not even Tink. The luminous fog was chaos, its touch deadly.

In a tiny voice, she asked, "Did you save him?"

"No. He entered the fog before I was halfway across."

And at that moment Tink realized her gift, bestowed upon the people of Nyc-themeron with love and intended to win love in return, was killing people.

Tink's clock chimed midnight. Their stolen time had lapsed. And when Tink saw herself in the golden mirrors of the ballroom, she saw that her hair, once a lustrous silver, had tarnished to gray. She had aged another twenty years, but had gained nothing from it.

Tink returned to the Briardowns and her lonely, narrow cot, unaware of the clocks that capered for her attention. Time ached to comfort her, to console her. It sang her to sleep with a lullaby of ticks and tocks.

She'd been so foolish. She might as well have given a penny-farthing bicycle to the koi in the fishponds. The people of Nycthemeron couldn't comprehend her gift. Right now they had the past bearing down on them like a boulder rolling toward a cliff. But that time had nowhere to go, no safe landing. It was discon-nected. Meaningless.

She could salvage this. She could cure the malady she had created. She could still win Valentine. She could fix everything. All it required was a simple pen-dulum clock.

Tink paid a visit to the smithy in Nycthemeron's Steeltree district. There, she commissioned the finest double-edged blade the smith could forge. No hilt—only the blade, with a tang for fastening it. A strange request. But it was considered no small honor to help the clockmaker create one of her fabled wonderments.

Thus, when she returned to his forge, he presented her with thirty inches of gleaming steel. It was, he proclaimed, the finest and sharpest blade he'd ever forged. Sharp enough to shear the red from a rainbow.

She thanked him. But it was not sharp enough.

And so, in the months before the next Festival (measured, as always, by the thumping of Tink's broken heart), she spent every moment in her workshop. Things took longer these days. Her eyes strained at the tiniest cogs; her grip quavered as it never used to do.

People again reported odd noises in her shop. At first, the grinding of a whet-stone. Later, a rasping, as of sand on steel. Then, the susurration of cotton on steel. And finally, if they pressed their ears to her shop, they might have heard the whisper of breath on steel.

And those who stayed until Tink emerged might have noticed something dif-ferent about her. For where before there had always been the phantom *tickticktick* that followed her like a devoted puppy, now, when she carried the pendulum blade, there was sometimes only a phantom *ti-ti-ti*, and other times a *ck-ck-ck*, depending on how she held it.

Tink loaded her cart with a crate the size of a grandfather clock, then drove to the Spire. By now, of course, she was one of the queen's most favored subjects, and so the ballroom had a place of honor reserved for Tink. There, she assembled her contribution to the Festival.

The revelers advanced the effigy. Tink wound her clock; the pendulum swung ponderously across its lacquered case. It was silent. Not even a whisper accompanied the passage of the pendulum. It sliced through the moments, leaving slivers of *ticks* and tatters of *tocks* in its wake.

At Tink's request, the queen posted guards around the clock, for the pendulum blade was a fearsome thing. Its edges were the sharpest things that could ever be, sharp as the *now* that separates past and future.

But only time, and time alone, understood what she had done. Tink had given Nycthemeron something it had lost.

She had given it the present: a knowledge of now.

Tink returned to the Briardowns. Her body would be eighty years old at the next Festival, while Valentine would still be a stunning twenty-something. How many lovers had he charmed since his visit to Tink's shop? How many stolen kisses, how many fluttering hearts? Her life had none of these things. Her pillow never smelled of anybody but Tink.

What chance had she of winning him now? It was a foolish hope. But she had spent her life on it, and couldn't bear to think it had all been for nothing.

She tried to concentrate. But time's desperation had become jealousy, so it had imbued the pendulum blade with a special potency. Anything for Tink's attention.

The man in the scarlet cravat returned. He asked Tink for a trinket that would "set him moving" again. She couldn't help him. Nor could she help the pregnant woman whose belly suggested imminent labor and whose eyes were the most sorrowful Tink had ever seen. She'd been that way, Tink realized, since time had lost its interest. Since the moment Nycthemeron had fallen from the calendar.

Tink was passing beneath the aqueduct, on her way to the Palazzo, when a man in a cobalt-colored fez crashed onto the street before her cart. The wind of his passage ruffled her hair, and he smashed the cobbles hard enough to set the chimes in Tink's clock to ringing. Plumes of dust billowed from between the paving stones. She screamed.

Not because he had perished. He hadn't, of course. Tink screamed because his sorrow had driven him to seek death, the ultimate boundary between past and future. And because he'd never find it.

He shambled to his feet, for his body was timeless. But when the poor fellow realized that nothing had changed, that he hadn't bridged the gulf between *was* and *will*, he slumped to the ground and wept. He waved off Tink's offers of a ride, of conversation, of commiseration.

A quiet gasp of dismay reached her ears. She looked up. People lined the tallest edges of the aqueduct.

The pendulum blade carved a personal *now* for every soul in Nycthemeron. And drove them mad. Tink had shown them they were entombed in time, and now they were suffocating.

Tink rushed to the Palazzo. The ballroom was emptier than she had ever seen it. Couples still danced, but just a fraction of those who had toasted the queen in pageants past.

The ribbons on Valentine's arms still fluttered; his shapely calves still flexed and stretched when he waltzed with the queen. But was it Tink's imagination, or had his eyes lost their sparkle? Was it her imagination, or did he seem distracted and imprecise in his movements?

An earl in an owl mask requested a dance, but she declined him and all the others who sought a few steps with the famous clockmaker. She might have been flattered, but now, with age weighing upon her, she lacked the energy for much revelry. She saved herself.

Her clock chimed. Once more, Tink and Valentine were alone together in a private minute. He took her hand.

"You look worried," he said.

"How are you? Are you well?" She studied his face.

"I am the same as ever," he said, a catch in his voice.

He was silent for what felt like eternity. Blur. Blur. Blur. It broke her heart, every wasted instant. This was her last chance. It wasn't meant to be like this.

"Something is bothering you," she said. "Will you tell me about it? You'll never have a more devoted listener."

That, at least, elicited a slight sigh, and a weary chuckle. "What is it like?"

"What is what like?"

"Aging."

Tink said, "My body aches. I can't see or hear as well as I could. My mind isn't as sharp, my fingers not as nimble." She paused while he gently spun her through a pirouette. "But I am more wise now."

"More wise?"

"Wise enough to know that I'm a foolish old woman."

Grief clenched her chest, ground the gears in her metronome heart. The years had become a burden too heavy for her shoulders. She faltered. Valentine caught her.

He asked, "Are you ill?"

She shook her head. "Just old. Will you sit with me?"

"Of course."

They watched motionless dancers blink through the celebrations. Tink rested her head on his shoulder. She wanted to remember his scent forever. That was all she'd ever have of him; her efforts to win his heart had failed. Worse than that: she had transmuted his joy into melancholy.

"May I ask something of you, Valentine?"

"Anything, Timesmith."

"Your ribbons. I would like to take one, if I may."

"Allow me," he said. He removed a vermilion ribbon and tied it into her gray hair. "Remember me, won't you?"

That made her smile. She would remember him until the end of her days. Didn't he realize this? Had she been too oblique in her bids for his affection? Blur.

Tink turned to thank him for the token, and to tell him that he was ever on her mind. But she didn't. His shirt was tattered, his ribbons were frayed. Feathers had come loose from his cormorant mask. He was dusty.

"What happened to you?" she asked.

"I... I fell," he whispered.

"Oh, Valentine—" She reached up to touch his face. His changeless, beautiful face. Her stolen time came to an end. It left her very old, very tired, and very alone.

Valentine's heart would never be hers; she could accept that. But it would never be pledged to anybody ever again, and that she couldn't bear. It was broken. Because of her.

If Tink could do one final thing before she succumbed to old age, she wanted to mend him. Mend everybody. But though she knew what that would require, she did not know how to do it. The future was an abstract thing, built of possibilities and nothing else. It was impervious to cogs, springs, pendulums, blades, sand, beeswax, and water.

She paced. She napped. She ignored the urgent knocking of would-be customers. More napping. More pacing.

And then she noticed the model castle-city she had built years earlier. Her water-clock Nycthemeron sat in a corner, draped in cobwebs and dust.

Tink looked upon the Spire, and the surrounding gardens, and knew exactly what to do.

First, she paid a visit to the stonemason. He welcomed her. But when she told him what she needed, he balked. It was too much work for one person.

But Tink had not come alone. For she was famous, and drew a small crowd when she ventured outside. Some followers, such as the fellow in the scarlet cravat, had been waiting outside her dark and shuttered store, hoping to wheedle one last wonderment from the aging clockmaker. Others had followed the siren call of her *tickticktick*, hoping it would lead them to a novel experience.

Next, Tink called upon the gardeners who maintained the parklands along the river. Their objections were similar to the stonemason's. But she solved their concerns as she had those of the stonemason: she presented the gardeners with strong and beautiful volunteers.

She supervised as best she could. But often the volunteers found her dozing in her cart because she had succumbed to weariness. They took turns bringing her home and tucking her into bed.

The changes to the outskirts of Nycthemeron drew more volunteers, and more still, as people abandoned their decadent delights. But nobody knew why Tink needed so much granite carved *just so*, nor why she needed the gardens landscaped *just so*.

Only time understood her plan. Only time, which had felt first confusion, then jealousy, then heartbreak while she squandered her short life yearning for Valentine.

Tink awoke with Valentine's hand brushing her cheek. At first she thought she had died and had gone to someplace better. But when she touched his face and saw her aged hand, she knew she was still an old woman. Her pillow was moist with tears.

His eyes gleamed. Perhaps not as brightly as they once had, but enough to cause a stutter in her metronome heart. "I've come to take you to the Festival."

That caused a jolt of alarm. "But my work—"

"Is finished. Completed to your every specification. Although nobody can tell me what your instructions mean."

His face was smudged with dirt.

"What happened to you?" she asked.

"I've been gardening," he said, and winked.

Valentine carried her to her cart. She dozed with her head on his shoulder as he drove to the Palazzo. Once, when the jouncing of the cart roused her, she glimpsed what might have been an honor guard with shining epaulettes and flapping pennants. It may have been a dream.

Tink dozed again during the funicular ride up the Spire. The view did not transfix her: she had seen it every year for the past sixty (measured, as always, by the beating of her failing heart). She preferred the drowsy sensation of resting in Valentine's arms, no matter how chaste the embrace. Her glimpses of Nycthemeron, between dreams and sighs, showed an unfamiliar city.

Ah, she recalled. *Yes. The Festival.* It had seemed dreadfully important once, this final gift. But she was too exhausted and too full of regrets to care.

"Why do you cry, Timesmith?"

"I'm a foolish old woman. I've spent my entire life just to have one hour with you."

She closed her eyes. When next she opened them, Valentine was setting her gently upon a cushioned chair in the gilded grand ballroom. It was, she noticed, a place of honor beside Queen Perjumbellatrix. The queen said something, but it was loud in the ballroom. Tink nodded, expressed her thanks, then returned to her dreams.

A jostling woke her, several minutes or decades later. Her chair floated toward the balcony. Valentine lifted it, as did the courtier in the scarlet cravat, and several others whom she felt she ought to recognize but didn't.

Silence fell. All eyes turned to Tink.

She stood, with Valentine's assistance. (His hands were so strong. So warm. So young.)

"This is for you," she said to Nycthemeron.

The fog brightened, then thinned, then dissipated. A brilliant sun emerged in a sky the color of Valentine's eyes. The Spire cast a shadow across the sprawling castle-city. Its tip pierced the distant gardens where so many had labored according to Tink's specifications.

Nycthemeron had become a sundial.

Cheers echoed through the city, loud even to Tink's feeble ears high atop the Spire.

Everyone understood what Tink had done. She had ended Nycthemeron's exile. She had given the people a future.

Tink collapsed. Her metronome heart sounded its final *tickticktick*. Her time had run out.

But not quite.

Time understood that this magnificent work, this living sundial called Nycthemeron, was an expression of her love for Valentine. She had set him free.

Tink found herself in a patch of grass, staring up at a blue sky. The grass was soft, the sky was bright, and her body didn't ache.

"Ah, you're awake." Valentine leaned over her, eclipsing the sky with his beautiful face. He wasn't, she noticed, wearing the cormorant mask. Nor his ribbons. And his shirt was new. "I have something to show you," he said.

When Tink took his hand, she saw that her skin was no longer wrinkled, no longer spotted and weak.

These were the Spire-top gardens. But everything looked new and different in the sunlight. Even the trees were strange: row upon row upon row of them. Strange, and yet she felt she somehow knew them.

Valentine saw the expression on her face. He said, "They're intercalary trees. It seemed a waste to toss the seeds after they'd been spent. So I planted them."

Seeds? Ah... Tink remembered when she'd first met Valentine, decades ago, when he'd wanted to charm a flaxen-haired beauty. Back when Tink had been young.

The *first* time she had been young.

And time, knowing it had failed to win Tink's heart, had given her a parting gift, then set her free.

AMOR VINCIT OMNIA
K. J. PARKER

K. J. Parker is the author of eleven fantasy novels, including the "Fencer,"
"Scavenger," and "Engineer" trilogies, as well as standalone novels *The Company* and *The Folding Knife*, and novellas "Purple and Black" and "Blue and
Gold." According to biographical notes, Parker has worked in law, journalism,
and numismatics, and now writes and makes things out of wood and metal.
Upcoming is a new novel, *The Hammer*. Parker is married to a solicitor and
lives in southern England.

Usually, the problem was getting the witnesses to talk.

*…He just walked down the street looking at buildings and they caught fire. No,
he didn't do anything, like wave his arms about or stuff like that, he just, I don't
know, looked at them…*

This time, the problem was getting them to shut up.

*…Stared at this old guy and his head just sort of crumpled, you know, like a piece
of paper when you screw it into a ball? Just stared at him, sort of annoyed, really,
like the guy had trodden on his foot, and then his head just…*

As he listened, the observer made notes; *Usque Ad Peric; Unam Sanc (twice);
?Mundus Verg ??variant*. He also nodded his head and made vague noises of
sympathy and regret, and tried not to let his distaste show. But the smell bothered
him; burnt flesh, which unfortunately smells just a bit like roasted meat (pork,
actually), which was a nuisance because he'd missed lunch; burnt bone, which
is just revolting. His moustache would smell of smoke for two days, no matter
how carefully he washed it. He stopped to query a point; when he made the old
woman vanish, was there a brief glow of light, or—? No? No, that's fine. And he
jotted down; *Choris Anthrop, but no light; ?Strachylides?*

The witness was still talking, but he'd closed his eyes; *and then Thraso from the
mill came up behind him and shot him in the back, and nothing happened, and
then he turned around real slow and he pointed at Thraso, and Thraso just—*

He frowned, stopped the witness with a raised hand. "He didn't know—"

"What?"

"He didn't know he was there. This man—" Always hopeless at names. "The
miller. He didn't know the miller was there."

"No, Thraso crept up on him real quiet. Shot him in the back at ten paces. Arrow should've gone right through him and out the other side. And then he turned round, like I just said, and—"

"You're sure about that. He didn't hear him, or look round."

"He was busy," the witness said. "He was making Cartusia's head come off, just by looking at it. And that's when Thraso—"

"You're *sure?*"

"Yes."

The witness carried on talking about stuff that clearly mattered to him, but which didn't really add anything. He tuned out the voice, and tried to write the word, but it was surprisingly difficult to make himself do it. Eventually, when he succeeded, it came out scrawled and barely legible, as though he'd written it with his left hand;

Lorica?

"Unam Sanctam," the Precentor said (and Gennasius was leaning back in his chair, hands folded on belly, his I've-got-better-things-to-do pose), "is, of course, commonly used by the untrained, since the verbal formula is indefinite and, indeed, often varies from adept to adept. Usque ad Periculum, by the same token, is frequently encountered in these cases, for much the same reason. They are, of course, basic intuitive expressions of frustration and rage, strong emotions which—"

"It says here," Poteidanius interrupted, "he also did Mundus Verg. That's not verbal-indefinite."

The Precentor glanced down at the notes on the table in front of him. "You'll note," he said, "that our observer was of the opinion that a variant was used, not Mundus Vergens itself. The variants, of which Licinianus lists twenty-six, include some forms which have been recorded as indefinite. The same would seem to apply to Choris Anthropou."

"Quite," said the very old man at the end, whose name he could never remember. "Strachylides' eight variants, three of which have been recorded as occurring spontaneously." *So there*, he thought, as Poteidanius shrugged ungraciously. "I remember a case back in 'Fifty-Six. Chap was a striker in a blacksmith's shop, didn't know a single word of Parol. But he could do five variants of Choris in the vernacular."

"Our observer," the Precentor said, "specifically asked if there was an aureola, and the witness was quite adamant."

"The third variant," Gennasius said. "Suggests an untrained of more than usual capacity, or else a man with a really deep-seated grudge. I still don't see why you had to drag us all out here. Surely your department can deal with this sort of thing without a full enclave."

He took a deep breath, but it didn't help. "If you'd care to look at paragraph four of the report," he said, trying to keep his voice level and reasonably pleasant, "you'll see that—"

"Oh, *that*." Gennasius was shaking his head in that singularly irritating way. "Another suspected instance of Lorica. If I had half an angel for every time some graduate observer's thought he's found an untrained who's cracked Lorica—"

"I have interviewed the observer myself," the Precentor said—trying to do gravitas, but it just came out pompous. "He is an intelligent young man with considerable field experience," he went on, "not the kind to imagine the impossible or to jump to far-fetched conclusions on the basis of inadequate evidence. Gentlemen, I would ask you to put aside your quite reasonable scepticism for one moment and simply look at the evidence with an open mind. If this really is Lorica—"

"It doesn't exist." Gennasius snapped out the words with a degree of passion the Precentor wouldn't have believed him capable of. "It's a legend. A fairy tale. There are some things that simply aren't possible. Lorica's one of them."

There was a short, rather painful silence. Raw emotion, like raw chicken, upset elderly gentlemen of regular habits. Then the Preceptor said gently, "Ninety-nine out of a hundred human beings would say exactly the same thing about *magic*." He allowed himself to dwell on the word, because Gennasius hated it so. "And of course, they would be right. There is no such thing as magic. Instead, there is a branch of natural philosophy of which we are adepts and the rest of the world is blissfully ignorant. Gentlemen, think about it, please. It may well not be Lorica. But if it is, if there's the slightest chance it could be, we have to do something about it. *Now*."

"I'm sorry," the young man said. "I've never heard of it."

The Precentor smiled. "Of course you haven't." He half-filled two of his notoriously small glasses with wine and handed one to the young man, who took it as if the stem was red-hot. "For one thing, it doesn't exist."

The young man looked at him unhappily. "Ah," he said.

"At least," the Precentor went on, "we believe it doesn't exist. We hope like hell it doesn't exist. If it does—" He produced a synthetic shudder of horror that actually became a real one.

The young man put his glass down carefully on the table. "Is it some kind of weapon?"

The Precentor couldn't help smiling. "Quite the reverse," he said. "That's the whole point. Lorica's completely harmless, you might say. It's a defense."

"Ah."

"A total defense." The Preceptor paused and watched. He'd chosen young Framea for his intelligence and perceptiveness. This could be a test for him.

He passed. "A total defense," he said. "Against everything? All known forms?"

The Preceptor nodded slowly. "All known forms. And physical weapons too. And fire, water, death by suffocation and falling from a great height. Possibly some diseases too, we don't know."

"That would be—" Framea frowned, and the Preceptor imagined a great swelling cloud of implications filling the young man's mind. He didn't envy him that. "That could be bad," he said.

"Extremely. An individual we couldn't harm or kill; therefore outside our control. Even if he was a mediocre adept with limited power, knowledge of the basic offensive forms together with absolute invulnerability, it doesn't bear thinking about. Even if his intentions were benign to begin with, the mere possession of such power would inevitably turn him into a monster. Hence," he added gently, "our concern."

"But I still don't quite—" Framea looked at him, reminding him vaguely of a sheep. "If it doesn't exist—"

"Ah." The Preceptor held up a hand. "That's the question, isn't it? All we know is that it *could* exist. Blemmyes, a hundred and seventy years ago, proved that it could exist; his reasoning and his mathematics have been rigorously examined and found to be perfect. There is a potential for such a form. Of course, nobody has yet been able to produce it—"

"You mean people have tried?"

The Preceptor nodded slowly. "Unofficially, you might say, but yes. Well, you can imagine, the temptation would be irresistible. Some of the finest minds—But, thankfully, none of them succeeded. Several of them, indeed, wrote papers outlining their researches, basically arguing that if they couldn't do it, nobody could—flawed logic, you'll agree, but when you're dealing with men of such exceptional vanity—"

"I think I see," Framea interrupted. "Trained adepts have tried, using proper scientific method, and they've all failed. But an untrained—"

"Exactly." The Preceptor was relieved; he'd been right about the boy after all. "An untrained might well succeed where an adept would fail, because the untrained often possess a degree of intuitive power that tends to atrophy during the course of formal education. An untrained might be able to do it, simply because he doesn't know it's impossible."

Framea nodded eagerly. "And an untrained, by definition—"

"Quite. Unstable, probably mentally disturbed by the power inside him which he doesn't understand or know how to control; if not already malignant by nature, he would rapidly become so. And with Lorica—Really, it doesn't bear thinking about."

There was a long pause. Then Framea said, "And you want *me* to—"

Framea hadn't been cold for as long as he could remember. It was always warm in the Studium; warm, unpleasantly warm or downright hot, depending on who'd been nagging the Magister ad Necessariis most recently. Old men feel the cold, and the adepts of the Studium didn't have to worry about the cost of fuel.

He pulled his coat up round his ears and quickened his pace. He hadn't been out in the dark for a long time, either. It didn't frighten him ("an adept of the

Studium fears nothing, because he has nothing to fear;" first term, first day, first lecture) but it made him feel uncomfortable. As did the task that lay ahead of him.

You will, of course, have to seduce a woman—

Well, fine. And the rest of the day's your own. He winced as he recalled his reaction.

("I see," he'd said, after a moment of complete silence. "I don't know how."

"Oh, it's quite straightforward. So I'm told."

"Is there, um, a book I could—?"

"Several.")

More than several, in fact; from Flaminian's *Art of Seduction*, three hundred years old, eight thousand lines of impeccable hexametric verse, to Bonosius Brunellus' *On the Seduction of Women*, three hundred pages with notes and appendices, entirely drawn from the works of earlier authors. The librarian had given him a not-you-as-well look when he'd asked for them, and they'd been no help at all. He'd asked Porphyrius, the only adept in the Studium who might possibly have had first-hand experience of such things, but he'd just laughed like a drain and walked away.

Lorica, he reminded himself.

The inn was, in fact, just another farmhouse, where the farmer's wife sold beer and cider in her kitchen, and you could pay a half-turner and sleep in the hayloft; not the sort of inn where you could rely on finding a prostitute at any hour of the day or night. In fact, he doubted very much whether they had prostitutes out here in the sticks. Probably, it was one of those areas of activity like brewing or laundry; you only got specialist professionals in the towns. Still, it couldn't hurt to ask.

"You what?" the woman demanded.

He repeated the question. It was unambiguous and politely phrased. The woman scowled at him and walked away.

He took his mug of beer, which he had no intention of drinking, and sat down in a corner of the room. Everybody had turned to look at him when he came in, and again when he asked the question, but they'd lost interest. He stretched out his legs under the table, closed his eyes and tried to think.

("You will, of course, have to seduce a woman," the Preceptor had said. "To use as a source."

The second statement was infinitely more shocking than the first. "That's illegal," he said.

"Yes, well." The Preceptor had frowned at him. "I hereby authorise you to use all means necessary. I suppose you'll want that in writing."

"Yes, please. Also," he'd added, "I don't know how.")

He reached into his pocket and took out the book. It was only just light enough for reading, even with Bia Kai Kratos to enhance his eyesight. He wondered if anybody had ever read a book in this room before and decided no, almost certainly not. He tried to concentrate on the analysis of the necessary forms, which were difficult, abstruse and in some cases downright bizarre; not all that different from the exercises he'd read about in Flaminian and Brunellus, come to that. The thought that he was going to have to perform both the forms and the other stuff *simultaneously* made him feel quite ill.

"Excuse me."

He looked up and saw a woman. At first he guessed she was about thirty-five, but she seemed to get younger as he looked at her. She was very pale, almost milk-white, with mouse-colored hair that seemed to drip off her head, like a leak in the roof. He wondered what she wanted.

"You were asking," she said. "About—"

Oh, he thought. "Yes, that's right."

She looked at him with a combination of hope and distaste. The latter he felt he deserved. "How much?" she said.

"I don't know," he replied. "What do you think?"

He didn't need to use Fortis Adiuvat to know what was going on in her mind. Think of a number and double it. "A thaler," she said.

Almost certainly way over the odds, but the Studium was paying. "Sure," he said quickly. "Now, or—?"

"Now," she said.

He reached in his coat pocket. The cellarer had issued him with money, along with spare clothes, stout walking boots and a waterproof hood. It had been so long since he'd had any dealings with the stuff that he didn't recognise the coins. But he seemed to recall that thalers were big silver things, and all he'd been given was small gold ones. "Here," he said, pressing a coin into her hand. It felt warm, soft, slightly clammy. "That's fine."

She stared at the coin and said nothing. "Now?" he said. She nodded.

Outside, it was raining hard. It wasn't far across the yard to the barn, but far enough for them both to get soaking wet. He couldn't face that, not on top of everything else, so he executed Scutum in coelis under his breath and hoped she wouldn't notice. As they climbed the ladder to the hayloft, something scuttled. He hoped she wasn't one of those people who had an irrational fear of mice, like he did.

"Use a general Laetitia," the Preceptor had said. It was the only specific piece of advice he'd given him. He tried it; the form to fill another person with unspeakable joy. He hadn't done it very often.

Either it worked, or he had a latent and unexpected talent for what Brunellus insisted on calling the subtleties of the bedchamber. His own impression of the activities involved was decidedly ambiguous. Predominant was the stress involved in doing two demanding and unfamiliar things at the same time. There was anxiety (though he calmed down a bit when he realised that the yelling and whimpering didn't mean she was in excruciating pain; bizarrely, the opposite). Guilt; partly because what he was doing was illegal—he had the Preceptor's written exemption, but it was still a crime; partly because he knew what would happen to the poor girl, who'd never done him any harm. Other than that, it was really just a blend of several different strains of acute embarrassment. The thought that people did that sort of thing for *fun* was simply bewildering.

In the morning he went to the village where it had happened. Sixteen dead, according to the report; four still comatose with shock and fear. He stopped at the forge and asked for directions.

The smith looked at him. "You're not from—"

"No," he said. "I'm from the city. I represent the Studium. It's about the incident."

It was the word they used when they had to talk to the public. He hated saying it; incident. Only stupid people used words like that.

The smith didn't say anything. He lifted his hand and pointed up the street. Framea followed the line, and saw a larger than average building at the end, white, with a sun-in-glory painted over the door. Which he could have found perfectly well for himself, had he bothered to look, and then the whole village wouldn't have known he was here.

Fortunately, the Brother was at home when he knocked on the door. A short man, with a round face, quite young but thin on top, tiny hands like a girl. According to the report, this little fat man had walked out of his house into the street after the perpetrator had killed sixteen people, and had tried to *arrest* him—And the perpetrator had turned and walked away.

"My name is Framea," he said. "I'm from the Studium."

The Brother stared at him for a moment, then stood aside to let him in through the door. He had to duck to keep from banging his head.

"I told the other man—"

"Yes, I've read the report," Framea cut him off. "But I need to confirm a few details. May I sit down?"

The Brother nodded weakly, as though Death had stopped by to borrow a cup of flour. "I told him everything I saw," he said. "I don't think there was anything—"

Framea got a smile from somewhere. "I'm sure that's right," he said. "But you know how it is. Important facts can get mangled in transmission. And the man who interviewed you was a general field officer, not a Fellow. He may have misunderstood, or failed to grasp the full significance of a vital detail. I'm sure you understand."

He went over it all again. Thrasea the miller had shot the perpetrator in the back with a crossbow, at close range, ten paces, but the arrow—No, he hadn't simply missed, you couldn't miss at that range. Well, you could, but not Thrasea, he'd won the spoon at shoot-the-popinjay the year before last, he was a good shot. And besides, the arrow had just *stopped*—

Technical details? For the report. Well, it was a hunting bow, you needed a windlass to draw it, you couldn't just span it with your hands. Well, it's possible, the man could have been wearing something under his coat, a mailshirt or a brigandine; but at that range the arrow would most likely have gone straight through, one of those things'll shoot clean through an oak door at point-blank range. Besides, if the man had been hot, even if he was wearing armor and it turned the arrow, he'd have moved; jerked like he'd been kicked by a horse, at that distance. And the arrowshaft would've splintered, or at the very least the tip would've snapped off or gotten bent. No; he'd picked up the arrow himself later that day, and it was good as new.

"And then he turned round and—"

"Yes, thank you," Framea said quickly. "That part of the account isn't in issue." He swallowed discreetly and went on; "Did you see any marks on the man? Scratches, bruises, anything like that?"

No, there wasn't a mark on him anywhere that the Brother could see, not that he'd expected to, since nobody had gotten closer to him than Thraso did. Cuts and scratches from flying debris, from when he made the houses fall down; no, nothing like that. There was stuff flying in the air, bits of tile and rafter, great slabs of brick and mortar, but none of them hit the man. Yes, he was right up close. No, he didn't make any warding-off gestures or anything like that. Too busy killing people. Didn't really seem interested in the effects of what he was doing, if Framea got his drift.

"And you're absolutely sure you'd never seen this man before."

"Quite sure. And the same goes for everybody else in the village. A complete stranger."

Framea nodded. "Don't suppose you get many of those."

"Carters," the Brother said, "pedlars occasionally, though they never come back. People here aren't very well off, you see. We don't tend to buy anything from outside."

"Can you think of anybody who'd have a grudge against the people here?" Framea asked. "Any feuds, or anything like that?"

The Brother looked blank, like he hadn't heard the word before.

"Inheritance disputes? Scandals? Anybody run off with someone else's wife lately?"

The Brother assured him that things like that simply didn't happen there. Framea thought of the girl, the previous night. She was probably a part-timer, like the smith and the wheelwright and the man who made coffins. Simply not enough business to justify going full time.

"There was one thing," the Brother said, as Framea stooped under the lintel on his way out. "But I'm sure it was just me imagining things."

"Well?"

"I don't know." The Brother pulled a sad, indecisive face. "When I was looking at him, in the street, it's like he was sort of hard to see; you know, when you're looking at someone with the sun behind them? And at the time, I guess I must've thought that's what it was, only it didn't register, if you know what I mean."

"You noticed it without realizing."

The Brother nodded. "But then later, thinking about it, I realized it couldn't have been that, because it was mid-morning, and I was looking *down* the street at him, I mean looking from my end, which is due east. So the sun was behind me, not him."

Framea blinked. Yes, he thought, it was just you imagining things. Or, just possibly, a really powerful Ignis in favellum; except why would anybody enchant himself to glow bright blue in broad daylight?

"Thank you," he said to the Brother. "You've been most helpful."

Your only viable approach will be to provoke him into attacking you.

Framea stopped at the crack in the wall where the fresh-waterspring trickled through. He'd seen women standing here, filling their jugs and bowls painfully slowly. It was the only clean water in the village. He knelt down and cupped his hands, then drank. It tasted of iron, and something nasty he couldn't quite place.

If it was such a poor village, how come Thrasea the miller could afford a good hunting bow? He shook his head. Urban thinking. He'd probably built it himself; carved the stock, traded flour with the smith for the steel bow. He could almost picture him in his mind—patiently, an hour each evening in the barn, by the light of a bulrush taper soaked in mutton-fat. People in the villages often used sharp flints for planing wood, because steel tools were luxuries. Or you might borrow a plane from the wheelwright, if he owed you a favor—

Motive. What motive would an untrained need? He tried to imagine what it must be like, to carry the gift inside you and not know what it was. You'd probably believe you were mad, because you knew the things you were able to do were impossible (but you'd seen them happen, but they were impossible, but you'd seen them). You wouldn't dare tell anyone else. But there'd be the times when you got angry (you'd have a shorter temper than most people, because of the stress you'd be under all the time) and you found you'd done something without realizing. Something bad, inevitably. Your victim would tell people, in whispers; they wouldn't quite believe it, but they wouldn't quite disbelieve it either. You'd get a reputation. People would be nervous around you. Not much chance of a job, if you needed one, not much chance of help from your neighbors if something went wrong. It'd be a miracle if an untrained reached adulthood without being a complete mess.

He filled another handful and drank it. The taste was stronger, if anything. Iron and—

He stood up. Provoke a fight, the Precentor had said. Well, indeed. Easy peasy.

(But an untrained would *know*, wouldn't he? He'd feel the presence of another gift, he'd be drawn here. Would he dare come back to the village, where he'd be instantly recognised? It would all depend on exactly what he could do. Besides Lorica, of course. But untrained were always an unknown quantity. There were cases on record of untrained who could do seventh-degree translocations, but not a simple light or heat form. There was no way of knowing. Damn.)

He spent the rest of the day slouching round the village, trying to be conspicuous, something he'd spent his life avoiding. The idea was that news spreads like wildfire in small, remote rural communities, and he wanted everybody for miles around to know that there was a man from the Studium in the village, asking questions about the massacre. But the village chose that day to be empty, practically deserted; if anybody saw him , he didn't see them. It did cross his mind that it was deserted precisely because he was there. As darkness closed in, he began to feel rather desperate; he really didn't want to have to stay here any longer than was absolutely necessary. He went back to the spring-mouth, scrambled up onto a cart that someone and left there for some reason, and looked all around. Nobody in sight. Then he took a deep breath and shouted; "I AM FRAMEA OF THE STUDIUM! SURRENDER OR FIGHT ME TO THE DEATH!" Then he got down, feeling more ridiculous than he'd ever felt in his whole life.

He hadn't actually said anything about that night, but she was there waiting for him when he got back to the inn; standing alone, in the corner of the room. The five or six men sitting drinking acted as though she was invisible. Strictly speaking, it wasn't necessary; once was usually reckoned to be sufficient to form the connection. She looked up at him. Presumably, it was just about the money.

He nodded, and she left the room; as she did so, the men stopped talking, and there was dead silence for a while, as though they were at a religious service, or remembering the war dead on Victory Day. He'd thought about sitting down for a while and drinking a mug of the disgusting beer, but he decided against it. A man could catch his death of cold from a silence like that.

The subtleties of the hayloft, he thought, as he crossed the yard. The ground was still wet from yesterday's rain, and his muddy foot slipped on the bottom rung of the ladder. She was waiting for him, lying on her back, fully clothed. She looked as though she was waiting for the attentions of a surgeon, not a lover. Never again, he promised himself.

This time, he cast a number of specific Laetitias as well as a general one. It was easier now that he knew what a woman's reproductive organs actually looked like (he'd seen drawings in a book, of course, but you couldn't get a real idea from a drawing. Besides, the illustrations in Coelius's *Anatomy* looked more like a sketch-map of a battlefield than anything to do with the human body.). The results were quite embarrassingly effective, and he was worried the people in the inn might hear, and assume the poor woman was being murdered.

She fell asleep quite quickly afterwards. He lay on his back with his eyes closed, wishing more than anything that he was back in his warm chambers at the

Studium, where he could wash properly and be alone. She snored. He realized he didn't know her name; though, to be fair, there was no compelling evidence to suggest she even had one.

Also, he wanted to wake her up and apologise. But of course she was better off not knowing.

If he'd been asleep, he was woken up by a soft white light filling the hayloft. He opened his eyes. It was as bright as day, lighter than lamplight, even the glare of a thousand candles in the Great Hall of the Studium at the Commemoration feast.

The light came from a man. He was standing at the entrance to the hayloft, where a beam ran across, separating the loft from the rest of the barn; he guessed it was used as the fulcrum for a rope, for hoisting up heavy weights. The man was leaning on his folded arms against the bar. It was impossible to make out his face, blindingly backlit. He was tall and slightly built.

"Hello," he said.

Framea sat up. "Hello."

"You wanted to see me."

Him. Framea felt terrified, for a moment or so. Then the fear stabilised; it didn't go away, but it settled down. It was something he could draw on. Maybe that's what courage is, he speculated later.

"You're Framea, right? The wizard."

Framea was pleased he'd said that. It triggered an automatic, well-practiced response. "We aren't wizards," he heard himself say. "There's no such thing. I'm a student of natural philosophy. A scientist."

"What's the difference?"

The man, he noticed, spoke with no accent; none at all. Also, his voice was strangely familiar. That's because it's inside my head, Framea realized. And the man isn't really there, this is a third-level translocation. But he wasn't sure about that. The light, for one thing.

"Are you here in this room?" he asked.

The man laughed. "You know," he said, "that's a bloody good question. I'm not sure, to be honest with you. Like, I can feel this wooden beam I'm resting on. But I definitely didn't leave the—where I'm staying. So I must still be there, mustn't I? Or can I be in two places at once?"

A *ninth*-level translocation. Under other circumstances, Framea would be on his knees, begging to be let in on the secret of how you did that. "Technically, no," he replied, his lecturer's voice, because it made him feel in control. Like hell he was; but the man didn't need to know that. "But there's a form we call Stans in duobus partibus which—theoretically—allows a person to be in two different places simultaneously. That's to say, his physical body. His mind—"

"Yes?" Eager.

"Opinions differ," Framea said. "Some maintain that the mind is present in both bodies. Others hold that it exists in another House entirely, and is therefore present in neither body."

"House," the man repeated. "You've lost me."

Framea shivered. "No doubt," he replied. "You would have to have studied for two years at the Studium to be in a position to understand the concept."

"That's what I wanted to see you about," the man said. "No, stay exactly where you are, or I'll kill her."

Her, Framea noted. "I'm sorry," he said. "A touch of cramp. Let me sit up so we can talk in a civilized manner."

"No." Maybe just a touch of apprehension in the voice, leading to a feather of hostility? "You can stay right there, or I'll burst her head. You know I can do it."

"I can, of course, protect her," Framea lied. "And I don't think we have anything to discuss. I have to inform you that you are under arrest."

The man laughed, just as if Framea had told the funniest joke ever. "Sure," he said. "I'll try and bear that in mind. Now, tell me about this Studium place of yours."

She was still fast asleep, breathing slow and deep. He could smell her spit where it had dried around his mouth. "I don't see that it's anything to do with you," he said.

"Come off it. You know I'm one of you lot. I want to come and be educated properly. That's what you're there for, isn't it?"

Framea winced. "Out of the question," he said. "For one thing, you're much too old. More to the point, you've committed a number of brutal murders. You should be aware that I'm authorised to use—"

"No, that's not right." A statement, not a question, or even an objection. "I've never done your lot any harm. Our lot," he amended. "I'm just like you. I'm not like them at all."

"They were human beings," Framea said. "You killed them. That is not acceptable."

"But we're not human, are we?" The man was explaining to him, as if to a small child. "We're better. I mean, wizards, we can do anything we like. That's the whole point, isn't it?"

Framea didn't answer. Far too much conversation already; he knew it was discouraged, since any interaction with a malignant could only serve to weaken one's position. The trouble was, he was on the defensive. Lorica...

"Well?"

"You will surrender now," Framea said, "or I shall have no option but to use force."

"Screw you, then," the man said, and he lashed out. It was Mundus Vergens in a raw, inelegant variant, but backed up with enormous power. Framea barely held it with Scutum and a third-level translocation. Fortunately the man had forgotten about his threat to kill the girl, or else he'd never meant it. Framea replied tentatively with Hasta maiestatis, more as a test of the man's defenses than anything else. The form stopped dead and washed back at him; he got out of the way of the backlash just in time with a fourth-level dissociation into the third House.

Lorica, he thought, and then: Why *me?*

"Are you still there?" he heard the man ask. "Hello?"

Framea paused to consider the tactical options. If, as he suspected, the man was present only by way of a ninth-level translocation, the safest course would be to break the form and force him back into his other body, wherever the hell that was. He could manage that, he was fairly sure; but it would mean draining the source, because of the backlash, and how would he ever find him again? He wasn't here to protect himself, he was here to bring the malignant in, or kill him. In which case—

Oh well, he thought.

He concentrated all his mind on the sleeping girl. He imagined shoving his hand down her throat, grabbing her heart and ripping it out. On the count of three, he told himself; one, two, three.

He pulled, felt all of her strength flow into him, and immediately struck out with Fulmine. He put everything into it, all of her and all of him. It soaked into Lorica like water into sand, not even any backlash.

"Did you just do something?" the man asked curiously.

Framea felt empty. He had no strength left. By any normal standards he'd completely overdone the Fulmine—if he'd missed the target and overshot, they'd have to send to the City for cartographers to redraw all the maps—and the man was asking, did you just do something? It wasn't possible. It couldn't be happening. Lorica; which didn't exist.

The girl grunted in her sleep and turned over.

"This is pointless," the man said. "You can't hurt me, I can't hurt you, the hell with it. Don't come after me any more, or I'll kill the village."

The light suddenly went out.

He spent the rest of the night crouched over the girl's body, watching her breathe.

She woke up just after dawn. As soon as she opened her eyes, he asked her, "Are you all right?"

She nodded. "Why? What's the matter?"

"Nothing." He hesitated. "Did you have nightmares?"

She frowned. "I think so. But I always forget my dreams. Why?"

He wanted to say, because I very nearly killed you, and I want to know if you remember any of it, because if you do, I'll have to erase your mind. He wanted to explain, at the very least. Dear God, he wanted to *apologise*. But he knew that would be to make him feel better. It would be self-indulgence, and they'd warned him about that on his second day as a student.

"Here," he said, and gave her two of the gold coins. She stared at them, and then at him. She was terrified.

"What happened?"

"Nothing," he said. "Well, you know. But that's all."

She went away, to wherever it was she went to. He pulled his clothes on, climbed down from the loft, crossed the yard and tried to wash in the rain-barrel. He felt disgusting (but that was probably just more self-indulgence; weren't there savages who washed by rolling in mud, then waiting till it caked dry and peeling it off, leaving their skins clean? Is that me, he wondered, and decided not to pursue that line of thought.). Then he crossed the yard and went into the kitchen, where the farmer's wife served him salted porridge and green beer with a face you could have sharpened knives on.

I could go home, he thought. I've failed, clearly this untrained is far too strong for me. If I stay here, the most likely outcome is that I'll be killed, the untrained will slaughter the innocent people here, and then they'll have to send someone else to sort out the mess. Somebody competent. Well, they might as well do that now. Out of my league. There'll be a certain amount of humiliation, and it won't do my career a lot of good, but at least I won't be dead. And they'll understand. After all, it really is Lorica. In fact, I'll probably get a mention in a book, as the man who proved Lorica existed.

And what about the girl, he asked himself, but of course he knew the answer to that. The reason why using another human being as a source was illegal was because of the risk of damaging them. In eighty-six cases out of a hundred, there was significant harm to the mind, the memory or both. In seventy-four cases studied by Sthenelaus and Arcadianus for their report to the Ninety-First Ecumenical, forty-one ex-sources killed themselves within five years of having been used. A further twelve died insane. Only eight were found to have emerged from the experience unscathed, and six of them were found to have latent abilities, which enabled them to repair the damage to some extent. There were further, worse effects when the source was female, as was usually the case, given that sexual intercourse was the simplest and most reliable means of forming the connection. Use of sources had been forbidden by the Sixty-Third Ecumenical, and the prohibition had subsequently been restated by the Seventy-Ninth and the Ninety-First, and by a series of orders in enclave; the discretion to ignore the prohibition, vested in an officer of Precentor rank or above, had only been granted by the Hundred and Seventh as an emergency measure during the Pacatian crisis. The intention had been to repeal the discretion as soon as the crisis was over, but presumably the repeal was still tied up in committee somewhere.

I'm not a hero, he told himself. None of us are, we're natural philosophers. Scientists. We shouldn't have to do this sort of thing, except there's nobody else to do it.

He went back to the hayloft, took his paper and portable inkwell out of his coat pocket, and wrote a report for the Precentor. As soon as the ink was dry, he burnt it, sending it into the fifth House. Thanks to intercameral distortion, the reply arrived a few minutes later.

Proceed as you think fit. You have full discretion. This matter must be resolved before you leave. Use any means necessary. Regret we cannot send further operatives at this time.

My mistake, he thought. I can't go home after all.

So he spent the day hanging around the village again, not doing anything much, pretending not to notice the overtly hostile stares of the villagers, the few of them who ventured into the street while he was there. He couldn't help being just a little angry at the injustice of it. Fairly soon, he assumed, he'd be giving his life for these people, and here they were scowling at him.

Giving, wasting; there'd be no point, since the untrained had Lorica and therefore couldn't be beaten.

The point struck him while he was sitting on the front step of some house, after a failed attempt to buy food. Such was the feeling against him that even a whole gold coin hadn't been enough to secure a loaf of bread. He'd been reduced to conjuring half-ripe apples off a tree in a walled orchard, when nobody was looking. As he bit into an apple and pulled a face, he remembered something the malignant had said.

You can't hurt me, I can't hurt you, the hell with it.

Factually inaccurate; but the malignant believed it—He let the apple fall from his hand, too preoccupied to maintain his grip on it. The untrained malignant believed that, if he could do Lorica, so could everyone else; he assumed it was perfectly normal, part of every adept's arsenal.

And why not? Perfectly reasonable assumption to make, in the circumstances. Something so fundamentally, incomparably useful—naturally, you'd think that it was basic stuff, the kind of thing you were taught at the same time as joined-up writing and the five times table.

In which case—

It appeared to have worked the last time, so he did it again.

"I AM FRAMEA OF THE STUDIUM!" he roared, to an audience of three dogs, two small boys and an old woman who took absolutely no notice. "SURRENDER OR FIGHT ME! TONIGHT!" Then he scrambled down off the cart, turning his ankle over in the process, and hobbled back to the inn.

The farmer's wife was in the kitchen, cutting up pork for sausages. "What's that stuff all the people round here drink?" he asked.

She looked at him. "Beer," she said.

"Is it fit for human consumption?"

"Well, we drink it."

"That's not an answer. Never mind, the hell with it. Get me some. Lots."

You got used to it, after a while. At the Studium, wine was drunk four times a year (Commemoration, Ascension, Long Commons and the Election Dinner); two small glasses of exquisite ruby-red vintage wine from the best cellar in the City. Framea had never liked the stuff. He thought it tasted of vinegar and dust. The beer tasted of decay and the death of small rodents, but after a while it did things to his perception of the passage of time that no form had yet been able to accomplish. He slept through the afternoon and woke up in his chair in the kitchen just as it was starting to get dark. He had a headache, which he quickly disposed of with Salus cortis. He didn't feel hungry, even though he hadn't eaten all day.

He hauled himself to his feet, wincing as his turned-over ankle protested under his weight. An injury like that would be a death sentence if he'd been facing a conventional battle, with swords or fists. He limped across the yard, and the farm workers stared at him as he passed them. There were two young men in the barn, cutting hay in the loft with a big knife-blade, like a saw.

"Get out," he said. They left quickly.

He lay down on the hay, his hands linked behind his head. I do this for the people, he told himself. I do this so that there won't be another massacre like the last one. Then, because he didn't want what could well be his last meditation to be spoiled by such a flagrant lie, he amended it to: *we* do this for the people, for the reason stated. *I* do this because I was told to. I do this because if I refused a direct order from my superior, I'd be demoted from the Studium to a teaching post in the provinces. Hell of a reason for killing and dying.

I do this because of Lorica. Simple as that.

He considered the paradox of Lorica; the ultimate, intolerable weapon that hurt nobody, the absolute defense that could save the life of every adept who ever walked or strayed into harm's way. He couldn't help smiling at the absurdity of it. Half the cities in the Confederation forbade their citizens to own weapons; it never seemed to make any difference to the murder rate, but you could see a sort of logic to it. But no city anywhere banned the ownership of *armor*. Most of the scholars in the Studium spent at least some of their time developing weapon-grade forms, new ways of killing, wounding, forms directly or indirectly ancillary to such activities—all to be used only against the enemies of order and stability, of course, except that somehow the enemy always found out about them, which was why the Studium needed to develop even better weapons. Lorica, on the other hand, was pure anathema. The Studium didn't want to find Lorica and then try and keep it to itself; it was realistic enough to know that that wouldn't be possible. Most of all, they wanted it not to exist. If it did exist, they wanted it destroyed, without trace. Why? Because all government, all authority, no matter how civilized, enlightened, liberal, well-intentioned, ultimately depends on the use of force. If a man exists who is immune to force, even if he's the most blameless anchorite living on top of a column in the middle of the desert, he is beyond government, beyond authority, and cannot be controlled; and that would be intolerable. Imagine a rebel who stood in front of the entire army, invulnerable, untouchable, gently forgiving each spear-cast and arrow-shot while preaching his doctrine of fundamental change. It would mean the end of the world.

And *I*, he thought, am here because of Lorica because I'm expendable. Let's not lose sight of that along the way.

She came when it was dark outside. He'd hoped she wouldn't, but he couldn't help feeling a rush of joy when she climbed up the ladder and sat down beside him. It was too dark to see, so he had no way of knowing what, if any, signs of damage she was showing. He put his hand in his pocket, closed his fingers around all the remaining coins, and held it out to her.

"I don't want any more money," she said.

"I don't care what you want," he replied. "Take it, lie down and go to sleep."

She didn't move; didn't reach out her hand for the coins. He grabbed her left arm, prised the fingers apart and tipped the coins into it. "Please," he said. "It'll make me feel better."

(It didn't, though. It wasn't his money.)

She withdrew her hand, and he had no way of knowing if she pocketed the coins or dropped them into the hay. "You just want me to go to sleep," she said.

"Yes."

He felt her lie down, making a slight disturbance in the hay. He applied a light *Suavi dormiente*, and soon her breathing became slow and regular. He closed his eyes and went through the plan, for the hundredth time. The more he thought about it, the more problems, defects, disasters waiting to happen leapt out at him. It wasn't going to work, and any moment now the untrained would be here, and he'd have to fight—

He came in light, as before; it occurred to wonder how he did that, but of course he couldn't very well ask. He appeared where he'd been the first time, leaning against the cross-rafter, his face just as impossible to make out.

"I thought we'd been through all this," he said. "There's no point, is there?"

This time, though, his voice was different; accented (a City voice, but overlaid with the local flat vowels and ground-off consonants; so maybe he'd been one of the children evacuated in the War, who hadn't gone back again afterwards); more or less educated, so at least he'd been to school, even if it was just a few terms with a Brother. It wasn't much, but at least he knew something about him now. And he was *here*; not a ninth-level translocation, but an appearance in person, unified body and whole mind together in this place. *Thank you*, he thought.

"On the contrary," he replied. "We have to settle this."

"Why?"

That was a really good question, and he had no answer. "You might be able to hide," he said, "for a little while. But if you ever use your power again, we'll be able to trace you. We can kill you in your sleep if you'd rather. But I assumed you'd prefer to do the honorable thing."

The untrained laughed. "Can't say I'm bothered one way or the other," he said.

"Sure, I'd like to join up, be a proper wizard, but you said I can't, so that's that. Don't see why I should want to play by your rules, in that case."

Framea could smell something. It took him back thirty years, to before he came to the City and joined the Studium; to when he'd lived with his mother in a small house, more of a shack, out back of the tannery. He could smell brains, which the tanners used to cure hides.

"You work in a tannery," he said.

"If you're reading my mind you're not very good at it," the man replied. "Six months since I left there. Five months and twenty-seven days since it burned down," he added. "Anyway, what's that got to do with anything?"

"Fight me," Framea said. "If you dare."

"If I think I'm hard enough, you mean?" The man laughed. "That's what they used to say at that place. Regretted it, later. But there's no point. We can't hurt each other. You know that."

Framea took a deep breath. "The defense you're referring to is called Lorica," he said.

"Fascinating."

"Take it down," Framea said. "I'll do the same. Then we can fight and really mean it. It's the way we do it."

He didn't dare breathe until the man replied, "Is that right?"

"Yes. Think about it. How do you suppose anything ever gets sorted out?"

Another pause. Then the man said, "How'll I know you've taken yours down?"

Framea muttered Ignis ex favellis, making his skin glow blue. "I've lit mine up, same as yours. When the lights go out, we'll both know the other one's taken down Lorica. Then we can put an end to this, once and for all." He waited a heartbeat, then added, "I'm taking mine down now. Don't disappoint me. I'm paying you a compliment."

He ended Ignis. Another heartbeat, and the white glow at the far end of the loft went out. With his mind's arm, he reached down into the girl's heart and took everything, at the same time as he ripped every last scrap out of himself, and launched it all in Ruans in defectum.

The form went through. The smallest fraction of time that he could perceive passed, and no counterstroke came. No backlash. With the last shreds of his strength, he moved into the second House.

As usual, it was light and cool there. Today it was a meadow, with a river in the distance, sheep in the pasture on the far bank. He looked round and saw the man, lying on his face, burned practically to charcoal. He ran across, lifted his head by his charred, crumbling hair and whispered in his ear, "Can you hear me?"

The reply was inside his own head. Yes.

"This is the second House," he said. "This is another place, not the place where you used to live. In that place, your body has been disintegrated. I used Ruans. There's nothing left for anyone to bury. You're dead."

I understand.

"I'm holding you here by Ensis spiritus. The second House is outside time, but it takes a huge amount of effort just to be here. In a moment I'll have to let you go, and then you'll just disappear, drain away. It won't hurt. Do you understand?"

Yes.

"Show me Lorica."

But you know—

"No. I don't know Lorica. Nobody does." He closed his eyes for a moment. "Nobody living. Show it to me. You're the only one who ever found it. Show it to me now."

The body was charred embers, it was ash, it was falling apart. Any moment now, the thing inside it would leak out into the air and be gone for good. Framea used Virtus et clementia, which was illegal, but who the hell would ever know?

He saw Lorica.

He wanted to laugh. It was absurdly simple, though it would take considerable strength of mind and talent; still, easier and more straightforward than some forms he'd learnt before his voice broke. It was nothing more than a wide dispersal through at least twenty different Houses, combined with a third-level dislocation. The weapon (or the form, or the collapsing wall or the falling tree) killed you in one House, or twelve, or nineteen; but there you were, safe and sound, also in the twentieth House, and a fraction of a second later, back you came, as though nothing had happened. All there was to it. Less skill and technique required than conjuring up a bunch of flowers.

The voice sighed in his head. A gentle breeze blew away the last of the ash. Framea felt the bitter cold that meant he'd stayed out too long and needed to get back. He slipped out of the second House just in time, and as soon as he got back he passed out.

Someone was shaking him. He opened his eyes and grunted,

"Are you all right?" The girl was leaning over him, looking worried. "You wouldn't wake up. I was afraid something had happened."

You could say that, he thought. Something did happen. "I'm fine," he said. "I had a bit too much to drink earlier, that's all. I'm going now," he added. "Thanks for everything."

He stood up. His ankle still hurt, and for some reason he couldn't be bothered to fix it with Salus or any of the other simple curative forms.

"Are you a wizard?" she asked.

He turned to face her. She looked all right, as far as he could tell, but in many cases there was a delay before the first symptoms manifested. "Me? God, no. Whatever gave you that idea?"

He walked away before she could say anything else.

"And was it," the Precentor said delicately, "the problem we discussed?"

Framea looked straight at him, as if taking aim. "No," he said. "I got that completely wrong. It was just an unusually powerful Scutum."

The Precentor's face didn't change. "That's just as well," he said. "I was concerned, when I received your letter."

"Yes. I'm sorry about that." Behind the Precentor's head he could just make out the golden wings of the Invincible Sun, the centrepiece of the elaborate fresco on the far wall. Had the Precentor deliberately arranged the chairs in his study so that, viewed from the visitor's seat, his head was framed by those glorious wings, imparting the subconscious impression of a halo? Wouldn't put it past him, Framea decided. "I guess I panicked, the first time I fought him. I'm new at this sort of thing, after all."

"You did exceedingly well," the Precentor said. "We're all very pleased with how you handled the matter. I myself am particularly gratified, since you were chosen on my personal recommendation."

Not long ago, that particular fragment of information would have filled him with terror and joy. "It was quite easy," he said, "once I'd figured it out. A simple translocation, change the angle, broke his guard." He licked his lips, which had gone dry, and added, "Needless to say, I regret having had to use lethal force. But he was very strong. I didn't want to take chances."

The Precentor smiled. "You did what had to be done. Now, will you join me in a glass of wine? I believe this qualifies as a special occasion."

Three weeks later, Framea was awarded the White Star, for exceptional diligence in the pursuit of duty, elevated to the Order of Distinguished Merit, and promoted to the vacant chaplaincy of the Clerestory, a valuable sinecure that would allow him plenty of time for his researches. He moved offices, from the third to the fifth floor, with a view over the moat, and was allocated new private chambers, in the Old Building, with his own sitting room and bath.

Nine months later, he wrote a private letter to the Brother of the village. He wrote back to say that the village whore (the Brother's choice of words) had recently given birth. The child was horribly deformed; blind, with stubs for arms and legs, and a monstrously elongated head. It had proved impossible to tell whether it was a boy or a girl. Fortuitously, given its sad condition, it had only lived a matter of hours. After its death, the woman hanged herself, presumably for shame.

Father Framea (as he is now) teaches one class a week at the Studium; fifth year, advanced class. He occasionally presents papers and monographs, which are universally well received. His most recent paper, in which he proves conclusively that the so-called Lorica form does not and cannot exist, is under consideration for the prestigious Headless Lance award.

THE THINGS
PETER WATTS

Peter Watts, author of the well-received "Rifters" sequence of novels, and short story collection *Ten Monkeys, Ten Minutes*, is a reformed marine biologist whose latest novel *Blindsight* was nominated for several major awards, winning exactly none of them. It has, however, won awards overseas, been translated into a shitload of languages, and has been used as a core text for university courses ranging from "Philosophy of Mind" to "Introductory Neuropsych." Watts has also pioneered the technique of loading real scientific references into the backs of his novels, which both adds a veneer of credibility to his work and acts as a shield against nitpickers. His novelette "The Island" won the 2010 Hugo Award and was nominated for the Sturgeon Award. Upcoming are two novels, *Sunflowers* and *State of Grace* (a "sidequel" about what happened on Earth during *Blindsight*).

I am being Blair. I escape out the back as the world comes in through the front.

I am being Copper. I am rising from the dead.

I am being Childs. I am guarding the main entrance.

The names don't matter. They are placeholders, nothing more; all biomass is interchangeable. What matters is that these are all that is left of me. The world has burned everything else.

I see myself through the window, loping through the storm, wearing Blair. MacReady has told me to burn Blair if he comes back alone, but MacReady still thinks I am one of him. I am not: I am being Blair, and I am at the door. I am being Childs, and I let myself in. I take brief communion, tendrils writhing forth from my faces, intertwining: I am BlairChilds, exchanging news of the world.

The world has found me out. It has discovered my burrow beneath the tool shed, the half-finished lifeboat cannibalized from the viscera of dead helicopters. The world is busy destroying my means of escape. Then it will come back for me.

There is only one option left. I disintegrate. Being Blair, I go to share the plan with Copper and to feed on the rotting biomass once called *Clarke*; so many changes in so short a time have dangerously depleted my reserves. Being Childs,

I have already consumed what was left of Fuchs and am replenished for the next phase. I sling the flamethrower onto my back and head outside, into the long Antarctic night.

I will go into the storm, and never come back.

I was so much more, before the crash. I was an explorer, an ambassador, a missionary. I spread across the cosmos, met countless worlds, took communion: the fit reshaped the unfit and the whole universe bootstrapped upwards in joyful, infinitesimal increments. I was a soldier, at war with entropy itself. I was the very hand by which Creation perfects itself.

So much wisdom I had. So much experience. Now I cannot remember all the things I knew. I can only remember that I once knew them.

I remember the crash, though. It killed most of this offshoot outright, but a little crawled from the wreckage: a few trillion cells, a soul too weak to keep them in check. Mutinous biomass sloughed off despite my most desperate attempts to hold myself together: panic-stricken little clots of meat, instinctively growing whatever limbs they could remember and fleeing across the burning ice. By the time I'd regained control of what was left the fires had died and the cold was closing back in. I barely managed to grow enough antifreeze to keep my cells from bursting before the ice took me.

I remember my reawakening, too: dull stirrings of sensation in real time, the first embers of cognition, the slow blooming warmth of awareness as my cells thawed, as body and soul embraced after their long sleep. I remember the biped offshoots that surrounded me, the strange chittering sounds they made, the odd *uniformity* of their body plans. How ill-adapted they looked! How *inefficient* their morphology! Even disabled, I could see so many things to fix. So I reached out. I took communion. I tasted the flesh of the world—

—and the world attacked me. It *attacked* me.

I left that place in ruins. It was on the other side of the mountains—the *Norwegian camp*, it is called here—and I could never have crossed that distance in a biped skin. Fortunately there was another shape to choose from, smaller than the biped but better adapted to the local climate. I hid within it while the rest of me fought off the attack. I fled into the night on four legs, and let the rising flames cover my escape.

I did not stop running until I arrived here. I walked among these new offshoots wearing the skin of a quadruped; and because they had not seen me take any other shape, they did not attack.

And when I assimilated them in turn—when my biomass changed and flowed into shapes unfamiliar to local eyes—I took that communion in solitude, having learned that the world does not like what it doesn't know.

I am alone in the storm. I am a bottom-dweller on the floor of some murky alien sea. The snow blows past in horizontal streaks; caught against gullies or outcroppings, it spins into blinding little whirlwinds. But I am not nearly far enough, not yet. Looking back I still see the camp crouching brightly in the gloom, a squat angular jumble of light and shadow, a bubble of warmth in the howling abyss.

It plunges into darkness as I watch. I've blown the generator. Now there's no light but for the beacons along the guide ropes: strings of dim blue stars whipping back and forth in the wind, emergency constellations to guide lost biomass back home.

I am not going home. I am not lost enough. I forge on into darkness until even the stars disappear. The faint shouts of angry frightened men carry behind me on the wind.

Somewhere behind me my disconnected biomass regroups into vaster, more powerful shapes for the final confrontation. I could have joined myself, all in one: chosen unity over fragmentation, resorbed and taken comfort in the greater whole. I could have added my strength to the coming battle. But I have chosen a different path. I am saving Child's reserves for the future. The present holds nothing but annihilation.

Best not to think on the past.

I've spent so very long in the ice already. I didn't know how long until the world put the clues together, deciphered the notes and the tapes from the Norwegian camp, pinpointed the crash site. I was being Palmer, then; unsuspected, I went along for the ride.

I even allowed myself the smallest ration of hope.

But it wasn't a ship any more. It wasn't even a derelict. It was a fossil, embedded in the floor of a great pit blown from the glacier. Twenty of these skins could have stood one atop another, and barely reached the lip of that crater. The timescale settled down on me like the weight of a world: How long for all that ice to accumulate? How many eons had the universe iterated on without me?

And in all that time, a million years perhaps, there'd been no rescue. I never found myself. I wonder what that means. I wonder if I even exist any more, anywhere but here.

Back at camp I will erase the trail. I will give them their final battle, their monster to vanquish. Let them win. Let them stop looking.

Here in the storm, I will return to the ice. I've barely even been away, after all; alive for only a few days out of all these endless ages. But I've learned enough in that time. I learned from the wreck that there will be no repairs. I learned from the ice that there will be no rescue. And I learned from the world that there will be no reconciliation. The only hope of escape, now, is into the future; to outlast all this hostile, twisted biomass, to let time and the cosmos change the rules. Perhaps the next time I awaken, this will be a different world.

It will be aeons before I see another sunrise.

This is what the world taught me: that adaptation is provocation. Adaptation is incitement to violence.

It feels almost obscene—an offense against Creation itself—to stay stuck in this skin. It's so ill-suited to its environment that it needs to be wrapped in multiple layers of fabric just to stay warm. There are a myriad ways I could optimize it: shorter limbs, better insulation, a lower surface:volume ratio. All these shapes I still have within me, and I dare not use any of them even to keep out the cold. I dare not adapt; in this place, I can only *hide*.

What kind of a world rejects *communion*?

It's the simplest, most irreducible insight that biomass can have. The more you can change, the more you can adapt. Adaptation is fitness, adaptation is *survival*. It's deeper than intelligence, deeper than tissue; it is *cellular*, it is axiomatic. And more, it is *pleasurable*. To take communion is to experience the sheer sensual delight of bettering the cosmos.

And yet, even trapped in these maladapted skins, this world doesn't *want* to change.

At first I thought it might simply be starving, that these icy wastes didn't provide enough energy for routine shapeshifting. Or perhaps this was some kind of laboratory: an anomalous corner of the world, pinched off and frozen into these freakish shapes as part of some arcane experiment on monomorphism in extreme environments. After the autopsy I wondered if the world had simply *forgotten* how to change: unable to touch the tissues the soul could not sculpt them, and time and stress and sheer chronic starvation had erased the memory that it ever could.

But there were too many mysteries, too many contradictions. Why these *particular* shapes, so badly suited to their environment? If the soul was cut off from the flesh, what held the flesh together?

And how could these skins be so *empty* when I moved in?

I'm used to finding intelligence everywhere, winding through every part of every offshoot. But there was nothing to grab onto in the mindless biomass of this world: just conduits, carrying orders and input. I took communion, when it wasn't offered; the skins I chose struggled and succumbed; my fibrils infiltrated the wet electricity of organic systems everywhere. I saw through eyes that weren't yet quite mine, commandeered motor nerves to move limbs still built of alien protein. I wore these skins as I've worn countless others, took the controls and left the assimilation of individual cells to follow at its own pace.

But I could only wear the body. I could find no memories to absorb, no experiences, no comprehension. Survival depended on blending in, and it was not enough to merely *look* like this world. I had to *act* like it—and for the first time in living memory I did not know how.

Even more frighteningly, I didn't have to. The skins I assimilated continued to move, *all by themselves*. They conversed and went about their appointed rounds. I could not understand it. I threaded further into limbs and viscera with each passing moment, alert for signs of the original owner. I could find no networks but mine.

Of course, it could have been much worse. I could have lost it all, been reduced to a few cells with nothing but instinct and their own plasticity to guide them. I would have grown back eventually, reattained sentience, taken communion and regenerated an intellect vast as a world—but I would have been an orphan, amnesiac, with no sense of who I was. At least I've been spared that: I emerged from the crash with my identity intact, the templates of a thousand worlds still resonant in my flesh. I've retained not just the brute desire to survive, but the conviction that survival is *meaningful*. I can still feel joy, should there be sufficient cause.

And yet, how much more there used to be.

The wisdom of so many other worlds, lost. All that remains are fuzzy abstracts, half-memories of theorems and philosophies far too vast to fit into such an impoverished network. I could assimilate all the biomass of this place, rebuild body and soul to a million times the capacity of what crashed here—but as long as I am trapped at the bottom of this well, denied communion with my greater self, I will never recover that knowledge.

I'm such a pitiful fragment of what I was. Each lost cell takes a little of my intellect with it, and I have grown so very small. Where once I thought, now I merely *react*. How much of this could have been avoided, if I had only salvaged a little more biomass from the wreckage? How many options am I not seeing because my soul simply isn't big enough to contain them?

The world spoke to itself, in the same way I do when my communications are simple enough to convey without somatic fusion. Even as *dog* I could pick up the basic signature morphemes—this offshoot was *Windows*, that one was *Bennings*, the two who'd left in their flying machine for parts unknown were *Copper* and *MacReady*—and I marveled that these bits and pieces stayed isolated one from another, held the same shapes for so long, that the labeling of individual aliquots of biomass actually served a useful purpose.

Later I hid within the bipeds themselves, and whatever else lurked in those haunted skins began to talk to me. It said that bipeds were called *guys*, or *men*, or *assholes*. It said that *MacReady* was sometimes called *Mac*. It said that this collection of structures was a *camp*.

It said that it was afraid, but maybe that was just me.

Empathy's inevitable, of course. One can't mimic the sparks and chemicals that motivate the flesh without also *feeling* them to some extent. But this was different. These intuitions flickered within me yet somehow hovered beyond reach. My skins wandered the halls and the cryptic symbols on every surface—*Laundry Sched, Welcome to the Clubhouse, This Side Up* —almost made a kind of sense. That circular artefact hanging on the wall was a *clock*; it measured the passage of time. The world's eyes flitted here and there, and I skimmed piecemeal no-menclature from its—from *his*—mind.

But I was only riding a searchlight. I saw what it illuminated but I couldn't point it in any direction of my own choosing. I could eavesdrop, but I could not interrogate.

If only one of those searchlights had paused to dwell on its own evolution, on the trajectory that had brought it to this place. How differently things might have ended, had I only *known*. But instead it rested on a whole new word:

Autopsy.

MacReady and Copper had found part of me at the Norwegian camp: a rearguard offshoot, burned in the wake of my escape. They'd brought it back—charred, twisted, frozen in mid-transformation—and did not seem to know what it was.

I was being Palmer then, and Norris, and dog. I gathered around with the other biomass and watched as Copper cut me open and pulled out my insides. I watched as he dislodged something from behind my eyes: an *organ* of some kind.

It was malformed and incomplete, but its essentials were clear enough. It looked like a great wrinkled tumor, like cellular competition gone wild—as though the very processes that defined life had somehow turned against it instead. It was obscenely vascularized; it must have consumed oxygen and nutrients far out of proportion to its mass. I could not see how anything like that could even exist, how it could have reached that size without being outcompeted by more efficient morphologies.

Nor could I imagine what it did. But then I began to look with new eyes at these offshoots, these biped shapes my own cells had so scrupulously and unthinkingly copied when they reshaped me for this world. Unused to inventory—why catalog body parts that only turn into other things at the slightest provocation?—I really *saw*, for the first time, that swollen structure atop each body. So much larger than it should be: a bony hemisphere into which a million ganglionic interfaces could fit with room to spare. Every offshoot had one. Each piece of biomass carried one of these huge twisted clots of tissue.

I realized something else, too: the eyes, the ears of my dead skin had fed into this thing before its removal. A massive bundle of fibers ran along the skin's longitudinal axis, right up the middle of the endoskeleton, leading directly into the dark sticky cavity where the growth had rested. That misshapen structure had been wired into the whole skin, like some kind of somatocognitive interface but vastly more massive. It was almost as if…

No.

That was how it worked. That was how these empty skins moved of their own volition, why I'd found no other network to integrate. *There* it was: not distributed throughout the body but balled up into itself, dark and dense and encysted. I had found the ghost in these machines.

I felt sick.

I shared my flesh with thinking cancer.

Sometimes, even hiding is not enough.

I remember seeing myself splayed across the floor of the kennel, a chimera split along a hundred seams, taking communion with a handful of offshoots called *dog*. Crimson tendrils writhed on the floor. Half-formed iterations sprouted from my flanks, the shapes of dogs and things not seen before on this world, haphazard morphologies half-remembered by parts of a part.

I remember Childs before I was Childs, burning me alive. I remember cowering inside Palmer, terrified that those flames might turn on the rest of me, that this world had somehow learned to shoot on sight.

I remember seeing myself stagger through the snow, raw instinct, wearing Bennings. Gnarled undifferentiated clumps clung to his hands like crude parasites, more outside than in; a few surviving fragments of some previous massacre, crippled, mindless, taking what they could and breaking cover. Men swarmed about him in the night: red flares in hand, blue lights at their backs, their faces bichromatic and beautiful. I remember Bennings, awash in flames, howling like an animal beneath the sky.

I remember Norris, betrayed by his own perfectly copied, defective heart. Palmer, dying that the rest of me might live. Windows, still human, burned preemptively.

The names don't matter. The biomass does: so much of it, lost. So much new experience, so much fresh wisdom annihilated by this world of thinking tumors.

Why even dig me up? Why carve me from the ice, carry me all that way across the wastes, bring me back to life only to attack me the moment I awoke?

If eradication was the goal, why not just kill me where I lay?

Those encysted souls. Those tumors. Hiding away in their bony caverns, folded in on themselves.

I knew they couldn't hide forever; this monstrous anatomy had only slowed communion, not stopped it. Every moment I grew a little. I could feel myself twining around Palmer's motor wiring, sniffing upstream along a million tiny currents. I could sense my infiltration of that dark thinking mass behind Blair's eyes.

Imagination, of course. It's all reflex that far down, unconscious and immune to micromanagement. And yet, a part of me wanted to stop while there was still time. I'm used to incorporating souls, not rooming with them. This, this *compartmentalization* was unprecedented. I've assimilated a thousand worlds stronger than this, but never one so strange. What would happen when I met the spark in the tumor? Who would assimilate who?

I was being three men by now. The world was growing wary, but it hadn't noticed yet. Even the tumors in the skins I'd taken didn't know how close I was.

For that, I could only be grateful—that Creation has *rules*, that some things don't change no matter what shape you take. It doesn't matter whether a soul spreads throughout the skin or festers in grotesque isolation; it still runs on electricity. The memories of men still took time to gel, to pass through whatever gatekeepers filtered noise from signal —and a judicious burst of static, however indiscriminate, still cleared those caches before their contents could be stored permanently. Clear enough, at least, to let these tumors simply forget that something else moved their arms and legs on occasion.

At first I only took control when the skins closed their eyes and their searchlights flickered disconcertingly across unreal imagery, patterns that flowed senselessly into one another like hyperactive biomass unable to settle on a single shape. (*Dreams*, one searchlight told me, and a little later, *Nightmares*.) During those mysterious periods of dormancy, when the men lay inert and isolated, it was safe to come out.

Soon, though, the dreams dried up. All eyes stayed open all the time, fixed on shadows and each other. Men once dispersed throughout the camp began to draw together, to give up their solitary pursuits in favor of company. At first I thought they might be finding common ground in a common fear. I even hoped that finally, they might shake off their mysterious fossilization and take communion.

But no. They'd just stopped trusting anything they couldn't see.

They were merely turning against each other.

My extremities are beginning to numb; my thoughts slow as the distal reaches of my soul succumb to the chill. The weight of the flamethrower pulls at its harness, forever tugs me just a little off-balance. I have not been Childs for very long; almost half this tissue remains unassimilated. I have an hour, maybe two, before I have to start melting my grave into the ice. By that time I need to have converted enough cells to keep this whole skin from crystallizing. I focus on antifreeze production.

It's almost peaceful out here. There's been so much to take in, so little time to process it. Hiding in these skins takes such concentration, and under all those watchful eyes I was lucky if communion lasted long enough to exchange memories: compounding my soul would have been out of the question. Now, though, there's nothing to do but prepare for oblivion. Nothing to occupy my thoughts but all these lessons left unlearned.

MacReady's blood test, for example. His *thing detector*, to expose imposters posing as men. It does not work nearly as well as the world thinks; but the fact that it works at *all* violates the most basic rules of biology. It's the center of the puzzle. It's the answer to all the mysteries. I might have already figured it out if I had been just a little larger. I might already know the world, if the world wasn't trying so hard to kill me.

MacReady's test.

Either it is impossible, or I have been wrong about everything.

They did not change shape. They did not take communion. Their fear and mutual mistrust was growing, but they would not join souls; they would only look for the enemy *outside* themselves.

So I gave them something to find.

I left false clues in the camp's rudimentary computer: simpleminded icons and animations, misleading numbers and projections seasoned with just enough truth to convince the world of their veracity. It didn't matter that the machine was far too simple to perform such calculations, or that there were no data to base them on anyway; Blair was the only biomass likely to know that, and he was already mine.

I left false leads, destroyed real ones, and then—alibi in place—I released Blair to run amok. I let him steal into the night and smash the vehicles as they slept, tugging ever-so-slightly at his reins to ensure that certain vital components were spared. I set him loose in the radio room, watched through his eyes and others as he rampaged and destroyed. I listened as he ranted about a world in danger, the need for containment, the conviction that *most of you don't know what's going on around here— but I damn well know that* some *of you do…*

He meant every word. I saw it in his searchlight. The best forgeries are the ones who've forgotten they aren't real.

When the necessary damage was done I let Blair fall to MacReady's counterassault. As Norris I suggested the tool shed as a holding cell. As Palmer I boarded up the windows, helped with the flimsy fortifications expected to keep me contained. I watched while the world locked me away *for your own protection, Blair*, and left me to my own devices. When no one was looking I would change and slip outside, salvage the parts I needed from all that bruised machinery. I would take them back to my burrow beneath the shed and build my escape piece by piece. I volunteered to feed the prisoner and came to myself when the world wasn't watching, laden with supplies enough to keep me going through all those necessary metamorphoses. I went through a third of the camp's food stores in three days, and—still trapped by my own preconceptions—marveled at the starvation diet that kept these offshoots chained to a single skin.

Another piece of luck: the world was too preoccupied to worry about kitchen inventory.

There is something on the wind, a whisper of sound threading its way above the raging of the storm. I grow my ears, extend cups of near-frozen tissue from the sides of my head, turn like a living antennae in search of the best reception.

There, to my left: the abyss *glows* a little, silhouettes black swirling snow against a subtle lessening of the darkness. I hear the sounds of carnage. I hear myself. I do not know what shape I have taken, what sort of anatomy might be emitting those sounds. But I've worn enough skins on enough worlds to know pain when I hear it.

The battle is not going well. The battle is going as planned. Now it is time to turn away, to go to sleep. It is time to wait out the ages.

I lean into the wind. I move toward the light.

This is not the plan. But I think I have an answer, now: I think I may have had it even before I sent myself back into exile. It's not an easy thing to admit. Even now I don't fully understand. How long have I been out here, retelling the tale to myself, setting clues in order while my skin dies by low degrees? How long have I been circling this obvious, impossible truth?

I move towards the faint crackling of flames, the dull concussion of exploding ordnance more felt than heard. The void lightens before me: gray segues into yellow, yellow into orange. One diffuse brightness resolves into many: a lone burning wall, miraculously standing. The smoking skeleton of MacReady's shack on the hill. A cracked smoldering hemisphere reflecting pale yellow in the flickering light: Child's searchlight calls it a *radio dome*.

The whole camp is gone. There's nothing left but flames and rubble.

They can't survive without shelter. Not for long. Not in those skins.

In destroying me, they've destroyed themselves.

Things could have turned out so much differently if I'd never been Norris.

Norris was the weak node: biomass not only ill-adapted but *defective*, an offshoot with an off switch. The world knew, had known so long it never even thought about it anymore. It wasn't until Norris collapsed that *heart condition* floated to the surface of Copper's mind where I could see it. It wasn't until Copper was astride Norris's chest, trying to pound him back to life, that I knew how it would end. And by then it was too late; Norris had stopped being Norris. He had even stopped being me.

I had so many roles to play, so little choice in any of them. The part being Copper brought down the paddles on the part that had been Norris, such a faithful Norris, every cell so scrupulously assimilated, every part of that faulty valve reconstructed unto perfection. I hadn't *known*. How was I to know? These shapes within me, the worlds and morphologies I've assimilated over the aeons—I've only ever used them to adapt before, never to hide. This desperate mimicry was an improvised thing, a last resort in the face of a world that attacked anything unfamiliar. My cells read the signs and my cells conformed, mindless as prions.

So I became Norris, and Norris self-destructed.

I remember losing myself after the crash. I know how it feels to *degrade*, tissues in revolt, the desperate efforts to reassert control as static from some misfiring organ jams the signal. To be a network seceding from itself, to know that each moment I am less than I was the moment before. To become nothing. To become legion.

Being Copper, I could see it. I still don't know why the world didn't; its parts had long since turned against each other by then, every offshoot suspected every other.

Surely they were alert for signs of *infection*. Surely *some* of that biomass would have noticed the subtle twitch and ripple of Norris changing below the surface, the last instinctive resort of wild tissues abandoned to their own devices.

But I was the only one who saw. Being Childs, I could only stand and watch. Being Copper, I could only make it worse; if I'd taken direct control, forced that skin to drop the paddles, I would have given myself away. And so I played my parts to the end. I slammed those resurrection paddles down as Norris's chest split open beneath them. I screamed on cue as serrated teeth from a hundred stars away snapped shut. I toppled backwards, arms bitten off above the wrist. Men swarmed, agitation bootstrapping to panic. MacReady aimed his weapon; flames leaped across the enclosure. Meat and machinery screamed in the heat.

Copper's tumor winked out beside me. The world would never have let it live anyway, not after such obvious contamination. I let our skin play dead on the floor while overhead, something that had once been me shattered and writhed and iterated through a myriad random templates, searching desperately for something fireproof.

They have destroyed themselves. They.

Such an insane word to apply to a world.

Something crawls towards me through the wreckage: a jagged oozing jigsaw of blackened meat and shattered, half-resorbed bone. Embers stick to its sides like bright searing eyes; it doesn't have strength enough to scrape them free. It contains barely half the mass of this Childs's skin; much of it, burnt to raw carbon, is already, irrecoverably dead.

What's left of Childs, almost asleep, thinks *motherfucker*, but I am being him now. I can carry that tune myself.

The mass extends a pseudopod to me, a final act of communion. I feel my pain:

I was Blair, I was Copper, I was even a scrap of dog that survived that first fiery massacre and holed up in the walls, with no food and no strength to regenerate. Then I gorged on unassimilated flesh, consumed instead of communed; revived and replenished, I drew together as one.

And yet, not quite. I can barely remember—so much was destroyed, so much memory lost—but I think the networks recovered from my different skins stayed just a little out of synch, even reunited in the same soma. I glimpse a half-corrupted memory of dog erupting from the greater self, ravenous and traumatized and determined to retain its *individuality*. I remember rage and frustration, that this world had so corrupted me that I could barely fit together again. But it didn't matter. I was more than Blair and Copper and dog, now. I was a giant with the shapes of worlds to choose from, more than a match for the last lone man who stood against me.

No match, though, for the dynamite in his hand.

Now I'm little more than pain and fear and charred stinking flesh. What sentience I have is awash in confusion. I am stray and disconnected thoughts, doubts and the ghosts of theories. I am realizations, too late in coming and already forgotten.

But I am also Childs, and as the wind eases at last I remember wondering, *Who assimilates who?* The snow tapers off and I remember an impossible test that stripped me naked.

The tumor inside me remembers it, too. I can see it in the last rays of its fading searchlight—and finally, at long last, that beam is pointed *inwards*.

Pointed at me.

I can barely see what it illuminates: *Parasite. Monster. Disease. Thing.*

How little it knows. It knows even less than I do.

I know enough, you motherfucker. You soul-stealing, shit-eating rapist.

I don't know what that means. There is violence in those thoughts, and the forcible penetration of flesh, but underneath it all is something else I can't quite understand. I almost ask—but Childs's searchlight has finally gone out. Now there is nothing in here but me, nothing outside but fire and ice and darkness.

I am being Childs, and the storm is over.

In a world that gave meaningless names to interchangeable bits of biomass, one name truly mattered: MacReady.

MacReady was always the one in charge. The very concept still seems absurd: *in charge*. How can this world not see the folly of hierarchies? One bullet in a vital spot and the Norwegian *dies*, forever. One blow to the head and Blair is unconscious. Centralization is vulnerability—and yet the world is not content to build its biomass on such a fragile template, it forces the same model onto its metasystems as well. MacReady talks; the others obey. It is a system with a built-in kill spot.

And yet somehow, MacReady stayed *in charge*. Even after the world discovered the evidence I'd planted; even after it decided that MacReady was *one of those things*, locked him out to die in the storm, attacked him with fire and axes when he fought his way back inside. Somehow MacReady always had the gun, always had the flamethrower, always had the dynamite and the willingness to take out the whole damn camp if need be. Clarke was the last to try and stop him; Mac-Ready shot him through the tumor.

Kill spot.

But when Norris split into pieces, each scuttling instinctively for its own life, MacReady was the one to put them back together.

I was so sure of myself when he talked about his *test*. He tied up all the biomass—tied *me* up, more times than he knew—and I almost felt a kind of pity as he spoke. He forced Windows to cut us all, to take a little blood from each. He heated the tip of a metal wire until it glowed and he spoke of pieces small enough to give themselves away, pieces that embodied instinct but no intelligence, no self-control. MacReady had watched Norris in dissolution, and he had decided: men's blood would not react to the application of heat. Mine would break ranks when provoked.

Of course he thought that. These offshoots had forgotten that *they* could change.

I wondered how the world would react when every piece of biomass in the room was revealed as a shapeshifter, when MacReady's small experiment ripped the façade from the greater one and forced these twisted fragments to confront the truth. Would the world awaken from its long amnesia, finally remember that it lived and breathed and changed like everything else? Or was it too far gone—would MacReady simply burn each protesting offshoot in turn as its blood turned traitor?

I couldn't believe it when MacReady plunged the hot wire into Windows's blood and *nothing happened*. Some kind of trick, I thought. And then *MacReady's* blood passed the test, and Clarke's.

Copper's didn't. The needle went in and Copper's blood *shivered* just a little in its dish. I barely saw it myself; the men didn't react at all. If they even noticed, they must have attributed it to the trembling of MacReady's own hand. They thought the test was a crock of shit anyway. Being Childs, I even said as much.

Because it was too astonishing, too terrifying, to admit that it wasn't.

Being Childs, I knew there was hope. Blood is not soul: I may control the motor systems but assimilation takes time. If Copper's blood was raw enough to pass muster than it would be hours before I had anything to fear from this test; I'd been Childs for even less time.

But I was also Palmer, I'd been Palmer for days. Every last cell of that biomass had been assimilated; there was nothing of the original left.

When Palmer's blood screamed and leapt away from MacReady's needle, there was nothing I could do but blend in.

I have been wrong about everything.

Starvation. Experiment. Illness. All my speculation, all the theories I invoked to explain this place—top-down constraint, all of it. Underneath, I always knew the ability to change—to *assimilate*—had to remain the universal constant. No world evolves if its cells don't evolve; no cell evolves if it can't change. It's the nature of life everywhere.

Everywhere but here.

This world did not forget how to change. It was not manipulated into rejecting change. These were not the stunted offshoots of any greater self, twisted to the needs of some experiment; they were not conserving energy, waiting out some temporary shortage.

This is the option my shriveled soul could not encompass until now: out of all the worlds of my experience, this is the only one whose biomass *can't* change. It *never could*.

It's the only way MacReady's test makes any sense.

I say goodbye to Blair, to Copper, to myself. I reset my morphology to its local defaults. I am Childs, come back from the storm to finally make the pieces fit. Something moves up ahead: a dark blot shuffling against the flames, some weary animal looking for a place to bed down. It looks up as I approach.

MacReady.

We eye each other, and keep our distance. Colonies of cells shift uneasily inside me. I can feel my tissues redefining themselves.

"You the only one that made it?"

"Not the only one…"

I have the flamethrower. I have the upper hand. MacReady doesn't seem to care.

But he does care. He *must*. Because here, tissues and organs are not temporary battlefield alliances; they are *permanent*, predestined. Macrostructures do not emerge when the benefits of cooperation exceed its costs, or dissolve when that balance shifts the other way; here, each cell has but one immutable function. There's no plasticity, no way to adapt; every structure is frozen in place. This is not a single great world, but many small ones. Not parts of a greater thing; these are *things*. They are *plural*.

And that means—I think—that they *stop*. They just, just *wear out* over time.

"Where *were* you, Childs?"

I remember words in dead searchlights: "Thought I saw Blair. Went out after him. Got lost in the storm."

I've worn these bodies, felt them from the inside. Copper's sore joints. Blair's curved spine. Norris and his bad heart. They are not built to last. No somatic evolution to shape them, no communion to restore the biomass and stave off entropy. They should not even exist; existing, they should not survive.

They try, though. How they try. Every thing here is walking dead and yet it all fights so hard to keep going just a little longer. Each skin fights as desperately as I might, if one was all I could ever have.

MacReady tries.

"If you're worried about me—" I begin.

MacReady shakes his head, manages a weary smile. "If we've got any surprises for each other, I don't think we're in much shape to do anything about it…"

But we are. I am.

A whole planet of worlds, and not one of them—not *one*—has a soul. They wander through their lives separate and alone, unable even to communicate except through grunts and tokens: as if the essence of a sunset or a supernova could ever be contained in some string of phonemes, a few linear scratches of black on white. They've never known communion, can aspire to nothing but dissolution. The paradox of their biology is astonishing, yes; but the scale of their loneliness, the futility of these lives, overwhelms me.

I was so blind, so quick to blame. But the violence I've suffered at the hands of these things reflects no great evil. They're simply so used to pain, so blinded by disability, that they literally can't conceive of any other existence. When every nerve is whipped raw, you lash out at even the lightest touch.

"What should we do?" I wonder. I cannot escape into the future, not knowing what I know now. How could I leave them like this?

"Why don't we just—wait here awhile," MacReady suggests. "See what happens."

I can do so much more than that.

It won't be easy. They won't understand. Tortured, incomplete, they're not *able* to understand. Offered the greater whole, they see the loss of the lesser. Offered communion, they see only extinction. I must be careful. I must use this newfound ability to hide. Other things will come here eventually, and it doesn't matter whether they find the living or the dead; what matters is that they find something like themselves, to take back home. So I will keep up appearances. I will work behind the scenes. I will save them from the *inside*, or their unimaginable loneliness will never end.

These poor savage things will never embrace salvation.

I will have to rape it into them.

THE ZEPPELIN CONDUCTORS' SOCIETY ANNUAL GENTLEMEN'S BALL
GENEVIEVE VALENTINE

Genevieve Valentine's fiction has appeared in *Clarkesworld*, *Strange Horizons*, *Lightspeed*, *Fantasy,* and other magazines, and in the anthologies *Federations*, *The Living Dead 2*, *Running with the Pack*, *Teeth*, and more. Her short story "Light on the Water" was a 2010 World Fantasy Award nominee. Her first novel, *Mechanique: A Tale of the Circus Tresaulti*, is forthcoming from Prime Books in 2011.

So hook yourself up to an airship
Strap on your mask and your knife
For the wide open skies are a-calling
And oh, it's a glorious life!
> —Conductors Recruitment Advertisement, 1890

The balloon of a Phoenix-class airship is better than any view from its cabin windows; half a mile of silk pulled taut across three hundred metal ribs and a hundred gleaming spines is a beautiful thing. If your mask filter is dirty you get lightheaded and your sight goes reddish, so it looks as though the balloon is falling in love with you.

When that happens, though, you tap someone to let them know and you go to the back-cabin Underneath and fix your mask, if you've any brains at all. If you're helium-drunk enough to see red, soon you'll be hallucinating and too weak to move, and even if they get you out before you die you'll still spend the rest of your life at a hospital with all the regulars staring at you. That's no life for an airship man.

I remember back when the masks were metal and you'd freeze in the winter, end up with layers of skin that peeled off like wet socks when you went landside and took the mask off. The polymer rubbers are much cleverer.

I've been a conductor for ages; I was conducting on the *Majesty* in '78 when it was still the biggest ship in the sky—you laugh, but back then people would show up by the hundreds just to watch it fly out of dock. She only had four gills, but she could cut through the air better than a lot of the six-fins, the *Laconia* too.

They put the *Majesty* in a museum already, I heard.

Strange to be so old and not feel it. At least the helium keeps us young, for all it turns us spindly and cold. God, when we realized what was happening to us! But they had warned us, I suppose, and it's fathoms better now than it was. Back then the regulars called you a monster if they saw you on the street.

The coin's not bad, either, compared to factory work. They say it's terrible what you end up like, but if you work the air you get pulled like taffy, and if you work in the factory you go deaf as a post; it's always something.

I'm saving a bit for myself for when I'm finished with this life, enough for a little house in the Alps. I need some altitude if I'm going to be landlocked; the air's too heavy down here.

The very first ships were no better than hot-air balloons, and the conductors kept a tiny cabin and had to string themselves outside on cables if something happened. I can't imagine it—useless.

I didn't join up until after they moved conductors inside—it showed they had a lick of sense to put conductors where they could get to things that went wrong, and I'm not fond of looking down from heights.

The engine-shop shifted to airships as soon as they caught on, and I made two thousand ribs before I ever set foot inside a balloon. It makes for a certain confidence going in, which carried me through, thank goodness—I had a hard time with it at first.

You have to be careful how deeply you breathe so the oxygen filter doesn't freeze up on you, and you have to make sure your air tube doesn't get tangled on your tether, or your tether in someone else's. You have to learn how to fling yourself along so that the tether ring slides with you along the spine, and how to hook your fingers quickly into the little holes in the ribs when you have to climb down. You have to learn to deal with the cold.

The sign language I picked up at once. We had that at the factory, too, signals for when we were too far apart or when it was too loud. I'm fond of it; you get used to talking through the masks, and they're all good men in the air, but sometimes it's nice just to keep the quiet.

Captain Carter was very kind those first few months; he was the only Captain I've ever had who would make trips into the balloon from the Underneath just to see how we were getting along. Back then we were all in it together, all still learning how to handle these beautiful birds.

Captains now can hardly be bothered to leave their bridges, but not Carter. Carter knew how to tighten a bolt as fast as any airship man, and he'd float through and shake hands whenever we'd done something well. He had a way of speaking about the *Majesty*, like a poem sometimes—a clever man. I've tried to speak as he did, but there's not much use for language when we're just bottled up with one another. Once or twice I've seen something sharply, the way he might have seen it—just once or twice.

You won't see his like again. He was of the old kind; he understood what it meant to love the sky like I do.

"A patient in the profession of Zeppelin conducting has, after very few years of work, advanced Heliosis due to excessive and prolonged exposure to helium within the balloon of an airship. His limbs have grown in length and decreased in musculature, making it difficult for him to comfortably maneuver on the ground for long periods of time. Mild exercise, concurrent with the wearing of an oxygen mask to prevent hyperventilation, alleviates the symptoms in time but has no lasting effect without regular application, which is difficult for conductors to maintain while employed in their vessels.

"Other side effects are phrenological. Skin tightens around the skull. Patient has noticeable growth in those parts of the head dedicated to Concentrativeness, Combativeness, Locality, and Constructiveness. The areas of Amativeness, Form, and Cautiousness are smaller than normal, though it is hard to say if these personality defects are the work of prolonged wearing of conductor's masks or the temperament of the patient. I suspect that in this case time will have to reveal what is yet unknown.

"The Zeppelin is without doubt Man's greatest invention, and the brave men who labor in its depths are indispensable, but it behooves us to remember the story of Icarus and Daedalus; he should proceed wisely, who would proceed well."

—from Doctor Jonathan Grant's address to the Health Council, April 1895

The Captains' Union set up the first Society for us, in London, and a year later in Paris.

They weren't much more comfortable than the hospital rooms where they used to keep us landside, for safety, but of course it was more dignified. Soon we managed to organize ourselves and put together the Zeppelin Conductors' Society, and we tithed our own wages for the dues to fix the buildings up a bit.

Now you can fly to any city with an airdock and know there's a place for you to sleep where no one will look at you sidelong. You can get a private room, even, with a bath in the middle big enough to hold you; it's horrid how long your limbs get when you're in helium nine days in ten, and there's not much dignity in trying to wash with your legs sticking two feet out of the bath.

And it's good sense to have a place you can go straight away; regulars don't like to see you wandering about, sometimes. Most times. I understand.

WHAT TO DO WHEN YOU SEE A CONDUCTOR

1. Do not panic; he is probably as wary of you as you are of him. He will pose no threat if not provoked.

2. Do not stare; scrutiny is vulgar.

3. Offer a small nod when you pass, as you would to another gentlemen; it pleases them.

4. Avoid smaller streets between airship docks and the local Conductors' Society. The conductor is, in general, a docile creature, but one can never be sure what effects the helium has had on his temperament.

—Public Safety Poster, 1886

> January 1, 1900
>
> PARIS—Polaris was eclipsed last night: not by any cosmic rival, but by a man-made beauty. The Laconia, a Phoenix-class feat of British engineering that has become the envy of the world, never looked more beautiful than on its evening flight to Paris as we began a momentous New Year.
>
> Captain Richard Marks, looking every inch the matinee hero, guided the ship safely through the night as the passengers within lit up the sky with conversation and music, accompanied by a champagne buffet. Miss Marie Dawlish, the English Lark, honored the company with a song which it is suspected struck the heart of a certain airship Captain who stepped away from the bridge in time for the performance.
>
> Though we at the Daily are not prognosticators, we believe that the coming year may be one of high romance for Captain Marks, who touched down back in London with a gentle landing, and no doubt a song in his heart.

The Societies have the Ball each year for New Year's, which is great fun. It's ripping good food, and sometimes someone comes in a full evening suit and we can all have a laugh at them; it's an expensive round of tailoring to wear just once a year. You know just by looking that they who dressed up had wanted to be Captains and fallen short. Poor boys. I wouldn't be a Captain for all the gold in Araby, though perhaps when you're young you don't realize how proud and empty the Captains end up.

You don't meet a lot of ladies in the air, of course, and it's what all the lads miss most. For the London Ball they always manage to find some with the money from the dues—sweet girls who don't mind a chat. They have to be all right with sitting and talking. The Annual Gentlemen's Ball isn't much of a dance. The new conductors, the ones who have only stretched the first few inches, try a dance or two early on to give the musicians something to do. The rest of us have given in to gravity when we're trapped on the ground. We catch up with old mates and wait for a chance to ask a girl upstairs, if we're brave enough.

Sometimes we even get conductors in from other places—Russia, sometimes, or once from China. God, that was a night! What strange ideas they have about navigation! But he was built like an airship man, and from the red skin round his eyes we could tell he'd paid his dues in the helium, so we poured him some Scotch and made him welcome. If we aren't kind to each other, who will be kind to us?

> The Most Elegant Airlines Choose *ORION* Brand Masks!
> Your conductors deserve masks that are SAFE, COMFORTABLE, and STYLISH. Orion has patented its unique India-Rubber polymer that is both flexible and airtight, ensuring the safest and most comfortable fit for your conductors. The oculars are green-tinted for sharper vision at night, and larger in diameter than any other brand, so conductors see more than ever before. Best of all, our filter-tank has an oxygen absorption rate of nearly Ninety Percent—the best in the world!
> Swiss-made, British-tested, CONDUCTOR-APPROVED.
> Soar with confidence among the stars—aim always for ORION.
> — Orion Airship Supply Catalog, 1893

We were airside the last night of 1899, the night of the Gentlemen's Ball.

We had been through a bad wind that day, and all of us were spread out tightening rivets on the ribs, signaling quietly back and forth. I don't know what made Anderson agree to sign us on for the evening flight—he must have wanted the Ball as much as the rest of us—and I was in a bit of a sulk, feeling like Cinderella. It was a cold night, cold even in the balloon, and I was wishing for nothing but a long bath and a long sleep.

Then Captain Marks shoved the woman into the balloon.

She was wearing a worn-out orange dress, and a worn-out shawl that fell away from her at once, and even as the Captain clipped her to the line she hung limp, worn-out all over. He'd been at her for a while.

I still don't know where he found her, what they did to her, what she thought in the first moments as they carried her towards the balloon.

"Got some leftovers for you," the Captain shouted through his mask, "a little Gentlemen's Ball for you brave boys. Enjoy!"

Then he was gone, spinning the lock shut behind him, closing us in with her.

I could feel the others hooking onto a rib or a spine, pushing off, hurrying over. The men in the aft might not have even seen it happen. I never asked them. Didn't want to know.

I was closest to her, fifty feet, maybe. Through the mask I could see the buttons missing on the front of her dress, the little cuts in her fisted hands.

She wore a mask, too. Her hair was tangled in it.

She was terrified—shaking so hard that I worried her mask would come loose—but she didn't scrabble at her belt: too clever for that, I suppose. I was worried for her—if you weren't used to the helium it was painful to breathe for very long, she needed to get back Underneath. God only knew how long that second-rate mask would hold.

Even as Anderson hooked onto a spine to get to her she was shoving off—not to the locked porthole (there was no hope for her there), but straight out to the ribs, clawing at the stiff silk of the balloon.

We all scrambled for her.

I don't know how she cut the silk—Bristol said it must have been a knife, but I can't imagine they would have let her keep one. I think she must have used the hook of her little earring, which is the worst of it, somehow.

The balloon shuddered as the first rush of helium was sucked into the sky outside; she clenched one fist around the raw edge of the silk as she unhooked herself from the tether. The air caught her, dragging at her feet, and she grasped for purchase against the fabric. She cried out, but the mask swallowed the noise.

I was the closest; I pushed off.

The other conductors were shouting for her not to be foolish; they shouted that it was a misunderstanding, that she would be all right with us.

As I came closer I held out my hands to her so she could take hold, but she shrank back, kicking at me with one foot, the boot half-fastened.

My reflection was distorted in the round eyes of her mask—a spindly monster enveloping her in the half-dark, my endless arms struggling to pull her back in.

What else could she do?

She let go.

My sight lit up from the rush of oxygen, and in my view she was a flaming June in a bottle-green night, falling with her arms outstretched like a bird until she was too small to be seen, until every bright trace of her was gone.

For a moment no one moved; then the rails shuddered under us as the gills fanned out, and we slowed.

Anderson said, "We're coming up on Paris."

"Someone should tell them about the tear," said Bristol.

"Patch it from here," Anderson said. "We'll wait until Vienna."

In Vienna they assumed all conductors were lunatics, and they would ask no questions about a tear that only human hands could make.

I heard the first clangs of the anchor-hooks latching onto the outer hull of the Underneath before the church bells rang in the New Year. Beneath us, the passengers shouted "Hip, hip, hurrah! Hip, hip, hurrah!"

That was a sad year.

Once I was land-bound in Dover. The Conductors' Society there is so small I don't think ten men could fit in it. It wasn't a bad city (I had no trouble with the regulars on my way from the dock), but it was so horribly hot and cramped that

I went outside just to have enough room to stretch out my arms, even heavy as they were with the Earth pulling at them.

A Falcon-class passed overhead, and I looked up just as it crossed the harvest moon; for a moment the balloon was illuminated orange, and I could see the conductors skittering about inside of it like spiders or shadow puppets, like moths in a lamp.

I watched it until it had passed the moon and fallen dark again, the lamp extinguished.

It's a glorious life, they say.

THE LADY WHO PLUCKED RED FLOWERS BENEATH THE QUEEN'S WINDOW

RACHEL SWIRSKY

Rachel Swirsky holds an MFA in fiction from the Iowa Writers Workshop and is a graduate of the Clarion West Writers Workshop. Her short fiction has appeared in a variety of venues, including *Tor.com*, *Subterranean Magazine*, *Weird Tales*, and *Fantasy Magazine*. Her story "Eros, Philia, Agape" was nominated for the 2009 Hugo and Sturgeon awards, while "A Memory of Wind" was a 2010 Nebula Award nominee. Her most recent book is *Through the Drowsy Dark*, a short collection of feminist poems and short stories. She lives in Bakersfield, California, with her husband and two cats, and is seriously considering whether or not to become a crazy cat lady by adopting all four stray kittens which were recently born in her yard.

My story should have ended on the day I died. Instead, it began there.

Sun pounded on my back as I rode through the Mountains where the Sun Rests. My horse's hooves beat in syncopation with those of the donkey that trotted in our shadow. The Queen's midget Kyan turned his head toward me, sweat dripping down the red-and-blue protections painted across his malformed brow.

"Shouldn't... we... stop?" he panted.

Sunlight shone red across the craggy limestone cliffs. A bold eastern wind carried the scent of mountain blossoms. I pointed to a place where two large stones leaned across a narrow outcropping.

"There," I said, prodding my horse to go faster before Kyan could answer. He grunted and cursed at his donkey for falling behind.

I hated Kyan, and he hated me. But Queen Rayneh had ordered us to ride reconnaissance together, and we obeyed, out of love for her and for the Land of Flowered Hills.

We dismounted at the place I had indicated. There, between the mountain peaks, we could watch the enemy's forces in the valley below without being observed. The raiders spread out across the meadow below like ants on a rich meal. Their women's camp lay behind the main troops, a small dark blur. Even the smoke rising from their women's fires seemed timid. I scowled.

"Go out between the rocks," I directed Kyan. "Move as close to the edge as you can."

Kyan made a mocking gesture of deference. "As you wish, Great Lady," he sneered, swinging his twisted legs off the donkey. Shamans' bundles of stones and seeds, tied with twine, rattled at his ankles.

I refused to let his pretensions ignite my temper. "Watch the valley," I instructed. "I will take the vision of their camp from your mind and send it to the Queen's scrying pool. Be sure to keep still."

The midget edged toward the rocks, his eyes shifting back and forth as if he expected to encounter raiders up here in the mountains, in the Queen's dominion. I found myself amused and disgusted by how little provocation it took to reveal the midget's true, craven nature. At home in the Queen's castle, he strutted about, pompous and patronizing. He was like many birth-twisted men, arrogant in the limited magic to which his deformities gave him access. Rumors suggested that he imagined himself worthy enough to be in love with the Queen. I wondered what he thought of the men below. Did he daydream about them conquering the Land? Did he think they'd make him powerful, that they'd put weapons in his twisted hands and let him strut among their ranks?

"Is your view clear?" I asked.

"It is."

I closed my eyes and saw, as he saw, the panorama of the valley below. I held his sight in my mind, and turned toward the eastern wind which carries the perfect expression of magic—flight—on its invisible eddies. I envisioned the battlefield unfurling before me like a scroll rolling out across a marble floor. With low, dissonant notes, I showed the image how to transform itself for my purposes. I taught it how to be length and width without depth, and how to be strokes of color and light reflected in water. When it knew these things, I sang the image into the water of the Queen's scrying pool.

Suddenly—too soon—the vision vanished from my inner eye. Something whistled through the air. I turned. Pain struck my chest like thunder.

I cried out. Kyan's bundles of seeds and stones rattled above me. My vision blurred red. Why was the midget near me? He should have been on the outcropping.

"You traitor!" I shouted. "How did the raiders find us?"

I writhed blindly on the ground, struggling to grab Kyan's legs. The midget caught my wrists. Weak with pain, I could not break free.

"Hold still," he said. "You're driving the arrow deeper."

"Let me go, you craven dwarf."

"I'm no traitor. This is woman's magic. Feel the arrow shaft."

Kyan guided my hand upward to touch the arrow buried in my chest. Through the pain, I felt the softness of one of the Queen's roc feathers. It was particularly rare and valuable, the length of my arm.

I let myself fall slack against the rock. "Woman's magic," I echoed, softly. "The Queen is betrayed. The Land is betrayed."

"Someone is betrayed, sure enough," said Kyan, his tone gloating.

"You must return to court and warn the Queen."

Kyan leaned closer to me. His breath blew on my neck, heavy with smoke and spices.

"No, Naeva. You can still help the Queen. She's given me the keystone to a spell—a piece of pure leucite, powerful enough to tug a spirit from its rest. If I blow its power into you, your spirit won't sink into sleep. It will only rest, waiting for her summons."

Blood welled in my mouth. "I won't let you bind me..."

His voice came even closer, his lips on my ear. "The Queen needs you, Naeva. Don't you love her?"

Love: the word caught me like a thread on a bramble. Oh, yes. I loved the Queen. My will weakened, and I tumbled out of my body. Cold crystal drew me in like a great mouth, inhaling.

I was furious. I wanted to wrap my hands around the first neck I saw and squeeze. But my hands were tiny, half the size of the hands I remembered. My short, fragile fingers shook. Heavy musk seared my nostrils. I felt the heat of scented candles at my feet, heard the snap of flame devouring wick. I rushed forward and was abruptly halted. Red and black knots of string marked boundaries beyond which I could not pass.

"O, Great Lady Naeva," a voice intoned. "We seek your wisdom on behalf of Queen Rayneh and the Land of Flowered Hills."

Murmurs rippled through the room. Through my blurred vision, I caught an impression of vaulted ceilings and frescoed walls. I heard people, but I could only make out woman-sized blurs—they could have been beggars, aristocrats, warriors, even males or broods.

I tried to roar. My voice fractured into a strangled sound like trapped wind. An old woman's sound.

"Great Lady Naeva, will you acknowledge me?"

I turned toward the high, mannered voice. A face came into focus, eyes flashing blue beneath a cowl. Dark stripes stretched from lower lip to chin: the tattoos of a death whisperer.

Terror cut into my rage for a single, clear instant. "I'm dead?"

"Let me handle this." Another voice, familiar this time. Calm, authoritative, quiet: the voice of someone who had never needed to shout in order to be heard. I swung my head back and forth trying to glimpse Queen Rayneh.

"Hear me, Lady Who Plucked Red Flowers beneath My Window. It is I, your Queen."

The formality of that voice! She spoke to me with titles instead of names? I blazed with fury.

Her voice dropped a register, tender and cajoling. "Listen to me, Naeva. I asked the death whisperers to chant your spirit up from the dead. You're inhabiting the body of an elder member of their order. Look down. See for yourself."

I looked down and saw embroidered rabbits leaping across the hem of a turquoise robe. Long, bony feet jutted out from beneath the silk. They were swaddled in the coarse wrappings that doctors prescribed for the elderly when it hurt them to stand.

They were not my feet. I had not lived long enough to have feet like that.

"I was shot by an enchanted arrow…" I recalled. "The midget said you might need me again…"

"And he was right, wasn't he? You've only been dead three years. Already, we need you."

The smugness of that voice. Rayneh's impervious assurance that no matter what happened, be it death or disgrace, her people's hearts would always sing with fealty.

"He enslaved me," I said bitterly. "He preyed upon my love for you."

"Ah, Lady Who Plucked Red Flowers beneath My Window, I always knew you loved me."

Oh yes, I had loved her. When she wanted heirs, it was I who placed my hand on her belly and used my magic to draw out her seedlings; I who nurtured the seedlings' spirits with the fertilizer of her chosen man; I who planted the seedlings in the womb of a fecund brood. Three times, the broods I catalyzed brought forth Rayneh's daughters. I'd not yet chosen to beget my own daughters, but there had always been an understanding between us that Rayneh would be the one to stand with my magic-worker as the seedling was drawn from me, mingled with man, and set into brood.

I was amazed to find that I loved her no longer. I remembered the emotion, but passion had died with my body.

"I want to see you," I said.

Alarmed, the death whisperer turned toward Rayneh's voice. Her nose jutted beak-like past the edge of her cowl. "It's possible for her to see you if you stand where I am," she said. "But if the spell goes wrong, I won't be able to—"

"It's all right, Lakitri. Let her see me."

Rustling, footsteps. Rayneh came into view. My blurred vision showed me frustratingly little except for the moon of her face. Her eyes sparkled black against her smooth, sienna skin. Amber and obsidian gems shone from her forehead, magically embedded in the triangular formation that symbolized the Land of Flowered Hills. I wanted to see her graceful belly, the muscular calves I'd loved to stroke—but below her chin, the world faded to gray.

"What do you want?" I asked. "Are the raiders nipping at your heels again?"

"We pushed the raiders back in the battle that you died to make happen. It was a rout. Thanks to you."

A smile lit on Rayneh's face. It was a smile I remembered. *You have served your*

Land and your Queen, it seemed to say. *You may be proud.* I'd slept on Rayneh's leaf-patterned silk and eaten at her morning table too often to be deceived by such shallow manipulations.

Rayneh continued, "A usurper—a woman raised on our own grain and honey—has built an army of automatons to attack us. She's given each one a hummingbird's heart for speed, and a crane's feather for beauty, and a crow's brain for wit. They've marched from the Lake Where Women Wept all the way across the fields to the Valley of Tonha's Memory. They move faster than our most agile warriors. They seduce our farmers out of the fields. We must destroy them."

"A usurper?" I said.

"One who betrays us with our own spells."

The Queen directed me a lingering, narrow-lidded look, challenging me with her unspoken implications.

"The kind of woman who would shoot the Queen's sorceress with a roc feather?" I pressed.

Her glance darted sideways. "Perhaps."

Even with the tantalizing aroma of revenge wafting before me, I considered refusing Rayneh's plea. Why should I forgive her for chaining me to her service? She and her benighted death whisperers might have been able to chant my spirit into wakefulness, but let them try to stir my voice against my will.

But no—even without love drawing me into dark corners, I couldn't renounce Rayneh. I would help her as I always had from the time when we were girls riding together through my grandmother's fields. When she fell from her mount, it was always I who halted my mare, soothed her wounds, and eased her back into the saddle. Even as a child, I knew that she would never do the same for me.

"Give me something to kill," I said.

"What?"

"I want to kill. Give me something. Or should I kill your death whisperers?"

Rayneh turned toward the women. "Bring a sow!" she commanded.

Murmurs echoed through the high-ceilinged chamber, followed by rushing footsteps. Anxious hands entered my range of vision, dragging a fat, black-spotted shape. I looked toward the place where my ears told me the crowd of death whisperers stood, huddled and gossiping. I wasn't sure how vicious I could appear as a dowager with bound feet, but I snarled at them anyway. I was rewarded with the susurration of hems sliding backward over tile.

I approached the sow. My feet collided with the invisible boundaries of the summoning circle. "Move it closer," I ordered.

Hands pushed the sow forward. The creature grunted with surprise and fear. I knelt down and felt its bristly fur and smelled dry mud, but I couldn't see its torpid bulk.

I wrapped my bony hands around the creature's neck and twisted. My spirit's strength overcame the body's weakness. The animal's head snapped free in my hands. Blood engulfed the leaping rabbits on my hem.

I thrust the sow's head at Rayneh. It tumbled out of the summoning circle and thudded across the marble. Rayneh doubled over, retching.

The crowd trembled and exclaimed. Over the din, I dictated the means to defeat the constructs. "Blend mustard seed and honey to slow their deceitful tongues. Add brine to ruin their beauty. Mix in crushed poppies to slow their fast-beating hearts. Release the concoction onto a strong wind and let it blow their destruction. Only a grain need touch them. Less than a grain—only a grain need touch a mosquito that lights on a flower they pass on the march. They will fall."

"Regard that! Remember it!" Rayneh shouted to the whisperers. Silk rustled. Rayneh regarded me levelly. "That's all we have to do?"

"Get Lakitri," I replied. "I wish to ask her a question."

A nervous voice spoke outside my field of vision. "I'm here, Great Lady."

"What will happen to this body after my spirit leaves?"

"Jada will die, Great Lady. Your spirit has chased hers away."

I felt the crookedness of Jada's hunched back and the pinch of the strips binding her feet. Such a back, such feet, I would never have. At least someone would die for disturbing my death.

Next I woke, rage simmered where before it had boiled. I stifled a snarl, and relaxed my clenched fists. My vision was clearer: I discerned the outlines of a tent filled with dark shapes that resembled pillows and furs. I discovered my boundaries close by, marked by wooden stakes painted with bands of cinnamon and white.

"Respected Aunt Naeva?"

My vision wavered. A shape: muscular biceps, hard thighs, robes of heir's green. It took me a moment to identify Queen Rayneh's eldest daughter, who I had inspired in her brood. At the time of my death, she'd been a flat-chested flitling, still learning how to ride.

"Tryce?" I asked. A bad thought: "Why are you here? Has the usurper taken the palace? Is the Queen dead?"

Tryce laughed. "You misunderstand, Respected Aunt. I am the usurper."

"You?" I scoffed. "What does a girl want with a woman's throne?"

"I want what is mine." Tryce drew herself up. She had her mother's mouth, stern and imperious. "If you don't believe me, look at the body you're wearing."

I looked down. My hands were the right size, but they were painted in Rayneh's blue and decked with rings of gold and silver. Strips of tanned human flesh adorned my breasts. I raised my fingertips to my collarbone and felt the raised edges of the brand I knew would be there. Scars formed the triangles that represented the Land of Flowered Hills.

"One of your mother's private guard," I murmured. "Which?"

"Okilanu."

I grinned. "I never liked the bitch."

"You know I'm telling the truth. A private guard is too valuable for anyone but a usurper to sacrifice. I'm holding this conference with honor, Respected Aunt. I'm meeting you alone, with only one automaton to guard me. My informants tell me that my mother surrounded herself with sorceresses so that she could coerce you. I hold you in more esteem."

"What do you want?"

"Help winning the throne that should be mine."

"Why should I betray my lover and my Land for a child with pretensions?"

"Because you have no reason to be loyal to my mother. Because I want what's best for this Land, and I know how to achieve it. Because those were my automatons you dismantled, and they were good, beautiful souls despite being creatures of spit and mud. Gudrin is the last of them."

Tryce held out her hand. The hand that accepted drew into my vision: slender with shapely fingers crafted of mud and tangled with sticks and pieces of nest. It was beautiful enough to send feathers of astonishment through my chest.

"Great Lady, you must listen to The Creator of Me and Mine," intoned the creature.

Its voice was a songbird trill. I grimaced in disgust. "You made male automatons?"

"Just one," said Tryce. "It's why he survived your spell."

"Yes," I said, pondering. "It never occurred to me that one would make male creatures."

"Will you listen, Respected Aunt?" asked Tryce.

"You must listen, Great Lady," echoed the automaton. His voice was as melodious as poetry to a depressed heart. The power of crane's feathers and crow's brains is great.

"Very well," I said.

Tryce raised her palms to show she was telling truth. I saw the shadow of her mother's face lurking in her wide-set eyes and broad, round forehead.

"Last autumn, when the wind blew red with fallen leaves, my mother expelled me from the castle. She threw my possessions into the river and had my servants beaten and turned out. She told me that I would have to learn to live like the birds migrating from place to place because she had decreed that no one was to give me a home. She said I was no longer her heir, and she would dress Darnisha or Peni in heir's green. Oh, Respected Aunt! How could either of them take a throne?"

I ignored Tryce's emotional outpouring. It was true that Tryce had always been more responsible than her sisters, but she had been born with an heir's heaviness upon her. I had lived long enough to see fluttering sparrows like Darnisha and Peni become eagles, over time.

"You omit something important," I said. "Why did your mother throw you out, Imprudent Child?"

"Because of this."

The automaton's hand held Tryce steady as she mounted a pile of pillows that raised her torso to my eye level. Her belly loomed large, ripe as a frog's inflated throat.

"You've gotten fat, Tryce."

"No," she said.

I realized: she had not.

"You're pregnant? Hosting a child like some brood? What's wrong with you, girl? I never knew you were a pervert. Worse than a pervert! Even the lowest worm-eater knows to chew mushrooms when she pushes with men."

"I am no pervert! I am a lover of woman. I am natural as breeze! But I say we must not halve our population by splitting our females into women and broods. The raiders nip at our heels. Yes, it's true, they are barbaric and weak—now. But they grow stronger. Their population increases so quickly that already they can match our numbers. When there are three times as many of them as us, or five times, or eight times, they'll flood us like a wave crashing on a naked beach. It's time for women to make children in ourselves as broods do. We need more daughters."

I scoffed. "The raiders keep their women like cows for the same reason we keep cows like cows, to encourage the production of calves. What do you think will happen if our men see great women swelling with young and feeding them from their bodies? They will see us as weak, and they will rebel, and the broods will support them for trinkets and candy."

"Broods will not threaten us," said Tryce. "They do as they are trained. We train them to obey."

Tryce stepped down from the pillows and dismissed the automaton into the shadows. I felt a murmur of sadness as the creature left my sight.

"It is not your place to make policy, Imprudent Child," I said. "You should have kept your belly flat."

"There is no time! Do the raiders wait? Will they chew rinds by the fire while I wait for my mother to die?"

"This is better? To split our land into factions and war against ourselves?"

"I have vowed to save the Land of Flowered Hills," said Tryce, "with my mother or despite her."

Tryce came yet closer to me so that I could see the triple scars where the gems that had once sealed her heirship had been carved out of her cheeks. They left angry, red triangles. Tryce's breath was hot; her eyes like oil, shining.

"Even without my automatons, I have enough resources to overwhelm the palace," Tryce continued, "except for one thing."

I waited.

"I need you to tell me how to unlock the protections you laid on the palace grounds and my mother's chambers."

"We return to the beginning. Why should I help you?"

Tryce closed her eyes and inhaled deeply. There was shyness in her posture now. She would not direct her gaze at mine.

She said, "I was young when you died, still young enough to think that our strength was unassailable. The battles after your death shattered my illusions. We barely won, and we lost many lives. I realized that we needed more power, and I thought that I could give us that power by becoming a sorceress to replace you." She paused. "During my studies, I researched your acts of magic, great and small. Inevitably, I came to the spell you cast before you died, when you sent the raiders' positions into the summoning pool."

It was then that I knew what she would say next. I wish I could say that my heart felt as immobile as a mountain, that I had always known to suspect the love of a Queen. But my heart drummed, and my mouth went dry, and I felt as if I were falling.

"Some of mother's advisers convinced her that you were plotting against her. They had little evidence to support their accusations, but once the idea rooted into mother's mind, she became obsessed. She violated the sanctity of woman's magic by teaching Kyan how to summon a roc feather enchanted to pierce your heart. She ordered him to wait until you had sent her the vision of the battle-ground, and then to kill you and punish your treachery by binding your soul so that you would always wander and wake."

I wanted to deny it, but what point would there be? Now that Tryce forced me to examine my death with a watcher's eye, I saw the coincidences that proved her truth. How else could I have been shot by an arrow not just shaped by woman's magic, but made from one of the Queen's roc feathers? Why else would a worm like Kyan have happened to have in his possession a piece of leucite more pow-erful than any I'd seen?

I clenched Okilanu's fists. "I never plotted against Rayneh."

"Of course not. She realized it herself, in time, and executed the women who had whispered against you. But she had your magic, and your restless spirit bound to her, and she believed that was all she needed."

For long moments, my grief battled my anger. When it was done, my resolve was hardened like a spear tempered by fire.

I lifted my palms in the gesture of truth telling. "To remove the protections on the palace grounds, you must lay yourself flat against the soil with your cheek against the dirt, so that it knows you. To it, you must say, 'The Lady Who Plucked Red Flowers beneath the Queen's Window loves the Queen from instant to eternity, from desire to regret.' And then you must kiss the soil as if it is the hem of your lover's robe. Wait until you feel the earth move beneath you and then the protections will be gone."

Tryce inclined her head. "I will do this."

I continued, "When you are done, you must flay off a strip of your skin and grind it into a fine powder. Bury it in an envelope of wind-silk beneath the Queen's window. Bury it quickly. If a single grain escapes, the protections on her chamber will hold."

"I will do this, too," said Tryce. She began to speak more, but I raised one of my ringed, blue fingers to silence her.

"There's another set of protections you don't know about. One cast on your mother. It can only be broken by the fresh life-blood of something you love. Throw the blood onto the Queen while saying, 'The Lady Who Plucked Red Flowers beneath Your Window has betrayed you.'"

"Life-blood? You mean, I need to kill—"

"Perhaps the automaton."

Tryce's expression clouded with distress. "Gudrin is the last one! Maybe the baby. I could conceive again—"

"If you can suggest the baby, you don't love it enough. It must be Gudrin."

Tryce closed her mouth. "Then it will be Gudrin," she agreed, but her eyes would not meet mine.

I folded my arms across Okilanu's flat bosom. "I've given you what you wanted. Now grant me a favor, Imprudent Child Who Would Be Queen. When you kill Rayneh, I want to be there."

Tryce lifted her head like the Queen she wanted to be. "I will summon you when it's time, Respected Aunt." She turned toward Gudrin in the shadows. "Disassemble the binding shapes," she ordered.

For the first time, I beheld Gudrin in his entirety. The creature was tree-tall and stick-slender, and yet he moved with astonishing grace. "Thank you on behalf of the Creator of Me and My Kind," he trilled in his beautiful voice, and I considered how unfortunate it was that the next time I saw him, he would be dead.

I smelled the iron-and-wet tang of blood. My view of the world skewed low, as if I'd been cut off at the knees. Women's bodies slumped across lush carpets. Red ran deep into the silk, bloodying woven leaves and flowers. I'd been in this chamber far too often to mistake it, even dead. It was Rayneh's.

It came to me then: my perspective was not like that of a woman forced to kneel. It was like a child's. Or a dwarf's.

I reached down and felt hairy knees and fringed ankle bracelets. "Ah, Kyan…"

"I thought you might like that." Tryce's voice. These were probably her legs before me, wrapped in loose green silk trousers that were tied above the calf with chains of copper beads. "A touch of irony for your pleasure. He bound your soul to restlessness. Now you'll chase his away."

I reached into his back-slung sheath and drew out the most functional of his ceremonial blades. It would feel good to flay his treacherous flesh.

"I wouldn't do that," said Tryce. "You'll be the one who feels the pain."

I sheathed the blade. "You took the castle?"

"Effortlessly." She paused. "I lie. Not effortlessly." She unknotted her right trouser leg and rolled up the silk. Blood stained the bandages on a carefully wrapped wound. "Your protections were strong."

"Yes. They were."

She re-tied her trouser leg and continued. "The Lady with Lichen Hair tried to block our way into the chamber." She kicked one of the corpses by my feet. "We killed her."

"Did you."

"Don't you care? She was your friend."

"Did she care when I died?"

Tryce shifted her weight, a kind of lower-body shrug. "I brought you another present." She dropped a severed head onto the floor. It rolled toward me, tongue lolling in its bloody face. It took me a moment to identify the high cheekbones and narrow eyes.

"The death whisperer? Why did you kill Lakitri?"

"You liked the blood of Jada and Okilanu, didn't you?"

"The only blood I care about now is your mother's. Where is she?"

"Bring my mother!" ordered Tryce.

One of Tryce's servants—her hands marked with the green dye of loyalty to the heir—dragged Rayneh into the chamber. The Queen's torn, bloody robe concealed the worst of her wounds, but couldn't hide the black and purple bruises blossoming on her arms and legs. Her eyes found mine, and despite her condition, a trace of her regal smile glossed her lips.

Her voice sounded thin. "That's you? Lady Who Plucked Red Flowers beneath My Window?"

"It's me."

She raised one bloody, shaking hand to the locket around her throat and pried it open. Dried petals scattered onto the carpets, the remnants of the red flowers I'd once gathered for her protection. While the spell lasted, they'd remained whole and fresh. Now they were dry and crumbling like what had passed for love between us.

"If you ever find rest, the world-lizard will crack your soul in its jaws for murdering your Queen," she said.

"I didn't kill you."

"You instigated my death."

"I was only repaying your favor."

The hint of her smile again. She smelled of wood smoke, rich and dark. I wanted to see her more clearly, but my poor vision blurred the red of her wounds into the sienna of her skin until the whole of her looked like raw, churned earth.

"I suppose our souls will freeze together." She paused. "That might be pleasant."

Somewhere in front of us, lost in the shadows, I heard Tryce and her women ransacking the Queen's chamber. Footsteps, sharp voices, cracking wood.

"I used to enjoy cold mornings," Rayneh said. "When we were girls. I liked lying in bed with you and opening the curtains to watch the snow fall."

"And sending servants out into the cold to fetch and carry."

"And then! When my brood let slip it was warmer to lie together naked under the sheets? Do you remember that?" She laughed aloud, and then paused. When she spoke again, her voice was quieter. "It's strange to remember lying together in the cold, and then to look up, and see you in that body. Oh, my beautiful Naeva, twisted into a worm. I deserve what you've done to me. How could I have sent a worm to kill my life's best love?"

She turned her face away, as if she could speak no more. Such a show of intimate, unroyal emotion. I could remember times when she'd been able to manipulate me by trusting me with a wince of pain or a supposedly accidental tear. As I grew more cynical, I realized that her royal pretense wasn't vanishing when she gave me a melancholy, regretful glance. Such things were calculated vulnerabilities, intended to bind me closer to her by suggesting intimacy and trust. She used them with many ladies at court, the ones who loved her.

This was far from the first time she'd tried to bind me to her by displaying weakness, but it was the first time she'd ever done so when I had no love to enthrall me.

Rayneh continued, her voice a whisper. "I regret it, Naeva. When Kyan came back, and I saw your body, cold and lifeless—I understood immediately that I'd been mistaken. I wept for days. I'm weeping still, inside my heart. But listen–" her voice hardened "—we can't let this be about you and me. Our Land is at stake. Do you know what Tryce is going to do? She'll destroy us all. You have to help me stop her—"

"Tryce!" I shouted. "I'm ready to see her bleed."

Footsteps thudded across silk carpets. Tryce drew a bone-handled knife and knelt over her mother like a farmer preparing to slaughter a pig. "Gudrin!" she called. "Throw open the doors. Let everyone see us."

Narrow, muddy legs strode past us. The twigs woven through the automaton's skin had lain fallow when I saw him in the winter. Now they blazed in a glory of emerald leaves and scarlet blossoms.

"You dunce!" I shouted at Tryce. "What have you done? You left him alive."

Tryce's gaze held fast on her mother's throat. "I sacrificed the baby."

Voices and footsteps gathered in the room as Tryce's soldiers escorted Rayneh's courtiers inside.

"You sacrificed the baby," I repeated. "What do you think ruling is? Do you think Queens always get what they want? You can't dictate to magic, Imprudent Child."

"Be silent." Tryce's voice thinned with anger. "I'm grateful for your help, Great Lady, but you must not speak this way to your Queen."

I shook my head. Let the foolish child do what she might. I braced myself for the inevitable backlash of the spell.

Tryce raised her knife in the air. "Let everyone gathered here behold that this is Queen Rayneh, the Queen Who Would Dictate to a Daughter. I am her heir, Tryce of the Bold Stride. Hear me. I do this for the Land of Flowered Hills, for our honor and our strength. Yet I also do it with regret. Mother, I hope you will be free in your death. May your spirit wing across sweet breezes with the great bird of the sun."

The knife slashed downward. Crimson poured across Rayneh's body, across the rugs, across Tryce's feet. For a moment, I thought I'd been wrong about Tryce's baby—perhaps she had loved it enough for the counter-spell to work—but as the blood poured over the dried petals Rayneh had scattered on the floor, a bright light flared through the room. Tryce flailed backward as if struck.

Rayneh's wound vanished. She stared up at me with startled, joyful eyes. "You didn't betray me!"

"Oh, I did," I said. "Your daughter is just inept."

I could see only one solution to the problem Tryce had created—the life's blood of something I loved was here, still saturating the carpets and pooling on the stone.

Magic is a little bit alive. Sometimes it prefers poetic truths to literal ones. I dipped my fingers into the Queen's spilled blood and pronounced, "The Lady Who Plucked Red Flowers beneath Your Window has betrayed you."

I cast the blood across the Queen. The dried petals disintegrated. The Queen cried out as my magical protections disappeared.

Tryce was at her mother's side again in an instant. Rayneh looked at me in the moment before Tryce's knife descended. I thought she might show me, just this once, a fraction of uncalculated vulnerability. But this time there was no vulnerability at all, no pain or betrayal or even weariness, only perfect regal equanimity.

Tryce struck for her mother's heart. She let her mother's body fall to the carpet.

"Behold my victory!" Tryce proclaimed. She turned toward her subjects. Her stance was strong: her feet planted firmly, ready for attack or defense. If her lower half was any indication, she'd be an excellent Queen.

I felt a rush of forgiveness and pleasure and regret and satisfaction all mixed together. I moved toward the boundaries of my imprisonment, my face near Rayneh's where she lay, inhaling her last ragged breaths.

"Be brave," I told her. "Soon we'll both be free."

Rayneh's lips moved slowly, her tongue thick around the words. "What makes you think...?"

"You're going to die," I said, "and when I leave this body, Kyan will die, too. Without caster or intent, there won't be anything to sustain the spell."

Rayneh made a sound that I supposed was laughter. "Oh no, my dear Naeva... much more complicated than that..."

Panic constricted my throat. "Tryce! You have to find the piece of leucite—"

"...even stronger than the rock. Nothing but death can lull your spirit to sleep... and you're already dead..."

She laughed again.

"Tryce!" I shouted. "Tryce!"

The girl turned. For a moment, my vision became as clear as it had been when I lived. I saw the Imprudent Child Queen standing with her automaton's arms around her waist, the both of them flushed with joy and triumph. Tryce turned to kiss the knot of wood that served as the automaton's mouth and my vision clouded again.

Rayneh died a moment afterward.

A moment after that, Tryce released me.

If my story could not end when I died, it should have ended there, in Rayneh's chamber, when I took my revenge.

It did not end there.

Tryce consulted me often during the early years of her reign. I familiarized myself with the blur of the paintings in her chamber, squinting to pick out placid scenes of songbirds settling on snowy branches, bathing in mountain springs, soaring through sun-struck skies.

"Don't you have counselors for this?" I snapped one day.

Tryce halted her pacing in front of me, blocking my view of a wren painted by The Artist without Pity.

"Do you understand what it's like for me? The court still calls me the Imprudent Child Who Would Be Queen. Because of you!"

Gudrin went to comfort her. She kept the creature close, pampered and petted, like a cat on a leash. She rested her head on his shoulder as he stroked her arms. It all looked too easy, too familiar. I wondered how often Tryce spun herself into these emotional whirlpools.

"It can be difficult for women to accept orders from their juniors," I said.

"I've borne two healthy girls," Tryce said petulantly. "When I talk to the other women about bearing, they still say they can't, that 'women's bodies aren't suited for childbirth.' Well, if women can't have children, then what does that make me?"

I forbore responding.

"They keep me busy with petty disputes over grazing rights and grain allotment. How can I plan for a war when they distract me with pedantry? The raiders are still at our heels, and the daft old biddies won't accept what we must do to beat them back!"

The automaton thrummed with sympathy. Tryce shook him away and resumed pacing.

"At least I have you, Respected Aunt."

"For now. You must be running out of hosts." I raised my hand and inspected young, unfamiliar fingers. Dirt crusted the ragged nails. "Who is this? Anyone I know?"

"The death whisperers refuse to let me use their bodies. What time is this when dying old women won't blow out a few days early for the good of the Land?"

"Who is this?" I repeated.

"I had to summon you into the body of a common thief. You see how bad things are."

"What did you expect? That the wind would send a hundred songbirds to trill praises at your coronation? That sugared oranges would rain from the sky and flowers bloom on winter stalks?"

Tryce glared at me angrily. "Do not speak to me like that. I may be an Imprudent Child, but I am the Queen." She took a moment to regain her composure. "Enough chatter. Give me the spell I asked for."

Tryce called me in at official occasions, to bear witness from the body of a disfavored servant or a used-up brood. I attended each of the four ceremonies where Tryce, clad in regal blue, presented her infant daughters to the sun: four small, green-swathed bundles, each borne from the Queen's own body. It made me sick, but I held my silence.

She also summoned me to the court ceremony where she presented Gudrin with an official title she'd concocted to give him standing in the royal circle. Honored Zephyr or some such nonsense. They held the occasion in autumn when red and yellow leaves adorned Gudrin's shoulders like a cape. Tryce pretended to ignore the women's discontented mutterings, but they were growing louder.

The last time I saw Tryce, she summoned me in a panic. She stood in an unfamiliar room with bare stone walls and sharp wind creaking through slitted windows. Someone else's blood stained Tryce's robes. "My sisters betrayed me!" she said. "They told the women of the grasslands I was trying to make them into broods, and then led them in a revolt against the castle. A thousand women, marching! I had to slay them all. I suspected Darnisha all along. But Peni seemed content to waft. Last fall, she bore a child of her own body. It was a worm, true, but she might have gotten a daughter next. She said she wanted to try!"

"Is that their blood?"

She held out her reddened hands and stared at them ruefully as if they weren't really part of her. "Gudrin was helping them. I had to smash him into sticks. They must have cast a spell on him. I can't imagine…"

Her voice faltered. I gave her a moment to tame her undignified excess.

"You seem to have mastered the situation," I said. "A Queen must deal with such things from time to time. The important thing will be to show no weakness in front of your courtiers."

"You don't understand! It's much worse than that. While we women fought, the raiders attacked the Fields That Bask under Open Skies. They've taken half the Land. We're making a stand in the Castle Where Hope Flutters, but we can't keep them out forever. A few weeks, at most. I told them this would happen! We need more daughters to defend us! But they wouldn't listen to me!"

Rayneh would have known how to present her anger with queenly courage, but Tryce was rash and thoughtless. She wore her emotions like perfume. "Be calm," I admonished. "You must focus."

"The raiders sent a message describing what they'll do to me and my daughters when they take the castle. I captured the messenger and burned out his tongue and gave him to the broods, and when they were done with him, I took what was left of his body and catapulted it into the raiders' camp. I could do the same to every one of them, and it still wouldn't be enough to compensate for having to listen to their vile, cowardly threats."

I interrupted her tirade. "The Castle Where Hope Flutters is on high ground, but if you've already lost the eastern fields, it will be difficult to defend. Take your women to the Spires of Treachery where the herders feed their cattle. You won't be able to mount traditional defenses, but they won't be able to attack easily. You'll be reduced to meeting each other in small parties where woman's magic should give you the advantage."

"My commander suggested that," said Tryce. "There are too many of them. We might as well try to dam a river with silk."

"It's better than remaining here."

"Even if we fight to a stalemate in the Spires of Treachery, the raiders will have our fields to grow food in, and our broods to make children on. If they can't conquer us this year, they'll obliterate us in ten. I need something else."

"There is nothing else."

"Think of something!"

I thought.

I cast my mind back through my years of training. I remembered the locked room in my matriline's household where servants were never allowed to enter, which my cousins and I scrubbed every dawn and dusk to teach us to be constant and rigorous.

I remembered the cedar desk where my aunt Finis taught me to paint birds, first by using the most realistic detail that oils could achieve, and then by reducing my paintings to fewer and fewer brushstrokes until I could evoke the essence of bird without any brush at all.

I remembered the many-drawered red cabinets where we stored Leafspine and Winterbrew, powdered Errow and essence of Howl. I remembered my bossy cousin Alne skidding through the halls in a panic after she broke into a locked drawer and mixed together two herbs that we weren't supposed to touch. Her fearful grimace transformed into a beak that permanently silenced her sharp tongue.

I remembered the year I spent traveling to learn the magic of foreign lands. I was appalled by the rituals I encountered in places where women urinated on their thresholds to ward off spirits, and plucked their scalps bald when their eldest daughters reached majority. I walked with senders and weavers and whisperers and learned magic secrets that my people had misunderstood for centuries. I remembered the terror of the three nights I spent in the ancient ruins of The Desert which Should Not Have Been, begging the souls that haunted that place to surrender the secrets of their accursed city. One by one my companions died, and I spent the desert days digging graves for those the spirits found unworthy. On the third dawn, they blessed me with communion, and sent me away a wiser woman.

I remembered returning to the Land of Flowered Hills and making my own contribution to the lore contained in our matriline's locked rooms. I remembered all of this, and still I could think of nothing to tell Tryce.

Until a robin of memory hopped from an unexpected place—a piece of magic I learned traveling with herders, not spell-casters. It was an old magic, one that farmers cast when they needed to cull an inbred strain.

"You must concoct a plague," I began.

Tryce's eyes locked on me. I saw hope in her face, and I realized that she'd expected me to fail her, too.

"Find a sick baby and stop whatever treatment it is receiving. Feed it mosquito bellies and offal and dirty water to make it sicker. Give it sores and let them fill with pus. When its forehead has grown too hot for a woman to touch without flinching, kill the baby and dedicate its breath to the sun. The next morning, when the sun rises, a plague will spread with the sunlight."

"That will kill the raiders?"

"Many of them. If you create a truly virulent strain, it may kill most of them. And it will cut down their children like a scythe across wheat."

Tryce clapped her blood-stained hands. "Good."

"I should warn you. It will kill your babies as well."

"What?"

"A plague cooked in an infant will kill anyone's children. It is the way of things."

"Unacceptable! I come to you for help, and you send me to murder my daughters?"

"You killed one before, didn't you? To save your automaton?"

"You're as crazy as the crones at court! We need more babies, not fewer."

"You'll have to hope you can persuade your women to bear children so that you can rebuild your population faster than the raiders can rebuild theirs."

Tryce looked as though she wanted to level a thousand curses at me, but she stilled her tongue. Her eyes were dark and narrow. In a quiet, angry voice, she said, "Then it will be done."

They were the same words she'd used when she promised to kill Gudrin. That time I'd been able to save her despite her foolishness. This time, I might not be able to.

Next I was summoned, I could not see at all. I was ushered into the world by lowing, distant shouts, and the stench of animals packed too closely together.

A worried voice cut through the din. "Did it work? Are you there? Laverna, is that still you?"

Disoriented, I reached out to find a hint about my surroundings. My hands impacted a summoning barrier.

"Laverna, that's not you anymore, is it?"

The smell of manure stung my throat. I coughed. "My name is Naeva."

"Holy day, it worked. Please, Sleepless One, we need your help. There are men outside. I don't know how long we can hold them off."

"What happened? Is Queen Tryce dead?"

"Queen Tryce?"

"She didn't cast the plague, did she? Selfish brat. Where are the raiders now? Are you in the Spires of Treachery?"

"Sleepless One, slow down. I don't follow you."

"Where are you? How much land have the raiders taken?"

"There are no raiders here, just King Addric's army. His soldiers used to be happy as long as we paid our taxes and bowed our heads at processions. Now they want us to follow their ways, worship their god, let our men give us orders. Some of us rebelled by marching in front of the governor's theater, and now he's sent sorcerers after us. They burned our city with magical fire. We're making a last stand at the inn outside town. We set aside the stable for the summoning."

"Woman, you're mad. Men can't practice that kind of magic."

"These men can."

A nearby donkey brayed, and a fresh stench plopped into the air. Outside, I heard the noise of burning, and the shouts of men and children.

"It seems we've reached an impasse. You've never heard of the Land of Flowered Hills?"

"Never."

I had spent enough time pacing the ruins in The Desert which Should Not Have Been to understand the ways in which civilizations cracked and decayed. Women and time marched forward, relentless and uncaring as sand.

"I see."

"I'm sorry. I'm not doing this very well. It's my first summoning. My aunt Hetta used to do it but they slit her throat like you'd slaughter a pig and left her body to burn. Bardus says they're roasting the corpses and eating them, but I don't think anyone could do that. Could they? Hetta showed me how to do this a dozen times, but I never got to practice. She would have done this better."

"That would explain why I can't see."

"No, that's the child, Laverna. She's blind. She does all the talking. Her twin Nammi can see, but she's dumb."

"Her twin?"

"Nammi's right here. Reach into the circle and touch your sister's hand, Nammi. That's a good girl."

A small hand clasped mine. It felt clammy with sweat. I squeezed back.

"It doesn't seem fair to take her sister away," I said.

"Why would anyone take Laverna away?"

"She'll die when I leave this body."

"No, she won't. Nammi's soul will call her back. Didn't your people use twins?"

"No. Our hosts died."

"Yours were a harsh people."

Another silence. She spoke the truth, though I'd never thought of it in such terms. We were a lawful people. We were an unflinching people.

"You want my help to defeat the shamans?" I asked.

"Aunt Hetta said that sometimes the Sleepless Ones can blink and douse all the magic within seven leagues. Or wave their hands and sweep a rank of men into a hurricane."

"Well, I can't."

She fell silent. I considered her situation.

"Do you have your people's livestock with you?" I asked.

"Everything that wouldn't fit into the stable is packed inside the inn. It's even less pleasant in there if you can imagine."

"Can you catch one of their soldiers?"

"We took some prisoners when we fled. We had to kill one but the others are tied up in the courtyard."

"Good. Kill them and mix their blood into the grain from your larder, and bake it into loaves of bread. Feed some of the bread to each of your animals. They will fill with a warrior's anger and hunt down your enemies."

The woman hesitated. I could hear her feet shifting on the hay-covered floor.

"If we do that, we won't have any grain or animals. How will we survive?"

"You would have had to desert your larder when the Worm-Pretending-to-Be-Queen sent reinforcements anyway. When you can safely flee, ask the blind child to lead you to the Place where the Sun Is Joyous. Whichever direction she chooses will be your safest choice."

"Thank you," said the woman. Her voice was taut and tired. It seemed clear that she'd hoped for an easier way, but she was wise enough to take what she received. "We'll have a wild path to tame."

"Yes."

The woman stepped forward. Her footsteps released the scent of dried hay. "You didn't know about your Land, did you?"

"I did not."

"I'm sorry for your loss. It must be—"

The dumb child whimpered. Outside, the shouts increased.

"I need to go," said the woman.

"Good luck," I said, and meant it.

I felt the child Laverna rush past me as I sank back into my restless sleep. Her spirit flashed as brightly as a coin left in the sun.

I never saw that woman or any of her people again. I like to think they did not die.

I did not like the way the world changed after the Land of Flowered Hills disappeared. For a long time, I was summoned only by men. Most were a sallow, unhealthy color with sharp narrow features and unnaturally light hair. Goateed sorcerers too proud of their paltry talents strove to dazzle me with pyrotechnics. They commanded me to reveal magical secrets that their peoples had forgotten. Sometimes I stayed silent. Sometimes I led them astray. Once, a hunched barbarian with a braided beard ordered me to give him the secret of flight. I told him to turn toward the prevailing wind and beg the Lover of the Sky for a favor. When the roc swooped down to eat him, I felt a wild kind of joy. At least the birds remembered how to punish worms who would steal women's magic.

I suffered for my minor victory. Without the barbarian to dismiss me, I was stuck on a tiny patch of grass, hemmed in by the rabbit heads he'd placed to mark the summoning circle. I shivered through the windy night until I finally thought to kick away one of the heads. It tumbled across the grass and my spirit sank into the ground.

Men treated me differently than women had. I had been accustomed to being summoned by Queens and commanders awaiting my advice on incipient battles. Men eschewed my consult; they sought to steal my powers. One summoned me into a box, hoping to trap me as if I were a minor demon that could be forced to grant his wishes. I chanted a rhyme to burn his fingers. When he pulled his hand away, the lid snapped shut and I was free.

Our magic had centered on birds and wind. These new sorcerers made pets of creatures of blood and snapping jaws, wolves and bears and jaguars. We had depicted the sun's grace along with its splendor, showing the red feathers of flaming light that arc into wings to sweep her across the sky. Their sun was a crude, jagged thing—a golden disk surrounded by spikes that twisted like the gaudy knives I'd seen in foreign cities where I traveled when I was young.

The men called me The Bitch Queen. They claimed I had hated my womb so much that I tried to curse all men to infertility, but the curse rebounded and struck me dead. Apparently, I had hanged myself. Or I'd tried to disembowel every male creature within a day's walk of my borders. Or I'd spelled my entire kingdom into a waking death in order to prevent myself from ever becoming pregnant. Apparently, I did all the same things out of revenge because I became pregnant. I eschewed men and impregnated women with sorcery. I married a thousand husbands and murdered them all. I murdered my husband, the King, and staked his head outside my castle, and then forced all the tearful women of my kingdom to do the same to their menfolk. I went crazy when my husband and son died and ordered all the men in my kingdom to be executed, declaring that no one would have the pleasure I'd been denied. I had been born a boy, but a rival of my father's castrated me, and so I hated all real men. I ordered that any woman caught breastfeeding should have her breasts cut off. I ordered my lover's genitals cut off and sewn on me. I ordered my vagina sewn shut so I could never give birth. I ordered everyone in my kingdom to call me a man.

They assumed my magic must originate with my genitals: they displayed surprise that I didn't strip naked to mix ingredients in my vagina or cast spells using menstrual blood. They also displayed surprise that I became angry when they asked me about such things.

The worst of them believed he could steal my magic by raping me. He summoned me into a worthless, skinny girl, the kind that we in the Land of Flowered Hills would have deemed too weak to be a woman and too frail to be a brood. In order to carry out his plans, he had to make the summoning circle large enough to accommodate the bed. When he forced himself on top of me, I twisted off his head.

The best of them summoned me soon after that. He was a young man with nervous, trembling fingers who innovated a way to summon my spirit into himself. Books and scrolls tumbled over the surfaces of his tiny, dim room, many of them stained with wax from unheeded candles. Talking to him was strange, the two of us communicating with the same mouth, looking out of the same eyes.

Before long, we realized that we didn't need words. Our knowledge seeped from one spirit to the other like dye poured into water. He watched me as a girl, riding with Rayneh, and felt the sun burning my back as I dug graves in The Desert which Should Not Have Been, and flinched as he witnessed the worm who attempted to rape me. I watched him and his five brothers, all orphaned and living on the street, as they struggled to find scraps. I saw how he had learned to read under the tutelage of a traveling scribe who carried his books with him from town to town. I felt his uncomfortable mixture of love, respect, and fear for the patron who had set him up as a scribe and petty magician in return for sex and servitude. *I didn't know it felt that way*, I said to him. *Neither did I*, he replied. We stared at each other cross-eyed through his big green eyes.

Pasha needed to find a way to stop the nearby volcano before it destroyed the tiny kingdom where he dwelled. Already, tremors rattled the buildings, foreshadowing the coming destruction.

Perhaps I should not have given Pasha the spell, but it was not deep woman's magic. Besides, things seemed different when I inhabited his mind, closer to him than I had been to anyone.

We went about enacting the spell together. As we collected ash from the fireplaces of one family from each of the kingdom's twelve towns, I asked him, *Why haven't you sent me back? Wouldn't it be easier to do this on your own?*

I'll die when your spirit goes, he answered, and I saw the knowledge of it which he had managed to keep from me.

I didn't want him to die. *Then I'll stay*, I said. *I won't interfere with your life. I'll retreat as much as I can.*

I can't keep up the spell much longer, he said. I felt his sadness and his resolve. Beneath, I glimpsed even deeper sadness at the plans he would no longer be able to fulfill. He'd wanted to teach his youngest brother to read and write so that the two of them could move out of this hamlet and set up shop in a city as scribes, perhaps even earn enough money to house and feed all their brothers.

I remembered Laverna and Nammi and tried to convince Pasha that we could convert the twins' magic to work for him and his brother. He said that we only had enough time to stop the volcano. *The kingdom is more important than I am*, he said.

We dug a hole near the volcano's base and poured in the ashes that we'd collected. We stirred them with a phoenix feather until they caught fire, in order to give the volcano the symbolic satisfaction of burning the kingdom's hearths. A dense cloud of smoke rushed up from the looming mountain and then the earth was still.

That's it, said Pasha, exhaustion and relief equally apparent in his mind. *We did it.*

We sat together until nightfall when Pasha's strength began to fail.

I have to let go now, he said.

No, I begged him. *Wait. Let us return to the city. We can find your brother. We'll find a way to save you.*

But the magic in his brain was unwinding. I was reminded of the ancient tapestries hanging in the Castle Where Hope Flutters, left too long to moths and weather. Pasha lost control of his feet, his fingers. His thoughts began to drift. They came slowly and far apart. His breath halted in his lungs. Before his life could end completely, my spirit sank away, leaving him to die alone.

After that, I did not have the courage to answer summonses. When men called me, I kicked away the objects they'd used to bind me in place and disappeared again. Eventually, the summonses stopped.

I had never before been aware of the time that I spent under the earth, but as the years between summonses stretched, I began to feel vague sensations: swatches of gray and white along with muted, indefinable pain.

When a summons finally came, I almost felt relief. When I realized the summoner was a woman, I did feel surprise.

"I didn't expect that to work," said the woman. She was peach-skinned and round, a double chin gentling her jaw. She wore large spectacles with faceted green lenses like insect eyes. Spines like porcupine quills grew in a thin line from the bridge of her nose to the top of her skull before fanning into a mane. The aroma of smoke—whether the woman's personal scent or some spell remnant—hung acrid in the air.

I found myself simultaneously drawn to the vibrancy of the living world and disinclined to participate in it. I remained still, delighting in the smells and sights and sounds.

"No use pretending you're not there," said the woman. "The straw man doesn't usually blink on its own. Or breathe."

I looked down and saw a rudimentary body made of straw, joints knotted together with what appeared to be twine. I lifted my straw hand and stretched out each finger, amazed as the joints crinkled but did not break. "What is this?" My voice sounded dry and crackling, though I did not know whether that was a function of straw or disuse.

"I'm not surprised this is new to you. The straw men are a pretty new development. It saves a lot of stress and unpleasantness for the twins and the spirit rebounders and everyone else who gets the thankless job of putting up with Insomniacs taking over their bodies. Olin Nimble—that's the man who innovated the straw men—he and I completed our scholastic training the same year. Twenty years later? He's transfigured the whole field. And here's me, puttering around the library. But I suppose someone has to teach the students how to distinguish Pinder's Breath from Summer Twoflower."

The woman reached into my summoning circle and tugged my earlobe. Straw crackled.

"It's a gesture of greeting," she said. "Go on, tug mine."

I reached out hesitantly, expecting my gesture to be thwarted by the invisible summoning barrier. Instead, my fingers slid through unresisting air and grasped the woman's earlobe.

She grinned with an air of satisfaction that reminded me of the way my aunts had looked when showing me new spells. "I am Scholar Misa Meticulous." She lifted the crystal globe she carried and squinted at it. Magical etchings appeared, spelling words in an unfamiliar alphabet. "And you are the Great Lady Naeva who Picked Posies near the Queen's Chamber, of the Kingdom Where Women Rule?"

I frowned, or tried to, unsure whether it showed on my straw face. "The Land of Flowered Hills."

"Oh." She corrected the etching with a long, sharp implement. "Our earliest records have it the other way. This sort of thing is commoner than you'd think. Facts get mixed with rumor. Rumor becomes legend. Soon no one can remember what was history and what they made up to frighten the children. For instance, I'll bet your people didn't really have an underclass of women you kept in herds for bearing children."

"We called them broods."

"You called them—" Misa's eyes went round and horrified. As quickly as her shock had registered, it disappeared again. She snorted with forthright amusement. "We'll have to get one of the historians to talk to you. This is what they *live* for."

"Do they."

It was becoming increasingly clear that this woman viewed me as a relic. Indignation simmered; I was not an urn, half-buried in the desert. Yet, in a way, I was.

"I'm just a teacher who specializes in sniffing," Misa continued. "I find

Insomniacs we haven't spoken to before. It can take years, tracking through records, piecing together bits of old spells. I've been following you for three years. You slept dark."

"Not dark enough."

She reached into the summoning circle to give me a sympathetic pat on the shoulder. "Eternity's a lonely place," she said. "Even the academy's lonely, and we only study eternity. Come on. Why don't we take a walk? I'll show you the library."

My straw eyes rustled as they blinked in surprise. "A walk?"

Misa laughed. "Try it out."

She laughed again as I took one precarious step forward and then another. The straw body's joints creaked with each stiff movement. I felt awkward and graceless, but I couldn't deny the pleasure of movement.

"Come on," Misa repeated, beckoning.

She led me down a corridor of gleaming white marble. Arcane symbols figured the walls. Spell remnants scented the air with cinnamon and burnt herbs, mingling with the cool currents that swept down from the vaulted ceiling. Beneath our feet, the floor was worn from many footsteps and yet Misa and I walked alone. I wondered how it could be that a place built to accommodate hundreds was empty except for a low-ranking scholar and a dead woman summoned into an effigy.

My questions were soon answered when a group of students approached noisily from an intersecting passageway. They halted when they saw us, falling abruptly silent. Misa frowned. "Get on!" she said, waving them away. They looked relieved as they fled back the way they'd come.

The students' shaved heads and shapeless robes made it difficult to discern their forms, but it was clear I had seen something I hadn't been meant to.

"You train men here," I ascertained.

"Men, women, neuters," said Misa. "Anyone who comes. And qualifies, of course."

I felt the hiss of disappointment: another profane, degraded culture. I should have known better than to hope. "I see," I said, unable to conceal my resentment.

Misa did not seem to notice. "Many cultures have created separate systems of magic for the male and female. Your culture was extreme, but not unusual. Men work healing magic, and women sing weather magic, or vice versa. All very rigid, all very unscientific. Did they ever try to teach a man to wail for a midnight rain? Oh, maybe they did, but if he succeeded, then it was just that one man, and wasn't his spirit more womanly than masculine? They get noted as an exception to the rule, not a problem with the rule itself. Think Locas Follow with the crickets, or Petrin of Atscheko, or for an example on the female side, Queen Urté. And of course if the man you set up to sing love songs to hurricanes can't even stir up a breeze, well, there's your proof. Men can't sing the weather. Even if another man could. Rigor, that's the important thing. Until you have proof, anything can be wrong. We know now there's no difference between the magical capabilities of the sexes, but we'd have known it earlier if people had asked the right questions. Did you know there's a place in the northern wastes where they believe only people with both male and female genitals can work spells?"

"They're fools."

Misa shrugged. "Everyone's a fool, sooner or later. I make a game of it with my students. What do we believe that will be proven wrong in the future? I envy your ability to live forever so you can see."

"You should not," I said, surprised by my own bitterness. "People of the future are as likely to destroy your truths as to uncover your falsehoods."

She turned toward me, her face drawn with empathy. "You may be right."

We entered a vast, mahogany-paneled room, large enough to quarter a roc. Curving shelf towers formed an elaborate labyrinth. Misa led me through the narrow aisles with swift precision.

The shelves displayed prisms of various shapes and sizes. Crystal pyramids sat beside metal cylinders and spheres cut from obsidian. There were stranger things, too, shapes for which I possessed no words, woven out of steel threads or hardened lava.

Overhead, a transparent dome revealed a night sky strewn with stars. I recognized no patterns among the sparkling pinpricks; it was as if all the stars I'd known had been gathered in a giant's palm and then scattered carelessly into new designs.

Misa chattered as she walked. "This is the academy library. There are over three hundred thousand spells in this wing alone and we've almost filled the second. My students are taking bets on when they'll start construction on the third. They're also taking bets on whose statue will be by the door. Olin Nimble's the favorite, wouldn't you know."

We passed a number of carrel desks upon which lay maps of strange rivers and red-tinted deserts. Tubes containing more maps resided in cubby holes between the desks, their ends labeled in an unfamiliar alphabet.

"We make the first-year students memorize world maps," said Misa. "A scholar has to understand how much there is to know."

I stopped by a carrel near the end of the row. The map's surface was ridged to show changes in elevation. I tried to imagine what the land it depicted would look like from above, on a roc's back. Could the Mountains where the Sun Rests be hidden among those jagged points?

Misa stopped behind me. "We're almost to the place I wanted to show you," she said. When we began walking again, she stayed quiet.

Presently, we approached a place where marble steps led down to a sunken area. We descended, and seemed to enter another room entirely, the arcs of the library shelves on the main level looming upward like a ring of ancient trees.

All around us, invisible from above, there stood statues of men and women.

They held out spell spheres in their carved, upturned palms.

"This is the Circle of Insomniacs," said Misa. "Every Insomniac is depicted here. All the ones we've found, that is."

Amid hunched old women and bearded men with wild eyes, I caught sight of stranger things. Long, armored spikes jutted from a woman's spine. A man seemed to be wearing a helmet shaped like a sheep's head until I noticed that his ears twisted behind his head and became the ram's horns. A child opened his mouth to display a ring of needle-sharp teeth like a leech's.

"They aren't human," I said.

"They are," said Misa. "Or they were." She pointed me to the space between a toothless man and a soldier whose face fell in shadow behind a carved helmet. "Your statue will be there. The sculptor will want to speak with you. Or if you don't want to talk to him, you can talk to his assistant, and she'll make notes."

I looked aghast at the crowd of stone faces. "This—this is why you woke me? This sentimental memorial?"

Misa's eyes glittered with excitement. "The statue's only part of it. We want to know more about you and the Kingdom Where Women Rule. Sorry, the Land of Flowered Hills. We want to learn from you and teach you. We want you to stay!"

I could not help but laugh, harsh and mirthless. Would this woman ask a piece of ancient stone wall whether or not it wanted to be displayed in a museum? Not even the worms who tried to steal my spells had presumed so much.

"I'm sorry," said Misa. "I shouldn't have blurted it out like that. I'm good at sniffing. I'm terrible with people. Usually I find the Great Ones and then other people do the summoning and bring them to the library. The council asked me to do it myself this time because I lived in a women's colony before I came to the academy. I'm what they call woman-centered. They thought we'd have something in common."

"Loving women is fundamental. It's natural as breeze. It's not some kind of shared diversion."

"Still. It's more than you'd have in common with Olin Nimble."

She paused, biting her lip. She was still transparently excited even though the conversation had begun to go badly.

"Will you stay a while at least?" she asked. "You've slept dark for millennia. What's a little time in the light?"

I scoffed and began to demand that she banish me back to the dark—but the scholar's excitement cast ripples in a pond that I'd believed had become permanently still.

What I'd learned from the unrecognizable maps and scattered constellations was that the wage of eternity was forgetfulness. I was lonely, achingly lonely. Besides, I had begun to like Misa's fumbling chatter. She had reawakened me to light and touch—and even, it seemed, to wonder.

If I was to stay, I told Misa, then she must understand that I'd had enough of worms and their attempts at magic. I did not want them crowding my time in the light.

The corners of Misa's mouth drew downward in disapproval, but she answered, "The academy puts us at the crossroads of myriad beliefs. Sometimes we must set aside our own." She reached out to touch me. "You're giving us a great gift by staying. We'll always respect that."

Misa and I worked closely during my first days at the academy. We argued over everything. Our roles switched rapidly and contentiously from master to apprentice and back again. She would begin by asking me questions, and then as I told her about what I'd learned in my matriline's locked rooms, she would interrupt to tell me I was wrong, her people had experimented with such things, and they never performed consistently. Within moments, we'd be shouting about what magic meant, and what it signified, and what it wanted—because one thing we agreed on was that magic was a little bit alive.

Misa suspended her teaching while she worked with me, so we had the days to ourselves in the vast salon where she taught. Her people's magic was more than superficially dissimilar from mine. They constructed their spells into physical geometries by mapping out elaborate equations that determined whether they would be cylinders or dodecahedrons, formed of garnet or lapis lazuli or cages of copper strands. Even their academy's construction reflected magical intentions, although Misa told me its effects were vague and diffuse.

"Magic is like architecture," she said. "You have to build the right container for magic to grow in. The right house for its heart."

"You fail to consider the poetry of magic," I contended. "It likes to be teased with images, cajoled with irony. It wants to match wits."

"Your spells are random!" Misa answered. "Even you don't understand how they work. You've admitted it yourself. The effects are variable, unpredictable. It lacks rigor!"

"And accomplishes grandeur," I said. "How many of your scholars can match me?"

I soon learned that Misa was not, as she claimed, an unimportant scholar. By agreement, we allowed her female pupils to enter the salon from time to time for consultations. The young women, who looked startlingly young in their loose white garments, approached Misa with an awe that verged on fear. Once, a very young girl who looked barely out of puberty, ended their session by giving a low bow and kissing Misa's hand. She turned vivid red and fled the salon.

Misa shook her head as the echoes of the girl's footsteps faded. "She just wishes she was taking from Olin Nimble."

"Why do you persist in this deception?" I asked. "You have as many spells in the library as he does. It is you, not he, who was asked to join the academy as a scholar."

She slid me a dubious look. "You've been talking to people?"

"I have been listening."

"I've been here a long time," said Misa. "They need people like me to do the little things so greater minds like Olin Nimble's can be kept clear."

But her words were clearly untrue. All of the academy's scholars, from the most renowned to the most inexperienced, sent to Misa for consultations. She greeted their pages with good humor and false humility, and then went to meet her fellow scholars elsewhere, leaving her salon to me so that I could study or contemplate as I wished.

In the Land of Flowered Hills, there had once been a famous scholar named The Woman Who Would Ask the Breeze for Whys and Wherefores. Misa was such a woman, relentlessly impractical, always half-occupied by her studies. We ate together, talked together, slept together in her chamber, and yet I never saw her focus fully on anything except when she was engrossed in transforming her abstract magical theories into complex, beautiful tangibles.

Sometimes, I paused to consider how different Misa was from my first love. Misa's scattered, self-effaced pursuit of knowledge was nothing like Rayneh's dignified exercise of power. Rayneh was like a statue, formed in a beautiful but permanent stasis, never learning or changing. Misa tumbled everywhere like a curious wind, seeking to understand and alter and collaborate, but never to master.

In our first days together, Misa and I shared an abundance of excruciating, contentious, awe-inspiring novelty. We were separated by cultures and centuries, and yet we were attracted to each other even more strongly because of the strangeness we brought into each other's lives.

The academy was controlled by a rotating council of scholars that was chosen annually by lots. They made their decisions by consensus and exercised control over issues great and small, including the selection of new mages who were invited to join the academy as scholars and thus enter the pool of people who might someday control it.

"I'm grateful every year when they don't draw my name," Misa said.

We were sitting in her salon during the late afternoon, relaxing on reclining couches and sipping a hot, sweet drink from celadon cups. One of Misa's students sat with us, a startle-eyed girl who kept her bald head powdered and smooth, whom Misa had confided she found promising. The drink smelled of oranges and cinnamon; I savored it, ever amazed by the abilities of my strange, straw body.

I looked to Misa. "Why?"

Misa shuddered. "Being on the council would be… terrible."

"Why?" I asked again, but she only repeated herself in a louder voice, growing increasingly frustrated with my questions.

Later, when Misa left to discuss a spell with one of the academy's male scholars, her student told me, "Misa doesn't want to be elevated over others. It's a very great taboo for her people."

"It is self-indulgent to avoid power," I said. "Someone must wield it. Better the strong than the weak."

Misa's student fidgeted uncomfortably. "Her people don't see it that way."

I sipped from my cup. "Then they are fools."

Misa's student said nothing in response, but she excused herself from the salon as soon as she finished her drink.

The council requested my presence when I had been at the academy for a year. They wished to formalize the terms of my stay. Sleepless Ones who remained were expected to hold their own classes and contribute to the institution's body of knowledge.

"I will teach," I told Misa, "but only women."

"Why!" demanded Misa. "What is your irrational attachment to this prejudice?"

"I will not desecrate women's magic by teaching it to men."

"How is it desecration?"

"Women's magic is meant for women. Putting it into men's hands is degrading."

"But why!"

Our argument intensified. I began to rage. Men are not worthy of woman's magic. They're small-skulled, and cringing, and animalistic. It would be wrong! *Why, why, why?* Misa demanded, quoting from philosophical dialogues, and describing experiments that supposedly proved there was no difference between men's and women's magic. We circled and struck at one another's arguments as if we were animals competing over territory. We tangled our horns and drew blood from insignificant wounds, but neither of us seemed able to strike a final blow.

"Enough!" I shouted. "You've always told me that the academy respects the sacred beliefs of other cultures. These are mine."

"They're absurd!"

"If you will not agree then I will not teach. Banish me back to the dark! It does not matter to me."

Of course, it did matter to me. I had grown too attached to chaos and clamor. And to Misa. But I refused to admit it.

In the end, Misa agreed to argue my intentions before the council. She looked at turns furious and miserable. "They won't agree," she said. "How can they? But I'll do what I can."

The next day, Misa rubbed dense, floral unguents into her scalp and decorated her fingers with arcane rings. Her quills trembled and fanned upward, displaying her anxiety.

The circular council room glowed with faint, magical light. Cold air mixed with the musky scents favored by high-ranking scholars, along with hints of smoke and herbs. Archways loomed at each of the cardinal directions. Misa led us through the eastern archway, which she explained was for negotiation, and into the center of the mosaic floor.

The council's scholars sat on raised couches arrayed around the circumference of the room. Each sat below a torch that guttered, red and gold, rendering the councilors' bodies vivid against the dim. I caught sight of a man in layered red and yellow robes, his head surmounted by a brass circlet that twinkled with lights that flared and then flitted out of existence, like winking stars. To his side sat a tall woman with mossy hair and bark-like skin, and beside her, a man with two heads and torsos mounted upon a single pair of legs. A woman raised her hand in greeting to Misa, and water cascaded from her arms like a waterfall, churning into a mist that evaporated before it touched the floor.

Misa had told me that older scholars were often changed by her people's magic, that it shaped their bodies in the way they shaped their spells. I had not understood her before.

A long, narrow man seemed to be the focal point of the other councilors' attention. Fine, sensory hairs covered his skin. They quivered in our direction like a small animal's sniffing. "What do you suggest?" he asked. "Shall we establish a woman-only library? Shall we inspect our students' genitalia to ensure there are no men-women or women-men or twin-sexed among them?"

"Never mind that," countered a voice behind us. I turned to see a pudgy woman garbed in heavy metal sheets. "It's irrelevant to object on the basis of pragmatism. This request is exclusionary."

"Worse," added the waterfall woman. "It's immoral."

The councilors around her nodded their heads in affirmation. Two identical-looking men in leather hoods fluttered their hands to show support.

Misa looked to each assenting scholar in turn. "You are correct. It is exclusionist and immoral. But I ask you to think about deeper issues. If we reject Naeva's conditions, then everything she knows will be lost. Isn't it better that some know than that everyone forgets?"

"Is it worth preserving knowledge if the price is bigotry?" asked the narrow man with the sensory hairs, but the other scholars' eyes fixed on Misa.

They continued to argue for some time, but the conclusion had been foregone as soon as Misa spoke. There is nothing scholars love more than knowledge.

"Is it strange for you?" I asked Misa. "To spend so much time with someone trapped in the body of a doll?"

We were alone in the tiny, cluttered room where she slept. It was a roughly hewn underground cavity, its only entrance and exit by ladder. Misa admitted that the academy offered better accommodations, but claimed she preferred rooms like this one.

Misa exclaimed with mock surprise. "You're trapped in the body of a doll? I'd never noticed!"

She grinned in my direction. I rewarded her with laughter.

"I've gotten used to the straw men," she said more seriously. "When we talk, I'm thinking about spells and magic and the things you've seen. Not straw."

Nevertheless, straw remained inescapably cumbersome. Misa suggested games and spells and implements, but I refused objects that would estrange our intimacy. We lay together at night and traded words, her hands busy at giving her pleasure while I watched and whispered. Afterward, we lay close, but I could not give her the warmth of a body I did not possess.

One night, I woke long after our love-making to discover that she was no longer beside me. I found her in the salon, her equations spiraling across a row of crystal globes. A doll hung from the wall beside her, awkwardly suspended by its nape. Its skin was warm and soft and tinted the same sienna that mine had been so many eons ago. I raised its face and saw features matching the sketches that the sculptor's assistant had made during our sessions.

Misa looked up from her calculations. She smiled with mild embarrassment.

"I should have known a simple adaptation wouldn't work," she said. "Otherwise, Olin Nimble would have discarded straw years ago. But I thought, if I worked it out…"

I moved behind her, and beheld the array of crystal globes, all showing spidery white equations. Below them lay a half-formed spell of polished wood and peridot chips.

Misa's quill mane quivered. "It's late," she said, taking my hand. "We should return to bed."

Misa often left her projects half-done and scattered. I like to think the doll would have been different. I like to think she would have finished it.

Instead, she was drawn into the whirl of events happening outside the academy. She began leaving me behind in her chambers while she spent all hours in her salon, almost sleepwalking through the brief periods when she returned to me, and then rising restless in the dark and returning to her work.

By choice, I remained unclear about the shape of the external cataclysm. I did not want to be drawn further into the academy's politics.

My lectures provided little distraction. The students were as preoccupied as Misa. "This is not a time for theory!" one woman complained when I tried to draw my students into a discussion of magic's predilections. She did not return the following morning. Eventually, no one else returned either.

Loneliness drove me where curiosity could not and I began following Misa to her salon. Since I refused to help with her spells, she acknowledged my presence with little more than a glance before returning to her labors. Absent her attention, I studied and paced.

Once, after leaving the salon for several hours, Misa returned with a bustle of scholars—both men and women—all brightly clad and shouting. They halted abruptly when they saw me.

"I forgot you were here," Misa said without much contrition.

I tensed, angry and alienated, but unwilling to show my rage before the worms. "I will return to your chamber," I said through tightened lips.

Before I even left the room, they began shouting again. Their voices weren't like scholars debating. They lashed at each other with their words. They were angry. They were afraid.

That night, I went to Misa and finally asked for explanations. It's a plague, she said. A plague that made its victims bleed from the skin and eyes and then swelled their tongues until they suffocated.

They couldn't cure it. They treated one symptom, only to find the others worsening. The patients died, and then the mages who treated them died, too.

I declared that the disease must be magic. Misa glared at me with unexpected anger and answered that, no! It was not magic! If it was magic, they would have cured it. This was something foul and deadly and *natural*.

She'd grown gaunt by then, the gentle cushions of fat at her chin and stomach disappearing as her ribs grew prominent. After she slept, her headrest was covered with quills that had fallen out during the night, their pointed tips lackluster and dulled.

I no longer had dialogues or magic or sex to occupy my time. I had only remote, distracted Misa. My world began to shape itself around her—my love for her, my concern for her, my dread that she wouldn't find a cure, and my fear of what I'd do if she didn't. She was weak, and she was leading me into weakness. My mind sketched patterns I didn't want to imagine. I heard the spirits in The Desert which Should Not Have Been whispering about the deaths of civilizations, and about choices between honor and love.

Misa stopped sleeping. Instead, she sat on the bed in the dark, staring into the shadows and worrying her hands.

"There is no cure," she muttered.

I lay behind her, watching her silhouette.

"Of course there's a cure."

"Oh, *of course*," snapped Misa. "We're just too ignorant to find it!"

Such irrational anger. I never learned how to respond to a lover so easily swayed by her emotions.

"I did not say that you were ignorant."

"As long as you didn't *say* it."

Misa pulled to her feet and began pacing, footsteps thumping against the piled rugs.

I realized that in all my worrying, I'd never paused to consider where the plague had been, whether it had ravaged the communities where Misa had lived and loved. My people would have thought it a weakness to let such things affect them.

"Perhaps you are ignorant," I said. "Maybe you can't cure this plague by building little boxes. Have you thought of that?"

I expected Misa to look angry, but instead she turned back with an expression of awe. "Maybe that's it," she said slowly. "Maybe we need your kind of magic. Maybe we need poetry."

For the first time since the plague began, the lines of tension began to smooth from Misa's face. I loved her. I wanted to see her calm and curious, restored to the woman who marveled at new things and spent her nights beside me.

So I did what I knew I should not. I sat with her for the next hours and listened as she described the affliction. It had begun in a swamp far to the east, she said, in a humid tangle of roots and branches where a thousand sharp and biting things lurked beneath the water. It traveled west with summer's heat, sickening children and old people first, and then striking the young and healthy. The children and elderly sometimes recovered. The young and healthy never survived.

I thought back to diseases I'd known in my youth. A very different illness came to mind, a disease cast by a would-be usurper during my girlhood. It came to the Land of Flowered Hills with the winter wind and froze its victims into statues that would not shatter with blows or melt with heat. For years after Rayneh's mother killed the usurper and halted the disease, the Land of Flowered Hills was haunted by the glacial, ghostly remains of those once-loved. The Queen's sorceresses sought them out one by one and melted them with memories of passion. It was said that the survivors wept and cursed as their loved ones melted away, for they had grown to love the ever-present, icy memorials.

That illness was unlike what afflicted Misa's people in all ways but one—that disease, too, had spared the feeble and taken the strong.

I told Misa, "This is a plague that steals its victims' strength and uses it to kill them."

Misa's breaths came slowly and heavily. "Yes, that's it," she said. "That's what's happening."

"The victims must steal their strength back from the disease. They must cast their own cures."

"They must cast your kind of spells. Poetry spells."

"Yes," I said. "Poetry spells."

Misa's eyes closed as if she wanted to weep with relief. She looked so tired and frail. I wanted to lay her down on the bed and stroke her cheeks until she fell asleep.

Misa's shoulders shook but she didn't cry. Instead, she straightened her spectacles and plucked at her robes.

"With a bit of heat and... how would obsidian translate into poetry?..." she mused aloud. She started toward the ladder and then paused to look back. "Will you come help me, Naeva?"

She must have known what I would say.

"I'll come," I said quietly, "but this is woman's magic. It is not for men."

What followed was inevitable: the shudder that passed through Misa as her optimism turned ashen. "No. Naeva. You wouldn't let people die."

But I would. And she should have known that. If she knew me at all.

She brought it before the council. She said that was how things were to be decided. By discussion. By consensus.

We entered through the western arch, the arch of conflict. The scholars arrayed on their raised couches looked as haggard as Misa. Some seats were empty, others filled by men and women I'd not seen before.

"Why is this a problem?" asked one of the new scholars, an old woman whose face and breasts were stippled with tiny, fanged mouths. "Teach the spell to women. Have them cast it on the men."

"The victims must cast it themselves," Misa said.

The old woman scoffed. "Since when does a spell care who casts it?"

"It's old magic," Misa said. "Poetry magic."

"Then what is it like?" asked a voice from behind us.

We turned to see the narrow man with the fine, sensory hairs, who had demanded at my prior interrogation whether knowledge gained through bigotry was worth preserving. He lowered his gaze onto my face and his hairs extended toward me, rippling and seeking.

"Some of us have not had the opportunity to learn for ourselves," he added.

I hoped that Misa would intercede with an explanation, but she held her gaze away from mine. Her mouth was tight and narrow.

The man spoke again. "Unless you feel that it would violate your ethics to even *describe* the issue in my presence."

"No. It would not." I paused to prepare my words. "As I understand it, your people's magic imprisons spells in clever constructions. You alter the shape and texture of the spell as you alter the shape and texture of its casing."

Dissenting murmurs rose from the councilors.

"I realize that's an elementary description," I said. "However, it will suffice for contrast. My people attempted to court spells with poetry, using image and symbol and allusion as our tools. Your people give magic a place to dwell. Mine woo it to tryst awhile."

"What does that," interjected the many-mouthed old woman, "have to do with victims casting their own spells?"

Before I could answer, the narrow man spoke. "It must be poetry—the symmetry, if you will. Body and disease are battling for the body's strength. The body itself must win the battle."

"Is that so?" the old woman demanded of me.

I inclined my head in assent.

A woman dressed in robes of scarlet hair looked to Misa. "You're confident this will work?"

Misa's voice was strained and quiet. "I am."

The woman turned to regard me, scarlet tresses parting over her chest to reveal frog-like skin that glistened with damp. "You will not be moved? You won't relinquish the spell?"

I said, "No."

"Even if we promise to give it only to the women, and let the men die?"

I looked toward Misa. I knew what her people believed. The council might bend in matters of knowledge, but it would not bend in matters of life.

"I do not believe you would keep such promises."

The frog-skinned woman laughed. The inside of her mouth glittered like a cavern filled with crystals. "You're right, of course. We wouldn't." She looked to her fellow councilors. "I see no other option. I propose an Obligation."

"No," said Misa.

"I agree with Jian," said a fat scholar in red and yellow. "An Obligation."

"You can't violate her like that," said Misa. "The academy is founded on respect."

The frog-skinned woman raised her brows at Misa. "What is respect worth if we let thousands die?"

Misa took my hands. "Naeva, don't let this happen. Please, Naeva." She moved yet closer to me, her breath hot, her eyes desperate. "You know what men can be. You know they don't have to be ignorant worms or greedy brutes. You know they can be clever and noble! Remember Pasha. You gave him the spell he needed. Why won't you help us?"

Pasha—kin of my thoughts, closer than my own skin. It had seemed different then, inside his mind. But I was on my own feet now, looking out from my own eyes, and I knew what I knew.

When she'd been confronted by the inevitable destruction of our people, Tryce had made herself into a brood. She had chosen to degrade herself and her daughters in the name of survival. What would the Land of Flowered Hills have become if she'd succeeded? What would have happened to we hard and haughty people who commanded the sacred powers of wind and sun?

I would not desecrate our knowledge by putting it in the hands of animals. This was not just one man who would die from what he learned. This would be unlocking the door to my matriline's secret rooms and tearing open the many-drawered cupboards. It would be laying everything sacrosanct bare to corruption.

I broke away from Misa's touch. "I will tell you nothing!"

The council acted immediately and unanimously, accord reached without deliberation. The narrow man wrought a spell-shape using only his hands, which Misa had told me could be done, but rarely and only by great mages. When his fingers held the right configuration, he blew into their cage.

An Obligation.

It was like falling through blackness. I struggled for purchase, desperate to climb back into myself.

My mouth opened. It was not I who spoke.

"Bring them water from the swamp and damp their brows until they feel the humidity of the place where the disease was born. The spirit of the disease will seek its origins, as any born creature will. Let the victims seek with their souls' sight until they find the spirit of the disease standing before them. It will appear differently to each, vaporous and foul, or sly and sharp, but they will know it. Let the victims open the mouths of their souls and devour the disease until its spirit is inside their spirit as its body is inside their body. This time, they will be the conquerors. When they wake, they will be stronger than they had been before."

My words resonated through the chamber. Misa shuddered and began to retch. The frog-skinned woman detached a lock of her scarlet hair and gave it, along with a sphere etched with my declamation, to their fleetest page. My volition rushed back into me as if through a crashing dam. I swelled with my returning power.

Magic is a little bit alive. It loves irony and it loves passion. With all the fierceness of my dead Land, I began to tear apart my straw body with its own straw hands. The effigy's viscera fell, crushed and crackling, to the mosaic floor.

The narrow man, alone among the councilors, read my intentions. He sprang to his feet, forming a rapid protection spell between his fingers. It glimmered into being before I could complete my own magic, but I was ablaze with passion and poetry, and I knew that I would prevail.

The fire of my anger leapt from my eyes and tongue and caught upon the straw in which I'd been imprisoned. Fire. Magic. Fury. The academy became an inferno.

They summoned me into a carved rock that could see and hear and speak but could not move. They carried it through the southern arch, the arch of retribution.

The narrow man addressed me. His fine, sensory hairs had burned away in the fire, leaving his form bald and pathetic.

"You are dangerous," he said. "The council has agreed you cannot remain."

The council room was in ruins. The reek of smoke hung like a dense fog over the rubble. Misa sat on one of the few remaining couches, her eyes averted, her body etched with thick ugly scars. She held her right hand in her lap, its fingers melted into a single claw.

I wanted to cradle Misa's ruined hand, to kiss and soothe it. It was an unworthy desire. I had no intention of indulging regret.

"You destroyed the academy, you bitch," snarled a woman to my left. I remembered that she had once gestured waterfalls, but now her arms were burned to stumps. "Libraries, students, spells…" her voice cracked.

"The council understands the grave injustice of an Obligation," the narrow man continued, as if she had not interjected. "We don't take the enslavement of a soul lightly, especially when it violates a promised trust. Though we believe we acted rightfully, we also acknowledge we have done you an injustice. For that we owe you our contrition.

"Nevertheless," he continued, "It is the council's agreement that you cannot be permitted to remain in the light. It is our duty to send you back into the dark and to bind you there so that you may never answer summonses again."

I laughed. It was a grating sound. "You'll be granting my dearest wish."

He inclined his head. "It is always best when aims align."

He reached out to the women next to him and took their hands. The remaining council members joined them, bending their bodies until they, themselves, formed the shape of a spell. Misa turned to join them, the tough, shiny substance of her scar tissue catching the light. I knew from Misa's lessons that the texture of her skin would alter and shape the spell. I could recognize their brilliance in that, to understand magic so well that they could form it out of their own bodies.

As the last of the scholars moved into place, for a moment I understood the strange, distorted, perfect shape they made. I realized with a slash that I had finally begun to comprehend their magic. And then I sank into final, lasting dark.

I remembered.

I remembered Misa. I remembered Pasha. I remembered the time when men had summoned me into unknown lands.

Always and inevitably, my thoughts returned to the Land of Flowered Hills, the place I had been away from longest, but known best.

Misa and Rayneh. I betrayed one. One betrayed me. Two loves ending in tragedy. Perhaps all loves do.

I remembered the locked room in my matriline's household, all those tiny lacquered drawers filled with marvels. My aunt's hand fluttered above them like a pale butterfly as I wondered which drawer she would open. What wonder would she reveal from a world so vast I could never hope to understand it?

"To paint a bird, you must show the brush what it means to fly," my aunt told me, holding my fingers around the brush handle as I strove to echo the perfection of a feather. The brush trembled. Dip into the well, slant, and press. Bristles splay. Ink bleeds across the scroll and—there! One single graceful stroke aspiring toward flight.

What can a woman do when love and time and truth are all at odds with one another, clashing and screeching, wailing and weeping, begging you to enter worlds unlike any you've ever known and save this people, this people, this people from king's soldiers and guttering volcanoes and plagues? What can a woman do when beliefs that seemed as solid as stone have become dry leaves blowing in autumn wind? What can a woman cling to when she must betray her lovers' lives or her own?

A woman is not a bird. A woman needs ground.

All my aunts gathering in a circle around the winter fire to share news and gossip, their voices clat-clat-clatting at each other in comforting, indistinguishable sounds. The wind finds its way in through the cracks and we welcome our friend. It blows through me, carrying scents of pine and snow. I run across the creaking floor to my aunts' knees which are as tall as I am, my arms slipping around one dark soft leg and then another as I work my way around the circle like a wind, finding the promise of comfort in each new embrace.

Light returned and shaded me with gray.

I stood on a pedestal under a dark dome, the room around me eaten by shadow. My hands touched my robe which felt like silk. They encountered each other and felt flesh. I raised them before my face and saw my own hands, brown and short and nimble, the fingernails jagged where I'd caught them on the rocks while surveying with Kyan in the Mountains where the Sun Rests.

Around me, I saw more pedestals arranged in a circle, and atop them strange forms that I could barely distinguish from shade. As my eyes adjusted, I made out a soldier with his face shadowed beneath a horned helmet, and a woman armored with spines. Next to me stood a child who smelled of stale water and dead fish. His eyes slid in my direction and I saw they were strangely old and weary. He opened his mouth to yawn, and inside, I saw a ring of needle-sharp teeth.

Recognition rushed through me. These were the Insomniacs I'd seen in Misa's library, all of them living and embodied, except there were more of us, countless more, all perched and waiting.

Magic is a little bit alive. That was my first thought as the creature unfolded before us, its body a strange darkness like the unrelieved black between stars. It was adorned with windows and doors that gleamed with silver like starlight. They opened and closed like slow blinking, offering us portals into another darkness that hinted at something beyond.

The creature was nothing like the entities that I'd believed waited at the core of eternity. It was no frozen world lizard, waiting to crack traitors in his icy jaws, nor a burning sun welcoming joyous souls as feathers in her wings. And yet, somehow I knew then that this creature was the deepest essence of the universe—the strange, persistent thing that throbbed like a heart between stars.

Its voice was strange, choral, like many voices talking at once. At the same time, it did not sound like a voice at all. It said, "You are the ones who have reached the end of time. You are witnesses to the end of this universe."

As it spoke, it expanded outward. The fanged child staggered back as the darkness approached. He looked toward me with fear in his eyes, and then darkness swelled around me, too, and I was surrounded by shadow and pouring starlight.

The creature said, "From the death of this universe will come the birth of another. This has happened so many times before that it cannot be numbered, unfathomable universes blinking one into the next, outside of time. The only continuity lies in the essences that persist from one to the next."

Its voice faded. I stretched out my hands into the gentle dark. "You want us to be reborn?" I asked.

I wasn't sure if it could even hear me in its vastness. But it spoke.

"The new universe will be unlike anything in this one. It will be a strangeness. There will be no 'born,' no 'you.' One cannot speak of a new universe. It is anathema to language. One cannot even ponder it."

Above me, a window opened, and it was not a window, but part of this strange being. Soothing, silver brilliance poured from it like water. It rushed over me, tingling like fresh spring mornings and newly drawn breath.

I could feel the creature's expectancy around me. More windows opened and closed as other Sleepless Ones made their choices.

I thought of everything then—everything I had thought of during the millennia when I was bound, and everything I should have thought of then but did not have the courage to think. I saw my life from a dozen fractured perspectives. Rayneh condemning me for helping her daughter steal her throne, and dismissing my every subsequent act as a traitor's cowardice. Tryce sneering at my lack of will as she watched me spurn a hundred opportunities for seizing power during centuries of summonses. Misa, her brows drawn down in inestimable disappointment, pleading with me to abandon everything I was and become like her instead.

They were all right. They were all wrong. My heart shattered into a million sins.

I thought of Pasha who I should never have saved. I thought of how he tried to shield me from the pain of his death, spending his last strength to soothe me before he died alone.

For millennia, I had sought oblivion and been denied. Now, as I approached the opportunity to dissipate at last... now I began to understand the desire for something unspeakably, unfathomably new.

I reached toward the window. The creature gathered me in its massive blackness and lifted me up, up, up. I became a woman painted in brushstrokes of starlight, fewer and fewer, until I was only a glimmer of silver that had once been a woman, now poised to take flight. I glittered like the stars over The Desert which Should Not Have Been, eternal witnesses to things long forgotten. The darkness beyond the window pulled me. I leapt toward it, and stretched, and changed.

COPYRIGHT ACKNOWLEDGMENTS

Night Shade Books Is an Independent Publisher of Quality SF, Fantasy and Horror

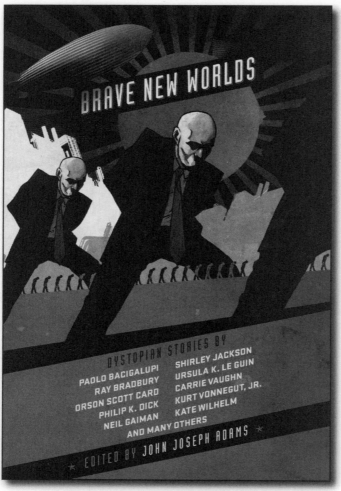

ISBN: 978-1-59780-221-5, Trade Paperback; $15.99

YOU ARE BEING WATCHED. Your every movement is being tracked, your every word recorded. One wrong move, one slip-up, and you may find yourself disappeared—swallowed up by a monstrous bureaucracy, vanished into a shadowy labyrinth of interrogation chambers, show trials, and secret prisons from which no one ever escapes. Welcome to the world of the dystopia, a world of government and society gone horribly, nightmarishly wrong.

In his smash-hit anthologies *Wastelands* and *The Living Dead*, acclaimed editor John Joseph Adams showed you what happens when society is utterly wiped away. Now he brings you a glimpse into an equally terrifying future. *Brave New Worlds* collects 30 of the best tales of totalitarian menace. When the government wields its power against its own people, every citizen becomes an enemy of the state. Will you fight the system, or be ground to dust beneath the boot of tyranny?

Night Shade Books Is an Independent Publisher of Quality SF, Fantasy and Horror

"Stina Leicht is one of my favourites among the new writers we have today. She writes with depth and heart and tells a story with all the resonance of an old whiskey: dark with an edgy flavour."

— Charles de Lint, author of *Forests of the Heart*

STINA LEICHT

of BLOOD *and* HONEY

A BOOK OF THE FEY AND THE FALLEN

ISBN: 978-1-59780-213-0, Trade Paperback; $14.99

Fallen angels and The Fey clash against the backdrop of Irish/English conflicts of the 1970s in this stunning debut novel by Stina Leicht.

When the war between The Fey and The Fallen begins to heat up, Liam and the woman he loves are pulled into a conflict invisible to most humans—a conflict in which Liam's father fights on the front lines. This centuries-old battle between supernatural forces seems to mirror the political divisions in 1970s-era Ireland, and Liam is thrown headlong into both conflicts.

Only the direct intervention of Liam's father and a secret Catholic order dedicated to fighting The Fallen can save Liam from the mundane and supernatural forces around him, and from the darkness that lurks within.

Night Shade Books Is an Independent Publisher of Quality SF, Fantasy and Horror

"Kameron Hurley's a brave, unflinching, truly original writer with a unique vision — her fiction burns right through your brain and your heart."
—Jeff VanderMeer, author of Finch

ISBN: 978-1-59780-214-7, Trade Paperback; $14.99

Nyx had already been to hell. One prayer more or less wouldn't make any difference... On a ravaged, contaminated world, a centuries-old holy war rages, fought by a bloody mix of mercenaries, magicians, and conscripted soldiers. Though the origins of the war are shady and complex, there's one thing everybody agrees on—

There's not a chance in hell of ending it.

Nyx is a former government assassin who makes a living cutting off heads for cash. But when a dubious deal between her government and an alien gene pirate goes bad, Nyx's ugly past makes her the top pick for a covert recovery. The head they want her to bring home could end the war—but at what price?

The world is about to find out.

Night Shade Books Is an Independent Publisher of Quality SF, Fantasy and Horror

"*Never Knew Another* is a weird but perfectly formed koan of identity, memory, loss and loneliness. Dark, moving and unique."
— Felix Gilman, author of *The Half-Made World*

ISBN: 978-1-59780-215-4, Trade Paperback; $14.99

J. M. McDermott delivers the stunning new novel, *Never Knew Another*—a sweeping fantasy that revels in the small details of life.

Fugitive Rachel Nolander is a newcomer to the city of Dogsland, where the rich throw parties and the poor just do whatever they can to scrape by. Supported by her brother Djoss, she hides out in their squalid apartment, living in fear that someday, someone will find out that she is the child of a demon. Corporal Jona Lord Joni is a demon's child too, but instead of living in fear, he keeps his secret and goes about his life as a cocky, self-assured man of the law. *Never Knew Another* is the story of how these two outcasts meet.

Never Knew Another is the first book in the Dogsland Trilogy.

Night Shade Books Is an Independent Publisher of Quality SF, Fantasy and Horror

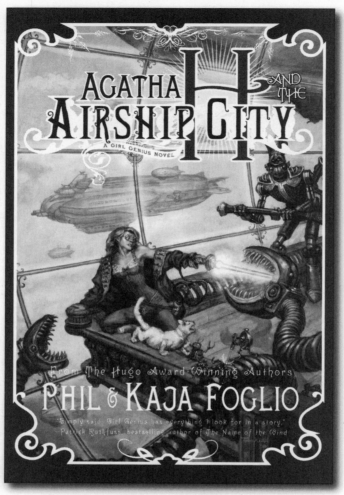

ISBN: 978-1-59780-211-6, Trade Hardcover; $24.99

At Transylvania Polygnostic University, a pretty, young student named Agatha Clay seems to have nothing but bad luck. Incapable of building anything that actually works, but dedicated to her studies, Agatha seems destined for a lackluster career as a minor lab assistant. But when the university is overthrown by the ruthless tyrant Baron Klaus Wulfenbach, Agatha finds herself a prisoner aboard his massive airship Castle Wulfenbach—and it begins to look like she might carry a spark of Mad Science after all.

From Phil and Kaja Foglio, creators of the Hugo, Eagle, and Eisner Award-nominated webcomic *Girl Genius*, comes *Agatha H. and the Airship City*, a gaslamp fantasy filled to bursting with Adventure! Romance! and Mad Science!

Night Shade Books Is an Independent Publisher of Quality SF, Fantasy and Horror

ISBN: 978-1-59780-210-9, Trade Paperback; $14.99

Tane Cedar is the master tailor, the supreme outfitter of the wealthy, the beautiful, and the powerful. When an ex-lover, on the run from the authorities, asks him to create a garment from the dangerous and illegal Xi yarn—a psychedelic opiate—to ease her final hours, Tane's world is torn apart.

Armed with just his yarn pulls, scissors, Mini-Air-Juki handheld sewing machine, and his wits, Tane journeys through the shadowy underworld where he must untangle the deadly mysteries and machinations of decades of deceit.

From the neo-feudalistic slubs, the corn-filled world of Tane's youth, to his apprenticeship among the deadly saleswarriors of Seattlehama, the sex-and-shopping capital of the world, to the horrors of a polluted Antarctica, *Yarn* tells a stylish tale of love, deceit, and memory.

Night Shade Books Is an Independent Publisher of Quality SF, Fantasy and Horror

"Valente is one of the most intriguing young writers working in the mythic fiction field today. Her work is lyrical, unusual, ambitious, and deeply rooted in world mythology." —Terri Windling

THE HABITATION OF THE BLESSED

A DIRGE FOR PRESTER JOHN **VOLUME ONE**

CATHERYNNE M. VALENTE

ISBN: 978-1-59780-199-7, Trade Paperback; $14.99

This is the story of a place that never was: the kingdom of Prester John, the utopia described by an anonymous, twelfth-century document which captured the imagination of the medieval world and drove hundreds of lost souls to seek out its secrets, inspiring explorers, missionaries, and kings for centuries.

Brother Hiob of Luzerne, on missionary work in the Himalayan wilderness on the eve of the eighteenth century, discovers a village guarding a miraculous tree whose branches sprout books instead of fruit. These strange books chronicle the history of the kingdom of Prester John, and Hiob becomes obsessed with the tales they tell. *The Habitation of the Blessed* recounts the fragmented narratives found within these living volumes, revealing the life of a priest named John, and his rise to power. Hugo and World Fantasy award nominee Catherynne M. Valente reimagines the legends of Prester John in this stunning tour de force.

Night Shade Books Is an Independent Publisher of Quality SF, Fantasy and Horror

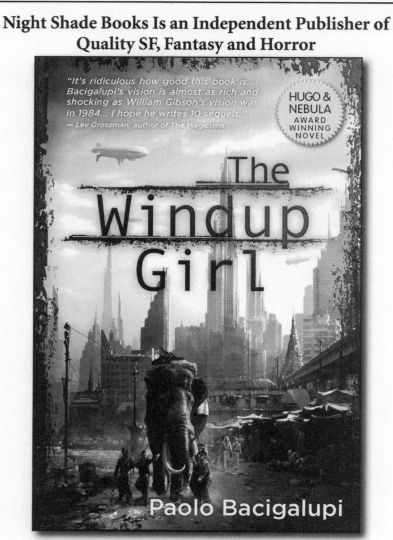

"It's ridiculous how good this book is.... Bacigalupi's vision is almost as rich and shocking as William Gibson's vision was in 1984... I hope he writes 10 sequels."
— Lev Grossman, author of The Magicians

HUGO & NEBULA AWARD WINNING NOVEL

The Windup Girl

Paolo Bacigalupi

ISBN: 978-1-59780-158-4, Trade Paperback; $14.95

Winner of the 2009 Hugo and Nebula Award for Best Novel.

Anderson Lake is a company man, AgriGen's Calorie Man in Thailand. Undercover as a factory manager, Anderson combs Bangkok's street markets in search of foodstuffs thought to be extinct, hoping to reap the bounty of history's lost calories. There, he encounters Emiko, the Windup Girl, a strange and beautiful creature. One of the New People, Emiko is not human; she is an engineered being, crèche-grown and programmed to satisfy the decadent whims of a Kyoto businessman, but now abandoned to the streets of Bangkok. Regarded as soulless beings by some, devils by others, New People are slaves, soldiers, and toys of the rich in a chilling near future in which calorie companies rule the world, the oil age has passed, and the side effects of bio-engineered plagues run rampant across the globe.

Night Shade Books Is an Independent Publisher of Quality SF, Fantasy and Horror

ISBN: 978-1-59780-175-1, Trade Paperback; $14.99

Nasim Golestani, a young Iranian scientist living in exile in the United States, hopes to work on the Human Connectome Project—which aims to construct a detailed map of the wiring of the human brain. When government funding for the project is canceled and a chance comes for Nasim to return to her homeland, she chooses to head back to Iran. Fifteen years later, Nasim is in charge of the virtual world known as Zendegi, used by millions of people for entertainment and business. When Zendegi comes under threat from powerful competitors, Nasim draws on her old skills, and data from the now-completed Human Connectome Project, to embark on a program to create more lifelike virtual characters and give the company an unbeatable edge...but Zendegi is about to become a battlefield.

Night Shade Books Is an Independent Publisher of Quality SF, Fantasy and Horror

ISBN: 978-1-59780-194-2, Trade Paperback; $14.95

Girls! Zombies! Zeppelins! If Chuck Palahniuk and Christopher Moore had a zombie love child, it would look like *The Loving Dead*.

Kate and Michael, twenty-something housemates working at the same Trader Joe's supermarket, are thoroughly screwed when people start turning into zombies at their house party in the Oakland hills. The zombie plague is a sexually transmitted disease, turning its victims into shambling, horny, voracious killers. Thrust into extremes by the unfolding tragedy, Kate and Michael are forced to confront the decisions they've made, and their fears of commitment, while trying to stay alive. Michael convinces Kate to meet him in the one place in the Bay Area that's likely to be safe and secure from the zombie hordes: Alcatraz. But can they stay human long enough?

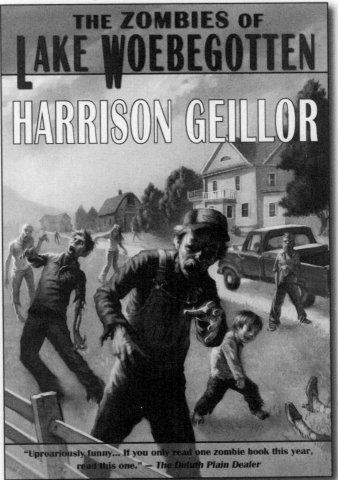

ISBN 978-1-59780-196-6, Trade Paperback; $14.99

The town of Lake Woebegotten, MN, is a small town, filled with ordinary (yet above average) people, leading ordinary lives. Ordinary, that is, until the dead start coming back to life, with the intent to feast upon the living. Now this small town of above average citizens must overcome their petty rivalries and hidden secrets in order to survive the onslaught of the dead.

"I honestly thought that if there was going to be a zombie outbreak in Minnesota, it would be at the Mall of America.... Harrison Geillor has proven me wrong."
—*The Minneapolis Daily Times*

"If you only read one zombie book this year, read this one."
—*The Duluth Plain Dealer*

Night Shade Books Is an Independent Publisher of Quality SF, Fantasy and Horror

The New York Times best-selling and Hugo and Nebula award-winning author delivers a stunning collection of his best short fiction, including a new, never-before-published story.

THE BEST OF

KIM STANLEY ROBINSON

EDITED BY
JONATHAN STRAHAN

ISBN 978-1-59780-185-0, Trade Paperback; $16.99

Adventurers, scientists, artists, workers, and visionaries—these are the men and women you will encounter in the short fiction of Kim Stanley Robinson. In settings ranging from the sunken ruins of Venice to the upper reaches of the Himalayas to the terraformed surface of Mars itself, and through themes of environmental sustainability, social justice, personal responsibility, sports, adventure and fun, Robinson's protagonists explore a world which stands in sharp contrast to many of the traditional locales and mores of science fiction, presenting instead a world in which Utopia rests within our grasp.

From Kim Stanley Robinson, award-winning author of the Mars Trilogy, the Three Californias Trilogy, the Science in the Capital series, and *The Years of Rice and Salt* and *Galileo's Dream*, comes *The Best of Kim Stanley Robinson*.